The Ronan:
Heir to Magrados

By: John Christopher

The Ronan: Heir to Magrados is dedicated to Donovan.
My best friend, my rock, my everything.

John Christopher's
The Ronan:
Heir to Magrados

This is a work of Fiction. All the characters are fictitious, and the events portrayed in this book are products of the author's imagination.

All rights reserved
Copyright © 2019 by Johnathan Moore
ISBN: 978-0-578-48641-3

This book is protected under the copyright laws of the United States of America. Any reproduction or unauthorized use of the material is prohibited without the express written permission of Johnathan Moore.

Edited by: Katherine Fanning
Cover art: Genel Jumalon

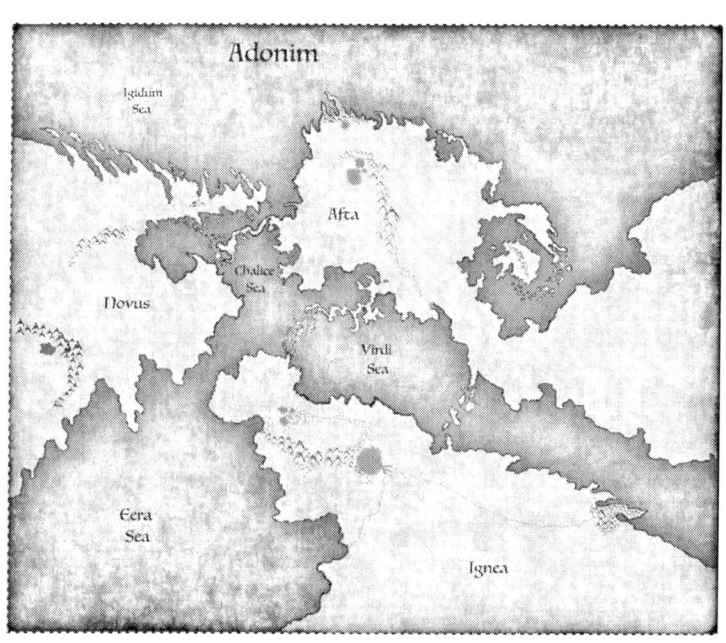

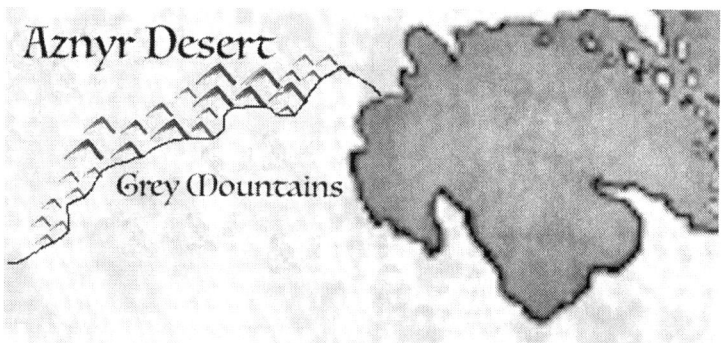

Aritian

Chapter One:

A Desperate Grief

Aritian's eyes opened slowly, flickering as his thoughts struggled to find consciousness. Within his mind a ruby coil stirred, pulsating with heady power. It prodded his consciousness from a deep exhaustion and endued him with renewed energy. Bolts of vigor shot through his limbs, and his heart pounded as sweat dripped from his brow. His skin burned hot with the bonfire that raged within.

Aritian's vision swam as a thick hand wiped a silken rag across his brow, cool and gentle. His head lolled as the room seemed to turn on its side, and he saw that the walls were made from tightly-woven wicker. The room dipped suddenly to the left and his head tipped back. Above, he saw supplies held against the ceiling by a heavy net and a crisscross of thick rope. A single, blue-paned lantern hung from the net by a hook. The lantern spun erratically, throwing pale light across the walls. Beneath him, he could feel plush furs that made it seem as if he lay on the softest of clouds. His head rolled to the far right as the room dipped again, and Aritian saw that two of the walls had been adorned with white drapes in an attempt to make the room seem more spacious.

Darkness flickered across his vision as Azera bent over him. Aritian blinked rapidly as he struggled to free himself from the fever that gripped his mind. The Titan was dressed in a red, silk top that was cropped just beneath her breasts and brown, leather trousers that were stitched with red geometric shapes. She leaned over him and gently poured cool water over his brow from the gooseneck of a yellowed glass pitcher. The half-giant's face was tight with concern. Groggily, Aritian noted that her wild hair had been rowed into long braids. Aritian tried to focus on the details, hoping that it would help center him, but his thoughts spun haphazardly, confused by her rich apparel. He smiled dazedly and thought hysterically, *Azera, the prettiest Titan to ever grace Inee.* The offhand thought smacked him in the face like a cold pail of water. *There is no Inee,* Aritian thought dumbfounded. *No,* he thought wildly, *that was a dream, a terrible dream of fire, smoke, and ash.*

Aritian tried to sit up, but his head spun and he fell back weakly, crying out. A deep voice spoke to him, and two more faces appeared floating in the wild light. A man, who had pale, shoulder-length hair and a hooked nose swam in the air to his left. Aritian didn't recognize him, and dimly wondered who he was. Beryl smiled weakly at him, his rosy complexion floating next to Azera's. Aritian saw their mouths moving, but the voices were muffled and it was as if they spoke to him through water. Aritian eyed them desperately, his gaze seeking succor. Wonderingly, he thought, *Where is she? Where is Razia? Where is my love?*

A memory, bold and scathingly honest, swirled out of flames of memory before his eyes. *He stood above and Razia crouched below. His hands rested on her shoulders. The flames were too much, too much to consume. Razia looked up at him and met his gaze. She nodded tightly, and flames boiled from his hands. Razia screamed as she drank in the wrath of Ignathra. Her voice held such torture, such pain, Aritian knew that no human could survive such a wail. He tried to let go, but Razia's hands snapped around his wrists, holding on even as her skin melted from her bones.*

Aritian jerked up and wailed in grief, flinging those nearest away as his heart died. He looked around wildly and knew suddenly where he was. He was within that basket, in the contraption that had been strapped to the chest of great bird who had flown from the ash ridden sky. The room dipped again and Aritian knew that it was not vertigo. *The Roc is flying and I am carried at its breast*, he thought knowingly. Aritian roared, bestially enraged. *They are taking me from my love*, he thought woefully, his mind torn by grief.

Aritian stood unsteadily, flailing around as the basket rocked and tilted, and shouted, "Take me back. Take me back to Inee. Let me go."

There was silence within the basket, as those within looked at him with fear and uncertainty. He saw that the young Dranguis sitting knee to knee, next to Rythsar and Ori against the far wall. They bowed their heads whispering supplications, but their hands were out turned toward him. The lorith looked at him with an unreadable gaze, his muscled legs taunt, as if he was ready to spring. Next to the tall lorith, watching his movements unfazed, sat the gnome. The creature eyed him entrapped, but seemed unmarred by fear. Ori looked at him with excitement. Aritian saw adoration in the young Titan eyes, and flinched away, refuting such an emotion.

Next to him Azera spoke, "Aritian, please," her voice shook, as she said, "Inee is gone. There is nothing for us to go back to."

Aritian turned to face her slowly, "Razia. Razia is there." He choked on his next words, "I killed her. I burned her." His voice fell and he whispered, "I never said goodbye. I never said..." His words trailed off and he looked up to the ceiling. Rage boiled in his breast, as reality lost all meaning. "I need to go back. I need to see her." He insisted, his eyes wide with desperation.

A voice spoke into his mind. It slipped within his thoughts like cool ice, jagged and penetrating. *Aritian you must calm your inner mind. My name is Selyni. I have come to help you.* A gust of wind punched into them and the Roc banked to the side, slipping beneath the gale.

Aritian's hands sprang out as he balanced. *Who is there? How... how can she speak into my mind*, Aritian wondered fearfully.

3

Aritian yelled, "Selyni!" His grey eyes were rimmed with a flickering blackness. Aritian looked down at his palms and saw that they burned with latent power. Those within the basket cowered as fierce wind tore from the palms of his hands. A red vortex rushed through the compartment, as the wind struggled for release, rippling along the silk walls furiously as it spun around them in a whirlwind

Selyni spoke on, her voice growing urgent. *Aritian your power is unstable from the Awakening; you must calm down. You cannot lose control.*

"Or what?!" Aritian screamed, and his eyes were lost beneath a swirling darkness. He clawed at his head, as he yelled into the air, "Get out of my head, Witch. Face me! Tell this beast to land. Now!"

A gust of wind slammed into the basket throwing those within against the carpeted floor. The Roc twisted mid-flight, flinging them all into the air. They fell against the ceiling of the compartment in a tangle of limbs, before rolling in a heap along the walls as Selyni barrel rolled through the air.

Aritian eyes snapped closed as Selyni's mind grappled with his own. Her grip burned his mind with clawing cold as she sought control. Aritian called out in pain as pale, blue light flashed before his eyes. For a moment he saw through her eyes. The scene before him was detailed with incredible precision. For a moment, Aritian forgot to breath as fear leapt to his breast.

The white clouds around them twisted wildly, as if tortured, and an unnatural gale swirled through the air with ferocious, deadly intent. The blue sky faded to steel grey as his power distorted the weather and booming thunder rocked the sky with shuddering vibrations. A downdraft smacked into Roc and flung them into a spiral. The Roc plummeted suddenly, her wings flapping desperately against the wind as she struggled to hold them airborne. The bird's wings crumpled beneath the pressure, and for a timeless moment they spun in the air like a leaf caught in the grip of a thunderstorm. Lightning crackled through the sky, dangerously close.

Aritian could feel what the Roc felt. He felt the straps and the weight of the basket clinging to her breast, and could feel her wings cramp with pain as wind crazily tore at her like a ravenous pack of wolves. Aritian could feel a saddle upon the bird's neck, and heard Namyr scream desperately as he clung to the pommel of the saddle. Namyr's words were stolen from his mouth as the clouds around them began to twist into a tunnel.

Aritian's face paled and his eyes flashed with fear as Selyni let out a piercing scream. The Roc folded her wings close to her breast, stretching her neck forward as she nose-dived toward the cloud wall. They hit the wall, like running into stone, and those within were dashed against the ceiling and floor. They punched through, wind flinging them head over tail.

Golden sand appeared, sprawling beneath them like a gilded ocean. They fell toward it at a breakneck speed. Spirals of grey wind shot from the sky and struck the sand. Three tornadoes rose, and danced around them. The tornadoes crackled with red lightning, as thunder railed against the horizon in an unending boom. The Roc's path was erratic as she dived through the trio of cyclones. The twisters transformed in color from grey to gold as sand was lifted into the air, and now the Roc was pelted with scathing waves of biting sand. The witch's mind went red as she screamed in pain. Desperately, Selyni ripped into to his mind like ten thousand lances, sending flashes of cold light. Aritian matched her scream with his own, and his body began to twitch and jerk as she tried to wrench away control of his magic.

Another power entered Selyni's thoughts. Aritian didn't understand, but all of a sudden an emerald light filled both of their minds. The light sprang between Selyni and her pain, shielding her. The glimmering light became tinged with a ruddy hue as it absorbed the brunt of the torturous wind. The Roc tumbled dangerously close to the ground, and Aritian began to panic as the dunes rose to meet them. The unknown presence engulfed his mind in brilliant light, stabbing like a dagger into the center of his thoughts. Aritian felt himself fall into dark unconsciousness.

Selyni wings snapped open a mere hundred feet above the ground. The Roc shrieked in pain as the muscles of her wings tore. She raced toward the ground, even as the magic-fueled storm died, fading around her as quickly as Aritian lost consciousness. The orange tornados sputtered, skirting up and down dunes drunkenly before the wind died and softly vanished.

Selyni slammed into the dunes and sand was thrown in all directions as her wings spasmed and crumpled. The Roc felt the basket beneath her splinter apart as it was crushed against the ground. Namyr was flung from the saddle when they made impact and was dashed against the side of a dune. Sand puffed outward with the impact, and Namyr rolled down the dune to lay unmoving.

The air around the Roc twisted and blurred, before shrinking, leaving Selyni's naked, unconscious form sprawled atop the remnants of the basket. Sand slowly fell from the sky, the plume of their impact settling with the hot air.

Caethe

Chapter Two:

The Tale of the Elder Fae

Caethe woke slowly as pale, jade light filled his vision. Cautiously, he looked around and found himself in the center of a small glade. He lay on a raised stone that was softened by a plush mattress of thick, green moss. The trees that surrounded him on all sides were gargantuan in measure, with trunks thicker than the greatest of castle towers and bark tinged a deep-green basil. Caethe craned his head up, tracing the trunks hundreds of feet until he saw the canopy above that was lost in a viridian glow. The air was thick with golden light, so copious that Caethe felt as though he merely had to reach out and he might catch the gilded motes. Caethe glanced down at himself and found that he had been dressed in a long, tightly-woven, shift of pale green. The cloth was strange, smooth to the touch, and looked to be made from diminutive, living vine.

A voice filled the glade suddenly, "Rest is good for the travel-worn soul, but the time to wake is upon you, Ronan." The Fae's voice was filled with vibration, as if he hummed beneath his words. Caethe sat up slowly, eying the Fae that approached.

The Elder Fae was tall, standing nine-feet in height and had a short coat of pure-white fur. Its limbs were overly long, lithe, and its waist was thin. It had long hands that held three, slender fingers that ended with hooked, brown talons. Its legs were similar to a man's, although longer, ending in three-toed feet that closely resembled split-hooves.

Caethe eyed the Fae openly, both curious and

apprehensive. The voice held no guile, but Caethe could feel the shadow of its powerful touch. Bowing his head, Caethe said, "I thank you for your hospitality, and am indebted to you for the care that you have provided." The Fae nodded in acquiesce, but did not reply. Caethe realized that it was observing him with an equal amount of interest. Carefully, Caethe remarked, "It would be easier to facilitate communication if I were provided a word with to address you by." Caethe knew better then to ask for its name.

The Fae's voice grew light, as it said, "You have knowledge of the Fae. I find this curious. It has been more than a millennium since one of your Coven has reached this forest." Caethe nodded cautiously and stood. The Fae froze at the edge of the glade, eyeing him suspiciously. Caethe halted, not wanting to startle the weary creature. Cautiously, the Fae said, "You may call me Arkyn."

Caethe gave Arkyn a small bow, and politely said, "My name is Caethe Aethyon William Ronan." The Fae's large amber eyes bubbled with inner light, and the halo of gold that floated above its long, pointed ears seemed to glow brighter.

Arkyn cocked his oval-shaped head to the side and his left ear twitched with surprise. Warmly, Arkyn said, "You freely gift me with you name. I am humbled by this show of trust." Arkyn stepped fully into the glade and strode toward him. Caethe found himself craning his head upward to meet the towering Fae's eyes. "You are quite young to travel such a harrowing path, but you paid the price of immortal blood to gain entrance and have thus gained my respect," Arkyn said, his gaze unblinking.

Caethe smiled and answered the hidden question, "I have come here for your people's wisdom and guidance."

Arkyn reach out and lightly touched Caethe's temple where his hair had turned white by the creatures of the Aelfmae Sea. In a whisper, Arkyn pondered, "To pay such a price as you have..." Arkyn looked down at him and Caethe became transfixed by the creature's brilliant, golden eyes. Slowly, Arkyn's eyes began to spin, and Caethe felt himself drawn into the luminance light that suddenly shone in the Fae's gaze.

Caethe knew in that moment that Arkyn was searching his mind, and shook his head slightly, in protest. The movement was so small it would be indiscernible had the creature not been touching him. It was the only movement Caethe could make. Arkyn whispered, "It would seem your need is great." Arkyn's hand fell away and the Fae took a step back. "I must warn you, young Ronan, I am bound by the Covenant of the Sanguis." Caethe nodded with excitement; it was not often that such ancient accords were so openly spoken of.

Caethe bowed low once more, and said, "I come on tides of prophecy and implore you to allow my impetuously brash tongue, indulgence. I am unused to the grace of the Fae and do not wish to give insult."

Arkyn nodded with understanding and Caethe thought he saw the edge of the Fae's dark lip curl with the hint of a smile. The Fae observed, "To know oneself is refinement in itself, but I thank you gladly for your care." Arkyn sat on the mound of moss so that they were on a more equal level, and said, "There are others of your kind that I have spoken to regularly, whose tongues are as equally clumsy. Fear not, I shall endure."

"You speak of the lost Covens?" Caethe asked in a hushed whisper, without thinking. Arkyn flinched at the bold question and Caethe cursed himself mentally for his incivility.

Arkyn bent his long neck, and answered simply, "I do."

Caethe's mind began to spin, and hastily he framed a question that was not a question, before saying, "If the Covenant of Sanguis was broken that would permit the Elder Fae to assist uninhibited by their oath."

Arkyn nodded in agreement, but frowned. Caethe could tell the Fae was uncomfortable by his line of thinking. The Fae's voice rolled with a buzzing hum, as he suggested, "I sense great curiosity within you. If you indulge me, I shall explain how we

Elder Fae came to this realm. Thus, we may avoid..." Arkyn paused as if searching for the proper politeness in which to express his discomfort, and then said, "any misunderstanding."

Caethe nodded, and said, "I think this would be wise." He sat on the ground by the Fae's feet, crossing his legs.

Arkyn turned his eyes toward the canopy as he remembered a past, long forgotten. In a rumbling voice, Arkyn said, "After the Dawn of Adonim the world was much changed. Humanity was wild, mere babes, and elves little more than children. Forests stretched across the land and magic flowed as free as a river, both swift and strong. Gods walked among us, shaping Adonim and those within. We Elder Fae were the first born, and for many centuries we lived alongside the child races. The age was wild, the spirit free, and time stretched naturally forward with the raw exuberance of youth. Magrados bridged the realms tying Adonim with the Aether, and they to it." Caethe was mesmerized by the Fae's voice and he drank in every word. Caethe knew that he was hearing an account from one who had experienced it firsthand and, for a moment, was overwhelmed by the antiquity of the creature before him.

Arkyn's eyes fell from the greenery above to rest fully upon the Ronan at his feet, as he said, "You must know, young Ronan, that before the Dawn of Adonim the world was dark, full of chaos and war." The Fae's voice deepened, sounding like a swarm of bees, as he warned, "Magic was a wild thing and the gods warred against one another for dominance. Thousands of races were born and fell before the eternal light was born. From the shadows, Adonim was wrought, and like all birth it was ugly, bloody and fraught with mortal danger. In time, the memories of the long night faded from all, even the elves, and life continued with blissful ignorance."

The Fae's voice rolled like the tide of a sea, as he said, "Light does not exist without darkness, and we Fae know this great and terrible truth. In time, Adonim once more felt the shadow of Chaos. Etta's time had come. Death was upon the elves god-born tree. Rot blackened Etta's silvery limbs, cracked its golden trunk and in death, corrupted its deep-reaching roots. In their desperation the elves sought succor." Caethe nodded, more to himself then anything. This part of the history was well known to the Ronan.

Arkyn spoke on, "Far and wide, the elves traveled across the land searching for one who could heal their soul and free them from their great fear. The time grew dark and soon they found a young magus whose power surpassed all those who came before."

Arkyn lip curled with bitter anger. When he next spoke, the words fell from his mouth in a growl, "Prophecy warned against such unnatural hopes, for life is not without death and to forestall such a fate is aberrant to nature. Mangus, the mage was named, and he refused the elven call." Sadness filled the Fae's gilded eyes, and his voice dipped into a growling whisper, as he said, "When the elves laid his daughter's neck upon the Bloodstone, Mangus wept, relenting, even as he cursed the cruelty of those who had once been so fair." The image of a silver-haired woman flashed across Caethe memory. *Ayfe*, Caethe thought knowingly. "To Adonim, Mangus brought a newly born god. She, who crawled forth from the Abyss and whose lips played promised aid, was named the Dark Lady."

Arkyn's eyes grew heavy with remembered pain, and his voice trembled, as he said, "Dark and severe, she demanded noble sacrifice for the cost of healing was high. Truly, Etta stood at the threshold of chaos, and wide the shadowed door of the Abyss waxed. While the elves wept for such a cost, in the end they acquiesced. The elven king Agsonath and his fair family paid the price. While weeping tears of joyful hope, the royal family crawled beneath Etta's roots and the Dark Lady danced, singing in the black speech of the Abyss."

Arkyn paused in his recount, his eyes rising to the eaves of the forest once more. The Fae struggled to contain his rage and Caethe was buffeted by the great emotion that rolled off of the

Fae in waves. The canopy above stirred with a wind and the air grew stifling hot. Caethe trembled before such wrath, ducking his head to his chest as he braced against the tumultuous power the Fae brought with his emotion.

The words seemed to torture to his tongue, but Arkyn spoke on, "The tree was returned to life, but deceptive was this revival, for the Elves had been deceived. Etta was corrupted beyond return. Malignant and foul, it spread disease across the land. Born from its roots the first Vampire crawled forth. The land blackened and the forest died, leaving naught but bare limbs and cracked ground. Horror struck the hearts of the fair folk, as they watched the corruption spread and their noble kin rise, undead, reborn from a dark chill."

Arkyn's ocher-gaze met Caethe's emerald eyes, and the weight carried in that stare made Caethe shudder. In a heavy voice, Arkyn said, "With revulsion, the elves choked upon the cost they paid. With fury, their retribution was swift and without mercy. Etta burned." Caethe watched as the Fae's eyes closed briefly. It seemed that Arkyn expended great effort casting the memories aside. The telling came at a great cost.

Arkyn stood, and began pacing across the glade. His long strides carried him quickly from one end to the other. The Fae's emotion changed from grief to anger, and glimmering waves distorted the air as his growing detestation boiled the air. Arkyn's voice dropped and grew guttural, as he said, "The Children of the Dark Lady walked in the night, for sunlight smote them. They needed no shelter from nature's wrath and survived wounds far beyond mortal men. They hunger naught but for the blood of their prey, so for two hundred years the Blood Wars raged; the Vampire hunted Adonim without release, killing millions, spreading their affliction to a hundred-thousand strong. Even the Fae fled before them, as their goddess's power crippled our own, even beyond the Unseelie's strength from a millennia past." Arkyn's heavy gaze met Caethe's pointedly, as if emphasizing his weighted words.

Caethe dropped his eyes to the moss-covered mound before him, unable to withstand the intensity of the Fae's stare.

The Fae's power brought Caethe's own magic to the surface and in its influence, swayed his very mind. Caethe felt an overwhelming need to jump to his feet and cry a wordless scream of rage, so strongly did he empathize in the wake of Arkyn's power. Caethe breathed heavily, nearly as furious as Arkyn. Arkyn voice softened suddenly, returning to normal and Caethe sighed in relief. "All the land wept, for with the Vampire, came the chill of the north and rivers ran red with blood. The black moon rose high in the sky, and the Dark Lady grew in power to rival the might of the Elder Gods. Corruption touched not only the land, but fouled hearts of all races. In the darkness, the Vampire armies rose."

Arkyn sat on the mound before him and his voice grew buoyant. Entrapped, Caethe felt his soul grow hopeful, reacting to the mood of the Fae words. "Those who walked in the light strove against the Dark Ladies forces. Our armies battled against the undead tide, but like a cracked dam our forces were overwhelmed by the vampire's ravenous hunger." Arkyn bared his teeth in a grin and met Caethe's eyes as he said, "Like a star shining in a dark sky of a moonless night, a prophecy was born. The words offered hope, but like all magic, the price was steep. Many screamed in defiance, but as the shadow stretched across the world there could be no divergence." Arkyn stomped his left foot into the ground, as if to drive in his point.

Arkyn explained, "The Covenant of the Sanguis was born. The lesser court of Covens would flee south and raise the Luxarma, safeguarding those who feared the dire repercussion of what must come. Those of fey nature would retreat in slumber or exile, and we who fled swore non-allegiance, no involvement, and no restitution. We would diminish so that Adonim could rise above the darkness that threatened." Caethe felt a shadow of a smile play across his face. He knew the moment he waited for grew close, but swiftly controlled his expression and the smile faded into a mask of attentiveness.

Arkyn spoke on, "The Trescoronam Coven remained, as did the lesser gifted and the elves. They alone would pay the price. What came next came to be known as the Great Sundering. A cataclysm of magestorms born from the destruction of the Bridge of Magrados. Magic was shattered across the land. The sea rose, swallowing cities and forests, drowning thousands. The mountains spewed fire and ash, and wind-fires danced across Adonim consuming all within their path. Stars fell from the sky and the heavens lost two moons in mourning. The elven forests were consumed by chaos, turning black and grey. Those left within were twisted beyond recognition. The Vampires retreated to slumber and the Dark Lady crawled to the edge of the Abyss where she waits in hibernation for magic to be whole once more. The lesser gifted perished instantly, the elves lost their magic, and the Trescoronam was nearly destroyed." Caethe nodded, it was a dark part of the Ronan history and one of three times that the royal Coven was nearly destroyed.

Arkyn words dripped with grief. "In the end we paid the ultimate cost, but lived on, secure of the promise that one day the Bridge of Magrados would be reborn in a brighter age. One, where we would be prepared to smite the Dark Lady back into the void from which she came and triumph over darkness. As we fey faded and fled the world of Adonim, elves and men bound together to hunt the Hives of Vampire, purging the land of the sleeping darkness. Now, nearly a millennium has passed in waiting." Arkyn's voice faded into silence. Together they sat, each digesting the words that had been spoken. Caethe heart pounded with excitement. He knew that he had received a gift far beyond the weight of gold and silver.

Caethe nodded to himself, purging himself of all emotions. Now was not the time for sentiments. *I must tread ever carefully*, he thought nervously. Tentatively, Caethe broke the silence, saying, "I know that this gift of telling was not without cost. You have honored me Arkyn, and for that I thank you."

Arkyn long neck curled in a small bow, but he did not speak. For a moment Caethe hesitated, not wanting to disturb the peaceful gaze that clouded the Fae's eyes, but Caethe had not come for history, no matter how glorious a telling it had been. In a murmur, Caethe whispered, "My journey here is tied to the words you have spoken, Holy One. I fear that you have been deceived." Caethe bowed his head; his long hair shadowing his face.

Caethe felt Arkyn's heavy gaze fell upon him with terrible scrutiny, and the Fae spoke a single word, "Deceived."

Caethe nodded tightly, keeping his eyes pinned to the ground before him. When he spoke, he allowed a feigned-grief to creep into his voice. "Yes Arkyn, deceived. I tell you this truly, Trescoronam and the lost covens beyond the Luxarma have no intention of upholding the Covenant of Sanguis. Your people's time to return to Adonim is nigh at hand. I speak with the words of an Oracle, for I have been shown the future. There is but one chance, one instant, one crux upon the turn of the age to succeed, and it is but a mere three years from this moment." Caethe felt the air grow cold as the Fae grew enraged. Caethe knew that he danced on the edge of a sword, but he had not risked coming here to hedge words. Caethe whispered words that would stab into the heart of the Fae like daggers. "Your people will be damned to this realm for all eternity, and the memory of your might will fade from history. Even now, you are but a shadow of a fable in the minds of the common folk."

In a dangerous whisper, Arkyn warned, "Your words are poisonous and should I find that you lie you shall pay with your life." Caethe nodded, knowing that the Fae's words were no mere threat. Caethe's eyes rose to meet Arkyns. The Elder Fae's face was twisted with bestial anger, his teeth were bared and his eyes burned with a fire that made Caethe tremble.

Caethe swallowed thickly, before continuing, "It is why I

have come, Holy One. There is a new prophecy, one that promises your peoples' return to the lands of Adonim."

Arkyn cocked his long neck, eying Caethe intently. Caethe had the sense that the Fae was debating on whether to attack or not. When Arkyn spoke his voice came in a hiss, "It is strange that you, unknown to me, would have me believe those who spilled blood in a sacred oath have loyalty now tangled with the vines of duplicity."

Caethe spread all four of his arms wide and bowed his head in supplication, as he responded in a firm but pleading voice, "I am strange to you, and you doubt my intentions. I do not begrudge this mistrust, for I understand the gravity of what I speak. I implore you to consider my rationale." Caethe met Arkyn's eyes then and though meeting the Fae's glowing stare brought him pain, he did not flinch away.

Arkyn gave him a slight nod, and Caethe sighed in relief. Caethe spoke on, "Without the rebuilding of the Bridge of Magrados, the Trescoronam Coven is left unchallenged by the might of gods and the multitude of those lesser gifted. The threat of the southern Covens becomes but a shadowed threat beyond an impenetrable barrier. " Caethe's eyebrows rose, and he stared intently, as he said, "The promise of the Dark Lady's second rising is killed before it has a chance to be born. Without your return, the Seelie inherit the lands of the Elder Fae and the holy lands of Amissa. I implore you to trust me Arkyn, for you have already been betrayed."

The Fae hissed angrily and stood. The halo of light above his head flashed, pulsating with glaring brightness. Arkyn snarled, "The avarice of humanity and the Lesser Seelie Court will be their downfall." Arkyn turned away from Caethe then, and Caethe watched the Fae's shoulders rise and fall as he tried to contain his fury. The Fae turned suddenly, and implored, "Surely our cousins will not let such a travesty take place." Arkyn grasped his upper arm in a bruising grasp, saying desperately, "You speak of the genocide of my people."

Caethe nodded forlornly, and whispered, "What power do the elves now have? With the death of Etta, all but the smallest of magics have abandoned them." Caethe shook his head in sorrow and met Arkyn's gaze with eyes brimming with tears, and said, "Only the Ronan, and only the royal Coven, have the power to grant your return. We are the last strength of Magrados on Adonim. Hear me when I say this: They do not wish it." Caethe concluded with finality, speaking slowly, emphasizing each word.

"Show me." Arkyn demanded, and Caethe knew he spoke of the prophecy that promised his people hope. Caethe nodded as he closed his eyes, and felt Arkyn's hands come to rest on either side of his temples. Arkyn's power thrummed through his skull, seeking entrance. The Fae's power shone brilliantly against the barriers of protection Caethe had erected. Caethe let a shaky breath out, and opened his mind. It was a risk, he knew, for there was many a thing he sought to hide, but there was but one path before him.

Arkyn's power flooded through him like a golden sun, its light illuminating his thoughts and mind with stark brightness. With concentration, Caethe brought the prophecy he had witnessed with Devaney to the forefront of his thoughts. Arkyn's power intensified, flashing with the light of the stars. Caethe gripped the grass beneath him and sweat dripped down his brow. The Fae was not being gentle as he examined the memory, searching it for any signs of tampering. Caethe knew that if Arkyn was displeased that he would soon be dead.

For a moment they were silent, the only sound their combined breathing. The forest had grown mute while Arkyn examined Caethe's memories, and it was as if the forest itself held its breath in anxious anticipation. When the images faded to darkness, Arkyn's hands fell away. Caethe breathed shakily, swallowing the echoes of pain that radiated from his temples to the base of his skull.

Caethe murmured, "Now you know the truth." Arkyn

nodded slowly. The shadow of what Arkyn had seen still danced in his eyes like a comet fleeing through a dark night sky, flashing brightly, before dying beyond sight. The Fae's chest rose and fell rapidly.

A time passed, what seemed like hours, but surely was only minutes. Caethe waited for the Fae to speak. Finally, Arkyn spoke, "I see the truth in you, Ronan, but I am unsure why you have come to the forests of the Fae. I am bound to this realm, and cannot bring the strength of the Elder Fae to bear."

Caethe turned away, and looked at the moss the clung to the trunk of a nearby tree. It was jade in color, and netted up the length of the tree like a cobweb. Caethe's mind sung with joy, but he let none of his emotion touch his expression. It had been a dire risk, and Caethe didn't quite believe that he had dared the feat, and more than that, succeeded. When he spoke, his voice was steady and calm, "The realm of Avalon spans beyond the Luxarma. I require something from beyond the shield and lack the power to walk beyond it."

In a low growl, Arkyn demanded, "Tell me what you require Caethe, Ronan of the Trescoronam Coven." Caethe reached toward the Fae and brushed his fingertips across the Fae's arm. An image passed from Caethe mind to Arkyn's.

The Fae's eyes grew wide with shock, and he pronounced with surety, "You demand a power that rivals that of a god. It will consume you."

Caethe shook his head and allowed a small smile to cross his lips, as he explained Ultan's machinations: "My physical body is entombed in amber, the antithesis to my Ronan power. The Covens themselves have been Cursed to exile. They wish to release me from my prison so that I may free them. There is but one way for them to do this."

Arkyn cocked his head to the side and murmured, "I see. The power to bind the Trescoronam Coven must be a strong one, unknown to me." His pointed ears twitched with curiosity.

Caethe explained, "They were bound by the powers of the

Elder Gods, a power now exhausted." Caethe paused, and then added, "There are other powers in Adonim which would be alien to one such as yourself."

Arkyn eyes flicked toward Caethe's lower set of arms and the Fae's forehead wrinkled in agitation. "You speak of those who entombed you." Arkyn said perceptively.

Caethe sensed the Fae's curiosity and spread his thin, veiny arms wide. Dryly, he said, "The curiosity of man is inexhaustible. This is," he flicked his four hands in a dismissive wave, and said, "but the least of their crimes against my person." Caethe's voice fell, and he warned, "Those who hold me captive are a great enemy, equal a threat as the Dark Lady. Known as the Ordu, their gods might rival that of the Elder Gods before the Sundering."

Arkyn's voice grew incredulous as he said, "That is impossible. Such power would be known to me."

Caethe explained in a low whisper, "Theirs is a god of man's collective unconscious, unbound by the constraints of immortal power." True fear colored his words.

Arkyn nodded slowly with understanding, and compassionately, said, "I sense you have endured much for one so young. You seek this prophesy with thoughts shadowed by revenge."

Caethe responded ambiguously, his voice hard as he said, "I seek it for many reasons."

Arkyn nodded, not questioning him further, and said with finality. "I cannot retrieve what you seek," Caethe's head snapped up in shock. The Fae smiled dangerously watching Caethe's eyes dance with heady power, before wryly saying, "But I can call one who will retrieve it for you." Caethe smiled, dropping his anger as fast as it had come. Before Caethe could speak, Arkyn's voice grew suddenly serious as he said, "You will submit yourself to the High Seelie Court. If they deem you pure of heart, I shall grant your request. I am but the voice of my kin, nothing more." Caethe nodded, knowing that the easy part was over. The true test would come next. Arkyn stood, and said, "Come, let us walk a short while."

Caethe stood, unfolding his legs gracefully. Nonchalantly, Caethe remarked, "My swords are not within the glade." He knew that he had pushed the Fae far with his directness, but he was loathe to walk this enchanted forest unarmed.

Arkyn had walked to the edge of the glade, but turned back to face Caethe. His expression was emotionless and his thoughts veiled, as he stonily remarked, "The Black Twins of Aegoth are not something I believed to ever witness within the forests of Avalon. Demonic weaponry shall not be allowed free within these hallowed forests. You may have the Soul Reapers when you depart." Arkyn gave him a long, measuring look.

"As you command, Holy One." Caethe whispered with a curt nod. Inwardly, he wondered how many souls of the Fae his swords held, but he knew better to contemplate such a thought with Arkyn nearby. The Elder Fae turned away, and walked past a tall oak tree. With a hidden smirk, Caethe followed after.

Selyni

Chapter Three:

The Threat of the Scarlet Witch

Selyni rolled onto her side and coughed raggedly; her lips stained red with blood. The sun glared down hot and Selyni saw that her usually-pale skin was flushed pink, her northern complexion unused to the harshness of the Ignean heat. Dazed, she shook her head trying to gain her bearings. Selyni did not know how much time had passed, but as she gazed up at the sun she saw it was still high in the sky. *Good, I haven't been unconscious for too long*, she thought with relief. Gingerly, she heaved herself to her hands and knees. A soft whimper escaped her lips as pain racked up the length of her arms, her muscles screaming in protest. Selyni eyed her trembling arms and saw that blue and green bruising laced up her arms from wrist to shoulder. Shakily, Selyni sat on her backside, pushed the pale hair that fell messily over her face to the side, and gazed around.

The wind had fled and the sky had returned to its peaceful, serene blue. The basket beneath her was broken against the sand dune. The part of the fame she sat on was all that remained of the top-most portion of the compartment. Sand spilled into the dark recesses beneath her. All was quiet; too quiet. Fear rippled down her spine and Selyni hurriedly slid down the side of the basket to fall into an ungraceful heap. Frantically, Selyni pulled pieces of the basket aside, throwing them behind her until she was able to crawl into the interior. Her hand touched something wet, and she blinked owlishly in the shadowed confines and raised her palm to her face. It was covered in dark blood.

The interior was a twisted mess. The walls of the basket had shattered and large fragments lay scattered everywhere. Silken canopy lay in heaps, half-drowned in sand. She turned to the left and saw the first body. Speedily she crawled toward it, bending beneath the folded ceiling. It was the female Titan. *Azera*, Selyni thought, correcting herself. Selyni crawled to her side and touched her dusky neck. There was a strong pulse. Selyni sighed with relief, but noticed that the half-giantess lay on something. With a cry, Selyni pushed the unconscious Azera to the side and discovered that Ori lay beneath her. Azera had tried to shelter the boy, but Selyni took one look at his twisted legs and knew the boy's back was broken. His breath came shallowly and a trickle of blood fell down his prominent chin.

Selyni closed her eyes briefly, forestalling the panic that threatened to consume her. When her eyes opened, her pale blue eyes were hard as ice. *Only one truly matters*, she reminded herself. She turned her back to the Titans and dug further into the wreckage. Selyni soon came upon the dwarf and the gnome. Both had bruised faces, and several deep cuts. The dwarf seemed fine, otherwise. *Thick boned creatures*, Selyni thought ruefully. The gnome on the other hand was in rough shape. His right leg was twisted awkwardly to the side and a pool of blood seeped from beneath his grey robes. Selyni pushed the robes up, exposing the gnomes pale leg and found that it was broken. Blood pumped from around the exposed bone that jutted from underneath his knee. Selyni ripped a long strip of white canopy that hung above her head and wrapped the length of silk around the gnome's thigh. She grunted as she tied it as tight as she could. The creature groaned weakly, but did not wake.

Selyni crawled over him and sped over wreckage as her eyes caught sight of a morbid scene. Laying half buried in the sand was Hector. Selyni knew instantly that the man was dead. Hector's neck was twisted awkwardly to the side and he was impaled through the middle by a two-foot wide section of wood. Selyni felt a tear trickle down her face, as her heart thundered with panic. He had been her guide in Ignea, and a welcome traveling companion. Her Mistress would not be pleased by his death. The thought made her heart pound with the rushing tempo of fear.

Selyni looked around wildly and saw the lorith. With a sigh of relief, she saw that Rythsar had wrapped his body protectively around Aritian. They lay in a heap, but she noted immediately that they both breathed. Aritian looked untouched; as if he were merely sleeping. The lorith looked worse for wear, but was in no danger of losing his life. One of the three horns that crowned his head was broken off at a jagged angle, and his long tail was noticeably broken at the base. *He will live*, Selyni thought with slight annoyance. To her surprise Selyni saw that the ground dipped beneath Aritian. A shallow crater had been punched into the ground, and within the depression she saw the young boys the dwarf had insisted they bring along. All seven were alive and while they carried superficial wounds from Inee, none had suffered in the fall. *Interesting*, Selyni thought in wonder as she eyed Aritian, *you shielded them but no one else. Perhaps the dwarf was right in bringing them along*, she thoughtfully mused.

Selyni crawled to Hector's side and pushed his limp body over until he rested on his back. Gently, she closed his dull eyes with a sad smile. Selyni shook her head clearing her thoughts. Reaching beneath his chainmail, she searched his chest and found a small satchel tied beneath his shirt. With a jerk, the thin leather ties snapped free. The pack was wrapped in black silk and made of supple dark leather. With shaking hands, Selyni removed the silk and opened the satchel.

Within, Selyni found a small hand-held mirror made from elegant silver. Vines twisted and crawled along its oval rim and met, twining around one another to form a small handle. The surface of the mirror was not reflective rather, the surface of the mirror was made from a lighter metal that swirled with shimmering specks. The metal was not of this world, Selyni knew, and the specks were motes of starlight that had been captured during the mirror's conception.

Selyni closed her eyes and used her nail to prick the palm of her hand. Holding her palm over the mirror she let three drops of blood hit the surface. The mirror's face hissed when her blood fell upon it, and the metal began to swirl as it turned liquid. Selyni whispered a short chant, her voice barely discernible from her rapid breath. Selyni fell silent, and opened her eyes.

The mirror now held an image, but it was not a reflection. Instead she saw a cavernous hall that was lost to shadow. The mirror had a narrowed vantage, and faced the only light in the room. Illuminated by pale orbs of swirling fire that hovered in the air, sat a throne. The throne was massive, made from pure gold, and crowned with a trio of golden spires that disappeared into the shadows above. Sitting on the throne was a beautiful woman, older than Selyni but with skin touched by the softest tan and long, inky-black hair that gleamed as it spilled down either side of her elegant face before falling to pool in her lap. Selyni bowed her head respectfully.

The woman's voice carried across the room and through the mirror, "Why Selyni, this is a most unexpected surprise. I assumed that you would be nearly here by now, and yet by your brazen nudity and disheveled appearance, I have the sense that I am about to be deeply disappointed."

Selyni flinched as if she had been physically rebuked, but replied evenly, "The young magus lost control of his power. This is no fault of mine, Maud. The power within him is highly volatile and too great for him to control."

Maud fingered the black-diamond wand she held as her large, burgundy eyes narrowed. Her words came clipped, as she said, "I told the Archmagus that sending a Changeling was a mistake. Your kind is not suited for such delicate tasks. Your ineptitude has been noted, Selyni. What is your location and is the child intact?" Maud asked curtly.

Selyni's pale face reddened with anger, but she restrained herself. This was not a woman to trifle with. *Bandying words now would serve only to gain me greater punishment in the future*, Selyni thought to herself, swallowing her anger. Selyni answered calmly as she was able, saying, "We are two-hundred and fifty miles southwest of Odium. I sighted the Golden Plain just before he lost control. The child seems intact, although there has been a casualty and there are wounded."

Maud raised a single, manicured eyebrow and asked in a deadly whisper, "Are any of mine among the dead? Does Namyr still live?"

Selyni hesitated, knowing that her answer would only anger the woman, but eventually admitted, "The boy has twelve companions, a dwarf, two Titans, a gnome, a lorith and seven humans. Of those that survived, all are injured. One of the Titans and the gnome may not survive." Selyni paused and Maud spun her wand lazily, waiting for her to continue. With a sigh, Selyni added, "Namyr wasn't in the compartment. He rode in the saddle. I haven't located him yet, but I believe he was thrown. If he has survived, then there can be little doubt that he is injured. Hector is dead. I am sorry for your loss, Maud."

Maud's bored expression evaporated as boiling anger crept across her face and she stood stiffly. The woman was dressed in a northern fashion, in a high-necked, flowing gown of the deepest scarlet that billowed outward at her hips. Black-lace clung to the sleeves and corset, and rubies had been stitched in the folds of her skirt. As she stood the precious gems winked in the dim light. In a scathing whisper, she said, "How you Changelings are considered equal members of the Coven is beyond me. You have failed in your mission Selyni, and resoundingly so. We can only hope your brother isn't as much of a disappointment as you have proven." Selyni nodded, knowing that to argue was futile. Maud glared at her for several long moments. Selyni made to speak, but hesitated, her voice catching her in her throat. Maud's dark gaze narrowed and she flickered her wand in an impatient gesture, saying, "Out with it."

Selyni grimaced and in a whisper, she said, "The Ronan child is unstable. During the fall of Inee he lost a companion. They were close..." Selyni gave Maud a weighted look and Maud nodded in consideration. Selyni continued, "I fear that if the child wakes and remembers her death then we shall all perish in his grief. Furthermore, I suspect that he is ignorant of the Ronan and the fact that he is one. We may already be compromised. His power was witnessed by hundreds and word spreads quickly. We may not be able to avoid a confrontation."

Maud took a deep breath and smiled coldly, before saying lightly, "Keep the Ronan child unconscious until you locate Namyr. If he lives, tell him: Vinea creeps most tightly when the wyrm distraughtly cries." Selyni nodded slowly in confusion. She knew the phrase carried a hidden message and ached to know what it meant. Maud continued coldly, "If he is dead, call on me and I will instruct you on what must be done. Tend to the wounded as best as you are able and set up a perimeter. I have your location locked through the mirror. You are beyond the edge of my reach. Travel northeast, and stay away from towns and villages. Once you have reached the southern edge of the Golden Plain I will arrive within twenty-four hours." Selyni's nodded tightly in response. She knew that getting that far on foot would be nigh impossible. Silently, she cursed her weakness, but held her face free of fear.

Selyni felt the hair on the back of her arms raise, as Maud said, "Selyni, any more blunders and I will make you rue the day you ever stepped foot on Ignea. Am I making myself perfectly clear?" Selyni nodded jerkily and fear rippled in the pit of her stomach. Maud's smile grew wider, and brightly, she said, "Good, I am glad we understand one another."

Maud's wand flicked outward and a bolt of black lightning struck the face of the mirror. With a crackle, the image faded and the silver liquid swirled to its restful slumber. Selyni let the mirror fall from her shaking fingers to the sand and clutched her face in her hands as tears fell from her eyes.

Aritian

Chapter Four:

Revelations of a Changeling

Aritian woke sluggishly, his mind clawing through a deep darkness. His tongue rolled thickly through his mouth. *I've been drugged*, he thought groggily. His thoughts were slow, as if rising through sap. The memory of his anger and furious grief struck him then like a scathing sword to the heart. He shook uncontrollably, tears falling down his face. *Razia is gone.* The thought echoed through his mind.

Aritian didn't know how he survived, couldn't understand how he had controlled the flames in Inee, or raised the winds that flung them from the sky. It was as if some beast lived inside him and when his emotions rose it filled him, taking away any semblance of control. Aritian kept his eyes shut, feigning slumber. Desperately, he asked himself, *what am I? What foul power lives within my breast? Am I possessed by some fell demon?* The questions raged through him, fiercer than any storm. Long moments passed before he felt some likeness of control over his fear.

Aritian listened closely to his surroundings, and heard dim voices talking in the distance and the deep breath of someone close by. By the heat that rolled in the air, he knew that they were no longer in Velon. The air was dry and far hotter than he had ever felt before. The ground beneath him was soft. He lay on a thick mat, but the ground beneath was silkier still. *Sand*, Aritian summarized.

Slowly, Aritian cracked open his eyes to two thin slits and glanced around. Lavender silk billowed gently in the dry air above him, and reams of tears dipped and danced as a hot wind played across the fabric. The tent was tall and the center post had been snapped and shoddily repaired with thick coils of rope.

Aritian tilted his head slightly, and saw Beryl. The dwarf wore a green tunic, an onyx studded belt, and dark green trousers. His flaming hair had been cut, and his beard neatly combed. He held an axe in one hand and slowly worked a wetstone across the blade's edge. Without taking his eyes off of the weapon, Beryl asked, "Are ye done pretendin' to sleep, or should I give ye more time to gain ye bearin's?" Aritian's eyes opened fully, but he didn't answer immediately. Beryl whispered, "There is someone here who wants to meet ye, if ye have a mind for such things. The others are in a right fit, waitin for ye to wake."

In a hoarse voice, Aritian asked, "Where are we Beryl? Was there truly a Roc in Inee?"

Beryl flashed him an apologetic eye, before saying vaguely, "Yes and no, to answer ye question pertainin' the Roc. My tongue be too clumsy to explain such wonders..." Beryl's brow creased as he explained, "We were rescued from Inee and have traveled far from that blackened ruin. We be in the Ignis Desert, Aritian." *The Ignis Desert!* Aritian thought in bewilderment. Aritian calculated the distance, cursing his own ignorance as he struggled to remember the world maps he had once seen in Jabari's barracks. His mouth fell open as he began to recall.

Aritian incredulously exclaimed, "The Ignis Desert is more than two months travel south by horseback. It's impossible that we have traveled so far." Aritian had forgotten to whisper. He stood, realizing that he was nude as a silver sheet fell away. Aritian made no move to conceal his nudity. He was a slave; modesty had never been a concern. He touched his neck, unconsciously seeking the smooth feel of metal that had rested there for as long as he could remember. He felt only the smooth skin of his chest. Aritian dropped his hand awkwardly. *A slave no longer*, he thought with astonishment.

Beryl's eyes turned back to the axe, and he rumbled softly, "Ye slept for a full ten days after the fall of Inee before ye first cracked ye eyes and it's been another two since then. I would have named any man a liar, to claim such, but we did not travel by common means."

The tent flap was flung aside. His voice had been heard. Sicaroo burst into the tent, followed closely by the rest of the Dranguis. The boys had been dressed in a motley of mismatched collection of fine silk and leather, and most of the clothing was overly large on their thin frames. The boys wore beaming smiles as their eyes fell upon him, and as one, they bowed.

Aritian felt his heart soar at the sight of them and a smile tugged on his lips. "I'm glad to see that you all are well. How did you make it out of Inee?" The question bubbled forth unrestrained from Aritian's mouth as he struggled to grasp his bearings.

Sicaroo clapped his hands and said excitedly, "We fled Inee on a great eagle, who is also a woman! She's wonderful Aritian, you must meet her!" Aritian smiled at his exuberance, but was confused by his words. He flashed Beryl an incredulous glance, but the dwarf simply shrugged. Beryl flashed Sicaroo a pointed glare that silenced the boy, but did little to quell his excitement. Sicaroo bounced on the balls of his feet with boisterous energy. Aritian saw that the young boy's tanned skin was touched with sun and his prominent cheeks were painted a cherry red.

Beryl spoke quietly, "Perhaps it would be best if we gave ye some privacy." He pointed to a large chest that sat next to a low table, and said, "There are clothes within. Once ye are decent, ye can come outside and meet the eagle that is not an eagle, but also a woman." Aritian cocked his head in question and Beryl concluded with, "As this younglin' so elegantly stated, she eagerly awaits meetin' ye. It is she, who ye should look to for explanation."

Aritian nodded and Sicaroo bounded out of the tent followed by his excited companions. Aritian heard them shouting, "He's coming. He's comes! I told you he'd want to meet you."

Aritian hesitantly asked, "Did Azera and Ori not come? I thought... I think I remember seeing them in the basket, but my memory is so foggy. Beryl what happened?" He was almost too afraid to ask, but his need for answers bested his fear.

Beryl's eyes found the floor and he ground the axe's butt into the sand. With hesitant awkwardness, he slowly explained, "Aye, they are here. We crashed Aritian. I don't know how or why...." The dwarf bustled to the tents entrance, and paused. Bright light spilled eagerly into the tent as he held the tent flap open. Without turning to look at him, Beryl said, "Ye have changed, me' friend. Ye saved us Aritian, be knowin' that." Aritian eyes narrowed. He could tell Beryl was close to tears. The dwarf's voice had grew thick with emotion as he continued, "Maybe ye have always been this way." He paused and Aritian knew he wanted to say more on the subject, but couldn't bring himself to. "Dress. There's a mirror in the trunk." With that, Beryl walked through the flap and the harsh light that had spilled through the entrance of the tent fell to muted lilac.

Aritian walked to the chest. It was large and made from soft, grey wood. The top was carved intricately with a striking collection of animals, each lovingly detailed. Aritian lifted the lid and found a collection of folded silk. A silver mirror rested on top.

Aritian lifted the small mirror by its thin stem, and nearly dropped it when he saw his reflection. The most jarring change was his lack of hair. Aritian surmised that it must have all burned off in the white flames that had surrounded him. He touched his newly bald jaw and found it to be rough with short, dark stumble. His light-gold skin gleamed in the dim light of the tent. *The fires had done more than scour the hair from my skin*, he thought in wonder. It seemed that all his physical imperfections had been burned away. There wasn't a scar, callus, or mar on his body.

Aritian hurriedly turned his head to the side and saw that the Dranguis brand had vanished. Relief flooded him, as he saw smooth skin. A weight lifted from his shoulders that he had not known he carried. Aritian stood straighter and in shock, realized that for the first time in his life that he felt worthy. The emotion was so foreign that he giddily laughed. The brand had represented his Master's claim and marked him as nothing more than property. For the brand to be gone, as if it had never been, brought tears to his eyes. Hurriedly, he wiped them away only to notice that his grey eyes were now pigmented with tiny flecks of ruby — only noticeable if you looked closely, but Aritian decided he was fond of the bold color.

Aritian dressed in the first clothes he found. He slipped a sky-blue tunic over his head and pulled on a pair of cream colored breeches; baggy in the style of southern nobility. Aritian quickly clenched the gold drawstrings at each of his ankles and then at his waist. He then tried on two pairs of shoes that rested in a corner of the chest. The first, a simple leather sandal was too small, but the second pair he tried fit well. They were styled in a richer taste then he was comfortable with. The silver slippers were pointed at the toe and the ties ended with small gold bells that tinkled softly as he moved. Aritian looked in the mirror, fearing that he would look ridiculous in such rich dressings, but found that he didn't look as foolish as he had feared. Aritian shrugged and dropped the mirror onto the pile of clothing.

Aritian brushed aside the tent flap and looked around. Wonder made his steps falter. The land beyond was breathtaking. The Ignis Desert, the largest desert in all of Ignea, spread before him like an arid sea, rising and falling in soft waves of sand. The sky was a brilliant blue and the sun sat at its zenith in the sky. The land was stark, but astounding in its raw beauty. Aritian inhaled the dry air, taking his first breaths as a free man and smiled.

Aritian tore his eyes from the sloping horizon. Their camp was situated on a tall dune and opposite him stood a tent of brilliant, azure silk. This tent had fared better in the crash and stood unmarred before the remnants of the basket Aritian had seen strapped to the Roc, little more than a heap of kindling now. The weave had burst at the bottom, the wood had fractured and sand spilled from its broken maw. Two posts protruded from the ground a dozen feet away from the site with a tattered, yellow canvas stretched between them to create a shaded awning.

A green carpet was spread beneath the awning and Aritian walked toward it, shading his eyes with a hand. Sand slipped beneath his footfalls and he felt the gritty texture fill the bottom of his shoes. He paused before entering.

His companions sat among large pillows that had been piled high in a circle. Rythsar was the first to notice him, and bowed his thorny head in greeting. Their hushed conversations soon fell quiet as they noticed him. Across the awning, languishing against a large pillow, sat a pale young woman in a sleeveless, blue silk dress. Her golden hair sparkled with pale streaks of silver and she wore a warm smile, but despite her breathtaking beauty Aritian found himself frowning in response.

Namyr sat cross-legged at her side. He wore a sheer, navy-blue silk robe, with a golden belt that hugged his hips, and black slippers the curled at the toe. He bit into a peeled orange with his sharp teeth, lazily eying Aritian. "Why in the name of Ignathra is he here?" Aritian asked bluntly.

The woman's voice was light and pleasant, as she said, "Please sit, Aritian. Be at ease, all is well." She gestured to an empty pillow next to Sicaroo.

Angrily, Aritian said, "I won't be at ease until that man's

head is freed from his shoulders." Namyr dropped the orange and raised his hands in feigned fear, his eyes dancing with laughter. Aritian felt power bubble toward the surface of his mind and the whites of his eyes began to swirl black. It was like rising emotion, churning through him with a physical reaction and like a fire catching spark, the power crackled awake.

"Enough!" The woman shouted as she stood. The woman's pale-blue eyes met his own, unflinchingly. She waved a hand elegantly toward the empty pillow once more and Aritian sat with a grimace. The power within faded as he sat.

Emphatically, the woman said, "I can understand and sympathize with your frustration toward Namyr, but you must know that everything Namyr has done has been at the command of his Mistress." Aritian made to raise an eyebrow in question, only to realize that he lacked any. The woman continued pointedly, "If you wish to place blame at someone's feet, then lay it at mine or at his mistress, but not him. Namyr has been nothing but a faithful servant." Namyr's face took on a mask of mock innocence and he smiled sweetly at Aritian, batting his long, dark eyelashes. The young Dranguis looked from Aritian to Namyr anxiously, but Aritian's eyes were locked on the woman before him.

Bluntly, Aritian asked, "Why?" Before she could so much as open her mouth he demanded, "Explain everything now, before I lose my patience."

Beryl placed a thick hand on his shoulder, imploring him wordlessly to calm down. The eyes of his companions flashed between Aritian and the woman as the tension rose between them, but she simply continued smiling gently in response to his anger.

Calmly, she introduced herself with, "My name is Selyni Ronan." Aritian's eyes narrowed, remembering vision of the woman who had appeared in his mind through a doorway of white fire.

Aritian spoke before she could continue, "You're a

magus." It wasn't a question, but a statement. Selyni nodded, although she cocked her head in bemused confusion.

Curiously, Selyni queried, "How is it that you know of the Ronan Magi?"

Aritian shook his head no, and said darkly, "You explain first and then I will decide if I wish to tell you."

Beryl laughed gruffly and said, "Boy's sharp Selyni, I warned ye." The dwarf sipped wine from a silver goblet, seemingly enjoying the exchange.

Selyni nodded her head toward the dwarf with a small smile, and said, "Very well, I will explain as fully as I am able. While I do so, I ask that you please hold your questions, and after I will try to answer any you have as succinctly as possible." She looked around, clearly indicating that she expected silence from them all. To his surprise, his companions nodded in agreement. When her eyes found his, Aritian nodded once in acquiesce.

Selyni adopted a formal voice. "Before the Dawn of Adonim, our world was darkened by the shadow of chaos. Humanity was little more than animals, and the elves were nothing more than wild roaming clans; a far cry from their modern, haughty elegance." At her casual mention of elves, Aritian flashed Beryl an incredulous look, but Beryl stared at Selyni entranced. "Many things were born in this time, as Adonim was forged into a land of life. Among those born first were the Ronan."

Selyni's brow scrunched as she considered the proper words. Her tone became dangerously close to what one might use when speaking to a child as she carefully elaborated, "First you must understand that our world is connected to other realms. These realms are the places where gods walk and places that, in humanity's limited understanding, are known as the heavens and hells." Aritian cocked his head, at her continued use of the word humanity. *It's almost as if she doesn't consider herself human*, Aritian thought, perturbed. "For the purpose of your immediate acceptance I will leave that lesson to rest for the time being. I'm sure you're eager to understand why this pertains to you." Aritian nodded, although he couldn't imagine what explanation she could give. The air was heavy beneath the ragged awning, for the woman spoke of dangerous things that challenged more than one religion.

Selyni lightly sipped her wine, before saying, "There is a power that ties all things together. Every culture has their own name for it... Han, the craft, dweomer, but it is most commonly known as magic. Its true name is Magrados." At this Rythsar straightened, his yellow eyes flashing with anger. "It's the lifeblood that flows through Adonim and every living creature, and connects us to one another and to the very gods themselves." Beryl nodded in acceptance of her words. Aritian caught Rythsar's eye, and saw that the lorith looked as skeptical as he felt.

Selyni seemed unabashed by the varied expression before her, and her gaze fell upon him then. Her eyes were startlingly pale, and it almost looked as if he stared into two chips of ice. When she spoke, she emphasized her words as if to express that she spoke a truth that was undeniable. "We, Aritian, are Ronan. We are creatures of Magrados made flesh. Born in the age of darkness, it was the Ronan who brought humanity through the Dawn. It is the very reason why humanity survived the chaos, while so many other races perished. We Ronan are able to influence the Magrados within us and around us, to channel it in ways beyond imagination." Her back straightened with pride and she exuded confidence that belied the impossibility of her words.

Aritian made to speak, but she raised her hand begging for patience. She continued, "The flame of our Coven is immortal: if one falls then another rises, and thus twenty-one walk the lands of Adonim at all times. You were born with this power." Selyni flicked her pale eyes toward Rythsar, before saying slowly, "It cannot be gifted or wished away, and was not bequeathed by any god." Her eyes flicked back to Aritian, and she said, "It usually lays dormant until maturity, although this varies from Ronan to Ronan. It can be brought forth earlier in severe circumstances."

Aritian frowned at this. He had been in extreme conditions before and he had never felt power like he had the night Shu set Inee aflame. Memories of his life flashed before his eyes. He recounted the countless beatings he had received while training in the Dranguis Guild and the scars he had gained when Tooru had brutally whipped him. The memory of the scathing bite of the drake's venom filled his mind and was joined by the desperation he had felt in Ignathra's shadow prison and the darkness of the mine shaft. Slowly, he shook his head in denial. *No, she is wrong*, he thought silently.

Selyni pushed on, "Namyr is an agent of one of the Ancients who have lived in Ignea for many hundreds of years." *Hundreds?* Aritian thought, *surely this woman is touched*. "She has searched for you long before you were even born. We are creatures of magic and often times, for reasons unknown, we find ourselves at the mercy of fate more so than others. You were lost." Selyni smiled, and shrugged easily. "Why? We cannot know." Aritian remembered the woman who had appeared to him from a doorway of white fire, and her words of promised destiny rang through his thoughts like a bell. Selyni continued, musing, "Perhaps you were destined to go through what you have, so that you might become the Ronan that Magrados needed."

How convenient, Aritian thought bitterly. He watched a slow smile spread across Selyni's face. *Are you listening to my thoughts?* Aritian thought staring at her, but the Ronan made no reply. The question echoed through his mind. It was a disturbing thought.

Selyni waved elegantly to Namyr at her side, as she said, "Namyr has suspected you of being a Ronan for some time, but without evidence could do nothing but watch vigilantly. We don't usually Awaken in such a volatile way, but perhaps that was a product of your childhood." Aritian rolled his eyes at her simplistic view of what she casually called childhood. "Now that you've been found, you must come with us. The powers you hold can be unpredictable and proper control must be learned. I will take you to the Ancient One and she will be your teacher."

Aritian blurted the first words that came to his mind, "You're insane."

Selyni smiled in reply and Aritian barked on, "I don't know how much Ebris smoke you've inhaled over the years, but this is nothing more than a pipe dream. Only the gods have such power. No man can do what I have done. You saw the fire as well as I, we were saved by the grace of Ignathra." Aritian looked at his companions for support. They eyed the carpet, not meeting his skeptical gaze. In disbelief, Aritian asked, "Surely you all don't believe this farce?"

Beryl's gaze rose from the ground and he looked at him pleadingly. Bluntly and desperately, he said, "Aritian, ye' held off that fuckin' hellfire inferno. Ye' saved us, boy. Certainly, ye' can see why this woman's words be makin' sense?" Beryl asked, his voice now soft. Aritian could hear the gratitude in his voice; mentally, Aritian recoiled. He had not intended to do anything. It had just happened.

Rythsar spoke in a low reverent hiss, before Aritian could reply, "Something transpired Aritian. That is undeniable. We would be ashes if it were not for you. I, like you, believe this to be a gift given by Ignathra. You are blessed Aritian, by His very flame." Rythsar's long neck curled in a bow and his tail flicked against the ground.

Selyni rolled her eyes at Rythsar's words, and leaned forward, asking, "You were plagued with terrible headaches for many months before that night, weren't you?" Aritian's head snapped up. Insistently, Selyni explained, "That was the cortex of your power struggling to wake itself from dormancy. It happens to all Ronan."

Aritian shook his head, denying the truth of her words. With a voice filled with quiet doubt, he asked, "What if it wasn't me? Ignathra was called upon by Shu, perhaps through me, He stilled her rage and spared us all."

Rythsar nodded slowly to himself and hissed, "He who commands the flames is surely a son of Ignathra. A child was promised."

Selyni shook her head warningly at the lorith and Rythsar growled low in his throat. Aritian had a feeling they had argued this point before. Selyni chided the lorith, "No Rythsar, I know it must seem like a prophesy of your people has come to life, but Aritian is a Ronan. What that means for your people's prophesy I do not know, but he is firstly and foremost a magus." Aritian saw Rythsar's lips curl in anger and she splayed her hands peacefully, adding, "I am not denying the possibility that he fulfills both roles, but for now... for Aritian's sake, at the very least, we must concentrate on one matter at a time."

Rythsar's conceded to her with silence, but Aritian could tell by the lorith's pinning eyes that he was not pleased.

Selyni turned back to Aritian and asked, "Can you feel the power within you still? I know you can. You nearly unleashed it when you saw Namyr." Aritian felt himself nodding yes, even though he felt that by doing so he was admitting to something he didn't fully believe possible. Selyni's face became grave, a strange expression for one of such beauty and one Aritian struggled to take seriously. Her words however, were anything but light. "You must try to remain calm until we reach the Ancient One. I do not have the power to contain your power. If you lose control, it could have devastating consequences." A sobering silence fell over those within the awning.

"How was I able, to do..." Aritian asked tentatively, struggling to put words to what had happened in Inee.

Selyni expression softened, and with sympathy she said "Acceptance will come with time, Aritian. I understand that this is all new for you." She leaned forward and explained gently, "When you underwent the Awakening your life was in mortal peril. Your unconscious mind innately knows your power and so it momentarily dominated your actions. You are not some hedge witch that must study all their life to do the most simplistic spells, nor an elementalist that must make offerings decade after decade to grow the spirit within. You are Magrados made flesh. You are magic. In short, fate would not be denied." She concluded, pushing her long hair over her shoulders.

Aritian considered her words. He didn't know what to believe. Everything the woman said seemed to be spoken genuinely, but the power he felt, he knew, was that of a god. Worry filled him suddenly, and he asked, "What happened to the others? Those who shared the observatory with us? Where is Azera and Ori? Trilithi and Nyox? Did they survive?" Realization dawned and a fearful thought fell from his mouth before he could consider it. "What did I do to Shu?"

Namyr rolled his shoulders with feline grace and replied cheerfully, "You burned her face to char. A fate most deserved if you asked me." Namyr chuckled at Aritian's horrified expression and added, "But do not fear; Selyni did not allow her to die."

Selyni shot Namyr an annoyed glare, before clarifying with, "What happened to Shu is an example of why it's important for you restrain your emotions." Her eyes fell to the carpet then, and her voice grew serious, as she said, "I tended Shu's wounds before we left. She will recover in time, but will forever carry the scar of your touch."

Rythsar spoke in a quiet string of hisses, "Trilithi, Nyox, and the other slaves who witnessed survived. The slaves were freed, allowed to leave the city. Trilithi and Nyox returned to our homeland with the retreating Horde. They carry word of your ascension to our people." Aritian studied the lorith's serious expression with confusion, not understanding what he meant.

Selyni pursed her lips and in a near whisper, said, "Yes, an unforeseen problem that must be faced another day." After a moment, she said, "Azera and Ori wait within the tent there," She waved to the blue tent, and said, "We have spoken for some time now and must make haste. The monsoon chases us south, and the road ahead is long." Selyni stood and stretched, before waving a hand to Beryl, saying, "If you would, please break down the camp and pack what provisions you may. Sicaroo, Bo, Hui, Mingyo, Rong, Shan, Yi," she gazed sweetly at the young boys and requested, "If you would, could you please aid him?" The young Dranguis nodded enthusiastically in response. Beryl stood and walked toward the tent that Aritian had woken in, and the Dranguis danced behind him cheerfully bombarding the dwarf with questions.

Selyni gave the lorith a nod of respect, before asking, "Rythsar, would you take Aritian to Azera and Ori, and then see to it that he has eaten and drank his fill?" The witch spoke with the easy air of command of someone used to getting their way. She turned to Aritian and touched his arm lightly, saying, "I am sure you are famished."

Rythsar stood, gracefully uncoiling. Aritian saw that his tail was bandaged with thick silk. Aritian eyed it worriedly, but the lorith waved away his concern, as he flicked his tail to the side. He led Aritian to the blue tent silently. Aritian followed in somewhat of a daze, his mind a tumultuous, spinning-tumble of thoughts. When they entered the tent Aritian was surprised to find a large spread of provisions displayed on a long, low table. He saw bowls of fresh fruit, white rice, and elegant, glass pitchers filled with cool water and dark wine. The table hunched along the left side of the room, while a partition of black silk lined the right side and back of the tent.

Aritian walked to the table as hunger suddenly clenched his stomach with a rolling growl. Aritian grabbed a bowl of rice, a blue-stained pitcher of water, and a large bowl filled with berries, grapes, and peeled oranges. Rythsar sat on one of the low pallets that lay on the ground before the table and Aritian joined him, chugging half the pitcher of water before eating with gusto.

Aritian's confused thoughts disappeared as he filled his stomach. He popped a blackberry in his mouth, the tart fruit cleansing and bright. Once sated, he asked, "Where did they get the provisions?" He looked down at the rich clothing he wore and pulled at the silk shirt as he asked, "How did they know to bring such finery?" Aritian eyed the rich surroundings of the elegant tent, and added somewhat tersely, "Coin seems to be of little concern to these people."

Rythsar nodded in agreement and responded in a low whispering hiss, "Namyr reported back to his Mistress often and thoroughly. Selyni claims that they wished to be as accommodating to your needs as possible, and from Namyr's reports, thought it unlikely that you would accompany them alone."

Aritian nodded, and said genuinely, "I am glad that you are here." The lorith dipped his head. Aritian observed that Rythsar's titian scales gleamed as if they had been polished. The dead scales that had clung to the lorith's scarring had peeled away, revealing brighter, newer scales.

Aritian hesitated a moment, considering, then asked in a low whisper, "What do you think of Selyni and all of this? Do you truly think Ignathra has blessed me?"

Rythsar's eyes remained fixed on the ground as he whispered, voice trailing, "Selyni frightens me."

Aritian looked at the lorith, perplexed. Selyni seemed nothing more than a young noblewoman, not someone you would fear. He then remembered her voice in his head and the power she had exhibited when grappling with him. He nodded slowly in agreement. Rythsar made to continue, but gold light spilled into the tent as the flap was pushed aside.

Namyr walked into the tent and with drollness, said, "As she should." Namyr plucked a grape from the table and popped into his mouth, smiling teasingly.

Aritian stood and ignoring the young man's sarcastic words, asked, "Selyni said you suspected me of being a Ronan for a long time. How did you come to have such suspicions?"

Namyr leaned against the table and opened a small black pouch that was tied to his belt. "Because of this." Namyr pulled a small, dark glass orb from its depths. Aritian eyed it warily, and stepped back in shock as the orb begin to swirl with inner light. The dark cinnabar liquid within was illuminated by a light that pulsated with growing brightness. Namyr stepped closer and the pulsating quickened, much like a heartbeat that had begun to race.

Guardedly, Aritian asked, "What in the nine hells is that?" Aritian took another step back and the orb's pulsating slowed.

Namyr's smile broadened as he explained, "There are only six realms that might be considered hell, but this is called a Sanguis Stone. My Mistress gave it to me before I departed. The blood within calls to its own." Namyr's bright eyes flicked from the orb to meet Aritian's mystified gaze. Namyr continued, his voice growing serious as he said, "You share the blood of my Mistress. She sacrificed much in this stone's creation, but it has proved most useful." Namyr held the stone out to him and apprehensively Aritian reached for it. Namyr dropped it into his open palm.

The stone was small, no larger than a marble. Its surface was smooth and cool to the touch. Aritian watched as the light pulsed in his palm. The rate had intensified as it came in contact with his skin, and raced faster than a terrified heart. Slowly, it began to grow warm and the beat became erratic and frenetic. Aritian raised the stone closer to his face, studying the swirling liquid that danced in waves, crashing in on themselves with each beat of light.

With a final flash, the Sanguis Stone shattered in his hand. Rythsar let out a startled yelp and Aritian jerked his head back in surprise, blinking his eyes as the harsh light faded.

Aritian looked down at his hand and saw that only dull, red dust remained in his palm. Aritian met Namyr's eyes and the youth smiled toothily as he murmured with triumph, "Now your identity has been confirmed and my Mistress notified."

Aritian glared at Namyr as he brushed the dust from his palm onto his silken trousers. Aritian took a step towards his companion, but light blared through the tent as the flap was pushed open once more. Beryl entered and said gruffly, "Let us attend Azera now." As he eyed the two of them facing off, he muttered under his breath, "And let us be quick about it before blood is spilt."

Aritian nodded, and Rythsar led him through the black partition that lined the right side of the tent. Azera sat in the dark, and turned to face Aritian as he entered. Her black eyes were rimmed with tears and her expression tightened as she caught sight of him. Laying at her knee was Ori. The young Titan's face was pale, almost milky white, and wet with sweat. Ori lay unmoving on a litter that had been constructed from wood scraps and ropes crossed his chest securing him in place.

Aritian fell to his knees. His mind had gone blank, but as he caught Azera's angry glare, he knew that he was responsible. He stuttered, "What... what happened to him?"

In a growl, Azera spat out, "You did. With the winds you called, you flung us from the sky like sparrows in a hurricane. We were thrown against the sand like glass upon stone." She strangled a cry in her throat, before choking out, "Selyni says his back is broken. Ori may not survive it."

Aritian shook his head as tears fell down his face. There had been too much death, too much taken from him. In a moaned, he protested, "No... this cannot be. I'm sorry. So sorry."

Azera shook with anger, and with venom, she retorted, "Keep your apologies to yourself you foul-tongued witch. Stay away." Aritian blinked slowly, struck dumb by her cruel words. Azera lunged toward him as she roared, "Stay away from us!"

What have I done? Aritian thought with despair. The power within boiled as he was consumed by guilt and grief. Aritian let the magic rise dangerously, uncaring as it roared toward the surface. Instinctually, he knew if he released all the power at once it would consume him utterly as easily as a flame consumes a moth, but Aritian was beyond grief. He couldn't control his emotions any more than he could control the insidious power that harbored in the deepest part of his being.

This power isn't a blessing from Ignathra, but a curse, Aritian thought desperately. *Burn then, poisonous river, smite my soul,* Aritian whispered to it in his mind. Magic rippled through him and Aritian's back arched as it rose. He could hear voices shouting at him, but could not distinguish the words. The beast within ruled him. Hungrily, Magrados surged toward the surface. Aritian smiled with relief as the edges of his eyes burned and darkness began to crawl forth.

Aritian screamed as his right pinky finger suddenly burned and a bolt of fire raced up his arm. The bolt struck the rising power and rendered it impotent; like a cowed dog his power retreated to the core of his being. Aritian looked down at his hand in confusion. Resting on his pinky finger was a simple, white-gold ring. The skin beneath the ring burned red-hot and was blistered, but the metal was cool against his skin. Aritian's breath came raggedly. His skull throbbed fiercely and it was as if iron bands were being tightened against his mind, squeezing without mercy. Shakily, he collapsed to the ground. Azera stared at him open mouthed, but her anger had been replaced by fear.

Namyr crouched next to him and in a low whisper, said, "Now, now, dear Ronan babe, there will be none of that." Namyr rolled the ring around Aritian finger with a light touch, and said, "This is what we call a Ring of Suppression, and with it round your finger you shall not escape this world so easily. Do not think to pry it from your finger either, for the pain will be so terrible you will be lucky if it doesn't drive you mad." Namyr straightened and pronounced loudly, "No one is in any danger from being near Aritian. He cannot use his power until my Mistress releases him." Namyr chuckled gleefully, before adding, "But Aritian, do feel free to let your emotions rage should you have the masochism desire to feel the ring's ire."

Beryl leaned down and helped Aritian to a sitting position. The dwarf glared at Azera, and said, "Azera stop, ye' anger is pointless and serves us naught. Ye' angry at the storm within him, not Aritian himself. If ye' wantin ye' brother to live we must make haste. Selyni has promised the boy has a chance now, but only if we reach the Ancient One in time. Focus ye' anger on gettin ye' ass movin, bloody brute."

Azera snorted, but made no other response. She did not look at Aritian; could not. She stood and bent to grip the ropes that were tied to the front of the litter. With a grunt, she dragged the litter from the tent, her powerful arms bulging as she strained against her brother's weight.

Beryl gripped Aritian by his elbow and pulled him to his feet. Aritian felt weak. His limbs shook and he tasted bile in his throat. He looked down at the ring and relieved, thought, *I can't hurt anyone.* A wave of euphoria settled over him as he realized the danger would be contained. The pain, while hideous, was no less than he deserved.

Rythsar stepped forward and steadied Aritian with an arm around his back. In a hiss, he said, "Beryl, call the human boys and finish packing this tent." The dwarf nodded. In a muted hiss, Rythsar asked, "Are you ok?" Aritian nodded jerkily. Rythsar lunged his neck toward Namyr and snapped his jaws. In a low voice, he warned, "To bind a god's power is folly. You should not have done this, Namyr." With Rythsar's help Aritian stumbled past the partition toward the exit.

Namyr replied lazily, "Your precious Spark would be dead, along with the rest of us had I not. Keep your forked-tongue still lizard, lest I hew it from your jaws." Rythsar stopped in his tracks and faced Namyr with a threatening hiss.

Beryl stepped between them, raising a hand toward either

one of them. In stern voice, he said, "Now lads, none of that. Just go in peace." Namyr and Rythsar stood staring at one another with deadly intent.

Namyr was the first to drop his gaze. He laughed lightly and bowed with a flair, before saying, "Yes dwarven Lord, as you wish. I will collect my slave and be out of your way." Beryl gave him a nod. Rythsar pulled back the tent flap, but Aritian ground his feet into the sand at the threshold. Rythsar cocked his thorny head at Aritian in question, but remained silent.

Namyr disappeared behind the silk partition once more as Beryl walked through the entrance, and barked orders to the young assassins. Namyr returned shortly, holding a length of gold chain in one hand. He jerked it lightly, pulling the gnome from behind the shaded silk. Aritian recognized it as the creature that had been in Shu's company. It blinked its large, black eyes owlishly as it was dragged into the bright light. It limped heavily as it walked. Its right leg had been splinted and was wrapped from ankle to thigh with thick canvas.

Namyr made to pass him, but Aritian stopped the man with a hand to his chest. Namyr looked up at him with slight surprise, and Aritian asked darkly, "Why are you keeping this gnome as your slave?"

Namyr shrugged nonchalantly, and said, "Gnomes are rare creatures known for their intelligence. My Mistress has few in her employee and I thought to gift him to her." Namyr yanked the chain forward and the creature was forced a step closer. It gripped the gold collar that circled its neck with its pale hands, desperately trying not to choke as it's dark eyes bulged and watered with pain.

Aritian's voice took on a dangerous edge as he uttered, "No." Sudden anger thrumming through him. Aritian felt himself begin to shake and Rythsar dropped his supporting hand, stepping back. The gnome eyed him with dumbstruck fear and raised a hand as if to shield itself from him.

Aritian felt his pinky began to burn, but he reached out

and touched the gold collar the creature wore. The gold chain and collar shattered outward, exploding in small shards that cut through the silk partition. Glass pitchers and platters exploded into fine dust, pelting them with sharp bites. Namyr shrieked in surprised and pain. Aritian closed his eyes, breathing rhythmically, slowly controlling the rage that swirled through him, before releasing a shaking breath.

Namyr frowned, and with dismay said, "You should not be able to do that." He took a hesitant step back, as if he feared Aritian that would attack anew, and true fear filled the man's eyes. Aritian's smile was tight. The heat of the ring cooled instantly as echoes of pain thrummed along his hand and shot up his wrist, making his arm go numb.

After a moment of silence Aritian stepped forward, and took the gnomes small hand in his own. The gnome looked up at him with disbelief. Aritian walked from the tent, dragging the limping gnome behind him. Rythsar and Namyr followed nervously behind.

Selyni stood at the far side of the dune and waved for him to join her. When Aritian reached her side, she was intently eying the dunes on the horizon. She murmured, "It's a pity, but we must travel over land now. I cannot make such a drastic change as the Roc so soon." She held out an arm without looking at him. The limb trembled as though the effort of holding it up was nearly beyond her strength, and Aritian saw bruising, black and purple, crawl across her pale skin from wrist to shoulder.

Aritian shook his head, perturbed, and asked, "What do you mean when you say, change into the Roc?"

A smile played across her pale pink lips, as she said, "You didn't think we rode a wild Roc, did you?" She looked at him out the corner of her eye and laughed. The sound was light and lilting. Aritian didn't know what to think. He hadn't known if the Roc had been a dream or real, let alone considered if it was wild or not. Selyni explained in a low voice, "Wild Roc are not so large nor able to carry the weight I can while in that form. Roc are quite difficult to control, and there is only one among the Coven who has succeeded at taming one." Selyni faced him, her light blonde hair danced in the playful warm wind. "I am a Changeling, Aritian. I can change my shape at will to any beast I've ever come in contact with."

Aritian turned away from her open gaze and looked out at the rolling waves of sand. To know one in particular, he asked, "How is that possible?"

Namyr answered in a tone that suggested he was speaking to a daft idiot. "She's Ronan, that's how. It's a rare gift, even among your kin. Selyni and her twin are the only ones in the Coven who have the talent." Namyr laughed at Aritian's befuddled expression.

Aritian tore his eyes from the desert and looked to Namyr as the youth stepped to his side. In a dulled voice, he commanded, "There will be no slaves, Namyr. He is not yours to give."

Namyr eyed the gnome sadly as if he were a spoiled sweet, before saying, "Very well, as you wish." Aritian turned back to Selyni and eyed her hesitantly, as he tried to digest what he had heard, but what his mind refused to accept. Internally, Aritian thought, *I walked the world secure in my naivete for nineteen years, and in a single day all I've known has been thrown aside. Now I find myself wandering into a fable.*

A voice, bright and clear as a bell, responded to his thought. *You haven't stepped into a fable; you've been reborn into one.* Selyni's voice faded from his mind as suddenly as it had come. For a time, Aritian simply stood there, his mind and thoughts frozen, as Ignathra glared down from above.

Selyni stepped away, and stood at the edge of the dune. The skin around her mouth and neck twisted, as muscle and tendons bulged outward. Her jaw elongated and her nose receded to thin slits. Aritian felt his stomach roll at the sight, and the gnome next to him shook like a windblown leaf.

Aritian placed a calming hand on the gnome's trembling shoulder. Selyni's transformation was over as quickly as it began, and soon her skin stopped blurring. She hadn't changed her entire appearance, only her lower face and neck. It appeared as if she had the mouth of a large, predatory cat. Her neck had thickened and along her throat, two vented slits had appeared. She looked over her shoulder, her azuline eyes dancing with delight as she purred low in her throat.

Aritian could not wrench his gaze from Selyni's face. His heart thundered in his chest, both with excitement and fear. The air was tinged with a metallic scent. Mirthfully, Namyr said, "She's laughing at you, you know?"

Selyni turned back to face the horizon. She tilted her head to the sky and called out in a series of loud, sharp barks that echoed across the desert.

Aritian looked at Namyr, and asked, "What is she doing."

Namyr laughed with wicked excitement, and said jauntily, "Calling our mounts, of course." Aritian turned back to the desert, his eyes scanning it for signs of life. He saw nothing. There was no movement, but the lethargic current of sand. Long minutes passed. Selyni called twice more and still the desert remained barren. Aritian turned to question Namyr, but the man pointed to the southeast. Aritian looked to where Namyr pointed and saw that between two dunes a trail of dust fled into the sky.

Aritian leaned forward, his eyes narrowing as he peered. The mounts appeared then, fleeing from between the mounds of sand. Aritian counted as they raced across a mile of land within a handful of seconds and saw that there were more than twenty of the creatures. They were feline in nature, but far bigger than any cat of the jungle. They had long bodies, tan skin that lacked fur, and had pronounced, thick chests. With their elongated jaws, hollow cheeks, and vented throats they were fearsome creatures. Whipcord-like tails whipped side to side as they ran, keeping balance. Selyni barked to them once more and they redoubled their speed, racing up the dune toward them. She called to them again and they stopped before her in a cloud of thrown sand. The gnome clutched at Aritian's arm fearfully. The cats stood six-feet in height at the shoulder and were easily double that in length. Their limbs were long and lean, and their hips narrow. Selyni barked a series of calls and the cats laid in the sand at her feet.

Aritian stuttered, "What manner of creatures do my eyes lay upon?"

Namyr chuckled, clapping his hands in appreciation, and joyfully called, "The Feligni, of course!" Aritian eyed the Feligni. He had never heard of these creatures. The Feligni's chests heaved with exertion, but the pride was at ease. Several rolled onto their backs, while others merely lounged in the sun. Their large amber eyes glowed with intelligence as they eyed the people before them with bored disregard.

Selyni turned, her face blurring as she did. Aritian heard bones snap and she hunched over, crying out as her face transformed back to normal. With her hands on her knees she met Aritian's gaze, and said, "Our mounts, Lord Aritian, have arrived." She smiled with satisfaction as she stood straight, and said, "Fear not, they shall not harm us." Aritian stared at her, and then the Feligni, and then back again in dumbfounded amazement.

Caethe

Chapter Five:

Judgment of the Celestial Crown

Arkyn led Caethe between two towering trees and they found themselves standing at the mouth of a sloping, green valley. Knee-high grass glistened with bright dew making the rolling hills sparkle as if dappled with precious gemstones. A mild breeze played across the field, making the grass bend and wave in greeting. Caethe eyed the valley in awe. Bright, golden light filled the air with rich, buoyant joy. A mile away, a ring of nine grey stones stood on a sweeping hill.

Arkyn waved toward the stones as he stepped among the long grass, and said, "A Celestial Crown marks our origin. We came to Avalon upon ships of starlight and this is the gate where we stepped through. It is a hallowed place." His voice softened, as he looked at the ring of stones with yearning. "It is a place of remembrance; a symbol of hope." His golden gaze fell upon Caethe as his words trailed away. Caethe could feel the longing within the Fae. It called to him, bore into his soul with need. Arkyn desperately wanted him to be their salvation. Caethe could feel that and smirked, thinking, *I shall be a hero among the Fae.* Arkyn turned away, and said, "Come, the forest has sung of your coming and the High Seelie Court awaits us."

They walked to the Celestial Crown leisurely. Caethe knew better then to try and rush the Fae. Time was paramount, but in this case, respect was more so. The stones were huge and dwarfed them both in shadow. The smallest stood thirty-feet wide and the largest ninety. All stood a varying heights, from the shortest at twenty-feet and tallest at sixty. Aritian studied the stones with curiosity. They were veined with a metallic, gold shimmer that crawled across the stones in miniscule streams. When he passed close, the veins of minerals writhed as if excited by his presence. Caethe smiled, recognizing the stone and their reaction. He ached to reach out and touch the rough surface, but resisted the impulse.

As he stepped inside the circle of stones he bowed low before the arrayed Seelie that stood along the edges of the circle. The center of the stones was clear of grass, and the ground was hard and bare. There was more than fifty gathered and, like Arkyn, they stood unadorned, lacking any decoration or clothing. However, they did not all appear in a form similar to Arkyn.

The majority shared his pale fur and deer-like ears, but a handful stood together that shared wide-set, blue eyes, and more delicate features. They were shorter than Arkyn's kin, standing at six feet in height and had an equine-like tail. They seemed to glow with an inner silvery-light, and had coats that came in an array of colors from ruby, to the palest shade of pink and argent, to the deepest auburn and the darkest, midnight black. Just above their eyes, sprouting from their foreheads, was a horn that glowed and shimmered like pearl. They were lean creatures, but muscle rippled beneath their skin. From the knee down their legs were horse-like, though more slender, and they stood on black hooves.

The third variation of Elder Fae were feathered with a golden plumage. They were short, no more than five feet in height, and had bodies covered in short, flat feathers, with necks plumed with long, elegantly-thin feathers. Their heads were triangular, their beaks small, and their black eyes wide. They had disproportionately thin legs, and their hands and feet ended in dark talons. All of the Fae were male, save one.

The female stepped forward boldly, her hooves clipping smartly against the hard ground as she approached Caethe. She had a mane of silver hair that fell to her waist and her ankles were tufted with white fur. She appeared neither old nor young, but rather timeless. Her deep, sky-blue eyes held a sparkle of deep memory, one that had witnessed the birth of glaciers and turning of the sea. The Fae waved for him to rise and Caethe straightened. He met her eyes steadily. In a deep voice, she spoke, "You may call me Ekogina. I am of the Unicorn clan. You stand before my kin, the gathered strength of the Divinus Hart and the clan of Sacti'Avem."

Caethe replied respectfully, "I am honored to stand before the illustrious court of the Seelie." He bowed once more, touching one hand to his heart as he did. Ekogina circled him slowly. Caethe was aware of the collective weight that measured him, but he did not falter. He knew he could not.

Ekogina's voice filled the circle of stone and echoed across the hills, as she said, "You come to the shores of Avalon reeking of Igris frost and the corruption of the darker realms. You come with words of poisoned betrayal. You seek our help, promising salvation in return." Caethe met her eyes with surprise and Ekogina smiled. It was a wild smile, one of vigor and exuberance. The air around her was electric, and sparks of energy crackled around her horn, like a thunderstorm threatening to break. Ekogina nodded knowingly, and whispered, "Yes, I can hear the whispers of the forest. I know why you have come."

Caethe nodded his head in deference, and said, "I seek freedom, the same as you."

Ekogina lunged forward so her that face was a mere inch away from his own. Her silver hair shaded his vision so that she dominated his view. Caethe did not flinch away from her aggressive stance, as he ached to do, and instead, by a force of will alone, held his ground. Her breath was hot against his cheek as she whispered, "We have heard your wicked prophecy. Arkyn's thoughts echoed throughout the collective." Ekogina and Caethe stood there, locked in a stare for a full minute. Her gaze was unblinking, as was his own.

Caethe broke the silence, and said calmly, "Then there is no reason for words."

Ekogina smiled cruelly and leaned away from him. In a resonating voice, she pronounced, "We shall see if your soul is as true as the words your tongue has weaved, young Ronan, or if you have spun a wicked tale of deception." The unicorn stomped her left hoof into the ground as if to accentuated her challenge. She galloped to the center of the stones, her silver hair streaming wildly in the wind behind her. The blue sky crackled suddenly with lightning.

The Fae around him leaped into action, dancing forward into the circle of stone as they began to chant. They ran in a dizzying pattern around Ekogina as the sky flashed with a thousand of bolts of cobalt-colored lightning. Caethe did not understand their chanting, for they spoke in the Celestial tongue. Their voices were sharp and booming, full of power and thunder. He closed his eyes briefly. *There is no going back*, he told himself, as fear tickled his mind. He opened his eyes and Arkyn took his hand in his own. The Fae led him to where Ekogina waited. Though the Fae danced wildly, Arkyn led him unerringly, and around them the chanting Fae whirled, flinging themselves first toward him and then bounding away in great leaps. Streams of light chased the Seelie, spilling from their horns, beaks, and halos of light that crowned each of their heads.

Ekogina swayed side to side in the center of the ring of stones, holding her hands above her as her long fingers wove runic patterns. The puffy clouds that floated in the sky rolled and twisted as they spun through arches of lightning. The very air hummed with the strength of the Seelie's might.

The sky suddenly cleared of dazzling luminance and the Fae froze in their dance. Dust rose into the air and hung suspended. Arkyn paused in his approach. His eyes had grown ravenous and wild, as if caught up by the spell. The Seelie around him smiled wide with anticipation, exposing sharp teeth. Caethe looked around, expectantly. Ekogina's head curled in a slow circle as she chanted fervently, and her pale horn pulsated with blinding light. The dust that hung in the air suddenly surged toward the center of the stones like a swarm of bees, and gathered before Ekogina. The dust warped in on itself, and the cloud grew smaller and smaller, until finally it stilled. From the dust that hung in the air, a grey altar had formed at Ekogina's hooves. Arkyn stepped forward, pulling Caethe along. The Fae around them linked hands and began chanting in hushed whispers as they swayed side to side.

The altar of rock twisted violently with veins of shimmering light. Tentatively, Caethe touched the stone. His eyes snapped open, as he felt the potent power within the stone react to his touch. He could not pull his hand away, for his arm had gone numb. The stones influence held him, thrumming through him with intoxicating strength. Ekogina towered over him and threw back her head as she laughed into the sky with manic joy.

Arkyn touched Caethe's shoulder with a gentle finger and his robe's fell away to dust. Caethe laid upon the altar of stone, naked. Ekogina knelt by his side and stroked his cheek tenderly. In a sweet whisper, she promised, "I shall crack a window in the heavens and spill the flames of truth from the Realm of Celestial Fire. This fire is born of starlight, it sees all, knows all. No shadow can hide before it. If it finds you true of heart and consecrates you as Avalon's salvation, you shall live. If it finds you false..." Ekogina smiled inhumanly, pausing dramatically, before singing, "It will burn away your soul to ash." Caethe nodded grimly, his eyes staring into the sky above him. In a low voice, Ekogina said, "The power has awoken. The choice has been made."

Ekogina stood and held her hands above her head. She began to chant in a thunderous voice that echoed across the realm of Avalon. Her voice grew deep as it rolled across the forests, valleys, and hills in a demanding call. Her pale hands grew white with strain as the sky twisted once more and a vortex of searing, blue light was born. Cerulean fire spilled from the sky, gathering, growing larger and larger with every passing second.

The blue fire exploded with a thunderous clap and struck downward. A pillar of flames scorched the air, spinning around the altar. Arkyn and Ekogina stood on the outside of the flaming gyre, watching unblinkingly. Caethe looked up and saw a flash of light fall from the sky. Its blinding light radiated scathing power across all it touched, and Caethe trembled as the light slowly floated to the ground to stand at his feet. Caethe was unable to move beneath the creature's terrible gaze. Its might held him, as surely as his thumb held an ant. The light flashed with piercing brilliance and Caethe screamed in pain as the Diamon's eyes fell upon him.

When it spoke its voice echoed from all directions, "I have been called to this realm in pursuit of ultimate truth. I see your Ronan blood, Caethe."

The light dimmed and Caethe could now look upon the creature without being blinded. The Diamon stood not three feet away, and looked to be shaped from clear crystal. Its face was small, rhombus-like in shape and roughly cut. Slit eyes of blue-flame gazed at him as its jagged mouth hung open displaying long, serrated teeth of crystal. The Diamon stood on four spindle-like legs that ended in points and had a twisted torso that seemed far too fragile to support its tall frame. Wings of pure cerulean flame swept behind its tall form, their definition lost beneath the harsh glare of light. In one clawed hand it held a white, crystal staff that was capped with flame that spewed refracted light. While it was a vision of frightening beauty, Caethe knew from the power that rolled across the stone that the Diamon could easily end him.

The Diamon spoke again, "You lay upon a Veritas Stone, and cannot lie." It stepped closer, coming to stand next to his head. The white crystal staff bent until the fire touched his chest where his heart lay. Caethe screamed as pain bloomed across his chest, and watched as sapphire flames danced across his skin. The flames licked down the length of him, before turning and racing over the exposed skin of his face. The fire burned, but did not scorch him. Only his eyes were left free of flame. The Diamon's staff rose, and the creature's voice cracked across the valley, "I come from a Sea of Cerulean fire, but that is not the true name of my realm." Its voice paused and then in sizzling hiss, it said, "You know this, Ronan, for this is not the first time you have encountered one of my kind."

A memory flashed across his mind, blooming with startling clarity. *Caethe sat at the foot of a black throne that rose above him, forty-feet in height. Around his neck he wore a chain of red fire. He sat in a pentagram, naked, his form hunched as he whispered an enchantment. Sweat dripped down his naked form and his pale skin was burnt a cherry red. Heat blisters covered his feet and hands, and wept down his shoulders. The land around him burned. The ground was cracked and scorched, but still flames danced upon it. The sky boiled red and the air glimmered with heat. Caethe looked up and his eyes boiled with red flame. His expression was wicked with triumph as he held up a black wand that was as long as he was tall. A massive hand fell from the heights of the throne and plucked it from his grasp. A voice spoke in the language of the inferno. Caethe bowed his head against the crackling command.* Caethe moaned on the stone and in denial, whispered, "No, that is not who I am."

The memory fell away, only to be replaced by another. *Caethe sunk through an orb of dark water and then fell through open air. The light within the Realm of Tenebrosaqa was a sickly green. He limply fell into another massive droplet that hung suspended in air. Caethe choked on the foul liquid, his tears mingling with the wetness around him. He struggled through, his arms and legs working desperately. He fell out of the droplet, his form falling head over heels through the air. A gurgling laugh filled the strange realm. He screamed, "No," as he plunged into another droplet.*

Another vision struck him. *Caethe landed on pliable ground that was blanketed with a spongy, grey moss. Caethe looked around and found himself in a realm of shadow. He was in Umbrael. Fog rolled along the ground twisting and curling, languidly reaching ever-upwards. As he looked across the barren expanse he realized that he was within the realms great plain. A translucent shield, gleaming with silver starlight, surrounded his wraithlike form with a quiet snap. The fog swirled outward in soft waves as it met his shield.*

Caethe fell to his knees as exhaustion overtook him. His chin met his chest and he closed his eyes, tears racing down his cheeks. Relief flooded through him, but it was fleeting. He felt his heart thrumming in his chest. His breath was shallow and broken. Opening the gate to this realm had sapped much of his remaining reserves. Caethe knew the end was near. He looked down at his hand and saw that it had became more translucent as the power within him flickered. Briefly, he considered fleeing back to his physical body, but he knew his consciousness wouldn't survive. I refuse to die there. No, if I am to be ended let it be here, Caethe thought desperately.

Barely heard whispers filled the air and Caethe raised his head as dark shadows flowed toward him. The darkness darted through the fog, quick and fleeting. Caethe didn't stand. The soft light of his shield flickered and began to fall. The shadows swirled around him once in a vortex of darkness, before growing still. The gathered demons had forms as substantial as smoke and appeared in forms of undefined pillars of darkness. They whispered to one another in a voice of ash and crackling embers. Coal-colored eyes formed in the pillar that stood directly before him and a humanoid form stepped forth from the smoke, trailing grey fog. Its features were blurred, but Caethe saw a reflection of himself born of shadow stand before him.

Tears spilled down Caethe's face as he stood shakily. The shadow touched the edge of his shield and it shattered like glass into a fine grey dust. The Daemon spoke in a dry, ruffled voice, "Long have you walked beyond the Shadow Realm, young magi, but we take heart in your return."

Caethe bowed his head in respect, even as he weakly wavered on unsteady feet. In a whisper, he said, "Lord Shethiyae, I am honored by your presence to witness my homecoming and final breathes."

The creature cocked its head in confusion. Death was not a concept the Daemons of this realm were used to contemplating. In a whisper it said, *"More than a hundred years have passed within the shadowed crux since we last felt your presence. Long has your emergence been anticipated. Have you succeeded?"* Caethe smiled, appreciating its candor. The Daemons of this realm were not known for expedited conversation. *It must sense my energy level,* Caethe thought to himself distractedly.

Caethe shook his head, and said mournfully, *"No, Lord Daemon, I failed. The son of Aethral survives and with him, the lock that contains the fragment of my soul."* Caethe shook his head even as the circle of shadow Daemons whispered with fervent worry. Shethiyae raised a shadow hand and the pillars of smoke fell silent.

The mirrored shadow studied his face intently before saying, *"Failure is but a delay before success. The Mother of a Thousand Eyes has seen you bring the balance. Her sight is true. Death is not an option. You must find another way, promised one."*

Caethe bowed his head as abject despair rent his thoughts. He knew that he had failed them and hated himself for it. Caethe whispered, *"My life is at an end, Shethiyae. Another life perhaps I will return and bring the balance. Now, the end comes."* The words left a bitter stain upon his tongue, but he knew the truth and felt no need to deny it.

The shadowed plain was silent. Shethiyae shook his head in denial as his shadowed face twisted with anger. The Daemon stepped forward and pronounced, *"Life is but energy. We have waited long for you and will wait no longer."* The shadow placed its hand on Caethe's chest. The essence of its being crawled along his skin, spreading across him until it enveloped him completely in a wreath of shadow. The Daemon whispered, *"The balance must be kept. One life for another. A sacrifice to keep the truth alive. I give this freely and will pass into the Chaos by my own accord. Find the way, Caethe."* Caethe nodded solemnly in response.

Potent power filled him, rushing through his skin where the smoke *of the Daemon touched. Caethe was lifted in the air by the pillar of smoke as the Daemon's form lost its shape. Caethe choked as the life force of the Daemon filled him, and shook uncontrollably as he was filled with pain and blooms of climaxing pleasure. Like a raging tide, the power drowned him as it sought to bind its power to his weakened cortex. For a moment his cortex, a flickering, steel-grey pillar failed; sputtering out. He fell still and Caethe's mind went dark. The Daemon's power rushed like a grey flaming sea, filling his mind. When the shadow met the deepest part of Caethe, his cortex bloomed anew and flared into existence. Caethe's magic sprang out like a ravenous wolf, consuming the Daemon's essence, and his green eyes snapped open as life filled him once more.*

The smoke surrounding him slowly faded and he was lowered to the ground. The shadowed face nodded in final farewell as an unfelt wind tore it from Umbrael. Caethe sat on the ground, suddenly consumed by both grief and relief. The pillars of smoke whispered in hushed tones before circling him three times and fleeing into the fog. Caethe watched them disappear from sight through bleary eyes.

A tingling sensation raced down his spine and Caethe knew with certainty that he was not alone. Slowly, he lowered his hands from his tear stained face. A silver shield snapped around him as quick as thought as Caethe turned to face east. A white light appeared in the sky above, shining as brightly as a star. Slowly, it descended from the grey clouds and met the plain. The shadowed fog recoiled like a cowering dog from the raw energy its light extruded.

Caethe felt his mouth go dry with fear and bowed low, displaying his hands before him in total submission. The Diamon stepped toward him. The light the creature produced was blinding and Caethe was grateful in that moment that his eyes were downturned. It stopped a dozen feet from him and a voice filled the air. "An immortal perished in this place. You are responsible." It was not a question.

Caethe voice was surprisingly steady, as he responded. "The life was given freely. I broke no law, Guardian." The light flared and Caethe felt its power thrum through his mind, seeking the truth. Memories flashed, faster than thought. Slowly, the light around the

Diamon faded.

When the Guardian spoke, its voice was soft and colored with sadness. "The life was not yours to take, Ronan. While you have the blood of the phoenix, you are not immortal in truth. The shadow within will change you."

Caethe bowed lower still, knowing that today at least, he would be granted leniency. "I understand the consequences. I was fading. The Daemon saved my life..."

The light flared again, tearing into his mind. Caethe screamed as it rifled through his thoughts. Its power was searing, like hot pokers that plunged deep into his mind. When it was finished, Caethe was coated in sweat and trembling. The Guardian addressed him, its voice crisp. "Fading, yes. Long have you walked the Shadow Realm of Umbrael. A place your heart calls home, but this is merely a deception you coddle yourself with." The echoing voice spoke with cold assessment, booming across the shadowed plain, as it said, "You do not belong here, child of Magrados. You have not passed through the Aelfmae. Your physical body remains on Adonim. But I have known of you." Caethe felt a shiver of fear race down his spine. Caethe tucked his lower to arms beneath his robe and slowly, his hands began to draw runes. The Guardian continued, "The one who walks through gates he should not. The one who wanders at the edge of Umbrael through the mists. You are he who once served Sabizael, son of Aethral. I smell Inferno along the edges of your spirit and see that your hands are stained with the blood of Demons."

Caethe spread his upper arms wide as he looked up to meet the Diamon's eyes. He knew that his next words would determine his fate, and said, "Your gaze pierces my soul and you can see the truth of who I am better than I know myself. I may have served Sabizael in my youth, but that was purely out of my desire to free my mortal body from the constraints laid upon me in the name of Ordu. I paid the price of my ignorance and sought to destroy Sabizael. I linger within the realm of Umbrael to escape the mortal bounds and salvage what's left of my sanity. The Daemons of shadow have granted me sanctuary here, within the forest of Umbrael."

The Diamon spoke without emotion, "You linger in Umbrael like a parasite, clinging to your mortality because you fear passing into the Aelfmae without truly living. The wound given by Sabizael, a Demon most-foul, marks the extent of your desperation. You have been corrupted, Ronan. There is no denying that fact."

Caethe flinched from the Diamon's cruel damnation, but his spine straightened with determination, as he said, "The Origin Glade is my birthright. You cannot claim otherwise, Diamon of Cerulean Fire. As I am a child of Magrados, you have no right to banish me. Umbrael is a neutral realm and by the shadow that clings within, it is evident I have been granted safe haven here." Caethe spoke the words forcefully, knowing that with only truth could he forestall reproach.

The Diamon seemed to consider his words. Its light slowly dancing across the plain of fog. Caethe stared unflinching into its eyes, despite the pain that it caused him. When the Diamon spoke, it bowed its head and its words were filled with warning. "I can see the deepest desire within your heart Ronan. Even if you succeed, you cannot truly leave the Astral Realms should Sabizael survive. He possesses a tattered portion of your soul. A demon of his potential cannot possess control of a Ronan." Caethe nodded in understanding and the Diamon studied his face intently, before saying, "The Umbrael Daemons believe that you could tip the balance. That you could right what was broken. I see this potential, but perhaps in their zeal they have forgotten that this can easily sway against their favor."

Flatly, Caethe said, "You can see my intentions as clearly as if they were your own. Help me, Guardian."

The Diamon considered his words, cocking its head to the side, before slowly saying, "I cannot intercede. Change only comes with great sacrifice. The Daemons have put their faith in you and that is telling. Meditate on the price of balance." The Guardian blinked heavily, its words weighted with intent. Caethe nodded slowly, his mind racing as he struggled to see what the Diamon was alluding to. "Success will come to you if it is truly meant to pass." The Diamon stepped forward and raised its clawed hand. It passed through his shield without effect, as easily as he would wave his hand through air. Caethe resisted the urge to flinch away as the Guardian rested its cold, stone hand against his cheek.

Caethe fell to his knees, his breath coming in great gasps as he dry-heaved. Pain boiled through his heart as the Diamon touched his soul. After a few tortured seconds, the guardian stepped back and reached into the flames of its staff. The Diamon stretched its hand toward him, presenting a tiny blue crystal that was delicately held between two talons. In warning, the Diamon said, "Even with your power rejuvenated by the shadow Daemon, your physical body will reject your consciousness. It is too badly injured." Caethe nodded, eying the small, clear crystal. In a clap of distant thunder, the Diamon said, "A Seed of Stella. Take it and ingest it before you reclaim your soul. It will light the way to righteousness."

Caethe bowed deeply. The Diamon turned, and waved it staff through the shadowed air. A ripple of blue flame formed with a crackle, splitting the shadow as a doorway formed.

Caethe sat up, splintering away from the wash of visions. His body was still encased in flame, and his breath came haggard as his gleaming eyes met the Diamon's. In a whisper that resounded over the bated breath of the Fae, he said, "Glory to the fires of truth, but my soul need not be interred by your light, for I have been judged by your kin before and have not faltered. I smote Sabizael to the depths of the Abyss and reclaimed my soul as I promised, resplendent with the Seed of Stella gifted by your own kin. I am the balance that has come to right what has been wronged. My path has been sung in the whispers that web the dreamland of Somnumexteri weaved by Aranya herself."

The Diamon eyed him coldly, and its staff rose in the air as if to strike him dead. Caethe cocked his head, his eyes gleaming with challenge. The fire that clung to his skin vanished and the Diamon stepped back. Caethe stood on the stone altar, and the Diamon held his gaze for a moment. Suddenly, the Diamon leapt into the air, its flaming wings pumping furiously as it fled into the sky. It plunged into the depths of the flaming portal and disappeared.

Caethe turned in a circle, daring the stunned Fae to protest. The pillar of flame that encircled him snuffed out suddenly, spilling smoke. Caethe smiled as he felt warm sunlight spill upon him. The sky had returned to its placid state. The portal was gone, as if it had never been.

Aritian

Chapter Six:

The Despair of Questions

They cut across the desert's rolling sea of sand with desperate haste. The Feligni were creatures of great stamina, and ran tirelessly through the day in an inverted V formation with Selyni leading at the crux. Sand and dust were thrown into the air, marking their path with a yellow plume.

Aritian hunched over the shoulder of his mount. The creature's muscles rippled fluidly beneath him, its massive head bouncing with the rhythm of its gait. The large cats were almost soundless as they moved, as their wide-padded paws muted their gallop as they crossed the hot sand. Their breaths came in great wooshes, indistinguishable from the wind, through the pair of vented slits that ran the length of their necks.

Though the feline bore his weight easily, the ride was any anything but. The Feligni had a tanned skin that was slippery-smooth to the touch, and Aritian was forced to grab handfuls of excess skin at the base of its neck to hold on while his legs trembled from gripping the cat's sides. The cats moved gracefully, and were agile, able to turn with sickening abruptness — hence the smallest of the caravan, Beryl, Mingyo, and Yi, unable to hold to the beasts with their legs, had all been thrown more than once. Inevitably, they had consented to the ignoble embarrassment of being tied, like the injured gnome, to their mounts.

And lastly, one Feligni ran free of a rider. It instead dragged a makeshift litter that had been constructed to carry Ori. Ori was sheltered with a light blanket to prevent his pale skin from being burned, but had not regained consciousness since the crash.

The land here seemed abandoned, and an oppressive quiet clung to the desert air. Sweat dripped down Aritian's face and his lips were chapped. They had ridden for nine hours without stop. None had suggested that they do, as all of them knew what was at stake. Ori's life hung in the balance. The young Titan stood with one foot over the threshold of Great Shadowed Door. The sun hung low in the sky, burning red as its light slowly died. Aritian looked over his shoulder, and in the distance saw that the sky was already fading to night.

Selyni raised a fist into the air. The woman rode tied to her mount by reams of silk, and clung to the Feligni's back with only her legs, preferring to ride upright as if she were riding horseback. She rocked in perfect synchrony with the beast beneath her as she scanned the horizon. Her serene expression had evaporated within an hour of riding, as she was forced to contend with her injuries and the sweltering heat. Now she rode with a grimace of determination that made her frail countenance seem etched in steel conviction. The Feligni slowed and their gait became more bouncing as they dipped into the shadow of a tall dune. Aritian leapt from his cats back before it had come to a stop and went to Mingyo's side. The boy was the smallest of the bunch, and could not have been more than nine. He was small for his age; just a thin waif of a boy. He had long brown hair that hung like a sheet down his back and sharp distinctive features. Aritian jogged, coming to his side, and the boy smiled gratefully as Aritian began to untie the ropes that held him in place.

The boy jumped down, only to stumble to his knees as his legs cramped. Aritian helped him stand, and said, "Mingyo, sit here in the shade a bit." He pointed to a shadow on the dune. "I'll have Sicaroo come around with the waterskin."

The boy sat in the hot sand, but shook his head stubbornly, saying insistently, "I am fine, Serpent. Save the water for the big one. The heat will kill him as surely as his wounds."

Aritian shook his head. The Dranguis were trained from a young age to look past pain, to strive past what the natural body could perform, but Aritian knew the young were the most susceptible to this heat. In a low voice he said, "No, you will drink as I have commanded. The Titan will live. Now rest." Mingyo nodded, and was soon joined by Yi, Shan and Rong. Bo, Hui, and Sicaroo had begun helping Beryl unpack the tents and their meager provisions.

Aritian walked to the litter. Azera crouched next to her brother and poured water tenderly between his cracked lips. She looked over her shoulder, hearing his approach, and stood. She eyed him wearily and asked, "What do you want?"

Tentatively, Aritian eyed Ori's prone form, and asked, "I just wanted to check on him. How is his condition after the ride?"

Azera grunted, spitting into the sand. In a dry monotone, she responded, "No different. There, now you have your answer. Go." She turned her back to him, her stance rigid.

In that moment, realization dawned on him. Azera's anger had morphed from blame to the beginnings of hate. Like a sheet, guilt and fear fell over Aritian as he eyed her quite fury. Pleadingly, Aritian said, "Azera, please you know that I didn't intend this. You know that if I could go back and change what's happened, I would." *So much I would change,* Aritian thought in despair. The image of Razia's face floated before his eyes.

Azera whirled to face him, her expression was dark and terrible, beyond rage. She yelled, "Well you can't! You have the power to hold back a hurricane of fire and call the winds, but you can't do anything for my kin." Azera chucked bitterly, and spat once more on the sand. "You have only destruction to offer, Aritian. You're cursed. Go." She waved a broad hand in his direction.

Aritian eyed her blankly for a moment as cold remorse

filled him like an insidious poison. He was stunned by the quickness in which she had turned from him, but as he gawked at her, he saw Ori behind her, still as death, and could hear the rattling gasps he took as he struggled to survive. *If Ori dies, I will have stolen the last family that is left to her,* Aritian thought with dismal panic. He spread his arms at his sides, and insisted, "Azera, you know me – please." Even to his own ears, his apology fell flat. *How can I show her how I truly feel? How can I make her see how horrible I feel, and how much I wish these powers had never came to me?* Aritian asked himself with anguished misery.

Azera's thick brow bunched and she placed her hands on her hips as she sneered, "Do I? In the mine I thought I did, but as soon as we were free I learned all sorts of things I'm not sure I like." Her dark, beady eyes narrowed as she whispered harshly, "You lied to us Aritian. Back in the mine you didn't tell us of the tunnels. You didn't tell us of the lorith's plan, and you certainly did not tell us of your demon blood." Her jaw clenched as she ground her teeth. Her underbite rode forward and back as she tried to control her emotions, but her voice cracked with sorrow as she uttered, "And now you've killed my only brother. The last kin I have in this world." She shook her head, her braids falling over her broad shoulders. "No Aritian, I do not know you."

Aritian flinched physically as her harsh words smacked him with resounding honesty. He stared at her back before walking away, cowed, eyes lowered to the sand. She spoke the truth; there was no sense in denying it to her or even himself.

The Feligni had all climbed the shadowed side of the dune and lay in the dim light, chests heaving laboriously from the long run. Their heads hung low and most lay unmoving, too tired to do anything other than sprawl in the scant shade. He stalked past them across the dunes and sat in the sun, staring at the glowing sand at his feet. Tears fell down his face, and he did not try to forestall them.

A shadow fell over him as Rythsar squatted in the sand at his side. The lorith seemed at home here, in the desert. The heat bothered him little and if anything, seemed to be invigorating. With a hiss, Rythsar rasped, "There cannot be light without darkness, Aritian. You know this. Many fall to shadow, their light snuffed from this world far too soon, but that is the eternal battle. The last battle. Those of us who survive must strive on to protect the enduring light of Ignathra."

Aritian shook his head and said with certainty, "Azera will never forgive me if Ori dies."

Rythsar snout rose in the air and his tongue flicked between his sharp teeth as he scented the air. Gently, Rythsar warned, "Maybe so, but the brightest of all lights cannot afford to host one whose heart flickers with the shadow of despair. They will invite only darkness, and doom all those who share company."

Aritian knew what he was implying, but Aritian couldn't contemplate the thought. In a strained voice, Aritian said, "Azera saved my life back in the mine. I cannot abandon her."

Rythsar's tail flicked the sand, throwing golden grains in frustration, and said, "Then save him."

Aritian leaned back and stared at the darkening sky. He sighed heavily, before saying, "I can't. I don't know what lives inside me. I don't know what these powers are, but it feels more like damnation." Rythsar exhaled sharply through the two nostril holes, making a huffing sound. Aritian continued, confessing, "Rythsar, I don't know who I am anymore."

Stonily, Rythsar said, "Your heart weeps for your mate, Razia." Aritian shook his head, closing his eyes. He could not speak of her. Not now, and maybe not ever. Rythsar spoke blandly, "You are blaming yourself for something that you cannot control. Razia made her choice. She embraced Ignathra. Do not grieve for one who sits within his kingdom, for those who are in His flame do not feel pain or sorrow. Look to the living, for it is they who suffer." Rythsar stepped in front of him, shadowing him from the sun's last rays. "Do not punish yourself in Ignathra's glare, he would not wish it."

In a slow whisper Aritian confessed, "Ignathra's eye no longer stings." He held his hand out, catching a lingering beam of sunlight, as he explained, "I can feel its touch, but it is no longer harsh." It was true. Through the day it was as if his body had grown with vigor as well. Instead of feeling tired after the ride, he felt stronger. His arms and legs that trembled as he rode stilled and steadied with strength the moment he stepped from his mount. Aritian had the feeling that he could endure riding far beyond what the large cats were capable of. It was as though he soaked in the very sunlight and instead of burning him, it filled him with potent energy.

Reverently, Rythsar hissed, "The Flame within wakens." Rythsar curled his long neck down so that he could look Aritian in the eyes. His voice thrummed with remembered amazement, as he said, "Aritian, you stilled Ignathra's flame. You saved hundreds." His voice fell lower still, "Yet you weep. Humans are not like the lorith. There is no shame in death for our kind. Many must be sacrificed for the greater good. This is Ignea. Here in the south, victory is paid by the blood of your enemies. You are not at fault. If you must blame something, blame the Shadow, for it is he that snuffs out the light of our lives."

Aritian's jaw tightened, as the memory of the thousands who died flashed through his mind like sparks of the flame that had consumed Inee. Angrily, he asked, "How many more, Rythsar? How many more must die until we are safe?"

A woman's voice interrupted Rythsar's response, saying, "None." Selyni walked to stand before him. Firmly, she said, "There will be no more death. The Ancient One will save Ori."

Aritian looked up at her, and her pale beauty reminded him once more of her heritage: a northerner. *She does not know the ways of Ignea*, Aritian thought resentfully, *she does not belong here.* Incredulously, Aritian asked, "How do you know this? How can you know that she can? Or will be even willing?"

Selyni crossed her arms. She wore a long blue toga that had been slit on either side for ease of riding. Her arms were still dark with bruising, but they had changed colors leaving her arms a muddy green. *They are healing*, Aritian thought with wonder, *and quickly*. Already they had lightened from this morning. Insistently, she assured, "She'll do it."

Grimly, Aritian shook his head and said, "You don't know that."

Selyni smiled, but it was not a kind smile. It was a smile of regret. With a quiet sadness, she said, "Yes, I do. I know her. She will do it and happily so, because she knows that by saving him you will owe her."

Aritian cocked his head to the side, and asked, "Owe her?"

Selyni nodded once, very slightly. Her voice shook with a slight tremor as she said, "Nothing comes without a price, magic most especially."

Aritian looked to the horizon and then back to the witch. Anxiously, he asked, "What if we don't make it in time?"

Selyni smiled slightly and replied confidently, "We traveled for forty-four miles today. Tomorrow we will stop at a small Oasis and resupply there. By the third day, we will stand before the Ancient One. She has promised to meet us on the southernmost edge of the Golden Plain."

Aritian looked to the shadowed dune. Darkness had already fallen and the sky was now a deep plum color, the way Selyni's arms had been this morning. All of the Feligni slept soundly, snoring softly through the vents on their throats. He waved toward them, and asked, "Will the Feligni be able to sustain such a pace?"

Dismissively, Selyni said, "The Feligni can survive two weeks without food and a week without water. They will be fine. These were fat and lazy when we caught them this morning. They will survive." She waved toward where the tents now stood erect. A small fire had been started between the two. She extended a hand to help him rise, and said, "Now come, let us take respite and turn in for the night." Aritian nodded and took her hand.

*****

Night ruled the sky, but Ignathra's warrior's dotted the black battlefield. The shining specks of starlight stood unfaltering as they warred through the night. Aritian admired their resolve as he sat before the tent on a small pillow. Most of his companions had gone to bed, but a few lingered around the dying coals of the fire. The heat of the day had fled the sands and now the air was cool. Their water had grown scarce, but they still had three full wineskins. Aritian took a heavy slug. The bright, berry bite hit his throat, but he no longer tasted the bitter aftertaste. The wineskin was more than halfway empty. The others left him be, studiously keeping their eyes from straying toward him while he steeped in his misery. His face was expressionless, even apathetic, as tears fell down his face, but he no longer cared to hide it. His mind, however, was like a sparrow caught in a winter storm who knew to land and grow still would result in a slow death. So he struggled on, never settling in anyone spot, flitting through the blizzard of grief to survive. Detached, he listened to his companions converse by the fireside.

Namyr idly played with a stick, running it through the hot coals to let the flame catch before removing it and watching it disappear. Wood was scarce in the desert, but they had scavenged a fair amount from the wicker contraption that morning. Namyr spoke in the quiet darkness, "Rythsar, I am surprised that you accompanied us rather than return to the horde. They would have accepted you back into the colonies with honor. You would have been hailed a hero, bringing word of the one promised in prophecy. Yet you left that to Trilithi and Nyox, why?"

Rythsar sprawled on his side, but his body tensed when Namyr spoke of his kin. He replied dryly, "I will not leave

Aritian's side. He is the one who was promised, and it is my sacred duty to protect him." His yellow eyes narrowed in dislike as he gazed at Namyr, but when he spoke his tone was casually enough, "Nyox was wounded. He knew he could only serve by acting as herald... as much as he railed against it."

Cautiously, Entah asked, "What is the nature of this prophecy that you allude to?" The gnome had spoken little and his eyes constantly watered from the pain of his leg. He bore his wound without complaint and Beryl had insisted he drank his fill of wine. The gnome had reluctantly complied, to Beryl's great amusement.

Rythsar hesitated for a moment, and then said, "It is foretold among my kind that a champion of Ignathra would be born, called the Spark. It is said that one day Ignathra will be split asunder and hew a child from his own flesh to rule the faithful and lead them against a great adversary." Rythsar sat up straighter as he continued, "He will be the one to protect Ignathra's immortal flame on Ignea. There is proof the prophecy is real. Nearly six-hundred years ago the lorith colony of Pateru was visited by a young human known as Aileen. It was she who gave my people this hope." His tail flicked toward Selyni as he continued, "The witch herself has confirmed that there is such a woman among the Ronan, some kin of Aritian's." The lorith looked over his shoulder at Aritian pointedly, but Aritian made no response. The lorith's words were too difficult to contemplate, especially with how he felt. Beryl, Selyni, Entah and Namyr all looked at Aritian at once, before hastily turning their eyes away. Aritian took another generous swig of wine.

Namyr laughed lightly and looked at Selyni in disbelief, as he asked, "You didn't tell him?" Selyni shook her head, gazing into the dying flames with a unreadable expression.

Namyr laughed again and flicked the flaming stick he held over his shoulder with a whoosh. "Aileen is madder than a Gillo in a plum wine bath. She is a raving loon." Namyr pushed onward, ignoring the lorith's annoyed expression, and suggested, "You would have been smarter to herald this news while the horde remains ignorant of the Augury's insanity. Who knows when they might learn the truth? You should have gotten while the getting was good, lizard. Your position among your kin is perilous at best."

Rythsar sat straighter with anger. In a low growl, he said, "I care not for the approval of the colonies." Namyr's eyebrows rose and he smiled broadly, displaying his pointed teeth as he moved to speak again.

Beryl glowered at Namyr and cut him off with a tone that said the discussion was ended. "Rythsar ain't goin' nowhere. He is accepted by us, and we by him." The dwarf flashed Rythsar a grizzled smile, and quipped, "Besides Namyr, you said you heard rumor of his mate..." Rythsar growled low in his throat, deep and threateningly. Beryl's next words died as he looked at the lorith with confusion, knowing that he had spoken out of place but not understanding why.

Namyr splayed his hands wide, and said innocently, "No need to get angry, Rythsar. I sympathize with you completely. Lorith mate for life, so it only makes sense that you wish to be reunited. I simply am trying to judge where your alliance lay. Is it with Aritian, or are you driven by more selfish motives? You may have to decide between them one day..." Rythsar looked as if he was nearly ready to spring upon the petite man.

"She's an albino, is she not?" The question was asked quietly and all eyes turned toward Entah.

Rythsar replied in a low whisper, "An Alba, yes." The lorith eyed the gnome curiously, momentarily jolted from his anger by the creature's perceptive question.

The gnome leaned forward, his large black eyes gleaming with orange light, and asked curiously, "This is why you were banished?" The gnomes voice was neutral, lacking all emotion, and Aritian had the feeling that Entah's interest was purely academic. Aritian had seen the gnome watching them closely.

He had the feeling that the gnome was studying them. Though why, Aritian could not imagine.

Rythsar shifted, uncomfortable by the conversation, and answered simply with a quiet, "Yes."

Bluntly, Beryl asked, "Why would her colorin' matter?" He raised a wineskin to his lips and drank heavily.

Rythsar replied quietly, annoyed, "You are not of the lorith."

Entah opened his mouth, as if he was about to ask for an explanation. Aritian stood. His head spun with spirit and he held his hands out to steady himself. He took a steading breath, and then queried, "Rythsar, where did Namyr say your mate was?" They all looked at him with surprise, for he had not spoken all night.

Rythsar bowed his head respectfully, and answered, "Namyr claimed that Aethara was in Mistress Simisola's company. That she is some sort of companion to this Simisola and that she, along with the Mistresses favored slaves, sail south along the Velox." Aritian frowned at the lorith's words. If the female lorith was with Simisola, of all people, she was far from safe.

Aritian gestured with a wave of the wineskin, and said with sincerity, "You can leave us at any time the mood strikes you, my friend. I will not keep you from your love and you owe me nothing." He couldn't imagine how the lorith felt after all these years to hear that his mate may still live yet.

The lorith slowly shook his head stubbornly and Aritian sighed, annoyed. They had treated him differently since that night in Inee. He hadn't noticed it fully before, but as the day passed he saw the subtle change in the way they looked and spoke to him. *I don't deserve this adoration*, he thought darkly.

Namyr smiled brightly, seemingly unbothered by the tension that hung in the air, and said cheerfully, "Luckily he won't have to. Mistress Simisola and Master Jabari are going the same place we are. They, like Selyni and I, are servants of the

Ancient One. They have been recalled to receive further orders, and will sail along the Velox until they reach Utarye and then travel north, overland, to the coast." Aritian felt his heart miss a beat at the mention of his old Masters.

Aritian voice grew tight as he asked, "How could it possible that you so coincidentally serve the same Mistress? Where are we going? And who is this woman, this Ancient One, that you speak of with such reverence?" He was tired of his ignorance and felt as though he was caught in some great web that stretched beyond his understanding. He felt sure that there was more going on than he knew, and this last connection seemed a bit too convenient to be called a coincidence.

Namyr's smile grew wide to Aritian's annoyance, and he said lightly, "Oh, I cannot speak her name for she forbids such casual mention. She is known among the powerful as the Mistress of Shadows. Heard of her?" Aritian should his head, no. "I would have been surprised if you had." Namyr drawled, as if pleased by Aritian's ignorance.

Aritian sat heavily on the pillow, his legs too wobbly with spirit to hold him any longer. Namyr spoke with the arrogance of someone who believed themselves to be a god; Aritian took another heavy swig from the wineskin. Loftily, Namyr said, "I can tell you that she has been in Ignea for more than seven-hundred years."

Aritian saw Beryl roll his eyes and Aritian smiled weakly, glad that someone else was annoyed by Namyr patronizing manner as he continued, "And she has spent much of her life consolidating her power here. There is a reason why her name is but a whisper in the shadows, a hushed rumor that plays on the tongues of kings and sultans alike, but that is for her to explain." Aritian didn't know if he believed the man's words, but he had seen too much to outright discount them. He shivered, and not from the chilly desert air. Namyr concluded brightly, "All you need to know as of now is that she is your kin, and her power is both wide and formidable. You will be safe with her."

"Where are you taking me?" Aritian asked again, noting that Namyr had danced around the question. The tension in the camp grew, and Aritian had the sense that his companions knew the answer, and knew that he would be displeased by it.

Namyr's answered was nonplussed. "We travel northeast, to the Collation of Odium, specifically Creuen. Really Creuen should be the capital, but the Emperor prefers the greenery of Victes."

Aritian bolted upright as panic filled him. Unnerved, he slowly asked, "You're taking escaped slaves to the capital of slavery in Velon?" Aritian stood shakily, and felt the edges of his eyes burn. *I've been betrayed too many times by this man to trust his intentions*, Aritian thought angrily. The ring on his pinky began to burn hot as it struggled to contain his power. Aritian whispered dangerously, "Why would you think I would go there without complaint? Do you think I am some dumb lamb to be led quietly to slaughter? I will not go there."

Namyr looked around with mock surprise, and said sweetly, "We must, Aritian, that is where my Mistress..."

Aritian raised a hand, cutting off Namyr's words, and shouted, "I don't give a goblin shit. We are not going to such a place."

Stunned silence fell over the camp. Aritian's chest heaved with vexation and his finger burned as if he had placed it in a forge, but he didn't care. Namyr had tricked him twice now, Aritian wouldn't allow the bastard to fool him a third time.

In the silence Selyni whispered, "You will if you wish for Ori to live." Aritian looked at her wide-eyed, but she didn't look up from the dying coals. Mildly, she commanded, "Get some sleep, all of you. I will stand watch." Aritian turned away and stumbled into the tent.

Devaney

Chapter Seven:

The Decadence of Revenge

High in the bright, blue sky above the wispy, white clouds flew a silver feathered Roc. Its wings cut through the air lazily. The wind currents rose graciously from the deep blue sea below, making it easy to glide with the tradewinds that blew from the west. Devaney clung to the bird's back, holding fistfuls of feathers as the muscles of its great shoulders bounced her up and down with the rhythm of their flight.

Devaney cracked a sightless, white eye, her magesight allowing her to see through her blindness. She felt her stomach twist as she saw the dizzying height that they flew. A handful of weeks had passed since they had left the rocky outcrop at the foothills of the Grey Mountains. They had flown south along the coast of Novus, stopping only at night and finding remote uninhabited land to recover. The farther south they traveled the less frequent these respites had become. Coastal cities had sprung up like gargantuan monoliths that buzzed with activity, and between these thousands of villages and hamlets clung to the coast. It was unavoidable, the flight across the Igidum Sea was too great an expanse so far north.

The flight felt perilous to Devaney so far; she was raw with nerves and each time they landed her heart raced with renewed fear. She knew that if they were discovered by the Ordu all would be lost. Lifoy seemed unfazed by the danger and brushed her concerns away as pointless worrying.

The further they flew south, the warmer the air had grown. Near the Grey Mountains, high in the sky, the air had felt thin and brittle with the promise of ice. Now though, Devaney had to admit, the air held a touch of summer. Fall had not yet come to this land, and absently she wondered how many hundreds of miles they had flown to feel such a drastic shift.

Two days passed, they had turned eastward. Lifoy had assured her that they had reached the southern rim of the Igidum Sea. Below her, the clear-blue waters danced merrily. To the south, clinging to the last edges of Novus's coast, gleamed a magnificent, white city. It rose along the coast, its mouth, a port that spilled thousands of ships. In the center of the city, like all cities of Ordu, a pyramid rose marking the might of Ordu. Devaney's heart skipped a beat as she took in the dark ships below.

The armada prepares. Soon the armies of Ordu will reach the shores of the Unified Free Kingdoms. Lifoy said into her thoughts. Devaney's eyes narrowed as she spotted the white sails of the ships. A sigil gleamed brightly on each; a golden fist that held a burning sun in its grasp.

Devaney spoke above the wind with a shout, "Do the people of the U.F.K. know of this doom?" Worry burned at her heart. Ordu had crushed all resistance on Novus, toppling more than a hundred kingdoms in the last four hundred years. Now Ordu turned its eye east, to the old country.

Lifoy tittered, laughing through her thoughts before saying kindly, *yes dear, they know. They have been preparing for this war for the last twenty years. I fear this cohort of ships are but the latest to sail into the Reena.*

"What's the Reena?" Devaney asked, puzzled. She knew little of the wider world. Before the Ordu had come to her hamlet's small valley, she had never left the foothills of the Grey Mountains.

Lifoy explained cheerfully. *The Reena is a Strait between Novus and Afta. It's where the Igidum Sea meets the Chalice Sea. Of late it has been called the Strife. You shall see soon. Keep your eyes peeled to the south. In a few hours we will reach it.*

The land beyond the shores of Novus had become dotted with islands. The small green gems bustled with teaming life. Docks circled many of the small patches of land and while some seemed rocky and too small to hold much, others were large, forested, and held rings of tall walls marking small cities.

They flew on. They had not stopped since they had turned east. Lifoy had said the land was too crowded and had promised safe landing soon. Unlike their perilous flight from the Grey Mountains, they were prepared. Lifoy had stolen provisions from unsuspecting towns and villages. A pack bulged behind her, tied tightly across the Roc's shoulders. Devaney loosened her white-knuckled grip and untied one of the many waterskins that was fixed to the pack. One handed, she opened it and drank the cool liquid before retying it to the pack. She clutched the feathers once more, closing her eyes against the dizzying scene beneath.

A vision rolled deep within her. Devaney felt it stir like a caged cat waiting to burst free, took a steading breath and coaxed it upwards, unafraid now of what she might see. In the darkness, light bloomed and she saw.

A battle raged before a long, twisting wall. Beneath it, a sparse forest of oak trees rose. The attackers wore white, with chests emblazoned with sun beams and a cruel fist. The defenders wore sky-blue capes, and rained death from the thirty-foot, stone wall. Arrows thudded into the ranks men that crowded below. Shields were raised, and a line of soldiers moved a long battering ram beneath a turtle-shield toward a small, iron bound door. From the top of the wall, a tall man screamed orders, and pitch was poured down upon the shields. A flaming was torch tossed after, and flames burst against the men below. Screams filled the air with the fragrance of charring flesh. The shield broke as men twisted to the ground blanketed in fire. An order was shouted, and arrows buzzed from below filling the top of the wall with death screams. Soldiers below raced to the fallen ram, unscathed by the pitch, and a new turtle-shield was formed. The ram boomed against the door once, twice, and thrice. Cracks formed along the door's surface as it buckled inward.

Suddenly, screams filled the top of the wall. It was not screams of pain, rather of shock and surprise. A small, wooden statue suddenly appeared on the lip of the wall. The vision zoomed in closer, and Devaney saw that it was not a statue – rather she found herself looking at a puppet. The puppet was made from a dark wood and stood two-feet tall, dressed in thick leather armor, and wore a sweeping blue-cape that matched the ones worn by the defenders. On its chest was painted a proud, white ship with blue sails and in its petite hand it held a thin, silver sword.

The puppet was joined by a second, identical puppet. Then another appeared, and another. Soon the lip of the wall was filled with hundreds, and then thousands, of small puppets. The lead puppet thrust its sword into the air, and the action was copied by its fellows. Arrows whizzed into their ranks, thudding into their wooden bodies. A few were knocked back, but most stood, ignoring the arrows that protruded from them. The puppets leaped down upon the attackers in a silent tide.

The puppets landed on the backs of those beneath and struck wickedly. Their thin, wooden arms working rhythmically as they plunged their needle-thin blades into soft flesh. The attackers fell back in surprise, screaming wards against evil. The puppets silently worked, running beneath soldiers and crawling over any who dared grow close, all the while cutting and slicing. Men fell as their hamstrings were cut, and gripped their bloody throats as jugulars were stabbed. They crawled desperately away, trying to escape as puppets swarmed over them. The men on the wall gave a reverberating shout of triumph. The door at the foot of the wall burst open, and a cavalry streamed out as a rout began. The Ordu fled through the forest. Those too slow were cut down by horsemen, and fell beneath a surging wave of puppets.

Men shouted in voices full of anger and fear as horns blazingly sung retreat. The screams of the dying rent the air as they cursed or pleaded with their god. The defenders screamed battle cries and cheered as the Ordu fled to the shoreline. Soldiers' boots splashed through the low tide as they raced to the roughly-made ferries that waited just off *the shore of the Reena, though they were pursued on horseback, and more men fell with blood-curdling screams as they were cut down from behind. The wood of the ferries groaned with the weight of the armored men and the screams of commanders filled the air as they ordered the soldiers to row. Puppets plunged into the rolling waves cutting down unlucky men who had yet to make it to the ferries, before disappearing beneath the red-tinged waves.*

A voice boomed over the slaughter, "Bowmen, nock and fire at will." The whisper of bowstrings filled the air a thousand times over, mingling with the grunts of men who pulled them. Arrows whistled through the air and the sounds of men screaming cascaded across the water. Heavy splashes filled the air as men fell from the ferries and were swallowed by the rolling waves of the Reena. The sea churned red with blood.

Devaney's eyes snapped open as she was released from the vision. She scanned below, and saw the Strife. The islands of Novus had been left behind and now she saw the strait fully. A deeper-blue water from the south met the cool, pale water of the north. The current was swift here, as the strait was narrow, no more than ten miles in width. To the east another string of islands waited, and she watched as Ordu ships sailed toward the ferries that were being pushed south along the coast. Dimly, Devaney could hear the soldiers crowding the ferries call desperately to the approaching ships.

Devaney screamed into the wind, "Fly swiftly Lifoy, a battle has taken place. We must aid the U.F.K."

Lifoy reply was muted compared to her passion. *King Paul has won the day. Look, the Ordu flee his shores.*

Devaney kicked her heels into the Roc's neck and tightened her grip on his feathers as she screamed, "Those men on the ferries, target them. Don't let them escape!"

Lifoy made to respond, but Devaney bombarded his mind with a wordless scream. Her mind swirled with rage and turned red as the need for revenge gripped her heart. Overcome, Lifoy dived from the blue clouds, and screamed a battle cry. The great

Roc's call echoed across the sky, and the men below looked up in shock.

Lifoy swooped over the first ship, his black talons extended. He raked the sails with his claws, shredding them asunder. Arrows whizzed by their head, and Devaney jerked back as one blurred past her nose. Sailors and soldiers below, ducked and dived, as the sail was torn away. Lifoy's great wings thundered furiously, and the water beneath danced with the wind he threw.

Lifoy rose in the sky, only to twist as he tucked his wings closed. Devaney screamed, clutching his feathers as they plummeted toward the first ferry. Several soldiers jumped into the water to frightened to face the Roc, but more raised swords in defense. Lifoy crashed his full weight among them, smashing those beneath in a spray of blood and splintered wood, before rising into the sky once more. The ferry broke apart and the armored men sunk beneath the waves.

The soldiers on the shore shouted in triumph. A wave of arrows filled the sky, as the men on the closest ferries tried to strike the Roc from the air. Lifoy nimbly dodged the arrows and circled above. There was a half a dozen ferries left and three ships sailing toward the shore unmarred. The ship they had attacked impotently listed in the sea.

There's too many. If I close again, we shall be hit. We had our fun, now let us return to the sky. Lifoy said into her mind. Devaney shook her head in denial. She wanted the Ordu to pay. All of them. A voice whispered in her mind. It was far away, almost unheard, but thrummed across a strand as solid as silver. The strand hummed with hungry promise. Devaney smiled wickedly.

Devaney raised her hands in the sky, and shouted, "Bulzaelar, come to the call of your Mistress!" Lifoy's wings pumped erratically as surprise ran down the length of him. He begged desperately into her mind to cease, but Devaney was beyond hearing. Her call had fled across the realms. A roar shook the sky and Devaney smiled.

The sky grew grey suddenly, twisting with darkness. From the heights above, a demon burst into the world of Adonim. Devaney gasped suddenly as energy was leached from her, and her breath came fogged with a chill.

Bulzaelar flew on wings of shadow and streamed through the air toward his mistress. His horned head rose as his long snout sniffed the mortal world. Another roar filled the sky. Devaney felt her limbs grown numb, and her grip loosen on Lifoy's feathers as she barely had the strength to hold on. Calling the demon had sapped her strength and drew from her every second that he remained in this realm. She pointed to the Ordu below, and screamed desperately, "Destroy the Ordu. Kill them all!"

Bulzaelar could not deny her command. The demon streaked across the sky past them, toward the nearest ship. The demon crashed into the side of the ship, ramming the wood with his black horns. The wood exploded with the impact and black fire danced across the ship's deck, consuming men and wood with equal vigor. Men screamed in horror. The demon burst from the center of the ship, throwing splintered wood in all directions. The ship lurched, and water sprayed after him, as it began to sink. His black wings pumped furiously as he flew to the next ship. The men on the shore fell into silent shock.

Bulzaelar landed lightly on the prow of the neighboring ship. Men raced toward him, raising swords to strike the foul beast down, but Bulzaelar merely laughed a hissing string of ash. The demon raised a hand and the ship was flooded with shadows, lost to darkness. Terrible screams filled the air, rising from the cloud-wreathed ship.

Devaney could see through the shadows, and saw her demon whirl across the deck, rending men apart with his claws and flinging them against the deck with enough force to shatter bone. His tail curled around the throat of a soldier before whipping out viciously, flinging the man over the deck. A soldier struck his chest with a sword and another stabbed his shoulder with a spear. Bulzaelar reared up on his hind legs, chuckling with a hiss of steam. He tore the silver sword from his breast with a snap of his jaws and the metal shattered beneath his teeth. He reached up lazily and grabbed the spear, yanking it free with a gush of green ichor, and flung it like a javelin. Two men who sought to flee were impaled. The spear shaft stuck between their midsections, and for a moment they struggled to free themselves from one another, but then the first man collapsed, dragging the man behind down with him. The demon returned to his dance of death. Shadows fell away from the ship when all had grown quiet. Bulzaelar stood atop the mast, his leathery wings spread behind him as he launched himself into the air.

Devaney smiled manically. She could feel her power bleeding from her, but did not care. She commanded, "Hurry Bulzaelar, strike them down." The last ship had turned its sails and fled south. Those on the remaining ferries rowed furiously back to the shores of the U.F.K. The soldiers on the shore waited grimly, ready to deal out death. Bulzaelar flung himself like a dark arrow across the sky and Lifoy followed.

Bulzaelar hovered above the last ship. Arrows darkened the sky beneath the demon, but he waved a casual hand. A dark wind surged from his leathery wings and the arrows fled to the left of him, before dipping down toward the sea. The demon reared up, and his claws grew dark. The demon began throwing bolts of black fire in a steady barrage. Wood exploded outward with the impact, and black fire danced along the ships deck. Men abandoned ship, preferring the watery grave of the sea to the unnatural flames. Bulzaelar hung in the air, throwing fireballs in an unending tirade. In less than a minute the ship had begun to sink.

Lifoy screamed into her mind. *Banish him, now! You cannot allow him to remain, he will drain you unto death.* Stubborn, Devaney weakly shook her head and grimaced. She did not call out to Bulzaelar with her voice, rather she sent her thoughts across the sky.

Bulzaelar pumped his wings furiously and made toward the listing ship. Blackness swallowed the ship and soon, it too was burning. Devaney lay on Lifoy's neck. She was so tired, her eyes fluttered as she fought of unconsciousness. In a whisper, she said, "Bulzaelar, I banish you to the Realm of Umbrael." Her eyes fell closed and her grip on the feathers grew lax as darkness took her.

The demon cried out in rage as a wind tore him from the grey sky. Bulzaelar was pulled upward into the swirling clouds, cursing and fighting its pull all the way. He flapped his wings desperately against the wind, but was soon sucked into depths and lost to sight. The sky cleared immediately. Lifoy sighed dramatically, and banked toward the shore of the Unified Free Kingdoms.

Aritian

Chapter Eight:

The Oasis

Ignathra sat high in the sky as the pride of Feligni trotted toward a green smudge in the distance. The foliage was some five miles away and floated hazily on the horizon. The land around it had flattened out. The dunes were no more than rippling dips and small hills now. They had left before sunrise and had ridden into the late afternoon.

Aritian wore a silken wrap over his head that shielded his face from the sun, though it had grown sodden with sweat. The young Dranguis seemed to fair worse this day. They all had to be tied on their mounts as their exhausted muscles couldn't bear to grip the cat's sides any longer. Despite this, they had made good time. They had stopped four hours ago to consume their remaining provisions and Selyni claimed they had travelled some fifty miles already.

Aritian nudged his heels into the great cat's side, edging it forward, but the feline ignored the command and stayed in formation. Aritian sat straight, keeping one hand secure in the fold of the cat's skin, and called, "Selyni." The blonde woman looked over her shoulder with a smile, and Aritian gestured to his mount and then to her. Selyni nodded, turning away. His cat bounded forward and Aritian threw himself forward, hugging its neck, as the beast leapt into a run. His mount weaved among the other cats and skirted the litter that spat sand, before slowing as it came to Selyni's side. "Do they listen to every command you give them?" Aritian asked, irritated. Selyni nodded. "Can they even think for themselves or have you taken their autonomy along with their will?" Aritian asked accusingly, sitting straight now that the felines wild run had slowed.

Selyni gave him a dark frown as she patted the wrinkled skin between her mounts pointed ears. "The Feligni will return to the desert unhurt. They will have little memory of us," she said quietly.

Aritian shook his head ruefully and bit back, "I'm sure you'll make sure of that, but you haven't answered my question."

Selyni sighed heavily, and explained, "No, they cannot think properly at the moment. You wouldn't want them to. Feligni are predators." She leaned down and touched her mount's long whiskers. The cat's jaw hung open, and Aritian saw that the cat's upper and lower jaws were lined with three rows of sharply curved teeth. The largest were more than four inches in length. Blandly, Selyni said, "They would rip us apart in mere moments if I released them, quicker than you or I could react." She smiled at his aghast expression, and said with a laugh, "Don't look so worried, I've placed them in a trance."

Wonderingly, Aritian asked, "How did you know they were close enough to call? Could you sense all the life that was out in the desert when you gazed upon the dunes?"

Selyni shook her head, and said "No." She petted the shoulder of her mount causally, before saying, "I knew they would be close. Their natural habitat lays between the Golden Plain and the Velox far to the south. They stalk the herds of gazelle that live in the Golden Plain, and find much substance along the jungle that clings to the river's edge. Life blooms for more than twenty miles either side of the Velox River as it flows through the heart of the Ignis. Isn't that amazing?" She asked, brightly. Her blue eyes flicked across the horizon back and forth. Aritian realized that she was barely paying attention to their conversation.

"Yes," Aritian said, nodding. "I never thought I'd see such

sights." He touched her arm, and she looked at him with surprise. In a low voice, he asked, "Why have we slowed?"

Selyni forced a smile and waved toward the land around them with a flick of her wrist, saying, "This part of the desert can be dangerous. There is a creature that stalks this land. The small village we go to is named Jade's Pond. Quite lovely." She raised a hand, forestalling his question, saying, "You'll see why when we get there. The people have been here for more than a hundred years, and have warned travelers to take care traveling this stretch of territory." Aritian look held doubts, and she said lightly, "I'm merely being cautious."

Aritian leaned close and asked in a whisper, "Why are you so afraid then?"

Rythsar spoke in a growl, "Death rides the air, that's why." The lorith had dismounted and ran alongside their mounts. His long legs carried him forward in a bobbing gait, and his tail flicked side to side, despite the thick bandage. Aritian watched him flick his forked black tongue between his lips with quick, repetitive flicks.

Aritian looked to him worriedly, and asked, "Rythsar, what do you mean?" In the bright sunlight Aritian could see that the lorith's dark scales were highlighted with brighter, cherry-colored scales that sparkled along the ridge of his back, and around his deep-set eyes.

He warned, "I smell the decay of many." Rythsar cocked his horned head to the side as if surprised, and asked, "You can't smell it?"

Aritian shook his head as he scanned the quiet desert, and said, "No, I cannot. Selyni, what is this creature you fear so greatly?"

Selyni beamed indulgently at him, and said brightly, "Nothing to worry yourself over." She waved toward the oasis, and said, "Come, let us make haste to the village. There are walls there and we will be safe."

Aritian made to speak, but his mount fell back into

formation by an unheard command. The pride tightened, so that they were running shoulder to shoulder, and their speed doubled as they cut across the open land. The Feligni ran like an arrow loosed on a windless day. Aritian hunched over, gripping the cat hastily as it galloped forward. Rythsar ran behind and incredibly, kept pace. Rythsar leaned forward with his arms clenched to his chest, snout before him, as his powerful legs ate the ground and dashed grit into the air. As they neared the oasis, its form lost its hazy glamour and the beauty of Jade Pond was revealed.

Greenery bloomed in the middle of the desert with dazzling opulence. The oasis sprawled for two miles, surrounded by towering palm trees and a thick cluster of foliage. This close, Aritian could see a white sandstone wall had been erected around the oasis and stood some twenty feet in height. Bushes towered at its base with wide-fanned leaves, and vines crawled along its surface so heavily that the wall beneath blended perfectly with lush flora.

Selyni raised her arm in the air and the pride turned, curling around the side of the oasis toward the east. The Feligni slowed as the entrance came into sight. Aritian eyed the bulwarks along the wall, but saw no guards. The village seemed empty of life and was ominously quiet.

A wooden door, bleached harshly by the sun, stood gaping wide. The Feligni walked through at a sedate pace. The air had grown thick with humidity — water was close, and a lot of it, but that was not what held Aritian's attention. The cloying stench of rot hung like a cloud in the air.

Beryl eyed the streets darkly, and whispered sarcastically, "Oh, what a cheerful welcome this be." The Feligni stopped a few feet inside, and Aritian looked around. Single story, stone buildings clung to the walls, netted in greenery. Small gardens sprawled along the villages wide pathways, and a fountain bubbled gently, spilling precious water in the center of a wide square.

Bodies littered the ground and walkway everywhere. Men, women, and children lay where they had been struck down. Their bodies were pale and bloated. Flies flew thick in the air, and birds pecked at muscle and fat revealing white bone. Several corpses were missing limbs completely, while still others looked as though they had been crushed by some great weight. Selyni dismounted and Namyr, Azera and Aritian followed her lead. Beryl made to speak again, waving to the rope that held him place, but Namyr shook his head no and pressed a finger to his lips commanding silence. Beryl huffed angrily, but nodded.

Aritian walked to Selyni's side as the woman crouched next to the body of a small child. "What did this?" He asked in a hushed whisper. He cast a worried eye back to the young Dranguis, but the child assassin's looked around with only silent curiosity. They had seen death before.

Namyr whispered to Selyni, "Even the livestock had been killed. Hogs, camel, and chickens all dead. This was not done by man. There has been no ransacking, nothing." Aritian looked around, and saw that Namyr was right. A stable lay to their left, and through the open doors Aritian could see a dozen dead camel and horses that lay in a splash of red and pale guts.

Selyni pointed to the small body at her knee, and whispered, "This child has been torn in half. Her legs and waist are gone." She pointed to the thin waist, and said, "See there," gesturing to the girl's tattered intestines. It looked as though a swordsmen had hacked her body in neatly spaced rows. Selyni pushed the girl's arms to the side, exposing her chest, and nodded to herself as she recited, "Deep lacerations running in grooves." She looked at Namyr meaningfully, before closing the girl's eyes with a gentle touch.

Namyr asked, "Do you think the beast did this?" His emerald eyes flicked here and there. Namyr was tense, with his legs slightly bent as if he were ready to spring into action and feared attack at any moment.

Selyni nodded, before quietly saying, "It most likely is gone having sated its hunger, but we must take care. These people couldn't have been dead for more than a week."

"What could do this?" Aritian asked, repeating himself as he eyed the dead girl uneasily.

Selyni explained, fear coloring her words with a harsh rasp, "An old creature, from an age past. In the north we call them wyrms. It's a serpent... a rather large one. There are less than a dozen left in the world. All the males died out, hunted to extinction more than five hundred years ago." Her smile was grim, as if she had remembered the hunt. Aritian eyed her closely and thought, *maybe she does*.

Namyr nodded with a frown, and warned, "If it is a wyrm, don't engage it. Run."

Selyni stood, and whispered, "The children should not see this, should not be here." She waved to all the dead around them, and then said, "Azera, take your brother and the boys out of here."

Azera responded in a low growl, "No. Those boys are of the Dranguis Guild. Put a weapon in their hand and they will slice up a small army before it knows what hit them. As for myself, I am a Titan. Titan's do not hide." She concluded, as though she needed no other explanation for her refusal.

Selyni looked as though she wanted to argue, but instead nodded curtly. "Namyr go untie the boys, and arm them." Selyni commanded quiet whisper. Namyr jogged silently to do as he was bid. Selyni waved toward the Feligni and the cats moved with synchronized grace until they circled the litter where Ori lay. "The Feligni will guard Ori. Azera you and I will search the houses for food. Aritian you take the boys to the hot springs and fill the waterskins. The springs lay at the center of the village. You won't be able to miss the fog. Namyr and Rythsar, take to the wall and scout the village. Call out if you see anything. We will all meet back here as fast as were able."

Namyr nodded, his black curls bouncing with the movement. He unsheathed his longsword and dashed up a stairwell, disappearing from sight. Rythsar followed him, but as he came to the top of the wall he lithely bounded in the opposite direction.

"What about me?" Beryl asked, gripping the axe he had scavenged from Inee. The dwarf sawed at the ropes that bound him, and slid down the side of the cat to land with a grunt.

Azera took one glance at Selyni's blank face and replied, "Stay and guard Ori. I don't trust these fucking pussy cats. If they look like they're about to turn on you, shave off a few whiskers." Beryl smiled broadly and gave her a nod.

Sicaroo stepped to Aritian's side, and presented him with a sword. It was of northern make, and straight. The weight was odd, the style unfamiliar, but he appreciated the comfort of steel in his hand. He gave the boy a nod. He saw that Yi and Mingyo had strapped the waterskins over their shoulders and carried small daggers in either hand. Bo, Shan, Hui and Rong had armed themselves with traditional curved swords, and clustered around him.

Aritian looked into each of their eyes. All were Velonian. They were short and slim, yet to coming into their manhood. Bo and Rong were the oldest at fourteen. Bo had flat features and his head was shaved. Rong had curly, black hair, and almost golden eyes. He had a cruel caste to his thin lips, and his eyes were narrowed to thin slits. Shan and Hui were close in age, and looked alike enough to be brothers. Both had fine features, dark straight hair that was tied at the nape of their neck and green eyes. Yi on the other hand, had pale brown hair that curled around his ears and dark eyes. Aritian gave them all a nod and a small smile, approving of their readiness.

Aritian signaled in a complex series of hand gestures, and waited for their cut nods before slipping away without a word. He jogged along the right side of the street while Rong and Bo crossed to the other side, crouching low as they ran. Sicaroo and Hui dashed ahead, their swords held across their chests at the ready. Yi and Mingyo ran at his side, eyes flicking to the dark alcoves of the buildings, and Shan covered them from behind.

They made their way through the village with haste. It was small and though they moved carefully it took them no more than fifteen minutes to reach the village's center. Jade Pond had been a wealthy village, but the further they went the greater the destruction was.

A building to their left had collapsed inwards; crushed by something heavy. Another three buildings to their right held heavy cracks, as if they had been beaten in by some great war hammer. Dead soldiers and men who gripped long spears littered the ground in scores. A stand had taken place here, and those of Jade's Pond had lost. Aritian raised his hand in the air, signaling for them to slow their course.

In the center of the village was a large circular building. The structure was large enough to be a gymnasium, and two stories in height. Steam flowed from wide archways in white billows and spilled from open windows. Its domed roof was made with clay tile that glistened wetly with condensation. Small canals had been cut in to the street and were tiled with white stone, and led from the building both west and north in a series of two dozen quick moving streams. Aritian walked to the nearest one, and Mingyo and Yi bent before him to fill the waterskins.

Bo and Rong stood across the street, and made a hand gesture. Aritian shook his head no, indicating for them to stay there. The boys worked quickly, filling a dozen waterskins, and Aritian kept his gaze shifting across the buildings. Sicaroo turned his head sharply, holding a deep frown, and pointed toward the dome topped building. Aritian looked toward where the boy pointed, and saw movement in the billowing clouds of steam. Aritian smiled.

He gestured to Sicaroo and made several quick hand gestures. The boy shook his head no. Aritian pursed his lips and then narrowed his eyes. Sicaroo nodded, and walked silently to stand before Mingyo and Yi. Sicaroo signed to them with a quick flash of hand gestures and then turned to face the building sword at the ready. Shan turned his back and guarded the opposite direction. Aritian snapped his fingers once, and the crack of the motion echoed through the dead city. Rong and Bo's heads snapped toward him, and he tilted his chin toward the building. They both smiled in answer.

Aritian stalked across the street, and Bo and Rong followed him as he crept around the side of the building. They jumped over several streams, before coming to a large window. Clouds of steam boiled out. The steam was hot and made his eyes water, but Aritian ignored this discomfort and peaked over the edge of the sill. Pools of jade colored water bubbled and boiled from the center of the floor before being diverted through channels to larger pools and soak tubs. The floor and walls were tiled in white, and gold leaf had been inlaid along the rim of the central spring. Ceramic planters hung from the ceiling, and spilled long tendrils of yellowstar jasmine. The vines were in full bloom, and the yellow flowers filled the hall with an intoxicatingly sweet aroma.

Bo crouched at Aritian's side and made a few gestures toward the right, his eyes flicking repetitively toward the back of the hall. Aritian had to bite down to keep from gasping aloud: there, resting its head on the rim of the pool was the largest serpent Aritian had ever seen. The snake's golden scales glistened in the dim light. The beast was over two hundred feet long and as wide as a wagon. Its long body coiled and looped around the pools of water. A pair of long horns curved backwards over its skull, and a ridge of curved spike ran down the length of its spine. Aritian stared transfixed, taking every inch of its magnificence in, but then jerked away from the sill in shock. *This beast is no snake*, he thought in astonishment. Its heavy jaw rested on a pair of short legs that ended in black claws that curved to hooked points.

They had seen its barbed tail languidly playing in the fog

that danced at the entrance. Rong nodded toward it with a wicked smile, and raised his blade slightly. Aritian blinked owlishly twice. Both of the Dranguis nodded in response. They turned back to the window. The wyrm's hooded eyes snapped open, revealing a blood-red gaze. Lazily, it rose on its short legs as its head turned this way and that. Its nostrils flexed as it scented the air.

Aritian felt a low vibration fill the bottom of his skull, and knew by Bo and Rong's wide-eyes that they felt it too. A song filled their minds and wordlessly banished all thought. Aritian felt all his fear, anger, and anguish fall away. The voice was rolling and sweet, like liquid perfume, and filled them with promise as it curled through their minds. Aritian felt his stance relax, and all three rose from their crouched position. Aritian found his emotions flooded with giddiness and he heard himself chuckle. A smile spread of his face as he drank in the wyrm's sweet melody.

Aritian felt his pinky begin to grow hot. Sharp pain raced up his arm to his shoulder like a brand of fire. The song grew urgent with need. It filled his mind with a fast paced tempo and dimly he realized it was the sound of two heartbeats as they raced toward climax. Aritian panted as desire touched him and he gripped the sill as he cried out desperately. The image of Razia's face flashed through the song that filled his mind.

Aritian's grey eyes were swallowed instantly by black power. His head snapped up and he found himself staring into the wyrm's face mere inches from his own. Dimly, with the speed of thought, Aritian studied the face. The scales of the monster's face were overlapping and each shining scale looked as if it had been forged from pure gold. Aritian saw rows of curved teeth, and noticed that its heavy jaw dripped with saliva.

Aritian reacted instinctively, and swiped his hand out. He watched, as if in slow motion, his fingernails stretch and curl into sharp points. He raked them across the closet eye. The wyrm reared back, and screamed. Its voice rung through his head like the call of a thousand horns. He clutched his skull, and heard Rong and Bo hit the ground. Both cried out, clutching their heads. Aritian leapt through the windowsill.

The wyrm retreated hastily, slithering across the room as it coiled its length protectively around itself. It waved its maw toward the ceiling in agony, as it blinked its red eyes. Aritian chased after, running lightly across the slick floor. When he drew close he whipped his blade across the wyrm's body, scoring against the thick hide. A few scales fell, cut loose, to clatter to the floor with the sound of coin. The wyrm lunged downward, reacting with startling speed, and rammed its bony snout against his chest. Aritian felt all the air huff out of his lungs as he was flung across the room. He landed in one of the pools with a splash. Aritian clawed at the hot water and gained the surface sputtering for breath.

The wyrm snaked after him, its claws clipping noisily against the tile floor as it charged. Aritian kicked furiously to grab at the rim of the pool. He looked up, and found the wyrm leering down at him. Its jaw hung open in a frightening sibilance of a smile. Its left eye was closed and leaking black blood. Aritian opened his mouth to shout, knowing that the wyrm was about to strike.

Bo and Rong jumped through the window, roaring a battle cry. The wyrm snapped its head around, seeking the new threat. The boy's attacked, swinging their curved scimitar against the end of its tail, gaining its full attention. Its tail slunk away from them in a flash, even as it clawed its way across the pools toward them. The wyrm hurled its head out and Rong somersaulted backwards in a series of flips, narrowly dodging the snapping of its jaws. Bo danced around its head, bringing his blade across its face and horns. The beast flicked its neck, and one horn slapped against the boy's head with a sickening crack. Bo hit the ground like a ragdoll. Aritian pulled himself from the pool.

Aritian called out, "Ware the tail!"

The wyrm slung its tail across the room, coming from

behind Rong. Rong looked over his shoulder, and threw himself backwards, springing over the tail with mere inches to spare. The barbed spike crashed into the wall, shattering tile. Rong sprinted to the left, and dropped to the floor as the tail blurred above his head. He slid on his side toward Bo, leapt up, and moved to stand in a defensive position. The wyrm snaked forward in a rapid, wriggling S motion. Her tail flicked away from the wall, independent of her body and came toward the Dranguis high.

Aritian shouted, "Well come on old gal, let's see what you got." Rong rolled beneath the swipe of the tail just as the barb whistled through the air where his head had been. Rong grabbed Bo's shoulders, and began pulling him toward the entrance. Aritian smacked his sword against the tiled floor with a crack, and the wyrm's head twisted toward him. Aritian taunted it, yelling, "That's it. I'm the one who poked your pretty eye out."

The wyrm lunged across the room toward him with the speed of a striking viper. Aritian flung himself to the side as the wyrm's head shot past in charge of mass, scales and sinew. He whipped out his blade backhanded and felt it thunk against the wyrm's neck. He didn't turn to see if he spilled blood. He hurdled over a pool, landing on both feet, but the footing was slick, and he pinwheeled his arms to catch his balance. He looked over his shoulder, only to see the spiked tail zooming across the room toward him. Aritian lunged toward the wall and kicked off, somersaulting above the barbed tail. The tail crashed into the wall with a boom, tile raining from the wall. Aritian landed and ducked, expecting the tail to be whizzing toward him, but saw that the spike had been lodged in the stone wall and was stuck.

The wyrm jerked it frantically, trying to free itself. Aritian strode forward and hacked with all his strength. His sword began to bow and awkwardly curve, so great was his blows. Black blood was flung along the length of the wall. He struck it three more times, scoring deep. The wyrm roared with pain, and its body convoluted toward him. Aritian dodged to the side, but the wyrm's body crushed him against the wall. Aritian clawed desperately upwards, freeing his head above its rippling scales, but the creature's muscles were like iron. The wyrm pinned him firmly against the surface with its full weight. His chest and legs were being crushed. He could not breathe.

The wyrm tore its tail from the wall, and turned to face him. Its eye had grown swollen and bulbous with pus. The wyrm spoke into his mind. Its voice filled his head with despair, as it commanded control of his emotions. Nastily, it accused, *Nails of poison. Milk of a snake.* Aritian cried out as his mind was filled with sorrow. The voice hissed and spat with fire, and Aritian tasted the voice of Ignathra in her melodious tones. *How? How does it burn so? No snake can harm me, and you are no serpent. How have you come across my child's venom? How have you grown fangs at your fingertips?* The wyrm demanded with burning fury.

Aritian could barely breathe, and his vision began to cloud over with dots of darkness. He choked out one word, "Ronan." The wyrm's remaining eye bugled in recognition, but she was too late.

Aritian's mouth stretched and he felt his jaw unhinge. His gums burned with fire as fangs pushed his canines free, and he felt his teeth fall from his bloody mouth. Aritian lunged his head forward and bit into golden scales.

The wyrm screamed with such terror that the very foundation of the village trembled. Aritian felt his eardrums pop, and his ears began to bleed. His fangs pushed into taut sinew as his mouth filled with dark blood. The wyrm wrenched away from him with a scream, and Aritian fell to the floor.

His breath came in great gasps as his tortured lungs felt the cool touch of air. He coughed raggedly, and spat wyrm blood onto the floor. The wyrm writhed across the room, away from him. The poison was working fast, and Aritian could already see where he had bitten her swell and grow. Her movements became disjointed, and her body slammed into the walls. Tiles fell in sheets from the wall, only to shatter as the met the floor with a crash. Her tail dipped into pools and flung water in a wild spray, as she thrashed in the last throes of death.

Aritian pulled himself to his feet and walked toward her twitched head. He looked down at her, his gaze was red and his pupils split like a snakes. Softly, he whispered, "I'm sorry."

The wyrm double lidded eye blinked erratically, but she could still speak. Her voice filled his mind with tortured pain. *Oh, how it burns with such rage. Oh, the pain, how sweet it is. How thrilling.*

Tears streamed down Aritian's face, for he knew he had killed something great, something magnificent, and knew that the world would be lesser for it. Aritian repeated himself, "I'm sorry. You were going to kill us. I had no choice. I'm so very sorry." Looking at her now, all he felt was regret. She was gorgeous. Her scales rippled like molten gold, and her horns were a fine ivory.

The wyrm's voice was fading. Her twitching had stilled and her mouth gaped wide as she asked, *Your name.... who killed Sythilia? Who? Who?*

Aritian laid a hand on her horn, and whispered, "Aritian."

Sythilia laughed, filling his mind with her mirth, and promised, *I will tell my Lord. I will tell him.* Sythilia paused and Aritian knew she was close to the Shadow. When she spoke, her voice had grown desperate. *Take the eggs. Take them. The eggs. The last of me...my children....* Her head lolled to the side, and she whispered *...clutch.* Images flooded his mind. Aritian nodded, understanding her need. Sythilia fell silent, and her eyelids flicked closed. The wyrm was dead.

Aritian closed his eyes as the magic within retreated. His eyes burned as they morphed back to normal, and he felt his fang's recede into his upper jaw. Aritian opened his eye when the power had settled, and felt his teeth. The fangs were still there, but only the tips remained outside the gum line. He shook his head. He didn't know what was happening to him, but all he could think of was how grateful he was that he had seen Razia once more. She had come to him, and even though the image had lasted but a fraction of a second, it had saved their lives. Aritian turned and looked around the room. He was alone.

Aritian looked down at his left hand. From pinky to elbow, welts crawled along his skin in red clusters. The Ring of Suppression had tried to contain his magic, but had failed. He had felt the burning, torturous pain, but had been able to swallow it as he had so many times before. It was a frightening thought. He knew that because of his training the pain would not stop him as it was intended to do.

He retrieved his sword from where he had dropped it and walked around the pools to Sythilia's side. She had unrolled her long body in the last seconds of life. She had known what must be done. Her underbelly was darker, almost bronze in color, and the scales were much smaller, no larger than a common coin. Aritian's blade was bent nearly to a forty-five-degree angle. He took a moment to brace the sword against the floor, and used his foot to straighten it out as best as he could. Carefully, Aritian sliced between the two center rows of scales and worked the blade downward. It was hard work. He didn't want to cut her too deeply, but her scales and flesh were four inches thick and tougher than cowhide.

When he was done, he pulled the cut open wide. Black blood wept from the wound as her purplish-pink entrails spilled out at his feet. The stench was horrendous, but in that last moment of the wyrm's life, he had made a promise. Aritian worked his hands through her, relying on the memory she had gifted him with. When he came upon a smooth, rounded surface, he tore the membrane open. Gently, he reached within, hands slick, and pulled the first egg free. It was black and the size of a small melon. The shell was soft and covered in a yellow mucus. Aritian pulled off his long cloak and laid it on the ground before setting the egg on it. He worked speedily, pulling twelve more eggs' free. He felt inside her, making sure he left none behind. When he was sure none remained, Aritian folded the silk around the clutch and tied it closed; forming a rough carrying sack.

He heard footsteps approach and turned to see Selyni, Azera, Bo and Rong step through the steam that rolled from the entrance. Aritian smiled with relief, glad to see that Bo was unharmed. They gasped as they caught sight of the dead wyrm. Mournfully, Aritian called to them, "Sythilia the Fiercesome is dead." His companions stood there, enveloped in clouds of steam, staring at the sight with mouths agape wide.

Caethe

Chapter Nine:

Luxarma

Arkyn and Caethe walked timelessly through the forests of Avalon. Caethe did not know how long they had walked, but he knew that in any other realm days would have passed. Here, time stood still; motionless in a perpetual day. The ancient forest spread around them in a warm, sprawling haven. Soft, golden motes of light played across the forest floor, dappled sparingly through the breaks in the canopy above to bath the emerald moss that cushioned their footfalls with honey-tinged luminescence. A peace settled over them both; one that was marked without conversation. The Forest of Avalon was a relic from the another time. Caethe saw no other creatures, man or beast or otherwise, but he felt the eyes of many crawl along his back.

Whispered flapping of fragile wings filled the air above, as pixies hovered among the lowest branches of the canopy. Caethe knew from his years of study that each of the diminutive creatures had wings perfectly formed as a precious gem, sheer enough to see veins, and colored in shades as varying as the sky, sea, and land. They whispered to one another above, filling the canopy with the tongue of the forest.

At the edges of his vision he spied elves of impossible beauty, ever hidden by the trees around him. They moved silently through the forest, following the man and Fae. Their inner-brilliance illuminated the deep shadows of the ancient trees with radiant light. All of the undying land had come to see the Ronan mage. Caethe did not strain his eye toward them, rather he adopted Arkyn's stoic nature of unerring concentration as they wound through miles of forest.

Arkyn's tall stature and long legs ate ground quickly and Caethe found himself jogging at the Fae's heels. The grace of the Fae's steps were as light as stags, making not a sound, and the longer Caethe watched the more in awe he grew of the Fae's magnificence. The forest reacted to Arkyn's proximity with familiar joy. The trees reached out their heavy green limbs, brushing Arkyn's soft pelt as he passed, and flowers bloomed at his feet here and there, spilling fragrant perfume into the air. Their path was littered with bright blooms of purple, orange, lavender, and soft pinks. Caethe felt a clumsy beast in comparison. His every footfall was heard, be it the crackle of leaves or the snapping of a twig, and his breath was huffing and puffing as he trailed in Arkyn's wake.

Caethe broke the silence that had been held comfortably between them after what seemed like a week had passed, his mind itching with incessant curiosity. "The one you call forth has the power to walk through the Luxarma." It was a barely veiled question. Arkyn glanced over his shoulder and gifted him with a small, indulgent smile.

Arkyn's voice hummed with amusement as he said, "You swam through the Sea of Aelfmae for no more the fifteen seconds, and the Rán pulled forth many dozens of years from your essence. Step within the Luxarma and you shall be consumed instantly and utterly. The power to walk beyond the Luxarma rests solely with the Elder Fae."

Caethe surmised, "Then you shall pass through to call the one forward." The Fae nodded, agreeing. "This one, this magus..." Caethe remarked with consideration. He knew that it must be one of his southern cousins the Fae spoke of, for no other walked the mortal world that possessed the power to retrieve what he sought. "...Can be trusted." It was again, a half question, but Arkyn seemed unusually at ease compared to all the accounts Caethe had studied. Ekogina had seemed a more typical representation of their notorious demeanor. He remembered her fierce challenge and smiled.

Again, Arkyn nodded, and said warmly, "The one I shall call, I know quite intimately. He is a prodigy of my people and one I trust above all else, save for my own kin." Caethe's eyes widened in surprise, knowing that to have gained such praise from an Elder Fae was nigh impossible. He felt a flash of jealousy. *To study at the knee of a Fae was an honor beyond imagination*, he thought excitedly. More questions burned through his mind, but Arkyn quickened his pace. Caethe followed silently and harkened after. They traveled in silence once more.

A glow began to fill the forest, facing their approach. The light was silver and pale as moonlight. At first it was a mere tinge thrown against the rough bark of trees, but soon it grew until the forest silhouetted starkly against its brilliance. The power of the light was not constrained to its origin, but rather rolled across the land for miles and miles ahead. Caethe had never felt such might before, and in its greatness he trembled. The air had grown overly thick and he felt his skin redden as he faced the light. Caethe shaded his eyes against the glare, squinting as he sought to see beyond. A hand fell against his shoulder forestalling his steps, and Caethe awkwardly looked up at the tall Fae.

Arkyn cautioned, "You can go no further, Ronan of the Trescoronam. We have reached the edge of the Luxarma where the world, as you know it, ends. Stand here and witness." Caethe nodded, acquiescing.

Arkyn strode into the light, his tall form unbent against the glare. The halo of light that spun above his head grew brighter as he walked deeper into the Luxarma. His form became dark, but not lost to shadow — rather he became well-defined. The Fae took his last step forward, and he saw the wall of light ripple in response. As he passed the shield, Arkyn all of a sudden grew blurry as if he stood beyond a fogged glass.

The Fae stopped next to a large tree, and Caethe watched as he reached into a deep hollow. Arkyn pulled forth a small silver horn. It was as long as a man's arm, but curved, and its trunk held filigree glyphs of power. Caethe heart thundered at the sight. *A horn of Magrados*, Caethe thought in wonder. *A key to unlock gateways and door's beyond. A call that can sing across time and space. A weapon that can bend and break the very fabric of reality.* The horn was raised to the Fae's mouth and when the horn sung, its power rippled across the land. It blared like a dragon's roar, powerful and demanding, erupting with a voice that could not be denied. Caethe fell to his knees, overwhelmed. He caught himself with his two upper hands and braced himself against a tree as the sound carried across the realms.

Arkyn returned the horn within the tree and took two more steps south. So deep within the Luxarma, his form was like a dark cloud before a glaring sun and nearly lost to sight. Time passed and Caethe stood, regaining his composure. It did not take long before a new form to appear. Emerald fire rippled as a portal formed, and from it, a man stepped forth. Caethe's heart hammered in his chest. It had been a millennium since any of the Trescoronam laid eyes upon one of the lost Covens. Even among the long memory of the Ronan, some believed them merely fables of the past. Caethe strained his eyes desperately trying to observe as many details as he was able. So deep within the Luxarma as they were, it was but scant distinctions made.

The form within the light was taller, like most Ronan, and stood merely a few heads shorter than the Fae. The man was well-muscled, both broad and light of foot, and had a form more akin to that of a warrior then a magus. Caethe watched the man bow to Arkyn. The magi wore scant clothing, consisting of a loincloth that glinted metallically, a fur cape made from animal skin, and red feathers that adorned his dark hair and trailed down his back. The man's skin was tan and covered in dark tattooed lines. Caethe stepped forward, peering closer. The Luxarma flashed in response, scorching his skin a deep-blistered red. Caethe cried out, waving his hands before his face and was forced to retreat two steps.

The pair talked for a short period, but their voices did not pass beyond the barrier and so Caethe was forced to wait in silence. The man bowed once more, and disappeared in a flash of harsh, green flame that sputtered out the moment he passed through it. Only a curl of black smoke was left in his wake. Arkyn turned toward Caethe and gave him a deep nod. Caethe nodded in return, knowing that he must settle in to wait. Sinking to the ground, Caethe sat with his back against a tall oak tree and folded his hands neatly in his lap. With concentration, he let his senses expand. Before him, rising like a wall of flame the Luxarma sped into the sky and beyond. Caethe closed his eyes and let his senses expand away from the shield.

The forest of Avalon was unending, stretching beyond all senses. It was said that not even the Elder Fae knew how far the great forest spanned. The forest was ancient, an undying realm that had been born at times inception. It had long been a sanctuary to the Fey Folk, a haven where they could endure their immortal lives without care. Evergreen, the realm stood in full spring. The touch of night never shaded the forests reaching branches, nor dimmed its fair blue sky. It was an intoxicating place. A place where, if one was not careful, one could slip into an unending dream. Waiting as he was, Caethe fought the slow, sleepy contentment that seeped into his mind. It was like a fog that sought to drug him, ever seeking to pull his thoughts from his cares and lull him into forgetting all that he was.

Caethe sharpened his mind against the seducing power. He knew that a number of his kin had lost themselves within the forests of Avalon. They were damned to never again cross the bridge back into the mortal world and forever lost to wander aimlessly, without purpose or thought, until their long years had finally been spent. *I will not be one of them*, Caethe swore to himself. To distract himself, Caethe pushed his senses deeper. He opened his eyes and the forest disappeared from his sight revealing the true nature of the realm.

The forest was interconnected with slim, silver and gold light that gleamed brightly, bared to his naked eyes. He could see leylines of power stretching from one tree to the next, weaving a net that twisted and intertwined through every living thing. The tendrils even reached beyond the canopy, spinning thinly into the air where it met the warm sunlight and spun energy from the sky.

To his surprise, he found himself surrounded by many hundreds of brighter lights that stood like tall pillars next to trees or gleamed brightly like small flecks of starlight in the eaves. There was just over a hundred elves no more than thirty-feet from where he sat, their spirits gleaming with purity and strength. Above, in a like number, pixies walked along long branches or hovered behind leaves. They were not afraid of him, rather something held them back and stilled their curiosity with caution.

Caethe reached out toward one of the elves with his mind slowly, so as to seem non-threatening and open in his greeting. The light of the elf was a shocking cobalt that danced like the heart of a flame. He spoke to it, but without words, rather with his thoughts. *Greetings fair one, I am known as Caethe Ronan. I mean your people no harm. You have no need to shield your face from me.*

Caethe felt the energy grow in intensity and he sensed that the elf was tasting his thoughts, seeking the essence of his true self. *Arkyn has commanded that we do not interfere and so we do not.* The elf thought in reply. The voice that thrummed through his mind was neither male nor female, rather an androgynous euphonious voice colored with the strength of iron. *You are a curiosity to my people, Caethe son of Magrados. You come from the lands of Adonim, do you not?*

Caethe flicked his senses toward Arkyn. The Fae was pillar

of golden light more brilliant and rich then the Luxarma that he stood within. To look upon him was to risk blindness, and so Caethe turned his eye from the Fae, blinking rapidly as dark spots danced before his eyes. Caethe had not sensed any communication between the Fae and any other power while they had shared company. In truth, Caethe was unsurprised. The power of the Elder Fae was alien to his own.

Aye, I hail from Afta, though I have spent much of my life a prisoner in the lands known as Novus. Caethe said truthfully, knowing that any deception would easily be seen while communicating in such a form.

The elf seemed to hesitate, but soon many joined its light as its kin sensed their interaction. The light that gathered varied in color from individual to individual, ranging from cerulean, to ruby, to emerald and all color's between. It was like looking at gemstones turned to flame, and for a moment Caethe was taken aback by their beauty. When the elf spoke, its voice had gained confidence and all wariness had fled, joined as it was, by the multicolored flames of its people.

Now when it spoke, its voice was tinged with commanding, imperious tones. *Speak what you know of the Elves upon the mortal world of Adonim. Most of our people did not flee to the realm of Avalon, and weathered the storm that was the Great Sundering.*

Caethe bowed to their will and spoke of what he knew, careful to convey a polite version of the blunt truth. *After the great cataclysm recorded history became blurred, such was the confusion that followed. What I do know is that the lands of the Illustusta forest were decimated beyond repair.* Caethe felt the mind he was connected to shudder in response to his words.

Slowly and carefully Caethe continued, knowing that he must be delicate lest he offend and anger the elves around him. *Now, it is known as the Aznyr Desert.* Caethe felt the minds of the elves reach out and join with the first. Their collective conscious was vast, and Caethe felt his mind dwarfed before such an assembly.

Caethe pushed on despite the unnerve that crawled along his spine. *Magestorms ravaged the land, uncontrolled, twisting all who had not fled beyond recognition. A black storm of chaotic power rolls across the land to this day, taking any who dare touch its shores to the Black Gate of Shadow. Waves ravaged the coast, drowning it, and much of the land has fallen beneath the sea. The islands of Mortemal now flank the coast of the broken land, ruled by fell creatures. The mountain Duladad has risen where Etta once proudly stood, spilling liquid fire and smoke that colors the sky ever-dark from its roiling clouds. There are no elves within these damned lands. They are ruled now by the great black dragon, Calnimor.*

The collective consciousness rolled with emotion, a tumultuous storm of anguish, wrath and deep melancholy. The overwhelming emotion was like a sea that washed away Caethe's stoic resolve. A trail of tears fell down Caethe's cheek as he suffered their grief.

The elf that he had first spoken too sent a wave of choked grief; an almost pleading query thundering through Caethe's mind. *You make our hearts and souls weep. Surely, the fate of our people survived beyond the hope given by these dire words?*

Caethe bowed his head and assured, *hope remained. Trust with faith, your people more than survived despite the loss of your ancestral lands.*

The elf's voice once more grew hard and demanding. *Tell us, our hearts sing with sorrow and ache for the succor of triumphant news.*

Caethe spoke rapidly, for the minds he was connected to dragged forth his thoughts as quickly as he was able to form them. *The magus known as Solomon led your people to safety. On fifty-thousand ships they sailed east across the north Igidum Sea. They made port beyond the Mondeus Mountain Range and there populated the lands of the Ilvarsomni Forest, Yamillia Forest, Allisosian Plain, Urobor Island, Greenwood Forest, Sandivi Plains, Stellum Isles, and the Emerald Islands. Their numbers have grown beyond even the might* of the elves before the Sundering, and there they live alongside the Lesser Seelie court.*

Joy bloomed like a great flower, bursting with bright colors through the collective minds. Caethe found himself smiling drunkenly and for a time he luxuriated in the pure beauty of those that surrounded him. The elf who addressed him directly, spoke into his mind. *Our people have spread and fractured, but we take heart knowing that we have recovered our strength.* Caethe nodded in agreement.

Another mind spoke, distinctly male, and Caethe turned toward the light. The light was fiery-red, flashing with deep ruby. The voice was incredibly deep and held tones that were gravely, nearly bestial in nature. *We thank you Ronan, for these good tidings. Long have we wandered these hallowed forests, our minds pinned toward the shadow of hope.*

Caethe responded reverently. *It was my honor to gift you with such favorable knowledge.* Questions bubbled forth from his mind and before he could temper his curiosity, he asked, *May I implore your indulgence? I must admit myself curious as to why you few choose to flee to this realm? To leave your home and people, to live in such isolating exile, could not have been a choice made with ease.*

The first voice answered him with thoughts pregnant with emotion and bitter resentment. *We did not choose to live in such exile, child of Magrados. We were but children at the time of the Cataclysm. We are the last Druids of the Fair Folk. Our elders knew they would pay the price of their lives to Sunder Adonim from the power of Magrados and thus defeat the Dark Lady. To save us, they sent us to this realm so that one day we may return the strength of magic to our brethren.*

Caethe found his thoughts racing. Those elves upon Adonim had all but been abandoned by magic. If these elves should return to Adonim, the strength of the elves would grow ever greater than the mighty supremacy the nation already held. Caethe replied simply, *I see.*

A lilting voice, musical and female, spoke to him. Her

voice was like the softest touch of lily petals and her light a sheer, apricot color, flecked with rose-gold accents. *We wish to know, does the Magi known as Solomon live still?*

Caethe shook his head, his memory stretching to a near forgotten history lesson given when he was a young child. After a moment of consideration, he answered. *No, he was killed a few centuries after the Great Sundering.* A collective cry filled his mind, as the elves reacted to the death of Solomon.

Does this foul enemy who stole his life still walk the lands of Adonim? The deep voice of the male asked, his thoughts ribbed with colors of blood and the promise of violence.

Caethe shuddered beneath his animalistic fury. There was something disturbing about the male who spoke to him. Caethe could sense a wildness in the elf, untamed and deadly dangerous. Caethe replied speedily, *Cornelius and his son Cain murdered Solomon. The former succeeded him on the Weirwood throne, but both have since been killed.*

The female's thoughts raced through his mind as quick as a warm, spring creek. *It spurns our hearts that their darkness no longer plagues the land, but we weep with sorrow that we were not there to protect the one who proved our people's savior. We will light the stars in his honor. Forevermore, the name Solomon will be held in the highest esteem.*

Thank you. Caethe said, unsure of what exactly she meant, but sensing that it was an honor.

The neutral voice addressed him, but the thoughts had grown distant. *The magus Xokipilli has joined Arkyn. Your time within this realm grows short. If you ever come to find yourself among our people on Adonim, say my name: Ibreal, and they shall grant you asylum. Farewell, Caethe.*

Caethe nodded and dropped the magesight, allowing his vision to return to normal. He stood and watched the pair beyond the Luxarma intently. The mage had indeed returned to Arkyn's side. *Xokipilli,* Caethe thought, tasting the foreign name on his tongue as he committed it to memory. Xokipilli stood before Arkyn with obvious exhaustion. His shoulders were slumped and he clung to a tall staff that he now carried, depending on it heavily to remain standing. Obscured as they were, Caethe couldn't be sure if the man was wounded or not. Briefly, Caethe wondered what the mage had gone through in the intervening time. It would not have been easy, Caethe knew, but he pushed the thought away. The man had done as he was commanded, as was right. Caethe was a Trescoronam Ronan, a member of the royal Coven, and Xokipilli owed him his fealty.

Xokipilli handed Arkyn an object and then turned to face Caethe. He bowed deeply, his tall stature folding gracefully. Caethe smiled, and gave the man a deep nod. The emerald flames once more appeared and the man limped into the flames and disappeared from sight.

Arkyn walked through the Luxarma toward Caethe. In his hands he carried something long and thin. Caethe waited eagerly, his legs trembling and his hands clenched with the force of his unveiled anticipation.

Aritian

Chapter Ten:

The Scarlet Witch

The Feligni ran smoothly across the barren land having left the dunes behind in the midmorning. Now, the sun sat low and red on the horizon. They had traveled some seventy miles during the day, and soon they knew they would come upon the entity known as the Ancient One. The land here was hard and cracked with thirst, and the wind played across the plain, coating them in a gritty, white dust. Aritian had remained mute on the death of the wyrm, but Selyni had lingered behind a few moment's eying the creature's corpse. After taking what provisions they could find, they had fled the village of Jade Pond and camped some twenty miles into the desert. No one had been keen on staying in that place of death.

Aritian rode crouched over, with one hand tightly gripping the cats loose folded skin and the other clutching the sling he wore across his chest. The weight of the wyrm eggs was heavy, but comforting. He had not told anyone about them, and only stared dumbly when asked what he carried. It was his secret, one he would guard jealously, and he felt no inclination to tell anyone. He had fashioned the sling from heavy canvas and padded it with reams of torn silk. When he felt the shape of the eggs beneath his hand, he heard the faintest trill of voices in his head. He smiled.

"Look there, a camp." Azera called. Her eyes were desperate as she turned toward Selyni, and asked, "Is it the Ancient One?" Aritian looked between the bobbing ears of the Feligni, and saw a dark stain on the horizon. A series nine black tents were pitched across a half a mile. The tents were nothing like the torn, ragged tents they slept within. These were massive structures that towered thirty-feet in height, each more than a hundred feet wide. The black silk was unmarked, without decoration or sigil. Aritian could see soldiers walking among the tents in the hundreds, and a line of a few hundred horse's stretched along the right side of the encampment.

Selyni nodded, and the Feligni doubled their speed as they fled across the distance. Ori's litter bounced and bobbed in the wild pace, and the blanket covering his face fell. Aritian's heart sunk at the sight of him. The boy had been unconsciousness for five days now, and Selyni claimed that it was only due to his giant blood that he had even survived this long. Ori's skin was sallow, and his blonde hair was slick with sweat. His eyes fluttered, but did not open. Aritian bent forward, urging his mount to greater speed.

When they came upon the camp, Selyni slowed their mounts and they entered at a casual pace. Their feline mounts' chests rose and fell hard, their vented throats rasping with a *whoosh, whoosh* sound. They were met by soldiers standing in ranks along the center of the camp. Their faces were covered with white silk, and they wore heavy chainmail over black tunics with scimitars and spears uniformly at their sides. The soldiers were silent, and made no move to bar their path, nor did they seem startled by their strange mounts. Beryl and the young Dranguis looked to either side of them, eyeing the soldiers uneasily. Namyr waved to the men, beaming cockily. Rythsar dismounted, and jogged to his side as Aritian sat up, not wishing to approach so ungracefully hunched over.

A tent stood at the center of the camp. This tent was different than the rest, circular and grand, with a peaked roof and a flaming-red sigil that depicted a large bird wreathed in flame. Tall golden spears had been planted into the hard ground, flanking either side of the entrance. Before the tent lay a rug that swirled with maroon and black geometric shapes, set with a small copper brazier and two wooden benches that held dark pillows. Namyr dismounted gracefully and bowed to the two soldiers who stood guard before the tent. He chatted animatedly with them, but Aritian couldn't hear his words as he dismounted. Aritian lifted the sling over his head, and handed the bundle to Rythsar. The lorith looked surprised, and Aritian gave the Rythsar a pointed looked. The reptilian nodded, stepping away.

Azera walked boldly across the camp to the rich rug, and asked, "Well, where is she? Where is this mysterious Ancient One?" She looked around with exaggerated worry, waving her arms in near panic.

Namyr beamed at Azera, and said arrogantly, "You don't have an audience."

Azera's eyes bulged with anger and in outraged, bellowed, "Excuse me?" Namyr shook his head and pouted in mock despair. Azera's shoulders shook and her expression grew tight as she roared, "I just rode a fucking cat across the Ignis in hopes of saving my brother. I must speak with her. Move aside." Azera stepped forward, raising a hand as she prepared to bat the small man from her path.

Selyni ran to her side, and grabbed her arm. Azera wrenched her arm away, but Selyni shook her head no, her eyes pleading as she warned, "Don't, you'll only get yourself killed." Azera's mouth worked voicelessly as she tried to control her emotions. Her arm fell then and she retreated a step back.

Namyr waved to Aritian, and said cheerfully, "Aritian will speak to her on your behalf. Your brother's life once again resides in his hands. If he manages to convince her, the Ancient One will save your brother. If he cannot..." Namyr let his words trail away as he smiled viciously.

Aritian walked forward. Sicaroo and Bo touched their brow in question, but Aritian shook his head and they stood at ease. He made to pass Azera, but the Titan grabbed his forearm with a grip of an iron-vice. Aritian could feel his skin bruise beneath her touch as Azera leaned down to growl in his ear, "Save him any way you can. If she refuses, kill her." Aritian nodded tightly, and Azera let go of his arm.

Namyr bowed with a flourish and stepped to the side. The soldiers pulled back the flaps of the tents entrance and Aritian stepped inside. The harsh sunlight faded instantly as the flaps fell closed, and the room fell to muted shadow. The massive tent was stark, lacking any décor but one: a woman sat on a throne, watching him silently. The throne was simple, but made of pure gold that shone softly in the dim light, framing her figure. The woman sat so still that Aritian would have thought her a statue of pure perfection had not her odd, red eyes flicked across his face in astute assessment. Aritian found himself entrapped by her gaze, and for a moment simply stared soundlessly at her.

The woman was dressed in a traditional kimono; a sign that he stood before Velonian nobility. The kimono was black, and richly made with long flowing silken skirts that spilled down the three dark wooden steps that lead to her throne. Her skin was warm as if merely kissed by the sun; hinting that she was at least half northern. A gold torque circled her elegant neck and her long, black hair was tied neatly atop her head in intricate braids trapped within a net of finely-spun, gold chain. Her face was delicate, crafted with small features and sharp cheekbones. Aritian didn't think he had ever seen a woman so desirable in all his life and stood awestruck in the face of such perfection.

When she spoke, her voice came in a low whisper, "Aritian of Inee, I am most pleased to meet you. I am known as Maud. We have much to discuss, you and I." Her voice was pleasant to the ear, the epitome of femininity, and held a soft, lilting pitch. Aritian imagined that he could listen to her voice for the rest of his life and never have another care in the world. Maud pursed her thick, red lips in annoyance, and said, "If you wouldn't mind gracing me with respect, we may proceed."

Aritian shook his head, clearing his mind, as his cheeks bloomed red. Aritian bowed, instinctively knowing that this woman was due such a courtesy. *Surely, this cannot be the woman Selyni spoke of*, Aritian thought with confusion as he eyed the youth of her beauty.

Maud did not smile, but held his gaze for a full minute. Aritian dropped his eyes to the floor, unable to withstand her red glare. When Maud spoke, her word measured. "Two years ago I sensed a blooming of Ronan power. Since that moment I have spare no expense or resource discovering the source. Ignea is a large continent, but I knew with time that I would find you. Now, here you stand in all your glorious wonder. My eyes have not laid upon a Ronan child for more than half a century." Maud let a shadow of a smile grace her lips as she took in his form. With a half-smile she said, "We are family, you and I, descendants of a most ancient bloodline. A bloodline that holds tremendous power, as you have discovered."

Aritian heart sang with wonder as he contemplated the thought that he might hold familiar ties to such a glorious woman. It was beyond reason. She was magnificent. Deep within him, he felt something between them sing with recognition. He looked at her awestruck, and her smile spread. Softly, she said, "In time you will come to understand what this means, but for now we must place pleasantries aside. I have come here at great personal risk." Her voice grew hard and cold, as she said, "You have no sense of control over your emotions or power." Aritian felt shame overtake him and he bowed under her stinging rebuke. "This cannot continue. You must understand that there is always, and I mean always, a consequence to using magic." Maud stood and Aritian looked up from his feet as her tone changed.

Aritian saw power brimming in her dark eyes as her might rose before him, invisible to the naked eye, but undeniably present. Its strength made his legs weak, and his heart skip. Never had he felt anything so formidable in his life, and he could only compare her presence to that of what he imagined a god would command. Evenly, she accused, "You killed my grandson, Hector, and your human lover too. Their deaths stain your hands and the weight of that responsibility is the price you must pay for your inability to control that which resides within. You have unleashed your power brashly Aritian, and that is unacceptable."

Her commendation stuck Aritian like a bolt of lightning. He wanted to speak, to deny her words, but he could not wake his voice. Grief screamed denial through his thoughts like a raucous chorus, but he knew without a doubt that Maud spoke the truth. Deep down, Aritian had held out hope that Razia had somehow survived the inferno. That she had been saved by Ignathra, or was somehow, somewhere still alive, anything and anywhere, but dead. It had been a silly thought, one born from desperation, but with Maud's cruel words, Aritian knew all hope for such fancy was lost.

Maud held his gaze as his emotions crashed down upon him and filled his eyes, drowning him beneath a tortured sea. Her eyes gleamed, daring him to challenge her word. Aritian closed his eyes, and the image of Razia floated before him in the darkness. *Razia, please forgive me*, Aritian thought as he reached in his mind for her smiling face. His hand nearly touched her cheek, but before he could touch her the image fled into darkness like wisps of smoke. *I'll never touch her again.* The thought coursed through him, and Aritian screamed internally as his heart burned with self-damnation. *It's all my fault, I killed you*, Aritian thought sorrowfully. Tears spilled from his clenched eyes.

When Maud spoke next, her tone had grown sympathetic, "You blame yourself, and while you must shoulder some of the responsibility, the fault is not entirely your own." Aritian shook his head, his eyes still closed. Maud continued, "You are Ronan, Aritian, ours is no easy burden and this will not be the last sacrifice you're likely to make. Mourn your human, but know this: you are not human and no matter how much you may wish it, you never have been and never will be." Aritian eyes snapped open at the pronouncement. Maud held a small smirk as she drank in his aghast expression. Aritian saw the arrogant contempt in her eyes, and knew then that she found his grief a weakness.

Aritian choked out the words, "Razia is dead." The words stuck to his tongue like viscous poison. He shook with fury and grief, as adrenaline pumped through his veins. His thoughts were jagged, as he cried, "I killed her, Maud. Whatever you believe about me doesn't matter." Maud let a single eyebrow rise at this declaration. "Don't you understand?" He asked wildly. "I murdered the one person in this world that mattered. I thought maybe...maybe that you would lift this curse from my soul. Take it away so that I may never hurt another." He held out a trembling hand, pleading.

Maud stepped before him and with no preamble, slapped him across the face with a crack. The force delivered from her petite hand knocked him to his knees and Aritian clutched his stinging cheek as he eyed her from the ground. Maud smiled down at him with a feral wildness, and callously whispered, "Your ugly display of emotion is over. You are not a babe to be coddled at the tit. You don't see me wailing at Hector's death, begging the gods for salvation. They were human, Aritian." The words were spat with barely-veiled disgust. "You will live a hundred human lives, if not more, and Razia will be forgotten as easily as a grain of sand beneath the heel of your boot." Aritian inhaled sharply at her promise, his mind screaming defiantly against her callous cruelty.

"How could your heart be so cold?" Aritian asked, gazing up at her, rivers of tears falling down his chin. Maud remained silent, and Aritian closed his eyes as he whispered, "I am disgusted by what I've done. I don't want these... these powers. This magic is some foul demonry, and if I could cleave it from my breast, I would."

The power sitting within the deepest part of him was no longer alluring; rather he looked within with revulsion.

"I don't want any of this," Aritian beseeched, and prayed aloud, uncaring of Maud's disgusted stare. "Ignathra, please, strike me dead. No god could forgive the act of killing your one true love."

Aritian's steel-grey eyes burned black, and power rippled through him. The walls of the tent flapped wildly as his power sought escape. The ring at his finger flashed with white light. Aritian collapsed to the ground, his back arching as he his body was rocked with spasms of pain. Maud smiled down at him, and rested a hand on his head.

Sweetly, Maud said, "Your melodramatics have come to an end. That path is no longer open to you. The choice is no longer yours. Your life is no longer your own. You are a Ronan and from this day forward you belong to the Coven." She patted his head with feigned sympathy, as one would when placating a child, before turning from him. Her skirts whispered across the wooden floor, as she took her seat on the throne once more. "The Ring of Suppression cannot be broken, for it was made by me. I sense great power within you, Aritian, but your magic is a mere babe compared to the might I command. The ring is a training mechanism that will prevent you from harming yourself and others."

Aritian laughed, but it was not out of humor, rather it was born out of virulent despair. In a low growl, he said, "So the chains pass from one Master to the next."

Maud shook her head, and coldly said, "I am not your Master, Aritian, but I am your elder. You will abide my word." With a wave of her hand she commanded, "Stand, so we may dispense with this foolishness and put this behind us." Maud did not wait to see if he complied, but waved toward the tents entry. The black silk that blocked the entrance fell to the ground as if by its own accord, and sunlight spilled into the tent.

Aritian stood, blinking in the bright light as men entered. Four soldiers carried the litter Ori lay upon and grunting, they set their heavy burden down before the throne. Aritian heart dropped when he saw Ori's face. Azera had made him keep his distance, and this was the first time Aritian was able to see the Titan up close. Ori lay as still as death. His pale skin was ashen, and his lips were touched with a hue of blue. Only the rattling wheeze of his struggling breath gave indication that he still lived. Aritian fell to his knees and gripped the young Titan's cold hand. Ori's hair had been brushed and braided neatly off his face, and while he looked to be taken by a chill, beads of sweat clung to his broad forehead.

Aritian looked up at Maud pleadingly, begging, "Please, if you are kin to me, save him. Save him and I will be obedient. Please." Aritian thought of Azera's whispered words. He knew he had no hope of triumphing over this woman. He could only beg her favor.

Maud stood and said, "Very well, but I will not save him alone. If you wish for this creature to live then you must be the one to bring him back from the threshold." Aritian shook his head fearfully, his eyes flashing with worry. *I am cursed. This power can only destroy,* Aritian thought with dread. Maud continued, "I will release your power from the Ring of Suppression and guide you. You must learn and quickly, or your friend will die." Aritian didn't know how he could learn such a thing, but he knew he would try anything if it gave Ori a chance.

"I will do whatever you ask, just please hurry." Aritian begged, his emotions brittle. Maud nodded, and stepped from the throne. She knelt at Ori's side, opposite of Aritian. Gently, Maud stroked Ori's face. Aritian was shocked by the compassionate touch. She had been callous just minutes before, and now she looked down upon Ori emphatically as if he were her own child. Aritian realized that the woman before him was more complex than he could hope to understand.

Maud met his eyes with her maroon stare, and whispered, "I must warn you, bringing someone back from the edge of death will require much power."

Aritian nodded. He had learned the price of power and its rebuke still stung. Forcefully, he whispered back, "I will give him everything I have, if that is what it takes."

Maud smiled lazily, and explained, "Brute force will not save him. He dances on the edge of a precipice. Push too hard and your power will kill him as surely as his broken back. Let me enter your mind. Lower your guard, and I will show you the way." The thought of Maud, or anyone, in his mind repulsed him. The image of the pale woman wreathed in pale flame and her warning flashed in his mind. Aritian knew he could not trust Maud. Instinctively, he buried the memory and banished any thoughts of doubt from his mind. He had no choice.

Aritian replied grimly, "I will try."

In a voice devoid of emotion, Maud warned, "It will change him." Aritian cocked his head in question. Sweat began to trickle down Aritian's forehead. The heat of the tent was stifling. Maud brushed a wayward strand of blonde hair off Ori's face, before elaborating. "He is no magi. His body won't acclimate to the power, rather the power will change him to ensure that he lives. Do you still dare to proceed?"

Wildly, Aritian thoughts raced as he tried to imagine in what way the Titan would be changed. In the end though, Aritian knew it didn't matter. He had no choice. Aritian nodded, saying, "I must."

The corner of Maud's lip twitched in a smile, and she said stonily, "Swear to me that in return for saving this life, you will serve the Coven."

Maud's eyes glowed with hungry, ruddy-light as she stared into his eyes. Aritian knew that making this oath he would be resigning himself to her rule. Briefly, he closed his eyes in prayer to Ignathra. His voiceless question for guidance was answered with silence. Aritian opened his eyes, and said emotionlessly, "I swear it."

Maud held his eyes in her strange gaze for a moment, before nodding. When she spoke her tone was light, and she gifted him with a warm smile, as she said, "Good, now let us begin." Aritian nodded with a grimace, knowing that her smile was triumphant. She had won. What game she played, he did not know, but he knew in his heart that he had lost.

Maud reached across Ori and touched Aritian's temple with the tips of her fingers. With the gentle touch her power thundered through him. For a time, his mind was lost in the sea of her influence. Like a flailing fawn thrown into a raging river Aritian struggled awkwardly to orient himself in the current of magic. Aritian looked into her eyes and saw that they rolled with darkness. He felt his own eyes burn with power, but the ring at his finger remained cool.

Hesitantly, Aritian released his power to her control. Maud wasted no time. She gripped his mind with the fist of her might, and drew forth his magic. His power swirled around him like a red hurricane, filling him with ecstasy. In his mind's eye, Maud's power was a dark, scarlet fire that swirled with perfect control as it coiled around his own with surety and grace. When their power met Aritian tasted her. There was no other explanation for it. It was as if her pure essence filled his senses, and he could feel the antiquity and vibrancy of her like an aged wine. It washed over him and he drank her in. Aritian had never before felt fear like he did then.

Aritian felt his arms move on their own accord. He rested his left palm on Ori's chest and his right hand on the Titan's stomach. Maud's hands left his temple. The connection had been made. Her hands floated above his own; close, but not touching. Quickly, like a puppeteer, she moved his mind, shaping his power. Aritian didn't understand the complex way his mind weaved, but he saw his hands begin to glow with a pure, golden light. The light began to glow brighter and brighter, as it gathered in strength.

Aritian felt energy rush from him, and his breath quickened as if he had run a mile-long sprint. Still the light grew until his hands were lost from sight in harsh, glaring light. Maud dropped his mind from her control, and ceased to sculpt his power. He felt the softness of her palms meet the top of his hands. Slowly, Maud's hands began to move forming symbols and shapes. To his surprise, Aritian found his own hands moving in synchrony with her graceful movements. Aritian eyes moved from the golden light and met Maud's steady gaze with surprise. Maud smiled, before blinking rapidly three times. Aritian vision flashed as his own eyes mimicked her own. When his eyes opened after the last blink, he looked down.

Ori was awash in a network of nebulous green light that raced up and down his body. Like veins, the light crisscrossed across his form, connecting with one another as they spun an intricately weaved network. Aritian looked closer and saw that there were splotches of darkness around Ori's body where the channels were stymied. As he looked down at Ori's body he saw that the darkness bloomed around his lower spine and radiated from there. Nearly all of the lines leading from the spine were black or darkening. Aritian felt his hands blur in movement.

Slowly, as if watching stars falling from the night's sky, the golden light sunk downward and banished the darkness. The nebulous network slowly drank in the power and new strands weaved across the voids of darkness, creating new patterns across the gaps of darkness. Instead of fading to green to match the light elsewhere in Ori's body, the light where the magic formed remained golden.

Aritian fell backwards to the heels of his feet as the power left his eyes and black spots danced across his vison. Aritian's heart raced rapidly and fatigue tore at his mind, threatening unconsciousness, and he braced himself upright with both hands. Maud smiled kindly as she stood.

Aritian's eyes flashed back to Ori. The glowing nexus was gone. His sight had returned to normal. As he watched the

Titan's skin took on a healthy glow, and the beads of sweat that had clung to his brow fled. Ori now looked as if he merely slept. In that moment, the day's darkness lightened, for Aritian knew with certainty that a miracle had taken place.

Ori's eyes flickered open. Aritian touched the boy's arm, and Ori's eyes settled on him. Hoarsely, Ori asked, "Aritian, what happened? The last thing I remember was Selyni falling from the air and then nothing, just darkness. Where am I?"

Aritian made to speak, but it was Maud who answered first. She had reclaimed her seat on the throne, and as she looked down upon the Titan she addressed him directly.

"We are within the Ignis Desert. As for what happened... well to be brief, you nearly died." Maud waved a hand toward Aritian, before adding imperiously, "Aritian used his power to bring you back from certain death. He healed your shattered spine, saving your life. You owe him, Titan."

Ori looked at Aritian with awe, and asked quietly, "Is this true? Did I truly almost die?" Aritian nodded weakly back. Gingerly, Ori sat up. He flexed his hands and feet, as he looked over his body for wounds. Hesitantly, he stood. Aritian had to choke back tears of relief. Beaming, the Titan looked down at Aritian, and said solemnly, "Thank you Aritian. Truly, I am in your debt." Ori bowed.

Aritian closed his eyes. *I did nothing! It was all her*, he thought desperately, wishing he could shout denials. Instead, he said, "Thank Ignathra, for it is by his grace that I have this gift."

Aritian saw Maud roll her eyes behind the Titan's back, but she didn't correct him. She looked to the soldiers who silently watched from the doorway, and ordered, "Escort Ori from the tent. I am sure that his sister is anxious to see him in good health." The soldiers saluted and Ori looked at the woman curiously, before looking back to Aritian. Aritian gave Ori a nod, and the boy joined the soldiers as they left the tent.

Aritian made to stand, but found himself too weak and settled for sitting cross-legged. They sat in silence for a time.

Aritian found himself struggling against a river of grief. He had healed Ori, but it was by no means a penance for what he had done to Razia. At the thought of her name, he felt his eyes begin to glisten, but he hurriedly wiped away the tears before they could fall. *I've shown too much weakness before this woman already*, he chastised himself.

Meekly, Aritian said, "I am sorry for the death of your grandson. I never met Hector, but Selyni said he was a good man." The words were empty, but Aritian knew he could not live with himself without apologizing. To take an innocent life was to take light from the world. Those he had killed before had been just a name, given to him by his masters. He had not known them. He had been a tool, a weapon of death. Even so, he had always atoned for his sins.

"A good man?" Maud asked in reply. She laughed, and said callously, "He was obedient if that's what you mean, but he was by no means good. No child of man is." Her dark gaze settled on him, and she said, "I meant what I said before. Do not hold yourself to ideologies of lesser creatures. Such laws do not bind you. No god can touch your soul. You are not human, and the sooner you come to terms with that the easier your mind will rest."

Aritian closed his eyes as his mind refuted her words. In a hoarse whisper, he asked, "What now?" He was unable to meet the witch's scarlet eyes.

Maud smiled lazily, and said, "Now we return to the city of Creuen. There, we will begin your training immediately. What you performed today is but a sliver of the knowledge you must learn." She stroked the golden armrest of her throne as she held him in her hungry gaze. After a moment, she added, "And then you will uphold your promise to me and serve." Aritian raised his eyes and held her gaze, before nodding tightly. Soon, he knew, he would learn the price of his oath.

Devaney

Chapter Eleven:

An Oath Sworn

Devaney woke slowly. Her eyes were crusted, and her throat burned with bile. She felt weak, so desperately weak. She moaned softly, and Lifoy was at her side. "Be calm Mistress of Demons, you are safe." Lifoy said gently. She felt his hand push away curly hair from her forehead.

Devaney opened her eyes, but saw only darkness. She was blind once more. A startled grasp clutched her throat and tears sprang to her eyes. With a moan, she said, "I'm blind again. I can't see." In a wail, she said, "Only darkness. Oh, the terrible darkness." Panic filled her heart and she struggled to sit up.

Lifoy pressed her firmly down, and assured, "It will return. Your sight will return. Be calm, now." Devaney settled, desperately clinging to his words of hope. Sternly, Lifoy said, "You should not have called that demon. You should not have known how to."

Weakly, Devaney croaked, "Why?"

In an exasperated voice, Lifoy explained, "Because, dear one, you didn't summon him in a circle. You did not tie the calling to the leylines of Adonim. I am surprised he remained in control at all. He fed solely off your strength. You're too young for such advanced magic. It was foolish." Lifoy's voice had grown tight with anger.

Devaney whispered, "The Ordu..."

Lifoy shifted at her side, and replied in monotones, "All dead, and us the honorable guests of King Paul Thoriston, the mighty ruler of Agos. You got lucky, girl. Usually priests don't accompany the navy, at least not among the first wave. If there had been, they would have destroyed the demon easily." Devaney smiled weakly. She was not sorry that the Ordu soldiers were dead, and knew if she came upon them again she would not hesitate to strike them down, priests or no priests. She felt sated. Devaney had tasted revenge for the first time, and it was delectable to her burning sorrow. Like an addict, she already felt her anger salivating for more.

Lifoy looked at Devaney with concern. Her blood lust for revenge had made her reckless. He only hoped he could keep her under control until they reached Shades Island. As he thought of his ancestral home, he grimaced. Ultan would not be pleased. Lifoy pushed all of his uneasiness from his voice, and said lightly, "We are now in the city of Greenshield under the king's esteemed protection."

Devaney waved her hands toward her face, fear ribbed her voice as she said, "My sight..."

"Will come back once you have recovered." Lifoy said confidently. "You have slept for three days."

Devaney nodded, closing her eyes as she fought the tears that threatened to spill. "I'm sorry, Lifoy." She said, knowing that she had put him in danger.

Lifoy whispered, "I know." Silence fell between them. Devaney fought to control her emotions, and Lifoy fought the words of anger that threatened to boil from his mouth. After a moment, in a gentle chastisement, Lifoy said, "Devaney, you must understand that we have remained hidden for good reason. Those of the Faith can bind us, should they learn your true name. The Ordu has learned our weakness and can imprison us with ease. They don't care if they have to spend a hundred men to subdue you. They'll pay it happily, and you will not be glad to share their company. You cannot do what you did, ever again... at least not until the Ronan are free from exile."

Devaney shrugged her shoulders, and asked, "How could

the Faith learn my true name? They do not know me. I am not of this land."

Lifoy warned, "They have powerful priests who can discern such things. We must take care." Devaney nodded, placating Lifoy. "Do not underestimate the Ordu. They have agents everywhere, living in secret ready to strike in their god's name. They would risk all to bring you to the motherland." Lifoy warned crossly.

"I will take care, Lifoy." Devaney promised. In her heart though, she smiled and thought, *First blood was spilt by you, Ordu, to your folly. I have struck now, and oh how delightful it felt. Soon we will meet again,* she promised the god.

A flash of thought filled her mind, and she sat up straight. In a hushed whisper, she said, "The puppets... there is another Ronan here!"

Lifoy nodded, and said excitedly, "Yes, I must leave your side and discover the source. You will be safe here."

Devaney's face twisted, as though she was trying to remember something from long ago. The memory came to her mind and she smiled, saying, "Find him in the tinker's shop, red door, on Cherry St..." Her voice grew sharp as she warned, "Lifoy you will not touch him. Just find him. Do not speak to him or tell anyone of his presence."

"You presume much." Lifoy admonished, his voice growing indignant.

Devaney frowned and turned her sightless gaze toward where she knew Lifoy sat. In a low whisper, she challenged, "You trifle with Prophecy."

Lifoy stood and glowered down at her. In a cold voice, he said, "I am under an obligation to bring him to the Archmagus."

Devaney matched his tone with a wicked smile, and promised, "Then I am under an obligation to call forth my demon and with my last breath command him to strike you down."

For a moment there was a struggle of wills. Neither wished to relent, but in the end, Lifoy said quietly, "Very well." He turned from her bed, and strode across the large room. He knocked on the door three times, notifying the guards that he wished to leave. Under his breath he muttered, "Damn Oracles."

When he had left, Devaney closed her eyes and sighed heavily. She struggled to sit up. Her head spun dizzily, and she sat for a moment letting her balance return. Her mind ached with pain, but she pushed it to the side. She threw off the blankets and stood. Carefully, she made her way across the unfamiliar room. Without her staff, her progress was slow going. She smoothed down the cotton shift she wore and reached out with her hands, tracing the length of the bed.

When she felt the bed end, her outstretched hands found a long, low desk. She traced its surface. A tidy pile of parchment waited, along with an inkpot and some leather-bound books. They were worthless to her. She could neither read nor write, and so moved on. She came upon a tall dresser and smiled. Briskly, she opened the wardrobe and felt inside. It seemed as though either Lifoy or her new host had outfitted her with several gowns. Devaney ran her hand down the length of the dresses and snorted, thinking, *definitely Lifoy*. The gowns were adorned with lace, frilled at the collar and sleeve. Around the collar she could feel that many of them beaded or set with gemstones. She shrugged her shoulders, resigning herself to the gaudy apparel and consoled herself that, at the very least, none required a corset.

Devaney choose one that seemed to have the least fills, and after discarding her shift, pulled it over her head. The gown was tight, well fitting, and swept to the floor. Devaney moved from the wardrobe with one hand before her, and with the other, ran her hand through her thick hair. She tripped over the pack that had been left in the center of the room with a startled gasp. Devaney flung her hands out before her as she landed, and only managed to dent the stone floor with her head. She sat up in a tangle of skirts, rubbing her forehead as she heard the door bang open. By the footsteps she knew that two men had entered.

"My Lady, we heard a fall. Are ye' ok?" A heavily accented voice said to her left. Devaney felt her cheeks grow red with embarrassment.

"Yes, I am fine. Only my pride had been bruised." She said tartly, and stretched out a hand.

Another young voice politely said, "Here, let me assist you." She felt a calloused hand grasp her own, and she smiled graciously as they helped her stand.

Devaney put her hands on her hips, and with frustration said, "Damn Lifoy left that in the middle of the room on purpose." The soldiers were silent. Smiling at them, she dropped the heat from her tone, and asked, "If it wouldn't be a bother, could you help me?" Again they were silent. Devaney waved to her face, and said, "I am a blind woman in an unfamiliar place. If you would please assist me in finding my boots..."

"Yes, my Lady." The men stammered in unison. With care, Devaney navigated to the bed and sat on the edge.

The man who had spoken first, called, "I think I've found em', here." He rushed to her side.

Devaney raised a foot from the floor, and asked, "Socks please? They should be in the pack." Devaney heard the men riffle through her meager possessions. Devaney considered the men. She wondered what their life was like here. *They would had lived with the shadowed threat of Ordu all their lives*, she thought sadly. Their accents were harsh and held a heavy twang that she had never heard before. She wondered about them, and asked, "What are your names?" She sensed them hesitate, and she said, "I am Devaney."

The second man spoke tentatively, saying "My Lady, if you wouldn't mind...we prefer to keep our names to ourselves."

Devaney cocked her head in confusion, and the man stammered, "We saw, what erm... you did...what you called forth. We were on the beach that day, you see."

Devaney laughed, her bright voice filling the room. The two men were silent, and Devaney cursed her blindness. The look on their faces, she was sure, was priceless. "Please." She said between breaths, "Fear me not. I mean neither of you harm and no one really, unless you bear the mark of Ordu. Your names?" She asked once more, her mirth fleeing.

The first man said, "My name be Charles Lavrine, I hail from the City of Bells."

The second man said, "I am John Kendy, of Farrin. We meant no disrespect, fair Fey."

Devaney smiled at them kindly, and said, "I am no Fey, good sirs, but a Ronan."

John fearfully asked, "You're a witch, then?"

Devaney nodded, and said, "Yes, I am. Fear not, I am a good witch. Now socks, and then boots." The men hesitated, and she sensed that they were giving one another weighted looks. Devaney wiggled her toes impatiently, and they jumped into to action. The pulled thick woolen socks over her feet, and then tied her boots with nervous fingers. Devaney stood, and held her arms open. "How do I look?" She asked.

John stammered, saying, "Frightenin' me witching Lady." Devaney dropped her hands with a sigh.

"That'll do." She said. She cursed Lifoy in her mind. She was sure she looked a fool, but there was nothing to be done. "Charles if you would, lend me your arm." She held her hand out expectantly, and she felt Charles step close. Devaney took his arm. He trembled beneath her touch. "Please John, if you would be so kind, I must speak to your King."

The two soldiers looked at one another fearfully. Both were young men, newly come to service. In the end, John shrugged, and said respectfully, "Follow me, if I be knowing the King right, he'll be in the yard trainin.'"

The soldiers led her from the room, and down a winding hall. Charles was an excellent chaperone, and guided her with a steady hand. Devaney knew that they passed many people, but none stopped or spoke to them. They paused at a landing, and Charles carefully led her down a flight of twisting steps.

Soon the ring of steel against steel filled the air. They stepped free of an archway, and Devaney felt the heat of the sun upon her pale skin. They paused there, waiting. Men grunted in strain, and she heard the slam of a wooden sword upon a shield, and smelled sweat. Slowly, they were noticed. Men spoke in hushed tones, and Devaney listened as they said, "There she be."

To the left she heard, "The Mistress of the Roc."

A man shouted fearfully, "She-demon."

To her right she heard a man whisper in awe, "The Bane of Ordu has come."

A deep voice called out, "Be still and silent, men of Agos." The voice was flush with warmth, and the man's breath came quick as though he had just finished a run. Devaney stood silently as the guards at her side bowed. Devaney did not bow.

"It is good to see that you have recovered, friend of Agos." The man said, stepping closer. Devaney could feel the heat of him now, and the voice was spoken some feet above her. Devaney looked up, not wanting to appear as though she was staring at his chest. The man continued respectfully, "I am King Thoriston of Agos, but you may call me Paul." Devaney nodded, and the two men at her side moved away, no doubt by a silent command of their king. "You have come at an auspicious time, and I thank you for the assistance in routing the Ordu. Many fell beneath your hand." Devaney could hear the unveiled admiration in his voice.

Devaney gave him a slight nod, and said in a bold voice, "I am Devaney Ronan, the Oracle, and I have come to help your people in the fight against the Ordu." Shocked gasps filled the courtyard, but they were stilled quickly.

Paul spoke in a polite tone, "Take my arm, and let us walk. I sense that you and I have much to discuss."

Devaney took the king's outstretched hand. His arm was thick and corded with muscle. It was bare and she assumed that he was shirtless. All of a sudden color touched her cheeks, but as the king walked from the courtyard her steps did not falter. The king led her through a long hall to a quiet garden. Devaney smelled sweet fragrance in the air, and felt tickling touch of petals as they walked down a winding path. Paul led her up several short steps, and helped her take a few steps up to a shaded gazebo. With one outstretched hand she felt a trellis wall that traced the gazebo, and sat on the wooden bench that waited within. Distantly, below she could hear the hum of the city and the roar of waves crashing.

Devaney heard wood creak as Paul sat on the bench across from her. The king did not bandy words, and his voice lost some of its warmth, as he asked, "Why have the Ronan revealed themselves to the world now, after all these years? I had thought you all bound in exile."

Devaney nodded, acknowledging the truth of his words, and admitted, "I was born after the war, in the lands of Ordu, and have only just escaped." She felt Paul gaze grow more intense. Mildly, Devaney said, "The time for hiding is over."

With consideration, Paul asked, "What of your kin, do they still languish on Shades Island and other prisons throughout the land?" This man was not an ignorant commoner, he was a king. He knew of the Ronan and the might she promised him, but he was cautious. He knew that allying himself with a Ronan was not without risk.

Devaney leaned forward to explain, "They do. I will seek them out and try to free them. Should I fail, fear not, I will not abandon the people of the Unified Free Kingdoms. I will not allow you to fall into the grasp of the Ordu." Her promise was passionate.

"You mean to leave us then?" Paul asked, quietly. Devaney

could feel the fear radiating from the man. He was strong of will and proud, but he stared into the face of desolation. He knew they waged a war they could not hope to win.

"I do." Devaney said in a whisper. She smiled sadly at the man she could not see, and said, "Banish your fear, good king, for darkness awaits you upon the battlefield and only those stout of spirit shall prevail."

The tinges of hope touched Paul's voice, as he asked, "You have seen it then, our triumph?"

Devaney shook her head slowly; she would not give the man false hope. "I have seen you survive what you must." Devaney's voice grew grim, and carefully she said, "Paul, no matter what happens you must hold Ordu at bay for at least three years from the turn of the New Year."

Paul grunted stoically as if he had just taken a mortal blow and could make no other noise. Minutes passed and she heard him sigh sadly. Despondently, he asked, "Alone, with no help? Such a feat is impossible, my Lady. You struck down four ships, but for every ship that fell that day there are ten thousand more." He continued astutely, "The Empire has the largest armies in all of Adonim and they amass on my doorstep. A single Ordu army has more men then I have man, women, and child, and the Empire has many dozens of armies. No, as much as my heart hates to admit it, I cannot prevail against such odds."

Devaney grimaced, and said sternly, "Agos does not stand alone. Take heart; all is not yet lost, and there are many tides to come."

Paul let out a huff of frustration, and she heard him sag against the rail of the gazebo. He was a large man, Devaney knew. She had seen him in her visions. Agitated, he contested, "The Council of the Unified Free Kingdoms is fractured. A bickering lot that can agree on nothing, but uniformly clings to their greedy self-centered advances. They are little help."

Devaney leaned forward, and said viciously, "Make them."

Her own frustration was spilling over. These men might have felt the bite of the Ordu, but they knew only rumors of the horrendous acts that the Ordu were capable of. They hadn't lived through it, hadn't had their kingdom and gods taken from them. *Or Mother and Father*, Devaney thought sadly.

"Make them do what?" Paul asked, his voice tinged with true confusion.

Devaney slapped a fist upon her knee, and said, "Make them bend the knee. Kill them if you must, raze their lands if you must, but Agos must rule the U.F.K by the end of winter."

Paul shook his head, and said coldly, "We fight against such tyranny."

Devaney's laugh was bitter as she said, "You fight to survive. If you don't know that yet, then you are doomed before this war has truly begun." Devaney's voice grew urgent, as she insisted, "Do what must be done or all that you hold dear will perish in ways unimaginable."

The king shook his head. He did not like the words this strange woman spoke, nor liked the promises she made, but in his heart knew that she spoke the truth. He would never had admitted it, but he had thought long into the darkness of night of these perils. Wearily, he said, "Our individuality, our freedom, is all that we have. If I take that away the people will revolt."

Devaney sat back and with a casual smile, said, "People are motivated by fear, love, and greed. These nobles who oppose you are no different. Show them the path and place what you confront before them as you do. Make yourself righteous before them, both as a caring lord and a man of iron resolve. Word will spread to the commons and they will see you as their only hope."

"What have you seen?" Paul asked cautiously.

Devaney stood and walked to the guardrail. She looked out over the sea that she could not see, contemplating her next words. A cool wind played across her face and with it, a gentle chill. This land was ready, she could feel the strength in her bones, but the people clung to spring like a child does its mother's skirts. The snow storm that was Ordu was coming, and they would either perish in the cold or strive to survive. Without facing him, Devaney said, "Marry the Queen of Nimfrael and the Queen of Krin. Together, you rule the three largest Kingdoms. Kill the two lords of Lafrey, and have new stewards appointed to Westland and Eastland who are sympathetic to the cause. If you control the majority, and the bread basket of U.F.K, the rest will fall in line."

In a hushed whisper, Paul asked," You have seen this." Devaney nodded. "How?" Paul asked, his heart beginning to pound with the promise of hope.

Devaney smiled, and said, "Lifoy will help you. I must leave soon. In the intervening time send me a trusted scribe, I will outline pertinent battles and details. I will send Lifoy back to you before the next moon rise and he will help you gain control." Devaney turned and faced him. She could not see the king, but she could feel the air tremble with his emotion.

King Paul Thoriston stood and bowed to her. In a humbled whisper, he said, "I will await his arrival, Mistress of Time." Devaney smiled thinly. She was taking a gamble, she knew, but nothing gained came without risk.

Aritian

Chapter Twelve:

Miscreant Queen

Aritian shifted in his saddle as the company slowed. Before them, the cracked thirsty ground of the desert fled into a plain of grassland. Stalks gleamed gold in the bright sun, tall as horse's chests, and swayed gently in the wind. The land here was plentiful with life, making a stark contrast to the barren desert they left behind. Aritian could hear the buzz of a thousand insects and saw flocks of tiny birds rising to the air only to settle among the gold-tousled stalks moments later. The horses plunged into the sea of grass.

Maud rode at the front of the company surrounded by more than two hundred men. The company thundered into the plains with a jangle of chainmail and the pounding of horse's hooves. Along the perimeter of the company, twenty men carried maroon banners adorned with flaming phoenixes that snapped smartly in the wind. Maud raised a black-laced hand and in unison the horses slowed to a trot. The ground beneath was loose here, and the footing unsure.

It was shocking to Aritian see so many men under the command of a woman. Outside the Order of the Flame, women were rarely afforded such respect. But one and all, the soldiers lived and breathed for their Lady. Maud rode a black stallion, casually holding the reins of her horse in one hand and calling to the men around her in a familiar way. She wore a gown of scarlet silk that trailing down the back of her horse and played in the wind behind her. Despite the long ride, she seemed at ease riding sidesaddle.

Aritian looked to the stallion he rode. The beast was magnificent, with a long blonde mane and a silvery-white hide that seemed to twinkle under the bright sun. The horse was not a breed native to Ignea. Maud had explained that they had been imported from the far northeast, from the lands of Afta. Despite the foreign land, the horses seemed well-adapted to the heat. Their hooves ate miles with surprising speed and for the last two days they had run with unerring stamina. Aritian was an unsure rider, having never ridden a horse before, but his mount was well-mannered and seemingly quite intelligent.

Selyni nudged her grey-speckled mount closer. Lightly, she touched his arm, pulling him from his thoughts as she remarked, "The Golden Plain." She waved to the grasslands around them. "It fills the land between here and Odium. Quite beautiful, isn't it?" She asked. Aritian nodded curtly. He was not in the mood to talk, but did not wish to be rude.

Selyni hadn't left his side since he first emerged from Maud's tent, and had shadowed his footsteps, never letting him out of her sight. Around her the young novice-assassins rode. They, too, had not left his side, but Aritian felt comforted by their presence. They were familiar, and unlike Selyni, knew when to leave him in peace. The young boys chatted animatedly together, eying the grassland with bubbling excitement.

Aritian let his eyes fall to his left to where Azera and Ori rode next to one another. There mounts seemed undaunted by their large statures. Both seemed to be in good health, and talked brightly to one another. Azera had still not spoken to him since Ori had walked whole from the tent. Ori had later explained that she was still shaken, but assured him that she would come around. Aritian knew it was a lie. *She has lost trust in me*, Aritian thought, somber. He saw Beryl kick his red mount forward to close the distance between him and the Titans, and cursed the horse as it over-shot and trotted ahead. A smile tugged at Aritian's lips, but died as darker thoughts swirled through his numb mind.

Rythsar looked up from Aritian's side, and flicked his tongue out tasting the air. His chest heaved, as he caught his breath from the long run. The lorith had flat out refused a mount, and to Aritian's surprise, Rythsar had no trouble keeping up with the pace of the horses' gallop. Between breaths, he remarked, "These Plains are not as abandoned as they look." The lorith's tail hung limply behind him, still broken, but bound tightly at the base with new canvas bandages that kept it somewhat immobile.

Aritian scanned the plain, but for as far as his eye could reach he saw only tousled gold grass and the smaller wildlife that lived among it. Selyni nodded, pushing her bright hair from her face as she said, "Yes, there are several colonies of Insectis within the plain. They shouldn't bother us. They aren't a brazen people and are fearful of humans."

"Insectis?" Aritian asked. It was the first word he had uttered since leaving the encampment. His curiosity was dull, but he knew his companions were growing concerned.

Selyni was quick to explain with excitement. "Insectis are a colony race. There are more than a dozen varieties, but uniformly each colony is ruled by a Queen. I suppose they aren't found in Velon..." She mused with consideration. "They can be fearsome and often war against neighboring colonies. Surely, you've heard of Mothos Silk?" Aritian nodded, affirming that he had. The silk was popular and known for its strength. It hadn't occurred to him that it was produced by another race. Selyni concluded, "Nearly all our clothes and tents are made from silk produced by the Mothos."

"Mothos are found in the Pomum. Gentle creatures." Rythsar remarked, eying Selyni darkly. "There are many kinds of Insectis found in the northern parts of the rainforest. They don't inhabit the southern edge of the Pomum, and most have never heard of Velon or even humans before." His tone suggested that this was preferable to the alternative.

Selyni gave Rythsar a pointed look, and said, "The ones

found this far south are not similar to the gentle Mothos." Casually, she added, "Still, so close to Creuen I doubt they'll attack. They will fear that we are slavers."

With sarcastic dryness, Aritian said, "Thank Ignathra for the slavers." His horse sidestepped, nervously eying the lorith at its side. Aritian patted its neck reassuringly.

Selyni's eyes shut as she realized the lack of tact in her words. Tentatively, she said, "Forgive me, Aritian. I did not seek to make light of your history in my explanation…"

Aritian waved her to silence, interrupting her as he bluntly said, "Don't concern yourself with apologizing to me. You weren't my Master, and my upbringing was no fault of yours." Aritian let his eyes glaze over as he looked around. The company was richly outfitted. The men were well-organized, and worked with a uniform purpose that was born out of long familiarity. It was odd. None of the soldiers were full Velonian, rather they, like Maud, they were all mixed. *Like me*, Aritian thought, knowing that there was some connection there, but not quite able to see what it was.

In a somewhat frantic voice, Selyni asked, "Are you thirsty, hungry? It's been five hours since we embarked and more than half the morning's passed. I'm sure provisions can be found while we travel at this pace." Her easy-mannered confidence seemed to have evaporated the moment they entered Maud's presence. Aritian could tell that she was desperate to keep him talking now that he had spoken.

Aritian shook his head, and said, "No, thank you." He waved to the company, and asked, "Why has Maud slowed us so? Even in the grasslands the horses should be able to safely canter."

Selyni's answer was soft, not wanting her words to carry to the soldiers flanking them on all sides. "She's scouting ahead. Can you not feel her power spread before us? She seeks the clearest way though."

Aritian nodded. Ever since he had met Maud he had been

aware of her power. It was like being near a bonfire that spilled waves of heat to pervade the very air around her. Even now, more than three hundred feet away, he could feel Maud's influence stretching all around. Her magic was as present as the air they breathed. Aritian nodded, and whispered, "Yes, I can feel it." Confused, he asked, "How did Maud find us so easily? The men said it took them but a day to reach that spot, and yet we have ridden two days and we still have another days travel at least before we reach Creuen."

Selyni eyed the tooled reins she held, and whispered, "Maud used her power to strengthen the horses and speed their way."

Aritian gave her a quizzical look, and asked, "Why does she not do so now?"

Selyni looked over her shoulder, eying the desert scape they had left, and said, "Your gnome is injured still and cannot ride at such a pace. Rythsar," she waved to the lorith, "runs with the horses, and it would be impossible for him to keep up." Aritian saw the lorith's tail twitch and knew if it hadn't been broken, it would have whipped side to side in irritation. "Besides, there is no need to rush. Maud has found what she has sought and we're safe."

"Are we?" Aritian asked dubiously. He continued, his mood darkening as he asked, "What of Namyr?" He pointed to the youth who rode on a roan-colored mare at Maud's side. "I see him riding boldly, but Sicaroo told me he was thrown from the saddle when we crashed upon the dunes. No man could walk away from such a fall untouched and yet Namyr sits as hearty as ever." Aritian was unsure why it irritated him so, but he knew in his heart that Namyr was not human.

Rythsar nodded in agreement, and growled in the back of his throat, before hissing, "He smells like no other man I have scented."

Aritian nodded, saying, "Nyox said the same thing." Aritian met Selyni's eyes, and elaborated, "In the four years that

I have known him Namyr has always appeared as he does now, a boy just perhaps reaching eighteen. He hasn't aged a day in all that time."

Selyni shrugged, uncomfortable by the subject, and Aritian could tell she struggled to find the proper words. Lamely, she said, "You have nothing to fear of Namyr. He cannot hurt people like you and I."

Aritian frowned in annoyance, and said, "That's not an answer."

Selyni shook her head, saying, "No, it's not. You must ask him if you wish to know. It's not my place to say." She waved him forward, saying brightly, "Come, Maud calls for the company to move out." Aritian could tell that she was relieved by the distraction. The horse beneath him pranced forward with a high-stepped gait. The pounding of hooves became a deep counterpart to the quiet whispers of the waving grass. Rythsar bounded alongside his horse, his bouncing stride matching the steeds' speed.

Aritian found himself detached and unable to rise above the murky darkness of his thoughts. He could only mire in the painful memories of the past year. They blared in ugly flashes across his mind and like whips scourged him with guilt. Aritian flinched from the horrendous thoughts, his soul too fragile to relive them.

Distractedly, he turned to Selyni and said, "There is much on my mind and the road is long. I find myself sorely lacking any semblance of footing. Please, don't look at me as if I am a child that needs coddling. I need answers and I need you to speak truly." He spoke in a near whisper, and his voice could barely be heard over the gait of the horses around them. His mount followed the rest of the herd. Aritian did little to steer it, rather he let the horse take the lead.

Selyni flashed him a sympathetic smile and nodded with understanding. Aritian eyed her with seriousness, hoping that within her he may see through the cloud of ignorance that hung over him. Selyni was dressed brown trousers and a light, blue blouse. Her pale hair was unbound and flowed behind her in the wind. She held herself with a perfect posture, and her pale cheeks were flushed with the heat of the day. Aritian realized she was at ease here, in the wilderness. "I am sure you have more than a few questions, and I am more than happy to explain," She hesitated, and smiled apologetically, adding, "If I am able."

Aritian nodded in thanks, and asked, "When I first met you, you mentioned that there was always twenty-one Ronan at any given time. Are they in Creuen as well?" The thought had been niggling at the edge of his mind since Selyni had first told him of the Ronan. *Let's see if she passes the test. I know that at least one isn't on the continent of Ignea*, Aritian thought, thinking of the pale woman who appeared to him during his Awakening.

Selyni shook her head, and Aritian saw sadness cloud her pale eyes. With surety, she said, "No. Maud, myself, and you are the only Ronan on the continent of Ignea. The rest reside in the north." A complex series of emotion crossed her face, and Aritian knew there was a reason behind her vagueness.

Aritian pushed on, saying, "Maud speaks as if the Ronan are more than man, and insists that we aren't human. To be honest this frightens me. I still feel the same as I did before the Awakening, but also completely different. No one has explained exactly what these powers I have are or why I have them?" He knew he was being venerable, but between Maud and Selyni he knew who he preferred to ask.

Selyni touched her chest where her heart lay, and said, "We are magic made flesh." She laughed lightly as his expression clouded with disbelief, and she explained, "It's a foreign, odd idea if you think about it too deeply. As you continue to grow in power you will see the truth." Aritian nodded, although he didn't completely believe that he would ever come to terms with such a thought. "We are governed by a power of balance. Magrados is within all living creatures, rules all aspect of life. As sentinels of Magrados, it is our responsibility to keep that balance." Selyni let her eyes fall forward and Aritian saw her gaze settle on Maud.

When Selyni next spoke, her voice came in a hushed whisper, "We are last remnants of the of the proud race of Magi. While in nature you find opposites like water and fire, we are ruled by the balance of three. The Coven is divided by allegiance. Arbiters of the Grey, dabble in both dark and light magic, are neutral. Those who wear white, claim allegiance to Albastella; a cohort of magi that only practice magic deemed moral, who are governed by a strict Covenant of honor. Lastly, there are those who are known as Ronan of Sanguis Nox. They delve into the arts many would consider immoral. Most Ronan have a natural inclination, bound by lineage, though each is different. We are not created equally. Some are stronger than others, while others have talents more narrowly concentrated." Selyni flashed him an easy smile, and assured, "Worry not, if you learn that you are Sanguis Nox that does not mean you are evil and likewise, if you find yourself among the Albastella that does not mean you must live under a strict dogma. Magrados is fluid, and you are only bound by what's within yourself."

Rythsar cocked his head, clearly listening to their conversation, and asked in a wheeze, "Care to guess where Maud's inclinations lay?" Aritian shivered, his instincts told him that she was no woman of the light.

Selyni shook her head, and said in warning, "Maud is an Ancient. To live as long as she, it grows more complex. Maud has fulfilled roles in all aspects of Magrados. The lines are not always distinct as you may think."

Aritian's eyes narrowed, and he asked, "Just how old is Maud? What constitutes as an Ancient?" The moniker was being thrown around, and he knew that to navigate properly he must understand who he was dealing with.

With a bemused smile, Selyni said, "A Ronan attains the title of Ancient One once they have lived a thousand years."

Aritian stared at her in disbelief. Selyni nodded her head, indicating that he had heard correctly. Aritian turned his eyes away, too stunned to form words. He tried to contemplate living so long. It sent shivers down his spine, and he struggled to swallow his fear.

Rythsar's yellow eyes were pinned on Maud. Quietly, he asked, "How does she remain so youthful?" It was evident that the lorith found such a thought as difficult to conceive as Aritian.

Aritian looked to the head of the train. Maud cut a swath through the grass, leading the way. As Aritian watched the grass before her horse's feet bent in a sweeping wave before her mount even touched it. *Magic*, Aritian thought in wonder. Maud's beauty made his heart thunder even at this distance. She wore a cloak of noble bearing that was both imperious and frightening.

Selyni explained with unease, "Ronan consist of what we call the Trinity Flames: Spirit, Mind, and Magrados. Outside these, all else can be manipulated." Selyni's fear of Maud was evident, and Aritian found himself sympathizing with the woman. Although Maud's beauty made him flush with warmth, he recognized a coldness in her that made his attraction to her even more unsettling.

Aritian thought it odd that body wasn't included, but he nodded to himself as he considered. Selyni was a Changeling; he had seen her body transform into something entirely different. Namyr had mentioned that Selyni and her brother were the only Changelings within the Coven. Aritian leaned toward her, gripping the horn of the saddle to keep his balance, and asked, "Is there such a thing as an Oracle?"

Selyni looked up at him in surprise, and asked, "Has one appeared to you, then? Is that how you knew of the Ronan when we first met?" Aritian nodded tightly.

To think that there was someone who could see the future made his heart skip. He considered what that would mean, what secrets she might hold and what things she may be able to reveal? He thought of her promise: *When the rains stop, come north and find me. I shall tell you your destiny then.* He looked to the sky. It was clear and blue, without a cloud in sight. There was no sign of the monsoon, but he knew it would flood the land within a week. They had outpaced the storms in their flight south, but it would come. Aritian craved for guidance and swore to himself that he would somehow find the woman.

Curiously, Aritian asked, "Is that a common gift, this foresight?" Secretly, he wondered if it would be something he might develop.

Selyni shook her head, and said, "No, it's quite rare. There is usually only one at any given time and often none at all. We live in a strange time. There are two that now walk the land." Selyni looked at him intently, and cautiously warned, "Most Oracles are not stable. They not only see the future, but also many times the past and present. Most are driven mad by the visions." Aritian could tell that she was nervous speaking of such things so candidly in the open. "Out of those within the Coven, Oracles are often the most dangerous. They can alter the course of the future. You must take care if you ever meet one again."

Maud raised a fist into the air, and the train veered to the left. The horses flowed after her dark stallion. Aritian felt his horse turn, and Rythsar had to leap to the left to avoid being trampled. Aritian peered ahead, curious of why they changed course. The grassland before them looked the same as it had before, an abandoned blanket of golden grass that swayed gently around them.

Aritian gripped the horn of his saddle tightly as the horse angled. It was an odd feeling, but slowly Maud's course straightened due northwest. When Aritian regained his balance, he looked to Selyni, and asked, "Have you met them? The Oracle's who lives now? Are they mad?" Aritian held his breath. The woman who had come to him had seemed lucid while they spoke, but Aritian had to admit that their conversation was more than brief.

Selyni smiled coyly, as if she knew a secret, and said, "I know of Aileen and Devaney. If there is any doubt of the insanity of the Oracle you met, then I know that you did not meet Aileen. Devaney is," Selyni paused, as if trying to think of the proper phrase, before saying, "different. She is young, newly Awakened, but powerful. Honestly, we don't know yet. We are still watching her." Aritian noted the woman's odd us of *we*, but didn't remark. Internally, he promised, *Devaney, I will find you*.

Aritian asked, "What's an Archmagus?" Aritian tasted the foreign phrase on his tongue, it had a northern flare.

Selyni flashed him a smile, and he realized that for some reason she found the question humorous. He could tell from her expression she wanted to tease him, but instead she gently explained, "The Archmagus is our leader. Ultan has led the Coven for the last seventy-odd years. You will meet him in time, and swear allegiance to him." Selyni saw his worried glance, and added, "It's a formality, nothing to worry yourself over, and won't happen for some time. It must be done in person."

A hundred questions came to his mind. "What is this Ultan like? Is he a man of honor? Why haven't I ever heard of the Ronan before?" Aritian asked, unable to still his own curiosity. It seemed strange to Aritian that he had never heard of magi before. *Surely, if they exude even a modicum of the power I unleashed in Inee they would be well-known?* Aritian thought with consideration. The question hung in the air between them, and Aritian had the sense that the answer was not something that he would like. Selyni opened her mouth to answer, but Aritian felt Rythsar stiffen at his side.

Rythsar's jaw hung open and his tongue began flicking out rapidly. The lorith leapt upward mid-step, and swung his large head around as he scanned the grassland around them. The lorith landed gracefully on his hands, and regained his pace without pause.

Worriedly, Aritian asked, "What is it Rythsar?" He could tell the lorith had scented something, something that disturbed him. He saw Selyni sigh in relief out of the corner of his eye.

Rythsar spoke in a low growl, as he warned, "We are being tracked; followed. There is a strange scent on the wind." Aritian thought to ask him more, but the lorith dodged to the left, leaving the train, and dove into the grassland. Rythsar's mahogany scales blended into the warm shades of the grass, and he swiftly disappeared from sight.

Aritian turned Selyni in concern, but the woman seemed calm. "Stay close to me, Aritian." She suggested. Anxiously, Aritian looked for his friends. They rode before him now, toward the left side of the company. Aritian jerked the reins of his mount and kicked his heels. The stallion reacted fluidly, surging forward into a gallop. Aritian heard Selyni call his name, but didn't slow his mount. The stallion reached Ori, Azera, and Beryl in mere moments, and they looked at him with concern as he frantically scanned the grasslands and tugged the reins to match their pace.

"What is it, lad?" Beryl asked, sensing that something was amiss. The dwarf sat awkwardly on the massive stallion he rode, with his short legs stretched wide. His stirrups had been shorted and they sat high on the stallion's stomach. It would have been comical, if not for the circumstances.

The train continued on without changing the course; Maud seemed at ease. Selyni's mount caught up with him in short order, followed closely by the Dranguis. Hastily, Aritian explained, "Rythsar sensed something. He left the train. I wanted to be close should anything happen."

Azera snorted in annoyance, and said, "Maybe we don't want you close should something happen." She pulled her horse's reins so that she rode between Ori and Aritian, and glared at him in warning.

Aritian's jaw fell open, surprised by her continued hostility, but it was Ori who replied. Indignant, he said,

"Aritian saved my life, you will not be rude to him in my presence." The young Titan bared his teeth in challenge. Ori's expression was deadly serious, and Aritian could tell that he moments away from losing his temper.

Azera shook her head and her jaw clenched stubbornly. Frustrated, she said, "Oh goblin shit Ori, don't you see I'm trying to protect you?"

Ori's eyes narrowed until they were mere slits, and he grumbled, "From whom? The man who saved my life or the man who led us to freedom?

Beryl sniggered rudely, and said, "Lad's got a point, gal." Azera flashed the dwarf a glare, but Beryl only shrugged.

Their attention was torn from their inner conflict as Maud yanked her reins, pulling her horse to a stop. The black stallion dug its hooves into the dirt, throwing clumps of mud as Maud's command carried across the grassland, "Halt! Wheel formation, circle the child."

The soldiers maneuvered their horses expertly, spinning their horses around and flowing around him in either direction. Aritian pulled the reins of his horse tight and his mount stopped abruptly, nearly throwing him from the saddle. Beryl's horse planted its hooves into the ground, and the young dwarf clung to the saddle horn as he was thrown forward into his mount's neck. Aritian looked at the horse's eyes and saw something dull and still within them, and knew then that they had been touched with Maud's magic.

Cursing, the dwarf regained his seat, wiggling backwards as his horse stood as still as a statue. Aritian met Maud's eyes and she nodded slightly. Knowing that she read his mind as easily as his thoughts came to him, he scowled.

Two circles of mounted soldiers quickly formed. The inner band of soldiers traveled clockwise around him while the outer traveled counter. The operation was both dizzying and stunningly organized. Maud and Namyr remained outside of the circles and Aritian saw that both were armed – Maud held a dark, glittering wand in one hand and Namyr had freed his northern longsword. His mount danced in a circle around her protectively.

There was a quiet for a time. Aritian scanned the golden sea around him, but saw only softly dancing grass and clear blue skies. Aritian turned to Selyni, and said darkly, "I am a trained assassin, not some child. If something comes I can fight alongside the other men."

Selyni's face twisted with concern, and she shook her head, saying, "No Aritian, as a Ronan you are but a babe. Please, leave this to Maud." Aritian was about to respond, but his attention was snatched away.

The thud of horses' hooves was soon overtaken as a buzzing sound vibrated across the plain, it was as if thousands of bugs sung in concurrence. Their voices were similar to a cicada's, but the pitch higher and far more intense.

The horses neighed in irritation, and Aritian clapped his hands over his ears. Beryl cursed, his face scowling as he glanced side to side, his words lost beneath the whine of the call. Ori and Azera wore grimaces, but were seemingly less affected than the men around them. Mingyo jumped from his horse, crying with pain, followed by Bo and Yi. Sicaroo joined them, and Shan and Hui ran to Aritian's side, shouting questions, but Aritian could not hear what they said. Rong was the only Dranguis who remained seated, and his dark eyes raked across the golden grass searching for the enemy.

The sound was so loud that Aritian could feel his bones vibrate. With a sinking stomach, he felt the power within roll, awakening from its slumber. "What is this?" Aritian asked desperately, shouting over the strange call.

Selyni pointed wordlessly to the horizon and Aritian saw what approached. Aritian knew instantly what they were by sight, despite never having seen one before. Thousands of Insecti stampeded from all directions. They were frightening creatures, colored in muted browns and pale greens. Their triangular heads consisted of three bony plates that met neatly in the center of their face. Red compound eyes glared angrily beneath their long twitching antennas.

As they charged across the grassland, Aritian saw that their legs were similar to grasshoppers, but situated more vertically as they were bipedal creatures. Aritian watched as their long, thin legs carried them forward in springing leaps, each bound traveling more than a dozen feet. They had hook-like arms that swung before them, scything the stalks of grass. Aritian had never seen anything of the like. Even in Inee, where you could find a myriad of races in the slaving markets, he hadn't seen anything similar.

They raced liked a brown flood from all directions. The piercing call increased in decibel as they approached and Aritian's horse began to dance nervously. Aritian closed his eyes as his ears popped, and he felt wet blood trickle beneath his hands. The power within welled up, a river that met an impenetrable dam. Aritian felt shooting pain lance up his arm and trembled as his power fought against the Ring of Suppression until he fell from his horse with a thud. The trampled grass softened his fall, but he lay prone, staring up at the sky.

His horse danced to the side, eyes rolling wildly as it began to panic. Selyni and Azera jumped from their mounts and fell to their knees at his side. Aritian jerked erratically as the pain raced through him. It was like being struck by an unending bolt of lightning. The power within him battled the Suppression Ring furiously, and the ring on his finger smoked and burned with blistering heat. Azera and Selyni's eyes met with measured concern. With a curse, Azera lifted Aritian into her arms and held him tightly as his eyes rolled and his body jerked in seizure. Aritian clung desperately to her as he rode the wave, unable to stop that what fought for release.

The Insecti closed on them fast, their legs covering ground with astonishing speed. Soldiers pulled their swords free, bracing themselves for the impact of the charge. The soldier's screams of challenge were lost beneath the ear piercing Insecti call.

Maud sat on her horse casually, seemingly unaffected by the noise, and watched the stampede with a nearly bored expression. When the Insecti were but forty feet away and closing, the tip of her wand bloomed with radiant red light that shot outward in a band across the grasslands. The grass bowed nearly to the ground, flattened by the rush of power, before snapping up in a wave. The sound of the Insecti stopped abruptly.

Aritian opened his eyes in confusion. The power within fell back suddenly, leaving him drained. It was as if he was a wet rag and all the water had been twisted out, leaving him devoid of energy. The Insecti came to a skidding stop as their war cry fell mute. Their long heads swung side to side in confusion and their antenna twitched erratically. They stretched their heads toward the sky and their sharp mandibles opened and closed with a snapping, chittering sound.

Maud smiled. It was a cruel smile that twisted her beauty into something unrecognizable. Azera's grip tightened around Aritian as she saw the change in Maud's face like ice freezing over a pond, and beads of sweat sprung upon his brow. The soldiers around them stilled their racing circuit and casual smiles played across their faces. They knew they were in danger no longer. Selyni spoke, but Aritian found his hearing had abandoned him. The only sound he could hear was the blood pumping through his brain.

Soldiers pointed to the left, and Aritian turned his head to see what had caught their attention. An Insecti approached and Aritian knew that he was looking at the Queen of the colony. She flew on green, iridescent wings across the plain and was larger than the males by nearly three feet. As she came to land gracefully before the gathered Insecti, Aritian could see that her abdomen was swollen with eggs. The Queen's bright wings snapped closed.

The Queen's thorax thrummed with vibrations, but no sound came. The million eyes of the colony turned to face their Queen. They swayed side to side on their long legs, bouncing gently in anticipation. Maud lifted her wand to her throat and her mouth hung open. A buzzing sound, not unlike that of the Insecti call, emitted from her throat. Aritian could see the skin of her neck vibrating. The Insecti antenna twitched wildly in response, and the Queen's wings fluttered behind her in shock.

The Queen grew still, as if considering. Her head turned side to side as she accessed the threat and her antenna twitched wildly. Aritian could see Maud reflected a hundred times over in the Queen's red gaze. The Queens four wings snapped open with the sound of ruffled parchment, and blurred as they carried her upward with dizzying speed. She buzzed above the gathered soldiers, circling three times, before coming to a stop. The Queen hovered above Maud a hundred feet in the air and her hooked arms snapped outward.

The Insecti reacted immediately to her signal. They flung themselves forward, their long legs stretching out as they charged toward the soldiers. Maud raised an elegant eyebrow in muted surprise. Aritian swallowed thickly and shakily regained his feet.

Selyni's voice reached his ears as his hearing slowly returned. "Be calm Aritian, you are safe." Selyni took his hand in her own, squeezing it reassuringly. Aritian watched as the first Insecti vaulted forward, sprinting a dozen feet above the grass only to land and leap again. Those that led the charge held their hooked arms outstretched, and Aritian could see that their arms were covered in a bony shell that was edged with curved spikes.

Aritian watched a male, spring forward, rising in the air to fall upon the soldiers that waited below. The Insecti burst in a sputtering flash of white light, instantly incinerated as it met an invisible barrier that stood a foot from the first soldiers. Light flashed all around them as the Insecti were consumed as quickly as a moth that flirted with an open flame.

Azera mouth fell open in amazement, and she asked, "What's happening?" The Insecti threw themselves against the barrier with abandon. It seemed as if they had no concern for self-preservation as each met the flaming death without hesitation. The soldiers stepped back, but laughed as the threat turned to ash before their eyes.

"The Queen of Loci has commanded, and so they listen." Selyni said, shaking her head. Aritian saw her blue eyes held a glimmer of sadness, and he gripped her hand tighter. She looked up at him in surprise, and he nodded, grim.

Beryl tore his eyes from the mass suicide and kicked his horse toward them. As he approached, he asked, "This be Maud's doing, isn't it?" Aritian nodded in response. He could feel her power radiating all around them. Ori watched the Insecti with fascination. The boy didn't seem to be upset by what he saw, and as his eyes found Maud they glowed with admiration. Aritian frowned at the expression. Mingyo had stopped crying, and Yi clapped his hands in excitement as they Insecti disappeared in a puff of brown clouds.

Maud sat on her horse calmly. Namyr tilted his head up and watched the Queen. The Loci Queen fluttered from side to side with evident anger. She made a quick spin around the invisible shield. Her throat hummed with vibration, and it was clear to all that if she were able to call off the attack that she would have. It was pointless though, for Maud had struck her mute.

More than half of the Loci were consumed in under a minute. The Queen raced back across the sky, her hooked arms tight to her chest as she prepared to attack. Her grief was evident and it made her reckless with desperation. With a fold of her wings, she dived toward Maud.

Maud didn't even watch the Queen approach, and Aritian felt his heart drop. There was no hope for the Queen. *There never really had been*, Aritian thought sadly. Namyr lithely stood on his mounts saddle, crouching low as he gripped his longsword with both hands, preparing to leap upward. The Queen was no more than twenty feet above as a dark blur shot across the golden grass. The blur sprang into the air and crashed into the Queen, together they toppled to the ground before Maud's mount.

Namyr screamed, "No fair Rythsar, I clearly had her marked as my own." Namyr pouted prettily and dropped to sit on his saddle, his shoulders slumping. Rythsar held the Queen to the ground, pinning her wings tightly. Several Insecti raced toward their fallen Queen, but they disappeared in a flash of white fire and crumbling brown ash.

In an emotionless whisper, Aritian said, "Maud allowed the Queen through." Selyni nodded sadly, and pulled Aritian along as she walked toward the fallen Queen. Beryl and a soldier grabbed the leads of their mounts, and followed after. The last of the Loci raced forward into the light, meeting their bright deaths and the grassland fell still. Three feet of ash circled the company in a thick, black ring and the sharp pungent smell of burnt flesh floated on the warm wind. Thousands had died in mere minutes.

Aritian looked at Azera in thanks and she met his eyes steadily. In a harsh whispered, she asked, "What in Ignathra's name happened? Bloody hell, why did you react in such a way?" Confusion filled her eyes and creased her brow, and she almost seemed fearful. But it wasn't fear of him, rather it was fear for him and for that Aritian was grateful.

Selyni answered stonily, "By Maud's command, Namyr placed a Ring of Suppression on Aritian's hand. His power is contained. He is no longer a danger to anyone." Aritian could tell the Selyni was none-too pleased with Maud's solution, but Aritian felt relieved. The pain had been excruciating, but he hadn't harmed anyone. Without the ring, he didn't know what would happened. Weariness tugged at him as he walked forward and sweat made his loose tunic cling to his skin

Sicaroo whisper scathingly, "You saw it before, Azera, when Aritian first discovered what happened to Ori, but you were too angry to care." Aritian shook his head no, and Sicaroo fell silent, grimacing with anger.

Aritian touched Azera's arm, and said, "I am sorry Azera, truly. I couldn't control myself when I first awoke. I should have, but I just couldn't. I put you all in danger and for that my heart weeps." Grief choked him as memories assaulted his mind.

Azera nodded slowly, as if in thought. Her eyes fell to the ground as she considered. When she met his gaze once more, Aritian knew she had forgiven him. Her eyes were warm with pity. She stepped close, protectively, as they reached Maud.

Maud flashed him a cool smile over her shoulder, and said, "You have done well Aritian, selecting this lorith. He quite skillfully caught our miscreant Queen."

Aritian nodded silently, as he took a closer look at the Queen. Despite the Queen's assault, Aritian found himself admiring her. She was beautiful in her own way. Her thorax was slim, and so dark it was nearly black, and her brilliant green wings seemed like delicate fragments of emerald glass. Rythsar held her deftly, but not harshly, in his clawed grip. Her hooked hands dug into the ground as she struggled for release, and her myriad of red eyes flicked in all directions, panicked. Aritian felt a pang of pity for the creature.

Maud waved a hand to the lorith, and said casually, "Very well Rythsar, if you would, kill her now. We'll harvest her wings. I know a most skillful dwarven jeweler who will absolutely go mad for such rare material." Namyr smiled cruelly in anticipation. Rythsar's yellow eyes rose to meet Aritian, as if asking for permission.

Aritian shook his head, no. Tentatively, Aritian asked, "Lady Maud, if you wouldn't mind, I would like to keep her." Maud pulled the reins of her horse to face him and cocked her head in question. Aritian continued, knowing that he must not directly contradict her command, and said, "I believe it would be advantageous if I could learn their language as you have. Besides, she carries a clutch," Aritian pointed to the Insecti's swollen stomach, and explaining, said, "it could be used to seed a new colony; one that we could use to our benefit."

Maud seemed to consider for a moment. Namyr rolled his eyes knowingly, and made to speak, but Maud raised a gloved hand forestalling the youth. She met Aritian gaze evenly, saying, "As a Ronan it is important for you to grow your retinue. We may be powerful, but often times we need more mundane forms of protection than you might think. I was going to speak to you about this when we reached Creuen." Maud's eyes flicked from Aritian to Azera, Ori, Beryl and then the young Dranguis, before she said, "You have selected well so far." She nodded to herself, before saying, "I am inclined to allow your instincts to guide you in this."

Aritian bowed his head respectfully. Maud lazily spun her wand in one hand, and called out to the soldiers around her, "Bind the Loci Queen with rope. She will accompany us to Creuen. Water your horses now, and take refreshment. We ride in two hours." Soldiers raced to do as she bid. Maud dismounted and her men hurriedly erected a small traveling tent.

Aritian sighed. There had been too much death on his hands of late, and when the lorith's eyes had met his own the Queen's life had fallen into his hands. *I will not allow those who look to me for life fall to shadow,* Aritian thought with determination.

Caethe

Chapter Thirteen:

The Pearl Gate

Caethe stood on the edge of a frozen lake with Arkyn at his side. Before them dripped a frozen waterfall of at least two-hundred feet that begun in a halo of golden light and spiraled down the side of a cliff in elegant rivets, arcs, and dips before meeting the ice below. The ice itself was not of common ilk — rather it appeared like melted moonstones, glimmering grey with beams of silver, lilacs, and faded rose. The air was warm, lacking any hint of chill, but fog boiled from the lakes icy face where it met the heat of the sun.

For the first time Caethe could see the sun of the Avalon clearly. It sat heavily, spanning across three-fourths of the sky. Orange, pink, and brilliant yellow tones rolled across its surface, spilling graceful light to the land below. The lakes edge was rimmed in greenery, for the forest crowded close and bands of roots humped along its icy edge before sinking into the frozen depths. Caethe knew that he would have never found this hidden marvel had Arkyn not led him to the secret heart of the ancient forest.

Together, they stood at the lake's edge in silence. Behind them, beneath the shaded eaves of the forest, stood the elves. They donned white robes of spun moonlight that glimmered, illuminating their forms within the shadowed depths of the forest's edge. Their faces shone with an inner radiance that this realm naturally revealed, and stood at varying heights depending on their race. The shortest was no more than four feet in height and the tallest stood nearly seven tall. Their beauty was raw and natural in a way that belied human constraints. Each of their forms were fit, slim, and well-muscled, with an androgynous caste that made determining their sex difficult. All, however, wore their straight silken-hair long, flowing down in a glossy sheets to their hips. Caethe tried to determine whom he had spoken to through his thoughts, but found the task impossible. They stood mute, their eyes fixed forward on the lake.

Arkyn spoke suddenly, "The Relic has been entrusted to you so that you might uphold the Covenant of the Sanguis. Betray us, and you will find that despite our exile there are ways that we can reach beyond this realm into the world of Adonim. Betray us, and we will end you." His voice was neither threatening nor warm. He was simply stating a promised fact.

Caethe nodded. The weight of the relic lay heavy upon his chest. The worn leather throng on which it hung pulled heavily forward, as if it carried a weight greater than iron. Arkyn continued, "Succeed, and you shall have the allegiance of the Elder Fae and all who call this realm home. We see into your mind Ronan, and your heart. More than you would wish, I think." Caethe looked up at the Fae, but Arkyn's eyes were fastened on the falling turrets of frozen ice. The words sent a shiver down Caethe's spine, but he remained silent. Arkyn continued, his voice soft, barely above a whisper as he said, "Succeed, and the Elder Fae will pledge our support to you and assist in the path of your true ambition."

Arkyn's eyes fell heavily upon him and Caethe matched the Fae's gaze with an emerald stare that was as hard as stone. Caethe bowed his head in respect, and replied ardently, "I shall not fail you, Arkyn of Avalon."

Arkyn raised his hand and a pixie flew from a branch of an evergreen tree. Small, the creature stood no more than eight-inches in height and resembled the elves closely. It flew on wings of the deepest green, so sheer they seemed like a cape of dark shadow that contrasted against its bone white skin, darkvined wrappings, and long hair. Its eyes were two chips of onyx, and its ears sharply pointed and extended past its head. In one hand the pixie held a small staff of polished oak that was crowned with a sparkling diamond that seemed to greedily catch the bright light of the day. It landed lightly on two of Arkyn's brown talons and eyed Caethe boldly.

Arkyn voice was laced with bitter anger, as he said, "I cannot take up staff and bow in defense of my people. Should I walk from this realm, the powers that bind Avalon would tear asunder." Arkyn shook his head in frustration and sorrow as he said, "My heart rages that I must impotently wait. Those who have betrayed us will face a reckoning, but that day has not yet come." Caethe felt a lance of fear, his very soul reacting to the heat of that promise.

Arkyn's voice grew softer, but lost none of its determination. "Instead, I shall send Solani. He is a warrior of his people, and adept in the magic of the Fey. I have power enough to bind your essence. I fear, without such a commitment, you will be lost in a sea of power that you cannot hope to control. Solani will ground you, protect you, and assist you in fulfilling your oath to Avalon. Do you consent to such a marriage?"

Caethe felt his mouth fall open in shock, not only in the face of such a proposition, but because the Elder Fae had asked him a blunt question. Caethe could see the displeasure that it caused the Fae to be so rudely bold, as it flicked across Arkyn's face in the curl of his lip and the tightening of his forehead. Such directness was rare, nearly unheard of with the Fae, and reserved only for times of great peril.

Dumbly, Caethe snapped his mouth closed, and looked out toward the lake as he considered. Gravely, he warned, "I cannot guarantee his safety, or even that of my own life."

"That is not the question that the Elder Fae ask of you." Arkyn said undeterred.

Caethe sighed, knowing that he had no real choice. Caethe

turned back to Arkyn, and nodded curtly.

"I consent," he whispered, regretting the words even as he spoke them.

Arkyn's face split with a relieved smile, and the tense muscles of his shoulders relaxed. Pleased, he said, "I am gladdened by your acceptance. It shows us that you are prepared to put your faith in the people of Avalon, just as we put our hopes in you."

Caethe bowed in response, before eying Solani. The pixie looked fragile, his limbs were thin, no thicker than a small twig, and his wings were as fine as those found on a butterfly.

Solani stared at him unblinking, measuring him with equal intent. "He looks like nothing more than a skeletal child. We should invest the fate of Avalon in a more powerful magus." Solani admonished, his voice was strangely deep for such a diminutive creature. Arkyn flashed the pixie a sharp look, and the air crackled with the threat of a storm. Solani bowed, and said respectfully, "But I shall place my trust in you, Elder. You have led our people unerringly since before the retreat."

Arkyn nodded and thrust his taloned hand toward Caethe. Reflexively, Caethe reached out and Solani lithely jumped from Arkyn's hand to Caethe's open palm. The weight of the pixie was scant; the small Fey weighed no more than a pound.

Arkyn did not hesitate — he strut around the pair and drug a toe deep into the ground; drawing a circle. The halo of light above his head began to pulsate, growing brighter and brighter.

Caethe found his eyes drawn to Solani's. The pixie's eyes were like two pools of black wine that drew him in with intoxicatingly, heady demand. Arkyn began to speak in the language of the Elder Fae, his words commanding and guttural, yet light and haunting. His voice was beyond Caethe's understanding; the most beautiful thing to ever touch his ears. Caethe felt himself drawn forward and felt a power growing between him and the pixie. Something within Caethe stretched, reacting to Arkyn's commands, and was drawn outward.

Darkness flashed through his mind and Caethe found himself blinking dumbly. What he saw startled him, and he flung himself backward a few steps. Looming before him stood a man with skin stretched tightly over bone and too-large green eyes that were haunted by black bruising. The man was rail thin and stood no more than five feet in height. Caethe looked down as the ground beneath his feet and realization struck him. Stalks of silver veined grass stood to either side of him, towering above. Behind the man, a tree stood, rising like a mountain to impossible heights.

I am looking at myself through the eyes of the pixie, Caethe thought, marveling. Humorous thoughts rolled through his mind and Caethe realized that they were not his own, rather they were Solani's. Caethe clenched his eyes shut as vertigo filled him. He fell to his knees as he lost balance. It was strange, because even as he fell he felt his wings flutter. They lifted him into the air gracefully and he hovered above his fallen form. *Not my wings, the pixies*, Caethe reminded himself.

The humorous thought stream ended abruptly as his mind began to spin erratically. He struggled to orient his identity. He was both in control of his body and the pixies, but not fully in either. The strangeness confronted his mind like a hammer and he felt himself spin uncontrollably from the air to land in the plush grass that hugged the lakeside. He lay there, dazed, against a root that rose above him like a ridge.

Solani's mind gripped his own with surprising strength, forcing him back into his own body. There was a connection between them, a minute thread that spun from his mind to the pixie's, but it was hardly immersive. He could hear Solani's thoughts rolling, but it was dimmed, like a low roar in the back of his mind. The physical control over the pixie's body was now firmly out of his mind.

Slowly, shakily, Caethe stood. Solani grasped his staff and his dark wings blurred as they carried him into the air, before he came to rest lightly on Caethe shoulder. Arkyn smiled, and said, "It can be quite an adjustment, this kind of bonding. Humanity is limited in their ability to mind-meld. If you were not Ronan, Solani would fully control both your mind and physical form." The Fae's halo of light dimmed to a subtle, spinning glow.

"Thank Magrados for my blood." Caethe said between heavy breathes. He quickly projected a shield between his thoughts and the pixie's. Caethe was near panic, unsure of what the creature had learned in its few seconds of control.

"In time, the connection will become second nature." Arkyn assured.

"One can only hope." Caethe said in a hiss, his annoyance scarcely veiled.

Your thoughts dance on the edge of a lie, Solani thought, projecting the words in a wave across the thread of their connection.

Sarcasm is but one complexity that you must come to learn if you ever wish to have a hope of understanding the flow of my thoughts. Caethe replied dryly. He felt Solani's mind roll the word *sarcasm* across his thoughts and then felt the pixie's mind reach out grasping for understanding. Caethe's shield flared between them, and darkly Caethe warned: *My mind is not a wild field of flowers, free for you to prance through at your leisure.*

Caethe turned his head toward the pixie and met the creature's dark eyes, ensuring that the pixie understood. Solani gripped his staff tightly, but nodded sharply; once. Arkyn watched their silent exchange with barely concealed humor.

Caethe met the Elder Fae's jubilant eyes with a glare, and asked, "Why do I have the feeling that I should have considered such a bond more intently before so easily accepting? I can already tell that this creature shall be a distraction."

Arkyn smiled, baring his sharp teeth, and said; "You shall know his worth soon enough, young Ronan."

Caethe nodded, but his sense of unease did not diminish. Arkyn turned toward the lake, waving Caethe forward.

Caethe joined his side, and Arkyn raised his arms into the air. Slowly and softly, the elven Druids began to sing. Their voices were haunting. Beauty and intensity, were weaved together harmoniously until they sung with a single voice. The voice, commingled with more than a hundred tenors, rolled across the forest with indomitable might. The voice rose, twisting and falling, ever growing in pitch. Caethe felt tears stream down his cheeks. He had never felt such purity touch his heart and he ached at the thought of its loss.

Gradually, their wordless voice woke the frozen lake before him. The ice began to glow with a metallic sheen until the liquid began to run in small streams, unbound by its frigid constraints. The waterfall began to drip, filling the icy face with a small pool of grey, lavender, and olive fluid that spread with speed. The elves voice grew higher still, and the waterfall began to crack. Huge sheets of ice fell into the lake, breaking the frozen surface with a *boom*. Glossy liquid was thrown and rainbows filled the air in a mist of magical droplets. Within moments, the waterfall flowed freely and the lake began to turn with a current.

The lake spun downwards, flowing counterclockwise. Faster and faster, it swirled nearly three-hundred feet down until the water spilled into a cloudy, grey sky. Caethe peered down, leaning over the edge of the lake with curiosity. The elves voice slowly fell, before finally falling silent. Caethe spared a glance over his shoulder and saw that the elves leaned against tree trunks and gripped one another as exhaustion overtook them.

Eagerly, Arkyn harkened a warning, "The Lake of Argent Waters has been awakened. The Pearl Gate to Umbrael has been opened. Go quickly now, for the door shall not linger long." Arkyn waved toward the tree line and Caethe saw the ground roll with roots. The roots crawled across the soft loam, splitting open at his feet. When the ground grew still, Caethe saw his swords buried in the dark ground. Caethe lifted the swords carefully. The power within them reacted to his touch and the light that hung in the air grew dim around him. Arkyn glared at the weapons with unease. A shadow of a smile touched Caethe's pale lips as he lifted the swords. Their weight was a quiet, but firm, reassurance. Caethe held the swords crisscross across his back and shadows amassed around him, forming a dark cloak. Sheath's formed from shadow and encased both blades.

Caethe looked to the Elder Fae, and bowed. When he straightened, he solemnly said, "I thank you, Arkyn of the Avalon Forests. I go with the promise that all I have sworn shall come to pass. When we next meet, it shall be in the lands of Adonim. Farewell."

Arkyn returned his bow with his own, and said, "Go in peace, son of Magrados." Caethe sensed thoughts pass between the Fae and the pixie. Caethe did not wait for their communication to end.

With a leap, Caethe dove into the silvery water. The liquid of Ardent Lake was not like water found upon Adonim. It was smooth, wet-less, and silken to the touch. Like a heavy boulder thrown into a bottomless ocean, they plunged rapidly through the lake's depths. The pixie clung to his ear with a soft pinch, and wrapped his other hand in Caethe's hair. Caethe ignored it, his mind pinned toward what lay beneath them.

The current was swift, and they circled the lake four times before they grew close to the rim that was the bottom of the lake. Caethe's robes and hair danced wildly in the current. The silver substance grew finer here, and they fell all the faster as the water rapidly grew less substantial. Caethe spied the rim. The edge of the bottom of the lake was craggy, dark and open. Water fell from its mouth, but didn't spill beyond the air, rather it grew into sheets of billowing grey clouds that boiled forth.

We pass from the lands of the Avalon, brace yourself, Solani warned, nervous thoughts bouncing across their connection like crackling sparks. Caethe smiled, sensing the pixie's fear. They were tossed more urgently now as the water bottlenecked toward the edge.

"Fear not Solani, for fear has no place at my side," Caethe shouted, daringly. With a wordless cry, he threw them into the current's center were the clouds met the lake's bottomless mouth. The air grew cold, stealing his breath as they freefell through billowing grey. Caethe spread his arms wide as they plummeted, exhilarating in the falling rush.

The wind of the Umbrael Realm was wild so high in the sky, and they were flung erratically. Caethe let the currents have their way, barrel rolling as gusts of wind threw them toward the north, and diving as it died. The grey clouds soon grew thin and the land beneath was revealed.

Umbrael was dark and ashen. The very air was stained a pale shade of shadow. Cracked plains filled the south in flat, unending stretches that rolled with fields of thick fog. Thin, dusty tornados danced across the densely-shrouded land, reaching beseechingly into the dark sky. The forests directly beneath them were dark with trees the color of pitch that stood tall, reaching toward the sky like fractured thorns. True fear rolled through Solani as he took in the grim visage. Caethe howled in delight as they were thrown by a harsh gust of wind to the left, and they fell head over feet through the air.

The pixie screamed against the harsh wail of the wind, "We must slow our fall Caethe, or we shall be smote against the ground." Caethe cackled wildly, and drew in his legs and arms tighter, gaining greater speed. They dived toward the ground like an arrow.

The forest raced toward them, growing larger. The trees loomed with dark grandeur. Even in the throes of death, the forest of Umbrael rose above all else. Trees raced toward the sky, standing proudly at the threshold of chaos, more than a thousand feet in height. Their trunks were wide, more than three hundred feet in circumference, crowned with a canopy of bare branches that clawed at the sky like black lances. Caethe and the pixie sped toward death, their fall so quick now that they cut the very wind. Any breathe they sought was lost, stolen from their lungs before they were able to draw it forth.

They were now but a hundred yards above the canopy and falling fast. Solani thoughts had grown blank with panic, and the pixie merely clung to him. Caethe eyes were narrowed in concentration and beads of sweat were flung from his brow. All laughter had fled in these last moments. All four of Caethe's hands twisted in the air, drawing runes of power with blurred movements.

With a jolt, a silver orb of pure energy snapped around them just as they slammed into the dark canopy. Branches snapped with the sound of thunder, and they were jolted from their free-fall to stillness with break-neck shock. Branches shattered under the impact, throwing shards of dark wood in all directions. The orb slowly lowered in the air until Caethe felt a strong branch beneath his feet. The silver light flared once, then sizzled into a silver dust that fell away to the depths of the forest beneath them.

Caethe smiled, satisfied, as he looked around. The forest spread in all directions as far as he could see. The branches of the trees were sharply pointed and leafless. Jagged, shattered branches surrounded them on all sides. A sap bled from the core of the broken trees, boiling with a soft hiss, greying the white scars that marred the branches. Beneath them, the trunks of the great trees descended into murky depths like black, marble pillars. Noting that the trembling pixie still clung to his neck, Caethe said dryly, "Mornings are a bit breezy here in Umbrael, but fear not; we won't linger long."

Lifoy

Chapter Fourteen:

The Chase

Stars glittered in a spray of twinkling around the yellowed moon over the two seas in the distance as a pale cat prowled across the thatched rooftops of Greenshield. It padded silently as it leapt from roof to roof, and slunk around smoking chimneys. Dark clouds rolled from the west and gently spilled rain with a soft tinkling as it met the cobblestone streets below. The cat flicked its tail in annoyance. It was soaked to the bone and its long fur clung in clumps to its lean form. It vaulted over an alleyway and landed gracefully on a slick roof before taking shelter in the crook of a stone stack, and shook with irritation.

The cat's green eyes glowed from the depths of shadow like pale lanterns as it watched the shutters open in the alley below. A boy appeared. He was dark skinned and slight, no more than twelve years of age, and dressed in dark robes that Lifoy noted were cut strangely for the north. The boy eyed the alley below nervously, and ran a hand through his thick, black hair. The cat resisted a chuckle. *Foolish boy*, it thought, *eyes are everywhere, not just the street below.* When the boy was confident that the coast was clear, he threw down a thick rope. It coiled down the side of the building from the second floor to the street below. In one hand he carried a large sack, and with the other he made his way out the window and down the wall.

The boy scampered to the mouth of the alleyway and eyed the abandoned street. The street was filled with darkened shop windows, and lonely carts that had been abandoned in the night. There was no one about at this late hour. Suddenly, the boy dashed down the street, his pace surprising in its fever. The cat sighed melodramatically, stretched, and surged across the rooftops anew.

The boys path was unerring, save for the scant guard that strolled lazily every half mile or so. The boy ducked into an alleyway as a pair of soldiers passed. The cat jumped down from the roof, to an awning, and then to a sack of potatoes that had been left beside the door beneath. The guards passed, giving the handsome, preening cat no more than a flicker of a glance; there were thousands of feral cats in the city, after all. What was Lifoy but yet another of them? *Albeit, the most handsome of them all*, Lifoy thought while absently preening. When the soldiers turned the corner, the boy was off, running down the street almost as silently as the feline that trailed him.

The boy made it to the outer wall before ducking into its shadow. Here, warehouses stood tightly locked. The city had prepared for the long winter, and the longer war. Chains crossed the dark doors of twelve massive buildings that filled the street here, guarding against thieves. The boy eyed the top of the wall and then splayed his hands across the surface of the grey, stone wall. Finding a familiar handhold, the boy climbed up and rolled over the lip of the wall. The white cat stalked under the wall, eyeing the rough surface before vaulting the twelve-feet into the air. It clung to a rocky handhold no deeper than an inch and then leaped again, mounting the edge of the wall as it pressed its stomach against the stone floor. The boy stood directly across it, looking over the edge of the opposing side.

Guards walked in pairs with torches to their left and right, but were far off. With their limited sight, they didn't see the boy thirty feet away tie his rope to a merlon and scamper over the wall. Lifoy purred and arched his back, impressed by the boy's daring. Lifoy had spent all morning, afternoon, and now deep into the night watching the boy. He'd appeared normal enough; a simple tinker's son. That was, up until he fled into the night in secret. Lifoy had to be sure he was the one.

The boy made his way down the side of the wall with ease, and dashed into the protection of an oak that stood fifty feet from the wall. A small forest of the large trees twisted upwards and all around. Their heavy crowns were still verdant, though the greenery had begun to yellow as the first touch of fall wafted from the north on the cold waters of the sea.

Lifoy followed the boy through the sparse forest to the very edge where loose loam fled into white sand. The boy crouched on the shore, eying a small puppet that lay discarded in the sand. Lifoy climbed a neighboring tree, and watched from a low hanging branch.

Reverently, the boy laid his hand on the chest of the puppets scarred, leather armor. The puppet's wooden face was chipped, missing great chunks of wood where a sword had hacked it. The boy caressed a scar that lined its torso and smiled as he felt the hard wood beneath his hand. The puppets were made of the same strong oak as the trees around them; the wounds were superficial. Lifoy crawled further out on the branch to gain a better vantage. As he watched the puppet twitched. The cat's white teeth flashed in the moonlight, as a mockery of a smile formed on its black lips. *Magic*, Lifoy thought in triumph, *the boy animates the tiny golems!*

His smile faded quickly though, as the puppet's head turned in the sand to stare at Lifoy. Its eyes were two chips of unblinking, black pebbles. Lifoy met its dull gaze and a tingle of anxiety raced down his spine. The boy turned his head, his eyes easily finding the cat in the tree. Lifoy flinched back, his back arching as he hissed. The boy's eyes were black as pitch and filled with heady power. A shuffling sound filled the woods and as Lifoy watched, dozens of puppets rose to their feet. More than a hundred lay where they had fallen, too damaged to rise, but they twitched with movement as they struggled to do their master's bidding.

The boy whispered to the puppet at his knee, "The pretty

kitty is stuck in the tree, go get it." Then to night, he whispered happily, "Papa loves cats."

Lifoy spun on the branch, skittering across the wide avenue as he scanned the woods to either side. Puppets raced to the tree from all directions. Dozens ran from the beach, their wooden bodies slick with sea water and feet encrusted with sand. He jumped to another branch as the closest puppet climbed up the trunk. Lifoy dashed to the edge of the limb and eyed the distance to the neighboring tree. The closest branch was far below, and a fair distance. Beneath him, surrounding the trunk, a mass of puppets swarmed. Their eyes were all turned toward him, staring silently. Lifoy looked over his shoulder, reconsidering the jump, only to find a puppet driving down its tiny sword toward Lifoy's fluffy tail, intent on pinning the cat to the tree. Lifoy yowled and leapt, and the sword thunked into the wood, tearing free a few strands of hair. Lifoy landed on the low branch, clawing desperately, as it bowed down toward the crowd of wooden men.

As quick as thought, the cat streaked up the tree, only to catapult himself to the next bough and then to the next.

The puppets learned quickly — or rather their animator did. Soon there were puppets waiting in the trees before him. Lifoy leaped and dodged, slinked through their quick jabs and bony arms as they sought to catch him. He reared back as a puppet swung its sword, nearly cutting off a tufted ear, and rolled off the branch to land on the tree limb beneath.

Briefly, Lifoy considered changing into something larger, but below, chasing him among his army of puppets, was the boy. He called to Lifoy in a sing-song voice, "Here kitty, kitty, come to me. Kitty, kitty, my puppets just want to play. Kitty, kitty." His string of calls repeated over and over, and Lifoy dared not reveal himself.

Lifoy's sight narrowed to the next branch, to the next dodge, to the next tree. He was quick, and while the golems were well-made, the cat was quicker. For twenty minutes, Lifoy ran through the gauntlet of deadly creatures. He spotted the wall before him and redoubled his efforts. A puppet reared up before him, having jumped from a higher branch to the one that Lifoy stood on. Lifoy vaulted over its open arms, and used its head as a springboard to launch himself into the open air. He landed in the clear ground between the forest and the wall but feared any pause, not even to look over his shoulder to gauge the pursuit. He hit the wall running and dashed up the vertical climb in seconds.

When he halted, he fully expected a puppet to grasp the edge of the wall behind him, but saw that the ground below was unmoving. The chase had ceased. Lifoy's eyes narrowed. In the shadow of the nearest oak tree, the boy stood gazing at him, distant and forlorn. At his feet stood half a hundred puppets. Lifoy shivered, flicking droplets of rain, and promptly dashed away into the city to savor his hard-earned success.

The youngest Ronan had been found.

Aritian

Chapter Fifteen:

Creuen

The company cut across the Golden Plain heading due north, and rising on the horizon sat a mighty city. Aritian blinked rapidly as the city became more than a hazy smudge, reassuring himself that his eyes saw true: the city was indeed colossal, and at least four times the size of Inee. Its sandstone walls sprawled before the coast for miles, and behind it, Aritian could see the glittering, green waves of the Virdi sea. A massive temple sat in the city's center, the apex towering above the walls by nearly five hundred feet. Every half-mile mark was met with a tower on the rim of the wall, culminating in dozens of them, all circular and with wide windows that peered to each of the four nautical directions. Their walls smoldered darkly, reflecting the dying light. To the northwest a long road, heavy with traffic, snaked before it became lost to sight. Aritian cupped his hands over his eyes and saw that the road exited the city fleeing south as well, traveling parallel to the coast.

Maud maintained their speed at a quick pace, as the soldiers around them shouted joyously when they caught sight of Creuen. The red standards they carried snapped crisply in the dim light, and they kicked their horses to greater speed as renewed vigor filled them. Aritian turned to Selyni, and in wonder, said, "You said the city was large, but I had no idea it was this gargantuan. Surely this must be the greatest city in all of Adonim?"

Selyni laughed, her bright voice filling the air like tinkling glass. She assured him, "In Ignea, Creuen is but the second largest city. The largest is actually the capital of Spres, known as the City of a Thousand Lanterns." She smiled warmly, and warned, "Ignea is just one continent. There are many cities in Afta and Novus quite a bit larger than both the Lantern City and Creuen." Aritian shook his head in amazement. The city that reared before them was so mammoth that Aritian couldn't comprehend anything being larger.

Beryl spoke abruptly, "In Afta there be a mountain range known as the Mondeus. It stretches thirty-five hundred miles in length, splittin' Afta in two. The Mondeus be the largest mountain in all of Adonim, both in height and length. Alone, it holds four of the greatest Dwarven Halls. In Darkryn Hall, where I hail from, there is a model of the largest: The Grimrath Hall. It holds three million of me kin, and would dwarf this little red rock." Beryl's voice grew wistful, his dark eyes holding a soft gleam, as he said, "To see such magistracy would be akin to standin' before Feryium himself."

Aritian looked at the dwarf in surprise. Beryl did not often speak of his homeland nor of his people. Selyni smiled at the dwarf kindly, and said, "Standing at the side of a Ronan, that dream may one day come true."

Beryl shook his head, and said gruffly, "No lass, I have been cast out." He pulled up the sleeve of his shirt exposing a branded X that scarred his bicep. Sadly, he said, "I'll never again be steppin foot within a Dwarven Hall."

Selyni smiled brightly, undeterred, and said, "You really don't understand who Aritian is. Ronan stand above kings, just below the Mortal Gods." Aritian shook his head in irritation; Selyni, like Maud, easily bore this superior mindset. "Trust me, Beryl, nothing is beyond your reach should you serve Aritian well." The dwarf looked up at Selyni cautiously, not knowing if she was jesting or serious.

Aritian spoke sharply, "These are my friends, Selyni — not my slaves and not my servants. They do not serve me nor will anyone. Ever." Aritian kicked his horse forward, leaving a frowning Selyni behind.

Rythsar caught up and ran at his mount's shoulder. His horse had grown comfortable with the lorith's presence and as they raced together, their gaits flowed with perfect synchrony.

The lorith spoke, hissing between breathes, "There is no shame in serving another, Aritian. Serving a worthy Master is all that most can hope for in this life. It is what that Master does with that loyalty that shows the merit of their faith." Rythsar continued, warning, "We all serve something, be it the Gods, a King, or Master. It is simply the way of the world. Don't be a fool; you know this." Aritian nodded, but he was uncomfortable by the idea that anyone might regard him in such a way.

The city's wall loomed before them, consuming the horizon; it was only a few miles off now. The grassland slowly gave way to greenery. There was freshwater close. An orchard fled across the gentle hills to the north with tall trees planted in neat lines. Even at this distance Aritian could smell the fragrant perfume of fresh fruit.

Aritian led his mount to Maud's side. The soldiers flanking her promptly fell back, allowing space for him. Aritian gave them a nod of thanks.

Maud, in turn, looked at him curiously. They had not spoken much over the last three days. Nervously, he eyed the guards that lined the walls. Without preamble, he asked, "Are you known here, in Creuen?" The city had been made with defense in mind and he could see little weakness in its construction. Bulwarks stretched between towers guarded by tall gargoyles that bent over the wall. He had seen their construction before. Their gaping mouths would spill boiling oil should the city be threatened. The parapets crawled with soldiers in the hundreds, so high above they looked no larger than ants.

Maud's eyes flicked to the city, and with a dry humor, said, "I am known within the city as Lady Suna of the House of Maud. Such deceptions are necessary, you'll soon find out, and innocent enough. Here I am known as a widower bequeathed with great wealth, and the reputation of a benefactor who occasionally influences trade and dabbles lightly in politics as needed." Her smile grew wider, as she asked, "But you're not asking that, are you?"

Aritian shook his head.

Maud elaborated lightly, "I am not known as a magi in this place. To reveal myself fully would be like lighting a beacon, drawing all my enemies like bees to honey. We must show caution." With her warning came a gaze of longing as she looked upon the city, and Aritian knew then that if Maud loved anything in the realm, it was this place. She continued lightly, "Only a select few outside my House know my true identity. You must take care that that fact remains true during your stay here in my home." Maud turned her head toward him and the easy smile fled her face.

In a flinty whisper, she uttered, "To do otherwise will only result in more unnecessary blood on your hands."

Aritian nodded. A frown followed, however, and he asked, "How will you explain to the guards at the gate why you were out on the Golden Plain? Surely a woman, even one who has a hand in trade, would be looked on strangely riding out of the wild."

Maud laughed brightly. It wasn't an unpleasant sound, rather it was infectious and Aritian found himself smiling like a loon, not knowing exactly what they were laughing about. Maud leaned over and patted his arm, saying warmly, "Oh Aritian, it's been such a long time since I've been around one who questions me as you do."

Aritian bowed his head, and said, "I apologize. I meant no disrespect."

Maud waved a gloved hand dismissively, and said, "No, it's quite refreshing. You are young and curious. There is nothing wrong with that." She waved to the wall that fled into the sky above them, and said, "They can't see us, for I have weaved a glamour around us. Besides, who said anything about entering the city by a gate? Now come, let us ride." She kicked her horse, calling for greater speed and Aritian felt his mount surge forward. He grabbed his reins tightly as his horse chased Maud to the wall.

The company reached the wall in minutes, and dismounted in its south-facing shadow. The wall was smooth with red rock fitted so seamlessly that it appeared as though it had been made from a single sheet of stone. Aritian eyed the ruddy material, but saw no way of entry. Azera and Ori reached his side and dismounted, handing their reins to a waiting soldier.

Brightly, Ori said, "What a wonderful city. Its beauty is unchallenged, Lady Maud." Maud flashed the young Titan a smile. Namyr dismounted from his mount and joined Maud.

Azera asked, "Why are we not at the gate? We aren't waiting for dark to enter, are we?" The rest of the company dismounted and milled close. Aritian saw a soldier lift Entah off of his mount. The gnome winced as his feet reached the ground, and he settled heavily on his left foot. Selyni walked to his side, took the gnome's arm, and helped him limp forward. The gnome's right leg was in a splint and he shuffled forward with obvious pain, his oversized eyes narrowed tightly. The long ride had not been easy on him.

Namyr laughed at Azera, and said, "No, you foolish brute, have patience. Maud will open the way." Azera grunted in annoyance, but she swallowed any reproach.

A soldier led a large, roan mare forward and handed its reins to Maud. Gently, Maud caressed the horse's cheek and leaning close, whispered to it in hushed tones. The horse turned its head to the side, exposing its neck. It was an unnatural position, and Aritian knew from its dulled eyes that Maud controlled it with her power.

The black-diamond wand appeared in her hand and without hesitation, Maud drew the tip of the wand across the mare's throat. Where the wand touched hide and flesh split, as if cut by a knife. Aritian inhaled sharply in shock. Mingyo grabbed Aritian's hand with a gasp, and Aritian squeezed it in reassurance. Blood sprayed across Maud's hands and soaked the sandy ground. Maud turned from the dying horse and began drawing runes along the wall with the dark blood. The horse didn't make a sound. It stood with its head hanging low until its strength failed it and its legs folded. Azera and Ori whispered prayers to Ignathra, honoring the horse's sacrifice. Beryl mumbled a harsh curse and displayed two fingers and his thumb; a dwarven sign against evil.

When it collapsed to the ground, the runes Maud had drawn took on a pale glow. The sun dipped beneath the horizon, shading them in a muted wash. Slowly, the red light of the spell spread across the face of the wall and formed the outline of a massive doorway. With a rumble, the light fled and the door of light became cut into stone.

In a voice humbled by shock, Aritian asked, "Did you have to kill the horse, couldn't you simply used your power?" Entah shuffled forward from Selyni's side and bent awkwardly to study the cut with obvious interest.

Namyr smiled wide, exposing his pointed teeth, and drawled, "I wouldn't think you of all people, Aritian, would be so squeamish by a little blood." Aritian shook his head. It wasn't that he was squeamish; the death just seemed senseless.

Cut into the stone above the doorway were runes, and Aritian eyed them nervously. When his eyes met them, he felt his pupils began to burn. It felt as if he stared into a harsh fire, and he hurriedly averted his gaze.

Maud turned from the wall and an iron door swung open. She pointed to the calligraphy and pronounced, "It's written in runes of the Inferno, a demonic language, and reads: 'Only blood pays passage to power.' Poetic, no?" The blackened clouds that filled her eyes faded, revealing her maroon stare. Ominously, she said, "There is always a price for power,

Aritian." She turned away with a sweep of her long skirts and disappeared into the shadows of the tunnel that waited ahead.

Aritian walked forward after Selyni, followed by his companions into the depths of Creuen.

The immense passage beyond was dark, but red orbs of light illuminated the air around them as Maud walked, leading the way. None of the soldiers seemed unnerved by Maud's obvious use of power, but Aritian heard Entah, Sicaroo and Yi gasp as they caught sight of the source of light. They walked in silence through the magic-born tunnel, unsure of what lay at the end of it.

Aritian stopped a few steps behind Maud as they stepped from the tunnel into what could only be described as a small palace.

Before them spread a mosaic courtyard that divided the compound in two. The stones had been artfully placed in a repetitive design of a phoenix, and the firebird could be seen a thousand times over. A tall, gold-filigree gate rested a half a mile in the distance, guarding the entrance that faced the interior of the city, and palm trees lined the wall, their heavy heads resting eighty feet in the air above a low wall.

In welcome, an elegant garden spread before the gate, gurgling with the sound of half a hundred fountains. To either side of the courtyard sat red sandstone buildings that were crowned with golden domes and wide verandas that stretched around the buildings to the sprawling balconies above.

With a nod from Maud, their guard disbanded and young stable hands raced forward to attend their horses and take them to rest. The company walked to the staircase that led to the upper levels above the stables, carrying heavy packs and talking in low whispers. Maud turned toward Aritian with a small smile and said, "Welcome to my home. I hope that here you find peace and respite." Maud waved a young man forward, and said, "This is Ibriham, Hector's son. He will see to all of your needs during you stay in Creuen."

Ibriham stepped forward and bowed. He wore a uniform similar to that of the servants, although he wore a rich golden pendant shaped in the form of a hawk's talon that seemed to set him apart. His face was long and his nose hooked, but he wore none of the weariness or lines that had marred Hector's face. He was young, no older than Aritian himself, and had a soldier's build similar to his father, though he lacked Hector's long hair. Rather, he kept his blonde hair cropped short on the sides and let the top curl wildly.

Internally, Aritian winced and wondered if the boy knew he was facing the man responsible for his father's death. A moment passed as Aritian stared at him, unable to tear his eyes away. "Is there a problem?" Maud asked with an innocent smile. She petted the boy's shoulder, as she asked, "Surely, my own great-grandson is a sufficient enough servant?" Aritian nodded, unable to form a reply.

"Good, tomorrow at sunrise Ibriham will guide you to me and we will speak." Maud turned to Ibriham without seeing if Aritian agreed, and commanded affectionately, "See to their every need, dear one." The boy bowed deeply. With that, Maud walked off to the left and disappeared beneath an arch, servants following her like an obedient tide.

Aritian realized that all but his companions, Selyni, and himself, had abandoned the courtyard.

"It's good to see you again, Ibriham." Selyni said with a polite nod.

Ibriham smiled warmly as he gave Selyni a bow of respect in turn. "It is good to see you as well. Your presence brightens the day, Mistress. We heard that your travels were fraught with peril." Ibrahim's dark brown eyes flicked toward Aritian and Aritian sighed, knowing with that look alone Ibriham was privy to exactly what had transpired. "I am glad you returned to Creuen as pure and beautiful as you left it."

Selyni chuckled lightly at Ibrahim's silken tongue and gave the boy a wink. She waved to Aritian, and introduced him,

"This is Aritian Ronan." She gestured to Rythsar who hovered at Aritian's side, and said, "Rythsar of the Pomum." She indicated the Titans who stood together behind him, saying, "Ori and Azera of Inee." Selyni turned to her left, and said, "This is Beryl of Dakryn Hall, and Entah," Selyni hesitated, but the gnome made no effort to speak, and so she said, "of Victes." She then beamed at the Dranguis and pointed them out one by one, as she named them, "Bo, Shan, Hui, Yi, Mingyo, Sicaroo, and Rong. All hail from Inee."

Ibriham nodded respectfully to each of them. Aritian noticed that he held his eyes downcast in respect, and didn't meet any of their eyes. It was common courtesy expected of a slave when in the presence of a Master.

Selyni made to speak on, but Aritian spoke first, "Ibriham, there is no need for formality between us. I was once a slave, and such customary glorification leaves me uncomfortable." Aritian smiled nervously, trying to break the serious tension that built between them.

"I understand, Master Ronan." Ibriham said politely, without raising his eyes.

Aritian sighed. "Ibriham, I am sorry for your loss. By all accounts, your father seemed like a good man. My friends spoke well of him...but I did not know him. I have no words to express the depth of my sorrow or my regret, but know that I will do all I can to right the wrong between us."

Selyni looked at him in surprise, and she spoke slowly, "Aritian, Ibriham has lived in Maud's shadow all his life. He understands that things can go awry when in the presence of a Ronan. I am sure he doesn't blame you."

Aritian felt his anger spike. He turned to Selyni and took her shoulder, turning her to face him. Quietly, he hissed, "Just because we are Ronan does not give us liberties over the lives of others. How can you speak so callously of a man's death?"

Selyni cocked her head, and pushed her long blonde hair over her shoulder as she beseeched, "Aritian I don't mean to be glib, I just..."

Ibriham stepped forward and bowed, interrupting them. "Lady Selyni is right. I am aware of the risks that come with serving a magus and do so gladly. As did my father," Ibrahim's eyes flicked up to meet Aritian's. He held Aritian's gaze for a second, before dropping his gaze once more. "All is forgiven," he said politely, "please do not trouble yourself over concern for me."

Aritian made to speak again, but Beryl stepped forward, and said gruffly, "Good, now that the unpleasantries have been dealt with," he smiled and gave Selyni a nod before prompting, "How about a hot plate and a large tankard of spirit? The road be long and a dwarf's thirst be great."

Ibriham nodded to Beryl, and said, "Of course, dwarven Lord. Please, if you all would follow me, accommodations have been prepared for your arrival." With that announcement, Ibriham turned on his heel and led them across the courtyard toward a stairwell. Aritian hung back to aid Entah as his companions ascended. The gnome was not talkative and Aritian found his quiet company comforting. With a hand hooked underneath Entah's thin arm, they slowly rose to the fourth landing where a large balcony waited. Entah nodded to him in thanks and leaned against the wall for support as he caught his breath.

Through the wide-spaced columns of the balcony, they admired the sprawling city before them. The city was aglow with thousands of tiny lights that banished the darkness of night. Aritian could hear the rumble of civilization, and found himself smiling at the familiar sound of it. He felt himself begin to relax. He was born to city life, and the long road here had been filled with a strange openness that hadn't allowed him to breathe comfortably.

The veranda was illuminated by pale, blue-paned lanterns that hung from the ceiling and filled with low couches that were piled high with plush, brightly-colored pillows. Potted plants sat here and there along the veranda, bringing warmth to the red stone. The wide, orange petaled flowers filled the air with heady perfume. Low tables stretched before the couches, and beneath these woven carpets lay, softening the hard floor.

Ibriham opened the double doors that stood past the first set of couches and waved them inside. Beryl, the young serpents, Ori and Azera entered eagerly, but Selyni touched Aritian's arm, forestalling him. Seeing that Aritian had stopped, Rythsar paused in the doorway, his yellow eyes reflecting the soft light as he waited by the door. Ibriham cast his eyes downward, and folded his arms, waiting patiently.

Selyni smiled cautiously, not taking her hand from his arm, and said, "Before I bid you goodnight I wish to apologize for upsetting you. It seems that it will take time for the two of us to grow accustomed to one another." Aritian knew that she was being genuine, but he shook his head.

Frustrated, Aritian replied, "We are from two different worlds and I am just not sure that I wish to live in yours yet. No matter how handsomely adorned it may be..." Aritian gestured at the rich trappings around them. His tone grew more serious, as he went on, "In my world, life is hard. You fight for every breath you take and each day you wake up alive is a blessing from Ignathra. I can't," he shook his head again, and repeated with determination, "I won't take another's life for granted." Aritian could feel Ibrahim's eyes settle heavily on him, but Aritian ignored him. He wasn't speaking to pacify Ibriham; he was speaking from his heart.

Selyni frowned, and said, "Aritian, Namyr told me that before you were in the White Mine you were owned by a Master in an assassin's Guild. I am sorry for it, but I seem to be confused by your sudden, newfound morality."

At that, Aritian smiled, which only made Selyni's baffled frown deepen.

"As a slave you have no choice of occupation; no choice in anything. You do as your commanded or you die. You misunderstand my sudden morality, as you call it, with the moral standards of my Master. I was a slave, Selyni," Aritian said bluntly. "My actions were not dictated by my will. I bought each day with blood and I paid gladly because I wished to live. I've thought a lot about my past on the road to Creuen, and come to the conclusion that I have spent much of my life no better than an animal. I've been bestial, driven only by my base instincts to survive."

Selyni nodded as if she understood, but Aritian knew she didn't. Darkly, he asked, "Can I be condemned for the will of my Masters?" He shrugged at his own rhetoric, not knowing the answer. "Perhaps, but only the light of Ignathra can reveal that. Now I have a choice, and I won't go back to that brutish mentality. I don't think I could live with myself if I were to. Not after Razia."

Selyni nodded in silence once more, and he saw pity fill her eyes.

Aritian shook his head, holding back his grief, and continued in a harsher whisper, "That last day on Inee changed things. The dreams I once had," Aritian gently pushed Selyni's hand from his arm, "the dreams that Razia and I once had, were not filled with killing or subjugating others." Aritian looked into Selyni's blue eyes and narrowed his gaze as he said, "If you wish to share my company you will not display such ugly tendencies towards superiority."

Selyni stepped back in shock, her face paling in the face of his condemnation.

"You may be Ronan, but Ronan bleed like any other man." Aritian held her gaze for a moment, before nodding his head in respect, and said, "Good night, Lady Selyni."

Aritian turned from Selyni to find Ibriham looking at him with open astonishment. The man's mouth hung open and his eyes were wide with shock. Whether it was because Aritian had spoken so openly before him, the words he had chosen, or the rudeness in which he had addressed Selyni, Aritian knew not, but he was beyond caring.

Rythsar nodded to him, his black lips curling into a smile, and Aritian walked past the lorith into the apartments where his companions waited.

Caethe

Chapter Sixteen:

The Chaos of Umbrael

"Cimexael, you're looking rather delectable today," Caethe said, eying the demon that stood before him. The forests of Umbrael were rife with noise, far more than what was natural to the quiet realm. Before him, adorned in fog, was a tall demon of a hazy, citron color. Her antennae swept the ground before her, feeling along the roots and trees to supplement her lack of eyes as her long, multi-segmented body twined along the path behind her.

"You know why I have come, Caethe." Cimexael replied in a voice that was filled with rattling clicks. Her mandibles snapped when her words cut off, flinging poisonous venom. Caethe dogged his head to the right, as the acid flicked past in a spray of spittle. Where the venom splattered across the trees, the bark smoked with a hiss and melted away.

"No, I honestly don't, but I suspect that you're about to tell me," Caethe said dryly. Solani tried to reach across the connection of their minds, but Caethe had slammed the door to his mind shut the moment the demon appeared. The pixie nervously gripped his staff, tilting the diamond tip toward the demon warningly.

Cimexael took a few tentative steps forward, her long, thin legs scissoring up and down the length of her. Each leg grew in size as it descended down her body, and as she came fully into view he was able to see that her thirteenth pair of legs stood more than twice the height of the first, resting just beneath the lowest branches.

"We thought you dead, long past. The realms sung with your fall from grace." She hissed, in a series of rapid clacking noises.

"I'm still breathing." Caethe spoke with a bold smile. Cimexael's long feelers reached toward him, and Caethe did not move. She brushed his face with the delicacy of eyelashes before prodding down the length of his body. When her feelers touched Solani, he smacked it away with his staff, the tip flashing with sparks. A moment later, when they touched Caethe's swords, they snapped back, standing rigidly above her head. The small, thin hands that rested just beneath her shovel-like skull clutched one another in fear and her long mouth twisted in a frown.

Cimexael bowed her head, and whispered, "For now. Even as we speak, my lord sends couriers to the Horned King."

Caethe chuckled, and said, "Aethral's fury will rage impotently, for when he finally rouses I shall long be gone."

Cimexael smiled then, revealing a mouthful of needle-like teeth. With a distracted hand, she swept her long, stringy hair from her face, and warned, "Already the shadow fills with fiends who seek your head in hopes of currying favor." Caethe knew that she spoke truly. Umbrael was rife with creatures that did not belong; they had seen signs everywhere, but had so far avoided any confrontations. Until now.

Caethe smirked, and said, "I would have thought you above such trifling intrigue. A demon of your age should not place herself in such dire straits."

Cimexael hissed angrily, "While the dark one slumbers, the Lord of the Inferno rules the Under Realms. You are no fool, Caethe. Your power is tied to the realms; your essence has seeped for far too long in the Aether for it not to be. Even if you escape, how long do you suppose you'll be able to resist the call? We will be waiting each time you come, and eventually we will have you."

"Have you come to simply bandy threats or shall we

proceed?" Caethe asked, tiring of the game. Beneath the folds of his cloak, his lower hands began tracing runes of power in the air.

Cimexael made a whining sound before snapping back, "I come to make an offer, Magrados. Not all of us who live in the Under Realms share such love for the Flaming Master."

Caethe looked at the demon in surprise. He had wondered why she stilled her hand, why she had not attacked, and now he knew.

"You want me to kill him? End him?" Caethe asked in a hollow voice.

"The Mother of a Thousand Eyes has told of Sabizael's defeat. What was done to a son can surely be done to his father." Cimexael said, bowing her long head to the ground.

"That spider should learn to keep her mouth shut." Caethe growled in irritation.

Cimexael stretched her thin hands before her, nearly beseechingly, as she said, "You ended a greater demon before, you could do it again."

Caethe shook his head, and said darkly, "Aethral is not his son. I will not become a champion of Barathrum. If you want the Emperor dead, do it yourself."

The demon drew herself fully, towering to her twelve foot height, and warned, "If you won't kill him, then you force my hand to service." When her words ended, her thin hands stretched wide, and two swords that glowed with violet fire slid from under her carapace into her hands. She whirled the blades casually, leaving a trail of light.

"I am not afraid." Caethe drawled, raising his own blades in defense.

"You should be." Cimexael hissed, with a tittering, clicking laugh.

Solani struck first. A beam of white light shot from his wand and lanced into the face of the greater demon. Cimexael chittered a scream and reared up, bracing herself against the trees to either side. She rushed up the trees halfway, standing on her last pair of legs, before diving toward them with her swords held high. Her speed made her a blur, and Caethe flung himself into the air with a backhanded spring, accentuating the height he gained with magic, before flipping head-over-heels in a graceful arc over her diving head. Caethe landed on her back hard and stabbed between two segments where two shell-like pieces of her met, twisting. Yellow blood sprayed his face as he wounded the demon.

Cimexael clicked with a loud popping sound, and shivered down her full length. Her back was slippery-smooth and Caethe fell onto his side. She shivered again, more violently, and he was flung to the ground to landed in a puff of fog. Solani took to his wings, flying above. The pixie shot beams of scathing light, as Caethe crawled to his feet. Caethe dived to the side, avoiding being punctured by one of her stomping feet, and made to stand. Cimexael spun around, hissing as she recoiled from the pixies onslaught and kicked out with a thin leg. The hairy appendage knocked Caethe with a glancing blow, but the demon hardly seemed to notice. Her skin bubbled and smoke in the places where the pixie's magic touched. She shook her head, her jaws snapping angrily as she recovered.

Cimexael spun her blades in a circle formation that made them look like shields of purple, and charged Caethe. Solani whirled in the air just behind her head, bombarding her with light, but the demon ignored the irritation. Caethe jumped toward her, and his swords met hers in a spray of white sparks. They danced together, blades whirling, meeting in a clash and then springing away to defense. Cimexael was an old demon, one of great renown. She moved with grace as her long legs carried her close and then bolted away. Caethe dived toward her face, seeing an opening, but Cimexael merely lunged backward, her legs carrying her up a tree beyond his reach. Caethe stalked beneath her, waiting as her antenna flicked and swayed.

Solani drew a glyph with a quick flick of his wand, and the air was seared with green fire. The pixie pushed the flaming rune toward the demon with a wave of his staff. The fire grew in size as it jetted across the air until a whirling fireball screamed through the forest. Cimexael's feelers wheeled in shock, and she threw herself further up the tree, even as the fireball smashed against the trunk. The wood groaned beneath the fire, splintering, and the tree began to topple over in a great crash.

Cimexael leaped from the tree, plunging down toward him, her body writhing as she fell through the flames. She landed on the ground before him with a dim boom, unburnt. She raised a sword as he fell back, and a bolt of violet liquid shot through the air. The liquid hit Solani, turned gummy, knotting his wings and hands, and then hardened like frozen webbing. The pixie dropped from the air like a stone. Caethe flung his hands out and the encased pixie slowed in its fall, before gently falling to a rest on a raised root.

Cimexael whirled, enraged, and Caethe flicked his hands outward and bathed her in red fire. The flames crackled and spit, and Cimexael hissed with pain, but she did not burn. All along her body, violet runes of power glimmered as her protection wards snapped around her. While the inferno flames burned, she could not escape. She screamed wordlessly and spat venom, but the viscous poison disappeared in puffs of black smoke. Caethe raised his lower hands, and the flame-encased demon was lifted from the ground. He flipped one of his right hands, and her body went rigid-straight. In this position she was nearly forty feet in length.

Caethe walked beneath her, eying her hard shell. Her many legs were stretched out flat. As he walked, Caethe swung his swords and lopped off the members as he went. Cimexael hissed in pain and the flames sputtered. Caethe hurried, knowing that even now she was working on a counter spell that would release her.

When he reached the barbed end of her body, he plunged

his sword into the crease that ran along the full length of her segmented body. Yellow blood rained down on him in a rush, and her skin began to flake and crust where his sword touched. Caethe punched his second sword into her, widening the crack. Sawing his blades, he walked toward her head. Guts, blood, and organs fell from her body, smacking wetly on the foggy earth. Cimexael gave a tortured, whining scream as he eviscerated her.

When he grew close to her head, he could hear her begging, "Please, don't. Stop. Please, I shall retreat in peace."

Caethe bellowed, "I shall have no peace while I remain under threat. You should have stayed in the Grotto Canyons, but you grew greedy."

The demon moaned in a series of long dragged out clicks. Caethe worked his blades just under her chest, crossed his swords and snapped them out. Her chest cavity cracked audibly. Cimexael angrily spat, "My Lord shall join the Horned King if you kill me. Together they will crush you, but if you let me live I will serve you well."

Caethe pulled his swords free, and a rush of blood splattered the ground as he came to stand before the demon. Cimexael had long abandoned trying to fight his flame, as her pain had grown too great. Even now, her yellowed skin began to brown and blacken as his fire consumed her runes of power. "I suspect that Lord Cyraque allowed you this chase, because he has his eye on a younger consort. You are nothing to him." Caethe promised, knowingly. The hierarchy of the denzies was no less complicated than a noble court of man, and Caethe suspected treachery.

Cimexael's thin hands shook as she reached out toward him, and swore, "No, I tell you true, I am his most favored. Please, don't kill me." Caethe hacked off one of the gangly limbs and it fell to the ground with a thud before curling in on itself as it was consumed by rot.

Caethe shook his head sadly, and said, "I'm not going to

kill you, I'm going to feed you to my swords. What hell lay within I do not know, but soon you shall find out."

"Not the Prison of Souls! No, kill me, kill me." Cimexael screeched.

"They have tasted blood, and now they must be sated." Caethe said with grim determination, raising his blades. He punched them into her head, just above her mandibles and angled them upwards. The glittering black runes that traced the length of the swords began to pulse as they slowly, agonizingly, began to drink in the demon's soul. In seconds, nothing but a husk of the greater demon remained. Caethe wrenched his swords out of the shell, and they flashed darkly once, before falling still. The ruby flames consumed the corpse in seconds, filling the forest with the stench of brimstone before winking out of existence.

Caethe walked to where Solani lay encased. The pixie looked as if it imprisoned in a hardened, white snot ball. With a flick of his hand, the rock disintegrated. Solani climbed shakily to his feet, and dipped his head in thanks. Caethe sheathed his swords in shadow, and lowered a hand and the pixie climbed on gratefully. "Come on, we still have far to travel." Caethe whispered, turning back to the woods.

*****

Caethe ran through the forest of Umbrael, his robes snapping behind him in tendrils of smoke. As he ran he dodged trees, dashed under sweeping branches, and leapt over raised roots. A gusting sound filled the air and with it, heavy footfalls; Caethe knew the noise was no wind.

A shadow flanking him surged ahead, and Caethe skidded to a stop. A lesser demon of Barathrum landed heavily on the ground before him, having dropped from a neighboring tree. Out the corner of his eye, Caethe saw a dozen more crawled along the tree trunks, skittering from one to the next.

Solani spoke into his mind. *There are more than twenty more behind. We are surrounded.* Caethe nodded curtly, but did not respond. *The will never allow us to reach the Origin glade,* Solani insisted.

The mucus-green demon bent low to the ground, its maw stretching wide as it sucked in the essence of the realm; scenting for him. The fleshy stands that connected its upper and lower jaw dripped with mustard-colored venom. Caethe could feel fear rising in his throat, threatening panic. He shook his head, dazed. He knew the feeling was merely the effect of the creatures around him.

A whine filled the air, and then another. Something heavy landed behind him with a thud. Caethe whirled around, pulling his swords free. A brilliant, banana-colored demon squatted in the dark fog, its long neck weaved side to side threateningly. Two blurs of green fled above him, as demons crossed the air above. The sound of long talons tearing at bark filled the air as demons crowded the trees around them.

Caethe smiled, his breath coming raggedly. They had run for many days since he had smote Cimexael, and demons had chased them relentlessly deep into the heart of Umbrael's great forest.

The demon before him charged, clawing at him. Its attack met a silver shield that spat angry sparks. The demon was repelled back a step, and its wide mouth waned open as it huffed angrily. Undeterred, the demon spat a thick wad of sickly-green venom that splattered across his field of vision before burning off the shield in wisps of smoke. The fumes of a swamp filled his senses and burned his nostrils.

The demon sprang backward with a strange whine, its three gangly legs carrying it back half a dozen feet. Its call was taken up by the demons around him until the very forest seemed to be moaning in chorus. A demon smashed into the shield at his back, knocking him forward a step, and tore viciously at the silver shield with long talons.

Solani tugged at his hair, and screaming fearfully, "Do something. We can't just stand here." A demon crashed from the dark heights, and smashed into the shield, forcing Caethe to his knees.

Angrily, Caethe said, "Don't you think I am?" Demons hit the ground, and skittered around them. The atmosphere around Caethe and Solani became blurred as the demons sucked in air feverishly. Caethe closed his eyes, and his form vibrated. Suddenly, there were nine of him.

All the Caethes smiled, and called, "Come and get me, fat little toads." The nine images of him dashed into the woods, leaping over the demons or dodging beneath them. The Caethes chuckled, taunting them as the demons went wild chasing after the images, running over themselves, and smashing into trees as they fought to capture him.

"Over here, goblin shit." One called from high in a tree. Three demons raced up the trunk after him, throwing black dust in their wake.

"No, get me." One called, standing on a tall root thirty feet away. A demon leapt upon the form, and it disappeared. The demon crashed into a thick thorny brush with a high-pitched scream.

"Snot ball, get me." One called dashing south, toward the plain. The Caethes fled into the forest, and the demons gave chase.

A bullfinch fled from a hollow, and flew toward the canopy with Solani at his side. The pixie's dark wings blurred as it struggled to keep up. *How long will that deception last?* Solani asked across their bond. Caethe eyed the pixie as they sped through thick spikes that rimmed the canopy. The pixie's voice held a degree of disapproval.

Caethe responded across the mind link. *Barathrum Demons are dumb. They aren't what I'm worried about.*

The finch suddenly dived behind a branch as a claw crashed through the canopy. Wood cracked with a snap, and the sound of heavy wings filled the air. *Watch yourself.* Caethe warned with a chuckle. The finch snapped a wing out, stopping the pixie from taking flight. Another claw dipped beneath the canopy, scaled and red. The air grew hot, and the bark around them curled and smoked as the clawed foot tore at the branches. *Mind the Inferno folk, they have a nasty bite.*

This is insanity, Solani said, raising his staff. A gold wind thundered from his staff and branches exploded outward, as his power was flung against those above. A high-pitched scream filled the air. Caethe looked up, and saw gold light punching into the grey sky in a jet stream. A pair of winged-demons spun in the light, head over tail. They were tall yet emaciated creatures with rounded head and fangs, and red capes in the form of leathery wings. Caethe snapped his beak in agreement and they took to the grey sky. The golden wind faded. They both flew as fast as they could over the canopy, keeping low.

Caethe looked over his shoulder, and saw that the demons had regained their wings and gave pursuit. The demons of Inferno had three sets of black eyes on either side of their face that rested beneath a ridge of short horns. All of their eyes were narrowed in anger and they flew like shooting stars, closing the distance. Their long black talons were outstretched and they cursed him in the dark tongue.

Caethe opened his beak, and a shadow spilled free. In a booming voice, Caethe spoke in the language of Umbrael, "Braugaethrael, Lord Leviathan, I call you forth as a child of Umbrael." His voice came like hissing ash and rustling leaves. He paused, and then roared, "Invasion!" The shadows slipped between his beak, curling down his throat.

Solani screamed at his side, "How can you speak so? You are no creature of Umbrael."

Caethe pumped his wings furiously, and in a wheeze, said, "No, I am not, but one lives within me. Come on."

A roar shook the sky. The call sang across the realm, shaking the very air with its fury. Those who gave pursuit paused, hovering in the sky. Steel-colored lightning filled the air, outlining the gloomy clouds above.

A dark shape rose from the forest like a mountain taking flight. It was massive and clothed in crawling, black shadows. A second roar shook the sky. Caethe's snapped his beak closed around Solani's ankle, and folded his wings as he dragged the pixie with him. They tumbled between tall branches as lightning crossed the sky once more, closer now. The demons behind them screamed as they were outlined in in bands of grey, sizzling energy, their smoking forms spinning until they crashed among the trees.

Solani cried out, and knocked Caethe's beak with his staff. Caethe let go and spread his wings, banking in a low glide just above beneath tree tops. Angrily, Solani said, "You can tell me through the bond. Don't do that again, Ronan."

Innocently, Caethe said, "Do what, save your life?" They flew on as the shadowed creature rose higher in the sky. Caethe looked back. Where the inferno demons had been were nothing but coils of black smoke. Wind rushed through the realm as the Leviathan gained greater heights. The plain to the south boiled with activity as the demons of the realm woke to their master's call.

Solani slammed into Caethe's side, and they fell to the left. A Barathrum demon burst from below, its arms swinging wide as it tried to snatch them from the air. Caethe gave Solani a nod, and they flew higher. Demons leapt from the black crowns of the trees, clawing at the sky, only to fall and crash among the canopy. Solani and Caethe flew above as the demons below gave pursuit on treetop.

You have started a war, Solani accused through their bond. His thoughts were dark and banded with purple and blue splotches of anger. *You should have never woken the Guardian. Your kin will have trouble reaching the Glade now that he is awake.*

The feathers on the bullfinch's head ruffled in annoyance, and sourly he thought back, *Well it's time they shared the risk.*

Come, I see the Origin Glade. The finch pointed a talon to a glowing hue ahead.

Before them, golden light broke the dimness of the realm. They dipped between silvery leaves into the warm glow. A heavy shadow passed above, but for now they were safe: they had reached the Origin Glade.

Aritian

Chapter Seventeen:

The Promise of a Gift

Aritian woke on a soft cloud of goose feathers, and luxuriated in the soft furs that lay over him. The room he lay in was bathed in warm light and breezy, open, with whitewashed walls and warm tapestries depicting Ignea's green forests and sweeping plains. Flowers, pink and orange, bloomed bright from the small wash table crouched next to the wardrobe with a fragrance of tart citrus.

Aritian stretched as he crossed the soft furs underfoot to a chest filled with piles of silk and bold jewels. He pulled on a sky blue tunic that hung to his knees and trousers before sliding his feet into the least-gaudy pair of shoes he could find.

When he was dressed, he looked in the silver mirror that hung above the wash basin. His hair was coming back in a dark shadow, and his grey eyes were well-rested and bright. He had slept well for the first time in a long, long time.

Smiling at his reflection, he noted that his canines were still wickedly sharp, and knew that with little effort he could extend the fangs. He touched the tip, wondering how he had gained the poison of the drake, and shrugged; his lack of understanding did not make him ungrateful.

He splashed water on his face from the black stone bowl that rested on the table. Without much hair, it was a quick affair to look presentable.

Aritian walked onto the balcony, and the view stopped him in his tracks. The city sprawled before him. Dawn had come mere moments before, but the streets were already packed with milling crowds trying to beat the heat of the day. The throngs chatter filled the air, carrying with it the stench of a half a million people.

Directly across from the balcony, a massive temple rose; the largest he had ever seen. The pinnacle gleamed solid gold more than seven-hundred feet in the air and its width stretched a quarter of a mile. It was a temple of Ignathra. Before it squatted a shorter temple, made from blue rock, jade, and white quartz. *Aqu's palace*, Aritian summarized, as he gazed at the patterns that danced across the temples walls in swirling waves. Flanking the central temple to either side stood two more temples. One was covered completely in greenery, and Aritian knew from its bright finery that it was dedicated to Naturye. While, the eastern temple was made of connecting geometric stone shapes, its face covered with thousands of brass-rimmed holes. As the wind played across the temple Aritian listened as the Goddess Cael sang.

The walls of Creuen cupped the city against the breadth of the bay and Aritian could see the Virdi Sea stretch into the distance beyond the temples. It was the first time he had ever seen the sea. He stood there in awe, taking in the vastness and the beauty of its rolling, emerald waters. Aritian could taste salt in the air and could hear the low roar of the waves two miles distant.

"Breathtaking, is it not?" A voice asked to his left. Aritian pulled his eyes from the green water and nodded to Ibriham. Ibriham placed a heavy wooden tray on a low table that was piled with pastries, meat, and bowls of fresh fruit. Ibriham bowed after placing the tray down.

Aritian admitted, "It is. I have only heard tales of the immensity of the sea, but never truly believed the bards until now."

Ibriham smiled politely and waved toward the delicacies, saying, "Please sit and eat your fill. We have some time before Lady Maud expects you." Aritian sat and his stomach growled as he eyed the rich spread before him. He plucked a berry filled pastry from the tray, but ate slowly, unnerved by having a servant watch and attend him. Aritian reached for the silver pitcher, but before he had a chance, Ibriham stepped forward and poured him a glass of cool water into a silver cup. Aritian nodded in thanks. He finished the pastry, gulped down the glass of water, and grabbed an orange. Aritian peeled a section, and made to take a bite, before setting it down.

He looked up at Ibriham realizing that he was being rude, and said, "Please, sit. You must be hungry and I hate for you to have to stand while I eat."

Ibriham bowed his head, and said formally, "I thank you for your consideration Master, but I have already eaten." He met Aritian's eyes with his pale, hazel stare, and asked, "If you wish for company I can wake your companions? Or if you please, I can bring you a selection of concubines and you may choose from among them?"

Aritian shook his head, taken aback. Razia's face flashed in his mind and he closed his eyes briefly, swallowing his grief, saying, "No, I cannot." Aritian opened his eyes and waved to the couch across him, insisting, "Please, if you won't eat then at least sit."

Ibriham nodded curtly, and said softly, "As you wish." He took a seat on the edge of the couch, his posture stiff and rigid.

Aritian took a bite of the fruit, and asked, "Ibriham, would you care to tell me of Creuen and your life here? This is all new and strange to me." He waved toward the city, adding, "Before a few weeks ago I had never left the northern city of Inee."

Ibriham cleared his throat, and said, "Creuen is one of three cities that make the Coalition of Odium. While the Coalition rests within the southern lands of the Velonian Empire, a high council of merchant princes and guild families rule the cities independently. Through their collective wealth they have gained this autonomy and pay a substantial tithe to the crown in return for protection and the continued security of their autonomous identity." His voice was proud, and Aritian could tell that he had a great vestment in the city.

The man continued, "Creuen is the greatest among the three cities, and geographically central. The success of the cities is due to their location, having access to both northern Ignea and the south, while each city being coastal to the Virdi Sea. Our sea trade with the northern kingdoms of Afta has flourished in the last decade, bring much wealth and prosperity." He waved in the general directions as he explained. "Land trade is expedited by the ingenious construction of the Onyx Ribbon, a road that spans five hundred miles, connecting the Coalition to one another, while reaching deep into Velon itself." Aritian had mentally noted the road yesterday, but he hadn't known that it spanned such a great distance.

Ibrahim's voice took on a wistful tone as he described further, "The city is prosperous and we live with plenty. The Coalition is known throughout the lands as the Three Gems of Southern Wonder, for such varied and exotic goods can only be found here. It is a good place." He concluded with a small smile, his strict formality cracking for the first time since Aritian had met him.

Aritian frowned, and said slowly, "It is my understanding that these cities are known throughout Velon as the capital of slavery." Ibriham matched his frown. Aritian cocked his head in question, and said stiffly; "I assume the slaves being exported and imported through these ports in the hundreds of thousands have a much different opinion then your charmed vantage."

Ibriham shook his head, and as if explaining something simple, said plainly, "Slavery is the backbone of the Empire; a necessary evil. Ignathra does not make all lives of equal brilliance and we must take heart in the light that we are each given."

Aritian's frown deepened with frustration. *It seems I am alone in my opinion*, he thought darkly to himself, before asking, "I see, and what of your life here? Are you content with the lot that you have been given?"

Ibrahim's chin rose at the suggested insult, and he replied, "I may hold the status of a servant, but I live better than some kings." He leaned closer, and asked, "Tell me, Aritian, the men say that you were once a slave? Before you discovered who you were truly, were you not content in the life you had been given?"

The question startled Aritian and before he could think, he spoke honestly, "I admit, before I was sent to the mines I did not think much about stepping beyond the trappings of my position."

"Yet you were a slave?" Ibriham asked insistently.

Aritian answered slowly, "Yes." He had the feeling that Ibriham was drawing him down a path that led to a trap.

Ibriham smiled triumphantly, and sat straight. With a smirk, he asked, "So even though you were a slave, commanded to kill men and women you had never met, you were content?"

Aritian shook his head, annoyed. The man before him knew nothing of his past, knew nothing of the pain that he had endured. Aritian's voice grew with the beginnings of anger as he said, "I didn't enjoy killing. I have sinned and the shadow of those sins lay across my soul for all time. I was content because I was in a community, one among brothers, and I was well fed each day, educated and housed."

Quizzically, Ibriham asked, "You assume the slaves here are not treated in the very same manner?" A single blonde eyebrow rose in question.

Aritian clenched his jaw, and replied stonily, "I don't assume anything, but free from the Master's constraints I see now how wrong it is to treat another intelligent being as property. Ignathra breathes the flames of our souls unbound and thus it should remain." Aritian concluded passionately.

Ibrahim's lips pressed together in a thin smile, before he said, "The world is not so fair a place, Master Aritian."

Aritian nodded, consenting defeat, and said, "No it's not,

but it should be."

A few minutes passed. Aritian put down the fruit that he had forgotten in his hand, no longer hungry. He stared out toward the sea lost in thought.

Ibriham cautiously asked, "May I ask a presumptuous question?"

Aritian laughed lightly, and answered with a nod, "Of course."

Ibriham did not return his smile, but instead grew more serious still, asking, "Why do you allow yourself to forgive the sins of your past, yet look unkindly at Lady Selyni? Is she not the product of those who command her? How much free will do you assume she has?"

Aritian was silent for a moment. He was confused by the man's accusation. Somewhat indignantly, he said, "I never said that I forgave myself, and I certainly didn't intend to condemn Selyni. You misunderstood what I said last night."

Ibriham gave him a pointed look, staring at him flatly, before slowly saying, "You're allowing yourself to reevaluate your morality and have gained the freedom to do so. If you haven't forgiven yourself then you're willing, at least, to put the past behind you. You seek to recast yourself in to the image of who you wish to be, free from the damnations of your past actions, no?" Aritian stared at the man, stunned by his astute assessment.

Ibriham pushed on with sudden confidence, "Furthermore, I do not believe I misunderstood. Selyni is first and foremost a soldier, and much like you in your past, acts only by the command of her superiors. If, by extension of that servitude, she has come to see the world through different eyes then you or I, then you have no right to judge her." Ibriham leaned forward, and his voice softened as he said, "Like all of us, we see truth only through the lens of our own experiences. Try to teach her a better way, if she is open to such, but do not try to force your own newly forged morality on her just because you have self-admittedly, and by all intents and purposes, suddenly decided to care about the lives of others." Ibriham plucked a grape from the fruit bowl and popped it in his mouth before sitting back against the soft pillows of the couch.

Aritian considered the man's words. His first reaction was denial and anger, to reject the hypocrisy the man accused him of, but time passed and his temper cooled in the silence. Aritian looked at the young man, and whispered, "Ibriham, you are perhaps one of the wisest men I have had the honor to meet. I admit that perhaps I have made assumptions with undue haste." Ibriham nodded, agreeing.

Ibriham stood then and bowed respectfully, before saying, "Perhaps then, you owe the Lady an apology." Aritian nodded dumbly. Ibriham beckoned him with a wave, and said, "Come now, Lady Maud does not take kindly to waiting on others. Follow me, Master Aritian."

Ibriham led him down the flight of stairs that clung to the outside of the building and down to the courtyard. They made their way toward the western side of the compound until they passed under a stone archway and found themselves in a larger courtyard.

Here, soldiers milled, training in mock fights. The clang of sword against sword rang through the air among the grunts of straining men, and barked orders. Aritian and Ibriham passed along the perimeter of the courtyard with little remark and walked up a flight of steps that led to a wide veranda. Black marble columns lined the face of the four story building, and together they entered one of the eight arched doorways that opened to a great hall.

The floor was made from the same marble as the columns, and the walls had been painted with bright frescoes. Aritian eyed the shady glades, and sweeping oceans with interest as they were filled with strange and foreign creatures that he had never seen before. To his right, among green, white-capped waves a strange creature swam. It had large dark eyes, a sharply pointed beak, and eight, bright orange legs that sprang from its long abdomen to curl outward into the waves. One of tentacle's gripped a green spear that's length was covered in barnacles, and the tip set with, what looked like, a sharply pointed coral. Aritian made to walk closer, taking in the great detail of its bulbous head and molted skin, but Ibriham lightly pulled on his arm, dragging him toward the back of the hall where Maud leisurely sat on a low, black-furred couch.

Surrounding her were a small crowd of advisors; most of them were old men with sharply pointed noses and light hair, but all shared a close resemblance to Ibriham. The eldest looked to be close to eighty and the youngest among them was a portly man in his early forties. The others were gnomes, to Aritian's surprise. For such rare creatures, he was astounded to see eight of them standing at attendance. All were male, and looked to be far greater in age then Entah. Their blue-caste skin complimented the dark robes they wore, giving them a majestic air. The gnomes turned their large dark eyes toward him and gazed at him with potent intelligence.

"Aritian, so good of you to finally arrive," Maud said, her tone light, but tinged with slight annoyance. She waved for him to sit on the couch next to her, and he sat gingerly. He was painfully aware the he was now the center of attention.

Maud flicked out a casual hand, and commanded imperiously, "Be gone. We shall speak later." The advisors bowed low and walked away in huddled groups. Maud smiled brightly and flicked her fingers outward, as she said, "You too, Ibriham. Aritian will find his way back to his apartments easily enough." Ibriham bowed and turned away without a second look. Maud turned to Aritian, and asked, "I trust that you found the accommodations to your liking?"

Aritian bowed his head, and said truthfully, "I did. I have never stayed in such fine lodgings. Thank you for your hospitality."

Maud stretched, before sitting straight, and said

dismissively, "It's nothing really. Besides, you and I are family. We should be good to one another." Aritian found his eyes drawn to her in a way he wished they would not. Logically, he found her callous and her great age disturbing, but physically he was entrapped by her.

Aritian locked his eyes on her face, lest they wonder, and asked curiously, "Are you speaking in actuality or figuratively? Did you know my parents?"

Maud smiled indulgently as she nodded, and said, "Yes, of course." She ran a hand down her long, black skirts, before saying, "Your mother was my granddaughter. She was named Baleya, after the yellow desert flower." Aritian felt his cheeks reddened. He had not expected this... not expected that they would be so closely related. His stomach turned with revolution as his attraction to her became vile. The thought of his mother made his head spin. He hadn't really ever given her much thought. As a child, he had been one among thousands of orphan children that flocked the streets of Inee.

Maud took his confused expression as a question and laughed, saying lightly, "Oh, she wasn't a Ronan if that's what you're thinking. Goodness, no. She was born without the gift, as so many are." Her voice trailed off, somewhat bitterly.

Aritian shook his head, perplexed, and blurted out the first questions that came to his mind. "What happened to her? How did I come to end up a slave in Inee, if you speak truly?"

Maud stood, and began to gracefully pace before him, explaining slowly. "Prophecy is an odd thing, a tempting tool that we Ronan often fall prey to." She turned to face him, her long train whispering across the floor with her every move, and said, "I sent several of my female descendants north in hopes of producing a Ronan with the magi who are found there. All failed and returned — all that is, but one: Baleya."

With a voice broken by skepticism, Aritian asked, "How do you know I am her son?"

Maud glided forward and leaned down to cup his cheek

with one of her small hands. She looked deep into his eyes, and with certainty, said, "I know you are her child because your blood sings to my own. I know its call as surely as I know myself." Aritian blushed deeper, struggling not to gaze at her low neckline.

Aritian swallowed thickly, and asked hoarsely, "What happened to her?" His imagination ran wild as he tried to think of why she would have abandoned him if she was connected to such a prestigious house.

Maud straightened, and returned to her pacing. She answered without looking at him. "She died, obviously. Her ship crashed as it returned across the Virdi Sea. I thought she had failed, as had the others, but she must have made it to land before giving birth, for here you are."

"What was she like?" Aritian asked, suddenly filled with a need to know her. *Baleya*, he thought, tasting the word, *my mother*.

Maud smiled, and said softly, "Oh, she was a great beauty. She had the golden skin of her Velonian father, and a delicate bone structure. Baleya was kind and intelligent, a rare combination in mortals. Many desired her and she was a prolific little thing; as most of my descendants seem to be." Maud added dryly, before explaining, "It is the reason I sent her north, for she bore three healthy children before I chose her."

"I have siblings?" Aritian heard himself ask, his mind numb.

Maud nodded as if it was of little consequence, and said, "Yes, two half-sisters and a half-brother. It is why I selected Ibriham. He is her youngest born, before you. He is just a few years older than yourself."

Aritian raised a hand imploringly, and asked in confusion, "Wait, I thought Hector was your grandson?"

Maud nodded kindly, as if explaining her complicated lineage was a simple thing, and said, "Yes, he was. Hector's father was the greatest love of my life. An elf named Aktymor.

We enjoyed many centuries of happiness before he passed, and we had thirty-seven children together. Hector's father is among the youngest of them. Baleya was the product of a brief tryst shortly after Aktymor died; I took a Velonian prince as my consort for a number of years."

Aritian felt his mouth go dry and he swallowed thickly digesting her words. In a whisper he asked, "Does Ibriham know?" Maud nodded, yes. Wonderingly, Aritian asked, "My sisters, are they here as well?"

Maud's expression grew closed, and her smile died. In a frail whisper, she said, "No, they have both passed."

Aritian felt as his head spin, dizzied by the abrupt revelations. The news of his mother and sister's deaths were but a momentary pang in his heart. He could not mourn women he had never known. In a hopeful whisper, he asked, "My father?"

Maud's face brightened, obviously glad for the change of subject. Excitedly, she said, "Hmmm, he could be any number of Ronan. I can't be sure. We won't know until we see where your gifts lay. Your father would be able to sense the connection between you, as easily as I, but as I'm sure you know the Ronan men are far from here." Maud sat by his side and her long hair pooled in her lap. She took his hands in her own, and said warmly, "Take heart Aritian, no Ronan have died in the years since your birth. Your father still lives." The thought ran through his mind like a blazing lance. He had never truly considered that he would have a parent still alive, and it filled him with considerations that he had never allowed himself to explore before.

Aritian shook his head, pushing his confusion to the side. He let go of Maud's hands, pulling them free, and asked, "When I first met you, you spoke of training and the promise I gave you. I wish to repay my debt and be free to do as I wish."

Maud stood once more, nodding to herself. She spread her hands wide, as she said, "You are a part of the Coven. You shall never again be a slave, but you will never be completely free.

With power comes obligation, without exception." She met his eyes, her red gaze suddenly hard, as she promised, "You will realize a breadth of freedom far beyond what you have ever experienced, but you owe allegiance to your Coven; your family. Do you understand?" The question was not truly optional. Aritian could sense her power rising about her. A hot wind blew through the arched doorways and played through the hall. Maud's skirts and hair were thrown as her power sung with promise.

Aritian bowed his head, and responded with a simple "Yes." The wind died instantly.

"Good." Maud said, pleased. "Speaking of your personal obligation to me, I only have one request."

Aritian looked up in anticipation, and said, "Name it, and it will be done."

Maud smiled brilliantly at him, and Aritian averted his gaze, suddenly uncomfortable. Maud's voice grew serious, "Nearly sixty years ago the people of Afta revolted against the control of the Ronan." Aritian looked up, surprised by the new vein in which the conversation had taken. Maud continued, undaunted by his apparent confusion, and said, "In their anger they called upon the Elder Gods of the Faith and learned the secrets of a Curse. This Curse binds us by our true name and we have remained in exile ever since. For a people that can live beyond a millennium you can imagine the fear of being consecrated to such a prison. Yet, for all our power and all our knowledge, the people succeeded in their endeavor."

Maud smiled kindly as she took in his bewildered expression and sat next to him. In explanation, she elaborated, "Afta is our homeland, the birthplace of the Ronan. When my brother took the Weirwood throne and was crowned Archmagus, he ushered in a new era — an era where we Ronan left our lives of isolation and discarded the soft guiding hand of our most ancient laws. Instead, Cain wished to rule the people of Afta as a god. He wished to be worshiped and hold absolute power; and so he did." Maud paused, lost in memory, shaking her head slowly. Aritian shuddered as her words fell like a hammer against his thoughts. Maud broke from her recollection, and smiled sadly as she continued, "When my brother was murdered by members of our own Coven, my son took his place."

She smiled then, despite the tears that suddenly filled her eyes, and said warmly, "Demetrius was such a bold boy. Truly, he was too young to take the crown. The weight of monarchy is a heavy burden. The Coven fractured under his rule, poor foolish boy," a tear fell down her cheek, but she continued, "Eighty years into his reign, the people of Afta began their war. The Great Revolt lasted a decade. I warned them all." She nodded to herself as she said this.

Maud did not look at Aritian now; such was the shame she carried. Rather, she stared at the light that spilled through the archways lining the far wall. "I told my son to relinquish power, for it was never our right to hold sway over mortal men." Her voice grew hot and angry, as she said, "The Coven sanctioned me and my son rebuked me, cursing me as craven. I refused the call to war."

Tears dripped freely down her cheeks now. Aritian sat as still as stone, listening to her raw grief. "He died, my handsome son..." She said this softly, and then softer still, "My Ronan son." She swallowed deeply and shook her head, smiling coldly. The sudden shift of emotion was jarring. Her voice grew hard as steel, as she said, "I sailed upon the Virdi Sea with such speed and haste, and oh, was my fury great." She laughed bitterly, her smile nefarious. "I made the people bleed for taking him. The rivers ran red with my fury, and the screams. Oh, how those sweet screams were a balm upon my anguished heart."

Silence fell between them at the conclusion of her vindication; a quiet snow flurry that froze a forest glade in the deepest of winter. Such a place held a sacred quiet and a similar oppression filled the hall as Maud struggled to banish her grief.

Her moment of fragility only made her dark beauty more enduring to Aritian, and he wished for nothing more than to reach out and comfort her. He dared not, for he did not trust himself, and so remained still.

Maud turned back to face him when her sentiments were contained. Now she wore an expressionless mask, and her voice came monotone as she explained, "The rumor of a weapon filled the land. A weapon that promised to bring the Ronan to our knees, a gift of the gods themselves. I fled then." Maud stared into his eyes unabashed by her words. "I have no shame admitting it. I fled south and didn't look back as my family was bound and cursed to exile. My son's wife and my sister died protecting me as I ran; foolish girls."

Maud stood suddenly and with her back toward him, said, "I knew that one of us must walk free to find the key of salvation. Many Ronan died in the Great Revolt. The power of Magrados is immortal, however, and the Coven — our Coven — cannot die." She turned back toward him, her skirts twisting about her, as she said, "I knew children would be born into the world. Ronan that would be unknown to the people and free to walk the land unbound. You are one of those children, Aritian." Maud met his eyes as she said this and her voice sung with the ring of truth.

Aritian spread his arms wide, and said cautiously, "I don't know anything of magic, curses, or spells, Lady Maud. I can see now what you shall ask, but I don't see how I can possibly help free them. I can't even control myself without this..." He raised his pinky, displaying the Ring of Suppression.

Maud nodded curtly, before saying, "Yes, I know you're ignorant of the Ronan power." She stepped closer, her voice warmer, as she said, "I do not ask this lightly, and have no intentions on sending you forth, alone, on some suicide mission." She brushed her hand across his bare scalp with surprising gentleness, and said, "You are not the only newly born Ronan. In the sixty years of Ronan exile, four Ronan will have been born and four more, besides myself, escaped the Curse."

"Is Selyni and her brother among the newborn?" Aritian asked, his mind now racing.

Maud shook her head, and said, "No, they were born before the war, but as Changelings their true names are in constant flux and so they cannot be bound." She smiled down at him, and assured, "They will, of course, assist as they are able." For a moment she stared at him as if studying his reaction, and then her hand fell from his head. Her voice took on crispness, as she said, "Chiefly, there is one among the unbound who will soon gain the power to break the Curse." Maud looked down at the floor and under her breath, whispered, "If he survives." Aritian strained his ears to catch her mumbled words.

Maud shook her head, and said, "The others will fall into place as Prophecy has promised. All I ask is that you travel north and when the time comes you lend your power to those who gather. Combined, your power will shatter the Curse that binds the Ronan."

Aritian nodded, he knew he had no other choice. *Besides*, he thought, *north is where Devaney lives. This is destiny*, he thought in awe. *I must find the Oracle*. Aritian met her eyes, and asked, "When would I leave?"

Maud's eyes gleamed with triumph and she breathed heavily, in a most distracting way. "In two months' time, when the monsoon season dies and Ignathra once more looks upon Ignea with his golden eye." She smiled kindly, and said sympathetically, "I know the thought of leaving your homeland might seem frightening, but after this you will be free from your promise to me. Your debt will be paid in full."

Aritian nodded. He had no fear of leaving Ignea. In fact, his heart bubbled with excitement. He asked, "What must I do to prepare?"

Maud smiled in a predatory way that gave Aritian pause,

and bade him to follow. She strode across the hall and Aritian followed after. They came to a large double door that was set against the far wall. The door seemed to be made from solid silver and its face crawled with runic script and geometric shapes. Maud laid her hand on its silver surface. Aritian could hear a hum vibrate the air before the door.

When Maud removed her hand, her palm was wet with blood. The skin of her palm had been torn away. Aritian looked to her with horrified concern, but she pointed a bloody appendage toward the door. The bloody handprint she had left, slowly began to move. Aritian watched in fascination as her blood crawled toward the center of the door where a large ruby was set in the center of a radiant of runes. When the blood met the stone, the ruby flashed with dark light and the door opened. Aritian looked at Maud with wide eyes and Maud smiled, holding up her hand. Aritian watched as the skin of her hand slowly began to knit together. Blood dripped down her wrist, but Maud seemed not to care. In seconds, the bloodied hand became whole; her palm unmarred and pink with new skin.

Aritian made to walk through the door, but Maud stopped him with a hand to his shoulder. Gently, she nudged the door wide with her jeweled slipper so that they could see what lay beyond. The doorway was blocked by a ruddy shield of energy that hummed and crackled softly with vibrant magic.

Aritian gasped in astonishment.

Beyond the shield lay the largest library Aritian had ever seen. The library was four stories high, and the walls were lined floor to ceiling with shelves packed with darkly bound tomes. The center was open, more than three hundred feet across and two hundred in length, and at the heart inlaid a silver pentagram. Red light danced from the circle's center, and soared to the ceiling inside a ruby pillar. Floating among the light was hundreds of small orbs of amethyst crystal, all glittered brightly as they sat suspended in a spiral. To the right of the column were long tables filled with scales, vials of liquid, and small jars filled with varied powders; to the left, scarlet couches of velvet and tables filled with crisp parchment and ink pots.

Maud whispered against his ear, "I have collected the greatest collection of grimoires outside of Shades Island. There," she pointed over his shoulder, and said, "in the center of the room is my most prized collection. The crystals are called Remembrance orbs, for they hold the memory of more than a hundred Ronan. Those are your teachers, Aritian, along with these books. You could grow great here, in this place." Aritian nodded, knowing that she spoke truly. The wisdom and knowledge in this room was far beyond what he could have ever expected.

Forlornly, he asked, "How could I hope of learning even a fraction of this in so short an amount of time?" Aritian was hungry for the knowledge that lay before him, and he ached to step into the room. He was tempted, so tempted, by what lay promised within. The humming shield forestalled his steps, and he eyed the crackling light uneasily.

Maud purred in his ear, "Ah, and there lays our conundrum. You have little time, and even a portion of this would take you years to learn, if not a mortal lifetime." She chuckled, her breath tickling his ear, as she said, "The bite of time... Such a slippery thing, a cruel and chaotic beast." Aritian felt Maud press against him from behind, and she whispered, "Do not despair, sweet child; I am no time witch, but I am clever. I have built a construct beneath this library that speeds the time within the light of this shield," Maud played a finger through the light and as she drug it through the light, her finger blurred. He blinked and her finger jumped across the light. Maud pulled her hand back and squeezed his arm, with a saccharine tone, she said, "Time is the most precious commodity, far greater in value then metals or gems."

Aritian could not pull his eyes from the ruby light. Transfixed by it, he spoke carefully, his thoughts slow" "How much faster does time work within this room?"

Maud promised, "Oh, quite a bit, though it is costly. You could not stay for more than five weeks. To do so would kill you. But in that time, sweet Ronan child, you can grow great. In that time, you could become a Ronan of great caliber." Her grip on his arm grew tighter.

Aritian repeated himself, "How much time will pass, Lady Maud?"

Maud played a finger up and down his arm, as she mused, "I have tied the spell to the passage of the moon and the four seasons of Adonim. For every day that passes within, it will be as if you have lived four months."

Aritian shook his head, as he tried to calculate how much time he would gain. When he realized the immensity, his words tumbled from his mouth, "Five weeks... in five weeks, that would be nearly twelve years." He eyed the pillar of Remembrance Orbs, and a smile spread across his lips.

Gently, Maud whispered, "Yes, in that time you could learn much. Your training would be far from over, but you'd gain the foundations of becoming a Master of Magrados. You would discover where your talents lay, and would gain the power to do things you never thought possible. You'd be able to leave Ignea without this." She tapped the Ring of Suppression with her nail, and leaned closer to him as she promised, "You would have the power to protect the ones you care for."

The voice of the Oracle, rang through his mind: *Those that come now you can trust, but the one they take you to, beware, for she has an ugly heart. She will help your power grow, but seek to ensnare you to her will.* Tentatively, he asked, "Why only five weeks?"

Maud's answer was foreboding. "None have survived beyond that. Time is being cheated, after all; should you linger but a minute too long, it will tear you asunder."

Aritian turned to face her and found Maud's face just inches from his own. Searchingly, he gazed into her eyes, and asked, "What's the catch? This power cannot come easily. Raising such a construct had to come at a terrible price."

Maud shook her head slightly, but did not drop his gaze as she responded, "No, my boy, power does not come cheap. I paid a great price to erect the Time Vortex, but I knew that you would come to me soon," she touched his cheek, and her voice fell as she said sadly, "and I knew what lay before you. I have paid gladly, and do not wish for your thoughts to linger on my sacrifice." Maud dropped her hand, and her eyes found the floor, as she said, "I cannot leave Ignea with you when you go forth. I have tied myself to this land for my own protection, and cannot step past the bounds I have set. In many ways I have cursed myself..." Maud shook her head casting such thoughts aside, and looked him in the eye. Her voice grew stern, as she said, "The price for one who steps within the Time Vortex is indeed high. You will age in accordance to the flow of time within. In five short weeks, twelve years of your life will be gone."

Aritian nodded once. He had known he could not walk away unscathed from such a gift. Measuredly, he said, "Ronan age more slowly than humans...that's what Selyni said."

Maud nodded, and said simply, "They do."

Aritian looked over his shoulder, and gazed longingly at the library. The pull to step into the room was strong. Pragmatically, he asked, "How would I eat in there?"

Maud laughed and said, "Of all the concerns! My, my, you are a man." She rubbed his arm with sympathy, and soothed, "I will provide you with everything necessary. I know this is a lot for you, and I do not wish for you to answer impulsively – but one leap of faith will lead you to not only freeing the Ronan from exile, but also knowing your father. Please, take three days to consider my words. Let your body and soul heal from the trials you have endured. Enjoy the city and all it has to offer; the riches of my house are at your disposal."

Maud concluded her magnanimous promise by shutting the door to the library, "Then make your choice."

Aritian bowed with respect, his mind whirling with conflict

as he replied, "You have given me much to consider. Thank you, Lady Maud."

*****

Aritian entered the apartments to find Azera and Beryl standing by the large dining table that dominated the entry room. Behind them, he saw Ori, Mingyo and Rong playing dice on the red and gold woven carpet that sat between couches. Beryl and Azera were arguing quietly among themselves in hushed voices. When he entered they fell mute and looked at him expectantly.

Beryl placed a hand on his hip, and asked, "Well, out with it, what did the witch say?"

Aritian shook his head, and said dismissively, "Nothing of importance. What are you two arguing about?"

Azera flashed the dwarf an angry glance, before saying, "Beryl wanted to open something that is not his." She stepped to the side. On the table sat two large chests made from a dark wood. They were wrapped with iron, but Aritian didn't see any lock on them. "Ibriham and a few men brought these after you left."

Beryl nodded, and pointed a pudgy finger at Azera as he indignantly said, "Yes and Ibriham said they were for ye' pleasure. This brute hasn't let anyone open em."

Azera swatted Beryl's hand away, and said, "Yes, I thought it proper that we wait for you, Aritian."

Beryl muttered under his breath, "Always a stickler for the rules, she is."

Aritian smiled, shaking his head, and said, "Well, let's open them."

Beryl shuffled forward happily and flipped both of the lids open. He stepped back with a gasp. Aritian stepped forward, blinking rapidly, unsure if his eyes deceived him. The chests were full to the brim with hundreds of gold coin. Beryl turned

with a manic smile, and whispered, "Gold. Wonderful gold."
Azera shook her head, stunned.

Aritian chuckled, eying the vast fortune. He had never seen so many gold crowns in all his life. In an excited whisper, Aritian said, "I think, my friends, it's time we had a lark. We deserve a bit of spoiling, wouldn't you agree?" They both nodded, wide-eyed, wearing ridiculous grins.

Devaney

Chapter Eighteen:

The Tinker's Son

Devaney walked down the wide thoroughfare of Cherry Street, where small shops lined either side of the lane and brightly painted signs hung over each, denoting in cheerful lettering the name of the establishment. Every window had its shutters thrown back, displaying wares across manicured tables. Painted clay pots and tall-necked vases filled one window, while another held tallow candles and delicately worked lanterns. Another still, held woven carpets and brass buttoned capes.

Lifoy walked at her side, and a crowd of three dozen men followed behind them. Devaney held Lifoy's arm lightly. Her sight had returned, thankfully, and now more than ever she took in as many sights as she could. She had cried tears of joy when the darkness faded the second day she woke. She hadn't fully recovered from calling the demon — still her limbs were wooden with weariness — but her spirits were high nevertheless. The street was bustling, though the people moved with worry in their eyes. They had heard the battle, and many had climbed the wall to see the destruction that had been wrought. They'd been met with the sight of the bloodied field, and puppets all along the beach unmoving, scarred by war. None had dared to touch them.

The war against Ordu had begun, and it was painfully evident to everyone in the city. Greenshield was not large; built at the foothills of the Jade Mountains, the city depended on the range that had protected Agos from sea incursions for many hundreds of years. The interior walls were made from grey-stone, and were built high and thick. The mountain rose to towering heights behind the city, and the wall clung stubbornly to its side.

Lifoy leaned down and whispered in her ear, "Are you sure all this is necessary?" Devaney looked at him out the corner of her eye, and Lifoy stubbornly pushed on, "We can take the boy and leave, and none would know it."

Devaney replied in a flat tone, "The boy shall remain here, for now."

Lifoy stopped and turned her, forcing her to face him fully. The men behind them paused in their step, waiting a respectful distance away. Lifoy cautioned, "You place him in great danger leaving him here. He is young, Devaney, and this war is going to be bloody."

Devaney arched an eyebrow, and asked, "You know this?" People had begun to stop and watch their quiet confrontation. Many had heard rumors of a white-haired witch who had decimated the ranks of Ordu. Hushed whispers began to fill the street, but Devaney paid them no mind.

"I read the scribe's notes." Lifoy said, crossing his arms.

Devaney gritted her teeth in annoyance, and said, "Those weren't for your eyes. Besides, you said he gave a merry chase." She paused, and teasingly mused, "What were the words you used, oh yes, 'The puppeteer was equal parts creepy and deftly adept at controlling his golems beyond what his years merit.' I think the boy can hold his own."

Lifoy pursed his lips and flipped his hair over his shoulder, before saying stubbornly, "He isn't some sword for you to wield. He is a Ronan. You have no right to abandon him."

Devaney laughed coldly and said, "I have every right." She pulled Lifoy along, and they returned to their slow stroll as she reasoned, "Besides, you will be back soon enough."

Lifoy frowned, and said darkly, "Yes, and thanks for volunteering me." Lifoy shivered thinking about the boy's wild chase. His voice grew indignant, as he said, "You know this is the very reason people revolted against us. We shouldn't meddle so." In truth, Lifoy wanted to have nothing to do with the disturbed boy. He couldn't explain why, but the boy filled him with trepidation. He kept his thoughts to himself.

Devaney shook her head, her resolve final, as she whispered, "No Lifoy, this is why we were born into this world. You were right, I shouldn't have called the demon. I do not regret it, but the people must learn to protect themselves and we, as Ronan, must lead them toward the path of victory."

Lifoy asked, angrily, "So you will make puppets of them."

Devaney smiled sweetly, and said, "No more then you or I are. We are all ruled by some power, and I seek not to rule them, but to win them their freedom."

"What makes you think Ultan will let me leave Shades Island? He may not, you know?" Lifoy asked, somewhat condescending.

Devaney replied confidently, "He will."

"How can you be so sure?" Lifoy asked in wonder.

Devaney flashed him a bright smile, and said lightly, "Because you will tell him of this child."

Lifoy looked at her askance, but couldn't argue with her logic. In a whisper, he warned, "Devaney I don't know why you brought us here, or what plans you have rattling around in that tangled mind of yours, but meddling with the future is a dangerous path. You must take care."

Devaney nodded, but did not meet his eyes as she said, "I do as I must, and explaining the path would only further tangle the prophecy I strive to navigate. For now, you must trust me."

Lifoy scoffed, annoyed. Devaney knew he wanted her to confide in him, but she dared not. She needed him, and didn't know if he would stay if he knew all that she intended. She eyed him seriously then, and added, "I know you believe that I seek to use the U.F.K as a shield for some selfish vendetta, but I see the present clouded with the knowledge of the future. I am doing all I can, the best way I know how." Internally she thought worriedly, *and I pray to every god that looks down upon this world that I have the strength not to falter.*

Devaney smiled thinly, and with forced cheerfulness, said, "Now come, let us visit this wondrous toy shop." They came to a small shop that had red shutters and a large sign above that read *Sogin's Toy Imperium.*

Devaney pushed the door open and entered without a word. Lifoy shook his head ruefully, and waved the men who followed to wait outside, before stepping through the door.

The shop was crowded with tall shelves and long tables, stacked with every imaginable toy carved out of wood and polished to a gleaming luster. The first table held rattles, spin tops, marbles, and small card decks sprawled out in neat display. The shelves along the left side of the room held small dolls with neat dresses, and toy soldier statues that held silver sabers. Along the right side of the shop stood beautifully painted rocking horses, complete with leather halters and supple saddles.

A tall man sat behind a long desk at the back of the shop. He looked up as they entered, and smiled in greeting. Lifoy whispered into her ear, "A Zharain man. He must hail from the deep south, beyond the Fervite Mountains. The boy's the same... this must be his father." Devaney waved Lifoy away from her ear, and flashed the approaching man a smile. She didn't care where they hailed from or what their breeding was, it mattered not to her.

The man gave them a bow, before saying, "Welcome, I am Sogin Amar Emeka. How can I please you this day?" The man spoke in a rich voice, tinged with a heavy accent. Sogin was well muscled and touching his late thirties. He had short-cropped black hair and wore teal robes designed in a fashion suited to the south.

Devaney smiled in greeting, and said, "My brother was just admiring the puppets you have there," she pointed back to the window, where several marionettes were strung in the likeness of a dance, before saying warmly, "and he simply had to come see your wares."

The man followed her gaze, and then did a double-take realizing that she was blind. He gave her a bow, hiding his rudeness, and when he straightened he was smiling. Pride filled his voice, as he said, "My son fashioned them. He is quite skilled at woodworking and the string." He waved toward the window, and said, "Come, let us find you a playful companion, they're much easier to maneuver then people would suspect."

Devaney shook her head, and said, "No thank you, but I would like to meet your talented son."

Sogin looked at her with uncertainty, and asked, "Adwin, why?" Lifoy tittered behind her, and Devaney flashed him a dark look.

Devaney asked, "Are you aware of the battle that took place ten days past?"

Sogin nodded, and backed away to stand before the desk. "I am," He said cautiously. "Terrible occurrence, I grieve for those who lost their lives."

Devaney eyed him unblinking, and said, "If you are aware of the battle, then you must be aware of the strange occurrences that helped shape the Agosian victory."

Sogin's eyes met her gaze steadily and he nodded knowingly, saying, "I had heard of a silver Roc that flew in our defense and upon its back, a terrible witch who called a dark fiend down upon those of Ordu."

Devaney smiled coyly, and mused, "I suppose then that you also heard of the cohort of some-thousand puppets that stormed the troops of Ordu just as they threatened to breach the wall."

A sweat had broken out on the man's dark brow and he wrung his hands that hid beneath the long sleeves of his robe, but his voice held steady as he said, "Another of your tricks, all of Greenshield says, and for that you have our thanks."

Devaney shook her head, tiring of the game. More crossly

now, she said, "I did not make these puppets nor did I animate them, and you know that."

Sogin's eyes flicked side to side, as if seeking escape. In a whisper, he said, "Forgive me, my Lady, but I must insist that you leave."

"No." Devaney said flatly, and then commanded in a cold voice, "Bring me your son."

Sogin shook his head; all fear had left his eyes. He squared his shoulders bravely, as he said, "She said you'd come, my sweet love did. She warned Sogin." The man pulled his hand from his sleeves and pointed a spiraled rock at her. It was white and nine inches in length. Sogin warned, "Ware, for upon this coral a fiendish spell has been wrought. Approach and I shall strike you down."

Lifoy laughed and muttered, "Foolish human." He took a few steps advancing, smiling wickedly. Sogin whispered a hushed command and a bolt of green lightning thundered through the shop to smack Lifoy across the chest. Lifoy was flung backwards and toppled into a table, scattering toys, before rolling to the floor.

"Lifoy!" Devaney screamed, but she did not move. Her eyes flicked back to the man, who stared angrily at her. "Where did you come by this artifact?" She asked in a whisper.

In a low growl, the man said, "I warn you once, white witch, come for me son and I will strike you dead." The man trained the tip of the wand at her chest.

Devaney laughed. It was forced, but the man did not know that. She hadn't a clue how the man was able to strike Lifoy so. He was no Ronan; she could tell that. Devaney threw all worry aside and adopted a casual, but confident tone, as she asked, "Do you suppose your little parlor trick will work on the likes of my demon?" The man paled, and Devaney chuckled low in her throat, before whispering, "I think not." Sogin began to lower his wand.

A boy burst into the room. He was dark skinned like his

father, with a black afro of curly hair, and slight features. He was thin with intelligent, honey-brown eyes that took in the scene with a brief glance.

"Da!" He called to Sogin, eying Devaney fearfully. "What's happening?"

Sogin replied to his son with a shaking, but firm voice. "Adwin, they have come for you. Run now! Out the back." Sogin raised the wand once more, aiming with a trembling hand.

"Adwin, please calm your father. We mean neither of you harm." Devaney assured in a calm, reasonable voice.

Adwin looked to either of them, frozen by panic. His thin hand reached into his pocket. Sogin shook his head, and yelled, "No Adwin, don't."

Adwin didn't listen. He pulled a small, silver hand mirror from the pocket of his bright robes and scraped a nail across his thumb. Blood welled swiftly from the small cut and he rubbed his thumb across the mirror. Devaney made to step closer, but Sogin whispered again and a bolt of green lightning streamed across her vision, smashing into the shelves. Flame drenched dolls were flung in every direction and Devaney had to duck, dodging them. "Witch, last warning!" Sogin screamed, his voice cracking.

"Mamma!" Adwin screamed into the mirror. Devaney straightened carefully, keeping one eye on Sogin and one on Adwin. The mirror in his hand began to glow with emerald light.

"What causes you such distress, my sweet darling?" A cool voice asked soothingly.

Adwin turned the mirror. Devaney took a step back in shock. Within the surface of the mirror a woman was reflected. She was pale, paler then Devaney, and her face was wide and her jaw heavy with jowls. Her head was crowned with a wreath of flaming-red hair that was strung with beaded pearls. The woman's brilliant green eyes narrowed as she asked, "I do not know you, but if you threaten my child I will kill you where you stand. Leave now!" Her shout came with anger, her cheeks reddening. Devaney took a step back and nearly jumped as Lifoy placed a steading hand on her shoulder.

Lifoy was laughing and the woman's expression softened. "Morgana, you sly, prolific woman," Lifoy said, teasing. "You should have told me I had a brother." Devaney looked up at Lifoy in shock, as did Adwin and Sogin.

Morgana spoke gently, "Turn the mirror so I may look upon you, sweet love." Slowly, Adwin turned the mirror. "Mommy is sorry. I should have told you that you had a brother..."

Lifoy chimed in brightly, interrupting Morgana, "And a sister. Don't forget Selyni now, dear mother."

Adwin's eyes bubbled with tears and he shook his head in denial. Morgana spoke on, "You were my secret, dear one, my youngest. I had to protect you. Do you understand?" She asked. Adwin nodded slowly, uncertain. Morgana pursed her lips, and asked, "Now do you remember how angry I was when you painted Da's cat blue?" Adwin nodded, his eyes widening. "Good." Morgana said happily, before saying, "I am far angrier at your brother now than I was then. Be a big boy and turn the mirror so I might chide him." Adwin nodded rapidly and turned the mirror.

Sogin had sat on the edge of the desk, his face in his hands. The coral wand lay discarded next to him and his shoulders shook with grief. Devaney had only the briefest moments to spare him sympathy for when Morgana faced them her anger had returned. In a deadly quiet whisper, she asked, "Lifoy, what in the name of the Abyss are you doing in Greenshield?"

Lifoy stepped next to Devaney casually, and replied vaguely, "Oh you know, ever at the whim of an Oracle." He gestured to Devaney, but raised a hand imploringly as Morgana opened her mouth to speak, and said wryly, "Mother, you have broken Ultan's law and kept a child of Magrados a secret. I am commanded by a higher authority then your own. You have placed me in an impossible position."

Morgana's face twisted with anger, and she screamed, "I don't give a damn what position I've placed you in. You have your tongue so far up that foul man's ass, it's a wonder you can see the light of day." Lifoy gawked in shock, his mouth working furiously. Morgana gave him a deadpan stare of unflinching contempt.

When Lifoy was able to talk his face had gone white, and he yelled, "Selyni...!"

Morgana shouted over his next words, her voice growing shrill, as she said, "Don't get me started on your whore of a sister. She's probably sleeping with him, while you stand there wishing it were you. No." She shook her head, her pearl and silver earrings tinkling softly as she warned, "Listen to me closely, boy. Ultan cannot know of Adwin. I am not asking. I am telling you."

Lifoy was beyond anger. His cheeks had grown splotchy-red and his hands curled into fists at his side. He waved to Adwin, and said, "Is this any way to speak in front of my child brother. Contain yourself mother. You know damn well that Selyni and I are right in the middle, just as you are." His voice grew dangerous, as he promised, "I will warn you only once. Do not speak so of my sister, for if you do I shall fly to the shitty rock you call a home and crush it with you inside."

Morgana chuckled, and said dismissively, "Bide your threats, boy, for one who quakes before the power of a Changeling. You will find me above such tomfoolery that you call magic."

Devaney screamed, "Enough! Both of you." This had devolved far quicker then she had ever thought possible. Both their eyes turned to her and she bowed her head slightly, lowering her voice she said, "Morgana, my name is Devaney. Please forgive our intrusion. We were unaware that Adwin was your son and thus under your protection." Devaney whirled to face Lifoy, and she chided, "Lifoy, now is not the time. Contain yourself, please." Lifoy lips curled into a sneer, but he remained silent.

Devaney took a deep breath, and said, "Now please, all of you listen." She made sure that she held their attention and met each of their eyes before saying, "Morgana, your son stands in mortal peril here at the edge of Ordu's power, but he can be of some help to the U.F.K. He must remain here for the time being and help them. Prophecy demands it." Morgana made to speak, but Devaney turned away to face Lifoy, as she said, "Lifoy shall return to Shades Island with me, and only then reveal that he has found a child of Magrados." Lifoy nodded contently, knowing that he would not be betraying his Master.

Devaney turned back to an angry Morgana, and said, "He will not say who the child is or that you are his mother. Lifoy will return here by Ultan's command and remain with Adwin, guarding him against any and all threats until the proper time has arisen for him to leave." Her voice dropped lower still and softened, as she said, "You must have known, Morgana, that you could not hide him away forever. He is a Ronan and he has a responsibility to the people." Devaney held the furious woman's gaze for a long minute, and then said, "I swear by Magrados that Ultan will not find him before you do."

Morgana snapped, "You will help Ultan then? In this plan he has?"

Devaney shook her head, and said, "Not directly, but you must. If you succeed, you will take the first step toward freedom. If you want to be free to walk Adonim with your son, you will do as I ask."

Morgana seemed to deflate; her shoulders slumped and the light in her eyes dulled. In a whisper she conceded, "It seems I have little choice in the matter."

Devaney spoke with sympathy. "Fate bows to no one's will, Morgana; not even the Ronan. Now please calm your son. My time here grows short." Devaney turned away from the scene and Adwin began talking to his mother. Lifoy made to speak to her, but she shook her head and said, "No, not right now. Instruct Adwin on our plan and then send the craftsmen in. I need some air."

Devaney walked out of the shop and down the street to a quiet alleyway. She leaned against a cobblestone wall and wept.

Aritian

Chapter Nineteen:

Fortunes Found in Regret

Steam rolled through the air in a thick, swirling cloud. Aritian luxuriated in the hot waters of the bathhouse, letting the heat wash away his cares. Plants hung above him dripping long perfumed vines and the noise of the city buzzed comfortably beyond.

The bathhouse was open to the street, separated by a line of white pillars and a small garden veranda. A servant woman bent at his side, smiling brightly as she dipped a silver pitcher toward his goblet to refill his wine. The woman was beautiful, with dark, dusky skin that marked her a child of Zhara, and wore a flowing toga woven from lilac silk. She touched her chest with her right hand as he nodded his thanks.

Aritian sipped at the wine. It was light, watered down by his request, and filled with small pieces of fruit. The liquid was cool as it spilled across his tongue. He sunk lower in the water and sighed in contentment.

A shadow fell over him and he looked up. Hui stood there, beaming down at him. The boy wore an oversized leopard-pelt cape and a brilliant, cherry-red toga. He gave Aritian a short bow, before saying excitedly, "Beryl has found a dwarven stall. He asks that you come at once." Aritian raised an eyebrow, and Hui insisted, "The short Lord says he needs you."

Aritian smiled lazily, and asked, "If it's a stall run by his kin, why does Beryl need me?"

Hui shrugged, and said, "I'm not sure, but he seemed most anxious. Shall I tell him your coming?"

Aritian nodded, and said regretfully, "Aye, I'll come. Where is he?"

Hui smile brightly, and said, "Eastern Bazar, by the Pelican Cottage. You can't miss it; the inn is huge." The boy bounced on his heels with eagerness, and said, "I'll run ahead and tell him that you're coming." Aritian nodded and Hui bounded off, skipping through the pillars and into the crowd.

Aritian stood, splashing water, and stepped from the pool. He gave the young woman a wave and she came to his side with a towel. Quickly, she dried him off and then dressed him in a simple white tunic that fell to his knees and plumed, white pants that clenched at his waist. The servant girl lifted his feet, one by one, as he stepped into his sandals and with deft fingers laced up the leather straps. Aritian raised his hands as she clinched his corded, silk belt and accepted his heavy pouch of gold with a nod. He slipped a single coin from the satchel and handed it to the girl.

She smiled and with a bow said, "Master if you will wait here, I will return with your change." Aritian was uncomfortable by her use of the term Master but offered her a kind smile.

He shook his head and closed the woman's hand around the coin, as he said, "No, you keep it."

The woman looked at him in astonishment that eventually turned into a broad smile. Gratefully, she said, "Thank you, Master, thank you," and bowed to him over and over as he left the bathhouse.

Aritian made his way through the streets of Creuen with speed. They had spent all morning in the winding and wide streets and Aritian had easily become familiarized with the area around Maud's palace. In less than twenty minutes he spotted Beryl underneath a shaded canopy that spread along the left side of a large Inn. A sign hung over his head and depicted a blue pelican. Beryl was eyeing the wrong side of the street, fidgeting from one foot to the next, when Aritian came up behind him.

"Beryl." Aritian said, while tapping the dwarf's shoulder.

The dwarf jumped and then smiled when he saw it was Aritian. Excitedly, he said, "Good, good, ye came. Follow me." The dwarf immediately stepped into the throng of people and Aritian was forced to jog to keep up with his quick pace.

Following behind, Aritian yelled over the crowd saying, "Hui said you found a stall ran by your kin." Beryl nodded absently, his head bent forward as he shoved past two women who haggled over a bolt of yellow silk. "Why did you need me?" Aritian asked with true confusion. The dwarf was acting strange.

Beryl eyed him out of the corner of his eye, and said insistently, "I want ye to go in there, o'course. Meet me folk... see the skill of me people." Longing filled the dwarf's voice as he said, "Oh, it's been so long since I laid eyes on a civilized dwarf. How magnificent they be. Ye will see, ye will see." He assured before pushing an elderly woman from his path. Aritian squeezed passed her and mouthed, *I'm sorry*. The woman shot Beryl a dark look, before turning back to a hawker who waved to the pile of dark spices that lay on the table before him.

Aritian smiled. He was happy to see Beryl so excited and knew it had been a long time since Beryl had the opportunity to feel true joy. He had worked the mines for many years and had found little welcome among his banished brethren. Warmly, Aritian said, "Well I look forward to the introduction."

Beryl stopped in his tracks and the crowd swirled around them like eddies in a river that danced around a boulder. The dwarf turned to face Aritian, his expression startled and pale, and pointed at his chest, as he asked, "Me?"

Aritian nodded hesitantly, unsure of why they had stopped. Beryl shook his head slowly, and said mournfully, "I can't be goin' in there." Aritian raised one eyebrow in confusion, and Beryl said, "I just spotted their stall by happenstance."

Aritian frowned and asked, "Why can't you?"

Beryl bowed his head, and in a low voice explained, "I'm banished. If I'm recognized they'll strike me dead." He looked up at Aritian, and grief colored his words as he said, "They be Darkryn Dwarves."

Aritian nodded with understanding, and promised, "I will recount all that I see." He couldn't imagine how hard it must be for the young dwarf to see his kin, but not be able to speak to them.

Beryl smiled, and patted his arm roughly, saying, "Ye a good lad." Beryl turned on his heel and led Aritian deeper into the Bazaar. After a few minutes, Beryl stepped under the shade of an herb stall and pointed across the street. He pointed to a black pavilion that stood between two long tables.

"There it be," he said, and then insisted, "Go, and see the wonders of me kin."

Aritian crossed the street and walked into the pavilion. Eight dwarven men stood at attention for the clientele within the stall. Most of the Dwarves were young and had dusky, olive-colored skin, marking them as dwarves from Darkryn. They wore kind smiles and boasted in booming voices as they waved to their wares. He tried to memories their faces for Beryl. *Maybe he will recognize a sympathetic friend*, Aritian though hopefully.

Aritian struggled through the packed stall to one of the long low tables that lined the side of the canvas tent and to his surprise, found himself exclaiming over the fine work. The table was covered in glass and beneath, riches beyond imagination lay. The jewelry was crafted with breathtaking expertise and hardly seemed comparable to their clunky peers of human craftsmen. *This was art beyond ornamentation*, Aritian thought with awe. Gold, silver, and platinum were all represented and polished to a gleaming perfection.

Around him men and women crowded, pointing out pieces with gleeful excitement. A young, black-haired dwarf dressed in rich robes of red and black approached. Introducing himself in a deep, but cheerful voice, he bellowed, "My name be Ra'vig Blackwin, of Darkryn Hall. If it pleases the Lord, I can assist with any interest."

Aritian shook his head, and said, "I merely look with endless appreciation, but thank you."

The dwarf nodded his head respectfully, and said, "If anything catches ye' eye, do not hesitate to call one of me kin over." Aritian nodded in thanks. A woman dressed in a rich, black-silk toga trimmed with gold lace immediately pulled the arm of the dwarf close. Ra'vig's head came to her shoulder, but he turned his head upward attentively as she began listing pieces she wished to try on, pointing them out as she did.

As Aritian lazily scanned the fine pieces, something caught his attention out of the corner of his eye. There was something curious here, he felt a presence not unlike when he felt the touch of magic. It was startling to feel outside himself and strange, as the feeling was quite different then his own suppressed power, but somehow of a similar likeness. It sung to him like a barely heard melody. Aritian felt himself walk to the back of the stall, drawn in a trance of concentration.

Aritian gazed down at the glass container and saw that it held a several of pieces laid gently on beds of black velvet. The craftsmanship was fine, but it were the stones themselves that held his gaze. Black, the piece seemed to both gleam with small specks of glitter and absorb the light around them. Aritian laid a shaking hand on the glass so that it floated above a platinum ring set with a large, jagged stone. He could feel something respond to his closeness. Aritian bent closer, eying it with awe. The band of the ring had spiraling tracery and the stone itself sat in a delicate cage surrounded by a half a hundred minuscule diamonds. Aritian's concentration narrowed and it felt as though the stone's song grew then. Aritian could feel it pulse with energy, not unlike that of a heartbeat.

A grey-haired dwarf stepped beside him, breaking the enchantment. The dwarf spoke in a low whisper, his voice resembling the sound of gravel grinding against stone, as he said, "Dragonbone, a most rare and precious gem, mined from the Hammerhold Hall." Aritian eyed the dwarf, and the dwarf nodded to the case, saying, "Only one place can this stone be found, the Sepulcrum of Bones that lay beneath therein dwarven hall." The dwarf smiled in greeting, breaking his ominous tone, and said, "My name be Morgtar Blackwin." He waved a pudgy hand toward the glass case and suggested, "Perhaps, I may interest ye Lordship with some of these fine pieces?"

Aritian considered for a moment and then pointed to the ring. He eyed the case and acting on instinct, pointed to a gold chain-link pendant that held a fist size piece of the bone within a fine, gold net. Lastly he pointed to an elegant dagger. The hilt was made with bright silver and the blade from bone. Aritian swallowed thickly. He could barely drag his eyes away from the case, as he said, "I shall take the three. I have never seen dragonbone before and cannot deny my attraction."

The dwarf's dark eyes gleamed with greed, and he nodded enthusiastically, saying, "Dragonbone be the true gemstone of kings and while the stone be dark, there is none of the like that can draw the eye so commandingly. Fine choices me Lord, indeed!" Morgtar eyed Aritian, and pulled at his beard before saying cautiously, "I must be warnin ye Lord, with this stone's antiquity and rarity, these pieces come at a dear price."

Aritian smiled slowly and pulled a white pouch free from his belt. He opened its drawstring, cupping the bottom in his left palm, and spilled a quarter of the contents into his right palm. Diamonds of the highest quality and clarity sparkled in the muted light of the stall. Beryl had suggested they find a bank, and convert the gold to diamonds and other precious gems so that their fortune could be carried with more ease. Morgtar laughed gruffly, his grey beard splitting with a broad smile as he eyed the precious gems. He opened the case and removed the pieces. Carefully, the dwarf slid the dagger into a soft black leather scabbard and wrapped the necklace and ring in layers of fine, white cloth.

When the dwarf was finished packaging the wares, he placed a black, velvet sheet on the glass case and motioned for Aritian to place the diamonds down. Morgtar set the items to the side and picked up the diamonds. He squinted his left eye while inspecting the diamonds, one by one, an inch from his right eye. Aritian had placed nearly a full fifty stones on the table. A few minutes passed and the dwarf grunted with appreciation, grumbling, "These stones be exceptional. They hail from our cousin in the north, the Dvan Hall."

Aritian nodded, Beryl had spoken at length about the subject this morning. Knowledgeably, Aritian said, "Yes, the Dvan Hall has long been known to have the purest veins of diamond. I would value the very smallest at twenty gold crowns a piece and the largest," Aritian pointed to a stone that was nearly the size of the tip of his pinky finger, and said, "at nearly two-hundred gold crowns."

The dwarf huffed and grumbled to himself as he calculated. He weighed the weights of different stones in his hand carefully. "Ye' estimates be nearly as exact as a dwarves'. Does me Lordship have one of me people in ye service?" The dwarf asked curiously, eyes gleaming under his heavy brows. Aritian smiled wolfishly, but did not answer. Dwarves were very wary of their people serving humans or any other race. Morgtar grunted, accepting his silence, and said, "For the dagger, pendant, and ring I suggest twenty of the smaller diamonds." Aritian was taken aback for a moment. The dwarf was asking an exorbitant price. He was valuing the three pieces at four hundred gold crowns. It was more than most wealthy merchants would spend in half a year.

Aritian's eyes narrowed, and he said, "I'll part with seventeen and you will have them delivered to my home." The dwarf considered for a moment, before nodding happily with a bargain well struck. He presented a small parchment and quill.

Aritian collected the remaining diamonds and tucked the pouch securely into his belt next to the other, which held a handful of coins. With hands that trembled with excitement, Aritian wrote the cross-streets of Maud's compound and instructions for delivery. Morgtar handed him a bill of sale and they shook hands. The dwarf's hands were rough, covered in calluses, and his grip surprisingly strong for his stature.

Morgtar bowed, and said, "May ye day be full and prosperous me Lordship, and may ye wear the dragonbone with honor." Aritian gave him a nod of respect. Aritian turned to leave, but Morgtar called after him, "If ye wish to part with more of ye wealth I have a cousin, Theo Blackwin, who owns a shop in the blacksmith sector. He might have stock ye be interested in." The dwarf smiled toothily at Aritian, and his dark eyes gleamed. Aritian raised an eyebrow and nodded, before leaving the pavilion.

Aritian crossed the street to an impatient Beryl. The dwarf asked, "Tell me, Aritian, how did ye find the fine dwarves of Darkryn?"

Aritian smiled at his friend, and said, "I will tell you on the way to the smithy district. Come along." Beryl looked at him strangely, but Aritian walked into the crowd. Slowly, with as much detail as he was able, he told Beryl of his experience. Beryl's grin grew wider and wider as Aritian told him of his magnificent kin.

Caethe

Chapter Twenty:

The Pool of Magrados

Caethe pressed his head against the golden bark of a tree and quietly whispered. Tendrils of grey magic bled from his hand as he gave sacrifice to the tree, and the glistening bark drank in his power and began to wake. The roots at his feet curled through the soft loam and the trunk glowed with radiant, golden light. Above, the tree's silver leaves rustled in greeting. Caethe bowed his head to it, stepping back. He walked to the next and began the process again.

Caethe stood in a sunken glade of light — the only true light within Umbrael. Above, darkness rose as the dead forest crowded close, but none could pass the metallic sentinels that stood guard. In a spiraling ring, the sentinels of Magrados circled downward in rings growing ever deeper, leading to the origin of Magrados.

Solani sat on his shoulder, and in a whisper, asked, "Must you wake them all?"

Caethe nodded, and broke his whispered chant to reply, "Yes, all must be awakened or the pool will not rise."

Solani warned, "You have little strength left."

Caethe eyed the pixie at his shoulder with a dark glare. Caethe limbs were leaden and his fingers twitched with exhaustion, but he knew he must push on. In a harsh whisper, Caethe said, "Maybe I will drain you for strength, you certainly look spry enough."

Solani pinched his ear with a sharp twist, and Caethe hissed. The pixie laughed, and said, "You jest with callous abandon. We both know the sacrifice can only be given by the supplicant."

Caethe nodded, and said dramatically, "Yes, but what a shame. Magrados would gain potent power, and I would find myself unburdened of a chirping sprite."

They moved to the next tree and Caethe laid his hands upon the smooth surface. Power fled his hands and Caethe felt a sweat break across his brow. "You're nervous," Solani observed, and then whispered, "You know that if you fail, you will meet the Chaos."

Caethe muttered a chant and stepped back. His head had gown dizzy. With a grimace, he nodded, and whispered, "Yes, and all my struggles will have been for naught."

Caethe could feel Solani's mind reaching tendrils across their bond. Caethe had sensed the creature attempts before. The shield he had erected between their minds flared, flashing silver light in both of their minds. In annoyance, Solani asked, "Why did you serve the Emperor of Infiri?" Caethe paused, with one hand outstretched toward a tree, but not yet touching it. Solani persisted, "Do not deny the fact. I saw into your mind. You have done many atrocious things, Caethe. I do not know how you passed the test of Cerulean Flames. You should have met your end." Caethe arched an eyebrow and looked at the Fey. Solani's pale expression was pressed with frustrated anger and his dark eyes danced with confusion.

Blandly, Caethe asked, "What bothers you more, that I served the Inferno or that I have taken immortal lives?" The pixies and the Fae were neither dark nor light; however, it did not mean that they did not hold others in abhorrence.

In a low hiss, Solani observed, "Such things are beyond most Ronan."

Caethe chuckled and placed his hand on the metallic bark. In a quiet voice, he assured, "I am not most Ronan, Solani." Caethe chanted in a hushed whisper and gave more of himself to the glade. The bark beneath his hand grew warm as Caethe stroked it softly with reverence. Caethe confessed, "I served him because I was angry. It took me eight years to learn how to pass the wards of the Origin Glade. When my mind fled the amber, I was kept safe here." He waved downward, to where the sunken glade opened up. Caethe shook his head and smiled sadly. Regret filled his voice as he explained, "I wanted out. I wanted more." His four hands curled into fists, as he recalled, "I was a slave at first, for Aethral gave me to his son as a gift. Sabizael was powerful in the magical arts and took great delight in torturing me." Caethe chuckled bitterly, and said, "More so than the Ordu ever did. Ultimately, each torture was a lesson. I survived, and in time, became a sort of pet to Sabizael. He taught me all he knew and for a time I was lost, as my life on Adonim faded and my powers grew." Caethe sighed heavily and his fists uncurled. He let the regret go, and then said, "Sabizael came to regret teaching me. It took me three hundred years to escape the Realm of Inferno, and another hundred and ten before I ended him." Caethe's eyes closed as he remembered. In a harsh whisper, he said, "I do not regret taking his life."

In a soft whisper, Solani said, "The Abyss is a cruel end, even for one such as him." Caethe nodded in agreement.

Caethe's voice grew strained and weakly, he said, "I needed Aethral to believe us both dead. It was the only way." Solani nodded in understanding. The pixie's shoulders relaxed and the thread between them stilled as his need dimmed.

Solani considered his words, and then asked, "How did he come to know that you live now?" Caethe noted how the pixie avoided using the Master of the Inferno's name. He smiled, assured with the knowledge that no words of power could escape the bounds of the Origin Glade.

Caethe's lips pressed into a tight smile as he said, "After, I returned to Umbrael. I was not welcome in the Upper Realms, for they could see the stain of immortal blood upon my hands and banished me. So I endured here. I met a young Ronan, newly born. I helped her, but her presence attracted attention.

Aethral does not know for sure that I live. He has only the word of his slaves, but he will not easily abandon the trail until he knows with certainty." His eyes flicked from tree to tree, seeking their strength. Those he had touched glowed with life and vitality. In a hushed voice, Caethe said, "If he does..." He trailed off. Nothing more needed to be said.

"Then little will save you." Solani concluded solemnly. The pixie's dark eyes scanned the forest that loomed above them.

They made their way down the winding trail, and Caethe became more and more weak. Every tree stole a small piece of him and he felt thin, thinner than he had in a long time. He was close to the end once more. He had felt the touch of death before and knew its familiarity well. He stumbled to the next tree, his steps coming in shuffled limps. His lower arms hung at his side, and his upper hands trembled as they lay across the rough bark of the tree before him. When he finished the spell he leaned against the trunk for support. Solani did not speak to him now. The pixie could feel how weak he had grown and grimly witnessed his sacrifice.

When they neared the last two trees, Caethe looked back along the winding line of golden trees with confusion. He shook his head, trying to recount. Exhaustion lay heavily upon him, and his thoughts were slow and thick. In a whisper, he said, "Mistaken." He shook his head once more and knew he was not.

"What is it?" Solani asked, nervously.

Caethe waved weakly up the line of trees and then toward the last two. "These last two hold the immortal souls of Glenda Ambrosia Ronan and Hannah Rose Ronan. Ambrosia was the last of our kin to perish in the Great Revolt, and Hannah shortly there after. Before them." He waved back up toward the hill that they had just traversed. "Petronilla Elaine Ronan, Osvir Augustus Ronan, and Gabriel Thomas Ronan." Caethe's voice became labored and he coughed heavily, spitting dark liquid into the grey fog at his feet. He straightened after a moment, and said, "Don't you see? The tree beside Gabriel's is Catania Rose Ronan. It should be Demetrious, the Archmagus who sat the Weirwood Throne before Ultan. He's not here." Caethe shook his head in wonder.

A tingle ran up along his spine and he knew he had discovered something of import. He eyed the tall trees before him. Catania died some hundred years before the fall of Demetrius. He eyed her slim trunk and the proud carriage that held thousands of wide-leafed, silver leaves above. The vessel that held her soul whispered to him now. Woken, she assured him in the rattle of her leaves and the groan of her shifting branches that indeed, Demetrious was not here. Caethe nodded graciously, thanking her.

"Are you sure? You work in a daze, perhaps you have merely glanced over him." Solani suggested, tentatively.

Caethe's lips tightened in a pout. Sharply, he said, "One does not glance over Demetrious. His spirit should be here and we'd know it. This is troubling indeed." His thoughts whirled at the implications. He had woken Cain, Demetrius's uncle, and Cornelius, his grandfather. Both had long been dead, and had stormed to wakefulness with potent power. *No*, he thought, *I'd have remembered if I felt the cruel touch of Demetrius.*

"Perhaps he did not make it through the Aelfmae," Solani said thoughtfully. Caethe shot the pixie a dark glare. Solani held a hand up imploringly as he said, "You yourself know what one can encounter there. Perhaps he has fallen victim to the Great Sea."

Caethe grimaced, and said, "No, there is only one place he can be if he isn't here."

Caethe felt the pixie on his shoulder tremble, and Solani whispered, "The Abyss."

The trees closest to them waved, as if by an unfelt wind, reacting to the fell promise of that title. Caethe nodded in agreement, and said, "Yes. It is said that he died at the hand of St. Christopher, the very man who was gifted the secrets of the

Curse. No man of Afta, however blessed, could hold the power to banish one such as Demetrious to the Abyss." Caethe shook his head, cursing his slow thoughts.

"If not him, then who?" Solani asked with detached wonder. Caethe knew the concept of death was not frightening to the pixie. Like the Ronan they shared an immortal soul, but unlike the Ronan they were reborn with relative ease compared to the rarity that a Ronan did. Both feared the Abyss above all, for if you fell within there was no hope, only the oblivion of Chaos.

A thought struck across his dulled mind like a ringing bell. It was a dangerous thought, but it sung with truth. In a whisper Caethe said, "There is one who gained much in the fall of Demetrius..." Caethe paused and smiled, as he asked himself, "But would he dare such a thing?"

Solani impatiently tugged on Caethe's hair, asking, "Who?"

Caethe shook his head and walked toward the last two trees. In a stern voice, he said, "Come, Magrados waits." As he walked his steps were lighter and a small smile played on his lips. Though he was tired beyond reason and stretched far too thin, he had learned a great secret this day. *One that could be used to great advantage*, he thought gleefully. He woke the last two trees, his mind spinning down dark paths.

When the last tree was woken, golden light filled the air and silver leaves danced in greeting. The trees of the Origin Glade spoke in a wordless chant. Caethe watched as the hills around him shimmered and sung with joy. His ancestors had woken and their timeless voice was indomitable.

Caethe smiled as he heard the tinkling sound of a spring waking from a long slumber. Magrados had risen. Caethe turned to the center of the glade and his skeletal features stretched and pulled as he beamed with joy. Tears fell down his face as he looked upon the majesty of the Pool of Magrados.

Devaney

Chapter Twenty-One:

The Wrath of the Chalice Sea

The night sky rolled with thunder and lightning, and the clouds spat fat raindrops in a heavy torrent, dappling the rising and falling waves of Chalice Sea. Lifoy flew through the thunderous rain, his wings heavy with moisture and his feathers' slick beneath Devaney's grip. It was a moonless night; the Roc flew close to the waves, climbing as the waves grew more than forty-feet high and gliding down as the ocean dipped.

"We have searched for hours, Lifoy, please take to the sky once more." Devaney begged, her eyes clenched closed. Her stomach twisted in knots and bile rose in her throat as they glided downward. Sea spray drenched Devaney to the bone.

Lifoy spoke into her mind, his thoughts light and cheerful. *Dearest Devaney, try and enjoy the ride. Look to the angry sky and see it twist and boil. Glance below, and see a rolling strength greater than all the elements of Adonim. We ride the wind and tame it like a wild, bucking stallion. Rejoice in nature. Let yourself luxuriate in her rawness.*

Devaney bent to the side and emptied her stomach as they chased a white crest upward. Lifoy's wing muscles powerfully bunched beneath her as he carried them with seemingly inexhaustible strength. Devaney laid further down and hugged the bird's neck, her arms burning with cramps. With a cry, she yelled, "This isn't funny Lifoy. Please, I'm begging you, let us find the ship tomorrow when the storm has cleared."

Lifoy chuckled wildly in her mind and the Roc cried out a shriek that made the waves beneath them ripple. *No, we must* find one tonight and soon. *You said you saw a Pontees deep-sea fishing ship. Trust your vision as I do.* He insisted, bending his neck down and soaring so close to the water that his talon's cut through the surface of a wave. In terror, Devaney screamed as the crest broke, spitting white foam, and the sea began to rise once more.

"We can't keep doing this. The sea will swallow us whole." Devaney said, tears of fear falling from her eyes.

Lifoy's thoughts grew serious, as he said: *You are the one that insisted on this detour. Had we flown directly east, and not stopped in the U.F.K, we would have made it to Shades Island by now and I would not have to do this in the middle of the sea.* The connection between their minds cackled with his irritation, and he continued: *You haven't the foggiest how much shit I'm stepping into by helping you. Now please, keep your eyes peeled. The ship must be here somewhere.*

Devaney cracked her eyes open and seawater immediately stung them. She wiped the pale curls that clung to her face to the side and scanned the waves. Another wave rose ahead and on it something dark bobbed wildly. "There!" Devaney said with a scream. "There's the ship."

Lifoy did not respond. Instead, he flapped his wings harder, throwing them across the surface of the raging sea toward the ship. The ship was large, but Lifoy in this form nearly matched it in size. The deck was dark and the ship's purple sail displayed three emerald shields sprawled across its center. Men shouted desperately as they worked to close the snapping sails as the wind clawed this way and that. The ship bobbed downward, flying down the wave.

Lifoy followed after, mere inches above the water. They had not yet been seen, so intent were the men at the task at hand. Just before the ship began to climb up the next rising swell, Lifoy threw himself upwards with a powerful stroke of his wings and they hovered above the back of the ship. As a crack of lightning crossed the sky, Lifoy transformed back into a man with a snap of muscles and disintegrating feathers.

Devaney and Lifoy fell from the sky to crash down upon a pile of crates and nets. Devaney cracked her head against a barrel, and black spots danced before her eyes. Luckily, she had not been cut, only bruised. Lifoy struggled beneath her, naked, tangled in nets and splinters of wood. Dazed, Devaney ungracefully rolled to the side.

Lifoy grabbed her hand, crouching next to her and yanked her to her feet. He looked around side to side, before whispering, "I don't think anyone saw us. Most of the men will be below deck waiting out the storm." Lifoy's eyes grew hard and he gripped her shoulders as he said insistently, "Stay here. You don't want to witness what happens next."

Devaney didn't know what he spoke of, but nodded, suddenly afraid as she caught the gleam in his eyes. Lifoy stealthily crept around the raised cabin disappearing from sight. Devaney looked around and found a two-foot piece of broken wood. She snatched it up and held it at the ready. She eyed the corner of a cabin, waiting breathlessly for someone to discover her. Her stomach was tight with nerves and long minutes passed as Devaney crouched silently in the rain too afraid to move, holding her makeshift weapon in a white-knuckled grip. A few screams rent the night sky, promptly swallowed by a crack of lightning that danced across the waves next to the ship and the rolling thunder that pounded above. Devaney crouched lower, her heart beating rapidly in her chest.

A figure walked boldly around the corner and Devaney stood with a shout, brandishing the wooden plank. "It's just me." Lifoy said, his eyes dancing with laughter as he held his hands up in mock surrender. The magi had found some clothes and wore ragged pants, knee high boots, and an overly-large white shirt that clung to his skin wetly. On his head, he wore a three-pointed hat that was capped with a sodden, sad plume of red feathers. "How do I look?" Lifoy asked with a broad smile, before bowing with a flourish. "I fancy myself the most handsome sailor in all the seas, wouldn't you agree?"

Devaney rolled her eyes and dropped the wooden plank with a clatter. Her limbs shook from adrenaline and cold. Annoyed, she said, "I think you look a fool." Devaney looked past him, but from this vantage could see little. The deck was quiet. Devaney had to stand with her footing wide as the ship rocked crazily. "What happened? I heard screams." She asked suspiciously.

Lifoy pouted, crossing his arms, and said, "Why don't you go have a look, Lady Porcupine?"

Devaney stalked around him and walked around the raised cabin. The deck was empty. Heavy nets hung unattended and the mast swung wildly, free in the wind. Devaney knew that soon the sails would tear free, half-open as they were and exposed to the vicarious wind. Devaney saw that the door leading to the cabin and deck below had been barred with two swords. "Where is everyone?" Devaney asked softly to herself, but deep inside she knew the answer.

Lifoy bounced across the deck, spinning with his arms open. The slick, wet deck and the rocking of the ship seemed to only encourage his graceful jig. Carefully, Devaney walk across the deck and gripped the rail as she looked into the swirling waves beneath them. Lifoy called to her merrily, "I sent them on their way. They seemed the kind who liked a good swim."

Devaney turned from the water, and cried, "You killed them? You said you wouldn't hurt anyone!"

Lifoy smiled brightly in the face of her accusations, and said, "I must have forgotten that little promise." He raised his hands defensively, and said, "Wait a moment now, before you get all grumpy, I didn't kill everyone. Those below deck still live."

Devaney crossed her arms, and sorrowfully accused, "You bought them maybe an hour, Lifoy. With no one guiding the ship it'll capsize and they'll all drown! Don't you care at all?"

Lifoy laughed and began clearing the center of the deck. He looked over his shoulder with a smile and threw an armload of net and rope overboard, as he said, "Honestly no, I don't care. No more than you did when you killed those Ordu men. So either help me, Devaney, or shut up."

Devaney stared at him, stunned by his callousness. These men had been innocent. They hadn't done anything to wrong either of them, and their greatest crime was being in the wrong place at the wrong time. *I did this*, Devaney thought suddenly, *he only found the ship because of my vision.* They had flown along the southern edge of the U.F.K for the last week, having departed Agos the day after they met Adwin. The boy had set about the task they had left him eagerly, almost too eagerly in Devaney's opinion. It had been a speedy trek and one she was trying to forget. She dashed the thoughts away and turned her eyes to Lifoy.

Lifoy worked speedily, rolling barrels of fish to the side and dragging nets free until a space of ten feet was cleared. Devaney did not move to help. Instead, she stood watching him, wondering what kind of man could kill with such cavalier ease. It was true she had no regrets killing the Ordu, but they were the enemy. These sailors were men of Afta, the people the Ronan had sworn to protect. *No wonder they hate us*, Devaney thought, *if Lifoy's attitude is of a typical Ronan, then they have every right to wish us ill.* Lifoy had killed the men with little regard, and by the way he sung a tune beneath his breath she knew he didn't feel an inkling of regret.

Lifoy used an apprehended sword to cut a circle into the wood of the deck, and worked briskly to draw a five-pointed star. He then carefully wrote rows of tiny lines of script around the edge of the circle. The action seemed well-practiced, and within a few minutes the pentagram was complete. Lifoy laid down in the center of the pentagram, gripped the blade in the palm of his left hand and jerked the hilt in his right, cutting himself deeply.

Devaney inhaled sharply, shocked as blood spilled from his hand. Lifoy began wiping his cut hand across the script to either side, filling the runes with his blood. Just as he was about finish, he said, "If I don't come back, throw my body into the sea."

"Lifoy wait..." Devaney said stepping forward, but Lifoy quickly wiped his hand across the last line. His body fell limp and his head lolled to the side, spilling pale blonde hair across the deck. His green eyes remained open, unseeing, and his chest stopped rising. He looked dead.

Braugaethrael

Chapter Twenty-Two:

The Guardian's Rage

The Guardian flew on wings of steel-grey shadow across the plains of Umbrael, cutting through the harsh wind easily as he dove between twisting pillars of wind. The tornados that crawled across the plain held the sweet stench of poison. Those who fell within the winds hungry grasp had but a moment of thought to know the breadth of their mistake before they were utterly consumed. The plain below was filled with rolling currents of fog that boiled across the land and he could spy dark shadows racing through it, fleeing his presence.

The demons were not what he sought this day, however, and so he ignored them. His wings flapped with silent, immense power, and he gained greater height. The Guardian gazed across the immeasurable distance of the realm, searching. Waiting.

There was a disturbance, a flash of power that was foreign to the land, more pure and rawer than the muted nature of the shadowed realm. The Guardian flew higher still, soaring a thousand feet into the air, his keen eyes narrowing on the anomaly. In anger, the Guardian raked the sky with his long claws as he saw a flash of energy.

A rent had opened on the plain and he saw a portal form, wreathed in indigo-colored flame. The energy stained the air with radiant corruption. The portal stood no more than eight-feet in height and was barely taller than the fog that rolled around it. The flames arched, forming a doorway. The energy of the tear boiled the fog around, casting it outward in rippling waves. High in the air, the Guardian watched as cloaked figures stepped forth.

The Guardian flicked its long, spiked tail in irritation. *Magi*, it thought in annoyance. He watched in growing anger as eleven figures stepped forth from the flames. Cloaked in robes of white, grey, and the darkest of black and richly adorned with jewel and fine cloth, the Ronan were a tall race. The Guardian's mind raced down long forgotten warrens of memory as he sought his knowledge of humanity.

It had been an age since he last felt such a presence. *Meddlesome maggots*, the Guardian thought with disgust; his mind slowly awakening from his long slumber. Those beneath him had proud faces of both sexes, their eyes dark and filled with heady power. The Guardian let his power flow forth, tasting each of their essences. It was like ingesting a mobocracy of chaos, so anarchic and diverse were their powers. The Guardian choked on their essence with abhorrence, but the displeasure was well worth the trouble for he learned much.

They were not here in truth, but rather in their weaker Astral forms. As he thought of that, he sighed in disappointment. *If only they had come in their physical forms, they would have sunk to the depths of the Abyss and troubled me not*, he thought, despondent. As he grew closer he could see that several of the weaker ones had diaphanous forms, looking as substantial as a ghost. The Guardian growled low in his throat, his scaled neck vibrating with hate as he remembered.

The realms could no longer support their full strength. If they were to try, the realm would buckle beneath their vast weight. *Not after what they have done*, he growled to himself. The memory of the mage-storms and the ruin the Ronan and elves had wrought upon the Astral Realms burned his mind. The disruption of the Sundering had been vast and caused more than one lasting war that further rent the fabric of the realms. Grey lightening filled the sky as his power raged with bitter fury and the tornados beneath him danced in agitation, flinging themselves across the plains with greeter speed as they drank in the metallic lightning that licked across the sky.

With a snap, he folded his wings and dove through the air toward the blue-flamed rent. The power that rippled from those who stepped forth was immense, but the Guardian fled downward undeterred. *Foolish magi, I shall send you to the Sea of Aelfmae for such an impetuous invasion*, the Guardian's thought enraged.

Just as the Guardian was about to break cloud cover magic flared to the south, and then to the north, and then westward. The Guardian's wings snapped open once more and he flung himself upward. Gaining height, he spied four new portals across the land open up, their blue flame singing with glaring brightness. He watched with his ashen glare as five more robed figures stepped into the realm that he was bound to guard.

A roar of fury tore from his throat to arch across the sky, and the clouds contorted, boiling beneath the threat of his rage. He called the shadow demons forth in a voice that cut across the lands, guttural, like a thousand flames hissing.

"I am the shadow of Umbrael, the first among the Leviathan. I call you forth to drink the souls of those who would trespass upon this realm. My voice commands your immortal souls. My tongue is the whip of hate and my glare sings the song of stirring. Awaken, brethren, awaken – Braugaethrael commands you forth to battle."

Braugaethrael's voice rang across the realm like a bell tolling, calling to the very blood of those born to this realm, the plains to the south and the forests to the north exploded with activity. It had been centuries since the call to battle had rang, but time had no hold on those who were immortal. The plains boiled with millions as daemon scoured the land for intruders, and the sky above the dark canopy filled with the whispers of tens of thousands of wings that soon grew to a roar as dark creatures took to the grey sky. Braugaethrael smiled ravenously, his maw dripping with poison as he promised himself, *Soon, soon I shall taste the blood of Magrados.*

Caethe

Chapter Twenty-Three:

The Heir to Magrados

Caethe knelt on a small, flat stone within a sunken glade, and before him a spring bubbled pure gold, gleaming with iridescent light. The land around the Origin Glade gradually sloped for more than six-hundred feet so that the very crown of the highest trees sat at the rim of the basin. The glade shone like a lone star beneath a grey, moonless sky. The hills on either side were filled with hundreds of massive trees, unbent against the dimness above. The reaching branches and monolith trunks glittered gold and their heavy boughs held great leaves of mercury shaped in the likeness of stars.

Caethe had carefully drawn an intricate, massive pentagram in the center of the glade. Nine lines of miniscule runes raced along the edge of the circle, meticulously written. At each point of the star and at the interior interceptions, a circle had been drawn and around each were six lines of grounding runes. The center of the pentagram held a triangle, each point marked by circles wreathed with three lines of runic script. Caethe sat within the center of the interior triangle, every inch of exposed ground around him covered with runes that tied directly into the vein of magic.

Slowly, with morbid precision, Caethe's eyes traced the lines of runes, reassuring himself of their perfection. Hidden beneath his oversized robes of shadow, the relic hung heavy around his neck. Solani's eyes peeked from his collar, his thoughts silent as he took in the mastery of Caethe's creation. They had spoken little in the time that they had taken preparing, merely allowing their consciousness to stream through one another. The pixie had been a sagely companion, and Caethe had been shocked by his depth of runic knowledge.

Caethe's concentration was broken as he saw the clouds open above and the sky fill with thousands of bolts of slate-colored lightning. A resounding boom filled the sky and rang on as a fell voice called across the realm. Caethe smiled. *Soon,* he assured himself, *they will come.*

With a direct thought from Caethe, Solani disappeared beneath his robes. He looked up to the rolling sky. The thick grey clouds hid all from sight, but Caethe knew the beast within — he had spent hundreds of years hiding from the Guardian.

A northern wind blew through the dark eaves of the forest with a high-pitched wail. The gale was powerful, concentrated in a horizontal tunnel that wound through the stiff branches of the canopy. It was a pale wind, sapphire in color, that sparkled with ice.

The branches began to disintegrate beneath the torrid and black dust rained down. The wind grew more powerful as it drew closer to the glade and shadows began rolling against it in a great mass. The demon's forms, in turn, grew more distinct as they struggled against the mighty power, revealing parts of themselves — claws, snouts, and wings.

Caethe saw portions of them, hints of their form, but never all at once. They were towering creatures, around ten-feet in height. Neither the wind nor the shadows touched the eaves of the golden glade. The wind gathered above the glade, spinning in a great loop, buffeting the shadows from the air like shot. Demons crashed into the forest all around and howls of indignant rage filled the air.

Caethe spied three forms within the wind. The first was a woman with faint, flaxen hair. She had a cold beauty, with strong cheekbones, harsh blue eyes, and softly-freckled, pale skin. The woman ran calmly through the wind with her white robes snapping behind and a sword brandished before her. She swung the silver blade in a blur toward any demon who dared draw close, and smote them from the sky with beams of teal light.

The woman was followed closely by a man who looked no older than twenty, and was both muscular and tall. He had hair the color of sunlight, dreaded in a thick mane, and a beard that reached his chest. He wore clothes similar in color to the woman, but had forgone the robe for heavy silver chainmail that seemed to weigh no more than cotton. He carried a sword sheathed at his hip, and strung a bow before him. Glowing white arrows stuck the tumbling mass of shadow to either side, and dark shapes fell beneath his tirade of death.

The third person was dressed in robes that shimmered first ruby in color, then yellow, emerald, then cerulean, and onyx before rolling back through a spectrum different then the first. He was young, with cheeks touched with the blush of youth and his long hair was a pale shock of spun moonlight that reached his hips. Caethe recognized Lifoy instantly.

The shadowed denizens chased the wind as it spun above the Origin Glade. The woman shouted a wordless cry and the wind exploded outward with crackling flames and spitting sparks. The shadowed Daemons were flung threw the sky, many tumbling to crash among the canopy, while others spun through the air only to snap great wings out and catch the air some two hundred feet away.

The trio of magi fell from the sky, gracefully avoiding the reaching branches before landing lightly inside the glade. They carefully stepped along the outside of the pentagram. Caethe gave them a nod of respect and they returned the gesture in kind. The dazed demons took to the sky once more and flew in a thick flock above the golden glade, but none dared breach the silvery eaves. Instead, they contented themselves by settling among the bare limbs of the dark trees that rested above the glade, hunching like massive crows waiting to harry the magi if they dared venture forth.

No sooner had they arrived did a woman walk through the tree line, quiet and ambiguous. Her form looked slick, as if she had just emerged from water. Her long, dark-red hair clung to her chubby face as did the grey sodden robes on her already-corpulent form. As she sauntered into the glade, her thick red lips curled into a smile as she caught sight of the Ronan who had arrived before her.

She bowed her head, as she said, "I thank you, Lady Gwynevere, for that most distracting display of power. I was able to pass into the Origin Glade unmolested." Despite her drab robes, the wet woman was outfitted richly. Pearls hung from her thickly-rolled neck; the largest was nearly the size of an eagle's egg. Crowning her head was a golden diadem set with a large stone of lapis lazuli, and each of her plump fingers were adorned with golden rings encrusted with precious gems.

The blonde woman held a severe expression, but it softened slightly as she gave the women a nod. "I am glad to see you, Morgana. It has been too long." Morgana smiled in response and joined them, her dark chocolate eyes flicking toward Caethe nervously despite the easy smile she held.

The grey skies were suddenly torn with black, ruby, and white lightning. A warren had opened and from its depth flew Ronan. Their forms were outlined in power of black, white, or grey as they crossed the sky as quick as shooting stars. The lightning they threw raced together, rolling around one another until it stuck a massive shadow hidden in the clouds. When the lightning imploded against the demon, its form was revealed. *The Guardian*, Caethe thought in wonder as the beast was thrown backwards. Thousands of shadows now took to the sky, shooting like arrows toward the revealed Ronan.

The Guardian was gargantuan, nearly two-hundred feet in height with leathery wings that expanded more than six-hundred feet to either side. Its neck was long and its snout held a heavy jaw much like that of a wolf. It was a dull-black in color and scaled like a lizard, with a head crowned with three horns that ended in wickedly sharp points. Its body was long and lithe, as if it had a spine similar to that of a snake, and it had four thick legs spaced along its torso with two arms tucked beneath its wings.

The black warren opened again with a wail, tearing the grey sky with a black scar. The demons closed on the Ronan and magic exploded, illuminating the dim sky with blooms of bright energy. The Ronan disappeared from the sky once more, entering the warren and leaving the shadowed creatures in confused abandon. The warren snapped close with a crack.

The Leviathan's form was revealed for no more than a second before the shadows that clung to its form banished the Ronan magic, but now Caethe could track it as it tumbled from the sky. The Ronan outside the pentagram exclaimed their shock softly, not wanting to draw more attention to the Glade then they already had. The ground shook miles away when the demon met the ground and a roar vibrated the very air as the beast screamed in fury. Morgana slapped her hands over ears.

A black rent appeared above the Glade with an unnatural tearing sound. It was a horrid sound, like wood being torn asunder by hand. The shadow demons that floated above the Glade screamed in harsh whines, defiant, but as the warren opened and the Ronan spilled forth, the waiting demons were sucked within by an unnatural wind. The warren once more snapped closed and those within were lost from sight. The Ronan descended through the silvery eaves.

In total the Ronan numbered sixteen, not counting Caethe himself. The power within the Glade was akin to that of captured hurricane in a small bottle. The air crackled with magical potency, and the stench of brimstone and ozone filled the air as competing powers met one another in an eternal struggle that had lasted through the ages.

Those that held friendly relations greeted one another joyfully — namely Lifoy and a young woman who looked so similar there was no doubt in Caethe's mind that this was

Lifoy's twin. Their robes flashed brightly with colors of pinks, soft yellows, and joyfully bright blues as they embraced tightly.

Those who held one another in disdain greeted one another with stark indifference, eyeing each other like rival packs of wolves, their eyes ever-searching for weakness. The divide among the Coven was easily apparent to any who bore witness.

Those who wore white robes numbered five, and met one another with tight hugs and friendly smiles while casting baleful glares to those in black. The group contained the woman who had arrived on the northern gale, the young man who had accompanied her, along with two women and another man. The two other woman shared such similar resemblance to Gwynevere that close relation was undeniable, and the second man had an expansive stomach and swarthy skin that belied a southern heritage.

Those who wore black had all arrived together and numbered six. These men and women had their hoods drawn forward shadowing their faces. Their manner was more sober and concentrated, as if they found this reunion a bothersome distraction. Their heavy hoods hid their features, but Caethe could easily pick out the men and women: an even split. What was odd was that the shortest man among them held a chain that led to one of the women, and Caethe could see heavy shackles binding the woman's wrists that crawled with runes of power.

When Caethe caught sight of her, his stomach fell. He knew that out of all here, it was she who had the greatest chance of seeing through his deception. She wore a cloak of black, but the hood of her heavy cloak was thrown back with a casual shake of her head. The Ronan had dusky skin and a long face. She was the tallest woman here, standing six-feet five-inches in height, but her stature somehow only accentuated her haughty grace. The insanity that danced in her pale eyes did not add to her appearance, however, nor did the wild smile that split her lips.

A few moments of clarity filled the woman's eyes as she glanced at Caethe, and a startled gasp emitted from her throat. It was a gasp full of grief and regret. Tears sprang to her eyes and her bottom lip trembled with suppressed emotion. Caethe turned his head away from his mother and she began to cry softly, clinging desperately to the chains that bound her.

The grey-robed magi stood between both those clothed in dark robes and those in white. Much like a buffer, they assumed a mixed demeanor and numbered five. They wore robes similar to Caethe's own, save for Lifoy and his twin. Shadows clung to their forms in the shape of flowing robes that moved by an invisible wind, ever-changing in shape and curling like a living thing. Morgana held court among them, dominating the conversation, and both of the taller men shared Morgana's brilliant red hair.

Caethe observed them with a racing heart. They were magnificent and powerful, his family. His soul sung to feel them so close, but he was an outsider. He was not greeted. In fact, most kept their eyes from his form, as if they feared that they were looking at something dead, something vile that made their eyes roll with fear. No, he was not one of them.

I am cursed far worse than they could even imagine, he thought drearily. He had become a creature of the realms; a parasite in their eyes. His green eyes flicked from one to the next, knowing that if his plan was discovered his life would be forfeit in an instant.

A second roar shook the air, and silver leaves cascaded among the magi as the trees around them trembled beneath the strength of the Guardian's call. The threat interrupted the joyful reunion and the Ronan voices fell silent as their eyes turned north.

Ultan stepped forth from among the dark-robed magi. He wore rich black, trimmed with dark wolf fur and his shoulders flared with raven's feathers. An aura of power settled around him and hung palpable in the air like a shadowed threat.

Caethe's met his steel-grey stare for a fraction of a moment, and then Ultan's gaze flicked away in dismissal. Caethe let a shaky breath escape between his cracked lips.

Ultan's voice was soft and silken, but it commanded the attention of all as he said, "The Guardian is the only demon powerful enough to breach the wards of the Origin Glade. We cannot afford any interruptions during the Binding. Lifoy, Selyni," The two multicolored-robed figures bowed their heads in respect when addressed, "Go forth and guard the glade."

Ultan pulled two metal disks from beneath his robes and tossed them onto the ground. Even as the Coven watched, the discs began to spin, unfolding and expanding with fierce quickness. They emitted a metallic, scraping sound, not unlike two swords clashing against one another with a loud whine. In mere moments, two fourteen-foot long swords lay on the ground, each looked to weigh upwards of two-hundred pounds. Their hilt guards were crescent shaped and their pommels riveted.

A silver-haired woman stepped forward, and forestalled the twins with a wave of her tall white staff. She addressed Ultan directly, saying, "The risk is too great, Ultan." *Ayfe*, Caethe thought in awe.

A towering man, nearly seven-feet in height, leered toward her and growled a warning low in his throat. Caethe peered closer, noting that something was strange about the bulky man. He was unknown to Caethe, and must be one of the young that had been born after the Great Revolt. Dimly, Caethe wondered if the man was bound. "You will address the Archmagus with respect, Ayfe." His whispered in a deep, rasping voice. Ultan raised his hand, waving the man back.

Ayfe was the eldest among them all and looked to all the world as threatening as a grandmother. She was draped in white robes that were over-large and made her small stature look even more diminutive. She had severe, sharp features, and wore her white hair in a messy bun. He knew this doddering visage was deceptive, and as he looked at her he felt her power rise around her with subtlety, tinged with such fierceness that Caethe felt his mouth grow dry with fear.

Ayfe gave a nod toward the twins, and said, "The power of the Leviathan far surpasses the might of these two." Ayfe turned back to Ultan, her lips curling in displeasure, and said, "They haven't a hope in defeating such a demon alone." The sound of heavy wings flapping could be heard in the distance as the Guardian took to the sky once more.

Ultan's thin lips spread in a kind smile, as if he was humoring an elder, but his tone brokered no argument as he said, "Only the strong survive, Ayfe. You and I both know this harsh truth all too well. Time grows short. We have heard your unending protests for many long hours. We know you disagree with this path, but I have spoken," he waved toward the bound woman behind him, and said, "and the Oracle has sanctioned our success." Ayfe made to speak, but Ultan raised a hand, cutting her words off before she could speak. Ignoring her, he looked toward Lifoy and Selyni, and commanded, "Be gone the two of you." The twins bowed their blonde heads in response.

As the twins stood their forms stretched, growing taller as their faces twisted in pain, but they endured the torment silently. Their thin forms blurred and their sharp features grew broad. To watch their transformation was nauseating, and many of the Coven turned away. The twins' bones expanded, rolling beneath their skin, banishing their frail beauty as their facial features became disjointed. They grew to stand more than twenty-feet in height, and their limbs grew thick and their skin bulged with muscle. Together, they bent in unison, as if their stomachs were twisted with cramps, and the skin of their backs tore, spraying blood as great, pale pink wings burst from their backs. They stood, flapping their wings experimentally as silvery-white and gold feathers sprouted from the pink flesh.

With their wings folded behind them, they gracefully bent

and took up a sword. Caethe watched them in awe, witnessing the might of the Changelings for the very first time. They had taken no form of any one race, but instead had blended a collection in a way Caethe had not known was possible. Without hesitation, they threw themselves in the air trailing soft down feathers and silver leaves thrown by the wind of their wings. The shadow demons that clung to the eaves of the dark forest above howled gleefully, giving chase.

As she cast a mournful gaze to the sky, Ayfe whispered, "So be it."

A woman dressed in black stepped forward and threw back the hood of her robe, spilling waist-length ebony hair. Her face was dusky and overtly seductive, holding a dark beauty that took Caethe's breath away. When she spoke her voice both deeper and softer than he had expected. Quietly, she warned, "Ultan, they will not withstand Braugaethrael long, we must hasten."

Ultan nodded, "Yes, Maud, we must." With a casual wave, Ultan commanded the Magi forward. They had prepared for this moment and there was no instruction needed. Ultan dragged Aileen to the nearest tree and looped the long chain around the tree's golden trunk. With a whispered command the chain fused itself together, binding the Augury in place.

The Magi gathered in the pentagram. The weaker stood on the five points along the exterior, while the others took their places at the five points of intersection. At the three points of the interior triangle stood Ultan, Ayfe, and Maud. They eyed Caethe stonily, unblinking, as he rose to his feet, careful not to step beyond the perimeter of the stone he stood upon.

Ultan met his gaze, holding his very soul trapped within his grey eyes as he commanded, "With this spell, we shall bind you. By this binding we gift you with power that shall be wielded against those who have cursed us to exile."

Caethe responded in monotones, his voice unshaken and solid, as he said, "A weapon I shall be forged and like a phoenix, my wrath unmerciful."

Ayfe spoke, her voice full of warning, as she asked, "Do you proceed forward sound of mind, knowing that we shall use the true name of an Ancient long past and bind his soul to your own?"

Without hesitation, Caethe said, "I consent." Ayfe nodded in defeat.

Maud spoke, drawing his attention away from the grief of his elder. Her voice was liquid wine that spilled from her tongue with sweet promise, as she pronounced, "With this binding you shall gain the power of two, and with his name we shall command you."

Caethe bowed his head in submission, and said, "I bend to the will of the Coven and summit willingly to the command of the Archmagus." Maud's burgundy eyes flashed with pleasure.

Ultan's voice snapped across the glade, his voice biting with question, "With this gift we grant you the power to free yourself. Do you swear to repay us in kind?"

Caethe met Ultan's eye's unflinching, his mind calm and blank now that the time was upon him. "I swear, freedom shall be yours." Caethe promised.

Ayfe's voice had lost all the softness and it was cold, as she said, "The risk of binding is great. To forge your souls together you must step into the Pool of Magrados itself. Such power is raw, wild, and the risk is not only to your life, but to your very soul." Her icy gaze met his, pausing for a second as she weighed him deeply, before asking, "Do you step forth fully aware of the sacrifice you make?"

Caethe nodded, and said, "I do."

Impatiently, Ultan said, "You have drawn the runes of this binding and by your own skill you shall succeed or fail. The Ronan will anchor you."

Softly, Maud whispered, "The Ronan will gift you with the power of our strength." Her lips parted in a smile of heady anticipation.

Ayfe promised, "The Ronan will sing your soul the song of

grieving should you fail."

A roar of pain sounded overhead and the Coven looked up as one. Selyni and Lifoy battled the great demon of Umbrael above. Small against the mammoth shadow, they flew around the Guardian in dizzying circles, dodging and throwing themselves from the path of his claws, tail, and wings. Their great silver swords swung, smiting the lesser demons that flocked around them like crows, flinging the defeated from the sky.

Confidently, Caethe broke the stunned silence, as he said, "I am ready and with the power of the Coven, I go forth eagerly. Freedom awaits us all." He ignored the battle above. All thoughts of failure had fled his mind the moment the Coven had stepped around him. A single thought rang through his mind like the chime of church bells: *Destiny*. The word rang through his mind, over and over, solidifying his conviction.

"Begin," Ultan commanded.

The spell was long and laborious, but Caethe drew strength from the Ronan around him. Gone was his weakness and the tremble of his hand. Now he worked with a flawless grip, moving the magic around him, channeling it into himself and the spell that lay written at his feet.

Caethe woke the runes he had carved into the ground, and they flashed as they began to pulsate with golden light. They granted him access to the leylines that fled the Pool of Magrados. He felt the deep power of its source, and his mind ran along the rivers that fled the realm into warrens that sprawled across the full breath of the galaxy. Once the power would have struck downward directly, and in a graceful arch, bridged the Astral Realms to Adonim. As his mind passed along the veins of magic he saw signs of where it would have diverted to the mortal plane, but the foundation was gone; corrupted so deeply the very network of streams had been altered beyond recognition.

The Ronan chanted in unison, and from each bled power

in ribbons of light that swirled through the pentagram toward him. Every Ronan was outlined in the color of their aura and their magic, pure in this form, reflected their very essence. Morgana stood in a moody-emerald light that sparkled with shimmering flecks of deeper blue. Her magic moved slowly, like the deeper currents of the sea as it swam through the air toward him. Beside her, Gwynevere stood brazenly outlined in sapphire light that screamed such terrible purity that her form was lost to sight. In that moment, Caethe learned more about his brethren then he could have in half a century. An aura could not lie, and as he looked out across the dappled light that spread across the pentagram he saw greatness, both good and terrible. One and all, they gifted him with the full strength of their magic.

Caethe looked to those closest to him. Ayfe stood like a pillar of starlight, blinding and full of warmth. To his left Ultan was bathed in darkness that seemed like the deepest crypt, but a pearly cobalt licked over his aura that leeched the very heat from the air. Maud stood across him, glowing a deep scarlet, her magic swirling in a tunneled hurricane. The collective magic bathed him in brutal power, but the grounding runes at the edges of the pentagram flashed in lightning arches across the storm of magic, filtering the chaos and converting the individual magic into raw energy so that when it met him, it was as if he commanded Magrados itself.

Caethe stood silently at the center of magic, with his hands spread above him. In his mind, Caethe whispered words that lowered his innermost shields, baring the cortex of his power and his soul to the energy that raged around him. The thread that connected him to Solani thrummed like an anchor, its strength unyielding, holding him centered. A golden gale spun around the pentagram, rustling the leaves of the great trees as a whirlwind of spells thundered through the Origin Glade.

The wind grew in strength and the golden light tunneled upward, shooting into the grey sky like a gilded hurricane. Shadow demons fled its light and even Braugaethrael took pause, snapping his wings closed and diving away from the torrid. The Guardian's mind tumbled with revulsion and awe as he witnessed the power the Ronan had brought forth this day. The two Changelings pressed their attack then as he became distracted, and they bloodied the elder demon, hewing great tears along the skin of his wings. The blows sent him into a tumbling, frenzied freefall.

The spell had grown to its climax and the chanting fell silent in a moment of suspended time. Ayfe drew forth a spherical, myrtle-colored diamond from the folds of her white robes, and pronounced in a high voice, "The eye of Mangus Aetherian Ronan." With a small toss, Ayfe threw the stone to Caethe.

With a feral smile, Caethe caught the diamond in the palm of his hand. In the same second, his robes of shadow disintegrated away, revealing his nudity and the secrets that lay beneath. Hanging from a leather cord at his neck was a black griffin feather. Long, the feather reached from his chest to his groin. The Ronan gasped in startled horror. Solani clung to his neck, hissing angrily as he raised his staff in warning. Caethe looked up at the grey sky and spread his four arms wide, opening himself to the souls held in the vessel at his neck and the one in his hand.

The true horror of his torture and mutilation was bared before all, and in his nudity, a testament to what he had endured was revealed. The lower arms, where they had been reattached to his torso, were corded with thick bands of scarring. His anatomy was emaciated and skeletal, pale skin covered in masses of overlapping scars, and his feet bloodied and bruised from the long journey that had brought him to this moment.

The sky suddenly cleared, and three moons appeared hanging heavy and low in the grey sky. One moon was black and rimmed with steel-grey light, another was blood red, and the last blazingly white. They shone with victorious brightness, filling the shadow realm with more light then it had witnessed in a thousand millenniums. The eyes of the Coven followed his and found the bared moons.

In the stunned silence, Aileen cackled, and screamed, "Three moons mark the heir of Magrados, and the binding of all Covens. Three eyes rise to witness his ascension, for he is the one promised by the whispers of fate when Adonim was forged. The one foretold before the very gods crawled forth from the Abyss, before the Elves and Man and Dwarf were woken." She rattled the chains that bound her to the tree as she crooned to the moons above.

Ayfe's mouth fell open, and Maud's eyes grew cold with fear. Ultan's face had grown as still as stone, and a tortured word escaped his pale lips, "No."

The Oracle flung herself wildly, shaking in ecstasy as her eyes rolled with madness. Aileen pointed toward Caethe, and yelled, "Look round his neck, a Fey-born clings. The Elder race have bent the knee, bent the knee! Behold, Ronan, behold our master, the three-souled King!"

Ultan screamed in wordless fury, and reached toward Caethe as he sought to disrupt the spell. Without hesitation, Caethe took a small leap toward the simmering golden water at his feet and entered the golden Pool of Magrados with a splash. As he entered the pool the great spell was triggered, and white light exploded from the pool in a backlash of power. The band of light hit the Ronan with vicious fury and they were flung from the Realm of Umbrael in a flash.

When Caethe's skin met the raw power of the pool it was like jumping into an ocean of a hundred-thousand bolts of lightning. Excruciating pain tore through him as Magrados gripped him in an indomitable fist, overpowering his strength and drowning him in a sea of energy. Magic permeated every iota of flesh quicker then thought. Caethe did not resist, even as his mouth opened to scream. No sound escaped him as he was utterly consumed. His physical body was lost in the storm that raged around him like a blizzard, biting into his flesh with cold magic. Like a flame, his body was snuffed out of existence, and only Caethe's mind and soul remained. The power penetrated him like a thousand blades and he was judged.

For a time, he was lost. Caethe's senses fled, as did time, and for a moment, even identity.

The Origin glade had grown dim as the golden light fled, leaving the forest bathed in shadow. Above, the three moons stood defiantly among the grey clouds, and like silent sentinels, they waited. After a time, the pool began to grow in radiance. White fire rose to the surface and boiled among coils of black lighting. Suddenly, silver beams shot across the surface of the water as life bloomed within. The golden light pulsated with a feverish intensity as a figure emerged, rising from the rolling power of Magrados.

A man stepped forth from the pool, reborn. Golden droplets of magic dripped from his smooth, pale skin. All of the scars that had once marred his figure were gone, and his skin was tinted with a golden sheen that made him appear as if his blood was gilded with gold. His figure exuded vigor, and the youth that had once clung to his face had fled. The man's lower set of arms had grown to equal size as the ones above and were a glossy black of the deepest shadow. On his forehead, a third eye rested. Split, the pupil was half black and half blue, and the eyes beneath gleamed emerald with speckles of gold.

With a casual hand, Caethe raised the small pixie he had sheltered against his chest to his shoulder as he gazed at the abandoned glade and smiled. Turning, he bowed to the Pool of Magrados with a graceful movement. Then, with a snap of his fingers, he evaporated into thin air.

*****

Minutes passed and the golden gleam of the pool dimmed, as if spent. The dark shadows that clung to the eaves above had fallen silent; stunned by what they had witnessed. The

Leviathan lay among crushed branches and shattered limbs in a small crater, his mind raging darkly as he crawled to his feet. Inky-black blood spilled from the torn wings that spread above him, and drenched the forest in a dark rain as he took flight.

A red archway framed in fire crackled awake in the center of the Glade. Black smoke boiled from the portal and became gilded in the light. The Origin Glade whined angrily at the intrusion, and the trees began to bend. Long limbs tore at the portal, and their leaves fell upon it with sparks of fierce, white lightning that exploded in a series of booms. The portal shrunk beneath the tirade, but a hunched figure pressed first its horned head and then its shoulders through, before tumbling out of the red flames.

Eyeless, the demon swung its long head this way and that as its forked tongue scented the air intently. The surface of the Pool of Magrados erupted like a pyre, and fire lanced across the glade. The demon's blood-red skin bloomed with golden fire as Magrados punished it for its impertinence. The figure cried out in pain, falling back a step, emitting a high-pitched, inhuman scream. The demon gained some semblance of composure, shaking its head, and rushed forward.

The glade exploded with light and magic. Trees whipped their branches across the glade with moaning groans, and leaves exploded in flashes of searing heat.

The demon's skin boiled black with blisters, and where the leaves touched great scars of torn flesh appeared across its scaly hide. The demon knelt, all four of its spiked legs bending, and plucked a single strand of crimson-colored hair between its clawed hands. The demon's tongue slithered from its long maw as it tasted the strand of hair. Leaves rained from the sky, like a hail storm, and the demon was lost beneath a halo of exploding light. The pools surface hissed, spilling black smoke, and with a roar the demon was lost beneath an onslaught of golden flames. The demon turned, screaming, and leapt a dozen feet into the collapsing portal and disappeared.

Devaney

Chapter Twenty-Four:

Oh, Lord Shepherd

Devaney gingerly walked to the side of the pentagram, crouching just outside of the circle. Panic set in, and she looked around wildly. *What if he really is dead?* She thought desperately to herself as he looked down at Lifoy. Blood pumped freely from his left hand where he had cut himself, staining the wet deck. There was no indication that Lifoy still lived. *This doesn't look right*, she thought worriedly. As long as Devaney stared, he didn't move to breathe or twitch to blink. The ship rocked downward and Devaney looked around and thought, *If he is dead then I will drown here, alone, in the middle of a sea.* Devaney looked back to the cabin and thought, *maybe I should free those men.*

Just as she was about to stand. Lifoy jerked. Blood burst along his ribs, staining the white tunic he wore. Then a cut spread across his chest, as if he had been cut by an invisible blade. Devaney sat back in surprise. *He's alive*, she told herself. Lifoy's body rocked violently to the side, and a massive, blue bruise spread across his forehead. She wondered morbidly, *but for how long? I wonder if you are killed in the Realm of Umbrael, do you die here?* It was not something they had spoken of when Lifoy informed her that he must travel to the Astral Realm, nor had they spoken of any contingency plans when the asinine plan was formed.

The ship hit the bottom of a wave and sea spray crashed down upon the deck, drenching them both. Devaney was knocked off her feet, and rolled across the deck as the wave receded. She grabbed at the wooden steps that led to the helm, clinging desperately as the wave fled back into the sea. The ship bounced upward and Devaney crawled to her feet. The storm was worsening and quickly; the night sky boiled overhead.

The ship began to turn on its side as the sail snapped fully open. The thick canvas sails ballooned as wind tore at it with hungry claws and ship raced across the swells. Devaney scrambled toward the helm, and saw that the wheel spun freely, whirring softly. As the wave rose, the ship glided sideways up the swell. Devaney looked around. She hadn't a clue what to do. She grabbed at the wooden spokes, and the wheel jerked her hands hard to the right. Devaney let go with a cry as the force nearly broke the bones of her wrist.

The ship reached the apex of the swell. Devaney watched wide-eyed as they plunged forty-feet downward. The sail tore with a morbid buzz as the wind ripped it from the mast, and fled with a whoosh into the dark clouds like a shadow fleeing light. The tattered remains snapping crazily, flailing this way and that. The ship spun slowly as they fell down the wave.

Devaney looked to Lifoy, but he remained lifeless. He had gained a black eye and his lip was badly split. Devaney screamed, "Lifoy!"

The ship hit the bottom of the wave backwards. Devaney fell against the cabin, smashing against it, as the ship went nearly vertical. Waves thundered to either side in sheets of blue foam and above, as water was flung into the sky with the impact. Devaney flicked her sodden hair from her face, and saw that Lifoy was still within the circle. Despite the height of the near vertical incline and the wild rocking of the ship, the magi lay as if stone, untouched and unmoved by the storm.

The ship leveled out, and immediately began to rise on another swell, racing up the wave backwards. Desperately, Devaney flung herself across the deck, running down toward the circle. She lost her footing, and slid down the deck as it grew steep. With a grunt, she grabbed a heavy anchor that lay to the left of the pentagram. Barrels of fish flew past her head and crashing into the decks rail, shattering and bouncing into the dark water with a splash.

"Lifoy." Devaney cried, "Lifoy, dammit wake up." The ship reached the apex of the wave, and Devaney hugged the anchor as the ship jetted down again. The ship spun, and Devaney knew as she watched the ocean race toward her that they would hit the bottom sideways this time. Transfixed, she watched as the dark sea rose toward her. *Please Shepherd*, Devaney prayed, *lead me to the green pastures of your rich domain.* The ship began to tilt at an angle, as if to offer the deck to the frigid waters. Devaney closed her eyes.

No time for death prayers, Lifoy said into her mind. Devaney's eyes snapped open as the ship crashed into the waves. Lifoy leapt across the deck toward her, and the ship began to roll. The sea chased the Changeling as he smashed into her. The waves swallowed them. The deck plunged beneath the water as the ship rolled upside down, and the hull cracked with a clap louder than thunder. Lifoy pushed them free of the deck, dragging her deeper into to the sea.

Devaney panicked. She could not swim, and the weight of the dress dragged her down. Holding her in his arms, Lifoy kicked determinedly downward. *He's going to drown us*, Devaney thought wildly. It was dark beneath the sea, but lightning streaked across the sky and she could see wreckage sinking all around them. Devaney opened her mouth to scream and water rushed into her lungs, choking her.

The ship disappeared beneath rolling waves, sinking toward her. In the seas tumbling current the deck splintered apart, cracking in half, spilling its guts to the cold water. In seconds the ship was destroyed, leaving only splinters of scattered wood floating on surface. The waves rose and fell.

A porpoise jumped free of the waves, arching a dozen feet into the air, and on its back an unconscious woman lay. As it leapt in midair, its form twisted and blurred, and just before it plunged beneath the waves again the Roc spread its wings. Lifoy's wings pumped powerfully, flinging water as he fled into the sky.

Aritian

Chapter Twenty-Five:

A Path to Power

Aritian walked through the night bazaar with Beryl and Azera at his side. Ibriham led them through the teeming streets, waving them forward, his voice lost beneath the raucous chatter of the crowd. This bazaar was found in a wide courtyard between the mercantile district and the temples thoroughfare. Hawkers stood behind low tables barking at the crowd and boasting boldly of their superior wares. The crowds snaked up and down the rows like the current of a greedy river.

The sky had grown dark early and rolled with angry clouds that made the hour thick and humid; Aritian knew that soon the rains would come, but for now, this afforded some cool relief. Aritian had let two days past without speaking of Maud's proposal, though he had thought of little else. He had wanted his friends to have time to enjoy the luxuries of Maud's wealth without their thoughts turning toward darker matters.

Ibriham walked ahead. He was dressed in dark silk robes of black, and wore a banded gold-torque around his neck. He waved him forward, and yelled, "Come Master, I have found the stall just as I promised." Aritian couldn't hear his voice over the roar of the crowd, but could read Ibrahim's lips easily enough.

Aritian nodded, and pushed through the crowd. Azera shoved a man to the side who had grown too close, before leaning down and asking in his ear, "Tell me again Aritian, why did you want us to come along for this late night stroll?" She eyed the thick crowds around them with annoyance, before complaining, "There's so many humans." Aritian flashed her a glare, and Azera shrugged, before saying defensively, "They stink."

Beryl took a deep gulp from a golden goblet, slushing dark beer down his beard, before he said, "Perhaps the lad wanted company, Azera. Ibriham is a squirrely feller. Why should Aritian trust em?" Beryl eyed a table filled with gold trinkets and small rings eagerly, and waved Aritian toward it.

Aritian shook his head and made his way past the hawker's table. Beryl begrudgingly followed. They had spent the last two days in the markets. Aritian had split the coin equally among his companions, to their joy and amazement, and now their apartment was so full with packages and bundled product that it looked as though they were holding a market themselves.

"I trust Ibriham." Aritian said, shooting Azera a glance, before saying, "I wanted you to come so I could speak to you alone." He pulled Beryl away from a hawker that held out rubies for him to consider. "You have enough gems and gold adornments, Beryl, come on."

Beryl sighed heavily and waved away the gems. The dwarf wore five, gold chains around his neck and had strung silver beading through his beard. He wore a handsome silk tunic under a dark-leather vest that was studded with emeralds. *He looks like a dandy*, Aritian thought with a half-smile; it had been a struggle this morning to resist laughing when he first caught sight of the dwarf, bejeweled and garnished like some spoiled whore.

Azera, on the other hand, had taken a portion of the gift and bedecked herself in fine armor and weapons. Over a white tunic she wore silver chainmail that had been fitted to her form, and wore an innumerable number of long daggers strapped to her leather pants, waist, and boots. Across her back sat a huge war hammer that she had pronounced to be the finest skull splitter in all of Velon. The handle was made from thick oak, lacquered with black stain, and bound by ribs of silver, with a curved blade a full three feet in length.

When they finally came to Ibrahim's side, he waved toward the merchant before him. The table was crowded with tightly, woven baskets corded with leather binding that secured the lids. The merchant was a young man, and his dark eyes flashed as he eyed their rich apparel. Ibriham pointed to the smallest baskets, and said, "The snake you seek."

The thin man danced toward the basket Ibriham pointed to and picked it up. Carefully, he held the basket before him, saying, "Ah, the fabled drake. A wonderful selection. The finest and most fierce of all Ignea's serpents. Small they may be, but deadly. A single bite contains enough poison to kill seven fully grown elephants." He smirked then, in a suggestive, mischievous grin.

Aritian dropped three gold coins on the table, and said, "I have met the fiercest of all serpents in Ignea and her name was Sythilia." The merchant looked at him with confusion, and Aritian asked, "How many species of poisonous snakes do you carry?" Azera eyed him questioningly, but Aritian ignored her.

The merchant set the basket down, and boasted, "Of all the stalls here, I carry the greatest variety." He spread his arms wide, gesturing to some fifty baskets that lined his table

Ibriham leaned forward, cutting off the merchant's fanciful words, and said coldly, "Yes we know, that is why I brought him here. Now answer the Master's question."

The merchant nodded slowly, eyes-wide, and before clearing his throat and saying, "Ah yes, of course." The merchant nervously eyed the gold coins on the table, as if he itched to snatch them up. He smiled at Aritian, dragging his eyes from the gold, and said, "Besides the drake, from the Pomum I have the horned viper, yellow cobra, and tiger snake. From the Ignis I have the black mamba, red rattlesnake, copperhead, and the king cobra. From the sea..."

Aritian held up a hand. "That's enough." He pulled four more gold coins from the pouch at his side, and said, "I'll take one of each, and the remaining coin buys your silence. We were not here."

The merchant nodded knowingly, and excitedly began placing baskets before them. Beryl leaned close to him, eying the baskets warily, and asked, "Planning on poisoning someone?"

Aritian smiled at the dwarf, and said vaguely, "You will see." He picked up two of the larger baskets and waved Azera, Beryl and Ibriham forward. They gingerly picked up the remaining baskets that the merchant had prepared.

Azera eyed the hawker suspiciously, and asked, "How do we know he isn't cheating us? I haven't seen one snake. There could be nothing in these baskets." Aritian shook the baskets he held and felt something move within. A string of angry hisses followed.

Aritian suggested, "We know where to find him should we discover his stock false." He flashed a charming smile at the nervous merchant, and said, "We will know the vibrancy of their sting, be assured of that." The merchant nodded with understanding and wiped his forehead with the sleeve of his robe. Aritian gave him a wink, before turning away. He said, "Ibriham if you would, lead us back to the manse."

Ibriham nodded and pushed through the crowd, while holding his baskets before him. As people caught sight of the baskets he held, the crowd hurriedly skirting from his path.

Aritian motioned Beryl and Azera close as they walked, and said, "I have something to tell you. Maud has offered a gift, but it does not come without a price. Once you have seen what I have shown you, you will understand why I must accept her offer." Quickly, he explained what Maud had presented two days past. They both were silent during his explanation, and Aritian concluded, "I have known you both for a short time, but in that time you have saved my life and I value your opinion. I know when I emerge that I will be different, but what choice do I have?"

Beryl frowned into his red beard, and said, "I don't trust this witch. What if she traps ye inside this construct and ye live your whole life in a matter of months? What if she be lyin' about how long ye can stand within this time bubble? Lad, that woman gives me the shivers. She's evil as they come, I'll be tellin ye that." Beryl said with surety, grimacing. They walked swiftly through the thinning crowd. The moon above smiled high in the sky. It was nearly midnight and Aritian knew he must choose by dawn.

Azera's expression was closed and her brows bunched in thought. When she spoke, it was hedging, "You said the Oracle said not to trust her, but it sounds as though you wish to disregard this warning. Why ask us, if not to soothe your own conscience?"

Aritian nodded, she was right of course. Stubbornly, he said, "She also said I would learn from her." They walked free of the Bazaar and came to a street lined with open-faced carriages, led by teams of camel. Ibriham gave a tall driver a handful of coppers as he took the front passenger seat, and waved them to climb in. The driver cracked his whip, the camel snorted rudely, and then began plodding forward.

Azera leaned toward him, and whispered, "Yes, and said you had to seek out corruption, but not speak its name or you'd die. Maybe this Time Vortex is the corruption? Maybe that is what you were supposed to seek."

Aritian eyed Ibrahim's back, wondering if the man could hear their hushed conversation, before whispering back, "Then soon I will be dead." Beryl and Azera looked at him fearfully and Aritian shook his head, and said, "No, I do not know if manipulating time is against the Coven's laws, but I do know it's not the evil I am supposed to find."

Beryl eyes were nervous, as he asked, "How do ye know?"

Aritian shrugged, and said, "I don't know for sure. I can't explain it. When the Oracle told me, there was this emotion that crossed between us. I could feel the darkness, this wrongness... I will know it when I feel it again. The library is not the corruption." Aritian said with surety. When he thought back on the Oracle's words his skin crawled. After they crashed in the Ignis her warning had nibbled at the back of his mind, and as they grew closer to Creuen there were very few moments that passed that he did not think of her dire words.

With narrowed eyes, Azera asked, "Why isn't the lorith here?" The carriage moved through the winding streets with relative ease, as there was little traffic here. This part of the city was filled with sprawling shops and neatly spaced craftsman houses. The streets were lined with tall iron poles that held oil lanterns that washed the street in a bright, orange glow.

Aritian shook his head, and admitted quietly, "I haven't told Rythsar yet, because I knew he would protest and I wanted you both on my side. There is great risk, but without the knowledge..." He shrugged, unable to explain, before saying, "This magic, this thing... It sits at the center of me like a coiling flame, ready to boil over at a moment's notice." He held up his finger displaying the Ring of Suppression, and said, "Without this, who knows what will happen, and I can't rightly leave Ignea defenseless. I must gain control. To risk using magic now... I can't." He trailed off, not wanting to think of the consequences that he had already faced.

Azera fingered a dagger in her hand, turning the silver blade this way and that to catch the light as she contemplated. With a grunt, she offered, "Why not go north, relying on your strength of arms alone? You're an assassin, you don't need magic. Besides, you'll have us and the Dranguis. That will be enough."

Aritian gave her a smile, but shook his head slowly. In a quiet voice, he confessed, "I had not dared ask if you would come."

Beryl smacked his arm lightly, and said, "Don't be daft boy, ye not leavin us here with that Scarlet Witch."

Azera nodded to herself as if she had just come to a

conclusion, and warned, "The others will want to come."

Aritian shook his head sadly, and said, "I don't think I can bring the Dranguis north. They're too young for so dangerous a journey. I will have to find someone I trust to leave them with." The thought had been on his mind the last two days. He knew if the northerners had found a way to quell the might of the Ronan than they were not a people to be taken lightly.

Azera growled low in her throat, and said stoically, "No, I mean they will want to join you, Beryl, myself and Ori in the Time Vortex."

Aritian shook his head, and pressed his lips tightly. He was afraid, but nowhere close enough to put his friends at such a risk. In protest, he said, "I can't ask that of you." Azera settled her dark beady-gaze on him, and Beryl chuckled low in his throat. Aritian looked at each of them, and exasperated, said, "Twelve years of your life would be gone, and for what?" Azera held her stare, and Beryl beamed at him with a toothy grin. Aritian crossed his arm, and said insistently, "No, I must do this alone."

Azera eyed Ibriham nervously over her shoulder, before whispering, "The northern lands are going to be fraught with peril. It's not just you who needs to prepare, Aritian. I agree the boys are just fledglings at this point and that it would be irresponsible for you to bring them north, but if you brought them with us in the Time Vortex the boys would be children no longer. They would be warriors."

Beryl patted his arm, and said earnestly, "Dwarves are long-lived, Aritian. Twelve years is like a nap to us. Let me forge ye weapons. I grew up at me father's side forgin' and no dwarf be quick to forget the smithin. Let me hammer beat bone, metal, and fire."

Azera had caught Beryl's infectious grin, and smiled broadly as she said, "Maud told you that you needed to grow your retinue. Maybe she didn't mean by number, but by maturity. When you're doing fancy magic you'll need to be guarded. Ori and I will train in the time bubble." Azera said fiercely, adopting Beryl's monicker of the time construct.

Aritian threw up his hands in frustration, and said, "The both of you aren't helping."

Beryl cocked his head sideways comically, and said brightly, "Ye wanted us on ye side, and we are. I will begin a list of supplies I shall be needin."

Aritian felt his resolve melting, and said mournfully, "I don't even know if you could survive the Time Vortex."

Beryl made to respond, but it was Ibriham who spoke. He turned in his seat, and said, "They can."

"Excuse me?" Aritian asked, startled by the man's words. Worriedly, he searched the man's face to see if he had heard their entire conversation, but Ibriham wore the same polite expression that he always held.

Calmly, Ibriham said, "They can survive."

Incredulously, Aritian asked, "How do you know?"

Ibriham replied blandly, "I've seen it." He turned back in his chair before Aritian had a chance to question him further, and said, "We have arrived." Aritian looked up and saw that they had indeed reached their destination. With a shout from Ibriham, the gates to Maud's manse swung open.

Beryl chucked, jumping down from the carriage, and said, "Well that settles it. Now it's time to break it to the rest of our company."

*****

Aritian stood with his back against the rail of the balcony. Before him, on the low couches, sat Beryl, Azera, the Dranguis, Entah and Ori, while Rythsar stood by the door with his arms crossed. They all looked at him expectantly, eyes wide with shock.

Ibriham had left them at the gate, and Aritian was glad that the man had allowed them their privacy for this. He didn't like always being shadowed by Maud's creature, and no matter what blood they shared, Aritian knew the man was her loyal servant. No one had yet spoken after the news.

While their tongues were still tied, Aritian released the leather strap that held the smallest basket closed. He lifted the basket into the light, flicked off the lip, and reached in. Aritian felt the sting of the snake's bite before he raised his hand from the depths of the basket. It burned like ice and his hand went numb instantly.

Aritian dropped the basket and cupped the length of the small, black snake in his hand. The boys reared back in fear, gasping, while Entah leaned forward eagerly. Rythsar started, hissing, "Aritian," and made to jump forward as he too realized what snake he held. Aritian raised his free hand, stopping him. Ori cried out, but Azera slapped his shoulder and gave him a measured look.

In a low, pained voice, Aritian explained, "Six months ago I was poisoned by the milk of a drake. Here, the serpent bites me once more. I didn't die from the first touch of the drake and I won't now, so please do not be alarmed." He grunted in pain. Even as he spoke his hand swelled. He squeezed the jaws of the snake with his free hand and it released its grip. Aritian held his hand in the light so all could see.

The hand that was bitten swelled like a fruit pastry and held ugly purple lines that raced up his arm. Aritian ignored the pain. His heart thundered and a sweat had broken on his brow.

"I was cut by a northern sword that had been coated in enough venom to kill a small village. When I was in the mine I faced death and took wounds that should have marked me for life, if not killed me, and yet I stand here untouched." Aritian met the Dranguis' eyes and gave them a small nod. They relaxed and smiled weakly, looking to one another in wonder. Aritian continued, "When I killed the wyrm, I bit her and poisoned her with the very same poison that now streams through my veins. It is how I defeated her."

In the silence, Rong asked, "Is that why you have fangs?"

The boy leaned forward now, with as much interest of Entah. Aritian nodded. He carefully bent and found the basket and its top. With shaking hands, he placed the drake back in to its cage and secured the lid. Rong sat back, and said, "I saw you. I watched from the window, but I didn't believe what I saw. I thought my mind was playing tricks on me, like when the wyrm sung."

Aritian smiled at him weakly, and said, "You saw truly." He looked at each of them with a weighted look, and admitted, "I am changing and I don't know why." Aritian looked down at the baskets that lay at his feet, and said, "I have purchased seven of the deadliest snake here." He pointed to the baskets at his feet, before saying, "If you doubt the poison of the drake, then I shall let them all bite me so I can prove the truth of my words."

They all as one, shook their heads in protest, and Azera said, "No, we believe you Aritian. You do not need to suffer for us to have faith."

Aritian nodded curtly, swallowing emotion. *They believe me*, Aritian thought in relief. Aritian could see it in their eyes. He gave Azera a grateful smile, and spoke quietly, "I am going north once the rains stops and I may never return to Ignea. Any who wish to come are welcome." Aritian found the lorith's yellow eyes, and said, "I am going to accept the Scarlet Witch's gift." The lorith hissed angrily, but Aritian held his gaze for another moment before turning away. Rythsar's black lips rolled as he swallowed his anger and his tail flicked side to side. Aritian knew he wanted to argue, wanted to convince him to change his mind, but Aritian couldn't see any path except the one presented.

Aritian sighed shakily and closed his eyes, saying, "Any who wishes to enter the Time Vortex with me, can, but at their own risk. I cannot protect you from what I do not understand. If you decide to, I will be very sad, for I know what will be stolen from each of you. This is not something that I want for any of you, but each of you have stood by my side and have earned the right to choose for yourself." Aritian hated saying those words, wanted to deny them the choice, but he would not dictate anyone's life or personal choice. If they were to go north, then they had the right to prepare themselves in the way they thought best, and Aritian would not deny them something that may one day save their life.

Aritian nodded to Beryl, and said, "Beryl has started a list of supplies and will pass it to Ibriham in two hours' time. Take your time choosing, but know this: No power or weight of blood will make you anything but an equal in my eyes." Aritian held up the hand that had been bitten by the snake. "No matter how different I may become." The swelling had fled, as had the ugly purple lines. Even as they watched the two bite marks faded.

Rythsar stepped forward, and in a low hiss, said, "I am with you, now and always. I shall not leave your side." Aritian gave him a tight nod, and closed his eyes briefly as emotion threatened to escape. When he gained control, Aritian opened his eyes.

Each of his friends gave him a nod: all would accept the Scarlet Witch's gift.

Caethe

Chapter Twenty-Six:

An Amber Tomb

Caethe swam upwards through the sea of syrupy-thick darkness that was unconsciousness. It had been more than sixty years since his mind had left his physical body, and the journey back was long and torturous. Like a man who had sunk too far beneath the waves of an ocean, Caethe swam furiously with panic-stricken need toward the surface.

Caethe's eyes snapped open. The light around him was warm and fractured, his gaze hazily colored with pale oranges and dark yellows. He stared from within the crystalized amber tomb. The massive pillar of raw amber had been erected in the center of a large courtyard atop a mountainside. Caethe's thoughts raced toward panic as he held his breath, knowing that he could not survive long now that his consciousness had returned to the tomb.

He flicked his eyes south, beyond the edge of the courtyard where the cliffside plunged four-hundred feet and saw that below, a city sprawled. Caethe flicked his eyes to the north and saw the pyramid of Imperial Mountain. The temple was made from grey-veined, white marble that had been mined from the very mountain that hunched imposingly behind it. The temple's face was adorned with a pair of gargantuan pillars and between them, stood a small crowd of priest's robed in rich, white cloth. A silver door, stamped ornately with a fist shrouded in beams of light, rose behind them more than thirty feet in height.

Looking at the temple made his eyes twitch and burn, so Caethe looked to the crowd of supplicants that had come to garner salvation from the great temple of St. Aleksandru. A long stairwell zigzagged down the side of the mountain, leading to the city. Caethe lost count as the number of people climbing the stair grew beyond the hundreds. It he had been able, Caethe would have shaken his head at their folly. These observations had taken no more than five seconds.

The time was now or never. The thread of consciousness he had with Solani thrummed with anticipation, and Caethe could feel the pixie pressed against the hollow of his stomach. Caethe closed his eyes and in his mind's eye, saw his power. His magic rose in a tower of crystalized silver, veined pure gold with the raw might of Magrados. Around the pillar snaked a crawling black fire that radiated such heat that it nearly smote the core of who he was, but between the fire and his cortex coiled white starlight that shone with startling radiance. The three magics thrummed with perfect synchrony, forming a power so mighty that Caethe quaked before it. He hesitated for a fraction of a second, daring himself to touch it.

Caethe reached out with his mind and gripped the power. His eyes snapped wider as he drank in the formidable force, his heart began to pound, and sweat poured from his skin. The source within submitted eagerly, both foreign souls knew that to live they must escape the amber prison. Caethe began weaving the power and the magic within boiled, growing and filling him until it shone with such brilliance that the outlines of his very bones could be seen like a shadow against the sun. Dimly, he could hear startled cries and the beginnings of fear ripple across the mountainside courtyard, but it was like an echo, only faintly heard. The amber resisted his power, subverting the magic, deadening its effect. With a scream, Caethe channeled more energy than he had ever dared use, and the amber stone shone with ferocity of a star. He could feel his skin crackle and burn as the magic screamed for release. A crack formed in the stone before his bulging eyes, and leapt downward toward the base of the monolith.

The amber exploded outward, sending shards flying into the crowd, and Caethe fell naked to the ground. His limbs were too weak to support him, having atrophied long ago, and so he lay prone in a crumpled heap. Solani instantly took flight. A thought that was not his own commanded his hand outward, and a burst of silver light flooded through his cramping fingers, wrapping the pixie in a protective shield. Screams erupted as people panicked. Shards of serrated amber had impaled more than three-dozen common folk, and blood had begun to seep in a stain across the white-stone mosaic that decorated the courtyard.

Caethe twisted his torso around, grunting in pain, as he faced the temple. Priests stared at him with open-mouthed, astonished fear. Quickly, their eye grew hard and their faces reddened with fury. First one, and then the entire cohort broke from their stunned hesitation and raced toward him, their long robes flapping wildly in the wind. The priests wore heavy amulets of amber, and grabbed for books of power that were tied to their waistbands by thick leather cords. Solani fled into the sky, and sunlight flashed off the shield as he disappeared into the white clouds above.

Another mind within wrested control of Caethe's body and anger spilled forth. Lightening, black as pitch, flooded from his left hand incinerating all those in its path. The bolt of dark power struck the stairwell with a boom. Burnt flesh filled the air and where the power had flooded, only dust remained. The crowd reacted by flinging themselves like rats over one another in their attempts to escape. The mortar of the stair cracked in a series of rumbling booms and the uppermost part of the stairwell crashed down upon the lower level's spilling people into the open air. Screams filled the day as half a hundred fell to their deaths far below. The stairs began to crumble fully now and sections of the mountain broke off, crushing those beneath with tremors that shook the air.

Soldiers poured from the temple's silvered mouth,

outdistancing the portly, out-of-shape priests in their haste to defend the people of Ordu. The priest's holy books began to glow with white light as they called their god forth. Bile rose in Caethe's throat as his body reacted to the vile power they called upon. Caethe struggled to sit up as a soldier closed in wielding a large broadsword. The man screamed a battle cry as he loomed down and Caethe lifted his upper hands before him. A gold fog pounded forth with a wail and lanced into the soldier's chest, throwing him back a hundred feet. He did not rise again.

The priests called the soldier's back with warning; a strong voice rising above them all.

"Back, men of Ordu! Your might of arm has no power against one such as this. Ordu protect us!"

The chanting of the priests rose, and white light flooded across the courtyard enveloping him in stark power. The stench of ozone filled Caethe's nostrils and made his eyes water.

Caethe did not resist as the power struck him like a ton of stone. He was flung viciously onto his back and his head smacked against the stone mosaic, cracking it. The weight of rushing wind held him pinned to the ground like the thumb of a god, and Caethe choked, unable to breathe as black spots overtook his vision fully.

Aritian

Chapter Twenty-Seven:

The Gift of Time

The Shadow had risen, and the clouds above boiled black and wrathful green. Rain fell from the sky in sheets, drowning the city with a sound that droned on and on, dominating all else. Aritian and his companions dashed across the abandoned courtyard and within moments of stepping beyond the shaded confines of the apartments were drenched to the bone.

Aritian clutched his long robes close to his chest as they were thrown about in the wind. They walked up the steps, between the tall pillars, and entered the wide hall where Maud had held court four days' past.

Aritian's stomach was knotted with nerves, and his hands shook from boundless energy that coursed through him. His mind buzzed, as his thoughts danced in a crazed tempo, too scattered to linger on any one thought for any true amount of time. He wiped rain from his eyes, and saw that the hall had changed drastically since the last time he had seen it. Dark silk was strewn from the four corners of the wall and hung from the ceiling to pool darkly on the red marble floor. As his companions stepped through the archways, men unhooked a waiting canopy that fell behind them, throwing the room to shadowed darkness. In the center of the room a pentagram had been drawn with black wax.

In the circle stood a thirteen-pointed star marked at each point by a tall, yellow candle. Maud stood at the apex, and was dressed in a cherry red, long-sleeved, kimono. Over her face she wore a veil of black lace and her long black hair tumbled free to her waist in a glossy, black sheet. The pentagram glowed brightly in the scarce light. Aritian's eyes flicked to the library, and he saw that the silvery door glowed with a deep, maroon power.

Jerkily, Aritian bowed. The motion was mimicked by his friends. They dripped puddles at their feet, but the water went unnoticed. They had all dressed in sky blue robes by Aritian's command; his color contrasted Maud's deep-red eyes and would let her know that though they would accept gift, they stood separate and apart from her. It was a silly protest, but with the words of the oracle haunting him, Aritian felt as though he must make some point to rebuke her will.

Maud gave them a deep nod in greeting and pointed to each of the star's points. It was obvious what she expected. After a nod from Aritian, they each took their place at one of the points of the star. Aritian stood across from Maud, and could see her red lips twitch in a smile of satisfaction beneath her dark veil. Aritian swallowed hard. He knew he was taking a risk. He knew that he could not trust this woman, but the gleam of power hung in the corner of his eye like a sweet promise. Aritian's jaw tightened and when his companion's eyes turned to him, he gave them a curt nod.

Maud voice broke the silence like thunder, as she said, "Be welcome, Aritian and friends, one and all. I have received your list of accommodations, and arrangements have been made to satisfaction." Maud turned in place, giving each of his companions a warm smile. In a whisper, she confided, "I am unsurprised by your fidelity to Aritian. Living at the side of a Ronan can bring wondrous joy, but is a deep responsibility. With this act of solidarity, you have proven yourselves. In return for your loyalty I can promise that you shall live a life that others can only dream of."

Maud addressed Aritian in a bold voice, "You have done well in selecting your retinue, Aritian. When you emerge, the Insectis Queen shall have hatched her clutch. I shall begin instructing you in her tongue then. For now, know that you shall find more knowledge than you can imagine beyond the doorway." She waved toward the library, and said, "Power is our birthright, but knowledge is my gift. I give this knowledge to you free of will, as you are blood of my own." They both knew she was giving him something beyond value, and he just had to hope that the price would be worth it.

Maud splayed her arms wide, and said, "To begin, I must perform a ceremony that prepares your body for the time shift. This is necessary, and each of you must submit of your own free will. Do you comply?"

Rythsar hissed, "I do." The lorith's head bowed and he stared at the floor. He had been quiet since pledging himself, and Aritian knew he was uneasy with the idea of trusting Maud.

Maud's eyes flicked to Beryl who stood next to the lorith, "I do." Beryl said, smiling with a grimace.

Azera nodded, and in a low rumble said, "I do." She was echoed by her brother who stood next to her beaming with excitement. Maud gave the young titan a small smile, before her eyes flicked to the gnome.

Entah nodded his head, shifting heavily to the side, as he said sheepishly, "I submit freely, though I curse my own curiosity." Aritian gave the gnome a wink, and the Entah's blue lips cracked into a shadow of a smile.

Sicaroo slapped his fist to his heart, and said confidently, "I give my will and life to Aritian, freely." His pronouncement was echoed by each of the Dranguis. They were young, but even now, standing before something as strange and wild as magic they did not falter. Aritian's chest swelled with pride.

When Maud's red gaze fell upon him, Aritian nodded as he said, "I submit freely, and place my life and the lives of those I love in your care. Treat us kindly, Maud. I am trusting you, and we both know how long a Ronan's memory can last."

Maud nodded in acknowledgement, her eyes gleaming beneath her dark cowl. In a soft voice, she said, "Then let us begin." Maud began to whisper fervently, so quiet her words were lost. She did not speak in the common tongue, nor any langue Aritian recognized. The light of the candles suddenly jumped so that they stood a foot above the wick. Red motes of light danced from Maud's open palms, spinning and floating among those in the circle.

Instantly, Aritian felt his head grow light and his eyes began to glaze over. A feeling of such contentment fell over him that he was surprised that he could stand at all. Lazily, he smiled to his companions and saw that they too had glassy eyes and easy expressions. Maud's chanting grew deeper, her voice dipping below what was humanly possible. The voice commanded their will, and Aritian felt his mind bloom like the petals of a flower. He drank in her influence, submitting eagerly.

Maud's chanting stopped abruptly and she smiled wide. She stepped from her point in the circle and walked to the center where a silver, ornate bowl rested. She picked up the bowl, and turned to face him with a sweep of her long skirts. Softly, she spoke, "In this bowl I have the fruit of the Passion Tree. Few in this world know of them." She held up a dried berry. It was lime green and small, nor larger than a raisin. Maud eyed it in contemplation, as she said, "They are found in the lost lands of Amissa." Her smile curled higher, as she stepped close. When she spoke, it was in a whisper, "I don't expect you to know of such a land. It lays far to the south, guarded by the Luxarma, and for the past thousand years has been beyond our reach. A shame really." Maud brushed her hand along his cheek and Aritian smiled drunkenly at her. Softly, she explained, "I studied there, when I was still a child, and these small fruit are all I have left of that strange land." She eyed the fruit between her fingertips with longing, before smiling coldly.

Maud placed the berry in his mouth. Aritian smiled dumbly at her, as the fruit burst upon his tongue. It was like nothing her had tasted before, citrus but spicy, the juices made his tongue and throat numb. She walked to Rythsar and stroked the lorith's jaw. His maw hung open and his long black tongue flicked out. Maud placed the berry on his tongue and with a gentle push, snapped his jaw closed.

Maud looked into the cloudy eyes of the lorith, and with sweet promise, said, "When you emerge, your mate will be in this city. If you behave I shall give her to you, but test me and I will flay her alive before your eyes." The lorith shook visibly as he struggled against the daze that gripped them all. His tail flicked wildly behind him and hit something solid. With a boom, a shield flashed red all around them, encircling the pentagram. Maud chuckled, as the shield fell back to its translucent state. She gently blew motes of light that floated in the air toward the lorith's face. The light met the dark scales of his face and were absorbed. Rythsar's shoulders slumped and his head hung heavy against his chest, as if he had fallen fast asleep.

Maud walked on, and one by one, gave them each a berry. She spoke at ease as she did, "These berries are known by another name by the Elder Fae. They call them the Fruit of Singularity." She smiled, and her face lit with such ambitious hunger Aritian felt his eyes roll with fear. She popped a berry into Mingyo's mouth, and promised, "They bring out a drive in you, pull resolve from the deepest part of your soul and, when commanded, those who have ingested their sweet nectar cannot be stopped. I have accomplished greatness with their help." Maud set the bowl in the center of the pentagram and returned to her place at the apex of the circle. "I hope that in time you will come to see the great investment I have made with this gift, for you are about to accomplish such great things."

Aritian felt the ring on his finger begin to warm, but he barely noticed the shooting pain that raced along his forearm. He felt drugged, like he had smoked opium, and his thoughts floated on ethereal clouds, unable to fully form. He stood swaying as Maud hands rose in the air. Red power crackled around her fingertips and arched out, striking them each. Together, those in the circle writhed as Maud's power crackled along the length of their bodies.

With a shout, Maud commanded, "I take from each of you your emotions. Let all of your grief, worry, despair, happiness, and love fall away." Aritian felt his mind grow cold and his spinning thoughts fell away. With a shout, she demanded, "I take from you your will. I cut the strings that move and stir your spirit." Aritian felt himself slouch and his head lolled to the side. "I take from you your morality." Aritian's heart slowed and became even, as his mind grew metallic and sharp.

Maud's voice fell lower still, as she whispered, "You are empty now, mere shells." A wicked grin touched her lips. She spoke rapidly now, saying, "I fill you all with greedy ambition, and an insatiable thirst for knowledge and skill. Conversation will be but a mere function in your quest for power. You will strive together, until your limbs grow weary and your heart grows weak. You shall not want for respite, nor sustenance, for the berry shall provide both. Time is precious and such basic needs are profligate. When you step forth you will be born anew, and like newly forged steel you will be hard and unbreakable." Maud's magic died and they breathed heavily, free now from the pain that had gripped them. They stood straight and their eyes filled with iron resolve.

Maud walked to his side and took his hand. Gently, she pulled the Ring of Suppression from his finger. The metal of the ring was cool to the touch. Her palm curled around it, as she stroked his face with her other hand. In a whisper, she said, "Go now, Aritian. Step into the Vortex of Time." She leaned forward on her tippy-toes and kissed his lips softly. When she stepped back, she said, "Make me proud."

Aritian nodded curtly, turned on his heel, and strode across the room. His companions followed without a word. Aritian lay his hand upon the silver door. The shield sizzled with heat, and he felt the skin of his palm melt away. The price of entrance was not cheap. He pulled his bloodied hand back from the humming door and it swung open wide. Without hesitation, Aritian stepped through the ruby light into the Time Vortex. When Rong passed through the door, he gave Maud one last look and she smiled cruelly, nodding in response. Rong gripped the door, his hand smoking as it made contact, and slammed the door behind him.

In the shadows Maud laughed long and hard, her voice echoing through the hall as she relished in all that she had wrought.

Devaney

Chapter Twenty-Eight:

Shades Island

The Roc slowly spiraled from the bright sky. Below, green islands waited like emerald gems among a billowing sapphire-blanket of water. Like great skirts of white, fog circled the three small islands in an unnaturally-perfect circle. The air was crisp so high, but with each passing second Devaney could feel the air growing warmer and sighed in relief.

As they dipped beneath the clouds, Devaney felt a sort of resistance that made her mind go blank and her breath catch in her throat. It was like passing through a shield of thick water that belied and bewitched the mind of its sense of self. For a moment, she felt some indomitable force grip her and she let go of the feathers to clutch her throat. The feeling passed in less than half a minute as the presence seemed to lose interest in her. Devaney looked wildly about for the source, but she could sense no others besides herself and Lifoy.

Gently, Lifoy spoke into her mind. *We just passed the prison walls of Shades Island. The Curse can be quite uncomfortable, but take heart, it knows not your name. Should you attempt to leave, it will let you pass freely.* Devaney nodded tightly. She had not expected to feel anything, unbound as she was, and for a moment wanted nothing more to command Lifoy to fly from this place. To distract herself from such thoughts, she looked down.

The smallest Island lay to the north and was the first they flew over. Less than a mile in length, it was dominated by sharp cliff that jutted out into the sea and from it, the land sloped south. Dominating the cliff side was a massive, five-hundred-foot statue. Devaney felt her mouth hang open in shock. It was like nothing she had ever seen before.

Made from white stone, the figure rose from the sea. Its expansive robes were stained green along it trim and crusted with pale-grey barnacles. The man's face was serene, with kind, sculpted eyes that were heavy with wisdom. His forehead was wide, but smooth, and a long beard trailed to his waist. He looked neither old nor young, rather he held an ambiguity of timelessness that clung about him. In one hand the statue held a massive chain out above the water, and at its end hung a twisting sphere of metal made of interconnected rings. From its center, a harsh, blue light emanated, illuminating the water below. In the other hand, he held a massive staff that plunged into the sea. The island was covered in a wild forest that crawled up the cliffside to cling to the statue's back.

"Magnificent." Devaney yelled into the wind as the statue passed beneath them.

Lifoy responded in her mind. *It depicts Mangus, our greatest Archmagus, and was erected in his memory after the Sundering by his daughter Ayfe.*

Devaney shook her head, and called into the wind, "I wasn't talking to you, Lifoy."

Lifoy's laughter rang through her thoughts and he spoke into her mind. *Are you still angry at me for that little dip in the Chalice Sea?* Devaney ignored him. They had almost died, and Lifoy had killed dozens of sailors. She had not forgiven him and had barely spoke to him over the course of the last week.

Lifoy dipped downward as they passed the island, and Devaney clung tighter to the feathers she held. She had not yet grown used to flying, but now at least she could manage without clenching her eyes closed, as she had before. Her stomach jumped as they banked wildly to the side, flying closer to the second island. This island was much larger than the first, spanning twelve miles in length. White sand beaches stretched along its exterior before giving way to plush forests and fallow fields. The woods were a riot of color, bursting with crowns of yellow, red, and orange.

The center of the island was dominated by a small mountain that sat beneath the largest castle Devaney had ever seen. The castle's tallest towers sat on the mountain peak in a tight cluster. Made from grey stone, the monument was filled with wide courtyards and square cut towers that held wide, stained-glass windows. The pyramid caps of each tower shone brightly in the sun and appeared to be made from a dark metal. Iron spikes traced the roof and between these, massive stone gargoyles perched. The castle rolled down the mountain side for two miles and was guarded by a grey-stone wall the circled the castle in an arch. Beneath the wall sprawled a large village that soon gave way to farmland.

Lifoy's thundering wings carried them toward the castle. As they flew over the wall, Devaney could see a road that led to the village and lining it on either side were twelve, eighty-foot, robed statues. The statues were made from the same stone that Mangus had been crafted from. Their flight slowed dramatically and Lifoy's leaned backward in the air, flapping his wings rapidly as they landed in a large, grey cobblestone courtyard that sat among several tall towers.

As Lifoy landed, he rocked forward and the movement nearly flung her from his back. Devaney unclenched her cramped hands and slid down the side of Lifoy's feathered neck. Her wobbly legs managed not to fail her, and she gazed around her with rapt curiosity. The courtyard was cobbled in light-colored stone, and the tower walls held iron brackets of magefire that crackled softly with pale, orange light.

Dozens of archways led deeper into the castle interior, each guarded by a stone golem shaped in various forms of fantastical beasts. The closest was a towering humanoid who held the horned head of a bull and brandished a black, stone axe with a snarl. Every muscle had been sculpted with incredible perfection, and he looked as though he could spring to life at any second. Another was shaped in the form of a giant horse that stood twenty-feet high at its shoulder, marbled in a pale-blue stone. To her left snarled a pack of hollow wolves whose gaunt forms leapt over an archway, and to her right she saw the bulbous form of a troll, its black maw hung open with undisguised hunger. All of them wore expressions of terrible anger.

A tall woman dressed in a long-trailing black gown strode toward them, her quick steps filled with purpose. Devaney smiled shyly in greeting, eying the woman. The gown she wore was expansive and overtly decadent. The skirt held hundreds of layers of gauze-like, black silk and the corset was bejeweled with thousands of tiny onyx gemstones that glinted darkly in the bright light of day. The woman herself was taller than any women Devaney had ever met; standing over six feet in height. She had a long, graceful neck that had been left bare, a face that held pointed, sharp features, and heavy too-large, olive-colored eyes. The woman crossed the large courtyard in moments, stopping a mere foot from Devaney and looked down at her with an expression akin to when you see a particularly nasty bug. Devaney felt her frail smile falter as she came under the woman's heavy-lidded gaze.

Devaney dipped her head ungracefully, and said, "My name is Devaney."

The *crack* of the woman's sharp slap filled the courtyard, and Devaney cried out as she clutched her stinging cheek.

"You will not address me with such boorish cheek. I am Aileen, the Augury of the Onyx Order."

Devaney eyed the magus in shock, not understanding what she had done wrong. She opened her mouth to make an apology for whatever affront she had made, but Aileen's face loomed down until her nose was but an inch away from Devaney's. "Silence, farm girl." Aileen nodded smugly and continued, "Oh yes, I know who you are. I know exactly what you are." Aileen's head jerked up as Lifoy's form spun and twisted, transforming from bird to man. Devaney took a step backwards, not wanting to be in the woman's reach. Aileen screeched loudly, her neck rolling on her shoulders, as she pronounced, "Imposter! Imposter!"

Devaney spread her arms wide and pled, "Lady Aileen, no..."

Aileen flung her hands out above her head, her voice growing more piercing as she screamed, "This woman has come to supplant me. Come to kill me. Help! Ultan, my love, where are you?" She began shaking her head side to side. "Her tongue is false. Her heart is false. She kisses the dirt covered feet of my traitorous son. Slut! I know you're trying to sleep your way to power," Aileen accused, taking another step forward. Devaney brought her hands up to fend off another blow. She could feel waves of energy rolling off the woman. It was dark and heavy, not visible to the naked eye, but present nevertheless.

Lifoy stepped to Devaney's side, and Devaney flashed him a relieved glance. He nodded with a smile and turned to Aileen. Nude, he seemed little concerned with his modesty as he admonished the tall woman, "Aileen stop this ugly display, you're frightening poor Devaney. Devaney is family now, a Ronan just the same as you or I."

Aileen gritted her teeth, her eyes rolling as her face filled with anger. Hotly, through gritted teeth, she whispered, "Don't you dare speak to me, you mangy mongrel. You are not my equal." Aileen pointed a boney finger at Devaney, and promised, "Born of no line known to Ronan. No blood kin to me." Aileen's voice grew sharp once more and she screamed to the sky, "Resurgence!"

A voice cracked across the courtyard, "Enough, Aileen. Be gone with you." Devaney looked past the woman and found herself looking at a middle-aged man. Dressed in steel grey robes trimmed with gold stitching, the man was red-haired, trim, and had soft brown eyes. The man stopped halfway across the courtyard, and said, "Aileen back to your tower. You know the Archmagus doesn't like it when you wander."

Aileen dipped her head in chastisement and clutched handfuls of her thick skirts. Hastily, with her head bent she fled the courtyard, whispering, "Just wait until I talk to him. That white-haired cunt isn't taking my throne. Betrayers of soot-colored blood, always interfering...." She continued muttering to herself as she disappeared through an archway that lay to the right.

The man smiled apologetically through his expansive beard, and said, "Sorry you were greeted so roughly. We don't often have visitors here on Shades Islands, and I ask that you forgive us for our lax manners." The man pointed to himself, and said, "I am Aedus, and I welcome you most warmly to the ancestral home of the Ronan. May you find Castle Magistrate a warm and welcome respite." He waved to the elegant towers around them, and pronounced, "Here you may rest easy knowing that you are safe from all worries and cares of the outside world."

Devaney attempted to curtsey, and blushed knowing that it had been a clumsy excuse for one, before introducing herself, "My name's Devaney. Thank you for your warm greeting."

Aedus nodded deeply, smiling broadly, and said, "We have waited a long time for our Coven to once again be whole. Your arrival marks us a step closer to that dream. Now come, I am sure you are weary from your travels and filled with questions beyond measure." Devaney smiled, and walked forward with Lifoy at her side. A flicker of a frown crossed the man's face, and he said, "Not you, Lifoy. The Archmagus has asked for you to report directly to him upon arrival."

Lifoy stopped in his tracks and looked from Devaney to Aedus. Devaney looked over her shoulder with concern, but Lifoy flashed her an easy smile and a nod, before walking off toward the archway that Aileen had disappeared through.

Devaney turned and gave Aedus an unsure smile. He wrapped an arm around her shoulders as they walked, and said,

"Worry not. I have been instructed to take you to your rooms so that you may get settled. Lifoy will return to your side shortly."

"Thank you." Devaney said genuinely. Aedus had a warm demeanor and she liked his kind smile. The thought of a warm bed and a hot meal made her steps light as Aedus led her under an archway and through a pair of double doors.

Inside, the walls had been whitewashed and Devaney found the grand hallway both open and airy. The floor was carpeted with a strange rug that changed colors as they stepped upon it. The weave transformed from a muted grey to a vibrant yellow as she took her first step and then like ripples on a ponds face, the color fled before her, transforming the carpet. Similarly, the carpet morphed into an early brown where Aedus stepped. Archways lined the right side of the hallway leading to elegant halls and large rooms that Aedus led her past without hesitation. The left side of the hall was decorated with massive paintings filled with picturesque scenes of nature. The works were made with massive scale, racing forty-feet up the wall and spanning twice as long. Their detail was incredible.

Devaney studied one as they passed. It depicted a huntsmen and his dogs giving chase through a winding forest. Devaney resisted reaching out and touching the canvas. She knew that it was just a play of artistry, but her mind swore that if she did, she would be able to feel the glossy leaves that graced the trees.

Aedus smiled, noting her awestruck expression, and said politely, "The tapestries are micro, pocket dimensions. If you were to touch them, you'd find yourself in the place they depict. All of them were crafted by the famed artisan, Cinvanth Vego. Sometimes if you look long enough, you can find him among them. Poor soul lost himself to his art." He cleared his throat, and said, "I must apologize again for Aileen's horrid behavior. She is not a well woman, and despite all the power collected here we have yet to find a way to heal her mind."

Devaney nodded distractedly, and eyed a painting filled

with a lake dappled with soft-feathered, black swans. Casually, she said, "I was warned of Aileen. I was just taken aback by her hostility." Metal sculptures twisted from the ceiling, and around these floated massive orbs of yellow fire. The sculptures moved, whirling in spins and arch's that she was sure held some secret knowledge. Aedus walked briskly and Devaney had to trot to keep up with him, and so she had no time to contemplate their mysteries. Devaney smiled as she walked down the hall, exhilarating in the open, breathtakingly magnificent display of magic.

Aedus nodded thoughtfully and agreed, saying, "Yes, she can be quite aggressive, but I am glad Lifoy gave you forewarning."

"Oh no, Caethe did." Devaney said in answer, craning her neck upward. Aedus paused mid-step and asked, "You know Caethe? How can this be?" He looked down at her, and frowned. Aedus was a muscular man, and even beneath his long robes Devaney could see the strength of his limbs. When she had studied with Caethe she had always assumed the magi were studious, mousey people, nothing like this towering man next to her.

Devaney closed her eyes briefly, knowing that she had revealed too much. Lamely, she admitted the truth, "I met him in my dreams." All the Ronan possessed power, and Devaney did not want to be caught in a lie. *Who knows, maybe he can read my thoughts?* Devaney mused nervously.

Aedus nodded sharply, and a frown formed beneath his red beard. Quietly, he said, "I see." He resumed walking.

Devaney hurried after, and asked in concern, "Have I said something wrong?" She knew that among the Ronan that Caethe was unliked; viewed almost as if he was a parasite. But that had been before he had betrayed them. Lifoy had nattered on and on about Caethe's pluck and the anger of the elders. Now Devaney wished she had considered convincing Lifoy to take her somewhere else, but she knew that he would have insisted they came here, and more, she knew that it was merely her fear waking these doubts.

Aedus shook his head and flashed her a weak smile, before saying, "Oh dear no, of course not. I am simply surprised. You must have great power within, if you're able to Dream Walk without formal training."

Desperately, Devaney wished to change the subject and blurted out the first question she could think of, "Do all Ronan on Shades Islands live within this castle?"

Aedus shook his head, and said, "No, there is a chain of three small islands. The one we are on now is the largest of the three and the home of the Archmagus. Most of the Coven live on the other two islands. We Ronan tend to like our space." He added with a tight smile, before stopping before a pair of double doors. He waved toward the doors, and pronounced, "Here we are."

The doors were made from a chocolate wood and glossed with a bright veneer. Carved on the face of the doors was a grove filled with dancing trees and naked women. There was something strange about the women. Either the artist had taken liberties, or these lithe women were not human at all. They had twining, branching hair that was dappled and strung with vines, leafed and flowered. Their faces too, held a strange textured pattern, and their long limps seemed nearly twice as long as what a common women would have. Aedus tapped the doors with his knuckle and they swung open.

They stepped inside and Devaney looked around stunned. The room was elegantly decorated in pale greens and earthy browns. Gold chandeliers hung from the tall ceiling and were graced with hundreds of yellow-wax candles that spilled a honeyed light. A massive painting hung on the left side of the room, depicting a quiet glade. In awe, Devaney stood transfixed. Looking at the canvas was like looking through window to a faraway place. The painting moved and as she watched, a fox rolled in soft beams of dappled sunlight at the foot of an oak tree. Devaney pulled her eyes from the scene and took in the rest of the room.

The entry was filled with low couches that squatted before a tall fireplace that roared with warmth. Bearskin furs covered the floor with plush softness and a small dining table sat on the far side of the room. Even from this distance, Devaney could see that it was set with gold cutlery that held platters of steaming chicken breast, slices of ham, and loaves of bread. A large clear pitcher sat among the platters filled with water, and next to it, a cut crystal decanter that bloomed red with rich wine. By the dining table were two more doors that led further into the apartments.

Devaney looked to Aedus with uncertainty, and asked with restrained excitement, "This...this is for me?"

"Why yes, of course. Your comfort is the Archmagus highest concern." Aedus said with an indulgent smile.

Devaney looked around at the rich trappings, and in wonder, said, "I've never seen the like before." For the first time, in a long time, Devaney felt herself relax. It was like releasing a knot that was tied around her throat that she hadn't realized was choking her and now, free of it, she could breathe freely. "I was a farm girl. We lived in a small cabin." Devaney said explaining vaguely, as she looked around. She turned to Aedus with a beaming smile.

The magi had raised his left hand and his thick fingers moved in an intricate pattern that tricked the eye. Devaney watched transfixed as his hands blurred, and suddenly a popping sound filled the room. Devaney jumped. All welcome and warmth fled Aedus and he looked at her with sudden seriousness. Worriedly, he whispered, "We can speak freely now, but just for a moment." Aedus warned, "I will not share what you have told me about Caethe or Dream Walking, and it would be wise if you told no one else."

Devaney looked at him blankly, her heart suddenly racing, and asked in confusion, "Why?" Fearfully, she whispered, "Lifoy already knows." She felt the knot of worry tighten around her throat and resigned herself to it and the fear that accompanied it.

Aedus nodded, his brown eyes holding her gaze, and said emphatically, "Lifoy can be trusted. I am sorry, my dear, I wish I could shield you from what is to come, but I am powerless to stop it." He shook his head sadly.

"Stop what?" Devaney choked out as panic began to set in. She hadn't a clue what this man was talking about, but she knew that the Ronan could be dangerous. Caethe had warned her of Shades Islands. He hadn't wanted her to come here.

Aedus gripped her arm and leaned in close, as he whispered harshly, "Tell them nothing. Act dumb, like a simple country girl. I would not let them know you can see through your blindness." He advised, perceptively.

Devaney shook her head side to side in denial. She had really believed that she would have some semblance of peace, some moment where she could catch her breath. *I have been a naïve fool*, she thought berating herself. "You're scaring me. What are you talking about?" She asked fearfully.

Aedus stared into her eyes, and she saw true sorrow fill them. In a raspy-whisper, he said, "The curse of an Oracle." He sighed heavily. "To be so young and so heavily burdened." His voice grew hard as he warned, "There will be trials that you must face to survive. Whatever you do, do not submit." Devaney stared at him stunned and he shook her shoulder gently, drawing her out of her bewilderment, saying, "You must know what I speak of, if you have been Awakened."

Visions and memories flooded through her mind. In despair, she thought, *I don't know which one waits. I don't know what I should fear. There's so many. How can I prepare if I don't know?* Devaney thought, cursing her inability to understand what she had Seen. Pleadingly, she asked, "Please, help me."

Aedus let go of her arm and stepped back, saying, "I cannot. Forgive me, I've said too much as it is. I must go." With a few quick steps, he left the room and the door boomed shut.

Devaney walked to the door and pulled on the golden handle. It was locked. Devaney yelled, "Wait." There was no response. Slowly, she turned from the door, whispering to herself, "Aedus, come back." The decadent room waited empty before her, its richness no longer held any joy.

Lifoy

Chapter Twenty-Nine:

Obeisance

Lifoy walked down the long reception hall toward the throne of the Archmagus. Some two-hundred feet above, orbs of dim blue-fire hung suspended in the eaves of the curved ceiling. The hall was gargantuan, stretching three-hundred feet in length and was more than a hundred wide. The floor was made from black marble and the walls, grey stone. Wide windows lined either side, but the shutters were closed, leaving that hall dark. His Master preferred the shadows. The hall was abandoned and sparsely decorated. In time of old it had been a warm place, inviting and full of good cheer, but all of that had been stripped away. Ultan was utilitarian, and preferred the bare coldness the hall now displayed.

Lifoy's steps echoed as he walked toward the Weirwood throne. He had dressed in loose, practical robes knowing that soon he would once more take flight. Lifoy hadn't bothered taking his time. He knew that to make the Archmagus wait was to risk his fury. Lifoy sighed wistfully, wishing for a few days' respite, but he knew that was a fanciful, deluded hope. *First things first*, he told himself, *walk out of here alive*.

Lifoy stopped before a towering throne and bowed. The throne, made of living wood, was sixty-feet in height and sat on a raised dais of black marble. The back loomed upward with sharp peaks of twining ivory branches that wove together like a lattice, and had remained leafless since the Sundering, but by the sharp, cinnamon scent that filled the hall, Lifoy knew it still lived.

It was there that Ultan sat, staring down at him unblinking with his chin resting on his folded hands. The Archmagus dressed in black, utilitarian garb that mimicked the hall — devoid of adornments and style — and his robes hung loosely on his thin form before pooling at his feet.

When Lifoy rose from his bow, he respectfully addressed his king, "My Lord, I have brought the Oracle here as requested. Even now, Aedus leads her to accommodations."

Ultan did not break his stare, as he commanded in an intoxicating whisper, "Tell me what you have learned."

To hear his voice was like falling into a cloud of opium, and Lifoy drowned in an insatiable need to obey. Ultan's influence swept away all of Lifoy's thoughts, and before he had a moment to think, he was already speaking, "Devaney is a power to behold. She is not like the others. She does not possess the frailty that Hannah held nor the madness of Aileen. She grips prophecy in both hands and weaves it with a finesse beyond her years. Already fate begins to bend to her will." Ultan raised a single dark eyebrow in appreciation.

The Archmagus leaned forward, his dark robes spilling down the stone steps with the gentle movement. Softly, he said, "I felt a disturbance in Agos, an influx of power. Tell me."

Lifoy choked out the words, his tongue working faster than his mind, as he said, "Devaney grew mad at the sight of Ordu soldiers. She would not relent, refused to listen to reason. I could not stop her..." Lifoy stopped himself, his words cutting off as he shut his jaw closed tightly. He did not wish to betray Devaney. A bead of sweat broke out on his forehead and trailed down his cheek.

Ultan beckoned with his hand, and said seductively, "Tell me."

Lifoy saw tendrils of shadow creep around the edges of his peripherals. Darkness spun from the stone floor and coiled around his legs. Lifoy wanted to scream but could not. He wanted to run, to transform into a bird and fly away, but he was paralyzed. The smoke curled up his body and settled around his neck. Ultan's hand clenched, and the shadows tightened with a vice-like grip. Ultan's expression did not change as Lifoy struggled in the smoke's grasp, nor when his face turned beat red.

Ultan's hand relaxed, and Lifoy gasped as the shadow relaxed its hold. Even as his chest heaved, his tongue worked as if by its own volition, "Devaney exposed us. She called on her power before humans..." Lifoy shook his head slightly, and his next words came out choked and indistinguishable.

Ultan's hand once more clenched and the darkness tightened, threatening to crush his windpipe. Tears spilled down's Lifoy's bulging eyes. After a full minute, Ultan once more moderated his grip. Breathlessly, Lifoy confessed, "A demon... I don't know how she gained mastery over it... She called it from Umbrael and destroyed the Ordu forces that had gathered in the Strife." Ultan's lips twitched with a smile. Lifoy last words came in a harsh whisper. "Without a circle." Ultan let go of his hold and Lifoy collapsed to the floor. He sobbed, clutching his neck as he sucked in the sweet succor of air.

Ultan leaned back on the throne considering, before saying, "An unusual move for an Oracle, perhaps we will come to appreciate one another. I tire of hiding; of this insufferable prison." He added with unmasked hunger, "Oh, how I long to have bore witness to her might... How did she fare?"

Lifoy shook his head, still gasping heaps of air with his hands braced on the floor. When he spoke, his voice came out in a tortured whisper, "All fell before her might... she herself fainted with exhaustion moments later. Days she slept."

"Is she allied with Caethe?" Ultan asked, staring into blue fire above with his pale, grey eyes..

"I know not..." Lifoy confessed. Ultan's steely gaze fell to the prone Changeling, and Lifoy held his hands up fearfully. Desperately, Lifoy said, "It's true he sent me to retrieve her, but I do not know the depths of their relationship."

Coolly, Ultan asked, "Did she know of his betrayal?"

This is it, Lifoy thought, *this is what he truly seeks. Do I dare tell him?* He knew what Devaney would face if he did and he paled at the thought. His mind raced, for he knew even if he could remain silent on the subject, Devaney would not tread an easy path to Ultan's trust. *If I don't tell him, and she confesses...* Lifoy shuddered at the thought and his imagination went wild as he contemplated the punishments he would face. Lifoy hesitated, and then said dully, "...I know not."

Ultan smiled now. It was cruel thing. He had a coldness about him that promised bloodshed if he should be displeased. With a playful air, he asked, "Have you switched sides, Lifoy?" Lifoy shook his head rapidly. "Do you walk with the light now, supplanting my every wish and desire?" Ultan asked, his voice suddenly hard as stone.

Lifoy shook his head, tears streaming down his face. In a weak voice, he said, "I am loyal to you Master and you..." Ultan stood, and the shadows fled from the corners of the room, suffocating Lifoy's next words. The smoke lifted him in the air and Lifoy was dragged across the room until he hung before Ultan, suspended in shadow. Lifoy could not breath, could barely see, but managed to croak one word, "Alone."

In a casual whisper, Ultan said, "I don't believe you."

Lifoy felt piss run down his leg, as terror overcame him. The shadows began to rise. He could barely see above the dark clouds that crept just beneath his bottom eyelashes. In a shrill shriek, he screamed, "There's another...!" The shadows paused, and in a rush, Lifoy said, "I found another Ronan child in the Kingdom of Agos."

Ultan flicked his hand, and Lifoy spun around in the air so that his back was to Ultan. The Witch King whispered in his ear, "If what you say is true, then I must confess myself confused. Where is this child? Do they hide beneath your robes? Why has my faithful dog not retrieved them for me?"

Lifoy trembled in fear, and said shakily, "The girl..." His

mind raced. He no longer thought of loyalty but survival alone. In a rushed whisper, he said, "She took too great an interest, and I knew not if she was allied with Caethe. It seemed foolish to risk recruitment."

Ultan seemed to consider his words for a few minutes. Lifoy could feel his heart pounding in his chest. He did not move even as the anticipation mounted. With a flick of his hand, Ultan flung the smoke away. Lifoy landed on the cold marble in a heap, some dozen feet away. In a calm voice, Ultan commanded, "Very well. Go at once, then, and retrieve the child."

Lifoy closed his eyes, and breathed a sigh of relief. He would not die this day. Now that the threat of death had fled, he realized what he had done. Bile rose in his throat. Lifoy stood unsteadily. Without turning to face the Archmagus, Lifoy tentatively asked, "Should I not look in on Devaney? She will grow suspicious if I do not go to her to say goodbye."

Ultan face twisted in a macabre sneer, and he snarled, "Leave the Oracle to me, Lifoy." His voice dipped lower still, and dangerously, he demanded, "You will prove your loyalty to me or you shall face the consequences of failure. Begone."

Lifoy yelped in fear, uttering a weak "As you command, Archmagus," before fleeing down the hall.

Selyni

Chapter Thirty:

A Solemn Vigil

Selyni sat in a small wooden chair before an open doorway. The hall she waited in was abandoned and dim, and outside, the rain pounded relentlessly. Selyni stared unblinking at the room beyond the blood-red, energy shield. Her pupils were fully dilated, and flicked side to side rapidly as she traced the quick movements of those within. The sight before her was dizzying. Those inside the library blurred as they flashed across the room. It had been arduous adapting her eyes to the rate of time within the vortex. It was not an adaptation she had ever tried before, but on the third day she had managed to accomplish the feat. What she saw made her wish that she hadn't.

Aritian sat in the center of the room before the column of suspended Remembrance Orbs. He rocked forward and backward with rapid, jerky movements caught in a trance. She watched as he lifted his hand, and an orb flew through the light toward him. He caught it deftly, snatching it out of the air, before returning to his hunched-over position. Seventeen Remembrance Orbs lay scattered around him, used and discarded with little care. The Orbs were dark now, the magenta light that had once filled them had been spent; in his learning, he had destroyed them.

Against the far sight of the room she watched Beryl work over a small forge. The fireplace had been converted by Maud's command. Coal flashed, orange and white, glimmering with heat as he smashed a hammer upon a dark metal. His hammer sung; *ting, ting, ting, ting,* three-dozen times over every heartbeat she took. His brow dripped with sweat, but he smiled like one crazed. He sped over to the bellows and gripped the handle, yanking it up and down. The coals ignited, heating the long sword he slaved over until it gleamed white. He returned to his hammer and the library filled with the sound of his manic swings.

Before Beryl's hastily-fashioned forge stood Entah. The gnome bent over a long table that was strewn with tomes, haphazardly stacked. He mixed liquids and power in glass beakers, grabbing and pouring from the hundreds of jars that lay scattered before him. His thin hands were covered in soot. As Selyni watched he dashed to a ladder, climbed it four-stories high, and began pulling down books, throwing those in the way over his shoulders to the ground. He found the one he wanted and slid down the ladder to run back to his work table. The gnome took a pinch of blue powder and sprinkled it into a glass beaker that was filled with orange liquid. He swirled the contents, and smiled as the liquid turned to a milky white. Even as she watched, Entah took a sip of the contents. His huge black eyes widened in disgust and he spat onto the floor. He gripped his chest as he coughed raggedly. Entah threw the glass beaker over his shoulder and it shattered behind him in a tinkle of glass. He grabbed a new beaker and the process started anew once more.

Selyni turned away, unable to watch his desperate moves, and her eyes fell upon the lorith, the Titan's, and the Dranguis. Selyni bit her lip at the sight. Already a few of the boys had sprang a handful of inches taller. They had discarded their clothes and spared with one another in the nude. Their lithe bodies were slick with sweat, and their hair clung to their skin. All wore bruises and a few sported cuts that had been left unattended. They fought against one another ruthlessly.

Mingyo and Yi whirled spears toward one another in blurs. They distorted as they dodged and rolled away from one another's blows with terrible speed. Sicaroo, Shan, and Bo faced

Rong and Hui, with wooden swords. The boys, working in teams, screamed battle cries as they leapt over couches and off tables toward one another. Rong did a triple backflip and landed on a coffee table where he battled away Sicaroo and Bo's blows. Her eyes jerked to the side as Hui took a blow to the head. A cut burst across his scalp and blood wept down his face. Shan stood over him in triumph, his chest heaving. Rythsar looked on, hissing commands, whipping his tail out in chastisement as he egged them on.

Next to them, closest to the door, battled Ori and Azera. They fought with such ferocity that Selyni felt a tear stream down her face. Azera's face had grown hard and her expression was dark as she shouted to her brother, encouraging him to attack. Ori smiled bloodily, his lip had been split by a vicious backhanded blow delivered just a few moments ago. Ori sprang toward her swinging upward with his heavy wooden sword, aiming at her chest. Azera's wooden axe swung between them and caught the blade. They strained against one another, eyes wild and veins on their face and neck bulging. Azera hooked his blade and flung it away. With a triumphant cry, she kicked out, catching him in the chest. Ori flew back ten feet and crashed against the shelves with a terrible crack. Books rained down on him, but he leapt to his feet undeterred, shaking his head as he roared in challenge.

"Has he shown any inclination toward a particular craft?" A voice asked behind her. Selyni jumped in her chair, startled, and her pupil's grew small as she lost her concentration. She stood and faced Maud.

Shaking her head, Selyni replied angrily, "This is wrong, Maud. This violates the Covenant. You must put a stop to it. Now."

Maud chuckled. She wore a long black velvet cape over a lace-netted gown that scantily covered her breasts, and left much of her tanned skin revealed. "You presume to give me orders?"

Selyni grimaced, and insisted, "They are going to kill

themselves in there. Whatever you gave them has driven them insane. They don't sleep or eat. They barely talk. They're getting more aggressive... especially the Dranguis. They're going to kill one another."

Maud gripped her chest in mock aghast, and said, "Please, tell me everything you saw. I am so beside myself with concern."

Selyni frowned. She knew the woman was taunting her, but didn't care. She looked over her shoulder. Without her eyes adjusted to the time of the library, all she saw was blurs streaking across the room. Deadpan, Selyni gave her report, "They have been inside the vortex for four days now; the equivalent of a year. Aritian has showed no inclination of note, and has little interest in the Grimoires, unless he is referencing something he learned in the Remembrance Orbs. He's on his eighteenth Orb, in less than thirteen months." *It should have taken him nearly twice the time to complete so many Orbs*, Selyni thought, unsettled. "As he progresses, each Remembrance Orb is left completely depleted." Selyni frowned grimly, and said, "I'm sorry Maud, but he is destroying your collection."

A look of irritation crossed Maud's expression as she eyed the library. The Remembrance Orbs were beyond priceless, and Selyni hoped that it would be enough to make Maud reconsider this plan, if only to save the precious histories. Selyni didn't allow herself to think of what this desecration told of Aritian himself. The orbs should not be so easily spent, and their destruction hinted at powers most unusual. Maud considered for a moment, and thoughtfully said, "Interesting, even with the Passion Berry he is accelerating far quicker than I would have thought possible. No matter, it is good news. Proceed in your report." Maud commanded, nonplussed by her dire warnings or the loss of her irreplaceable artifacts.

Selyni nodded curtly, and said, "Beryl is forging some sort of dark metal. I'm not sure what it is. I haven't seen it's like before, but he's been working on the same sword since the beginning. He seems obsessed with perfection." Dwarves were known to be the finest craftsmen in all of Adonim, but still, his obsessive behavior was odd. *He could have forged ten swords in that time*, Selyni thought knowingly.

Maud smiled, and said, "Dwarves always are when they work dragonbone."

Selyni's mouth fell open, and incredulously, she asked, "Where in the world did Aritian come by that?"

Maud shrugged dismissively, and admitted, "I'm not sure. In the markets, obviously. A curious choice, I'll admit. It must have called to him, for he took a sizable amount in."

Selyni shook her head with confusion, and asked, "How could a mere slave afford such a material? Dragonbone is worth more than diamonds." Maud smiled teasingly, and Selyni frowned, nodding to herself. *Of course, you gave him coin in an attempt to win his affection*, she thought in vexation. In a quiet voice, she continued, "The gnome has me greatly concerned. He's an alchemist or some such. He is constantly mixing and brewing different concoctions. It's odd. I thought they were tinkers?" Selyni asked, perplexed. She worried for the gnome. *Drinking so many concoctions could not be good for anyone.*

Maud nodded, and said dismissively, "Some are, some aren't. They are fascinated by the deeper sciences and mechanisms. Entah is of noble blood, and would have been trained in the most secretive of arts." Selyni cocked her head to the side in question, and Maud explained, "The gnomes in my retinue are historians. They know such things and are confident in their assessment. What color is the concoction?"

Selyni eyed the ceiling of the hall, considering. She had seen him make hundreds, if not thousands, of variations. Thoughtfully, she said, "He seems most pleased when it turns white, but has never been happy with the result."

Maud grinned, and with excitement, whispered, "So the ambitious little creature is trying to recreate his people's famed Elixir of Life. I wonder if he does so willingly or by the command of Aritian?" She asked the air, looking past Selyni into the library.

"Elixir of Life?" Selyni asked, her brow creasing in wonder.

Maud's eyes flicked back to Selyni and filled with contempt. Acidic, she spat, "My word, for someone as well travelled as you, Selyni, you certainly haven't learned much." She adopted an overtly sweet voice, and asked, "Have you ever seen a young gnome?"

With a shrug of her slight shoulders, Selyni said, "Entah seems young."

Maud shook her head, and clarified, "No, I mean a babe." Selyni shook her head, she hadn't. Maud pointed toward Entah, and said blandly, "That gnome is more than twenty-thousand years old." Selyni shook her head in denial. *Such a thing is impossible*, she thought wildly. Maud insisted, "He wouldn't feel like he was or even know the truth. Gnomes go through cycles, a few hundred years they're awake, and then they hibernate for some thousands of years. When they rise from hibernation they have no memories beyond what they have recorded on paper and, as they migrate seemingly at random across the world, these recordings are often lost. The elixir is how they survive the suspended animation and extends their life span. It is one of the few notable pieces of knowledge that they retained from their homeland."

At Selyni's blank stare, Maud explained, "Adonim does not have the proper environment for successful gnome breeding, and they would have long ago gone extinct without it. My advisors say that it is very rare for more than one noble to be awake at any giving time. Currently, there are three active. This is a sign or turbulent times ahead." Selyni stared at Maud with glazed eyes, too stunned to speak.

Maud laughed arrogantly, before asking, "By Magrados, can't you recognize something not of this world? It stands before you there." She pointed once more to Entah. Selyni turned and looked. The blue-haired creature seemed normal enough to her. *Not of this world*, Selyni thought in awe, *where did the gnomes come from then?*

Selyni admitted, "I had no idea." She ached to ask Maud more, but knew the woman wasn't likely to elaborate. Maud enjoyed lording her superior knowledge over those she viewed as lesser.

"No, you didn't." Maud said, in clipped tones. "Entah will most likely fail. Do not concern yourself about him. I will consult my advisors and discern the threat he poses." Selyni nodded distractedly, still watching the gnome. Impatiently, Maud commanded, "Well, continue."

Selyni drug her eyes from the gnome, and said, "Rythsar trains the Dranguis, and does so with little regard to their person. I doubt very much that, at this pace, they will all survive."

Maud flicked a hand out dismissively, and said impatiently, "Only the strong deserve to. What of the Titans?"

Selyni shuddered at Maud's cold apathy and wished she was brave enough to protest further, but instead, said, "They train desperately. Azera seems to care little about the pain she inflicts upon her brother, but Ori is growing in skill quickly. He, much like the oldest of the Dranguis, has grown considerable. In a week, or less, he will tower over his sister. He's going to be large for a Titan." Selyni said, eying the tall blur that fled past her field of vision.

Maud nodded, smiling contently, before saying, "Good, good. I am pleased with your observations."

Maud made to turn away, but Selyni asked, "Maud, how did you get Aritian to agree to this, knowing the cost of such magic?"

Maud replied bluntly, and with little care, saying, "He doesn't know. He believes that giving up twelve-years of life is cost enough." She laughed, shaking her head, and said, "The boy is a fool, but he is young and by the time he emerges he may yet become wise."

Selyni felt as though the floor fallen out beneath her, as

her stomach twisted. In a disgusted whisper, she asked, "You lied to him?" Maud's smile held, unmoved. Selyni warned, "You will be sanctioned by the Coven for this."

Maud barked a laugh, and asked, "Who do you think gave me the idea?" Maud stepped closer, and her voice fell to a whisper, as she said, "The Archmagus is no fool. Do you really think he'd allow Caethe to deceive us, and that we would not put our own weapon into play?"

Selyni shook her head no, and asked, "Aritian has a pure soul, what makes you think he will join you?"

Maud's red-gaze found Aritian and she smiled with pride. She watched him for several minutes in silence. When she spoke, her voice was confident, "Aritian is my grandson. He is of Sanguis Nox. Besides, you have only to look to his father to see what kind of magic he will one day wield. The boy was born to darkness, his blood runs as black as my own."

Angrily, Selyni said, "You're wrong, Maud. When he learns the truth he will never forgive you." She knew Aritian was trying desperately to reform, that he wanted to become a good person, and was striving to leave his dark past behind. *He will not submit to your manipulation*, Selyni thought with brittle hope.

Maud replied simply, "We shall see." She wore a casual expression, as if the outcome meant little to her.

In a low whisper, Selyni cautioned, "The Albastella will pursue you, even if Aritian accepts the truth and all that you wish for him comes true."

Anger flicked across Maud's placid expression, and when she spoke, her voice filled with vehement passion, "We who choose the crooked path sit the Weirwood throne. It is by our strength we have survived through the Sundering and endured the following ages. Let the Albastella come. I will end them if they dare challenge me." Selyni bowed her head against the woman's might and stared at the floor, unable to meet Maud's terrible gaze.

"Show me. I must bear witness." Selyni said weakly.

Mildly, Maud nodded and said, "As you wish."

Maud led her across the hall to a staircase. The stairs swirled around and round, as they descended. When they walked into the shadow of the stairs an orb of fire materialized over Maud's shoulder. They walked down a hundred steps, and then another hundred more, before coming to a landing where a large iron door waited. Maud walked to it and placed her hand on its cool surface. The door glowed for a moment and then the light faded. Maud pulled the door open, and together they stepped within.

Selyni gasped in horror. Before her, a golden pentagram was inlaid across the red-marble floor. The room was cavernous, the edges of the room lost in darkness. In the circle's center was a thirteen-pointed star. At each point of the star was a raised altar. Men and women lay in slumber upon the stone beds, and at the center of the star whirled a spinning ball of emerald energy. The energy twisted like liquid and had a core of white. A beam of pure-white light shot from the energies center toward the ceiling above where another ball of energy waited, swirling in a second pentagram. The ceiling was bathed in red crackling lightning, and hummed with such ferocity that it shook stone and rattled her bones. White energy bled off of the human sacrifices, pulled from their chest's in a ghostly blur, swirling in a slow vortex toward the heart of the pentagram. Even as she watched those who lay on the altar's aged; their bodies growing thin and their skin darkening, as their faces grew lined and hollow. The stench of the room was copiously horrible.

Maud smiled as she drank in Selyni's horrified expression, and shouted over the hum of energy, "I didn't expect them all to join Aritian in the Time Vortex, and we've ran through quite a number of humans." Maud waved her hand through the air, and the orb of light flew across the room to hover over a pile of mummified corpses that had been thrown in a heap against the far wall. There were more than three-dozen bodies. Selyni cried out, clutching her mouth, as tears streamed down her face. Maud smiled wickedly in the brilliant glow of the Time Vortex.

Devaney

Chapter Thirty-One:

Lilith's Sweet Touch

Devaney sat nervously at the richly-dressed dining table, with a gilded plate of uneaten food before her. Worry gnawed at her stomach far more desperately then hunger. The decanter of wine sat half empty and she held a full goblet halfway to her mouth, but had not drank any for the last hour. She had been left here, in this gilded cage, for four days now. The morning had long fled and still she waited at the table.

A movement flicked in the corner of her eye. Devaney looked at the painting, and nearly gasped. A red-haired man slunk beneath the boughs of a willow tree. His movements were fugitive and fast. He had a thin face, and his green eyes flashed fearfully as he hunched beside a small brook. *What strange clothes*, Devaney thought, peering closer as she stood. The man was dressed in buckskin trousers, an open fur vest, and wore strange slippers that seemed to be made from some sort of animal hide.

Devaney walked to stand before the painting, as the man bent and slurped water from the stream. Tentatively, Devaney touched the canvas painting. The world spun then, and her vision twisted in a blur of pastel colors. When her sight cleared, Devaney found herself standing before a tall oak tree. The fox that seemed to perpetually play in the sunlight rolled over as it caught sight of her and dashed away into the woods, and the man spun, wide-eyed; water dripping down his chin.

"Hello there," Devaney said warmly. She offered a gentle smile as his head flicked side to side fearfully. "You're

Cinvanth, aren't you?" She asked, taking a step closer.

The man stood fully then, and his mouth twisted into a sour frown. Though he was rail thin, he towered over her.

"Why have you come?" He asked in a tense hush. Devaney made to walk across the small glade, and the man screamed, "No! Stay away!" He waved his hands in front of his face as he folded into a crouch.

Devaney froze in her steps. "I'm not going to hurt you," she promised emphatically.

The man peaked out from behind his hands and Devaney saw that tears streamed down his face. "You already have!" He accused in a strangled voice. He hugged himself, and began muttering under his breath.

Devaney looked around, confused. The forest seemed to go as far as her eyes could see, but there was something strange about the land. The trees had a blurred nuance to them and the stream that flowed behind the man seemed blurred almost. Devaney looked down at her hand and saw that her skin appeared patchy and smudged. *Almost as if I had been painted,* Devaney thought in realization. Her observations were broken as the man, barked, "Or have you forgotten?" Devaney shook her head, and Cinvanth moaned, "I told you what I knew of the Grails... I told you." He looked up at her then, his eyes bubbling with tears, and asked, "Why did you have to kill me? Why?!" His bottom lip trembled, and he hugged himself tighter, as he said, "I was helping you."

Devaney held her hands before her in a placating manner, and said, "I'm sorry..."

Cinvanth interrupted her, standing abruptly, his face suddenly swelling with a beaming smile. "You aren't her." He shouted, as if the thought had just dawned on him. "You aren't her!" He said again, as he did a little hop and jig.

Cinvanth began dancing beneath the willow tree. He grabbed some of the long branches that dripped from the tree, and swung himself around as he sang under his breath,

"A tridecagon star, magic old and new
Beneath the plumgrass dappled with eastern dew
The glyphs of Magrados will smite those reviled
The rays on Adonim will see it break
The star, the elder, the enemy's child
Such noble sacrifice they shall make..."

He's mad, Devaney thought. *I suppose I would be too, if I was stuck in such a place*, Devaney mused sadly, as she wondered how long the magus had been here. "I'm sorry, I don't know who you are talking about, but I certainly did not kill you Cinvanth. Please, I need your help."

The magus stopped swinging on the branch, and a look of such terrible anger fell across his face that Devaney felt herself take a step back. He pointed a thin, trembling hand at her, and screeched, "You asked me once before for help and look at what you've done! You locked me away, away, away. How can an artist work without the tools of his craft? All the centuries alone, all alone." He whimpered, as he was overcome by tears again.

Devaney shook her head, and said, "Cinvanth, please whoever hurt you, that isn't me. I swear it." She looked him in the eyes earnestly, trying to will the man into believing her. *This man had lived in the tapestries of Magistrate for who knows how long, surely he will know a way for me to escape*, Devaney thought desperately.

Cinvanth shook his head, and screamed, "No, there is only one reason why you'd come back. You want to do it again, don't you?" His expression grew dark as he accused, "Don't you?!"

Devaney held her hands wide, and said, "I don't know what you're talking about." Cinvanth made to speak, but Devaney shouted over him, "Please, listen. I am a captive of Ultan, the Archmagus. I'm being held here against my will. Tell me how to escape, please, tell me."

Cinvanth cocked his head to the side, his stringy hair falling over his face, as he asked, "You are trapped?"

Devaney sighed in relief, and nodded, saying, "I am."

Cinvanth clapped his hands gleefully, and said, "Good!" He chuckled manically, and said, "Good, serves you right. Now go away. Go!" He waved his hands at her, as if shooing her away, and said, "I helped you once before and it cost me everything. I hope this Ultan makes you suffer." He waved his hands again, and from his fingertips the very air began to swirl like wet paint.

Devaney could feel her vision twist, as the magus threatened to banish her from the dimension, and she yelled, "No please, you're mistaken..." Her mind did a mental twist and she found herself stumbling back from the tapestry. Devaney was back in her rooms.

Devaney sighed, and returned to her chair at the table. Cinvanth had lost his sanity in the untold centuries he had been kept prisoner in his own artistry, there was no doubt of that in Devaney's mind. *But who did he think I was?* She wondered. She grabbed her goblet, and took a sip of wine.

Suddenly, the doors to her apartments boomed open. Devaney jumped, spilling wine across the white-crocheted tablecloth. A woman sauntered into the apartment and the doors closed of their own accord behind her with a quiet snap. The woman was young and looked no older than Devaney herself. She was tall and had long free-flowing black hair that framed her heart-shaped, tanned face. She was dressed like a man, in loose black pants and a tight blouse of maroon silk that exposed the uppermost part of her full breasts. She sauntered in with confidence, swinging her hips in an easy, seductive manner. She smiled when she met Devaney's timid eyes.

The woman paused in her approach by the couch, and with narrowed eyes, said, "Aedus said something." It wasn't a question. Her voice was soft, high-pitched, and sounded like it belonged to a little girl. "Don't deny it. I can see the fear written across your face."

Devaney shakily set the goblet down. "I know your face." Devaney whispered, and indeed she had. She had seen this woman in one of her visions. "I know you, Lilith." Devaney said. As she named the woman, Devaney stood and painted on a brave expression as she met the woman's dark eyes.

Lilith pouted prettily and said, "Oracles truly are no fun. They take all the suspense out of life."

Devaney walked to the closest doorway, tracing her hand across the wall for support. The door led to a lavish bedroom. A heavy four-poster sat in the center of the room, and next to it lay a stone fireplace. A thick, green quilt stitched with a repetitive pattern of a phoenix lay across the bed, among supple furs made from strange animals she could not name. The dark fur was red, nearly russet in color, and the fur long and luxurious. Devaney imagined that the beast must have been large, for the fur was three times as long as she was tall. She sat lightly on the edge of the bed, with one hand braced against one of the bed's tall posts. The woman had followed her into the room and watched her from the doorway.

"Skipping to the best part I see?" Lilith asked, leaning against the doorway, a soft trilling chuckle escaping her red lips.

"There is little that I can do to stop you and I see no reason to try." Devaney reasoned dryly, and stared at her blinking with white, sightless eyes. Lilith's gaze flinched away, unnerved.

Staring at the stone floor, Lilith murmured, "I have nothing against you personally Devaney, and hope that you can understand why I must act as I do."

Devaney laughed, surprising both herself and Lilith. In a low voice, Devaney admonished, "Don't be coy now, Lilith. I know you enjoy it."

Lilith met her gaze and smiled, before admitting with a nod, "I suppose I do. I just want you to realize my position. I would never break the Accords by my own violation…"

"Nor would you defy Ultan." Devaney said interrupting her. Bravely, Devaney smiled. Internally, she screamed in panic, but she did not wish to waste the moment. Instead of letting a scream of fear escape her lips, she spoke in a self-assured whisper, "You stand there, putting on this show of the unwilling participant, because you know that if I survive this place you will have made a dangerous enemy."

Lilith grimaced, and whispered to herself, "I fucking despise Oracles." She frowned, considering a moment before nodding to herself, and pronouncing, "Due to the fraught times we live in, and the betrayal of Caethe, the Archmagus has commanded me, Lilith Circe Ann Ronan, to interrogate and search your mind for any treasonous thoughts or intent. Once cleared you will be free to join the Coven on equal standing, unburdened by any question of loyalty. If found guilty, you will be subjected and held in accordance to the law. Do you understand and comply with the Archmagus's command?" Lilith concluded in question, meeting Devaney's eyes.

Devaney smiled grimly, and said, "I do not comply. I do not submit. This is a breach of one of the nine Accords of the Sacred Commandment. By commanding such, Ultan himself is damned in the eyes of our people."

Lilith laughed, long and hard. When she stood upright and had her mirth under control, she gave Devaney a warm smile, and said, "I like you. In any other circumstance we would be fast friends." Devaney gave her a jerky nod. Lilith warned, "Prepare yourself, Devaney." Devaney met Lilith's eyes and saw her green gaze full of respect. It did little to quell Devaney's terror. Lilith nodded once, and all amusement fled her face. Lilith stepped forward and placed her hands on either side of Devaney's head. In a whisper, she said, "Don't resist, it will only make things more painful."

Without looking up, Devaney responded in a whisper, her breath already heavy with anticipation, "I will fight you with everything I have."

Lightning, pure black, radiated around Lilith's hands and Devaney's head tilted back as she let out a blood-curdling scream. Lilith's power tore through the flimsy shields of her mind like the claws of a wolf, and reached into her mind like insidious roots. Images flashed before her eyes.

Devaney reached up a hand to claw at Lilith, but the woman blinked once, and Devaney's hands slammed down to the bed. Lilith's control on her body was complete in its supremacy. Devaney had never known such fear, such constraint, or such overwhelming power in all her life. She mentally stilled her own fear. This was her first test. *I will not fail*, she promised herself mentally. Lilith's laugh rang through her mind.

Devaney did the only thing she could. She filled her mind with thousands of contradictory thoughts just as Caethe had taught her. He had warned her that should she ever feel Lilith's touch, she wouldn't stand a chance of resisting. Lilith grunted in annoyance, and dug deeper. Lightning crackled across Devaney's forehead burning her pale skin with a fiery bite. Devaney screamed again, and it was as if her mind was being torn apart by thousands of tiny needles. Lilith worked methodically, peeling away layers of thoughts and delving deeper to where she knew the prophecy lay. Devaney's breath came sharp and labored. She would have fought the woman physically if she could, but Lilith allowed no such movement.

They battled one another for hours, Lilith clawing deeper, peeling layer after layer back with cold precision, and Devaney bombarding the Inquisitor with random, nonsensical trite that muddied the memories. When it ended, neither was satisfied. Lilith dropped her sweat-soaked hands from Devaney's head and stepped back.

Devaney fell back on the bed, her chest heaving as she caught her breath. Her head felt as if it had been struck over and over with a hammer. The pain was beyond imaginable. She heard the receding footsteps of Lilith, and Devaney's heart sang with relief. Gingerly, she touched her forehead and gasped as pain rolled across her forehead at the slight touch. Tears fell down her cheeks and for a moment she let herself dissolve into a fit of self-pity. She submitted to it fully, wailing softly as she tore at the beds rich silk dressing. Pain seared through her eyes suddenly, and her back arched upward as her power thundered through her in a wave that gagged her with exquisite pain.

A wagon rolled through crowded streets, drawn by four prancing stallion's dressed in black and white parade apparel. Circling the wagon was a cohort of smartly-dressed soldiers who kept the crowd from overturning the wagon, but did little else. The street was wide and lined on either side with well-kept, four-storied grey buildings, and snaked through a maze of twists and turns. Devaney felt vertigo clutch her stomach as she soared through the air at a rapid rate.

Beneath her the street was filled with thousands of people. The crowd's faces, young and old, men and women, rich and poor, wore the same mask of twisted anger. They screamed in a roar of collective hate. As the wagon passed, the crowd pushed forward with furious intent, their eyes filled with hysterical malice. Stones, shit, and vegetables pelted the wagon in a steady torrid.

The wagon bed carried a large metal cage and within, a man crouched. He was a dirty thing, covered in filth and weeping cuts. His dark hair was twisted in sweat-drenched bands, despite the chilled fog his breath produced. His green eyes glimmered with fever. The only adornments the man wore was an amber collar, and silver shackles that circled his wrists and ankles that were studded with orange stones.

Caethe leered at the people with contempt. With bestial fury, he rattled the bars of the cage, screaming with a hoarse voice, "All of you are dead by my hand. Fuck the Ordu. I will murder your god. I will kill your kin." He spat into crowd, and the crowd shrank back in horror. "You're all dead." A stone smashed into his forehead, cutting the skin above his eye with a nasty gash. "You will feel my wrath soon, zealot pigs!" Caethe promised wrathfully, as he wiped the blood from his eyes and flung red droplets into the crowd. Women screamed and children cried in fear.

Devaney broke from the vision screaming.

Aritian

Chapter Thirty-Two:

The Singular Pursuit of Power

Aritian stepped within the circle that was inlaid on the floor before the pillar of red light. The pentagram was a simple seven-pointed star. Dimly, in the back of his mind, Aritian registered the sounds around him and out of the corner of his eye, saw his companions moving about the room. He did not care. He discarded the distractions as useless.

His eyes were wide and brimmed red, and sweat lay across his brow. He raised his left hand, and an orb that floated at the top of the pillar began to glow fiercely. Aritian nudged it gently with his power, and the orb flew from the light to his palm.

The candles at each point of the star bloomed awake in unison, their yellow light flashing, before settling quietly. A shield of silver energy snapped along the edge of the circle and arched over Aritian's head, encompassing him in its protective power. The surface of the shield was translucent, but dappled with a frosty shimmer of sheer-silvery liquid that moved in languid swirls.

Aritian took comfort in the isolation the shield as welcoming silence enveloped him. Aritian closed his eyes and found himself before a door that arched above him, suspended in darkness. White, the door was made of crystal, but was illuminated from within by a pulsating red gleam. The current of the magic quickened as he drew closer and light bled along the edges of the door, ever reaching, seeking his touch. Aritian felt himself smile. Only in the security and seclusion of the Haven Circle was did he permit himself to crack the door, and taste the saccharine touch of his power.

Aritian laid a hand on the door's surface, and magic crawled along the doors edge collecting around his palm before shooting through his arm. It was both painful and titillating. Like lightning in ice, it raged through his arm, biting with raw cold that made his back arch with sweet pleasure. Aritian pulled his arm from the door and opened his eyes. Dark heady power rolled across his pupils, clouding them with an inky river of magic.

Aritian brought the Remembrance Orb close to his face and studied the dark purple crystal. He let his eyes trace the complex lines that filled the refracting, multifaceted structure. Aritian let a stream of power flow between his fingertips and dance upon the Orbs surface. Crimson light filled the mirrored facets and Aritian felt his mind do a mental twist as his consciousness fell into the confines of the Orb.

Aritian found himself standing in a crystalized tower, hexagonal in shape. He looked down and saw hundreds of mirrors that rippled with ruddy light. The ceiling rose above him, soaring, before ending in a sharp peak. Light illuminated the apex of the ceiling with such intensity that the crystal tower was filled with harsh, stark-whiteness.

Before him, a man stood dressed in black robes. His form was nebulous and nearly as translucent as the crystal around them. He wore an ancient style of robes that met the floor, and each shoulder of the robe came to a point that was capped with a metal spike. He wore a black, wide-brimmed hat that ended in a point, and in one hand held a black staff that was capped by an electric-blue crystal. The man's face was angular, almost feline in nature, with a scar that ran from the corner of his left eye to the top of his lip — the only mar on his otherwise handsome face. Brilliant green eyes studied Aritian lazily and his thin lips curled with an arrogant smile.

The man spoke with a rich, bold voice. "I am Nagfari, first son of Mangus. Despite being born to the sacrilegious defiler, who we call Archmagus, I have the delectable distinguish of having Sanguis of Nox running through my veins, thanks to my dear mother, Circe. I have committed to this Orb my memories and instruction in the dark arts. We will begin on the subject of the Astral Realms and the varied wonders of walking the innumerable warrens. Who comes before me to learn the craft?" Nagfari asked, his tone imperious.

Aritian's bland disposition withered, and a cold calculating desire bloomed in his heart. Aloofly, he thought, *walking physically among the realms was impossible now, but to have knowledge of such an ancient practice could prove applicable in many other ways.*

Aritian smiled cruelly, and gave the magus a short nod of respect. "I, Aritian Ronan, come to learn all the knowledge that you possess."

Nagfari returned his short bow of his own. The form before him had no conscious mind and was simply a memory placed within the Orb so that future generations could learn from the ancients long passed. It was one of several ways that Ronan perpetuated their knowledge through the ages, the laborious and masterful feat of creating a Remembrance Orb.

Aritian eyed the man critically before him. Nagfari had been young when he created the orb; Aritian could see youth bubbling in the man's arrogant gaze, but still, even in his calculating state, he begrudgingly admired him.

The memory spoke, "I trust that you stand before me, of Sanguis of Nox, in good faith." Aritian made no reply. He knew that in ancient times the Ronan were a divided people who guarded their knowledge and power with jealous avarice. It would be sacrilegious for one outside of their own Order to receive such teaching. This however, fell out of practice after the Great Sundering, which belied the antiquity of the Remembrance Orb. Aritian had yet to pledge his heart or mind to any one faction, and instead studied all he could find in Maud's collection.

Nagfari began the lecture, "To travel the Astral realms is not something one can do with cavalier abandon, but instead must be done only in times of great peril or need. A detailed knowledge of all realms must be understood before attempting this form of travel, for the realms are not bound by the laws of Adonim and each are uniquely different.

Nagfari turned on his heel, and let his heavy gaze fall upon Aritian, before clarifying softly, "By this, I mean that each of the realms are incompatible with the necessary elements and groundings for human or Ronan survival." The man raised an eyebrow when he said this, and smirked. Aritian felt a corner of his lip curl, and he thought knowingly, *in other words, you mean that to travel there unprepared is to risk sinking to the depths of the Abyss.*

Nagfari began to pace, his form rippling slightly as the light shone through his translucent body. "The realms are where what we call Demons, Daemons and Diamons originate from." *Man's devils, angels, djinni, ghouls, imps, and fiends*, Aritian thought with contempt. The humans had dozens of words to describe the indescribable. Aritian preferred the practical approach of the Ronan to the dogmatic, ignorant classifications of the masses.

Nagfari paused in his speech, and his hands spun through the air. Light trailed after his fingers as his hands weaved, and hung there when his hands grew still. Before them were thirteen glowing orbs, representing the worlds tied to the Astral Realms. Thicker lines of light held them in position as they whirled slowly around thirteen, flat discs that represented the individual Astral Realms. With a last wave of his hand, tiny runnels of light fled through it all, like knotted string, until the worlds and realms were lost beneath a mass of woven light.

Aritian watched, stunned, for he had never seen such a straightforward example of the galaxy before. Even in his detached state he knew he was witnessing a great truth, one that seemed lost to the world of Adonim. Aritian smiled with lust as he drank in the knowledge before him.

Nagfari touched the nest of light, unraveling a length, as he continued his lecture, "These realms are connected to one another by thousands of warrens, and each of these are singular as well. A comprehensive knowledge must be known of the perils one might face before entering unknown or little-traveled warrens for many gods erect their domains herein. The realms are beyond mortal understanding, but a Magi can find sources of great power here."

The memories expression grew serious as he waved a hand, dispelling the galaxy of light. He crossed his arms, and warned, "Beware, for these places are where the very gods walk, and few who come upon them survive to tell the tale."

Nagfari smiled dangerously, and butted the end of his staff to accentuate his next words, "To travel there with your conscious mind is a perilous task, which requires a vast number of safeguards, protections, and an innate ability. This takes years of study and practice, and should only be attempted after receiving your full status as a magi of the Coven."

Nagfari held up a hand of warning, and said, "Should you find yourself drawn there in your dreams, be calm." He smiled disarmingly, and explained, "This often takes place when one is young and untrained. I counsel all who find themselves beyond their physical body without proper training to stay in one position until you wake. Seek out your mentor or the closest Master of the arts for the learnings of grounding one's soul, and your wandering mind shall cease to move beyond without your explicit will. The magicks are a learned art that must be dictated by a calm and measured mind."

Nagfari's voice grew whimsical, as if he spoke of a treasured memory. "What I speak of now is an entirely different animal. To walk the realms with your physical body is something only an adept at the height of their power should ever dare to attempt. Should you fail, the consequences are worse than death." A cruel smile touched his lips when he said this, and advised softly, "I caution any novice or even master leveled magus against such practices, and suggest returning to the idea only once you've reached the highest form of your art and passed the Adept trials." Nagfari paused dramatically, and his expression grew stern. It was as if he found these cautionary statements boring and Aritian smiled, feeling a kinship with the man.

Nagfari adopted his lecturing voice again, and said, "The most basic understanding of the realms can be described easily. There are six ascending and six descending realms, with a single realm between. The realm between is known as Umbrael and connects all others by warren or gate. Umbrael is special, for it is the realm that directly connects Magrados to our world, Adonim. Many ecclesiastical institutions group these realms into two broad categories: Heaven and Hell." Nagfari turned to raise an elegant, brown eyebrow in skepticism, but the memory chuckled.

"This is, of course, is an overly simplified and quite ignorant classification," he continued on. "Although, this base understanding does give indication to the nature of the planes you might find yourself within. The realms are known as such, in order from the lowest hell to highest heaven: The Abyss, Inferno, Somnumexteri, Barathrum, Tenebrosaqa, Igris, The Sea of Aelfmae, Umbrael, Avalon, Requiem of Uventae, The Celestial Realm, Cerulean Fires, Castitate, and The Zenith Crown." Aritian found himself nodding, he had knowledge of each, and he found himself sighing. *It seems Nagfari was a man who enjoyed the sound of his own voice*, Aritian thought, resigning himself to the long lecture.

One of the few downfalls of learning from Remembrance Orbs was that you could not interact with the memories or communicate your own knowledge. The lectures were as long as they were and there were no shortcuts that could be found.

"To travel to any realm, one must first enter the Shadow Realm..."

Aritian found himself thinking of the man lecturing, rather than the lesson at hand. Nagfari was a man from a different age and the more Aritian thought of the name the more details bubbled to the surface of his mind — son of Mangus, the most powerful Magi to ever grace the lands of Adonim. Mangus and Jyre, along with the Trinity following a prophecy, bore sixteen children in hopes of defeating the Dark Lady without shattering of the Bridge of Magrados. They had failed.

Alas, Aritian found himself annoyed with his limited knowledge, and resigned to discovering more about him. Nagfari seemed both confident and elegant, and his understanding of the deeper powers was evident. Aritian wondered what brought the intelligent magi to his downfall.

It was like that, in this state. His unconscious mind, the Magrados, seemed to know what he needed to learn far more than what logical thought could dictate. Aritian had let the power guide him from one subject to the next. He was a leaf in a hurricane of knowledge and he freely let himself be thrown hither and there, all the while growing in the art that was named magic.

Aritian blinked his eyes owlishly as his vision returned to the library. The shield fell around him with a hiss and the candles were extinguished in a curl of smoke that held a cinnamon scent commingled with the harsh bite of pine. Aritian breathed in the potent yet refreshing fragrance, clearing his mind. He stood, stretching his cramped legs.

In a sharp voice, he called, "Entah." The gnome looked up from his work table, and Aritian commanded, "Entah, pull anything on Nagfari Ronan, sixth age, son of Mangus. Concentrate on scripts that focus on his demise."

The gnome nodded, leaving a smoking beaker, and walked stiff-legged to the shelf. The floor was littered with Grimoires, and discarded books that either Entah or himself had read. The closest one lay on its spine, wide open. It had yellowed pages and tiny diagrams drawn with meticulous care. Aritian flipped it closed with his foot, and read the title, *Ten Thousand Applications for the Common Gemstone*, by Glenda Ambrosia Ronan. Aritian had flipped through the tome and found it derivative of half dozen older manuscripts, but it did hold the dubious distinction of holding the vast majority of collections bound in a single book. Closed now, the tome was almost as thick as his knee was tall.

While Aritian waited, he closed his eyes. In his mind's eye he stood before a black-stone maze that raced for miles in every direction. Aritian stood above it on a hill, and raised his hand. The walls to the east rose, pulled from the depth of his consciousness as they twisted into the air. He exerted his will and they began unfolding upon themselves, expanding and racing across the darkness of his mind. He raised his hands and they doubled back, springing upwards as they raced across his vision to the west and then back again. Over and over, he concentrated on raising the bulwarks outside the center of himself, until he had created a labyrinth of dizzying proportions.

He raised his hands and the walls he created trembled. They grew until they soared a thousand feet in the air. Holes burst from the newly formed towers, and stone shattered as he created a dizzying path of tunnels through the thick walls. Shafts melted in the interior, dripping downward, ensuring that any intruder would be thrown to the open air above a bed of spikes that spread across a field like upright lances. Above it all, the door to his power rose, growing greater with every moment that passed.

Aritian blinked three times and the air around the door burst with dazzling sparks of light as he freed motes of power. His battlements expanded with it, and he began weaving nets of power that circled the maze, some unseen, while others glowed with murky redness; one in the same, they promised death to all who dared enter uninvited. Tighter and tighter, he weaved spells, and each strand vibrated with a deadly trap, quivering with potent power. *No one will touch my power, but me. No one,* he thought with grim satisfaction.

Aritian blinked three times and fell out of his trance. The gnome stood before him. Aritian did not know much time had passed, nor did he care. The gnome bowed his blue head and held a tome before him. Aritian waved a hand for him to speak. The gnome's pale, lapis-colored skin was nearly ivory with exhaustion, and his black lips were cracked. In a hoarse voice, Entah said, "Nagfari never met the embrace of the Hooded One."

Aritian did not respond with surprise, rather he nodded in acceptance. Aritian inquired, "If he did not die, then what fate did he share? He is no longer a Ronan." Aritian said this with confidence. He knew this, for he had read Maud's recorded recollection in a catalogue that detailed all surviving known Ronan and their personal histories. He chuckled, wondering if they knew she kept such detailed archives.

Entah nodded in agreement, and recited, "Nagfari was one of the Magi who betrayed Mangus and the Allies of Light. He joined the forces of the Dark Lady and eventually became a Lich Lord of great power. During the rite of corruption, he died, becoming undead and far greater than any common Ronan."

Aritian raised an eyebrow at this. To choose such a path was beyond thought. Even in his manipulated state, his mind flinched away from such an act. It was reprehensible, abhorrent to Magrados.

Entah continued without pause, "It is said that his very presence was enough to turn a battle during the Blood Wars, as men would fall to despair and flee the field at the very sight of him." Entah said this dispassionately, concluding with, "Maud has noted in the margins that she believes he lays in slumber, hidden from the light of day in some dark hole, waiting for his mistress to wake." Entah pointed with a long black nail to a spiky-script that ran along the side of the page. A circle had been drawn next to her comments and an arrow pointed north. Aritian nodded, and waved the gnome away.

Aritian returned to his place within the pentagram, and for a month did not move from his position. When he finally did rise, he wore a grin. It was not a smile of warmth, but one of devious excitement. He looked across the library searching. When his eyes fell upon the seven men who spared against one another to his left, his smile grew broader. Aritian did not recognize them, but out of his peripheral vision and at some deeper level he had been aware of their growing skill in arms.

They will do, Aritian remarked silently.

Lifoy

Chapter Thirty-Three:

The Ladies of Nimfrael

The forest of Nimfrael stretched west nearly three hundred miles in a blanket of evergreen trees. Even now, as fall touched the land, miles and miles of greenery sprawled between the pale Igidum Sea and the murky-blue waters of the Chalice Sea. The forest was ancient, greater than its sisters of common ilk, for it had been touched by enchantment. Here, the trees grew densely and towered to impressive heights while their roots sought ever-deeper depths. Lifoy had left Shades Island and flown to the rolling hills of Pontees. He had reached the forest's edge within a week, and had flown tirelessly west for the past three days.

In avian form his eyes were sharp and he easily spied the Palace of Gemma hidden in a break of canopy. From the ground, however, it would seem as though the castle had appeared out of nowhere. He spied twisting spires of elegant grey stone and dipped below the tallest two, banking to the left to circuit the structure. A snaking wall, bent and bowed around trees, guarded the small city in a misshapen circle. Tall pines stood just within the walls, and still deeper in, were permitted to sparsely fill courtyards to further betray the eye. It was a brilliant defensive design, and one that made finding the city devilishly hard. The outer wall was made from roughly-hewn stone that was covered in sheets of lichen and bearded with green moss. fortifications, disguised as rocky outcrops, guarded the hidden gate.

Lifoy giggled to himself and folded his wings. He dropped from the sky and flew faster than an arrow between two towers, and heard men shouting in surprise behind him. *No doubt the lax guards cursing their own laziness*, he thought smugly. He gracefully glided over a battlement and landed lightly in the castles central-most courtyard. Nimfrael was the easternmost kingdom of the U.F.K, and he would have to deal with them first before moving onward.

Soldiers filled the battlements and cleverly hidden arrow slots that lay along the grey stone tower nearest him. Soon the walls of courtyard bristled with arrows all aimed at the Roc who had so brazenly landed in the heart of their home. Lifoy preened casually, rustling and flapping his wings as he did, sending gales of wind rushing through the courtyard. A horn was sounded, clear and bright, as Lifoy settled himself. In the distance, he could hear the clank of armor as men raced through the small city toward the interior.

Five women burst from an arched entry at the base of the tower. They were all dressed in fine gowns colored in spring, but one and all held longswords gripped in their pale hands. They were women beyond beauty, as only those with elven blood could be, with fair features and impressive stature. As they came upon him their steps slowed, eying his mammoth size. Two of the women had dark hair that streamed down their back, while one had hair pale as the moon, and the last pair wore brilliant, fiery locks. They shared similar features as only sisters would. *They're pretty, but still quite dull compared to myself*, Lifoy sighed.

One of the brunette half-bloods raised her hand, preparing to command her men to loose a volley. Lifoy groaned and thought, *Always in such a hurry*. His beak dipped and his wings hunched as he relaxed his hold on the form of the Roc. Rapidly, but with excruciating pain, he twisted into his true form. Lifoy stood before them within seconds, nude, shaking white down feathers from his long hair.

Soldiers began to curse and shout with fear, but the woman who had nearly instructed them to attack forestalled them with a single command, "Lay down your weapons and return to your posts. We are visited by a Ronan. There is nothing to fear."

Lifoy smiled at her confidence, and to his surprise, the men retreated without a word of protest.

"I am Lady Yamiel," she said before turning to her left and introducing the rest of her brethren. "These are my sisters," she gestured to the other raven-haired woman, and listing, "Lady Raelwyn," then to the pale-haired half-blood, "Lady Caereena," and finally to the fiery redheads, "Lady Ugrael and Lady Netheria."

Lifoy gave them a deep bow, and said, "I am honored to be in your esteemed presence. I am Lifoy Ronan of Shades Island." The women each gave him a respectful nod; these were queens in their own right and he expected nothing more. Ugrael and Netheria still held their swords at the ready. As he eyed the naked steel, he smiled casually, and said, "Ladies of Nimfrael, I come before you to humbly offer you a most handsome proposition."

Lady Yamiel did not smile, and coldly, she asked, "What is it you wish of us, Changeling of Magrados?"

Lifoy bristled at her impetuousness, and raised an eyebrow, as he said stiffly, "I see that you are short on time and cannot indulge in pleasantries, but no matter, I will speak bluntly. One of you will marry the King of Agos and stand as the sole monarch, and thus voice of Nimfrael."

Immediately the women exclaimed in anger.

Ugrael took a step forward and leveled her sword at his heart, asking hotly, "You dare presume to give us orders?"

Lifoy smiled broadly, and rested his pointer finger on the tip of the sword. "I know your story, Semumrae." Ugrael's face paled with anger, hearing the elven term that described her watered-down blood. Lifoy continued casually, "I am a patient man, but I confess myself unaccustomed to such impropriety." He flicked his finger down and the sword clattered to the floor.

He had flung it from her tight grasp with little thought. Her mouth opened and closed, as she glared at him, enraged.

Netheria stepped to her sister's side, and stood in a defensive pose. In a scathing whisper, she challenged, "Excuse me? What did you just say?"

Lifoy put his hands on his hips, and said dryly, "I said you're being rude. You should speak with care when a Ronan stands in the heart of your house."

Ugrael gripped her sister's arm as if to keep herself upright. In a bold voice, she yelled, "Threats will not..."

Yamiel cut her off, saying, "Silence sisters, be calm." She stepped next to Ugrael and Netheria's side to put an arm before them, shielding their anger. With a serene smile, she asked diplomatically, "Why do you come, honored Ronan, to our humble home bearing such dire tidings? Surely, you can see have been on edge as of late. The threat of Ordu looms near, and in our position, one can never be too careful when entertaining an unknown guest."

Lifoy replied soberly, "It is for that very reason I have come. King Paul of Agos stands alone while the rest of the U.F.K bickers among themselves, nitpicking over the number of men you'll each provide, taxation sanctions, and other frivolous nonsense. You need to unite and now, before the full force of Ordu gathers."

The anger slowly faded from the women's faces. Ugrael and Netheria sheathed their swords as Yamiel gave them a slight nod.

Lifoy spread his arms congenially. "I know this is all a little unorthodox, and that each of you is respected and honored by your people, but Nimfrael calls for one voice." He added ruefully, "Besides, if one of you agree, Paul will have two queens — I rather doubt that he could handle six."

Caereena glided forward, and while she spoke softly, her ire was evident. "Two queens? Explain fully, magus. Our patience is coming to a rapid end."

Lifoy bowed to her and when he straightened, he explained at length the plan that Devaney had set forth. By the end of his tense update, the fury in their expressions had dwindled until they were pale and thoughtful.

Yamiel asked, "Why would we consent to this, besides the reasoning that the U.F.K needs a united voice?" She glanced to her sisters who crowded close to either side, and said with honesty, "I do not believe that any of us would be willing to step aside."

Caereena's pink lip curled into a sneer, and with barely concealed disgust, she said, "Especially to share rule with a mere man."

Lifoy beamed at them, and said brightly, "Ah, my delightful friends, I thought that might be a tiny concern. You see, the lady who remains will actually gain the least, I believe, for those who step aside will be offered great sanctuary."

There was quiet as the women waited for him to elaborate. Lifoy enjoyed the tension too much, however, and waited until one asked warily, "Sanctuary? Where?"

Lifoy's pleasant smile grew even wider. "Within the Ilvarsomni forests, of course."

The women gasped. They understood immediately the gravity of the gift he offered, and could hardly believe his words.

Ugrael shook her head in denial. She whispered, "You cannot promise that."

Netheria's mouth tightened in a grimace. She spoke with blatant disbelief, "Lord Gythlear will never permit it."

"How can you speak with the King's voice?" Caereena asked stepping forward, her blue eyes wet with hope.

Lifoy raised a hand, and said cheerfully, "Ah, I see the prospect excites you! I said I knew your story. It is of my opinion that you should not have to bear the shame of your father, and as I am a Ronan, my voice carries heavily in the leafy, sylvan halls. I can and will secure your sanctuary, but only if," he held up one finger as he promised, "one remains in exile."

The half-bloods retreated to stand in a small tight circle, and conferred in animated whispers. After a few minutes, Yamiel approached him. She gave him a full, deep curtsey, and said with polite warmth, "My sisters and I will be discussing your proposal at length. Thank you for your efforts, Ronan friend; your journey has been long, so for now, please let us ease your burdens."

The kindness in their offer swelled in Lifoy's chest, and he nodded in grateful acceptance of their hospitality.

*****

By the next morning, he took flight just as the sun began to rise. *You're welcome Paul*, Lifoy thought smugly, as his wings carried him over the treetops.

The allegiance of the first kingdom had been won, but there were five more to visit.

Devaney

Chapter Thirty-Four:

The Tomb of Toutha 'Da Fae

Devaney sat before a roaring fire, staring with detachment at the dancing flames. She was dressed in a simple white shift that she had found in the chest that laid at the foot of her bed, and around her shoulders hugged a brown, bear-skin throw. It had been three days since Lilith had come and she had been left in seclusion since. Devaney did not know what Lilith had gained, but she did know that the woman hadn't obtained all that she wished.

She had tried to find Cinvanth in the painting afterwards, but found the glade empty. Even the small, red fox had fled. Devaney wished that the warmth of the fire could reach her, but she remained cold. Thoughts flew through her mind like a snow flurry. She could not quell the storm within, but outwardly she held a placid expression that gave nothing of her inner turmoil.

The doors opened, but Devaney did not look up. A man nearly seven-feet in height stepped into the room, strange in appearance. *This one is not fully human,* Devaney thought knowingly. The man had a more pronounced skull than was common to man, with bone-white skin, and twin horns that curved above his brow. He was hairless — both his head and face were smooth with a thick, muscular stature. He glared down at her with inky black eyes that were shaped like a snake's. To her he looked more akin to a military man then a magus, dressed as he was in a sweeping red cape lined with white fur over a smart, black uniform. At his belt her wore a sheathed broadsword, and sticking out of his boot, Devaney saw the golden hilt of a dagger.

"You must come with me, girl." The man said in a voice that was startlingly deep. His shadow loomed over her as he stepped close.

Devaney let her eyes flick upward, but did not let them rest upon the man. She knew now that they didn't know she could see, and so she let her gaze hang too far to the left, toward the mantle that sat above the fireplace.

She let a cool smile cross her face as she dipped her head in greeting and finally said, "Welcome to my prison cell, Lorchan." Devaney's smile broadened as he stiffened in surprise, and she said, "Bastard child of a Dracadalis, born from the corruption of Calnimor himself and the seed of a Ronan." Devaney smiled, and whispered, "Few can claim such a lineage, My Lord."

Lorchan looked at her with muted shock. His overly long tongue flicked out in a nervous habit, but he did not remain shaken long. In a growling voice, he warned, "If you know of me, Oracle, then you know it would be best for you to comply willingly, and not force my hand."

Devaney sighed heavily and stood. Lorchan gave her a nod, and with a heavy arm on her shoulder, led her from the room. He guided her through the decadent halls for what must have been an hour. They passed by a few servants here and there. Men and women who wore grey uniforms stamped with the sigil of the phoenix, but their numbers were surprisingly sparse for such a large place. Devaney walked without truly seeing.

Internally, she was fearful, and her heart pounded in her chest. Lorchan did not speak to her once nor did his hard grip lessen as they walked. They rounded a bend and came upon a flock of richly dressed courtiers that milled in the hallway, having just spilled out of a large reception hall. Devaney spotted more than a dozen sigils and crests, denoting houses far and wide across the breath of Adonim. *Ultan is mustering his allies*, she thought knowingly. Lorchan paused, waiting for the nobles to notice them. When they did their reactions were one in the same. Fear lanced across their expressions, and they bowed or curtsied before him with sudden silence.

Devaney's eyes flicked desperately through the crowd and found the pale-sapphire eyes of a young woman. The woman was short and dressed in a dark, navy gown that clung to her form before blooming at the floor in an expansive train of delicate lace. She was pale, but her cheeks were flushed red and she held features as delicate as a doe. She was more beautiful than any person Devaney had ever seen in her life.

Devaney smiled when she spied the long, pointed ears that sat delicately beneath the net of gold that contained her dark hair. The woman met her gaze steadily, unflinching. Devaney closed her eyes, projecting a torrid of thoughts across the hall. The woman stumbled back a step, confused, and her eyes flashed with sudden fear. When Devaney's thoughts stilled, the elfin maiden nodded with a slight bow, turned, and strode down the hall without a word. The dignitaries around her watched her flee, whispering questioningly to one another.

Lorchan shoved Devaney forward, making her trip a few steps as the courtiers scurried from his path. They walked for several more minutes until they passed beneath an archway. The room was bare, and Devaney soon realized that the space was merely an oversized landing. She was coming to realize that everything here in Magistrate castle was overly-done and larger than life.

Lorchan grumbled at her side, "We shall descend stairs in a few steps, take my hand." He commanded. Devaney reached her hand out before her, and Lorchan took it wrapping her entire hand in his thick grasp. His skin felt strange, and as they walked forward Devaney tried to think of why.

"Step down." He said, guiding her into darkness. The stairwell was twisting and they walked in silence for twenty minutes ever-downward. There were no more landings. Torches on the walls whispered quietly every thirty steps or so, their light meager in such oppressive darkness.

Torchlight fell upon Lorchan's hand as she stepped gingerly down a narrow step. With a soft gasp, Devaney suddenly realized that his skin was not like a man's, but made up of minuscule scales. *A gift from his mother, I suppose,* Devaney thought in wonder. She had heard rumor of strange creatures beyond the Grey Mountains as a child, but never in her wildest dreams did she ever think that she would one day meet the product of one. *Pa always said that only fools crossed the narrow path to the north side of the mountain, where fell devils reigned and winged men haunted,* Devaney thought, lost in memory. She remembered the long winters where the snow had grown too deep for them to leave, and her father's tales of beasts and magic. They had thrilled her as a child, *but seem more and more real every day,* she thought grimly. *Oh, how I miss you Pa,* she ached.

"The steps are at an end." Lorchan pronounced into the darkness some minutes later. The stone steps gave way to a bare, dirt floor. The walls and ceiling were rounded, and filled with ribbons of thick, white roots. The air was musky and smelled stale so far beneath the ground. "We enter the catacombs now," Lorchan said, before leading her forward through one of the nine open tunnels that faced the landing. There were no torches here; instead, a small orb of red flame bloomed to the left of Lorchan's head and hovered there, bobbing softly. The light was weak, and only illuminated a few steps before them. Mentally, Devaney committed to memory that they walked through the third tunnel from the left.

Lorchan led her down a winding maze. The floor was rolling, falling first downward and then inclining. Several times she found herself tripping on a raised root, only to have Lorchan steady her. The large half-breed was surprisingly gentle and didn't rush her now that they were beneath ground. The tunnel splintered off dozens of times, but Lorchan led her unerringly through them, turning down a tunnel, passing half a dozen openings then doubling back. The deeper they walked, the more Devaney realized that she couldn't hope to remember all of the turns and twists as her memorized map grew haphazard. After an hour of walking she abandoned the effort. Fear clutched her then and she thought, *I'll never escape this place.*

Lorchan turned down a tunnel that sat against the dirt wall to her left, and they walked a dozen paces until they came to a large, circular room. Dozens of dark tunnels led to the room, their shadowed maws wide with devious promise. When they came to the center of the room, Lorchan spoke in a whisper, his voice tinged by reverence, as he said, "Here lays the Tomb of the Toutha 'Da Fae, the westernmost Sidhe of the Shining Folk." Devaney looked around stunned. So deep beneath the ground, shadows held reign here. Even Lorchan's meager magelight barely penetrated the gloom, but in the scant light Devaney could see a domed, gold-leaf ceiling glinting softly overhead and altars interred beneath a blanket of dust.

Those that rested their heads upon the massive slabs of black-stone were lost beneath twisting roots, their forms hidden from all eyes, but Devaney ascertained that the creatures were far taller than man.

"You shall remain here," Lorchan said, stepping away from her.

Lorchan's pale hands curled before twitching in a quick pattern that belied the eye. The ground began to rumble and tremor, as roots snaked closer, twisting this way and that along the floor like a hundred snakes. Devaney stepped back, her eyes wide with fear. Roots suddenly burst from the ground and reached toward her like pale, clawed hands. She screamed as the roots caught her wrists and began to twists around her arms painfully. The roots retreated suddenly, yanking her to the floor and Devaney smashed face-first into the ground. She coughed, spitting dirt as the roots entwined tighter, cutting into her skin. When she was finally able to sit up, Lorchan was gone. In the darkness she struggled against the roots, sitting on her backside trying to yank them free, but there was no hope of escape. The roots were ancient and strong, and bound her as surely as iron shackles.

Selyni

Chapter Thirty-Five:

Sentinel of Immorality

Selyni scrutinized the library beyond the glowing doorway with growing horror. She had not moved for the past two days as she watched those within the Time Vortex. Her pupils were dilated and wide. Dark circles hung heavy beneath her eyes, and she gripped the edge of her chair with such panic that her nails bit into the wood. She wanted to scream, to call out, to put an end to this sacrilege, but she knew if she tried Maud would not hesitate to remove her from the equation.

"You called for me?" Maud whispered behind her. Selyni was not startled, for she was beyond fear.

Selyni nodded in reply, not taking her eyes off of the room before her. In a whisper, she said, "Yes, this must end now. Aritian has spent the last several weeks preparing some spell. I fear he means to do something terrible."

"What has you so terrified?" Maud asked amused.

Selyni eyed the pentagram Aritian had drawn. It crawled along the left side of the library. The edges of the circle were lined with complex runes of power, and within the circle he had drawn a seven pointed star. At each of the stars points stood Hui, Shan, Sicaroo, Rong, Mingyo, Bo, and Yi. The boys' youth had fled and hard men stood in their place. They wore expressionless masks, and stood motionless with faces painted with black lines of script. The pentagram had been drawn in blood: Aritian's.

"I think he is attempting a binding." Selyni described what she saw, and then added, "In the center of the pentagram he has seven dead snakes. I can't tell what kind they are. They died a long time ago." Selyni's voice grew more desperate, and she said, "Maud, you were wrong. Entah succeeded in creating his elixir. Aritian stands in the center now and holds a decanter full of it."

Selyni heard Maud exhale a hiss of surprise, and then Maud asked, "How much did he manage to brew?"

Selyni grimaced, and said, "The decanter is full." She hesitated, and then said, "It's a large decanter."

Maud didn't speak for a moment. Selyni wondered what she was thinking, but dared not turn away. When Maud spoke, she mused, "I have spoken to my advisors. It seems that Entah comes from a more prestigious family then first believed, but he was not supposed to be wakened during this age. When his people's ship crashed off the coast of Victes, all aboard were brought from their deep slumber to save them from drowning. All the records they carried were lost to the sea. He should not have succeeded."

Selyni shook her head, and with irritation, said, "Well, he has."

Maud's voice grew icy as she commanded, "Describe as you witness."

In a hollow voice, Selyni asked, "You can't be serious?" Selyni watched as Aritian began to chant. In a whisper, she begged, "You must stop this."

Maud's voice grew hard as she said, "We wanted the organic product of Aritian's power. I will not stop his progress for the sake of a few humans. He must be allowed to become who he is truly meant to be. Now recount."

Selyni nodded, and as she watched the spell progress she recited what she saw in a low voice. Aritian placed the dead snakes in a golden bowl. Carefully, he poured a quarter of the gnome's elixir into the bowl. He set the decanter at his feet and held the bowl before him. His chanting grew deep and he spoke in the tongue of the Rán. The voice was melodious, whispering, and his baritone vibrated with a demanding cadence. Aritian held up a long dragonbone dagger and sliced the length of his wrist, spilling blood into the bowl. The bowl hissed, bubbling with metallic smoke, before bursting with emerald fire.

Selyni watched as the dead snakes writhed in the flames, coming to life. Aritian shouted in triumph, and the snakes spilled from the edges of the bowl to the floor. The slithered to the seven points of the star, and crawled up the men to wrap themselves around the assassin's necks. Aritian shouted a command in the language of Ignathra, his voice hissing and popping as he stoked the snakes' hunger.

The serpent's reared back, hissing with passion as their dripping fangs extended. Greedily, they lunged forward in a blur and plunged their fangs into the assassins' jugulars. The men fell to the floor, writhing as their faces swelled and purpled. They screamed as their blood turned to fire and clawed at their necks. The snakes, spent, burst into flames and fell away in puffs of black ash. Aritian chanted and walked from the center of the pentagram. He knelt beside each man and forced his wrist to their mouth, making them drink his blood. When he was finished, he spoke in a hushed whisper, repeating the feverish words over and over. Slowly... very slowly, the men recovered.

They stood smiling, exposing sharp fangs and split eyes that gleamed yellow. The men's' tanned skin took on more color; ribbons of dead skin peeled away revealing patterned scales beneath. Aritian spoke a quiet command, and the men fell to their knees and bowed low before him. A master had been born, and those who prostrated themselves were now true serpents.

Aritian spoke another command and the men retreated outside the circle. Aritian waved his hand, dripping blood. Where his blood fell, gouts of emerald flames burst from the floor, consuming his essence in wisps of black smoke. Aritian called to the others in the room, and they jogged to stand before him. Aritian bent, picking up the crystal decanter, and beckoned them forward.

Maud stepped to Selyni's side, and reached out a hand. *Yes,* Selyni thought, *stop this madness.* Maud's hand fell to her side, and she whispered quietly to herself, "No."

Desperately, Selyni said, "You said you were hoping that at least half of his companions would die when they stepped forth and faced the backlash from the time spell. 'A hardening of the soul.' I believe are the words you used. If he gives them the elixir they all might survive."

Maud shook her head, and she said, "In the last three weeks, Aritian has grown greatly in power and wisdom. He is no longer a fool. While he is not ruled by loyalty or love for his friends now, he has become practical. He has come to know, or at least guess, that they have a slim chance of escaping the Time Vortex unscathed, and so takes precautions, nothing more. They have become valuable assets; he is too pragmatic to lose them now."

Selyni watched as each knelt before Aritian. Aritian tipped the decanter against Azera's lips and she drank the milky potion thirstily, her dark eyes dull. Aritian stepped to the side and gave Ori a drink, and then Rythsar, Beryl, and finally Entah. When each had a drink the decanter was still a quarter full. Aritian handed the elixir to Entah, who received it with a bow. Aritian returned to his place before the pillar of light and reached out his hand for the next Orb. Selyni blinked her eyes, letting her sight of time fall. Her eyes burned with strain and she sighed with relief, closing them briefly.

Maud turned toward her, and said, "You will leave Ignea tomorrow. I have prepared a ship for you."

Confused, Selyni hesitantly asked, "Should I not wait for Aritian to emerge? I thought we were to travel north together."

Maud's jaw tightened in annoyance, and she said, "The Archmagus needs you now. Aritian still has two weeks within the Time Vortex. When the seas are safer, and the monsoon has died, I will send him north. Worry not for Aritian, for by the time he emerges he will be a greater magus then you could ever be." She smiled, and said sweetly, "The Archmagus has a task for you that requires some degree of subtlety."

Selyni frowned, and asked, "Should I not be searching for the last, lost Ronan? It's been sixty years since the last Ronan died; surely all of them must be born."

Maud shook her head, and said sternly, "No, Ultan will use the Oracle to find them."

Selyni looked at Maud incredulously, and asked tentatively, "Aileen? I hardly think she is up to such a..."

Maud interrupted her words, and said bitingly, "No you fool, not Aileen. Devaney. Don't think I don't know that you and your brother Lifoy can communicate without a mirror." Selyni fell back against the chair in shock. *No one knows that*, she thought, suddenly frightened. Maud continued, "Lifoy took Devaney to Ultan, and Lilith has seen into her mind. Devaney knows where the last child is. It will be only a matter of time before Lilith breaks her, and they learn his whereabouts."

Selyni's mind raced. She ached to speak to her brother, but dared not. For a moment the image of the young blind girl flashed through her mind. She had seen Devaney through Lifoy's eyes. Momentarily, she felt a pang of pity for the girl. Lilith was not a friendly companion. Quietly, she asked, "Where is Ultan sending me?"

Maud swept her long black skirts around her as she turned and stalked across the hall, over her shoulder, she said, "Molveria." Maud left the hall, stepping into the heavy rains and disappeared from sight.

Selyni eyed the library before her. She knew when Aritian emerged there would be a reckoning, but she didn't know of which kind. He would be changed, though she knew not how. She wished she could stay, to help him reorient his identity. Who he had been before and the man who now lived within the bubble of time were not the same person and the melding of the two personalities would be a forging of severe pain. Selyni stood, and whispered, "I'm sorry, Aritian." The Changeling fled the hall.

Aritian

Chapter Thirty-Six:

Emergence

Aritian stood before the glowing red door. He wore black robes of light silk that flowed to the floor and around his neck hung a dragonbone pendant. Behind him, his companions waited silently. They were adorned in fine cloth, armored, and held weapons at the ready; all of their blades gleamed with the dark, dragonbone. Even their armor, finely wrought by Beryl, held the dark glamour of bone, augmenting the strength of silver and steel. Beyond the energy shield Aritian could see Maud standing, waiting patiently for him to emerge. Aritian eyed her coldly.

Maud was dressed in a blood-red gown that was made from lace that clung to her form like a second skin, seductively revealing, before blooming outward at her knees like a blossoming Dahlia. Maud's hair rolled to her waist in soft waves of inky darkness and around her neck, she wore a pendent displaying a phoenix that flew in the center of a golden, flame-wreathed pentagram. Her physical form was pleasing, but that was not what held him entrapped.

Maud was powerful in the magical arts, domineeringly so, and the air around her vibrated with potent energy. What had been just beyond his senses was now fully seen. The woman was more powerful than she ought to be, more akin to a force of nature then a magus. Aritian lifted his nose and smelled. There was a strange scent that hung about her. His dark eyes narrowed as he cast his magic toward her. His power rolled through the shield quicker than thought, and streaked toward her in a cloud of poppy-red smoke. A black shield rippled around Maud, buffeting his sparking magic to the side, but it didn't matter. Aritian could feel what crawled within the magic of her shield. He smiled cruelly. When Maud materialized from the cloud of smoke, she matched his smile, undeterred by his aggressive display. She beckoned him forward with a curl of her hand.

Aritian stepped through the shield that guarded the Time Vortex, and instantly energy was rung from every pore of his being. As he stumbled with sudden weakness, the door within his mind cracked open, spilling crimson energy. Waves of magic coursed through him, basking him in raw power, renewing him. The spell's cost had been high and he felt strangely lightheaded.

Aritian looked up and saw that Maud extended a hand to him. He took it, standing straight. Maud nodded toward the door, and Aritian looked over his shoulder. His companions had followed him through, and had fallen in a heap of tangled limbs and lay prone on the ground. Aritian let a tendril of magic curl from his right palm, and it slunk across the ground in a wisp of bright smoke. Aritian felt their life force. They had been drained in the backlash of the Time Vortex and were dangerously close to death.

Aritian turned back to Maud and shrugged. *The strong will survive*, he thought. Maud smiled brightly, and her voice came in a breathless whisper, as she said, "I see the Passion Berry and my enchantment lingers still. Worry not, it shall soon fade, but first, come..." She turned away, still holding his hand, and led him toward the back of the hall.

They approached a stairwell and quickly descended into darkness. When they reached the landing, Maud opened the door that guarded the room beyond. They stepped within and Aritian looked around with muted curiosity.

The room held twin pentagrams; one on the ceiling and one on floor that were echoed versions of one another. As he watched, the raw energy that spun in the center of each began to slow in rotation. Altars ringed the lower pentagram, and the humans who lay upon the stone choked on their last breaths. The pale energy that bled from them winked out of existence, as the last rattle of breath escaped their lips with a hiss. The sacrifices were decrepit, barely more than skin and bones, with hollowed cheeks and yellowed eyes. As the spell drew the last of their vitality, their skin greyed and their forms shrunk, leaving them mere husks of bone and cured, leathery skin. Aritian looked at the runes that crawled across the room, admiring Maud's work. It had been a powerful spell — one that even now he would not dare attempt.

Aritian looked at the witch before him with new admiration and she smiled, pleased that her skill was being appreciated. The room began to fall to darkness as the energy died. In the dim light, Maud whispered, "You have impressed me beyond my wildest imagination. You are unique Aritian. The breed of your magic has not been seen in Adonim for many thousands of years." Maud's voice shook, as she whispered, "To stand in the presence of a Deveron magi is likened to standing before the Abyss itself, or so it's whispered in the histories."

Maud eyed him with open desire, and said, "I shall the mourn the loss of the Remembrance Orbs, but I will console myself for you are a far greater prize. You have greatness in your blood and it calls so very sweetly to me." She stepped closer and looked him in the eye. Aritian cared nothing for her accolades and merely nodded in response.

The room fell to darkness as the whirling light of the Time Vortex crumbled to ash. In the sudden silence, Maud whispered in his ear, "I have a present for you... A reward for all your hard work. I think you will take great delight in it." Maud waved her hand and a five-foot sphere of swirling, scarlet light sprang from her hand to hover in the center of the room. The harsh light chased the shadows of the room away, leaving them awash in bright starkness. Aritian looked around without speaking. Mummified dead were piled from floor to ceiling along the edges of room, numbering in the hundreds. It was a macabre sight, but Aritian barely glanced at them as he looked at what lay on the opposing side of the pentagram.

Two naked figures were chained to iron hooks that were anchored to ground. Aritian's lip curled with vicious glee as they looked at him with bald fear. They were old, but far younger the dead sacrifices around him. Their dark eyes flitted across the room searching for escape.

Aritian called to them in a bold voice, "Jabari, Simisola, how good of you to join us. I had not expected to find my quarry so easily, but I thank you, Maud, for this magnanimous gift." Aritian took a step toward the prisoners, and purred, "I can't express the joy that fills my heart at the sight of you two wrinkled raisins."

Aritian stalked around the pentagram, careful not to step within its gilded bounds. Jabari raised his hands before him, and begged, "Please, have mercy."

Aritian laughed, loud and long. The man's scarred body was thin and the proud demeanor that had so arrogantly clung to his persona had fled. Simisola was no different. The woman was battered, covered in bruises, and was missing two of her front teeth.

"It seems you have been taking great care of our esteemed guests." Aritian remarked to Maud as he sauntered around them, drinking in their pitiful forms.

Maud remained on the opposing side of the pentagram, her dark gaze watching his every move. Quietly, she replied, "They failed me. I wished to save their final breaths for you, but I'll admit easily that I extracted a modicum of punishment."

Aritian looked down at his old master. The man was covered in scars, repetitive K's lined in white. Aritian could now see now that even the soles of his feet bore scars. "I always wondered at these scars," Aritian looked over his shoulder, and asked, "your doing I presume?"

Maud smirked, and said, "The Dranguis guild has existed for nearly five hundred years. When I first came to Ignea, I was cautious and patient. I let my power spread slowly, like disease that lays dormant, waiting to ravage these southern kingdoms." She smirked softly, and explained deeper, "I married a wealthy prince, assumed his wealth, and then married another, and another still. I moved from kingdom to kingdom under different names, leaving the stain of my presence on each. I find the underworld, the criminal side of culture, has an equal, if not more sweeping influence on a populace."

Maud smiled cruelly. Contemplating, she added, "Especially after one begins to destabilize the noble houses. Fifty years ago, one of my sons gained the great acclaim of being named Dragon." Maud's scarlet eyes found Jabari, and her lips became pale, as she said angrily, "Jabari here was a native in Victes with quite an ugly disposition. He killed my son, one of my last half-elven sons, nearly risking my hold on the guild. I paid him a little visit and left my mark." She waved to the man, and said, "A scar appears each time he has killed someone in my name." She smiled down at Jabari, and said, "I promised you that your skin would be a canvas displaying my grandeur for all to see, didn't I?'

Jabari grunted, and said, "You did, and I have spilt rivers in your name. None can claim the authority in which I exerted your will." He slapped his chest proudly and stared at her brazenly.

Maud chuckled, and said mirthfully, "You silly, silly man. You still don't get it, do you?" She shook her head, as if amazed, before saying, "I have mentored dozens of men, just like you, and all have met a fate similar to your own." Jabari shook his head silently, as if he could deny her words by the action. Maud dismissed him with a final look, and met Aritian's eyes with a smile, as she said, "You see Aritian, loyalty can be exchanged in many forms of commerce besides love. Jabari's was born out of penance." She said, waving to the man with all the care that one would when pointing out a sack of grain.

"I know you, witch, and you're a nothing but a grasping

black-hearted harlot. I should have killed you and your nest of devilish spawn." Jabari whispered, fuming at her disregard.

"Can a mouse know a lion?" Maud asked, shaking her head sadly. She smiled, tight-lipped, and said, "I think not... you live such short, tragic, little lives." Jabari's hands curled into fists as he raged in impotent silence.

"And Simisola? How did she come to your service?" Aritian asked, looking down at the old woman. Without her jewels and finery, she was truly a sad looking thing. Her back was hunched with age and her limbs were spindly thin. As she crouched there, like some dog, her breasts hung to her belly button, wrinkled and shriveled.

With a flick of her hand, Maud said, "Jabari's sister, a prostitute he begged me to get off the street. In the end she's nothing more than what I found her: a whore, albeit an old whore, but a whore nevertheless."

Simisola held out a hand beseechingly, her chains rattling, as she cried, "Lady Maud, please spare me. I have served you faithfully for forty-seven years, let me continue your great work. I shall not fail you twice." She promised ardently.

Maud eyed the woman coldly. "No."

Simisola wilted, rocking side to side as she hugged herself weeping. Maud's voice cracked across the room like a lash, "You have disappointed me beyond measure, both of you." Maud words crawled with furious anger, as she said, "You let Inee fall, and my hold in the north has weakened considerably because of it. You're old and pathetic. I have replaced you both." Jabari and Simisola both stared at her wide-eyed as the last vestiges of their pride died.

Maud smiled sweetly at them, as she asked conversationally, "Jabari, you remember Berko? He has taken your place and even now travels to the Capital." Jabari gripped his chains with furious anger, but Maud ignored him turning toward the old woman as she lightly chided, "Dear Simisola, don't fret. Mistress Saleena has taken your place in Futu."

Aritian met Maud's gaze and she gave him a curt nod.

Aritian grabbed Jabari by his mane of black hair and leaned in close. The stench of the man was palpable. He smelled of sweat and piss. Maud had let them languish here in their own filth, surrounded by the dead. In a whisper, he said, "I admit myself disappointed. I was so looking forward to hunting you both, to chasing you to the very ends of Adonim if that's what it took to bring my wrath down upon you."

The man eyed him coldly, defiant to the end. Aritian smiled, as he said, "Jabari, you discarded me like a lame horse, but I see now that my hunt would have be far from satisfying. I want you to know that I do not look at you like some beast of burden, too far gone to save. I look at you as manure and after this day, I promise that I shall give you no more thought then shit deserves." Jabari pursed his lips as if to spit at him, but Aritian shoved him away and the man crumpled at his feet.

Aritian pulled a dagger from his waist and displayed the dark blade before their eyes. "This blade is most curious, made from dragonbone, it is. Did you know dragons are creatures of magic?" Aritian asked as he stroked the blade with a finger, cutting his skin shallowly. Where his blood touched emerald fire bloomed, crawling up the length of the blade hungrily.

Aritian promised confidently, "You will wish that I tortured you... that I had taken hours to extract the last exquisite drop of pain from your twisted bodies, but I will not." Aritian promised shaking his head. Jabari and Simisola shook with fear, and cowered away him.

Aritian smiled wickedly, exhilarating in their fear, before explaining, "You see how the bone glows with flame? This fire is special; not of this world. The blade is connected to another realm — the Aelfmae Sea to be precise. Your souls will find no refuge within the god's paradise nor suffer in their hell. You will endure in my hell. Your souls will be bound to this blade, and through the millennia you will languish in the fires of the Aelfmae. Don't fear, you shan't be alone. The spirits there will delight in keeping you company."

Aritian grabbed Jabari by his silvery-black hair and slid the knife across his throat. Simisola screamed. Blood poured from Jabari's mouth and as it did, the fire flashed brightly, drinking in his soul. Aritian flung the man's body to the side and grabbed Simisola. She struggled mighty, screaming. Aritian grabbed her by the throat and lifted her off of the floor. She kicked and scratched at him desperately. Aritian looked her the eyes intently and she fell silent.

Aritian's whisper was hoarse and thin: "This is for Razia."

Simisola's eyes widened with shock and Aritian stabbed the knife into her skull to the hilt, and then yanked it out, tearing her soul from her body. He threw her corpse to the floor, and she crumpled into a heap at his feet.

Aritian stood there breathing heavily, smiling with manic fever as their blood pooled across the stone floor. *Why do I care so much?* He thought in detached wonder. He turned away from them, nearly disgusted by his heightened emotions, and found Maud standing in the center of the pentagram.

As he watched Maud drug a nail down the front of her gown. The lace split, cut by her touch. Maud stepped free of the gown and nude, stood before him in all of her glory. Aritian breathed hungrily. She curled a hand toward him, summoning him. Aritian felt heat touch his cheeks and he sneered at his own passion. He stepped within the pentagram and grabbed her by the hair. Aritian bent her neck down with a vicious twist of his fist and kissed her hard. Maud's hands snaked around him and she pulled his clothes off with need. Aritian bent his head lower as he kissed her breast and took her small nipple in his mouth. Maud leaned back, sighing with pleasure. Aritian tossed her to the stone floor and sunk into her open arms. Their powers swirled around them as they fell into the sweet embrace of passion, sinking into sex with bestial need.

*****

When Aritian woke, it was as if he had woken from a long dream that had lasted far too long. Groggily, he opened his eyes and saw that Maud lay in the crook of his arm. She was naked. Aritian looked down and with horror saw that he was too. He looked around the room as memories flooded through him. His heart raced and his mouth grew dry as he remembered. Aritian screamed with such rage and grief that cracks crawled across the stone walls. Aritian turned to the side and vomited, only to lock eyes with the eyeless stare of a corpse. He stood jerkily, pushing Maud away from his bare skin, as panic thundered through his head.

Maud sat up, lazily stretching in the tattered remains of their clothes. She watched lustily as all his emotions, will, and morality crashed like a wave across his eyes. Gently, she whispered, "The come down from the passion berries can be traumatic, but fear not," she played a hand seductively across her taut stomach, before smiling deviously, and saying, "You have repaid me with the greatest gift a Ronan can give."

Aritian shook his head in the deepest denial, and Maud laughed.

Darkness took him as he slumped to the floor.

Devaney

Chapter Thirty-Seven:

The Promise of Darkness

Devaney sat in darkness. Time passed, but she had no sense of how long. She had long ago abandoned thought of water and food. Her stomach had grown quiet and the thirsty need for water had fled as the weeks passed. In amazement, she found that she had not grown weaker. Instead, her eyes had filled with the heady darkness and she was sustained far beyond any mortal sustenance. Devaney looked around wildly, bracing herself.

A darkness rolled, a shadow among the deep dark that pulled her attention. Devaney saw it not with her eyes, but sensed it with her power. The cloud sent tendrils toward her, and Devaney raised her shaking hands before her in defense. The shadow struck her face and she was knocked onto her back. The tendrils of smoke snaked down her throat, choking her, and her eyes snapped wide. Red fire rolled across her pupils, and Devaney screamed as a vision bombarded her mind—

Devaney knelt before her brother, and Britton smiled down at her manically. He punched with a mailed fist, and Devaney's head snapped back as she tasted blood. Britton leered toward her, wrenching her head up by her hair as he placed a blade at her neck. "Before you burn, witch, you're going to serve Ordu," Britton said with vicious promise. He wrenched her neck back further, and said, "Boys, take what pleasure you can from this whore." Men who hung around them laughed. Devaney cried out as she felt callused hands tear her clothes free.

Devaney screamed, and the tendrils of black shadows fled

her throat, leaving her gasping and choking. A woman laughed, hidden in the darkness. Devaney crawled weakly to her hands and knees, and glared into the black. She could see nothing. She spat into the dry dirt, clearing her throat of the cloying power that had violated her. "Show yourself Aileen, you wicked coward. Face me!" Devaney screamed into the dark.

Aileen cackled behind her, and Devaney spun around only to see darkness. Aileen's laughter filled the cavern to her left. "Treacherous is your path, young Ronan. Join Ultan and he will protect you from the darkness that waits for you. Cast yourself from the will of the Coven, and you will only find despair."

Devaney shook her head in denial, and said shakily, "What you show me is false prophecy. You are trying to scare me into submission, but you will not succeed, Aileen."

Aileen's laugh echoed through the tomb, and she chanted in a sing-song voice, "Oh, the twisted darkness! Oh, the shadow of lust that lays upon your kin's heart! Woe, you'll cry as he corrupts your purity and a dozen more times after with Ordu's stain before slicing you open and spilling your vein."

Devaney screamed, "You lie!" She whipped her head side to side, trying to catch a glimpse of the woman who danced around her. Devaney tried to stand, but the roots bit into the raw skin of her wrists and became slick with dark wetness as she struggled.

Aileen's voice grew indignant, and she screeched, "Me, a liar?" The woman laughed heartily, before saying knowingly, "No, Aileen but sings the joyful shadowed truth. The path that lays before you and behind. Stalking your shade, waiting, and hoping for you to trip. Should you fall, it shall reach up and choke, tangling you in its webbed promised death. Behold, sweet babe of prophecy, the curse of the Oracle." Devaney felt shadows rise around her.

A black wind spun around her, throwing dirt and dust. Devaney felt her heart skip a beat. Devaney could feel Aileen's hot breath suddenly upon her neck. The Augury whispered in her ear, "One who sees the past, present, and future often stumbles as they look to the road their own feet travel. Deceptive and vague, maddening your obscured sight will be as you strain to see your future self. Wicked is Magrados, in its teasing taste of power's first bloom, but clarity falls like a pall across the eyes as the witch walks from child to woman."

Devaney twisted around, wrenching herself away from Aileen. Tears fell down her cheeks, and she ripped at the roots again. "No." She whispered, "No." Inwardly she thought, *could this be true? Has my vison began to fade as I look to my own future?* It was a frightening prospect, and one Devaney had never considered.

Aileen laughed from a distance, and said, "Yes, my little sphynx, it is true. You never should have betrayed the Archmagus. You never should have helped Caethe rise to such power. Now you must suffer. Now you must see all that awaits you should you not join Ultan's righteous rule." The shadows exploded outward, swallowing Devaney in darkness. Fire bloomed across Devaney's eyes as she clawed at her own throat.

Britton stood among a company of men in a white cobblestone courtyard. A line of ragged men stood before them. Koal stood among them, his face beaten and swollen, and his blonde hair shaven in haphazard patches. Britton stepped forward. His bright armor gleaming in the blazing sunlight. He lowered the long spear he held. Koal looked up, his blue eyes dull with defeat. Britton lunged forward and the spear punched into Koal's chest. The boy reached his thin hands up, gripping the spear as tears of betrayal spilled down his face. Britton twisted the spear with a jerk and blood pumped from his brother's chest. Britton grunted, as he tore the spear free. Koal fell to the ground, dead without a sound.

Devaney shook her head in horrified rejection, but a hundred more images filled her mind. All of them showed her darkness, all of them brought the promise of pain and stung her heart.

Hours later, Devaney lay on the ground. Tears fell from

her eyes, and deep scratches raced across her neck born from her own fear; leaving her chest and hands crusted with dried blood. *I'm going to die here*, Devaney thought. The promises that Aileen had chanted echoed in her mind. Desperately, she cursed Caethe for not warning her. *If I survive this place, I must learn to trust only myself*, she thought darkly.

"That's the first intelligent thought that you have had since being brought here." A soft voice said to her right. Devaney turned her head toward the sound, recognizing the voice, but too weary to be surprised.

In quiet whisper, Devaney asked, "How long have you lingered in the dark, Lilith? How long have you luxuriated in my pain?"

Devaney heard the woman sigh heavily and then heard her stand. Devaney did not move from her prone position even as the woman knelt beside her. Lilith's hands floated over Devaney's neck and her dark fingers glowed with soft, cerulean light. Devaney sighed as she felt sweet power sooth her skin. An orb of sapphire fire swam from Lilith's hands and floated above the woman's head, bathing them in pale light. Slowly, the cuts on her neck stitched themselves closed, and Devaney felt her hot, burning skin grow suddenly cool. "Cuts and infections can not kill us easily, but they can leave a lasting mark." Lilith said in a whisper, her dark eyes meeting Devaney's.

"Why are you helping me?" Devaney asked, her voice coming out in a harsh whisper. Devaney barely recognized her voice, so raw and angry.

Lilith shook her head, and said sadly, "I'm not. I cannot."

Devaney turned her head away from the woman, and said, "Leave then."

For a moment neither spoke. Then in the darkness, Lilith whispered, "Lifoy asked about you before he left. He sought to find you, to say farewell, despite Ultan's command. He risks much for you."

Anger bloomed in Devaney's heart, and angrily, she said,

"I don't know what game you're playing, but I can't imagine that selfish popinjay giving me a second thought. You can tell the bastard to spare me his mockery and save his feigned sentiments for the theatre he so loves."

Devaney could hear the smile in Lilith voice, as she said, "Lifoy told me what happened on the ship. He said how fierce your anger was, but I didn't believe him." Lilith laughed, before asking, "You really don't get it do you?" Devaney remained mute, staring off into the darkness. "Humans are nothing. They are but a passing rain drop in a sea of faceless waves. Do not turn your heart from his care; Lifoy was only trying to help his family."

Devaney cocked her head in the dirt, and recited, "Ronan are foremost guardians of humanity against the tides of darkness. They shall not seek to rule, nor may they subvert any free of will. They stand and watch as sentinels while the ages pass as a parent would watch their child, and steer only through influence of spirit and champion of heart. Second law of the Ronan Commandment." In a harsh whisper, Devaney swore, "Lifoy, and all the rest of you, are no kin to me. I'll throw my lot in with the rain drops and guide them until they rise in a wave of such terrible heights that all those corrupt shall be swept aside."

Lilith eyed her with bemused dismay, shaking her head slowly. Standing, she laughed lightly and said, "Maybe you will. Or perhaps you'll rise like the rest of us and in the sky call demons down from the heavens to smite your enemies." Devaney flinched at the memory, and cursed Lifoy three times over for telling Lilith. "Who knows?" Lilith mused, "Maybe one day you can free me from the bonds that bind me as surely as those roots do you." Lilith raised an elegant black eyebrow, and whispered, "But first you must free yourself." Devaney stared blankly in confusion, mulling over the woman's words.

Lilith walked to the nearest tomb and whispered softly to herself. Devaney saw her bow her head in reverence, before plucking a sprig of root from the altar. Cupping the white root in her hands, Lilith began to whisper a chant. So soft was her voice that Devaney could not distinguish the words nor language. Blue light bloomed before flashing a bright white color. Devaney blinked rapidly, the glare of the light stinging her fragile eyes. The light fled, as did all the light in the tomb. Devaney heard Lilith approach, but remained motionless. Lilith laid a white lily on her chest, and whispered, "Sleep well, cousin."

Devaney listened with confusion as Lilith soft footfalls faded away. Devaney sat up and plucked the lily from her chest. Gently, she brushed her calloused thumb across a silken petal. Dark heady power filled her eyes and Devaney sighed, surrendering herself to the power. This time was different, however, and as her head met the dirt floor, she felt her eyes flutter close and fill, not with prophecy, but with something entirely different.

Devaney found herself standing in a field of lilies. It was night, but a moon hung in the sky filling the land with soft, luminescent light. Burial mounds filled the fields around her, each guarded by a large boulder. Devaney squinted, and saw that the boulders were lined with runic script.

The nearest of them shifted, exposing a burrow within, and a black, furred creature stepped forth. *A Divinus Hart of the Elder Fae,* Devaney thought, her mind frozen by shock. Around its head floated a halo of indigo light that spilled across the plush, green grass around it. Where its light touched, flowers burst from the ground, and freshly bloomed lilies traveled behind its trail. Devaney eyed the creature nervously. It was naked, long of limb, and with perky breasts that bounced slightly with each step of its narrow feet. Its large, blue eyes found Devaney's.

Devaney whispered with reverence, "Forgive my intrusion Elder Fae, I did not know where my sight would bring me." She bowed her head.

Devaney felt a taloned hand lift her chin so that she stared straight into the Fae's eyes. The Seelie smiled serenely, exposing sharply pointed teeth, and said warmly, "The woes of the mortal realm cannot reach you within my dream. Take respite from you cares and be welcome, Devaney. You may call me Folsa." *How does she know my name?* Devaney wondered, enchanted by the creature.

Devaney smiled, and she felt the weight of sorrow fall from her mind as she breathed in the heady perfume that clung to the air. Gratefully, she said, "I thank you, Shining One, I had not thought to find such beauty, alone in the dark as I am."

Folsa leaned her long neck backward until she stared at the bright moon above and spread her hands, as she pronounced, "Darkness cannot survive without light, child. You linger in darkness, but now you see the light." Devaney found her eyes drawn to the moon. It was no moon of Adonim, she felt sure. It lacked all craters, facets or any only mar and gleamed with the smoothness of a pale opal. "If you have a spirit of purity, no shadow can touch you," Folsa promised warmly.

Devaney smiled, her heart lifting with hope, as she said, "I confess my mind has been rent of late. So much has changed in so short of time."

Folsa met her eyes, and the Elder Fae's voice purred with sympathy, "Death and sorrow has touched an innocent heart. If it is your wish, I may teach you the ways of the Elder Fae. To bathe in our power is to be purified of all darkness, and in the clarity that follows starlight shall guide you through the murky depths of deaths reaching grasp." Devaney nodded enthusiastically, but Folsa raised a hand in warning, saying, "To commit to such a path is not one for the weak, nor does it come freely. There is always a price for power, Devaney."

Devaney considered the Seelie's words for a moment, and then said, "I pay the price gladly and hope that I can prove myself worthy of your teaching."

Folsa smiled savagely, her expression animalistic, as she

cocked her head to the side. She whispered, "Do not speak an oath before you know the price, for to speak too quickly your heart may come to weep."

Devaney nodded and thought for a moment, trying to phrase a question that was not a question. Caethe had instructed that when dealing with the High Seelie Court you must never ask a direct question, as to them it was the highest form of insult. After a moment, she said, "I am alone, without friends, or allies near…" She paused clumsily, unused speaking with such poetic grace, but struggled on, "In an unfamiliar place, under the weight of torture. My heart bleeds with sorrow and sings with joy that hope might be found."

Folsa nodded in approval. Her long doe-like ears twitched as if listening to a far off sound. She leaned down, her blue gaze hovering before Devaney, as she chanted, "I alone walk through dreams while the fair maidens of my kin slumber, but I have power to wake the balance. The male comes now, running beneath the smiling moon, seeking, ever-seeking, a weighted boon. To gain free of his solemn vow, he shall come. An oath, a weighted promise, his soul-bound word made at the birth of starlight and Etta's first bloom. When the seas churned grey and Magrados sung, an oath was promised and with it, the Fae born. He, first among us, heard the oath between star, tree, and Magrados and betwixt the three he was so charged. Perhaps it is you. Perhaps you have come to give succor to our god-given king." Folsa stared at her expectantly.

Devaney didn't know what the Fae spoke of. Instinctually, she reached out and touched Folsa's soft cheek. Devaney saw, she witnessed, and then knew. The Elder Fae were born of Etta's flesh and starlight. Magrados had bound them, but a debt was owed. Her hand fell to her side as her nervous heart began to pound.

Knowingly, Folsa said, "You love him." Devaney nodded jerkily. Folsa smiled, and said, "Then there can be no greater love." Devaney nodded once more, knowing that the Fae spoke the truth. Folsa turned away and looked across the field. Devaney followed the Fae's gaze.

A black stallion ran through the hills. Its coat gleamed darkly in the starlight and its long mane flew behind it in an ebony sheet. From the horse's head, a horn sprouted. A dark grey pearl, the horn glowed with moonlight. A unicorn in its truest form galloped across the land. It came to a stop, snorting as it scented her, and pawed at the ground before rearing up with a high-pitched scream. Its body blurred, and before her stood a Fae in its humanoid shape. Its eyes were black and lined with age. The unicorn's mouth was curved in a grimace, as if it bore all the weight of the worlds upon his shoulders, but he stood straight, unbent against the will of time. His hair fell to his waist and his horn pulsated with bright light as he gazed at her. The unicorn's body was taut with muscle, and his dark gaze rolled wildly as he pranced in a circle around her. Devaney spun, trying to keep her eyes upon him. She was afraid, more afraid then she had been in her entire life. The power that radiated off of him was colossal. The very air hummed with his might, and his ever-graceful steps were marked by overwhelming masculinity.

In a deep voice he addressed her, "I am Primis of the Toutha 'Da Fae, High King of the Seelie Court. You will dance with me under the moonlight, and under her eye we shall weave a spell of such magnitude that no realm or world has ever bore witness to. Then my oath shall be done, and I free. Come, child of Magrados. Come." He held out hand. Devaney did not think. Already his magic swirled around her with heady demand. She could not have resisted if she had wished to. Devaney took his hand, and together they sojourned across the lily-strewn hills.

Aritian

Chapter Thirty-Eight:

Backlash

Aritian stood like a statue, his mind blank and devoid. Runnels of tears streamed down his red-rimmed eyes unnoticed. He stood in a hall of mirrors brightly lit by standing candelabras and dripping chandeliers that glowed the with light of hundreds of candles. It was a bright room, and the gold-rimmed mirrors that ran from floor to ceiling reflected the flickering light a thousand times over so the room shone with warmth. Twelves stone altars lay before him, and those upon them lay beneath light sheets.

Ibriham stood next to him. For the past hour, neither had spoken. Tentatively, Ibriham cleared his throat, and whispered, "Master Aritian, here in the Hall of Revelations your friends will find peace." Aritian did not respond, could not. His mind had fallen into a void of numbness. Ibriham spoke on, his voice hushed in respect, "It is a sacred place. Many years ago it was used for prayer. I think," he paused, hesitating, but then cleared his throat and spoke on, "I know that time has passed, but I am confident that the essence of spirituality still lingers, and that perhaps..."

Aritian interrupted him, saying, "No." Ibriham jumped at the sound of his voice. It had been three days since he had spoken, and his voice was raw and hoarse. Aritian turned to Ibriham and grabbed the man's shoulders. Aritian swallowed hard, as he was filled with sudden desperation. In a fervent whisper, he said, "Ibriham, take them from this horrid palace." Ibriham looked at him in surprise, and Aritian closed his eyes, as he whispered, "Somewhere, anywhere, but here." His voice came out ragged, as he said, "They deserve to rest easy away from the eyes of the one who did this to them."

Ibriham's eyes filled with concern, and his expression grew strained, as he asked, "Master are you sure? I thought, you might want to..."

"No." Aritian shouted over him. "I can't." Aritian whispered softer. He met the servant's eyes then. The blank mask Aritian had worn slipped then, and Ibriham saw the tortured pain crashing through Aritian's eyes. Aritian's gaze took on a feverish glow and his hands trembled as he gripped Ibrahim's robes desperately. "Ibriham, I am trusting you, please brother, do as I ask." Aritian begged, as his shoulders began to shake with emotion.

Ibriham nodded curtly, and promised in a soft whisper, "Your will shall be done."

Aritian nodded tightly in response and took a shaky breath as he dropped his hands from the man. Without looking up from the marble floor, Aritian walked across the hall. When he came to the arched doorway he paused, fighting the urge to look back. With a shake of his head, he stepped into the pounding rain.

The courtyard he stepped into lay off of the garden and was close to the gate. Waiting in the downpour was a covered carriage that was strung to a team of horses. Aritian walked slowly through the rain, unmindful of the downpour. A servant stepped forward, and bowed as he opened the door to the carriage. Aritian barely saw him, as he moved in a fog and climbed into the rich carriage.

The interior of the carriage was black and the benches to either side had been lined with plush furs. Maud waited within and gifted him with a small smile as he sat across her. The carriage began to roll forward as soon as the servant shut the door with a quite snap. The rain was muted inside, but still the tempo thundered on, dim but insistent.

Aritian did not look at Maud, would not. Instead, he stared at his hands folded in his lap. It was strange, because his mind felt disjointed, almost as if he was having an out of body experience. He knew consciously that these events were happening to him, but felt apart, almost as if he was watching someone else's life. He could not wrap his mind around the strangeness and so lingered in limbo, neither fully present nor detached.

Maud spoke suddenly, saying, "I have made arrangements for you." The Scarlet Witch did not look at him, but rather stared out of the carriage window as she spoke. "I understand, Aritian, that you are upset. As one who has felt the backlash of the Passion Berries, I too know how you feel."

"You don't know anything about me." Aritian answered in a quiet whisper. His voice held no rage nor emotion, but rather came monotone as he stated the fact.

Maud smiled slightly, and said lightly, "Oh that's not true. You forget yourself, young Ronan. I know you very well."

"You sicken me." Aritian said, without looking up from his hands.

Maud looked at him then, and whispered gently, "I know." Her voice took on an edge, as she said, "In time you will see that I have done all this only for your benefit."

Aritian looked up slowly, first seeing the black skirts of her long gown, then her slim waist, until his burning eye finally found her perfectly structured face. With narrowed eyes, and in a wrathful whisper, he said, "You self-righteous bitch."

Maud laughed teasingly, and she nodded, as she said encouragingly, "That's it, get angry. Let your emotions spill over."

Aritian looked away from her then, and his voice fell to a barely heard whisper, as he said, "I will not submit."

Maud touched his knee gently, and said, "You will in time." Aritian jerked his leg away from her touch. Maud returned her gaze to the window, and said, "As our true identities must be kept a secret, I have prepared an alibi for you." Maud paused, as if to see if he would react, but Aritian merely stared unseeing, barely hearing her words. After a moment, Maud spoke on, "You are my nephew and your parents were murdered by thieves who sought the treasures of your family's house. I took the liberty of selecting a suitable family that is well-known and connected to the House of Maud. No one will suspect our deception."

Aritian's head snapped up, and he asked, "You killed people in my name so you could protect this farce?"

Muad nodded, and said lightly, "Appearance is everything, Aritian."

Aritian felt his mind spin in that moment. His tanned skin suddenly paled as all the blood drained out of his face. He felt as though he was close to passing out and the rocking carriage seemed to spin. Aritian bent over and threw up. Maud carefully scooted a rubied slipper out of the way as Aritian emptied his stomach. His tears came then and Aritian could do little to stop them as he hunched over, hugging his stomach.

"You are ill of heart, but you will heal in time," Maud whispered with surety. She looked out of the window as the carriage bounced to a stop. "We are here." She announced, as the carriage doors opened. Maud stepped from the carriage and Aritian followed her out into the rain. Attendants opened lacey, silk umbrellas and shadowed their steps as they walked up a wide set of sandstone steps. Aritian looked up and saw a great temple rise above him.

A small man, dressed in long robes of maroon greeted them before a pair of golden doors. He was grey-haired and slim, and smiled wide as he said, "Welcome to the Temple of Flame. I am Nath, and I welcome you most warmly to this sacred temple of Ignathra."

Maud waved to Aritian who stood several steps behind, and said, "This is the boy I spoke to you about. Aritian, my sister's son."

Nath hobbled forward with the help of a cane. He was a petite man, far shorter than Aritian, and as he came to stand before Aritian, he had to peer up to gaze into his eyes. He nodded to himself, and said, "I see that your mind is troubled, my son. Your eyes are wreathed with the cloud of shadow, but fear not — as a champion of Ignathra, I shall take up the flaming sword in defense of your eternal soul."

Aritian looked into the man's kind, dark eyes and something crumpled within. Faced with the faith he had once held dear, he could no longer hold the wellspring of pain that threatened within. Aritian fell to his knees before the priest and sobbed like a child.

Maud stepped to his side, and whispered, "I fear his mind has fallen to darkness. As a widow myself, I understand the trials of grief and as piety above all, rules the house of Maud, I could think of no better place to bring him for succor. He does not sleep or eat, barely speaks. Please, return him to the light, holy one." She implored, with feigned emotion.

Nath patted Aritian's head, and whispered gently, "There, there, my boy." Aritian gripped the man's robes, and Nath placed a hand protectively on his shoulder. "Lady Suna, I swear to you that I shall do all that I can for him. Soon, his soul will burn bright with Ignathra's flame." Nath said with fervent promise.

Caethe

Chapter Thirty-Nine:

Beyond the Aether

Caethe floated among a galaxy of color that swirled and spun around his suspended form in a timeless rotation. Molten stars, colorful worlds, and nebulas of swirling gas filled the darkness. Some loomed large and seemed so close he felt he as though he could merely reach out and touch them, while others seemed so far away that he had to squint to even see that they were there. All of them were beyond his touch, and he knew those who magnitude rose in grandeur were merely closer than those who seemed far distant and small. He knew millions and billions more fled into the great beyond. Comets blazed passed him, spilling fire and light as they fled across the great expanse of darkness.

Floating amongst it all were gigantic, crystalized beings of light. They were spindled in form, with millions of thin webs of light that radiated from their center. Wings of misty shimmer held them in place, slowly flapping, filling the beyond with the wind that gave motion to the galaxy. Their triangular heads turned slowly, bequeathing the thirteen planets with their heavy gaze. Gracefully, they turned the eons of time, weaving stars, realms, and worlds. The dark pits of their eyes held the knowledge of eons and eons. The closest to him stretched tens of thousands of feet above and far below.

This was a place beyond realms and warrens, an expanse above the great grey mists that expanded across time. Caethe sensed a presence close and spun in place, his mouth falling open in shock as he found himself face to face with the sightless eyes of a pale, ethereal girl.

"It's not often I find myself in such a heaven. You must tell me how you reached this realm, Caethe." Devaney turned toward the closest Behemoth of Tempus, and a small gasp of appreciation escaped her lips.

Caethe glared at the young woman as he swallowed his irritation and forced himself to relax. He was unwilling to display how unnerved he was by her stealthy approach. Slowly, the fog that clung to his mind fell away. His heart beat rapidly at the thought of how easily he had allowed his mind drift. Silently, Caethe berated himself for his carelessness. When he addressed her, all traces of languorous peace had evaporated, and his voice came sharp as he said, "Devaney, such an abrupt appearance could have unwittingly devastating consequences. You must learn to take care when presenting yourself to a Ronan. Surely, the small courtesy of announcing your arrival isn't beyond you? Even hailing from such provincial roots, one would expect you to know something of decorum."

Devaney smiled, floating closer, and said brightly, "Not at all Caethe, but seeing you jump out of your skin was quite worth the risk." Innocently, she queried, "Why are we within the Astral Expanse?"

Caethe frowned. He was not in the mood for casual conversation. With a sigh, he said, "When I was a small child, before I was entombed in amber, I often came here to escape the trials of the mortal realm."

"Have you come here for escape once more?" Devaney asked, suddenly serious. Caethe turned from Devaney, unwilling to answer. Devaney reached out a thin hand and touched a thread of light that drifted from the Behemoth above.

A scene burst before Caethe's eyes as Devaney used the power of the Tempus to force him to bear witness to what was happening on the physical plane. *A large room filled his sight, white and circular, it was domed with a clear, glass roof. His body lay in the center of the room upon a stone altar. Hooded, white-robed priests surrounded him on all sides.*

Caethe flinched, struggling against the vision. He did not want to see the ruin that was his physical body, but Devaney compelled him to. Light flashed through his mind with resounding power, momentarily blinding him, and then he saw: *The priests wore heavy gold pendants emblazoned with a white, clenching fist that held a sun in its grasp. The sun was represented by an inset of amber. The sigil of Ordu made his stomach roll with fear.* Caethe struggled wildly against the grip of the Oracle's power, but with the strength of the Behemoth augmenting her own, he was powerless against her grasp.

The white light flashed once more and he found his vantage closer. Now, he hovered above his body. With a silent scream, Caethe relented to the power with resignation and gazed upon his physical form. *His eyes were closed, and his chest barely moved. He was collared in amber, and each wrist and ankle bound by the same orange stone. Finely-wrought amber needles covered the entirety of his skin, sinking dulling poison into his bloodstream. A grey-bearded, thin priest stepped forward and between his fingers he delicately held a long, amber needle. The priests around the alter chanted in unison, their voices rising with anticipation. The priest slowly inserted the needle into Caethe's ear. His body flailed and bucked wildly as the needle dove deeper. Blood wept from his ear in a red river and spilled down his pale neck. The priest's dark-brown eyes glinted brightly as he watched, and slowly a smile filled his face as he inched the needle in deeper.* Caethe knew his body's reaction was physical only. By all accounts, the shell that they looked down upon was brain dead, but the pain echoed through him. Caethe screamed in horror. White starlight flashed once more and Caethe found himself free of Devaney's power.

Caethe clenched his stomach, his breath coming in great gasps as he dry-heaved. The horror that was being inflicted upon him was great, but no worse than what he had experienced before. Devaney rested a gentle hand against his arm, and he did not pull away. Softly, she whispered, "That none other than

I know the true sacrifices you make is enough to make one's heart bleed with sorrow."

Caethe shrugged his shoulder, pulling away from her touch, as he regained his composure. "It is by your word that I suffer so." Caethe said tightly through clenched teeth.

Devaney floated lazily in the darkness, and said casually, "True enough. Did the pixie escape?" Caethe nodded tightly. "What of the souls bound to your mind? Did you leave them to suffer?"

"No," Caethe growled. The limit of his patience reached its end, as he snarled, "I hid them deep within. They slumber... in a manner of speaking."

"I'm impressed that you were able to control such powerful spirits with such ease. Do they not resent your power?" Devaney asked, her voice dripping with disbelief.

Caethe rolled his eyes, and said dryly, "Resent? Greatly. They endlessly natter and bicker with one another. They challenge my control at every turn, and buck against my will relentlessly." Caethe smiled ruefully, staring blankly, as he added, "Luckily enough, they hate one another more deeply than they do me. For now, I remain in control."

"Make sure it stays that way." Devaney said in warning, giving him a pointed look.

Caethe looked at Devaney darkly, and irritated, he asked, "Why do you bother me so?" He had come here for sanctuary, to be at peace. He had not come for an interrogation. "You have seen the torture inflicted upon my body. Why have you come to inflict my soul as well?"

Devaney's pale lips became pressed in annoyance. She wagged a thin finger at him, as she said, "Do not forget how you came to be, Caethe. You and I have an alliance. Communication is a part of that. We must stick to the plan. There is no room for you to go rogue, and if you lose control..."

Caethe interrupted her, waving his hands in the air, as he said, "I won't, dammit. What do I need to say to get you to leave me be?"

Devaney clucked her tongue, and said, "Testy, testy! Very well, I'll get to the point. Did the Elder Fae believe your deception?"

"Which one?" Caethe asked sarcastically, and then added, "I assume you're referring to the little deception that this turn of the millennia is the last opportunity they have to return to Adonim? Or are you alluding at one of the half dozen other lies I told?" Devaney nodded, indicating that yes, this was the question she sought an answer for. Caethe spat his response, "Obviously they did or I would not have gained the soul of Dileethues."

"Good. I'm impressed by your skill in partitioning your mind, that's no easy feat." Devaney said, nodding to herself in contentment.

Caethe spun to face her, his stance wide, as he glared at her. "What do you know of it? You only know what I tell you. Lying to an Elder Fae marks your soul. You cannot deceive one so pure without lasting effect." Devaney balked, her face paling in the face of his anger. "You have cursed me to bear this burden and talk so cavalierly, yet know nothing of its weight." Caethe accused angrily.

Devaney eyed him with concern, and said, "It was barely a lie. They could wait another thousand years or a thousand beyond that, but the world would be much changed. We Ronan would have long faded, and they would have failed to turn the tide against the Ordu. We could not risk that, Caethe." He ignored her pacifying words, and she continued, "I do not know the weight of lying to the Elder Fae, for you have not told me. I am still that ignorant girl you saved." Caethe barked a laugh, and she said insistently, "We had no choice, Caethe."

Caethe shook his head, and looked away from her. In a murmur, he said, "I will never again step within the forests of Avalon. If we succeed and the Fae are returned to this world, they will know my treachery and may the gods have mercy on us that day."

"Wouldn't they be simply grateful that they are returned to the mortal world?" Devaney asked quietly.

Caethe looked at her then, and said seriously, "No, they will not be. They escaped to Avalon to return only when we had the power to face the Dark Lady and win. I stole that surety away, and told them that their return was now against the threat of the annihilation of their entire race."

Devaney frowned grimly, and asked, "Where did you hide the memory?"

Caethe waved a hand through the air, and explained, "The Elder Fae's power permeates the land, the very air around them, but it has been a long time since they were last connected to Adonim and new powers have arisen that the Fae are unfamiliar with." Caethe gave her a weighted look, and Devaney's eyes flicked down to his second set of arms. "I buried the memory within my first recollection of Ordu's power. Arkyn could neither examine nor touch these, for he has no knowledge or connection with the man-born god."

Devaney's white gaze met his own, as she asked worriedly, "And the gaps in your mind, how did you explain such a thing?"

Caethe smirked with cocky confidence, and confessed, "No explanation was needed, for no gaps existed. The mind of a Ronan is a curious thing; I crafted illusions tied to real emotion and layered them in such a way that even Arkyn could not sense the deception."

Silence stretched between them. Both stared at the galaxy before them, taking in the sheer majesty and enormity of what they witnessed. After a time, Devaney broke the silence, and murmured, "The path to power is not paved in mincing actions. Fate does not come upon you and grace you with a gilded path. You must hammer your destiny from the very stars."

Caethe crossed both sets of his arms and chuckled at the irony of this role reversal, before saying, "Rich, coming from an Oracle."

Devaney's smile wilted, and she said, "Oracle's see only possibilities and branches of futures that could be. Only in the past and the present can we see solidly what has been forged with the hammer of truth." Devaney raised a pale eyebrow, as she asked, "I would have thought you would be grateful? We've changed the future fate had dictated you."

Caethe smile grew feral, and he said plainly, "And had I not stumbled upon a child running through Umbrael frightened of visions beyond her control, you would be in a grave rotting next to me."

Devaney sighed with a huff, but Caethe could tell her mood could not be dampened this day. She spoke lightly, "Yes, we saved one another. I simply thought we could celebrate our success. We've entered a branch of Elder Prophecy, a time of greatness, foretold by Maeve herself." Her voice took on an edge of wonder as she said this wistfully.

Caethe found her good cheer intoxicating, but resisted it. A cloud of knowledge hung over him, and he said, "Do not mistake my gloomy demeanor for a lack of conviction. It's easier for you." The words came out harsher than what he wished, but his mind was heavy on the path before him. "You do not share in the fate that awaits me."

"No, I do not, but with luck you'll survive." Devaney said, her expression flat. Caethe turned slowly to look at her in shock. She held the face for a few seconds before it cracked, and burst out laughing.

Caethe smiled despite himself, and asked, "Why are you in such a good mood? I would have thought being Ultan's prisoner would put a damper on anyone's spirit." Caethe looked at her then — really looked at her. There was something different, but he could not put his finger on what. She seemed lesser, changed, but in other ways far greater than she had ever been.

"Oh! Why, I have found new allies," Devaney said with a secretive smile.

"Who?" Caethe asked in confusion, but then realization

struck him and his smile broadened. "How did you learn to speak with them?"

Devaney beamed, and lied with ease: "I had a vision of myself in the future falling to sleep and finding myself in the Seelie's dream. So I laid my head down upon the hard roots and dreamed. I am learning much."

"Truly I am pleased for you, but be careful, the Seelie Court has their own agenda. As for Ultan, you're not the first Oracle who thought to escape him." Caethe said in warning. Silence settled between them once more, and Caethe took Devaney's small hand in his own. She squeezed it lightly, reassuring him.

Suddenly, Devaney said, "I must go now. Remember what must be." She cupped his cheek with a gentle hand, and turned his head so that he looked at her directly. In a passionate whisper, she said, "Do not let your hope fail even as darkness descends. You are the future of Magrados. If you fall, we all fall." Caethe nodded and flashed her a brittle smile. He was not shaken by her apparent need for departure. The life of an Oracle was ever-twisting with demand. *Shaping the world is no easy task*, Caethe thought even as she faded from sight.

Lifoy

Chapter Forty:

The Queen of Krin

Waves rolled in swelling crests and rose to new heights as a large, dark ship glided down the grey water with liquid grace. Rain poured from the grey sky, dappling the ships blood red sails. As the waves rose behind the ship, dozens more ships crested the foaming peaks and followed after. Queen Katherine of Krin stood at the bow, leading her navy south through the Igidum Sea. She was dressed in a soldier's uniform that lacked any adornment. Over her heavy tunic, she wore a sealskin cape, and her feet were adorned with dark boots. Her short, blonde hair was slicked to the pale skin of her thin face. She was tall for a woman and as broad as any of her men.

The sails snapped noisily behind her and sailors scattered to turn them. Suddenly, the ship surged forward with the wind as it caught, and they dashed up a swell at breakneck speed.

With deference, the soldier beside her bellowed, "Reports have streamed in and word is dire all around. The Seahog is merely the latest to give news. Ordu ships gather in the Strife in the hundreds."

"Their numbers, Captain Gustav?" Katherine shouted over the rain.

Gustav stood taller than his queen, with pale hair dreaded and braided into a knot, and dressed in similar ilk. At his waist he wore an axe and across his back, a sword. His face and hands, left bare to the cold, sea air, was rampant with the black ink of tattoos. Gustav dipped his head and yelled, "The daring Captain Ravnik, who sails the Bleedingwidow, engaged the first ships while returning from southern trade. He reported some three-hundred soldiers and a handful of those wicked priestly bastards on the ship they boarded."

Katherine smirked, and asked, "He escaped unscathed?"

Gustav nodded, and replied bluntly, "Aye, though he lost nearly half his men."

"The enemy?" Katherine asked, with a raised eyebrow.

Gustav chuckled, and said proudly, "He fucked em' bastards good, milady. Sunk himself three ships, killing nearly a thousand men." He spat to the side, before saying, "The fat skiffs these Ordu sail aren't built worth a salt lick."

"Indeed." Katherine nodded.

They rode another surge upward and both of them shifted with it, keeping their balance with ease. Gustav asked, "What'll it be, milady — do we sail to the Reena or turn tail to safeguard our coast?"

Katherine stared at the storm-turned sea before her with a steely blue gaze. Gustav remained silent as his queen considered. They both knew what this news meant. It was merely a matter of when they became engaged, rather than if. A movement in the sea caught her eye, and she watched a dark shape move in the water. She leaned forward, studying its form.

The creature burst from the water in a spray of foam and landed on the ship's deck. Katherine leaped back, as Gustav sprang forward pulling his sword free. The ray was large, nearly seven feet long. Its wings flapped noisily on the deck and its whipcord tail flicked side to side as it wiggled forward. *Strangely pale, but mayhaps it's ill*, Katherine wondered.

She laughed when Gustav turned back to her with wide eyes. With a smile, she asked, "Have you shat yourself, Captain?" Sailors ran toward them intent on seeing the threat themselves.

"By his smell, I'd say his pants are yet unsoiled, but that fact remains to be seen in the next few seconds." A mirth-filled voice said. Both Katherine and Gustav's head's snapped toward the voice. A naked man stood where the ray had once been. Lifoy bowed low, and said calmly, "Before your soldiers attempt to hack my wondrous physique apart, allow me to introduce myself. I am Lifoy Ronan, and I've come to have words with you, Queen of Krin."

By this point, the deck swarmed with movement as soldiers bared steel in defense of their queen. Katherine and Gustav stood on the starboard side, while Lifoy remained portside. A ring of men filled the area between the sails and bow, ignoring the violence of the storm.

Katherine did not hide behind her Captain. Instead, the queen stepped forward and hefted the axe from Gustav's waist. She pointed the tip of the weapon at the thin man before her, and said, "You're either incredibly stupid or have a death wish. One false move and you will be chopped into bloody chum. If you have come for me, then you know by reputation that I do not make this threat idly."

Lifoy bowed gracefully, and as he straightened, said, "I am aware of your bloodthirsty disposition, my Lady, but I fear that I must disappoint your hematic lust. The time has come, fair Queen: Ordu has set his eye on the kingdoms to the east, and I must beg an audience with you."

Lifoy smiled weakly in relief the moment Katherine nodded slightly. Gustav flung his hand forward and a dagger whirled toward Lifoy's heart. Lifoy grabbed it mid-flight, smiled, and flung it back in a blur. The dagger buried itself in Gustav's throat and the man fell to his knees spitting blood. Her nod had not been for him — rather it had been a signal to her captain.

Katherine's expression grew dark with rage. Her soldiers made to charge him, but Kathrine whipped out a hand, stopping them with the silent command.

Lifoy smiled lazily, and with a pout, said, "No need for such naughtiness, darling. I can paint this deck red if you'd like, but your struggle would all be for naught. We are having this little chat surrounded by your armed men or by their lifeless corpses. Either way, we will speak." Lifoy smiled broadly, and crooned, "It matters little to me which you choose."

Katherine grimaced, her jaw tightening with restrained anger, and commanded, "Speak, Changeling. You have thirty seconds before I bury my axe in your skull."

Lifoy shrugged his shoulders, and said simply, "You and all of your kingdom will be dead if you don't listen to me."

Katherine waited for him to continue as the seconds ticked by, but Lifoy remained silent. In a bark, she asked, "That's it? That's your big pitch to save yourself?"

Lifoy smiled and held his hands splayed wide, as he said, "Any other words would be extraneously superficial. At the end of the day that's the skin of it." He nodded at her, and said encouragingly, "Come now, along with a reputation for killing senselessly, you're well-known for not bandying words."

Katherine eyed him with narrowed eyes, but answered softly, "Very well." She turned toward the crowd of men, and in a booming voice that carried across the water, she commanded, "Get back to work before we all drown." She eyed the dead man at her feet with disgust, and ordered, "And clean up this mess." Katherine nodded to the bow of the ship, and with a wave of her hand, suggested, "Lifoy, if you would."

Lifoy gave her a flourishing bow, and said, "As you command, my Lady."

Katherine gave him a dark look, and warningly said, "Be careful with that pretty mouth, or I'll fuck it bloody. Now, out with it."

Lifoy gave a mock shudder as he leaned against the rail of the deck, and wistfully mused, "Copulations with a Queen would be a great honor, though who would be on top I wonder?" Katherine's hand blurred and the axe blade appeared at his neck. Lifoy held his hands up in submission, and said, "Very well, I see the fun is at an end." Katherine held his gaze for a moment, and then lowered the axe to her side. Brightly,

Lifoy explained, "I have come to you with a proposition." Katherine nodded with irritation, and Lifoy continued with a beaming smile, as he said, "One that entails your marriage to the King Paul Thoriston of Agos."

Katherine's eyes flashed with anger and a blush of color flooded her pale cheeks. In a low growl, she spoke, "The Kingdom of Krin has been ruled by a Queen for the last three-hundred and seven years. What makes you think that I, Katherine Vulvanna, will be the first to bend the knee to some limp dick with a crown?"

Lifoy leaned forward confidingly, and said, "I can't verify the lackadaisicalness of His Majesty's member, as I've had no personal relations, but I can assure you he is the best chance anyone within the U.F.K has in surviving the tide of Ordu. Even now, he gathers together the council to forge a unified cohort under his command." Lifoy straightened, and all humor left him, as he said dryly, "You, more than most, know what you will face. You can't face it alone, and separate, you will lose. Come now, you're a commander, you know the Unified Kingdoms need a single voice to lead them." Lifoy chided reasonably.

Katherine leveled him with a stare, and in a deadpan voice, asked, "Why do you not rally the seven Kingdoms around my banner? Do you think that just because Paul is a man that he is more suited to lead us against the great enemy?"

Lifoy flicked a hand to the side dismissively, and said, "I do not think anything. We, all of us including Paul, dance to the tune of a newly born Oracle. It is she who has seen him triumph, and I can assure you with all confidence that she gives little care to the sex when judging character. I don't even know if the poor thing knows she's a girl." Lifoy said in mock aghast.

Katherine spat into the swirling waves, and angrily said, "So the Ronan seek to rule us once more. Have your kin learned nothing in all their long years of exile?"

Lifoy barked a laugh, and replied loftily, "Forgive me,

Katherine, but we *are* superior beings. Do you really think the gods' little slap on the wrist was going to change the opinions of the Coven? Please, you're more intelligent than that. All you did was piss us off."

Katherine grunted in acceptance, and Lifoy was forced to admit admiration of her stoic practicality. "This new Oracle, she acts by the will of the Archmagus?" Katherine asked astutely.

Lifoy shook his head, and wiped a lock of sodden hair from his chin, as he explained, "Oh no, Devaney has little love for the elders of our Coven. She is, even now, being held under suspicion of treason herself."

Katherine smiled thinly, and said, "Sounds like a woman after my own heart."

Lifoy nodded, and assured, "The pair of you together would send any man into a faint of their own piss."

Katherine studied the waves in silence, before asking, "What do I get out of this? Or am I supposed to be content bending at the knee?"

Lifoy smiled gleefully, knowing that she was at least considering the proposition. "Oh not at all, in fact the Oracle has a message for your ears only – come closer." He leaned close, and whispered into her ear.

When Lifoy was finished he leaned back and gave her a curt nod. Katherine turned away, gripping the rail tightly for support. In a whisper, full of hushed emotion, she said, "I see." When she straightened and made to speak, Lifoy flashed her a smile, climbed the rail and dived into the swirling blue waves without another word. Katherine stared after him, but the magus was gone.

She shook her head, and turned to face the deck. In a booming voice, she called to her subordinates, "Men of arms, bare southward with all haste to the Strife! War is upon us! Prepare yourself for battle. We go forth, riding the waves like wolves of the sea. Let us paint the water red with Ordu's blood!" The men screamed with battle cries. A sailor climbed up the mast to the crow's nest and a lantern was lit. With mirrors, he signaled to the ships that followed, and soon the waters echoed with the bloodlust of Krin.

Aritian

Chapter Forty-One:

Ignathra's Rebirth

Drums pounded in rising and falling cadence from the summit of the Ignathra's High Temple to reverberate in a thunderous tempo over the boisterous clamor of the busy streets below. People swarmed in celebration and great parades pushed through the streets in snaking processions in dozens of places all over the city. The commoners dressed in multi-colored silks and wore masks painted gold. It was the longest night in the month of the Coyote and with sunrise, the official last day of the monsoon season. Each year, Ignathra was reborn on Aqu's solstice, marking that end of the long night of Shadow's Reign. Even still, rain poured in a soft mist from the dark clouds above. The celebration had lasted all night and with dawn coming, was nearing its climax.

The temple, a great pyramid, rose above all other structures in the city. It was the greatest of its kind found in all of Ignea. At the apex of the temple stood six great pillars, twelve feet in height, and these held a smaller pyramid made of solid gold and crowned with a ruby; the temple's blood-stone. Among the pillars, a great circle of people had gathered and within the circle stood an altar of gold. A silver enameled pentagram was inlaid upon the sand-stone floor, and seven censers graced the exterior of the pentagram, each crackling with great plumes of fire. The censers were serpentine in design, beautifully and lovingly depicting images of dragons, serpents, wyrms, and fire lizards. The kindling within the statuesque censors had been mixed with different elements so the fires varied in color;

flashing gold, red, green, blue, and indigo.

Drummers, bare-chested and painted in red and orange, stood between the multi-colored flames keeping tempo. Orators stood along the edges of the pentagram, chanting supplications to the fire god with booming voices. Those within the circle were painted cerulean, white, and orange and writhed atop the temple in a great hedonic orgy. Their sex honored the God's reproductive power and blessed his eventual rebirth, while the children born of the night's festivities would one day become High Priests of Ignathra.

Aritian led the supplication in the center of the orgy, chanting, as he rhythmically swung a small golden censer by a short chain. A bright white trail of sparks followed the censor's path. In his other hand, Aritian held a long, sharp dagger that was shaped in the form of a dragon with rubied eyes. Aritian was dressed unashamed, in gold. Bright chains adorned his neck, arms, and ankles and feathers dyed red were strung through his waist-length, black hair. The oil that coated his skin highlighted his bodies definition dramatically as the fires light licked across his form.

Upon the altar lay a young woman adorned with hundreds of pieces of gold jewelry. Dozens of necklaces sprawled along her chest, writhing like snakes among her breasts. Each of her slender finger held three rings, all crusted with rubies, and atop her head she wore a ruby encrusted crown. No older than sixteen, she was a vision of beauty with long black hair that spilled around her like a black sea upon the golden altar and a perfect physic oiled with incenses pleasing to Ignathra. *A vision of sacrifice, she is flawless*, Aritian thought.

The tempo of the drums increased. The darkness that had once held dominance on the night slowly began to lighten. Sixty-six slaves were held by chains along the edge of the pyramid steps and as the sun began to rise, the slaves were forced to their knees. Painted in all black, the slaves were a multitude of races captured or bought by the priesthood for this very night. All heretics, the slaves represented the Demon of Shadow in which Ignathra battled against eternally. As the first light crested the Golden Plains to the south, human, goblin, lorith, dwarf and a half a dozen other species found upon Ignea, were forced to bend their necks to the edge of the steps.

"May the blood of these infidels grant you the spark of light and their lives, the flame of vigor!" Aritian shouted as light spread across the land that lay beyond the city walls like a sea of golden hope. "Today marks return of Ignathra in all his brilliance! He comes! Blessed be his light." As his words left his mouth, the slave's throats were cut in unison, painting the steps of the temple in a crimson river. "As the shadow flees this world, we welcome you, Ignathra, your most humble servants in Ignea!"

The streets all throughout the city exploded in jubilation. Trumpets, horns, and whistles sung a screaming welcome to the Sun God. The participants of the circle writhed quicker now as they climbed toward culmination. The drums pounded at a furious rate. Finally, the sun emerged from its slumber, climbing the horizon and was born into the world fiery-red like a newborn babe. As the first rays reached the temple, its light touched the ruby that adorned the golden pyramid above, and the jewel flashed fiercely like a red star awakened by Ignathra himself. The circle began exhaling in pleasure as the priests reached their climax.

Aritian placed his palm upon the young woman's chest, sliding golden chains aside as he exposed the skin above her heart. He could feel it beating rapidly beneath his palm. Aritian silently sent a prayer to Ignathra to let his blade fly true, his lips moved silently as he held his eyes half-closed. The young woman smiled at Aritian, unknowing of the pain she would soon endure to reach her Lord.

"A sacrifice! A martyr! A gift of flesh to Ignathra!" Aritian yelled, plunging the dagger deep into her chest. The blade disappeared within her, leaving only the golden hilt exposed.

The dragon's maw was stained red and the woman coughed, choking as blood pooled from the corners of her mouth to run down her chin. Her breath came erratically now as her body struggled to survive, and her brown eyes darkened with pain. Aritian raised the golden-dragon censer he held. Tipping it slowly, he spilled white liquid fire from its laughing mouth down the length of her. The oil she was coated in ignited with a *whoosh* and the woman was consumed in a matter of a minute, leaving nothing behind but ash and boiling black smoke.

Only remnants of fire remained, licking the oil-coated altar with greedy tongues of flame. "Ignathra has accepted our tribute! Long may his light shine upon you!" Aritian shouted. Heralds repeated his words throughout the city and the streets of Creuen went wild as the people reveled in their god's return.

Aritian walked from the cloying smells of the altar to the edge of the steps. Looking down upon the city before him, his heart soared with joy. Crowds spread across the city filling every street, and all their faces were turned upward as they basked in the sun's newborn brilliance. Aritian's heart thudded rapidly as he inhaled the exuberance of the crowd. The warmth of the sun shone against his back; casting him in golden light. Blissfully, Aritian thought, *this is the touch of our god.*

An attendant dressed in all white approached him with a bow, and presented him with a teal, silk robe and a pair of silvered slippers. She balanced a small, brass bowl filled with water in her other hand. Aritian took the silver bowl and the cloth she presented. Quickly, he washed his hands free of blood and then his face of paint. The cool water trickled down his neck in a refreshing way. The robe was triple-layered from the waist down, allowing some form of modesty and intricately-stitched with gold repetitive-pattern of a phoenix. Aritian allowed the woman to dress him in the fine material. The crowd atop the pyramid began to disperse down the steps toward the lower-levels, and Aritian made to follow suit.

A black-laced, gloved hand reached from behind the

shadow of the pillar he stood next to. Aritian suppressed the instinct to jump, and instead bowed low. Maud was dressed in a dark maroon kimono and black veils, and lingered casually in the shadows. Aritian looked around and realized that Maud's timing had been impeccable — the summit of the pyramid was deserted. Even the servants had left, trailing their masters as they sought refreshment and shade. The sun had broken the heavy clouds above, and the misty rain filled the warming air with sticky humidity.

"Your performance was quite spectacular, Aritian. I was so deeply moved by the ferocity in which you took that young slave girl's life. To think, my grandson, the theatrical type." Maud whispered as she smiled beneath her veils. "I take it you quite enjoyed yourself?" Maud asked lightly, her voice teasing and filled with humor.

Aritian eyes narrowed, and in a harsh whisper, he replied, "The ceremony and sacrifice is anything but theatre, Maud. It was a great honor to be chosen to lead Ignathra's rebirth. I completed the sacrifice as it was written and give thanks to Ignathra for the strength he provided."

Maud voice dripped with mirth, as she asked, "So you'll kill for a supercilious, aloof, elemental god, yet hold the highest disdain for any such practices when it comes to your training and the growth of your power? My, my, what circular, hypocritical delusions you suffer." Aritian felt anger rush through his body, but the only sign of his emotion was the slight curl his hands as they rolled into fists.

Accusingly, Aritian asked, "Was it not your idea that I join the priesthood of Ignathra, here in Creuen, and become a follower of the Lord of the Flame?"

Maud stepped from the shadows and walk lazily toward the altar. Aritian followed. Maud was silent as she traced its golden edge with an elegant finger. When she spoke, her voice was contemplative. "Yes, I did indeed. You were so lost when you emerged from the Vortex of Time. You were so angry and filled with such doubt. I thought the familiarity would help you regain your inner peace. I thought you would return to your glorious climb, not become mired in dogmatic ignorance." Maud turned to face him, and he knew that she smiled beneath her veil.

Maud adopted a tone of surprise, as she said, "Never in my most wild predictions would I have thought that you would convert back to being a true believer. I thought after Razia's death you had abandoned your naivety. A Ronan, succumbing to such a base emotions as blind faith." A small chuckle escaped the dark veil, and she continued softly, "I wanted you to recognize the gift that I have given you. I believed, surrounded by the unwashed and ignorant, that you would come to see that you were better than them; of a higher conscious and power." Maud's voice lost all mirth, as she said bitterly, "I was wrong. I should have kept you in seclusion and forced you to face what you have become instead of allowing you to bury your guilt in deluded fantasies."

Maud's voice grew pragmatic as she confessed, "I do not admit such fallacies easily." She stood across him now, and bluntly, she said, "I am commanding you now, abandon these tribal whimsies." She paused, waiting for a reply, but Aritian remained stubbornly silent.

Maud chuckled to herself, and her voice grew contemplative, as she said, "You must understand, Aritian, I raised these lands from barbarity over seven-hundred years ago. That is what Ronan do. All things have their purpose, even this silly, little ceremony."

Maud stood at the apex of the altar and whispered hushed words. She traced symbols in the flame-touched oil, and Aritian watched her movements closely. His heart burned with fury at her casual dismissal of his faith. It was all he had from his past, and he clung to it with brittle fragility. Maud reached into one of the deep pockets of her gown and pulled a large triangular ruby from its depths. Aritian's heart plummeted and a sour stone filled his stomach.

The stone was identical to the holy bloodstone that rested high above them at the pyramid's apex. Maud placed the stone on the golden altar in the middle of the symbols she had drawn. She whispered a few more words and the stone shimmered. The light around it refracted oddly, as it vibrated with such intensity that the very air around it was distorted. Dark red fog rolled from the stone, billowing over the surface of the altar before dripping down the sides in lazy swirls. The stone was lost within the ruddy fog for a few seconds, before both the fog and vibrations dissipated.

A stone sat upon the altar just where Maud had placed it, but Aritian knew with certainty that this was not the same stone. No, in his heart, he knew that this stone before him was in fact the one in which had been blessed during the ceremony. Aritian found himself shaking. The realization of what he had just done slowly sunk into him as surely as he stabbed the ceremonial blade into the young sacrifice. A tear fell from his cheek as he realized that his beliefs and morality had been twisted, tainted by Maud's influence. *Maud has used the ceremony to power the bloodstone, with all the city inhabitants contributing, and me, the contributor of the life force to bind it all,* he thought dimly.

Maud walked around the altar and casually wiped his tears away with a laced finger. Aritian stood as still as stone as his thoughts screamed damnations that named him a fool. Maud placed the stone carefully into a pocket of her gown, and said gently, "Your refusal to use your birthright is ended. You were not chosen by the High Priests, nor the flame of Ignathra to lead the rebirth ceremony. I choose you and made the proper preparations with Nath. That simpleton's mind was nearly too easy to influence. I am the only true power here, in Ignea." Maud chuckled, and whispered, "I even chose that dark-haired beauty, the one who looked so similar to your dearly departed Razia."

Aritian swung his fist toward Maud, but her power stilled

his hand and froze it in place. They struggled against one another, and the air vibrated with the force of his anger. Maud smiled at him, before slapping his fist away with a nod of her head. Aritian turned away from her. He couldn't look at her, couldn't face what he had been about to do. *I cannot touch my power*, he thought determined, *no matter how hard she pushes me.*

Maud spoke on as if there hadn't been an interruption, saying, "Ignathra is a blind god, an elemental as pure and as focused as the element is dominates. It cares nothing for you or any other priest groveling and spilling blood in the dirt. Wake up, Aritian. It is the Ronan who rule this world. Your sense of morality is merely a symptom of your continued belief in your own humanity. You are not human, Aritian." Maud said this calmly, matter-of-factly, but Aritian flinched as if he had been stuck. "Your Covenant Trial looms. Before you depart Ignea, you will face the Coven and display the power you have become. I have let you linger in this fancy longer than I should have. The Archmagus grows impatient. You have two weeks to prepare."

Aritian's mouth suddenly went dry, and woodenly, he asked, "How soon shall I leave after the trials?"

Maud smiled, and said, "Morgana, our little sea witch, has prepared transport. It will be waiting for you at the old docks the very night you preform. You will meet ambassadors from Ignea upon the open sea, who sail to Molveria for the High King's jubilee. You will assume the identity of a diplomat and await further orders."

In a low whisper, Aritian asked, "If I refuse?"

Maud smiled spread with feral glee, and she whispered just as softly, "If you continue to refute your power, then in the name of Magrados, what is the purpose of your continued survival?" Maud chuckled to herself as she walked away from him and disappeared down the steps of the pyramid.

Aritian stood still, letting the storm of emotions rage through him, cursing the ease in which Maud manipulated him.

For him, it was as if twelve years had passed, and though he had learned much in that time, he had come no closer to grappling with Maud's subtle manipulations. Aritian felt like a fool, and the tattered happiness he had clung to these last few weeks was whisked away. The images of the young sacrifice danced before his eyes. The girl's deep brown eyes had locked with his own with such trust. Aritian closed his eyes tightly as he tried to banish her gaze from his mind.

Anger and confusion ran through Aritian in a torrid of dark emotion. Maud's voice echoed laughingly in his mind, stripping him of his fragile hold on his belief. Aritian had felt such honor and acceptance when he had been called from the young group of priests chosen above all to bring forth Ignathra flame. Now the memory was tinged with the knowledge that it has been Maud's doing all along.

Aritian's eyes snapped open and blackness filled them as he struggled to contain his power. Rage fueled his power and like a flood it threatened to escape the bounds. *No*, he told himself, *you will not use this disgusting power. It is nothing but corruption and death.* Self-hatred ripped through his breast as his heart pounded.

Aritian fell to his knees and slowed his breathing. All thoughts of Maud's betrayal were pushed aside as he fell into meditation. After what seemed like an eternity Aritian rose, his body was covered in sweat, but his power and emotions were firmly in control. A mask of perfect composure fell over his anguished face. Aritian allowed himself to hold a small smile, as would be expected of one so honored. Then, walking to the edge of the pyramid, he allowed his mind to concentrate on the one thing that had always forestalled him from falling to despair: revenge.

Devaney

Chapter Forty-Two:

The River of Souls

Devaney stood on a tall hill overlooking a dry riverbed. Folsa stood next to her, and whispered, "Long ago, when the realms of Aether were connected to Adonim, a river of souls traveled through my dreams. I am the third of my kin to hold such a doorway within my mind. The first was Aolosia, our king's mate. All souls godless, forsaken, and beyond the touch of the divine flowed here, from Adonim to the Aelfmae sea."

The hills around them bloomed with white lilies that had grown thick around the bank of the dried up river. Tall willows stood long dead, blackened and cracked, dotting the land in a long snaking line, bordering the once, raging river. Devaney tried to visualize the place when it was alive, but imagination failed her.

"It would be good to know why such a place exists," she whispered back. Above them the bright moon hung across the sky, bathing them with such brilliance that Devaney had to shade her eyes. The moon within this dreamscape seemed to grow larger and smaller. Devaney assumed that it depended on Folsa's mood. *This was, after all, happening in her mind*, Devaney considered mentally.

Folsa nodded, and said, "Aolosia, like Primis, made an oath to the Creator." Devaney looked at the Fae with confusion. Folsa didn't seem to notice Devaney's astounded expression, as she eyed the sand bed that snaked through the hills with a gaze laden with sadness. In a murmur, she said, "We are starlight and the flesh of a god. We cannot die, and so need a way to return to the mortal world when our physical bodies are destroyed."

"The creator's touch seems to have fled Adonim," Devaney replied, too overcome by what she was hearing to form a proper statement, rather than a half question.

Folsa met her eyes, and nodded solemnly. The Fae seemed to see the bitterness that lingered in Devaney's eyes, for she said, "The Creator birthed a thousand-thousand children with the chaotic abysmal powers and then left this world. He has sired other worlds, birthed other gods, and traveled to places beyond our imagination, for that is his nature." Devaney frowned at this as Folsa smiled, flashing her pointed teeth. The aura of light above the Fae's head flashed gently, as she said, "We cannot begrudge something's nature, nor could you or I understand such an entity's motives, for such knowledge is beyond even the immortals.'

Devaney nodded unhappily as she eyed the hills. "It must have been a great honor to be chosen." Devaney said, waving her hand through the air indicating the lands around them.

Folsa chuckled softly, with the sound akin to a hummingbird's wings and the buzz of a bumblebee. "Honor... duty, these words are mortal constructs. When Aolosia was destroyed by Aramubaer, the field of Fonsylia bloomed in Ophelia's mind. Many centuries later Ophelia met her end at Calnimor's hand and the wellspring of our people awoke in my mind. It is the cycle that flows eternally," Folsa explained quietly.

Devaney tried to imagine what it would be like to hold a place like this in her mind, not of her own volition, but simply because that was what was destined to be. Devaney imagined it would be a heavy burden, an invasion of the most intrusive kind, but she knew that Folsa did not think as she did; could not.

"Aramubaer and Calnimor must be fearsome to have defeated an Elder Fae." Devaney said tentatively. It was hard for her to imagine a Fae dying. They were somehow more than man, as if their bodies held more spirit, more purity or grace, than a mere mortal. They were a part of nature and it was abhorrent to Devaney to think of their blood being spilt.

Folsa's voice dipped low, and she spoke with the electric hum of a thunderstorm just before it was about to break the sky. "Aramubaer is the Unseelie King. He is a fell creature that has plagued Adonim before the Dawn. Long ago, the clans warred against the Unseelie for untold centuries. Even we immortals cannot remember how long the war lasted for so many were born only to die again in the same war. I thank the Creator each and every Turn that the dark court is held imprisoned in Carcere." Devaney let silence settle between them. Folsa had a strange effect on her. Whenever she was feeling a strong emotion, Devaney felt it too. Right now they were both overcome with grief. Devaney wiped away the tears that trickled down her face as she waited for Folsa's emotions to subside.

"Calnimor..." Devaney said, trailing off. She couldn't, in this state of mind, think clearly enough to form an elegantly crafted statement that would covey her wish to know more or even attempt a half-question.

"A black dragon, born from a most heinous brood. Long has he languished in the darkness. Of all the dragons, only he has not retreated to exile. He chose a darker path, one far more perilous. He sits at the center of dark storms that roll across the Aznyr Desert and channels the chaotic power to remain awake when all others of his kind have fallen to the long slumber," Folsa said, her voice the sound of frozen leaves crumbling away to nothing.

Devaney laid a hand on the Folsa's arm. Her dark fur was as soft as velvet. "I am sure it was a gift to receive Ophelia and Fonsylia when they were reborn." She said, trying to lift the Fae's spirits.

Folsa turned away, and walked toward the river bank.

"Neither have touched my mind. The cost to hold this gate within is great. Their souls will never be reborn. It is as if they have never been." Folsa whispered sorrowfully, without turning.

Devaney stood on the hill, her limbs frozen by her tumultuous mind, and said, "I admit myself curious about those who would have come here, but cannot now that the Bridge of Magrados is broken."

Folsa looked over her shoulder, her long neck twisting so that she could face Devaney. Sadness clouded her eyes, as she said, "I confess my knowledge lacking, too, but I fear their spirits are trapped on the mortal plane, unable to cross over. Some, like the Ronan, can travel more difficult paths to the Aelfmae, but like all things it is not without a price."

Devaney nodded, and thought aloud, "Adonim must be rife with spirits too weak to make the crossing."

Folsa nodded, and turned away, making her way further down the hill. On a soft wind, Devaney heard her response. "Yes, a terrible sadness, and even now I feel the gods' power weaken. It comes with only great effort to bring their chosen souls home to their respective dominions, and soon even that power will be beyond them. Adonim is dying, Devaney; without Magrados, all will be lost."

Devaney shuddered as fear rippled down her spine. Silently she prayed, *please Shepherd, guide Momma and Papa to your green fields. They were faithful and deserve the peace of your promised sanctuary.* Devaney stood there, half-expecting the god's voice to fill her mind, for here in such a hallowed place, why not? But she heard nothing from the divine, only the ramblings of her own worried thoughts. Devaney followed the Fae, and forgetting herself, asked, "Folsa, why did you bring me here?"

Folsa's long ears twitched with irritation at Devaney's rudeness, but when she answered her voice was placid enough, "While the River of Manemia has held no souls for a millennium, it has not run dry. The eternal waters endure. If the Bridge of Magrados is repaired, all the souls who died on the mortal realm who are destined to these shores will return in a flood."

Devaney eyed the dry river before her skeptically, she could see no water nor a current. The riverbed was dry and cracked, as if it had bleached in the sun. "You have swum in these waters before Devaney." Folsa said, turning to look at her with a graceful crane of her neck.

"You mean…. you're saying that I died before?" Devaney asked, stuttering over her disbelief.

Folsa nodded, and said, "Yes, but you had a different name in the past. You are not her, any more than she you." Folsa came to her side and rested a hand on Devaney's shoulder. Gently, she led Devaney through the thick lilies that crowded the bank, and said, "Ronan are born from ancient blood lines that harkens back to the beginning of time. Fifteen hundred years before the Sundering, Mangus murdered all but himself and four of the Trescoronam. All the living Ronan today hail from Mangus, Jyre, Glyrna, Circe, and Maeve. He made this sacrifice on the hopes of a prophecy, one that promised the Coven the strength to defeat the Dark Lady without breaking magic. He failed, and Mangus along with most of his Coven perished in the Sundering." Folsa gave her a measuring look as they came to stop at the edge of the bank, and said, "You do not hail from any of their children. You are a Resurgent."

Devaney shook her head and with uncertainty, said, "Caethe mentioned this possibility the first day I met him and to be honest I haven't thought about it since. I don't see how or why it would matter." It was true, she hadn't spared a thought about it. *Caethe didn't make a big fuss over it, so why should I?* She thought, anxiously.

Folsa looked into her eyes intently, and said, "It is crucial, vital. You were not born out of a Ronan coupling, your very soul was chosen by Magrados itself."

Suddenly, standing on the bank the dead river, Devaney felt very afraid. Her voice trembled as she asked, "Who am I?"

Folsa smiled, and said warmly, "You are Devaney, and no other. The question you must ask the Manemia, is who were you."

Devaney eyed the sandy river bed. Cracks ran along it, some falling to shadow, while others seemed shallow. She didn't say the obvious, that there was no water, but instead asked, "Will it change me?"

Folsa's smile broadened and it took on a feral gleam. Hauntingly, Folsa said, "You cannot step within the river of souls and not be. Your name is in flux, still being forged. What you do, and what choices you make, will determine who you shall be. Knowing your past will help you discover the path, and either you will embrace it or turn away. The choice is yours alone." Devaney nodded. It had been a stupid question; no magic came without a price.

Devaney walked to the very edge of the bank. She gently brushed her hands across the lily petals as she crouched. The petals were soft, almost slippery and she felt the barest touch of moisture. It was like feeling the last hint of a morning dew, just before the heat of day whisked it away. Devaney closed her eyes. She had been trusting her visual sense over her common sense; the Elder Fae cannot lie. Just because she could not see something did not mean that it was not there.

As Devaney knelt in the crowded lilies as she listened. A gentle wind played across her neck with a cool touch. The long-stemmed flowers bowed and dipped, their leaves whispering as they swayed. She could hear her own breath. It came quick and fast. Beneath this, at the farthest reaching of her hearing she thought she heard an echo of a tinkling sound. It was like hearing a river miles away while standing in a bountiful forest. You knew it was there, you believed that it was, but you couldn't quite separate the sound of rushing water from the thousands of sounds that filled the woods.

Devaney took a deep breath and smelled the perfume of the flowers around her. They carried a light scent that held a citrine undertone beneath the sweet aroma that dominated the air. She could smell Folsa. The Fae smelled like cinnamon and lemon, and honeyed-milk. Devaney could smell herself. She stank of dirt, sweat, and her own filth. Her own scent clogged her nose and she winced at the foul note she brought to this tranquil place. She was a discord that rankled against the lilting beauty of Folsa's mind. She did not belong. Devaney bent her head lower and caught the scent of water. It was a crisp, clean smell. It reminded her of the deep snow that capped the Grey Mountains and the cold springs that fed her valley. It smelled cleansing and she was filled with a sense of renewal as she breathed it in.

Devaney reached out her hand before her, but did not open her eyes. She merely took a leap of faith and trusted what her senses told her was there. She believed in what she had been born with, rather than what had been gifted. She gasped as she felt the bite of ice, cold water. This was not the water born of a deep spring, for this water was far colder; beyond freezing. She could feel the current swift and rolling, as it flowed across her hand. The cold crept into her very bones and sunk in to her soul. When she exhaled, her breath came fogged. Devaney knew then what death felt like.

As the river flowed over her hand, she felt something happen. She caught something, or rather felt something draw close to her hand. It was a memory. Here in the Manemia, souls were cleansed of their past life so that they might be born anew, unburdened by the woes of the past. The memory that clung to her fingertip knew her, for it was one she had long ago possessed. Devaney opened her eyes and she saw.

It was strange for she did not see through her own eyes as she had expected, rather she saw the memory as if from above. *Devaney sat on the back of a horse. She knew it was herself, but not. There were subtle differences between them. This woman had more pointed features, dark hair, and was far taller than Devaney. She was dressed in furs, and her hair was wild and long. She was older, far older than Devaney was now. Devaney was nearly startled out of the vision as she recognized the woman as someone she had seen during her Awakening. She hadn't drawn the connection then, but seeing her now, and knowing what she knew, the resemblance between them was undeniable.*

Two men were mounted on horses on either side, both were dressed in animal hides similar to her own. One held a spear and a bronze shield, and the other held a strung bow. The one on her left held the reins of her horse. They stood on a hill that looked out over a sea of death.

A battle had taken place. Tens of thousands littered the field below. Devaney saw that this war had not been just between men, for she saw beasts of far darker origins. Black-winged creature of inhuman beauty lay in craters, riddled with hundreds of arrows. Next to these were thousands of men, all who had taken their last breath in hopes of defeating the darklings. The blood-soaked ground was scorched black, and riddle with ice shafts that stuck haphazardly into the air. Giants slumped in great heaps here and there, making the dead around them look as small as mice. Dark-furred beasts were caught halfway between man and wolf as they clawed at the sky in death. Mammoths lay in a bloody line where they had died in a powerful charge and bled rivers of dark blood. Beyond this line, the dead changed drastically. Thousands, tens of thousands, of elves lay fallen, never to rise again. Their bright armor sparkled beneath the grime of dirt and blood that splattered them, but even beneath such filth their beauty was unmarred.

"Are you sure were in the right place?" The man who sat on her right asked. He held his bow strung tight, and his blue eyes flicked side to side.

"Yes, Mangus." Devaney heard herself say.

Mangus nodded with a grimace, and said, "Jyre, he trusts you above all others. It must be you who strikes first."

The man who held her reins nodded. He was a thin man, grey haired, but he smirked with a cocky confidence that belied his weak appearance.

Devaney felt herself about to speak, but she swallowed her words with a smile as the air before them rippled with black fire. A portal tore the air and from it, a white-haired man stepped forth. He was old, terribly so, with a beard that hung to his knees. His back was crooked and bent from being broken more than once, and he hobbled from the dark fire with a heavy limp and the help of a tall staff. He hesitated as he saw them there waiting. A long black griffon feather crowned his staff, and danced wildly in the wind.

The black fires snapped out of existence with a huff of smoke and the stench of brimstone. The old man leaned on his staff, and asked, "My son, I thought I told you to wait with the rear guard."

Mangus bowed his pale head in respect, and then met his father's eyes. "The army must turn back. The elves will crush us, Father; we cannot hope to defeat their might. This war is naught but for your own greed." He said hotly, his anger barely contained.

The old man looked side to side dramatically and cackled. "Turn back?" He asked indignantly, before barking, "You fool, look behind me and see what we have wrought. The elves have called a retreat. We must press them now while we have the advantage." He said, with a poisonous sneer and a dismissive wave to the field of dead behind him.

Devaney saw herself kick her horse forward, and heard herself say, "I have Seen too much blood spilt. We cannot hope to win this war without destroying the world you seek to rule." By the way the woman held herself, Devaney knew that she was blind in truth. She looked in the old man's direction, but did not rest her eyes upon his face.

The old man spread his arms wide, as he said, "Then I shall be king of the ashes." The black furs he wore bristled in the wind as he turned away from her. "Jyre, my old friend, is this what you wish for? Defeat? Surrender?" He asked in disbelief.

Jyre bowed his head and said solemnly, "Archmagus, we must look to the future. I happily joined this war, but you had painted a far different picture then the death you now promise."

The Archmagus's cheeks had grown blotchy with redness as a terrible anger consumed him. Sourly, he asked, "So you stand against me?"

"Father, please listen to reason." Mangus said, dismounting and taking a step forward. He demeanor was submissive and his voice pleading.

The Archmagus shook his head, and boasted, spittle flying, "No! I will win this war with or without you. None came stop me."

Jyre blurred in action. The spear he held suddenly glowed with golden light and he flung it with all his strength. It whistled with a howl as it sped across the air and punched through the Archmagus's chest, the point burying itself into the ground behind him. The Archmagus dropped his staff and stood there, pinned to the ground by the spear shaft. Blood pumped from his chest, but the Archmagus seemed only angered. He roared, "Betrayer!"

The light that illuminated the spear began to flicker and the Archmagus smiled with cold malice. He gripped the shaft with either hand, and the spear burst into flames. "I can't hold him much longer!" Jyre screamed.

Devaney watched herself calmly dismount and stride forward. In a whisper, she said, "I can." White light flooded over both of them and for a second the Oracle and Archmagus were lost in the glare. When Devaney stepped back, the ground was littered with blue ice and the Archmagus stood frozen where he stood. As Devaney watched she could see the Archmagus's dark eyes flick about with desperation, but frozen solid, he could not move. Devaney turned away from the man, and said sternly, "Mangus, do what you must. This darkness cannot be allowed to survive. We must choose another path."

From the far corners and no direction at all, the Archmagus's voice boomed, "You will diminish us! The elves will rule this world. Ware, a dark time is coming. I can feel it in my bones. Without me, you all will perish!"

Mangus strode forward, and knocked his bow. "Maybe so, Father," Mangus whispered grimly.

Devaney saw the Archmagus's eyes find his staff and he suddenly smiled with feral triumph. The ice of his face cracked and shattered with the expression, but Mangus loosed his arrow. The bolt hit the Archmagus right between his eyes and buried itself into his brain. Mangus whispered something under his breath, and the Archmagus's *body suddenly grew grey and ashen. Before their eyes his body decomposed rapidly, until seconds later nothing but a skeleton remained, held upright by the spear that protruded from its chest.*

Aritian

Chapter Forty-Three:

A Champion's Cause

Hours later Aritian milled through the crowded terrace, flashing polite smiles here and there to men and women of import. He was not a priest in his own right yet, merely a novice. While Aritian sought to become true believer, he had always known at the back of his mind that Maud would never allow his retreat to become a permanent one. It was a shame, because he had not felt such communal and mutual respect since he had shared quarters with his brothers in the Dranguis Guild. When he had awoken after emerging from the Time Vortex, he had truly been lost. Nearly mad, he had found refuge in his religion, and the light of his god had led him from the darkness.

A woman brushed against his arm, and he turned to apologize. His words caught in his throat as his eyes fell fully upon her. She was slight, barely stood at his chest height, and had dark hair that freely flowed to her waist in loose ringlets. She was dressed in a gown of soft pinks and pastel-yellow silk, and a thin veil rested just beneath her eyes shading her face from view. She was pale, starling so, with milky-white, flawless skin. It was her eye's, startlingly clear and sapphire that captivated and stole his tongue. He found himself staring at her dumbly, too overcome by her enchanted gaze to find his voice.

She gave him a slight nod, and blinked her eyes, releasing him from her thrall. In a lilting voice, she said, "You wonder among the celebration with a shadowed façade. You are somewhere else, far from this temple."

Aritian blinked, shaking his head slightly as he absorbed her strange words. When he was once more the master of his tongue, he asked shakily, "Who are you?" He eyed her up and down. Everything about her appearance was wrong. She was not Ignean nor was she a priestess. She wore rich clothes of a noble, but somehow they seemed drab on her thin frame. There was something about her that was off, something about the way she so fluidly and gracefully moved. Something in her soft voice that belied the ear, and those eyes... Quietly, without thought, he accused, "You do not belong here."

The woman's eyes laughed, and in a quiet whisper, she agreed "No, I do not, but neither do you, Aritian." Aritian looked at her blankly. *How does she know my name?* Aritian thought wildly. In the silence, she said, "You may call me Dellacindrael." She gracefully brushed her hair over one ear, exposing a pointed tip for a fraction of a second, before her hand dropped to her side. "I hail from the Forests of Ilvarsomni far to the east. Yet, I do not come on behalf of my people – I was beckoned south by fate's own hand."

She is an elf, Aritian thought bewildered as his mind began walking down paths of memory, methodically pulling any mention of the elves from his time of study. He looked side to side, scanning the cheerful expressions of those closest to them, nervous that someone had seen her swift revealing motion. There were too many people around.

Aritian touched her arm lightly and led her down fifty paces to a less conspicuous portion of the terrace. The elf followed him easily enough, allowing him to guide her. Wine and refreshment waited to their left, piled high on long tables beneath shaded awnings of deep blue, purple, and maroon silk. The awnings were topped with wooden sun emblems painted gold, and were thankfully, only sparsely crowded.

In a hushed whisper, Aritian warned, "Velon, most especially Creuen, is not safe for the likes of you." His eyes flicked back to the nobles and priests who shared the temple terrace, before he asked hurriedly, "Why have you come here, if not on behalf of your kin?" He couldn't imagine what would have brought a fair maiden so far from her shaded forests, but he knew that she would be a prize to any slaver or Master who learned of her. He had heard rumors of slaves with a quarter of elfish blood costing more than twenty rubies, and could only imagine the vast fortune a full-blooded one would bring.

Dellacindrael seemed at ease though, and little concerned with the swirling crowd around them. Her mesmerizing eyes never left his own. Aritian was unnerved by her, but he forced himself to meet her eyes. In a soft whisper, she said, "I have come to help you, Aritian."

Aritian felt as though his feet had fallen from beneath him, as he remembered her first words. *Beckoned south by fate*, he thought. His heart skipped a beat, as he breathlessly whispered, "The Oracle."

Dellacindrael nodded, and said, "Yes, we met briefly on Shades Island where I act as an ambassador for my people. She spoke into my mind and filled my thoughts with images of you."

Aritian didn't know what to say. His mind was awash with emotions. Quietly, he remarked, "You have come a long way."

Aritian raised a hand as a slave approached, forestalling her next words. He picked up a silver goblet and allowed the servant to fill his cup to the brim. Aritian sipped the wine. Dellacindrael watched him curiously, before hesitantly lifting a goblet from the banquet table, and holding her glass out expectantly to the short goblin. They stood at eye level with one another.

The goblin was a rare Banoot specimen, uncommon to the slave trade. The creature watched their reactions closely with intelligent, half-lidded, yellow eyes. With leathery, muted-green skin, elongated pointed-ears, and slits where normally a nose would be it looked rather odd in the white toga it wore. Nevertheless, it held the heavy silver pitcher steadily in its three-fingered, taloned hands and poured the dark red liberally. Aritian gave it a nod of appreciation and dismissal. With a bow, the goblin departed silently to attend another guest.

Dellacindrael waited a moment, letting the goblin fade into the crowd, before she said simply, "I have."

Aritian asked the only question, in his estimation, that mattered, "What help does the Oracle believe I need so gravely that she would risk sending one of the fair folk to me?"

Dellacindrael smiled beneath her veil, and her eyes twinkled, however her response was devoid of mirth, as she said, "I have come to bring you forth from the darkness, and return you to champion the light as you were born to be." Aritian made to speak, but she shook her head ever-so slightly, stalling his protests. "First, we must attend an errand. You must call transport, and we must depart for the dwelling of the witch known as Maud."

For a moment, Aritian wanted to ask a thousand questions, but in the end none seemed very important. He could not deny that his heart had fallen to shadow. These last few weeks he could barely look at himself in the mirror without cringing. The Oracle had given him hope, a direction before, and it seemed she would not allow him to be waylaid by his own internal struggle. Aritian nodded, once.

At his nod, Dellacindrael placed her still-full goblet on the banquet table, and took his hand. *This woman isn't human*, Aritian thought uneasily. Aritian resisted pulling from her slight grip and allowed himself to pulled through the throng of priests. Mentally, he reminded himself that the Oracle had sent her. It was difficult for Aritian to place trust in anyone, but Devaney had been the hope at the edge of his horizon for some time now and he decided he hadn't yet lost all faith. Aritian downed the remainder of his wine in a gulp, thinking he would need the fortitude, and hastily handed the cup off to a servant as they hustled into the interior of the temple.

There were nine levels within the temple, each with an

exterior terrace. Dellacindrael led them through the brightly-lit halls with obvious intimacy, passing nearly twenty small antechambers before reaching one of the four main staircases. Aritian looked at the elven woman with surprise, but he didn't ask her how she knew the interior maze of the sacred temple. *I don't want to know*, he told himself.

The temple was made with masterful design. All four corners of the temple held a staircase that led to the upper and lower levels, allowing for ease of access in navigating such a gargantuan building. The interior perimeter held alcoves for personal prayer, libraries, and small rooms dedicated to honoring champions of Ignathra throughout history. The center of each level was left open, providing space for mass prayer and reception halls where the woes of man were pleaded before wise priests. The walls had been sanded down, and mosaics made from painted, clay chips flowed across the walls in great expanses, depicting the power and laws of Ignathra. The temple was nearly four-hundred years old, and it was said that it had taken just over ninety years to complete at the cost of some fifteen-thousand slave lives.

The halls were mostly deserted, as most of the priests remained along the terraces celebrating, while others who had performed in the ritual all night had retired to recuperate. Dellacindrael led him to the nearest stair and downward. After nearly twenty-minutes of descending they finally reached the base of the temple.

They stood within the antechamber that held the staircase as attendants and young acolytes bustled up and down the stairs and milled through a large, red-painted door. The room was lined with cherry-colored wood benches cushioned with small burnt-red pillows stitched with gold lines of scripture. The floor was tiled intricately in a design of a coiled red dragon, and purple and blue flame spiraled from its maw to surround the beast in a bath of Ignathra's glory. A heavy brass chandelier, made in the shape of a flame, hung from the twelve-foot high ceiling.

Aritian warned the elf in a whisper, "The crowds will still be thick around the temple until nights' end. The Temple of Flame is the center of the Festival of Light. How do you suppose we manage through the crowds?" Aritian could hear the hum of the tens of thousands through the thick stone walls of the temple.

"There will be litters and slaves in abundance. Did you not take one to reach the temple, yesterday?" Dellacindrael asked plainly. Aritian nodded reluctantly. He eyed the elf closely, dismayed that he had been followed unnoticed.

Dellacindrael clapped her hands and one the younger acolytes stepped forward hurriedly, nearly tripping over the long, red robes he wore. In a friendly voice, Dellacindrael asked, "I am in need of a litter. Can you apprehend one?" The boy nodded his shaven head solemnly, eyeing their rich attire, and gave them each a respectful bow before spinning on his heel and fleeing through the red doors.

While they waited, Dellacindrael asked, "Is this merely a cloak to hide your identity or are you a true believer?" She eyed his robes appraisingly.

Aritian was surprised by the question, but answered honestly, "I am trying to be a true believer, as I once was before. A life in the service of Ignathra is my greatest desire, but that dream seems more and more remote as the seconds pass. I have taken sanctuary here, these last few weeks."

The elf studied him with an unreadable gaze, before she carefully said, "It is rare for your kind to show such an affliction." Aritian nodded, he knew that. Dellacindrael stepped closer, and her voice became hollow as she asked, "You killed a woman today. Do you weep for such a loss?" Aritian could hear the revulsion in her voice.

Aritian replied proudly, "Truly, being the Flame Bearer in Ignathra's rebirth was the greatest honor that I have ever fulfilled in my life thus far. I do not pity the girl, rather the opposite in fact." Dellacindrael arched her eyebrow in disbelief. Aritian continued, "Born with the blood and fire of the south, she knew there was a price for salvation and paid it gladly. Today, she basks in the presence of Ignathra at a place of highest honor. I have fallen out of faith before, in my darkest of moments, and never wish to feel such loneliness in my soul again. I only hope that Ignathra sees my conviction to the faith as one of true consecration."

Dellacindrael considered his words thoughtfully for a moment, before she said, "There are hundreds of gods whose heavy gaze fall upon Adonim, and I do not presume to understand yours. My own faith honors life as the most precious miracle and to take life, for any reason, is an absolute abhorrence. Even among my kin there are varying faith, so I am not unused to being confronted by conflicting convictions. Your religion is your own, and I seek not to cleave you from it, but you must forgive my discomfort."

Aritian nodded in understanding and Dellacindrael's stance seemed to relax. They stood in silence, both deep in thought. Moments later, the young acolyte rushed toward them and bowed, saying, "Master, Mistress, your litter wait upon the steps of the temple; red canopy, Gaour goblins, third litter in the train. Would you wish for me to provide escort?" Dellacindrael nodded, and the boy led them out of the antechamber into the bustling great hall of the temple.

The entrance to the Temple of the Flame was expansive. The walls sloped slightly upward at an angle, steadily rising sixty-feet. A massive brazier, made from hammered copper, dominated the center of the reception hall in the form of a Wyrm. The Wyrm coiled in hundreds of looping bands and rose thirty-feet in height, with its horned head graced with glaring rubied eyes that stared appraisingly at all those who entered. Fire lit the beast at hundreds of points and the bright light that rippled along its beaten copper scales made it appear as though it was alive with movement. It had been a gift from

King Leopold Darkryn – Lord of the only Dwarven Hall found in Ignea nearly a hundred and sixty years previously when the dwarfs first colonized Ignea. It had been a masterful political overture that won the Dwarven King trade agreements with the Collation of Odium.

Priests bustled hurriedly here and there carrying baskets of food, small wooden toys, and jugs of wine and water out of the temple doors. Another line of priests snaked in a steady stream in, carrying empty baskets to the tables along the back of the hall that were brimming with provisions. Outside the masses thundered like a dull roar.

They followed the young acolyte through the throng of robed priests and out of the ironbound, double doors to the steps of the temple. A courtyard spread for two acres before the sanctuary and was paved with black pebbles famously mined from the same area that provided the stones for the Onyx Ribbon road. Thousands filled the courtyard, and twelve snaking lines led from the street to temples entrance where the crowd waited to receive the gifts of Ignathra. The boy eagerly led them down the left side of the temple steps to a long line of grandly-opulent litters. The boy spoke excitedly as he led them, gesturing to the crowds, but his words were lost among the noise of the masses.

The servant boy waved toward one of the largest palanquin that waited among the train. All were garishly decorated in bright colors and filigreed with gleaming gold. The one the boy indicated was made from a pale wood, with walls that held wide-windows. The palanquin lacked a solid roof, but was draped liberally with a red canopy of fine silk. Spokes lined the side of the litter and round poles, set at intervals, allowed the goblins to carry the litter across their broad backs.

The Gaur wore white wraps around their thick waists, a leather harnesses that was fitted with heavy shoulder pads, and a metal collar that attached them to the palanquin by a length of thick chain. The young acolyte rushed before them and opened the small door that was set into the side of the litter, and then motioned them in with an excited wave of his hand. Aritian caught Dellacindrael glancing at the bulky goblins with narrowed eyes, but when she noticed his attention she quickly entered the litter.

Aritian walked to closest goblin. The beast stood over him, nearly a half a foot taller, its warm breath hit his face with pungent stench of raw meat. "Southwestern sector, Scorpion Street. Do you know the place I speak of? Da?" Aritian asked, keeping his tone neutral and pronouncing each word clearly. The beast let out a few lines of guttural language to his companions, shifting his flat feet in the dark gravel, before turning back to Aritian and nodding. The beast's yellow eyes seemed dull and bored, and for a moment Aritian pitied the creature. Although the monsoon season had just ended, the sun would soon banish the cool mist that fell from the lightening sky. Ignathra's glare was scathing and soon these goblins would suffer.

"Da," it said, the word for assent in goblin langue, before it said in a chirp, "We know." Aritian nodded and entered the palanquin, shutting the small door with a click. The interior of the litter was heavily padded with large pillows and throws. Aritian sat across Dellacindrael. The elf sat stiffly, her light eyes flicking this way and that, like a startled stag that had caught the scent of a wolf. The sound of chains rattling filled their ears, as the goblins bent and placed the support spokes upon their shoulders. The goblin lifted the litter up with little effort and the litter rocked gently with each plodding step they took.

Conversation was impossible as the goblins pushed through the crowds. Dellacindrael and Aritian both eyed the teeming streets in silence from their prospective window. Aritian found himself enjoying the ride. *The south is like no other*, he thought. Ignea held a myriad of people, and was true melting-pot of races. Here, in Creuen among the crowds, there was a true testament to diversity.

The poor and rich alike sought to gain closer access to the temple, and dozens of species of goblins thronged at the heels of their masters; their color and size changing with their perspective subspecies. The smallest were colored brightly and sung from the shoulders of many in the crowd. No larger than a small cat, these small creatures were kept as playful pets of the wealthy. Aritian eyed the Gillo with contempt. The largest, the Gaour stood like silent pillars guarding perfumed men dressed richly in bright silks. The peoples' painted faces were sweat streaked and smudged, and the crowd was wild, drunk, and adoring. As their litter cut a direct path through the courtyard, people bowed and pleaded for blessings.

Dwarves wearing heavy tunics crowded here and there in small pockets. Their beards were dyed bizarre colors of pink, green, and blue and decorated with silver and gold bells. Visiting from the Fervite Mountain range, these dwarves were merchants and craftsmen. Aritian was glad they had experienced such an honor. He held three fingers up, signaling respect, and the dwarves bowed their heads in return as he passed. Their cheeks and eyes were red from the dark wine, common and well-loved in Creuen.

A crowd of young naked children ran past the litter, forcing the goblins to pause a moment in their path. The children lacked any fear of the Gaour, laughing and dancing through the crowd passing within touching distance of the towering creature.

Passage through the crowd was slow and grew only more ponderous as they entered the streets beyond the courtyard. Merchant stalls lined the streets selling everything imaginable. Men dressed in white tunics and loose flowing trousers manned stalls filled with silver fancies, sparkling jewels, fine tapestries, dark oils, and luxurious silks. Swords winked at their hips, and goblins stood along the front of the stalls watching the crowds closely with narrowed, lidded eyes, on the alert for quick-fingered thieves.

They passed Yithla, who chirped brightly in their fluttering language, admiring the feel of a bolt of rich silk. Their long necks bobbed in appreciation, as they shifted their long legs in excitement. They fingered the fine material in their grey, three-fingered hands, their touch gentle so as to not tear the fine silk with their black talons. The Gaour carrying the palanquin pushed several out of the way of the way, which elected a piercing string of angry squawking from their sharp beaks. Their oval-shaped heads weaved with annoyance as their brilliant-colored expression contorted with outrage. The Gaour ignored the strange creatures and continued along their path.

Carts piled high with fruit, meat, and jugs of water and wine dominated the area. Wafting aromas of cooking meat and fresh bread filled the air. Crowds congested heavily around these, knowing that the tally of the day's sale of food and drink would be covered by the illustrious Order of the Flame.

Lorith thronged among the crowds in great numbers, each with a flaming sun painted upon their scaled foreheads, and wore cloaks of red that touched the dusty streets. Jubilant, high-pitched screams rent the air as they raised their snouts in celebration. Humans gave the lorith a large berth as the reptilian creatures wildly danced in joy. As the litter passed, a small group of lorith stepped forward bowing low, their hissing language filling the air with whispers as they honored Ignathra's chosen.

Aritian eyed them with slight nervousness. Lorith were plentiful here in Creuen, and not just as slaves, but as peaceful merchant princes that had left their tribal society for the richness of human culture. *These are not the lorith who harry Velon's border to the north*, Aritian chided himself mentally, as he flashed them a small smile and bowed his head in respect.

Rumors had filled the streets of great battles and dozens of villages burned in the north. Aritian had pressed Maud for information, but she had waved his fears away dismissively. She claimed that the Emperor had raised a great army and that the war would be ended soon. Still, rumors of bloodshed flooded south in a steady stream.

Music clamored for attention as small bands rode through the streets in groups of a dozen or more on backs of richly decorated camel and elephants. The animals were dressed in silks as gaudy as their owners', wearing skirts of bells on every limb, jangling with each step they took. Musicians skillfully played pipes, flutes, drums, and trumpets, filling the impassioned celebration with a menagerie of sound.

It was nearly an hour before they reached streets clear enough that the litter didn't pause every few steps. The sound of celebration dimmed at the outskirts of the city.

Aritian broke the silence between them, and said, "Ignathra," and then stopped, realizing that he was shouting. Dellacindrael smiled beneath her veil, as he continued in a normalized tone, "Ignathra will be most pleased." The elf nodded her head and seemed to genuinely impressed by the celebration. Aritian had seen her watching with great curiosity and he imagined it was radically different here than in her homeland in the north. She seemed entranced by the sheer foreignness of it all. Aritian broke her unblinking stare when he asked, "What errand must we attend at Maud's manse?"

The elf settled her unnerving gaze on him, and asked, "Do you know anything of the southern Warlords that rule the region along the Velox River?" Aritian shook his head no, and Dellacindrael continued, "The Velox spills from the Pomum Rainforest and floods south, cutting through the breadth of Velon. It then rushes through the northern edge of the Ignis Desert and runs southward, parallel to the eastern coast, stretching nearly four-thousand miles in length." Aritian blinked owlishly, slightly startled by her precise understanding of Ignea's geography. "The only habitable lands in the Ignis Desert flank the river. It is a territory volatile in nature, as a never-ending battle for supreme right endures between fifty of the most prominent Warlords." Aritian knew a cursory knowledge of the region she spoke of, but the elf's knowledge far surpassed his own. Aritian listened intently, but not without some degree of confusion, as she said, "It seems that Maud has summoned one of the more powerful Warlords to Creuen."

Aritian shrugged, and said flatly, "Why would that be of any interest to an elf from the eastern forests of Afta or even me? Forgive me, but I seem to be missing the importance of all of this."

Dellacindrael cocked her head, and with perplexity, asked, "Are you not curious?" Again, Aritian shrugged. He saw little reason why this should be of any consequence. Maud often met with officials, merchant princes, and indeed many from far and close lands alike. She grew her fortune with a deft eye. It took work, and it was one of the few tasks of her household that she did not delegate. The elf persisted, "If nothing else, does it not seem odd to you that Maud has enough influence to call a Warlord here like some errand boy?"

Aritian admitted, "Perhaps it's a bit strange, but not enough to raise any eyebrows. Maybe you are underestimating her scope of influence? Who is this Warlord?" He was more curious of the Dellacindrael herself than the dull negotiations of some trade agreement.

Dellacindrael waved a hand toward the left, and said, "Qurin One Eye, king of Utarye. He rules a territory some hundred miles due south."

Aritian nodded, he had heard of the man's reputation, but little else. Impatiently, he asked, "Is that supposed to mean something to me?" Aritian had the feeling that the elf thought differently than he did. Not that she inherently knew more than him, rather that her mind simply worked in ways his did not. He suspected that she followed paths and drew connections that were simply beyond him. As he stared into her inhumanly, intelligent eyes he had little doubt of his assessment.

Dellacindrael patiently asked, "What was the task the Oracle gave you the day you Awakened?"

Aritian felt himself jerk. The change of subject had been abrupt. The words of the oracle rang through his mind. *Find the corruption, but do not speak of it lest you wish lose your life. The right time will come for all things to be revealed, never fear.* Aritian felt a sweat break upon his brow that had nothing to do with the growing heat. Aritian swallowed thickly. In a whisper, he asked, "Do you know the nature of this corruption?" Dellacindrael shook her head no.

In frustration, Aritian said, "It seems to me that you know more of the situation than I. Why does the Oracle need me to discover such a truth when you have proved an adept envoy of her every wish?" Dellacindrael stared at him blankly. Aritian continued, his anger mounting, as he said, "You penetrated a sacred temple with disarming ease and you seem to know the political temperature of the south far better than I. Why should you not take this task on? Does Devaney think I do not have enough to concern myself with?" In truth, Aritian didn't want to have anything to do with the Ronan intrigue. They and his power had brought him pain far greater than he had ever experienced as a slave.

Dellacindrael stiffened, and flatly, she asked, "Like refusing to use your power?" Aritian closed his eyes. He didn't know how she could know that and supposed it didn't really matter. He clenched his jaw in a grimace, but did not respond to her accusation.

In the silence, Dellacindrael spoke, "Do you know of the Accords of your kin?" Aritian nodded that he did. He had read them when he was in the Time Vortex. At the time he had viewed them as an inconvenience to his pursuit of knowledge, and after, he had tried to forget everything and anything he had learned within. He hadn't been able to. The Accords had been odd. When he read them, the words seemed to brand themselves to his soul. He knew that he could recite them now, with little effort.

Dellacindrael leaned forward and touched his hand.

Aritian wanted to recoil away from her, but as he met her eyes, he found that he couldn't. In a demure whisper, she explained, "I was shown the future, but in fragments and only in a way to help you. Right now your heart has turned toward hatred. You keen for revenge. I can feel it as easy as I feel your hand beneath my skin." Her eyes seemed to grow more intense and Aritian flinched away from her searing, sapphire eyes. Calmly, Dellacindrael said, "I am leading you toward a dangerous secret, and yet you seem intent on ignoring the very key to what your heart yearns for."

"Is it something that can harm her?" Aritian asked, his attention now unwavering.

"Yes." Dellacindrael said, in a voice that seemed filled with sadness.

"I see." Aritian said, as his mind raced. He was still stinging from Maud's latest manipulation and would not proceed with haste. He hedged his excitement, and asked, "I thought the Oracle commanded you to bring me from the darkness, toward the light? I wouldn't think revenge was the proper mechanism to bring about such an evolution."

"Every champion needs a cause." Dellacindrael said mildly. Her eyes narrowed, and with surprise, she said, "You are suspicious of me." It wasn't a question, but a statement.

Aritian nodded, he didn't see the point in denying it. "How do I not know that this is some trick of Maud's? For all I know this could be another form of humiliation that she has designed to show me the error of my ways."

Dellacindrael leaned forward, and her voice grew hard with an edge, as she said. "The Oracle said that you would challenge my intent. I was instructed to tell you this: Indulge the command of the Oracle, Aritian, and Devaney shall tell you how to bring Razia back to the world of Adonim."

Aritian felt the edges of his vision blacken as he nearly fainted. His mouth went dry, and his heart began to race. His suspicion died. He didn't care if he was being a fool. Hope once more breathed life into his heart. Breathlessly, he whispered, "What must we do?" He didn't care what he had to do, after those words, he would do anything, absolutely anything the elf commanded.

Dellacindrael nodded to herself, and said curtly, "Maud and the Warlord of Utarye are set to meet in less than a candlemark. We must be there and we must not be seen."

Aritian

Chapter Forty-Four:

Qurin One Eye

They reached the southwestern sector in short order, and here the buildings grew in size and splendor. They had left the crowds in the center of the city and Creuen's great wall loomed to their left. This was a quiet corner of the city; a place where the wealthy retreated and where the masses were barred from entry. Gates lined the front of each manse, guarding against intrusion with gilded gold and cold iron. Quaint shops filled the spaces between the gates of the grand houses with storefront patios elegantly displaying fountains and blooming gardens. Soldiers patrolled the white cobblestone streets in pairs, wearing smart leather armor, canary capes, and dark cowls. They rested their hands casually on the pommels of their short-swords as they strolled the quiet, well-manicured avenues.

The palanquin turned a corner and stopped. Aritian opened the flimsy door and stepped down, turned and held a hand out to assist Dellacindrael. The elven lady took his proposed assistance after a moment's hesitation. She eyed the opulent manses and manicured shops with a cursory gaze, and seemed less than impressed with grandeur of the wealth around her. Aritian gave the goblin he had spoken to a polite nod, pulled a gold crown from a pocket sewn into his robe and flicked the coin to the goblin. The Gaur caught it deftly and exclaimed it with a bright, guttural chatter.

Dellacindrael watched the exchanged with surprise, but didn't remark. Aritian didn't have a second thought on spending the coin. It was, after all, not his wealth he squandered. but that of his Mistress. They turned to face Maud's manse.

Situated in the shadow of the city's wall, the manse looked more like a small temple then a house. As one of the oldest structures in Creuen, it had been converted several times throughout the years for new use. Maud claimed that it had stood here before the creation of the very city itself, and had once been a place of worship of a long forgotten goddess.

The manse was at odds with the architecture of rest of the city, with its golden spires that punched the sky from its domed roofs, its many pillars, and the sheer scale of it. Land was a premium in Creuen, and while each manse held a decorative garden retreat, none other held a flame to the grandeur displayed here. Everywhere in the south, but especially so close to the Ignis, water was at a premium. Maud's palace lavishly gurgled with the sound of dozens and dozens of fountains, all who held wide-basined pools so large they played home to hundreds of coy fish or crocodile.

So perhaps she told the truth, Aritian thought. There were other signs, like frescos of strange rituals that sprawled in halls that could only be compared to a sanctum of worship. These were spread throughout the manse, but were numerous enough that Aritian hazard that if it had been a temple that it could have held some ten thousand supplicants at any given time.

Just within the walls sprawled a luscious garden filled with exotic plants brought from all corners of Ignea. The compound was divided by a long mosaic courtyard that flowed from the gate to the guard tower, and the gold-leafed roofs glittered softly in the light drizzle. The gated entrance rested on Phoenix Street and on Scorpion Street, where they were now, lay the far side of the garden.

Dellacindrael waved toward the wall where date trees lined both the exterior and interior. Where the elf pointed to stood a tree that curved toward the street from the interior. Without waiting for him, she gracefully jogged to the closest trunk and shimmied up. Her soft pink robes seemed to hinder her only slightly as they caught on the rough bark several times. Once she climbed to a height just above the wall, she lightly stepped to it and crouched, grabbing two handfuls of date fronds and gingerly lowering herself to the interior of the estate. Aritian blinked with surprise, somewhat impressed by this clandestine skill and followed quickly after.

Once over, they both crouched low among the small bushes that crowded the shady base of the palm. Aritian turned to ask why they hadn't entered through the gate, but Dellacindrael made a quick motion with her left hand, indicating for silence. The elf crept forward, keeping low among the greenery around them, and Aritian followed, careful to move without a sound. Dellacindrael stopped beneath a thick fern and bent a leaf down to reveal the shady paths of the garden.

It took only a moment for the Warlord and Lady Maud to appear. The pair were strolling casually through the sizable garden and passed a large fountain some three-dozen paces from where Aritian and Dellacindrael hid. Qurin One Eye, king of Utarye, was a large man. He towered nearly a foot and a half taller than Maud, was broad of shoulder and thickly-muscled. He had tanned skin, tinged an almost sallow-green, and wore ceremonial robes of navy and silver. His face was younger than Aritian had expected, though heavily scared, and over his right eye he wore a silver patch. He walked with the natural rolling gait of a predator and wore a scowl, with his large hands clasped before him as if to keep himself in check.

Lady Maud wore a dark maroon gown of sweeping silk that trailed behind her, a silvered circlet, and a white lace veil that hid all but her eyes. Next to Qurin, she seemed diminutive, but she walked with a commanding air that was intimidated by no man. Aritian wonder why and when she had changed from this morning, but he disregarded it as superficial intimidation. Maud was a master at creating a visage that suited whatever purpose she pursued, and she used her beauty with no less care then she would a sword. It seemed like a weird quirk to Aritian, to be so detailed when presenting yourself, but Maud had lived a thousand years and he could not deny that she was a master of subtlety.

Dellacindrael leaned close, and her breath whispered on his cheek, as she quietly commanded, "Come, the bubbling of the fountain hides their words. We must gain a closer vantage."

Aritian shook his head, and in a hushed whisper, said, "She is guarded against intrusive ears. She will feel our presence."

Although Aritian desperately wanted to comply, he had no wish of being caught eavesdropping. Dellacindrael smiled disarmingly and pulled a thin chain from beneath the neckline of her gown. A pendant rested in her palm. A fat, droplet-shaped amber gem winked warmly in the soft shade. Aritian recoiled. He knew from his studies the devastating effect the gem could have on a Ronan. Dellacindrael dropped the pendant carefully beneath her robes and made a placating gesture with her hands. Aritian nodded, but eyed her uneasily. With the presence of amber, Maud would not feel their presence.

They crept among the date trees, careful to keep as much foliage as they were able between them and the path. It was more a matter of staying low, as the bushes along the paths edge grew quite thick, allowing them to remain hidden easily.

As they approached Maud's voice filtered through the trees. "... a Warlord of your stature. I suggest you continue to provide your services as we agreed. I hardly think it's necessary for me to remind you, Qurin boy, of where you would be today without my most generous assistance." Maud's voice held little emotion, just slight inflections allowing you to know the veiled meaning behind her polite demeanor.

"I have more than enough scars, Lady Suna, that any further reminder from you would be garish." Qurin's tone was as cool as ice, and Aritian could tell he was suppressing a furious anger. For a moment Aritian empathized with the man. The warlord's tone was tight, as he explained, "These are times of tenuous peace. To be seen procuring such copious amounts of weaponry and war stock would be seen as most provocative. My kingdom needs to remain as placatory as possible if we are going to see a full year without another war. I don't think..."

Maud held up a white, gloved hand lazily, cutting his words short. When she spoke, her words were colored by thick sarcasm. "My Qurin, I never knew you to be such a man of reconciliation, especially when it came to your cousin Warlords." Qurin gritted his teeth audibly. "I am humbled by your sentiments, truly I am, but in Ignea we all have our roles to play, Lord Qurin. You are expected to indulge the game when those in greater position demand it. If it relieves you of unease, know you have the full support of the Odium Collation. Should your..." Maud paused as if trying to stifle a laugh, then continued amused, "kingdom be threatened, we will give assistance. Your fears are groundless, young King, truly." Maud concluded simply, as if pacifying a child.

In a flat voice, filled with unveiled doubt, Qurin asked, "What assurances do I have that you speak the truth?" The pair now stood nearly directly in front of Aritian and Dellacindrael, although their backs were to them. Maud stopped to admire a delicate blue flower that grew on the opposite side of the path.

Maud's voice filled with notes of surprise, as she said, "Why Qurin, you have my most sincere pledge of honor." Maud cupped the small flower in her palm and bent close, breathing in its aroma. "Has my word ever failed you before?" Maud asked quizzically.

"No." Qurin admitted, shaking his head. Resentfully, he asked, "Why is this distribution so much greater than the last?" Maud did not deign to answer and Qurin made to place a hand on her shoulder to turn her toward him, but he recoiled his hand before touching her. Gruffly, he asked, "You're asking me to actively put my people in harm and for what? To carry weapons to some deserted city some hundred miles into the desert. Why and to what end, do you keep asking this of me?" Maud turned to face him and gave him a weighted glare. Qurin's shoulders sagged as he sighed and after a moment under Maud silent stare, he meekly asked, "How am I to accept that you speak for the Collation?"

Maud smiled, and replied in a near whisper, "You know how, Lord Qurin, you know." For a moment, the two of them stared at one another silently and then Maud took Qurin's large arm in her own. Brightly, she said, "Come now, in a week's time you will have fulfilled your agreement and this will all be just a slightly distasteful memory." They resumed their stroll along the path, and Maud made a sweeping gesture toward the gardens, as she said, "I have three more fountains I wish for you to see. The gardens are exceptionally gorgeous this time of the year, so plush after the heavy rains, and we simply cannot allow this afternoon be spoiled by trifling negotiations." Qurin grimaced, but nodded. Maud began chatting cordially about her garden and the weather.

Aritian and Dellacindrael sat silently for what seemed like an hour, both absorbing what they had heard. *This corruption must be a living thing or else Maud is outfitting soldiers to protect it*, Aritian thought. He searched his memory for a map of the outlying desert beyond the city, but he found his knowledge lacking. No map he had ever seen had noted ruin's close to Creuen.

Dellacindrael broke the silence first, speaking in a harsh whisper, "We must now speak to the man known as Ibriham. He knows of the ruin we seek. It is where your half-sisters perished and it is there that the corruption will be found."

Aritian looked at the elf in surprise. Dellacindrael's eyes were narrowed with determination, but he could see a glimmer of fear in her eyes. Aritian nodded, not arguing. If that is what the Oracle revealed then he would not doubt her. In a whisper, he said, "Tomorrow." Dellacindrael nodded in agreement. Aritian hesitated and looked away. Weakly, he said, "I have to show you something first. There is an Inn called the Red Fox, just north of the Gilded Bazaar. Meet me there tomorrow, just after dawn."

Dellacindrael cocked her head in question, and warned, "Time is of the greatest importance." Aritian nodded, but said nothing. Dellacindrael smiled thinly to herself, her eyes downcast and whispered, "Bring this Ibriham with you. We must learn this secret, and soon."

Adwin

Chapter Forty-Five:

Bend the Knee

The sun crested the horizon and blearily gazed through the copious fog that clung to the coast of Agos. Adwin stood on the wall gazing eagerly through the grayness. The white sand beaches below lay abandoned in the distance and the oak trees dotting the land between the sea and the wall stood silently, almost nervously twitching in the cool sea breeze.

A heavy pall of anticipation hung over the city. It was obsessive, and stifling to most. Men along the wall shifted from foot to foot, their armor clanking as they prepared themselves for the coming assault. Many a man's face dripped with sweat, and many more talked in low hushed voices between slugs from dark wineskins. Adwin's heart raced, but it was not from nervousness. He stood next to the king, his king, and as he gazed up at the living mountain of royalty, his chest swelled with pride.

King Paul Thoriston was a bear of a man, standing over six feet tall, and was as broad as two common men. He had coarse black hair, a hawk-like and clear blue gaze, with a square jaw lined with dark stubble. He wore his heavy silver armor like a second skin, and his pale-blue cape swept from his broad shoulders to stir at his feet restlessly. The king's eyes never left the rolling waves of the sea. They could all hear the drums. The pounding had relentlessly grown steadily for the last three hours until it was a roar that rose above the crash of the tide.

Lifoy stepped to his side, and peered out into the murkiness of the fog. Adwin looked at him apprehensively. His brother was tall, but rake-thin, with pale skin common to the north. *We look nothing alike*, Adwin thought in excitement, *but we are the same*. He had watched his brother spiral from the sky, weeks past, descending in the form of a giant, silver Roc. He had seen his brother transform from beast to man. To even think of such a thing made Adwin's heart skip with excitement. *I don't understand why Mother would hide such a magnificent truth*, Adwin thought as he gazed at his brother with both awe and joy.

Lifoy had returned to Agos in a foul mood. Adwin couldn't think of why, but he hoped desperately that it had nothing to do with him. "There," Lifoy pointed to the left of where they stood, toward the thick wisps of fog that stubbornly obscured their view. "Can you see the light?"

Adwin stood on his tiptoes, and dutifully peered over the grey wall to where Lifoy had pointed. He saw indeed. Even now, men along the wall began to whisper frantically. "I see it." Adwin said in a hushed whisper. From the fog a massive shadow emerged. A huge lantern hung from the bow of the ship and its harsh, yellow light burned away the obscurity of the fog. The ship's deck glittered metallically in the dim light, as ranks upon ranks of men in white capes and silver armor stood ready for war. In the center of them, men wearing little more than rags beat barrel-sized drums keeping tempo. Another ship emerged from the fog, the white clouds billowing apart as it cut through the sea, then another, and another still.

The king spoke in a hushed voice, "Adwin, the time has come." Paul glared at the ships, with terrible anger. Adwin nodded yes, his stomach twisting with anticipation. The king bellowed, "Light and arm!"

Activity bubbled behind the wall, as the men scurried to do the king's bidding. Lifoy touched Adwin's shoulder lightly, and in a whisper, advised, "Wait until they have reached the highest point of the arch. No need to strain yourself."

Adwin nodded. Behind him he could feel his father's eyes

boring into his back disapprovingly. Adwin knew his father hated what must happen, despised that these men sought to use his son as a weapon, but Adwin had stood firm. These were his people and he wanted to fight to protect them. "Loose!" The king roared, in a voice that carried across the beach.

Catapults thrummed and wood groaned as the sky was filled with tens of thousands of small wooden projectiles that shone with sparks of fire. They arched over the wall, and soared through the air. Adwin watched, craning his head, gripping the edge of the stone wall with sweaty hands. His eyes narrowed in concentration. The small wooden items, streamed through the fog like a miniature meteor shower; raining fire. They passed the beach and streamed toward the water. More than twenty more ships had appeared in view, pushing through the fog with unerring arrogance.

"Now!" screamed Lifoy. Adwin grunted, but didn't hear the noise. The veins of his forehead stuck out as he strained desperately. The flying objects snapped out of their fall. Their leathery wings burst open, flapping like bats as the marionette birds flew in a dark cloud toward the sails of the ships. In their talons, each grasped a glowing brand.

The puppets were roughly-hewn and pale. They had no time to cure the wood, and their shapes were mismatched and made by the hands of many. The men on the ships yelled in warning; many beseeching their god against such unnatural apparitions.

The first birds plunged into the sails of the ships, and orange flames rippled across the white sigil of Ordu. Adwin lifted his left hand and the flock rose above the first sails. The golems had no eyes and so he flew them blind. His thin hands shook and even releasing the first few, it did little to lessen the burden of the flock. The brands cut through the fog, exposing the armada below. Two thousand ships choked the waters of the Reena for as far as the eye could see. Adwin cried out in despair.

The front of the flock folded their wings and flung themselves down upon the ships. Arrows filled the sky, punching into the wooden birds. A half a hundred spun from the sky to fall into the blue water below with a hiss, but more fell upon the crowded decks of the ships, burning men and wood.

King Paul turned toward the council of U.F.K that stood behind him. In a cold voice, he pronounced, "The finger of the Ordu has come to test us." He raked his eyes across the faces of men and women who stood before him. They were dressed in the vestments of their respective houses and kingdoms. None had come prepared from war. Many looked nervously to the approaching armada and more than a few looked to the boy who wielded powers only whispered of in their parent's last words. "Today, Agos stands alone. This cannot be. You all have refused me troops, refused me supply, and yet it is I who stands like a shield before the threshold to all the lands of the United Free Kingdoms." Paul said with restrained anger.

Adwin rose his right hand, and the flock banked west, dodging the dark wave of arrows that flooded the sky. Dozens of birds dropped, free of his control, and crashed into the ships below. Men raced across the decks, screaming orders as they tried to put the fires out. The sea burned behind the king as he bared down on the nobles before him.

Paul waved a hand, gesturing to the approaching navy, as he said, "This is but a trifle to the grand army of the Imperial Ordu and even still, we shall be hard pressed to win this day." Paul's hawk-like gaze bore into the faces of the aristocrats before him with bald contempt. The king's voice had grown hard as he said, "Alone, Agos shall be defeated and after, it will be just a matter of years before the Ordu delivers you the same fate. The United Free Kingdoms must act with haste to bind under one rule for the singular purpose of survival. We must make a stand here at the threshold and stop them. We must unite and truly so, for if we don't our doom will come, and one by one each of us shall fall."

A tall man who wore silk robes of pale-green and gold stepped forward into the silence that had fallen over the crowd. He was a proud fellow with greying hair and a sour expression. His face twisted with anger, as he said, "I came here, bullied by your winged herald, but I shall not be browbeat into surrendering my lands to an Agosian King."

Lifoy smiled mischievously. He had taken great delight in sweeping down upon each capital, scattering people with fear as he landed in their wide, sweeping courtyards. It had been too long since he had rattled so many cages, and had come as a great relief to his impotent frustration and bruised ego.

Another man, younger than the first, but wearing robes that mirrored the man, spoke reasonably, "I must agree with the honorable Lord of Westland. Lord Richard speaks truly, for we would be remiss in our duties as stewards of Lafrey if we simple surrendered our independence. Is that not the very reason we formed this alliance, to remain free and independent of another Lord's will?"

A few other men began to nod their agreement, but a woman stepped away from the crowd and their muttering grumbles stilled. She wore a teal-colored gown and the points of her slightly-pointed ears rested just beneath the rim of her heavy, golden crown. She was beautiful, in a haughty way, with deep-blue eyes that were nearly back, and long raven-colored hair that swept to her waist. As a half-elf, she walked with a grace that the human eye could not properly appreciate, and despite her short stature, commanded the eye of every noble who bore witness. With a sweep of her skirts she turned to stand at Paul's side, and accepted his arm gratefully.

She addressed the crowd in a calm voice, "As Queen of Nimfrael and eldest of my five sisters, I, Lady Yamiel, speak for my people. I insist that you banish your fears and look to survival. I have pledged my Kingdom's allegiance to my husband and have committed my troops to our mutual defense." The woman looked at the two balking men with a kind smile, and said, "I implore you, Lord Richard and you, Lord David, to reconsider your stance of opposition and see reason in this promised hope." The men and women in the crowd stilled with shock, before erupting in hushed, fervent whispers.

Lord David's pudgy face paled with rage, and he roared, "Husband?" He shook his head, the heavy jowls of his chin jiggling drolly, as he yelled, "I see now that Nimfrael, along with Agos, seeks to rule us all!" He turned back to the nobles of the U.F.K, and beseechingly said, "Please, Lord and Ladies, do not listen to this farce. We seek to defend our freedom, not gift it away before the threat of the great enemy has reached our shores. Why else then, would we not simply bow to Ordu?" Many of the crowd had stopped conferring with one another and seemed to consider his words.

Lord Richard nodded sagely, and counseled, "Lord David is right, we shall not barter away our rights in the face of fear. The Kingdom of Lafrey bows to no power, not to Ordu and certainly not to Agos and its whore." He said, spinning angrily to face Paul and his bride. He spat to the side with disgust.

Lord David's eyes flicked nervously to his fellow ruler, dismayed by his companion's disrespect, but threw his worry to the side as he looked over his shoulder. The power of the council stood behind him. He spread his arms wide, and said angrily, "Lady Yamiel, this is outrageous. You are but one of five ruling members of your Kingdom. Surely, your sisters must be consulted? I am confident that many would never willingly forfeit their sovereignty..." He let the implication hang in the air for a moment, before smiling widely, and suggesting, "Let us call a meeting, and let all the Ladies of Nimfrael speak."

Yamiel matched his smile with a feral grin, and in a cool, emotionless voice said, "That you would imply that I gained my autonomy through some form of treachery is beneath you, Lord David. My sisters have ceded rule of the Kingdom to me peacefully, of their own free will. They too see the need for unity and in that spirit, understood the necessity of stepping aside. Nimfrael speaks with one voice now." The crowd gasped in shock, and the whispers resumed even more frantic then before.

David stuck out a pudgy finger at the queen, his many rings winking in the newborn light that had begun to break apart the heavy fog, as he indignantly said, "I will seek out the Queen of Krin. We will make assurances that will ensure that you stand alone in this desperate grab for power. She will oppose this insidious plot and with us, withstand both you and the Ordu."

Richard nodded, and said eagerly, "Yes, Lords and Ladies, see this deception for what it is, I beg of you. Why isn't the great Lady of Krin here?" He looked at them, his brown eyes wide with question. The whispers fell silent. Richard whirled on the united rulers, and said, "These two conspirators knew she would hear nothing of this and in fact, would have struck you down for your impertinence."

King Paul smiled and took a single step forward. His easy smile seemed to break the man's confidence and Lord Richard retreated a step, seeing the open threat for what it was. In a congenial voice, Paul said, "Take care Lords of Lafrey, you stand in my lands and I shall hear no threats upon my person or that of my Queens." He held the two men's gaze for a half a minute, before dismissing them with a flick of his eyes. The Lords of Lafrey shook with impotent rage.

"Queens?" Richard barked in question.

The King of Agos swung around with a laugh, and pronounced in a roar, "Look to the sea and you shall see where Krin's allegiance lay."

The sky had grown clear of the wooden birds. Adwin clung to the wall weakly, watching the ships burn below. The Ordu armada had lost last half of its sails and several ships listed abandoned, the fires left free to rage across the decks as they slowly sank. Sogin knelt at his side, supporting his son with a strong arm. The first row boats had been lowered to the sea and hundreds of Ordu soldiers paddled toward the shore.

Streaming from the north, cutting across the placid blue waters was hundreds of ships bearing the blood-red sails of Krin. Blaring with blue fire, stood the proud, golden trident of the Queen's sigil stamped upon the full length of the billowing sails of the ship that led. The ships in her armada had been stained black and the bows had been carved in the likeness of a snarling wolf. The Ordu's left flank began to turn to face the incoming threat.

Richard came to the wall, and bellowed, "What foul magicks have you worked on the fair Lady Katherine? The unbending Queen would never have agreed to this of her own free volition!" He turned to face Paul, pulling free his ornamental sword as he did so. King Paul eyed the free blade casually. The crowd of nobles had grown deadly quiet, and even Lord David dared not speak. The soldiers along the wall eyed the scene appraisingly, but made no move to intervene.

Adwin had turned from the sea, and nervously eyed the two men. *How dare that old man threaten my king?* He thought enraged. He stood, trembling with weakness and made to throw himself before his king, but Lifoy lay a restraining hand on his shoulder and shook his head.

King Paul waved a hand to the armada of Krin, and said lightly, "No spell lays upon my wife's heart, but that of love. Lady Katherine has agreed to take my hand in marriage. Agos, Nimfrael, and Krin stand united." Paul and Richard sputtered in outrage, but the crowd now only had eyes for King Thoriston.

A fat man in rich robes of purple stepped forward. Gold chains wrapped across the breast of his expansive doublet and his white hair stood in wisps above his golden crown. Nervously, he wiped the sweat from his brow with a green kerchief, before asking, "If the kingdoms of the U.F.K bowed to

Agosian rule, as have Krin and Nimfrael, what assurances would you give that you shall relinquish power should we gain victory?" He smiled weakly at Paul, and said, "As the King of Vale, I am not too proud to say that I have hopes of leaving my lands to my sons, as my father did before me and his father before him, and so on for the last three-hundred years."

Paul nodded in understanding, and said reasonably, "A treaty will be signed and all power shall be relinquished the moment the war has ended. Together, we will succeed..." He paused, making sure to meet each of the noble's eyes once more, before he said insistently, "But only if we are truly united can we win. There cannot be seven armies, seven navies, and seven generals. There must be one."

The crowd dissolved into hushed conference once more. Yamiel stepped forward and raising her hand, called for silence. The queen gained it easily. Her mask of serene calm broke, and with passion she said, "I beseech you, Lords and Ladies, listen to reason. We all wish to keep our independence, but to do that we must concede that a united front is the only logical way to gain victory. To think otherwise is akin to suicide." The nobles considered her words.

As one, a crowd of twelve men and women stepped forward. They were dressed in colors of grey, and their vestments were the simplest and least gaudy among the crowd. They varied in age and standing. A plump woman with curly grey hair stepped forward. She paused a moment, her green eyes searching the eyes of the two rulers before her, and then bowed. In a strong voice, she proclaimed, "The council of Ferrum will bend the knee." The council members behind her each dipped their heads conceding power.

A man in his thirties stepped forward. He wore armor gilded with gold. On the chest of his breastplate was the sigil of a raven perched on a silver branch. He had pale blonde hair and ruddy cheeks, but stood straight as he said, "I am not too arrogant to say that my heart is not filled with fear and trepidation, but I can see the sense of such a course. After review of said treaty, I, King William Roth of Tenese, will relinquish my rule." King Paul gave the king a nod of respect and the man stepped back.

The fat king minced forward again, and though he did not look pleased, he relented, "I too, must see this treaty or have a hand in its writing, but I bow to the ever-wise counsel of Lady Yamiel." He nodded to the half-elf with respect, and she flashed him a brilliant smile. In a bold booming voice that shook his great stomach, he swore, "I, King John Kent of Vale, will join your forces with my own."

Richard looked at his peers with dumbfounded perplexity. He shook his head, as he said, "I cannot fathom this."

David's face had grown red with rage, as he accused, "You all are fools."

Richard nodded, and said sharply, "The Kingdom of Lafrey will resist this insidious usurper." He gripped his swords hilt as though he wished to strike them all down.

David smiled cruelly, and warned viciously, "You will starve without our crops."

Paul nodded with a sigh, and said sadly, "Yes, we would..." he eyed the two men sorrowfully, and whispered, "if you two still lived." The men froze in panic, their eyes flicking side to side for support, but not one noble met their eyes. In a hoarse whisper, the King of Agos said, "Forgive me, but I will not allow the United Free Kingdoms to fall."

Paul's broadsword flicked from his scabbard with a hiss, blurring as it swung left to decapitate Lord David before the man had even a chance to react. The man's round head rolled away and his thick form collapsed to the floor.

Richard's face twisted in a snarl and he leapt forward, brandishing his sword. Paul met him, dancing lightly to the side with surprising swiftness. He batted the man's wild swing aside, and Lord Richard's sword clattered to the floor. Paul clutched the man's throat, meeting the man's eyes as his face purpled.

The King of Agos slipped his broadsword into the man's chest, holding Richard up as the life faded from his eyes. Paul released his grip and the man slid off the sword and landed in a heap.

For a moment, the battlement was stunned to silence; the approaching army but a distant thought as they stood transfixed. The moment broke, and Paul turned to a guard who waited within ear shot. Paul called to him, "Have the men of Lafrey, who escorted the Lords, been restrained?"

The caption saluted, and said, "Yes, my King."

King Paul nodded, and said, "Inform them that their Lords are dead, victims of Ordu." The caption saluted once more, whirled around, and raced down the narrow stairs to the courtyard below. Paul turned to the woman at his side, and said kindly, "Lady Yamiel, if you would?"

She nodded, her expression tightening as she promised in a cold voice, "My army waits on the edge of Lafrey's border. I will escort the guard back to their kingdom and meet my sisters. We will secure Lafrey and send word when it's done."

Paul gave her a short bow, and said, "I thank you and please, go with care." She nodded curtly. There was no love between these two, for they were bound together for mutual benefit. She followed the captain at a sedate pace.

The King turned back to the wall, and his voice boomed through the air, "Men, prepare yourselves! The Ordu have reached the shores!" Hundreds of rowboats littered the beach, and the Ordu had begun to organize themselves into columns. "Catapults, fire!" The king bellowed.

Wooden groans filled the air, and tons of rock and pitch streamed above. The wall watched as the burning stone crashed into the ranks of Ordu with a sickening crunch and the hiss of flames. Tortured screams filled the air, and Paul commanded in a shout that rose above the bloodied Ordu, "Arrows nocked!" He held out a hand, as the soldier's beneath shouted a war cry and began to march forward. "Hold, for the approach."

Paul turned from the line for a moment, and bowed to the

nobles with a curt bend. In a moderate voice, he said, "Honorable guests, if you would, an armed guard waits below to escort you away from the battle." They nodded as one and turned from the battle, each nervous to flee the impending assault and grateful for having been released. The King of Agos turned back to the battlefield.

Adwin tugged on Sogin's billowing robes and asked, "Papa, can I stay? I wish to watch."

Sogin frowned, and said sternly, "No, my son, you do not wish to see the bloodshed that soon shall come. Let us return to the safety of our shop." He tugged on his son's hand.

Lifoy came behind the boy and gave Sogin a smile. He punched Adwin in the back of the head and the boy crumpled to the floor, knocked-out cold. Sogin bridled with anger, and horrified, asked, "Why did you do that? What the seven hells is wrong with you?"

Lifoy smiled down at the prone form at his feet, and said, "Your son has helped as promised. The Ordu will be hard-pressed to return home with half their ships ablaze. Krin will capture many ships, which we may outfit for the coming war, but Adwin's part in this is finished." Lifoy's eyes flicked up to meet Sogin's gaze, and with a mocking pout, he said, "I fear I must spirit him away now."

Sogin shook his head in denial, and shouted, "You cannot do this! You cannot take my son." He turned to face the king and fell to his knees, as he begged, "My King, please, I implore you to intervene."

Paul grimaced, for he had known all along what was to come. Sadly, he shook his head, and said, "He is a being of magic. Surely, good man, you understood this would come to pass."

Sogin whirled to face Lifoy, and warned, "I shall call Morgana." His hands searched his robes frantically.

Lifoy chuckled and pulled the man's missing mirror from his pocket. He leaned back and shattered the mirror on the stone lip of the wall. Sogin's shoulders slumped and he looked close to tears as his desperation grew.

Callously, Lifoy said, "My mother knew this day would come. It is the very reason she bade your ship close and ensorcelled you to her bed." The man's eyes had grown wild with despair, and he shook his head once more. Lifoy's voice softened, and he said, "You were used, my friend, and now your use has expired." Lifoy bent over Adwin and pulled the unconscious boy into his arms. His back exploded with a burst of muscles and feathers as white wings tore free. Sogin fell back with a shout as Lifoy flapped his wings experimentally.

With a chuckle, Lifoy said, "Good day." Lifoy flung himself into the air, carrying the youngest Ronan in his arms. A howl of grief followed him, and below, ships burned and the sea churned as Krin and Ordu clashed. The Ordu army marched up the beach to war and from the wall, death rained down in a cloud of a thousand arrows. The second battle of the Reena had begun.

Aritian

Chapter Forty-Six:

Revelations of Regret

Aritian sat cross-legged on a small bamboo mat, staring at the flames that snaked into the air before him. He was not alone. Three-dozen men and women sat around a great fire that dominated the center of the room. The room was pitch black, save for the dancing fire. Neither the walls nor the ceiling could be seen, lost beyond the light within the shadows that crowded close. All were nude save for a simple loincloth, and their oiled bodies gleamed with high definition. All of their eyes were dilated, locked unblinkingly on the rippling blaze.

The flames crackled and twisted, dancing far above them with unnatural strength. The black wood that fed the fire was strange. It eagerly burned, but seemed to give little of itself in the process. The smoke curled in black tendrils from the mouth of the copper, sun-shaped censer and filled the room in rolling, languid waves. All of them breathed deeply, rhythmically, taking the smoke within them. The smoke twisted through his body, making him feel light and numb, yet more aware at the same time.

Aritian was deep within a trance and allowed the flames to consume all thought as he studied its intricate dance and subtle, hidden patterns. The fire was hot. Sweat beaded along his brow and intermingled with the sharp pungent smell of the oil. They had been sitting in quiet concentration for more than an hour. A pair of drums, lost beyond the shadows, picked up a slow tempo.

A man to Aritian's left began to speak. "Let the flames of

Ignathra guide your mind's eye. To see what is beyond yourself, you must give yourself utterly to the flame. Ignathra is all that is light in this world and no shadow can stand before His glaring eye." His voice was worn and came in a harsh whisper that complimented the hiss of the fire. "The flames are Ignathra incarnate, a gift that gives us life and yet also is the hand of the destroyer. Those most in tune with Ignathra will see clearly that he is a God of enlightenment." Aritian did not take his eyes from the flame, but he pictured the man who spoke.

Nath was a small man, with a thin frame, long grey hair and bronzed skin. He had a wrinkled face that held kind green eyes. It was a face that Aritian had grown to know well in the last several weeks. Nath droned on, "We soldiers of the Flame bring truth to the people and act with a singular purpose. We raise the ignorant from the depth of the Shadow and into the light. All men have darkness within their soul, but with the flame of Ignathra we may burn away this taint and purge ourselves of darkness. Each of you carries His flame within you, for He fills all life. Those who can train their mind to see the flame are truly blessed and thus responsible for those who cannot."

Memories flashed through Aritian's mind. He remembered the moment he took the Vertalian prince's life, the betrayal of Jabari, the mine shaft with its insufferable darkness, and the bloody dawn that brought retribution. The tendrils of the smoke he had inhaled gave his mind a clarity and concentration free of distraction. The image of the great calamity burned through him, and he remembered the searing heat of the flames that consumed the city and the stench of death that curled through the air.

"The fire before you today are but a symbol of the inferno that lays within your souls." Nath paused, stressing the importance of his words. Aritian's mind turned from the memories of the inferno. He knew what happened next and dared not think of Razia's death. He flinched away, and found himself contemplating his time in the Time Vortex. Years had passed. His grief of Razia had been purged from him, as had all emotion save for his thirst for knowledge. He had learned devastating knowledge, grown with terrible power, but when he stepped forth, dual personalities seemed to battle for supremacy. He was torn. He didn't know who he was anymore.

Like a candle in the darkness, Nath guided their minds now. "Look not with your eyes at the flame, but look within your mind and seek the core of yourself."

Aritian let his mind follow the High Priest's words, and soon found himself walking in a warren of dark tunnels. Aritian's conscious mind knew where the maze led, but it was his unconscious mind that carried him unerringly forward.

Nath continued speaking, his voice remaining low, "Each individual must walk their own path of enlightenment as each flame found within is unique from any other. Some call this flame the spirit, while others call it the soul. Both are wrong. Those pieces are separate, and along with the flame, make one whole. We call this the Trinity of Man. The spirit represents your passion, your will, all that drives and motivates you. The soul represents your sense of morality. It dictates your actions and inactions, and tells you what is right from wrong. The flame is something different entirely." Nath's voice hissed with pleasure as he spoke. "It is what connects you to the world beyond yourself. It is the invisible sense that gives voice to your intuition. It is the way you can find yourself worlds beyond our fleshly confines, a place where you can touch and be touched by Ignathra."

Aritian's unconscious mind raced through the maze with surety and speed. The maze was convoluted, designed to trick the mind and trap those foolish enough to dare its treachery. Aritian's conscious mind tried to slow his pass, to take a misstep that would allow him more time, but it was all for naught. The maze had been created for him, by him. He was the architect, even as his mind raged against such a thought. *That was not me,* he screams internally. Like an arrow shot from a bow on a windless day, he fled unerringly towards his destination.

Nath's words cut through him, as he said, "Many are unaware that such a flame exists. Many fear it. Most however, go through life too preoccupied to care of its existence, aware or not. The few that walk through that flame and withstand its touch are the truly rare men of completeness. They are people who are one with the world, themselves, and god simultaneously. These are men of true enlightenment. They are free of the lies of culture, heart, and home. They can see the world around them for what it truly is. Their minds are clear of self-doubt, ambition, and vice. They can hear the word of god. Do not walk your path to the flame clothed in the shadow of this world, rather step forth unburdened, for it is then that you shall find your way unscathed."

Aritian stepped from the maze within his mind. The flame before his eyes danced blood-red with bright, cherry warmth, but paled like a dim, dying coal, compared to the light within his mind's eye. Before him stood a door that stood suspended in nothingness. It arched above him, ascending beyond his sight into darkness. Along the edge of the door crimson light gleamed like a star from the heavens, blazing with blinding brightness. The door was covered with runes that crawled in intricate lines across the roughly-hewn crystalized surface in tight, small lines. Aritian paused before the door, his hand an arm's length from its surface.

Nath spoke again, his voice had grown warm, "Do not lose heart should your journey take time. We all walk different paths. Should you find the flame before you, rejoice, for you have found something that many do not touch until their last breath."

Aritian's unconscious mind reached toward the door with longing; the power beyond screamed for release. The light shone with greater intensity the closer his hand got to the door. Aritian knew what lay beyond and the exquisite pleasure that it would bring. His hand began to glow and crackle with ruddy electricity as the power beyond beckoned him close with sweet promise.

Quicker than thought, Aritian snapped his eyes open. The fire before him was lost to darkness and the door within his mind faded like an after image as he recoiled in revulsion. Aritian's breath came raggedly and he shook with the strength of restraint it took to abstain. Slowly, his breaths evened out and slowed. The power of the smoke, and the trance that had held his mind, fled. Aritian turned his head to the left and caught Nath's steady, knowing gaze. The old man's lips curled slightly in approval and he gave Aritian a slight nod, before turning his eyes back to the flames. Aritian let his eyes wander the room, never letting the fire hold his gaze for more than a moment as he listened to the remainder of Nath's sermon.

*****

After, Aritian walked from the temple into the breaking of dawn. The darkness of the sky was fleeing in purple and pink stains. Rain poured from the sky as he walked down the temple's great steps and the burgundy robes he wore soon became soaked, but Aritian didn't mind. The rain's cool touch soothed his hot skin and cleared the incense from his mind. Aritian made to walk across the wide courtyard when a soft voice called out his name. Aritian turned to see Nath descending the temple steps. The old man was assisted by a dark wooden cane and wore matching robes of red.

"Slow your steps young acolyte, you have no need to flee these temple grounds." Nath said breathlessly as he walked a measured pace to meet him. "I wish to speak with you before you depart. Let us walk the courtyard." Nath said, turning from him and walking toward the far side of the courtyard.

Aritian had no choice but to follow. "I would be honored, what is it that you wish to discuss?" Aritian asked respectfully, keeping his tone neutral.

"You stood before the door again, did you not?" Nath asked his tone displaying no emotion. Aritian knew the priest was not asking, but rather stating a fact. Aritian had confided his inner turmoil, but had not been so specific as to name it. The priest had been wise enough not to pry. Aritian simply nodded in response. "I find it most curious that you are able to find your flame at such a young age and yet, are unable or unwilling to open the door to enlightenment. What is it that you fear?" The question fell between them. Aritian wished that he could confide all, but he dared not risk it. He knew exactly what would happen if Maud discovered his indiscretion.

Aritian remained silent as he contemplated his answer. *It is odd*, Aritian thought, *that Nath now broaches the subject when this very question tortures my soul.* Aritian supposed that the old man could sense his confusion, and admitted to himself that he was doing a shoddy performance of hiding his misery. Never before had he felt emotions so raw, and yet he supposed that this was because had had always believed that he knew himself. That was no longer a question. He was lost, his identity as veiled as a strangers.

The morning day was quickly brightening and the noise of the city was beginning to stir. Aritian spoke carefully, "I am unsure. Certainly for more than one reason, but if I had to choose one that I fear above all else, it would be the thought of assimilation. What lays beyond will change me, and I do not wish to lose control of myself or allow it to dominate my actions."

The old priest contemplated his answer silently as they walked along the edge of the courtyards wall. A few moments passed, and Nath said quietly, "The power that lays within is both you and the essence of beyond. It is wise for you to understand the distinction however, I must warn you that you will never truly be whole until the door is open and you accept it fully. God is all, and you must embrace him fully to know yourself. Fear has crippled and stagnated your enlightenment." The priest's words hit Aritian like a hammer, despite the soft tone in which they were delivered. The man was right, Aritian knew. He was at a crossroads and he had to choose and soon, sitting in the ambiguity of his two halves was tearing him asunder.

Aritian replied honestly, "I am not sure I am worthy of enlightenment, nor the powers that might lay beyond."

Nath chuckled and took Aritian's arm, as he said warmly, "It is for that very reason that you are worthy. You are new to Creuen, but not Ignea. It is a cruel world we must suffer through in our path to absolution, but it is that very road that brings us our salvation."

Aritian considered his words, before cautiously saying, "A path has been presented to me, one that promises to bring me fully into the light, but I fear it." Nath looked at him askew, but remained quiet. "I fear that this path will force my hand... that it will take all that lies within me to succeed and I know not if I have the strength." He looked pointedly at the old priest, and said, "It is a path I have forsworn, but I fear equally inaction, lest I compromise my own morals by withholding..." Aritian trailed off, but silently continued, *these dark powers within.*

Nath shook his head, and said sternly, "It doesn't matter. If the path is righteous and true, then you must persevere." He smiled crookedly at Aritian, and said, "Promises made to oneself are the ones we most often break. Do not despair, for this shows your resolve in forging yourself anew in a light more pure than yesterdays."

The pair fell into a contemplative silence as they walked. Aritian knew that he should depart, that if he didn't leave soon the elf would be left waiting. At last, he bowed his head and turned to the priest. Respectfully, he said, "I must leave you now Nath, but I thank you. As always your wisdom proceeds with cool logic that undeniably banishes my selfish fears."

Nath dipped his head, accepting the compliment, before

saying, "I see greatness in you, Aritian, such that can be used for great good or evil. Let your heart champion your actions, for I sense there that Ignathra burns truest." Aritian gave the priest a small smile, and took his leave.

Aritian made his way through the city toward the Gilded Bazaar. The streets were still manageable, but soon he knew that slaves and nobles alike would fill the street in an effort to beat the heat of midday. He soon found himself beneath a white sign that depicted a prancing red fox. The inn before him was large, set back from the road, and faced with a sprawling herb garden. Aritian walked up the wooden steps and entered.

He found himself in a large dining hall. Along the back of the room a bar ran the length of the inn and behind it, immaculately kept shelves filled with bottles of spirit and racks of goblets. Tables filled the large space, each set with four to ten matching chairs depending on size and shape. All were empty, but Aritian could smell a sweet aroma wafting the kitchen that promised a delightful breakfast. Soon the inn would be packed. Aritian waved to the thin man who stood behind the bar and climbed a large flight of stairs that sat to the left. When he reached the landing, he walked down a narrow hall and came to a door that had been painted turquoise. He raised a hand to knock, but hesitated.

Aritian didn't want to go into the room, didn't want to face what was within. He sighed and leaned his head against the door. He straightened as he heard soft footsteps behind him, turned and saw Dellacindrael appear on the landing. She wore long, white robes, and a head wrap that hid her dark hair and pointed ears. She flashed him a small smile and dipped her head in greeting.

"Have you been following me?" Aritian asked, surprised to find her at the inn so soon. The elf nodded. "You thought I wouldn't come?" Aritian asked incredulously.

Her delicate features remained neutral, as she replied, "No, I knew you would. Where is Ibriham?"

Aritian waved a hand toward the door. "He's within." Dellacindrael made to enter, but Aritian placed a hand on her arm, stalling her. She looked at him blandly, dropping her arm from his touch. "What's within..." He trailed off, as he struggled to find the words. "It brings me great shame."

Dellacindrael met his eyes and nodded once. Her expression was unreadable. Aritian sighed, and knocked on the door three times fast and two times more after a slight pause. The door swung open and Ibriham bowed as he stepped back. Ibriham was not in his usual livery, but instead wore loose fitting robes of a design found among commoners. Ibriham eyed Dellacindrael with curiosity, but of course remained politely mute.

Aritian stepped into the room. His heartbeat quickened, as it did each time he came here, and stepped to the side so the elf could see. The main room had been converted from its original use. Instead of a dining table and low couches, there was five large beds equally spaced along the walls. Ori, Azera, Entah, Beryl, and Rythsar lay on one each. Their eyes were closed and they lay under light sheets of white linen. They did not stir, nor did their breath quicken at the sound of company. They lay as still as one in a deep slumber. Seven men stood around the room and who snapped to attention as Aritian entered. They wore soldier uniforms of black pants, tights tunics, and thick leather armor. All were armed, and heavily so. Their hands grasped the hilt of their weapons, ready to spring forward. They eyed Dellacindrael intently, their split, yellow eyes following her every movement as their forked tongues flicked between their thin lips; scenting her.

A lorith sat next to Ori, and as she used a wet towel to brush the sweat from his brow. When she saw Aritian, she stood and bowed her slim neck in deference. Aritian gave the albino a nod. The lorith's scales were pure white without a mar or stain and her hooded eyes glinted red beneath her boney brow. "Friend, it is good of you to come," Aethara said in a soft hiss. She was slim and petite for her race, standing barely four-feet in height.

"Has there being any change in their condition?" Aritian asked curtly. He waved his hand at his waist, and the Dranguis relaxed, falling back against the walls and retreating to the balcony to guard the street vantage. Aritian wished that they would temper themselves, but they didn't seemed capable of lowering their guard. It wasn't in their nature. *At least not anymore*, Aritian thought bitterly.

Aethara shook her head minutely, and said, "No, my friend, no change. They remain asleep." The lorith was deferential, no doubt due to her years of slavery, and demure in nature. Her voice was heavily accented with hissing sounds, more so than most lorith who lived alongside man. Aritian watched, guilt-ridden, as she retreated to stand next to her mate and tenderly cooed into his ear. While Maud had easily produced the lorith when Aritian demanded her, Rythsar and Aethera hadn't truly been able to reunite. *It's all my fault*, Aritian thought wretchedly.

Dellacindrael had taken in the room with a glance and stared at him unblinking. Aritian felt the weight of her judgment and struggled to explain. "I did this to them..." He closed his eyes, trying to find the words, before saying. "Well, it wasn't truly me."

Aritian described what had happened over the course of the last three months. He didn't hold anything back, nor tried to hide anything. Aritian felt shame creep into his words and more than a touch of grief. He explained how Maud had taken his morality, and how in turn he had strived for nearly twelve years towards power without a thought or care; sustained only by the unending need for mastery. He told her how time had passed so swiftly within the Vortex and yet only a few months passed in reality. Aritian admitted the cost and what had followed his emergence with burning cheeks. It was the first time he had confessed fully.

He told her of the brutal training the others had undertaken, too, struck by the same enchantment as he. He explained the forging of the Serpents, and how he made them into ultimate weapons, and how he had asked Entah to extend their life so that they may serve him beyond their normal span of years. It was hard to say such things. Harder still for him to even believe what he said was true and to admit what he had done. All the while Dellacindrael listened without remark. Her expression was placid, unmoving, and as still as stone. Aritian choked out, "Now they remain in a comatose state, unable or unwilling to waken."

When he was finished he wiped the tears from his face, annoyed that his emotions had once more claimed hold of him. The elven woman held him in her gaze easily. Aritian waited for her damnation, ached for it, but Dellacindrael merely asked, "Have you brought healers?"

Aritian nodded, and said, "I have, more than a dozen, but all offered me only befuddled explanations."

The elf nodded as if to herself, and then took a step forward. She hesitated, waved toward his fallen companions, and asked, "May I?"

"Please." Aritian whispered desperately. Dellacindrael walked to Beryl's bedside and laid a pale hand on his brow. She leaned down and listened to his chest, and then sat next to him. She closed her eyes and placed a hand on either side of his temples. A few minutes passed. Ibriham and Aritian walked closer to observe, while Aethera watched with pinned concentration from Rythsar's bedside.

Dellacindrael took a deep breath after a few minutes and opened her eyes. In a whisper, she said, "So far away." Her eyes met Aritian's, and she said, "They are mortal and should not have been taken within that spell. They are lucky to be alive." Her eyes flicked toward the closest assassin, Sicaroo, and she added, "I suspect by whatever connection these creatures have to you that these men are no longer human, and thus were spared from the brunt of the backlash."

Aritian nodded, and he beckoned Sicaroo close. No longer was Sicaroo a child. He had grown up and stood as a man in his late twenties. He was muscular, tall, and his skin had a reddish hue, and appeared subtly scaled. His eyes, golden, were split and emotionless. Aritian reached into his mind with the slightest touch and Sicaroo nodded, assenting to his silent command.

Faster than the eye could follow, a dagger blurred from Sicaroo's hip and appeared in his hand. Sicaroo turned to face the elf and she flinched. His hand whipped up as the elf's eyes widened in fear. Sicaroo's blade cut across his own throat. The blade cut deep, striking bone, splitting his windpipe wide. He choked for a second as blood poured down his neck and trickled from the edges of his lips. He staggered, but did not fall.

Dellacindrael tore her eyes from Sicaroo's and looked to Aritian with voiceless question. She gasped. A matching wound had appeared on Aritian's throat, but even as she watched the flesh of his neck began to stitch itself back together. Her eyes flicked between them as the twin wounds closed, and watched as the blood retreated into the fading cuts.

Aritian turned from her, and said, "You see. They are not easily killed or wounded."

Dellacindrael found her voice after a moment, and in a strained whisper, she said, "The others will recover in time." Aritian waved Sicaroo away, and the man retreated to his position on the wall, replacing his weapon without a word. The elf's voice grew in strength as she stood, and said, "A few weeks, maybe less, and they will waken."

Aritian sighed in relief and felt a weight lift from his shoulders. He steadied himself against the wall with his hand, fearing that his legs might give out. Dellacindrael walked to stand in front of him, and said, "You could have discerned that yourself had you bothered to try." It was the first time Dellacindrael had spoken with a hint of emotion, and it was filled with disgust. Aritian shook his head in slight denial, and Dellacindrael lifted his chin with a firm hand, forcing him to look into her eyes. "You cannot place blame on yourself when you were senseless beneath the weight of a spell. You had no choice, your will was stolen. You are not to blame for this." The elf said this with such finality that Aritian wished that he could believe her words.

    He leaned back from her grasp, and his voice grew strained, as he asked, "Am I not?" His eyes grew wild as he looked at Sicaroo. "Look at what I did to those children." He pronounced, waving toward the assassins. He felt the ring on his pinky finger grow hot as his magic threatened to rise. Maud had lessened its hold, allowing him some use of his power without pain, but what sought release now was far beyond such limits. Aritian swallowed the power, gasping.

    Dellacindrael nodded curtly, and in a stern voice, said, "You have taken their lives that is true, but with great sacrifice can come unparalleled good. Just because they were conceived with evil intent does not mean they must be used to such effect." She looked into his eyes, and promised, "They are powerful and if you had the mind, could be used for righteous good." She shook her head sadly, and said gently, "There is no going back. No reversing the damage done. They are gone, Aritian." Aritian nodded, and suppressed a sob that threatened to escape. The elf continued, her voice an ever-flowing stream of calm, as she explained, "Hate yourself if you must, but no matter the depth of pain you plunge yourself will they ever be whole again. Instead of sulking like a child, you must become powerful in your own right and prevent such acts from ever occurring again." Dellacindrael held his gaze, and Aritian found he could not tear his eyes free.

    "You want me to use my magic." Aritian said in a flat tone. He wanted to scream, to explain all the wrath and terror that it brought, but he knew that it mattered not. She cared not for his past, only his future, and she had traveled here to ensure that he would walk the path the Oracle demanded. In that moment Aritian resented her, and wished that she had never came. *You fool, if she hadn't you would never know of Razia*, he screamed internally.

"Discarding your magic will only make you weak and defenseless against such perilous evil. I will not let you become a puppet of power." Dellacindrael said this icily, emotion once more creeping into her voice. Aritian understood all at once. She would not allow him to fall under Maud's control. The path of light was the only path she presented, the only one she would allow him to tread. In a dangerous whisper, Dellacindrael said, "You have a choice, make it now, for I shall not ask again." The threat was obvious, and for a moment he knew fear. It was strange coming from such a delicate creature, but looking into her eyes, Aritian found himself believing that the elf was not merely bluffing.

Aritian's mind whirled. The sweet embrace of death would be easy. *Too easy*, he thought. Slowly, his resolve began to form. In a whisper, he said, "I can't...I must prevail for Razia's sake." Dellacindrael nodded, once. Aritian felt his past fall away. It was strange. Once he had decided, he found he could let the guilt fall away. It was surprisingly easy, and for a moment he thought himself a fool for the cage he had locked himself within. He cast the thought away and turned toward his half-brother.

"Ibriham."

The slave had not spoken the entire time and had observed their exchange without comment. His head rose sharply, startled that he had been addressed.

"Where did our sisters die?" Aritian asked in a whisper.

Ibriham paled and his eyes flicked toward the door as if he would flee. Rong casually slinked along the wall until he stood before the door and smiled cruelly, exposing his dripping fangs. Ibriham shuddered, and said, "I do not know what place you speak of."

Dellacindrael frowned, and snapped, "I can hear the lie in your words. Do not think that I am susceptible to such deception."

Ibriham turned away from the elf's burning gaze and shook his head. In a quavering voice, he said, "Master... I cannot, you know that I can't."

Aritian noted the fear in his brother's eyes and nodded. Plainly, he asked, "Ibriham, did you love our sisters?"

Ibrahim's mouth dropped open indignantly and he his voice grew angry, as he said, "Aritian, of course I did. How could you ask such a thing?" Ibrahim's back straightened, and in a firm voice he said, "I have been commanded to not speak of such things by my Mistress."

"Bound by magic?" Aritian asked, a single eyebrow raising. Ibrahim licked his lips, and Aritian knew that he had not. "Ibriham, please, you lack no intelligence – surely you see Maud's evil?" Ibrahim's eyes found the ground stubbornly. Insistently, Aritian continued, "She cares only for the cultivation of her own power. You are nothing to her. You see that, don't you?"

Ibrahim's eyes flashed and his mouth tightened. In a hash whisper, he asked, "Is that why you slept with her?"

Aritian felt his stomach roll at the thought, and he swallowed bile. Carefully, he said, "I was not myself."

Dellacindrael stepped forward while Aritian choked down his revulsion. She looked into Ibrahim's eyes, and in a kind voice, said, "I can see the good within you. Do you not wish to resist such darkness? To stand aside is akin to perpetuating such evil yourself. Come to the light, gentle soul." The elf's voice was tinged with the barest hint of magic and her words brought an irresistible desire to surrender. It was a small magic. One of the few talents he knew the elves still possessed. Dully, Aritian wondered if she had used this influence on him.

"I am of her flesh." Ibriham said stubbornly as he crossed his arms.

"As is Aritian." Dellacindrael said dismissively. She peered closer, her emerald eyes dancing with light, as she said, "You know something. You know what we will find there."

Ibriham flailed his hands before his face, and wailed, "Stop. Get out of my head." The elf stepped away, bowing her head.

Aritian extended a tendril of power toward the man, and touched Ibrahim's mind. Aritian was shocked by the depth of emotion that swirled behind the man's defiant plea. He reached deeper, the rims of his eyes burning black as he wrested Ibrahim's emotions from his control. Aritian brought the man's guilt, sadness, and fear bubbling to the surface. It boiled like an insidious storm, rolling through the man like a fever. Ibrahim's face twisted with anguish and he choked down a sob. Aritian dropped the power, shocked by how easy it had been for him to manipulate his brother's mind. Aritian felt a trickle of sweat roll down his forehead. In a whisper, Aritian said, "Kiara and Layanna would want you to help us."

Ibrahim's face crumpled and fell into his hands. His shoulders shook as he lost all sibilance of control. Between sobs, he said, "I sought the very information you seek once before, just after the Mistress departed with Kiara and Layanna." Saying their names seemed to have given him strength, and Aritian recognized a new resolve rise within Ibriham. Ibriham wiped away his tears of grief and his jaw tightened in a grimace.

Ibrahim's voice grew steady, as he said, "This was five years ago. I knew my sisters would not return. All the men here know that when the women are taken, they never come back. What befalls them, we know not nor do we speak of such things. My Father..." Ibriham trailed off. Aritian did not speak, knowing any words he might offer could break Ibrahim's resolve to betray his Mistress.

After a moment, Ibriham continued, "Da...." He paused, his head shaking side to side as he cast away the memory. "Hector found me in the Manse library. I was rifling through the records, searching for answers.... For anything, something that could explain why they were taken. He beat me bloody and was terribly angry, or so I thought at the time. Now I know he was just afraid. He told me after. He told me...." Ibriham trailed off.

Ibriham sighed shakily, and closed his eyes, as he said, "The dead city lays in the desert southeast of Creuen. The path is marked by a Cobra statue along the Onyx Ribbon. Head due south from there and you will find the ruins." He looked away, unable to meet their eyes. Aritian hung on his every word, committing them to memory.

Ibriham continued in a fear-laden whisper, "The ruins are named the Halls of Darth. Once they were a great monastery dedicated to the Master of Death, but the ruins were deserted nearly a century ago. The monastery had been built on an oasis, but it dried up. No one goes there now. That is all I know; all that I was told. My father made me swear to never speak of it and to forget my sisters, but I cannot, though I know in my heart that they are dead."

Aritian took a step forward, and asked, "Will you help me? We mean to stop this evil." Ibriham met his eyes, and Aritian saw in them the reflection of an emotion he knew all too well: hate. Steadily, Aritian asked, "What are you willing to sacrifice for revenge?"

Ibriham bowed his head, and in a hoarse whisper, he said, "Everything. Tell me what you need, Master."

Within an hour they had gathered what was required. Aritian had drawn a white pentagram on the floor in chalk and stood at the apex of the star, while Ibriham stood nervously in the crux of two points at the star's base. A tall floor mirror stood between them and a candle stood before them each, one on either side of the mirror. The orange flames coiled and flickered higher than was natural, and their mirrored reflections shifted erratically in the light. Aritian took a deep breath and then touched the door that lay in the center of his mind. As the power rushed through him anew, Aritian began to chant.

Aritian

Chapter Forty-Seven:

The Onyx Ribbon

The moon shone full in the night sky, casting the streets awash in pale light. Aritian waited by the Red Swan Inn across from the eastern gate tower. The inn itself was one of the more prosperous, having three stories and a wrapped porch set with hookahs and low couches. A large outbuilding squatted behind it with enough stalls to house more than a hundred mounts. The Inn clamored with noise and was filled with southern traders who had made the long journey from Futu and beyond. Wagons, carriages, and litters lined the side of the inn, from the very humble to the most ornate. Guard dogs were tied to several, and lay in the shadows beneath, their ears twitching at the boisterous noise of the inn.

Aritian stood in the shadow of a large wagon, holding the bridle of a white stallion. The horse was magnificent, and silently Aritian congratulated himself on purchasing it. It was an Ignis breed, bred for the harsh conditions of the desert. It was smaller than northern breeds, with wide hooves adept at traversing the hot sands of the Ignis. It wore two heavy saddle bags on either side of its back and a saddle made from dark, supple leather.

Aritian wore long, white robes and beneath, leathers and light chainmail. At his waist he wore his dragonbone dagger and across his back a dark sword rested in a black scabbard. He pulled his hood forward as several men staggered out of the Inn, and ducked his head as they passed.

Within minutes, Dellacindrael appeared riding solitarily

down the quiet street on the back of a red mare. She was hooded, dressed in dull robes of grey, and men's breeches. The moonlight illuminated her pale face, highlighting her elegant features. Aritian hurriedly mounted his horse as she approached, and edged his mount alongside hers as they made their way toward the towering sandstone walls of the South Gate.

The tower they reached was set with large, double doors that were bound with two cross-guards of thick iron. The way lay open, but was guarded by a dozen soldiers who wore dark armor and yellow capes.

"Stop." A soldier commanded.

"What business do you have traveling the Onyx Ribbon at such an hour?" A guard asked stepping forward. His dark mustache dripped to either side of his chin, and bobbed distractingly as he talked. Another soldier drew close and grabbed the bridles of their horses. Soon they were surrounded by the city watch. Aritian eyed the watchmen nervously; more than one held a smile and he saw emptied bottles leaned against the gate wall. The men were drunk and bored. Inwardly Aritian sighed as he thought, *it seemed escaping the city unnoticed was a vain hope.*

Before Aritian could respond, Dellacindrael gave the guard a tight-lipped smile, and pulled a heavy purse from one of her side packs. Casually, she dropped the purse to the ground and the loose strings fell open spilling gold crowns at the guard's feet. In a whisper, she said, "We were never here. Our business is our own and your shift was uneventful."

The soldiers seemed to consider for a moment. A tall, thickly built man rubbed his bald head, eying their packs greedily. Aritian met the eyes of the captain with a hard gaze, his threat silent, and the man gave him a curt nod. The captain waived his companions away, saying, "It seems that some thoughtless traveler dropped some coin, next round's on me boys." The men snickered and gave a weak cheer, as the captain bent and began picking up the spilt coin.

Aritian kicked his horse forward, leading with a quick canter, and Dellacindrael followed as they set upon the Onyx Ribbon. Beyond the gate, the road was paved with black gravel. To the left of the road lay a sparse jungle of bright green ferns and tall, dense bamboo. After a few hours, the greenery gave way and the coast was revealed. The Verdi Sea rolled in an unending line against the craggy shore and white beaches, the water stretching into the horizon in an emerald blaze. To their right, the plain's land quickly opened up to a forlorn, desolate expanse, cracked with heat and sparsely dotted with tall cacti. They rode for another four hours without a word.

After a time, Dellacindrael slowed her horse to a measured trot and Aritian followed suit. The road was abandoned save for themselves and the presence of the moon's watchful eye sharing the dark road with them. The only sound that could be heard was the dim roar of the ocean and the soft plodding of their horses' hooves.

Dellacindrael broke the silence, asking, "How long do we follow the Onyx Ribbon before we take to the plains?"

Aritian considered a moment, thinking back to the maps Ibriham had shown him, and said, "We travel a half a day along the Ribbon, but soon after daybreak we will leave the road. According to Ibriham it had once been a well-traveled route. We should spy the route marker with ease. The ruins are a full two days' ride south from there."

Dellacindrael nodded, and said, "Lady Maud's courtier is well chosen. The ruins fall along Qurin's path home, to the lands of Utarye." Aritian nodded agreeably. The Velox was two hundred miles south of where the ruins were supposed to be. Utarye was the northernmost territory claimed by the southern Warlords, and dominated the land where the Velox River spilled from the green lands of Velon. "What do you think we will find?" Dellacindrael asked softly. She sat in her saddle at ease, seemingly at home along the road, but Aritian could hear an edge in her voice that betrayed the perfect calm her expression exhibited.

"If I had to wager, I would surmise that some force will be there to meet the Warlord for an arms deal of some sort. Though for what purpose, I know not." Aritian said honestly.

Dellacindrael nodded as though that were obvious, and said, "There are few who call the Ignis Desert home so far north. If the oasis has run dry then the ruins must simply be a meeting place. When we grow close you should be able to sense the corruption. If you do not, we will be forced to follow whoever meets the Warlord back to whatever hole they have sequestered themselves in." Dellacindrael warned thoughtfully.

"Dellacindrael, can I ask you something?" Aritian edged his horse closer to her own, and the elf nodded. "I find myself at a loss as to why you would acquiesce to the Oracle and come to Ignea. The south is no place for an elvish Lady," Aritian said darkly. He wondered if she knew of the perils of Ignea or was simply ignorant of the dangers that existed here. "Was it out of fealty to the Ronan or to Devaney herself that made you take such a dire risk?" Privately he wondered, *Maybe this is simply a distraction to wile-away the boredom of her long life.*

Dellacindrael raised an eyebrow and smiled. Mirthfully, she asked, "Do you fear that ferocious Ignea will swallow me in some pit of fire? That I am too delicate to survive such a place?"

Aritian shrugged, noncommittally. In truth, that is exactly what he thought. He eyed her, though she rode with undeniable grace she seemed frail to him. Her limbs were willowy thin, and her face was slight and held a countenance of purity too innocent to the brutality of the south. She was more petite even than the diminutive women found in Velon, and lacked the hard-worn strength that glinted like iron in the eyes of those native to the land.

Dellacindrael met his assessing stare boldly, and said, "You love this land, and take pride in the strength that is required to survive here." Aritian nodded; he could not deny her word nor could he adequately describe or explain why he felt so, but he did. The humor fell from her voice, and she spoke with sudden seriousness, "Do not fear for me, child of Magrados, for I am not so fragile as you might believe." She held his gaze, and within her cold stare he saw the age of her unending memory. Aritian gave her a curt nod and looked away.

A few minutes of silence passed and Aritian eyed the stars above. The sky was a black field and gleamed with a thousand-thousand bright gems. He had found that since emerging from the Vortex that he could see far better than he could ever before. Now when he gazed upon the glinting lights, he could see variances in their color and even size, that he could have never distinguished before. In the city, the unending glow of humanity had prevented such distinction, but here, the stars' grandeur was undiminished. As he took in their splendor, he felt small, and smiled; glad for such a humbling reminder though he had grown greatly, he was still but a tiny iota in a galaxy vast and far greater than himself.

Dellacindrael spoke suddenly, "The elven nations pay no fealty to any power but our own monarchs." Aritian dragged his eyes from the sky at her words, and the elf continued, "I am unique, as I have spent many centuries outside the enchanted Sidhe of the far east. Most of my kin, as you seem to realize, don't wander far from our lands." She flashed him a wistful smile, and said, "In a way I feel a kinship to the Ronan, for there are so few races who live as long as we do. Even fewer now, after the Great Cataclysm."

Aritian fiddled with his brindle uncomfortable with the turn of topic. He had not yet accepted such a fate, and to even think of it made him grow with a panic that he did completely not understand. Dellacindrael continued, "I came because we elves owe a debt to the Ronan, though most of my kin do not share my sentiment." She smiled sadly, and explained, "Many of the elves do not accept the burden of truth or seek to blame the Ronan for the Sundering, but this is merely shame in its most indecent form."

"Were you there... I mean alive, to witness the Great Sundering?" Aritian asked tentatively. Dellacindrael nodded sharply, and turned away, becoming suddenly tense. Her back straightened and her hands had gripped the reins with a white grip, as if she dared not fully remember that time. Aritian burned to ask her more, but he could tell that she did not want to speak of it. He swallowed his curiosity and changed the subject briskly, asking, "Why do the fair folk sequester themselves so? You are the first I have met, and to be blunt, many in the south believe you are no more than fables whispered in the fancies of a children's tale."

Dellacindrael voice became tight with restrained bitterness, as she said, "Humans call our lands 'the wilds', but your lands are far more savage than our own could ever be." The elf looked over her shoulder, and her gaze cut his lingering stare. In a dull voice, she said, "I am sure as a male of your species you can guess as to the dangers a female of my kind might face? Even our males are coveted. Look to Ibriham, he is a Semumrae."

"What's a Semumrae?" Aritian asked, interrupting her.

Dellacindrael's eyes grew pale, as she whispered, "A stain, a corruption of elfish blood. Man has a hungry need to dominate; all the half-bloods of the world can attest to that." She concluded in a sorrowful voice.

Aritian thought back to when Maud had first told him of his blood relation to Ibriham, and asked, "Did you know Aktymor, the elf that Maud was in love with?"

"Love?" Dellacindrael asked, perplexed. She turned her mount to face him fully and Aritian was forced stop his own horse. Aritian watched as restrained emotion rolled just beneath the surface of her serene mask. After a moment, the elf whispered, "Aktymor Shanaid was Maud's prisoner; a slave. After decades of enduring her rape, he finally escaped and fled upon the sea. Maud cast a storm and drowned him, rather than see him free."

Aritian's eyes fell to the dark road. He could not hold her burning gaze. In a muted voice, he said, "I didn't know."

The elf turned in her saddle and did not look at him. She kicked her horse back into a trot, and Aritian followed. In a curt voice, she said, "You are naïve." Aritian bristled at her tone, but Dellacindrael continued, "I mean no offense, for it is not due to a lack of intellect." Aritian cocked an eyebrow, but remained silent. She continued in her assessment, "Maud has been careful in what she has allowed you to know and has used your ignorance as a weapon against you." Aritian nodded, knowing that this at least was true.

With a grim chuckle, Aritian admitted, "She isn't the first. I seem to have a knack for falling prey."

"Why do you think that is?" Dellacindrael asked quietly.

Aritian shrugged, and said honestly, "I am not sure."

For a moment the Dellacindrael was silent as they rode through the darkness. A wind blew from north and on it, Aritian could taste a salty brine. After a time, Dellacindrael counseled, "You must learn to think for yourself. You do not trifle with simple nobles and cutthroats anymore. You are not beholden to a Master's will." Aritian sighed away his pride with a huff. Dellacindrael seemed to know a great deal about him, but he buried the resentment that welled up. Instead, he decided that he would take heed and try to learn, for whether he liked it or not the elf was right. "You must learn to be observant of the motives of those around you. Only then can you divine why they act as they do. People are motivated by hidden desires and secret ambitions. Humans especially, are duplicitous creatures. It is by no fault of their own, it is simply their nature. If you watch closely, you may glean what drives them, and then foresee what actions they might take." Dellacindrael turned toward him and gifted him with a gentle smile, as she said, "You are young."

Aritian bowed his head, and said, "I am trying."

Dellacindrael nodded emphatically with understanding,

and asked, "Allow me propose a question?" Aritian nodded, and she continued, "I bribed the tax collector at the export bureau and discovered that Maud, through Qurin, has purchased fifty-thousand gold crowns worth of supplies and arms." Aritian eyes widened with shock as he heard the exorbitant number. "Furthermore, I was able to gain access to the records. I did not have much time, but I was able to discover that over the last eighty years alone a sizable fortune has disappeared from Creuen through various Warlords who have controlled Utarye; some three-million crowns worth, spread over the last eight decades. Qurin is not the first warlord Maud has used. What does that tell you?"

Aritian realized his mouth hung open, and snapped it shut. His mind went blank, and he said the first idea that came to his mind, "That Maud has been gathering her strength for some time." That was obvious, and Aritian cursed his dimness. He had no wish to appear stupid to this elf, especially after all the trouble she had gone through to be at his side.

The elf nodded, and patiently asked, "For what purpose?"

Aritian shook his head, and said hesitantly, "Invasion."

Dellacindrael pressed on, asking "Of who?"

Aritian thought for a moment, and then said, "There can only be two options, Velon or the territories to the south. The Collation of Odium sits in the crux between the two great powers. There are no others worth taking within close proximity."

Dellacindrael nodded, and explained, "Two hundred years ago, southern Ignea was ruled by a sultan of incredible power. His empire stretched the length of the Velox, from the eastern coast to Utarye. When his kingdom fell, the territories fractured and have remained so to this day."

Aritian wasn't surprised by her recount. Many nations, great and small, had fallen in the history of Ignea. It was the way of the south, he supposed. Aritian cocked his head, and asked, "You think Maud means to resurrect this Empire?"

Dellacindrael nodded, but said noncommittally, "Perhaps, but it would be difficult. There is strength in the Warlords, even divided as they are. Even so, they would be easier to quell than Velon."

Aritian grunted, acknowledging her words, but then worriedly said, "Velon is under attack. The lorith horde bloodies the empire's northern edge."

The elf smiled at him, pleased by his insight, and said casually, "Yes, Velon has been wounded. The lorith have not retreated, and even now they push close to Jerilo." Aritian grimaced at the dire news. Jerilo was sixty-miles southeast of Inee. The lorith were pressing closer to the heart of the Empire.

Aritian considered aloud, "I would have thought that after Inee they would have retreated. They suffered heavy casualties."

"Maybe this isn't a holy war." Dellacindrael suggested. Aritian could tell that she had already drawn her own conclusions, but was leading him to find the answers on his own.

"You think Maud has a hand in their actions." It wasn't a question, but a statement.

"Who could say?" Dellacindrael said with a shrug. "Either way, it would seem that she has been gathering strength for some time, to strike at either the Warlords of the Velox or the Empire of Velon."

"Or both." Aritian said dismally. "The numbers would have to be monumental." Dellacindrael nodded, agreeing, but he sensed that she was waiting for more. Aritian looked off toward the desert as he considered the predicament. This was all new to him. He had been a slave, and had made little choices that were truly dictated by his own will. Hidden agendas and political intrigue had always been the Master's expertise, and he but the weapon they wielded their deliverance. The baked ground fled as far as his eye could see in a sallow field of dead land. The moon was high above them and soon would begin its descent. After a time, he replied with frustration, "But there is no such force. The desert is abandoned and any sizable force would have been noted. Maud cannot hide so great an army."

"Can't she?" Dellacindrael asked with a smile. Aritian could tell she was enjoying herself, but he tried to take her goading at face value. She was trying to get him to think. Dellacindrael spoke on, seeing that he was lost, and said, "I doubt seriously that the Scarlet Witch is simply stocking the ruins of Darth with an armory that she does not intend to use. I would say that the question of how she is hiding the force, irrelevant."

With a frown, Aritian proposed, "Then logic would bring us to the question of what or who? Is the very corruption we seek, the who? Or is it a weapon a more common foe seeks to use?"

The elf nodded in agreement, and said, "We will have to wait until the ruins to discover the truth. There are too many variables to contend with." There was a tension to the air that clung to both of them. They would be going in blind and neither of them were comfortable in their ignorance, but no amount of speculation or debate would reveal the truth.

Aritian quickened his horse forward, as a sudden need for haste filled him, and his white robes billowed behind him as his horse surged into a gallop. Dellacindrael matched his speed, her own robes flapping in the wind like dark wings as they raced along the lonely Onyx Ribbon deep into the night.

Caethe

Chapter Forty-Eight:

The Beast of Fear

Caethe blinked foggily as the room came into focus. He was in a small, white stone cell. It was stark in décor, holding only a thin straw pallet and large clay bowl that squatted in the corner. The four walls were close, leaving him only enough room to lay fully stretched out along the back wall, and was less than half as wide. A heavy door, barred with iron and set with amber gemstone, stood across him. A single barred-window allowed beams of bright light to fill the room, and a cool draft swirled from the window, making the air crisp with the cold bite of winter. The floor was clean, and near his head rested a small clay pitcher of water and a loaf of bread.

Weakly, Caethe struggled to sit up. His head pounded as his consciousness settled into the shell that he called a body. Rapidly, his power rushed through his weakened body, renewing it and healing the damage that had been done. Thousands of small cuts faded from his pale skin, even as blue-green bruises fled his arms, legs, and chest. Caethe felt his swollen eyes sink and dully eyed the room as his full sight returned to him.

Caethe felt as though his mind and limbs were weighted, dim, and muted within his physical form; bound hand, foot, and neck in amber as he was. An overwhelming fear clutched his mind as he once more settled into weakness. It was a clawing, desperate fear, animalistic in nature. For a time, it blinded his mind and he sat there shaking as it consumed him. Caethe crawled to the clay bowl and vomited bile.

Painfully, he caged the beast of panic and in time, killed it. The frail illusion of control returned and his pounding heart evened out. Mocking laughter filled his mind as those within sneered at his weakness. When he sat up, he wiped his mouth before spitting into the clay bowl. He returned to the pallet and crossed his legs, resting his bare back against the cold, stone wall. With his upper hands he combed through his knotted hair and with his lower left hand he picked up the pitcher. Carefully, he sipped the water, knowing that if he gulped it he would only make himself sick. The cool water hit his dry, tortured throat and he sighed in relief.

Caethe grabbed the small loaf with his lower right hand as he set down the pitcher. He passed the bread to his upper, more dominant hands, and tore the bread into tiny bites. The bread was plain, made of an unflavored grain, but it tasted decadent to his salivating tongue. With care, Caethe slowly ate and drank. The tight, growling knot that was his stomach slowly loosened and when he finished he felt sated despite the meagerness of the meal.

For more than an hour he sat in silence, letting his body adjust and heal. He knew with certainty that he would not be able to jump beyond the confines of his body for some time. He was too weak now, and his magic was needed to retain his hold on the imprisoned souls within. The closeness that he had come to death was but a muted fear. Far too often he felt death's claws, and its threat had become but a numb shadow that fleeted at the corner of his peripherals. Caethe rubbed his chest as pain flared. *Battling within and tortured on the outside*, Caethe shook his head, knowing that lingering on such thoughts were for naught.

Caethe stood and walked shakily to the window. He stood with his left two hands braced against the wall for support and with his right two hands he held the cold iron bars that lined the window. The first touch of true winter had come to Novus. The window sat high in a tower, one among many that rose from the massive temple below. The temple itself was grand, situated on top of a cliff that jutted proudly into the center of the sprawling city. A white marble dome dominated the pinnacle of the pyramid, and surrounding the dome on all sides were fifteen towers. Bridges connected the towers at intervals, gracefully arching across the crisp air in fine torrents, making the dome appear caged in a rising pillar of marble.

Caethe's vantage granted him sweeping city views, and he eyed it critically. The city was made from grey-streaked white granite, pulled from the mountain that towered above it. A wide, hundred-foot tall wall cupped the land for four-miles against the foothills of the Imperial Mountain Range. The city was neatly organized in a geometric maze, with white cobblestone roads, yellow thatched roofs, and uniform buildings that slowly rose in height as they neared the deepest part of the city. Snow fell from steel-grey clouds, blanketing the city in white. The sun's light was muted behind the heavy blanket, but Caethe could tell that it was midmorning. The city bustled beneath as thousands trudged through the slush-filled streets, bundled in dark wool.

A thousand bell towers tolled brightly, filling the air with a thunderous cadence. Caethe watched as the city froze. Crowds stopped and fell to their knees facing north, and a chant rose in the air. The words were lost to the wind, but Caethe could hear the dim hum of a million prayers in unison. Goosebumps traced Caethe's skin, and he turned away from the city with a shiver. He sat on the pallet and pulled his knees to his chest, wrapping his four arms around himself as he huddled against the chill of ignorance.

It did not take long for the large iron keyhole to be rattled, jerking Caethe out of his fog of misery. With a metal hiss the iron bar was lifted and the door was pulled open. A man stepped within, his grey eyes widening in surprise. The priest was dressed in white robes, a long and crisp cape lined with grey fur, and well-fitting leather gloves. He was just past middle age and his cropped-short hair was grey and combed neatly to the left. Slowly he smiled, displaying his yellowed, crooked teeth. His reddened cheeks bunched with the expression, and he idly smoothed down the front of his vestments as he eyed Caethe.

The priest stepped within the room, and slowly shut the door, as he said, "I see that you have returned to us, creature." Caethe fought the urge to flinch as the man's deep, rumbling voice filled his ears. A thousand memories threatened to overwhelm his thoughts at the sound, but Caethe pushed them to the dark recesses of his mind. The priest's eyes flicked to the side, as he recounted, "Forty-three days you've huddled within the flimsy shelter of your mind, hiding from the righteous wrath of Ordu." He stepped closer, his large frame towering over Caethe. His voice grew lighter with disbelief, as he said, "Many believed you lost to us, your soul devoured by the void, but I warned them against such a hope." The priests voice grew dry, and his smile spread wider as he said, "Evil does not die so easily, I said, and here you are, a devil amongst us, crawling forth once more to test the Faith."

Caethe eyes narrowed, and he whispered back, "I am sure your fellow priests feared that their curious experiments were coming to an end." Caethe did not look at the man. His eyes remained stubbornly on the stone floor before him, as he asked, "Is that why you made them stop, Grigori?" Grigori's smile sputtered and died, falling into a frown. Caethe pushed on, "I know it was you who stilled their delicate ministrations, don't bother denying it." Caethe looked up at the man from beneath his pale lashes, meeting the man's cold gaze with his own. Slowly, Caethe licked his lips seductively, and anger bloomed across the priest's face painting it red. Caethe whispered seductively, "Have you come to think of me fondly in the cold, lonely nights just as your grandfather did so long ago?"

With a crack, the priest's hand swung across Caethe's face with enough force to bloody his lip. Caethe pushed his long hair from his face and gingerly felt his stinging cheek. Grigori, smiled and said sanctimoniously, "Ordu guides my hand, beast." His voice grew deeper, as he chanted, "May Ordu cast His light upon you and smote your foul tongue. He, who is just, sees clearly through the murk of corruption, and He, who is mighty, strikes them down."

Caethe's mouth tightened as his power raged within, impotent the storm screamed for release, but to no avail. It could not break free of the amber bindings that locked it away. *Not yet*, Caethe whispered silently to himself, *you must wait*.

A dark thought whispered promises of revenge into his mind. *Release me, and I shall send him to the foulest hell.* Caethe shook his head, ignoring the voice.

Caethe spat blood on the stone floor and glared at the priest. In a bored voice he asked, "Are you finished? Why have you come, Grigori?"

Grigori straightened, and adjusted his gloves slowly, before saying formally, "I am the watcher. As your keeper, the state of your health is my responsibility. Food and drink will be brought shortly." His grey eyes flicked down Caethe naked form with disgust, and with a sneer, he said, "I am sure your body has grown weak, fasting for so long. I will mark the records that you emerged successfully." The priest turned to leave.

Caethe asked, "What day is it?" He hated the desperation that he heard within his own voice.

The priest replied without turning to face him, "Three hundred and ninth, you've awoken just in time for the new year."

"Will the torture resume?" Caethe asked, the words falling from his lips before he could think. Internally, he screamed rebukes at himself for showing such weakness.

A calm voice within him assured him. *Weakness is momentary, and those who rise above such fear have true strength.*

A deeper voice screamed in his mind. *Fear is as binding as these amber chains, break the collar of doubt, free me and I'll raze this city to the ground.*

The priest turned back to face him fully, his long cape sweeping across the floor with a whisper. He raised an eyebrow, and asked lightly, "You mean the rites of cleansing?" Grigori watched Caethe closely, noting the trembling of his hands and shifting of his nervous eyes. A minute passed and the question hung in the air between them. Grigori frowned suddenly, before finally answering in a whisper, "No, his Holiness has something quite different in mind." The priest raised a finger, wagging it in chastisement, as he said, "I warn you, think not of retreating to whatever dark hole you have within. If you do, I have been given leave to kill you." The priest turned back to the door and opened the cell door.

Caethe stood and spoke in a soft, dangerous whisper, "I don't retreat within my mind, foolish human." Anger suddenly boiled through his mind, silencing the incessant chatter of the voice's within.

The priest whirled as his patience neared its end, and spat, "Where is it that you go, then?"

Slowly, a manic smile spread across Caethe's mouth until he was beaming at the man. Grigori, glared at him darkly in warning. Caethe crossed his lower arms and whispered, "Hunting."

Grigori's thick eyebrows rose, wrinkling his forehead with deep furrows, as he asked incredulously, "Hunting? Where? To what purpose?"

Caethe met the priest's grey eyes with his own. Caethe let the smile fall from his face, and let the full visage of his rage fill his expression. The change of expression was rapid and Grigori's eyes widened in shock at the ferocity in the man's face before him. Caethe replied in a venomous whisper, "I hunt the lands of gods. Soon, it will be Ordu who bleeds."

Silence fell between them as emotion raced across the priest's face. Grigori cheeks grew blotchy and a vein pumped furiously near his left temple. *You mentally fucked the ignorant worm*, the deeply-aged voice whispered in his mind, cackling with violent humor.

Slowly, in a voice shaking with rage, Grigori swore, "There is but one god, and He is Ordu. A demon you may be, but you have no power against His Holy might. You are nothing more than a heretical creature of the Void sent to Adonim to test the spiritual purity of humanity. My faith shall not falter!" Grigori screamed in conclusion, shattering his calm demeanor as his hate and disgust bled through.

Caethe barked a laugh, but it was humorless. His response came out in a growl, "There are thousands of gods and compared to the Elder Ones, Ordu is no greater than a worm crawling through cow shit in a fallow field."

A lie, but spoken as a truth that he cannot refute. The calmer voice reasoned pragmatically.

The priest stepped forward and grabbed Caethe by the throat. He yanked Caethe off the ground and slammed him by the neck against the wall. Caethe's head cracked against the stone and he could feel the tickle of blood creep down his neck. The priest was surprisingly strong for his age and in his weakened state Caethe could do nothing to stop him. Caethe struggled for breath as the priest leaned in close, and whispered in his ear, "I wonder how long it'd take your body to regrow your tongue? Keep spouting your wicked corruption and you will face the wrath of Ordu."

Caethe tore at the priest's hands with his upper arms and beat his chest with his lower ones, but to no avail. The priest tightened his grip and Caethe vision became distorted as dark spots darted before his eyes. Grigori leered closer, watching as Caethe face slowly turned dark red. Caethe's flailing hands grew weak and fell to his side limply.

Grigori threw him to the ground and Caethe collapsed, choking raggedly as he gasped for air. Grigori mused, as if speaking to himself, "It took four years for your arms to grow back, or so the records state. I think the lower ones only took two years to become fully functional once we sewed them back on." The priest barked a laugh, and said with a sneer, "But, of course, it could have been three? The histories are quite murky on that point."

Grigori looked at him with disgust and kicked him in the gut with a heavy boot. Caethe writhed as his lungs contracted, struggling for breath. Crowing merrily, the priest said, "The records however, are quite clear on how excruciatingly painful the process was." Grigori kicked him again and Caethe cried out. Grigori smiled down at him as he suggested, "Maybe a third leg will be next."

Burn him until he is nothing but ash. The gravely-aged voice screamed with fury, sending lances of pain through Caethe mind in admonishment. Caethe scratched at his forehead, tearing bloody furrows down his face as he begged the magi to stop.

Grigori walked to the door and swung it wide. He turned back to Caethe as he left, and promised in a harsh whisper, "By the time I'm done with you, the grotesque corruption within will be reflected by the macabre monstrosity I create on the outside." The door slammed shut with a bang and the iron bar slammed down. Caethe flung himself at the door clawing at it with vicious abandon, tears falling freely, as wrath burned his soul with chains of bitter frustration. He did not stop until the door was covered in blood.

Aritian

Chapter Forty-Nine:

The Horror of a Shadowed Wing

Dawn filtered through the night's sky with rich shades, relentlessly pushing the shadows across the horizon. Nearly an hour after daybreak they were joined on the road by teams of merchants traveling westward. Aritian and Dellacindrael rode silently, giving polite nods as they crossed paths with the fellow travelers. The merchants eyed them curiously, but without fear. The Onyx Ribbon was a well-patrolled road and few dared to raid its inky path. Those who did were hunted down relentlessly, and the continued security had garnered the road a famous reputation for being the safest trade route in all of Ignea. By midday, the road would be thick with travel.

Aritian called out to a merchant group who led a team of twelve heavily-burdened spice camels; he had smelled them for nearly a mile before they crossed paths. The traders looked at him from beneath their heavy hoods with coal darkened eyes, and dipped their heads in response.

"How far until the nearest trade post? Have you seen any route markers?" Aritian asked politely.

An older man with almond-color skin wrinkled as a raisin, but a straight back and easy gait answered gruffly, "Aye, Marisfa be about ten miles south east. It's a fair size town, and the largest you be likely to find 'tween Creuen and Futu." The older man spat upon the dusty ground, and said, "There's been a route marker every two miles, boy. Black post with numbers on it, you couldn't have missed 'em." The man explained with some amount of annoyance.

Aritian replied evenly, "I talk of markers leading to the Golden Plain, south. A particular one, an old statue shaped in the form of a cobra."

The merchant eyed them more wearily now, and said, "Eh, I know the one ye' speak of. Less than a mile east of here." The old man glanced at the bright clear blue skies. The rain had fled the sky, a rarity in this season. "I give ye' warnin, young travelers, the Golden Plain is the southern nesting ground of those great birds...those Rocs. Troublesome creatures..." He spat to the side again, and grimaced sourly as he said, "They carried off nearly forty pack animals in the last week or so." The man rubbed the side of the camel's neck he led, and nervously glanced at the sky again. "I know not what business ye' have in the Golden Plains, but if you're traveling south, I'd follow the Onyx Ribbon a fair number of miles before delvin' into the Ignis. A longer route, skirting the plains, but far safer." The merchant advised reasonably. Aritian gave the man a deep nod in thanks before kicking his horse forward.

Dellacindrael followed close behind, and once the merchant had traveled some distance away, she spoke worriedly, "The nesting season of the Roc is the very reason why little inhabits the Golden Plain. We cannot match the might of one of the great birds should they decide to attack, and should we fall under the attention of the flock..." She trailed off nervously. Aritian looked at the elf in surprise, shocked by the apparent fear she displayed.

Aritian rode quietly for a few minutes, considering their options, before saying, "The Roc primarily attack livestock and those who provoke them. We are neither, and pose little threat nor do we have great appeal. I say we travel on unencumbered by this knowledge." Aritian kicked his horse forward despite Dellacindrael's continued attempts to broach the subject. The birds were a hindrance and nothing more; he would not waver from their path.

Aritian spotted the cobra-shaped statue soon thereafter. It

stood along the edge of the road, about chest height. Its grey surface was worn and cracked, and a dark, yellow grass crawled along its base. The cobra curled in eight rings before rearing, its mouth agape with fangs exposed. There was no path leading from the statue, but Aritian led his horse from the road onto the sandy dirt. Dellacindrael hesitated at the post for a moment, but with a heavy sigh edged her horse forward.

They rode for two hours and then, like a yellow stain, the Golden Plain emerged from the horizon. Aritian thought back to the first time he had come upon the grassland. It had been mere months ago in reality, but for him it seemed far in the past. They were further south now, and he hoped, free of the lands claimed by Insecti. They plunged into the plains land, and the grass swayed and rippled, whispering as they passed.

Gold fields of grass flowed like an ocean of pale yellow before them from horizon to horizon. The grass was higher now, after the monsoon season, and stood nearly as tall as the horses they rode. They rode in silence for three more hours and all the while the sun rose steadily in the sky. The grassland, at first glance, looked deserted, but when peering closer the signs of life were evident all around. Small brown birds flitted here and there over the grass, rodents dived from their horses' hooves into dark holes, and the hum of insects filled the air.

"Let's set camp here, rest during the day, and then continue during the night," Aritian suggested. They had ridden all night and well into mid-day. The horses walked at a slow pace, and Aritian knew they needed water.

Dellacindrael stood in her stirrups and scanned the grassland that fled into the horizon, before nodding, and saying, "Very well, this place is as good as any." Aritian dismounted, and when his feet reached the ground he hissed in pain. Instantly, his legs cramped. He walked around awkwardly for a moment, before letting a tendril of magic escape the door of his mind. He sighed as the pain washed away.

Aritian opened one of his horse's side packs and began

unloading their compact, camping gear. Setting up camp was laborious work. After the horses were freed from the packs, Aritian and Dellacindrael led them in small circles, stomping the grass down, creating a clear area. They set up the small dome tent in short order, and soon had a campfire lit. Both of them were sweating profusely and in the end, the camp was serviceable if not the most elegantly constructed. Aritian was surprised to find that Dellacindrael was far more experienced than he. He wasn't sure why this surprised him, and begrudgingly admitted to himself that his reasoning had been based off groundless assumptions.

Aritian filled a wooden bucket from one of the large water casks and opened two sacks of crushed grain for the horses. The horses eagerly drank the water and ate with loud, content munching. Aritian tied their leads to one of the deep stakes of the tent. After, he drank deeply from a waterskin, before spilling the water over his head. His hair had regrown after the long years in the Time Vortex, and he quickly rewove his loose braid before wiping his sweat-streaked face with edge of his robe.

Dellacindrael climbed into the shade of the tent, and said, "I will take respite now. I have not taken Reverie in the last few weeks, and I fear that I will need all my strength for what is to come. Wake me in three hours and I'll take watch so you may sleep." Aritian nodded in response.

Aritian waited long minutes, eyeing the tent every so often waiting for the elf to fall asleep. To his surprise, Dellacindrael did not close her eyes and instead, seemed to have fallen into a deep trance. Her breath evened out, and occasionally he saw her eyes flick side to side as if she was dreaming. He shrugged, figuring that if she was not unconscious she was at least too deep into her meditation to fully realize her surroundings.

Aritian wanted privacy, free of any distractions, and let himself fall into a light trance. Closing his eyes, he almost instantly found himself standing before the door that held his power at bay. He eyed the symbols that traced its weathered surface, and watched as crimson light crackled along its edges.

He reached for the door. Like stretching an unused muscle, Aritian pried it open with little effort. Power furiously tore through the crack, bursting through his mind like a river spilling over a dam as the door slammed open. Aritian's back arched and his hand clenched at his side. The pain was exquisite. You can only deny the body for so long something that sustains it, and his body reacted to the magic like a man dying of thirst. His body drank it in, but it was painful process.

Aritian gripped the edge of the door and struggled to close it. For a moment, the door resisted him and the runes he had drawn flared with blinding light. With a great effort he slammed it shut, cutting off the avalanche of magic. It had been far too long since he allowed any true amount of power to escape. The power raged behind the door like a wild beast, furious at its imprisonment.

When Aritian opened his eyes, they were black and rolling with power. The magic spread through him like a heady wine, washing away the aches and pains of the day, refreshing him with potent energy. No longer was he tired from travel nor would he feel exhaustion for the foreseeable future. The pink redness of his skin, marked by the hot sun, faded to its natural golden tan. The muscles that had been cramped with tightness were loosened and rejuvenated.

After a few minutes Aritian rolled his neck and smiled. It felt good to embrace his power. A feeling like nothing else he had ever experienced, better than sex, spirit, and drugs. The crippling fear of being human was thrown aside. All of the insecurities and trepidations he had been feeling fell away, discarded. Aritian felt powerful and as his smiled grew broader, he thought, *As I should.*

Aritian let his senses spread in an invisible wave in every direction. He blinked rapidly and his sight blurred for a moment. When his vision cleared, he could see the natural energies of the land all around him, and could sense every living creature within seventy miles. Back along the trail that they had come snaked a line of bright energy — it was the people who traveled along the weaving path of the Onyx Ribbon. The city of Creuen shone as brightly as a star. The millions of living creatures living within illuminated the city with a flurry of activity brighter than fire. Aritian turned his eye from the cities overwhelming light, and searched the Onyx Ribbon. He did not sense the presence of the Warlord.

The power allowed him to see the auras of individuals, and each person's energy was unique. Qurin would be traveling among a cohort of soldiers; soldiers who had killed before. Such acts left marks on one's soul that he could easily spy, but no party along the Onyx Ribbon was large enough or held enough distinctive markers that would distinguish them as the Warlords regiment. Either the Warlord was still in Creuen or he was ahead of them.

Aritian turned his eye, letting his senses rove across the plains. To the northwest he felt energies beneath the ground. The Insecti tunnels weaved across the westernmost end of the Golden Plain, twisting like a giant ant maze beneath the ground. The energy was muted by the land that lay between them and the surface.

He looked south, and felt a field full of energy that rose before him like a towering wall. The energy was spread out, and flared before his eyes a mere twenty miles from where he stood. *The Roc nesting ground*, Aritian thought. The nests stretched twenty-five miles south, forty miles west, and sixty to the east. *A day to push through south, no more*, he considered.

Aritian expanded his search and smiled. Less than a day's travel before them lay the camp of Qurin One Eye. It lay situated along the western edge of the Roc nesting ground. The Warlord had taken the longer path around the dangerous territory of the Roc. Instead of striking first east and then south, he had struck immediately south from Creuen and had been forced to circle west to avoid the nests.

Aritian let his senses fall and his eyes cleared of darkness. Aritian walked to the white stallion and the beast neighed with fear, sensing the power that radiated off of him. Aritian touched the mind of the horse and it calmed immediately under his tranquil touch, growing unnaturally still. Aritian walked slowly around it, before placing the palm of his hand along the horse's shoulder. He let a bolt of energy flow into the animal, rejuvenating its lagging strength. Aritian began tracing runes along its neck with his pointer finger. It was a complex spell that took time, but little energy. After he finished with his stallion, Aritian repeated the process on Dellacindrael's mare. When he was finished he sat down on the folded stalks of grass and waited for Dellacindrael to wake.

The midday sun had fled and the sun had descended fat and orange at the edge of the Golden Plain. Thunder rolled in the distance, and Aritian knew that soon it would rain. Aritian turned his eye to Dellacindrael; the elf had meditated soundlessly through the day, and he hadn't bothered waking her for a watch; he required no sleep.

Darkness rolled like a storm through his eyes as he observed her aura. Pure, jade-colored energy radiated off of her, dappled with brilliant orbs of golden motes. She nearly looked like a precious gem turned to flame, but he did not sense Ignathra's will within her — no, it was something else entirely, something alien beyond his comprehension. He had never looked upon anyone with such a dazzling presence. The humans he had turned his eye upon had all been cast with pale energy that now seemed somewhat diminished compared to the soul he gazed upon. He stared, transfixed. *She's beautiful*, Aritian remarked.

As if sensing his eye, the elf stirred. Aritian blinked away the sight and turned away from her hurriedly. She rose from the tent and eyed the sky. He could tell that she was irritated to find that she had rested the day away, but made no comment.

Aritian rose, fleeing her gaze, and broke down the camp.

Within a candle mark, they were in the saddle and the horses were trotting through the tall grass. They rode cautiously, mindful of their mounts' limited sight and the unsure footing of the loose ground, through rest of the day's light in casual silence. After a few hours, rain began to fall from the now-dark sky. Fat raindrops pummeled them and they ducked beneath the shelter of their heavy hoods. Lightning began to lance across the sky in purple bolts of brilliant fury and thunder shook the plain. Dellacindrael gazed at the sky and her horse stopped of its own accord. The elf raised her hand in warning and Aritian slowed his mount.

"What is it, Della?" Aritian asked, and the elf looked at him with slight annoyance. Aritian smiled lightly, and thought, *It seems that my elven guardian has woken in a dark mood.* She frowned and pointed to the sky. Aritian looked up, and realized that she wasn't irritated by his shortening of her name, or rather, it wasn't why her eyes flashed with fear.

Aritian craned his head and scanned the night's sky. In the flash of lightning he could see feathered beasts of mammoth proportion. Their forms were indistinct against the darkness, but occasionally wings obscured the moon or shadowed the stars. The flock flew in lazy rotations, rising and falling above the nesting grounds below.

Aritian looked at Della and she pointed straight ahead. Aritian strained his eyes and saw that before them, a hundred yards away, the plain suddenly changed. The grass flattened in a blunt line that expanded for miles. Shadows crossed the field racing with a speed close to the crackling lightning that streaked above, before disappearing into the darkness. The wind spun in crazed currents here, and the horses snorted nervously as they caught the musky scent of the birds.

The plain was dotted with great mounds of grass and twigs, each towering more than a dozen feet in height and more than twenty-feet wide. *Nests*, Aritian thought in wonder, as he looked at the thousands of great mounds that populated the flattened expanse. In the dim light of the moon, the flat plain made for a strange landscape amid the golden grassland.

Dellacindrael's eyes were wide with fear as she pointed to the nests. In a harsh whisper, she said, "We have made a grave error traveling here. We will never pass unmolested. The flock is agitated by the storm." A piercing scream cut the air, as if accentuating her dire words. The elf hunched down, cowering as she begged, "We must flee to a safe distance now." Aritian edged his horse toward her, and gripped the reins of her horse.

Aritian whispered to her in an assertive, but calm tone, "No. We will go forward silently and carefully. We will pace the horses slowly through the nesting ground and with luck, reach the edge of the Ignis Desert by morning. I have touched the horses with magic, shielding from sight for as long as we remain unobtrusive." He smiled recklessly, enjoying the peril they had found themselves in. He felt powerful, untouchable with his magic pumping through his veins. The Ring of Suppression flashed at his hand with searing pain, but Aritian ignored the ache; he was used to it.

Dellacindrael shook her head violently, and whispered back, "Are you daft? Roc are not to be trifled with, especially nesting mothers. I have seen Roc take to the field carrying the enemy upon their back. I have seen them dive from the sky, carrying men and horse with ease to soaring heights only to dash them upon the ground." Aritian could see her body trembling with fear. She was like a rabbit who feared a hawk, who kept their eyes pinned to the sky, bracing themselves for the claws of death. *She doesn't trust my magic*, Aritian thought, *and thinks I am a cocksure fool.*

In a low whisper, he said reasonably, "This is the only way. If we backtrack now to circumvent the nesting ground, we will be a full day's ride behind Qurin. We will miss the exchange and all this would be for naught." *I will not let that happened*, Aritian thought with determination.

Without another word, Aritian kicked his horse forward. The horse walked slowly, cautious of the great birds who dominated both the sky and the plain before it. Aritian touched the mind of the mare the elf rode and encouraged the horse to move. Without any direction from Della, the mare followed behind. Aritian glanced back at Dellacindrael. The elf clung to reins of her mount with a white-knuckled grip, her body rigid as she scanned the night sky, but she did not voice her protests further. Aritian smiled slyly and thought, *She knows to argue now would only result in discovery.*

The first step beyond the border of flattened grass was the most difficult. The horses, despite his calming touch, didn't want to leave the shelter of the tall grass and in the end Aritian had to take command of their minds and force them. He kept his hood drawn forward, carefully holding his concentration on the magic that it took to shield them and directed the horses in a straight line, cutting the quickest path through the nesting ground.

The area closest to the standing grass was clear, but the grassland quickly became crowded with the gargantuan nests. The air was putrid with the stench of rotting flesh and the acidic bite of bird shit. Feathers lay upon the ground in a multitude of shades of grey, black, mottled brown, and pure white. Down floated thick in the air, spinning haphazardly along the ground as the storm blew across the plain. These smaller tufts of feathers were no larger than an arms-length and irregular in form. The larger feathers that graced the wings of the great birds reached more than ten feet in size and were structured in precise patterns. Bones bleached white by the bright sun lay strewn across the ground with flesh and tendons still hanging from the shattered fragments.

They passed a nest closely; a mere three feet from its woven side. The nest shook with the weight of the Roc that nested within. The Roc glared at the horses, watching them with dark suspicious eyes. Only its head peaked over the rim of the nest.

Its skull alone was nearly the size of the horses themselves. As it watched their progress, its head bobbed back and forth as if were confused. Its beak was black and sharp-looking, and the bird chittered softly with clicking sounds. White lines ran along the edges of its beak, small fractures formed from crushing bone.

The horses began to shy and Dellacindrael's horse neighed fearfully, causing her to whimper in sheer panic. Aritian tightened his control of the horses and kept them walking at a slow, but measured pace. Sweat trickled down Aritian's neck. It was as if time was slowed for a tension filled moment. Aritian kept his eyes pinned on the movement of the bird, just as it gazed unblinkingly at them. It could not see them, but it could hear them. In the end, the Roc dismissed them and readjusted itself, rocking the nest as it settled itself more comfortably.

The night stretched like an eternity with anxiety-ridden slowness. In time, the horses became adjusted to the Rocs' presence and looming nests. Aritian was grateful, because the strain of holding their minds so tightly was causing his hand to burn with the backlash of the Ring of Suppression. Aritian had glanced down at his hand once and saw that it was covered in boiling, red blisters.

Hours passed as they traversed the nesting grounds. They moved at a slow and measured pace, each quiet step garnering them closer to escape.

Della didn't speak a single word as they rode. Tears trickled down her face from wide, fearful eyes. Not for a single moment did she let her guard down. All through the night, noiselessly, she mouthed prayers to whatever god lay claim to her elven heart. Like a mantra that kept her from screaming in fright she repeated hours of gospels, over and over. Aritian pitied her, but knew there was nothing that he could reasonably do to placate her; there was no turning back now.

Their nerves were frayed as the black night lightened to purple and dim grey. The rain had stopped, and the far horizon become painted in soft oranges and pinks. The Rocs began to become distinct in the sky as the dim shadows of night lightened and the sun threatened to crest the horizon. It was a magnificent sight to witness the flock of Roc in the soft light of sunrise.

They flew with feral grace and liquid speed as they glided in the gilded light. Their wings spanned more than sixty feet as they played in the downdrafts of the warming air. Their shape, much like an eagle's, was streamlined and slim. Their black talons gleamed wickedly sharp and was matched by a hooked beak. The flock flew in a great circular arch that rose and dipped in a wide vortex of their dark wings. When one bird landed in their nest, another rose to take its place and thus they protected their young from both above and below.

Aritian edged the horses into a gentle gallop, encouraging greater speed. In darkness, Aritian knew the spell he had laid upon the horses would make them appear less threatening and blur their sight, but in the bright light of day he wasn't so sure. As they rounded a nesting Roc, the bird squawked, annoyed by the noisy pounding of the horses' hooves. The air was filled with the sound of rustling wings as the Roc warmed themselves in the dim light.

The ground soon became grainer and the grass slowly disappeared. Nests became less frequent now and were spaced further apart. The Ignis Desert lay before them, sand flowing in frozen waves of rising and falling dunes. Aritian nudged the horses' minds and their mounts took off in response. The sun climbed the horizon, just as they weaved between the last two nests, and spilled brilliant light upon the white sand. For a full ten minutes, they rode at the breakneck pace, both the horses and their riders glad to be free of the dangerous territory. The horse's hooves threw up plumes of sand in their wake and Aritian smiled brightly as he offered a prayer of thanks to Ignathra.

Della slowed her horse and Aritian pulled the reins of his

stallion, turning it just as Della's mare came to a halt. Dellacindrael leapt from her saddle, tears flowing freely down her face. The elf fell on shaking legs to her knees and bent her head taking in great gasps of air. Aritian was shocked to see her so rattled, but couldn't blame her; his own nerves were shot. Aritian gazed back along the path they had taken and his heart plummeted to his stomach.

"Dellacindrael get back on your horse, quickly now!" Aritian shouted. A single, black-feathered Roc flew high in the sky. It had trailed them from the nests and the moment Della had leapt from her horse, the Roc had seen her for what she truly was: a threat. With a great cry, the bird flapped its wings furiously, cutting across the sky toward them. Della's head whipped around wildly as the scream rent the air. Unmoving, as shock rippled through her body, Della stared at the bird with wide eyes as the blood drained from her pale face.

"Dellacindrael! Get on the fucking horse!" Aritian screamed at her, jolting her from her frozen panic. Aritian eyed the large bird. It was massive, even among its own kind, nearly a third larger than any of the others. *A male*, Aritian thought. It was rare for a male Roc to migrate south, for only the females and their young made the long journey to the nesting ground. *It must be an adolescent*, Aritian thought. Muscles rippled along its back as it tore the air gaining greater speed. It looked nothing short of terrifying and like a harbinger of death, it screamed a dark challenge.

Aritian drew a rune on the neck of his white stallion, removing all traces of his spell, exposing their true form to the Roc. Aritian reached to his side and pulled his sword from its leather scabbard. Silently, Aritian thanked Beryl for his craftsmanship.

The sword was freed with a hiss. The sword was long and black as shadow. Its hilt was made in the form of a serpent and its guard in the shape of wings that folded over his hand in a protective fashion. Aritian brandished the sword high in the air as his horse reared in challenge. The horse surged into a wild gallop and they passed Della in a jet of thrown sand. The stallion wanted to protect its master, and its mind gleamed with golden bravery. Aritian smiled at its single mindedness.

The Roc screamed again as it folded its wings tight against its body and free-fell to meet him. Dimly, Aritian could hear Della screaming his name. Aritian ignored her as he opened the magic that was locked within his mind. The Roc became larger as it plummeted from the sky and loomed above him now. Its dark eyes were pinned as it focused upon its prey and its beak hung open hungrily. Aritian matched its smile with a daring smirk.

Aritian let it come. The beast was no more than fifty feet above him when its wings snapped open with a crack louder than thunder. Its black talons extended toward him and within seconds, it was upon him. Aritian held the stallion's mind tightly as the bird closed in. Just as the bird was on top of him, its black wings blotting the light of the sun, Aritian commanded the horse to leap. Aritian swung his sword, clipping a talon, as the horse flung them to the left. The Roc's wings bounced off a silver shield that suddenly surrounded Aritian and the stallion, throwing sparks as it was battered.

The Roc landed and threw sand as it twisted deftly toward him, its yellow, speckled beak snapping against his shield. Its eyes were dark and the feathers of its face were puffed outward; making its head look larger than what it truly was. Aritian bellowed and a bolt of red lightning roared from the tip of his sword, striking the Roc between its eyes. The Roc jerked its head back, arching its wings in dismay. Aritian's power thundered into the Roc's brain like a lightning bolt, striking the bird deaf, blind, and mute.

The Roc went wild as it was suddenly deprived of its senses. It dove blind toward where it thought he was, slamming its head into the ground with a thunderous thud to the right of the horse, spraying sand. The stallion leapt again, escaping the whirlwind of its wings. A wild talon rent along the length of the shield, spraying sparks of brilliant white light. The horse retreated, dancing between the black, whirling wings as the beast flung sand in all directions.

Aritian pulled the stallion to a halt a dozen feet from the bird. Senseless, the Roc flung itself with abandon, furiously throwing a tantrum as it sought its prey. Its beak lashed out in random directions with loud snapping sounds. Voiceless, it could not call out, although it raised its beak to the air many times, its throat vibrating rapidly as it attempted to scream. Its chest heaved with great bellows and the black, glossy-feathers on its head crested wildly in challenge.

Aritian reached out to its mind casually. *That's right, great raven of the sky,* Aritian thought mockingly. *I have taken from you.* Aritian flashed an image of himself into the bird's mind. *Forevermore, you shall remember who championed your defeat.* For a moment, the Roc froze, startled by the voice within its head. Understanding passed through its mind and it screamed with voiceless rage. Its mind turned red and Aritian's presence was driven from its thoughts. The Roc tore at the sand with its sharp talons and flung its wings in great, sweeping arcs. The flock several miles away took no notice of the beast's silent fury. Aritian tugged the reins of his stallion, skirted the raging sandstorm of the Roc's wild anger, and emerged from behind the cloud of dust unscathed.

Aritian kicked his horse into a canter and raced toward Della. She was mounted and held a slim blade in her left hand. She stared at him stunned and made to speak, but Aritian waved south and she twisted her reins and kicked her mount to follow his own as he thundered past.

In a quiet voice, she said, "I am sorry, I let my fear claim my heart. It will not happen again."

Aritian nodded, pressing his lips together. In an angry whisper, he said, "You must learn to trust me. I am no fool. Try and look past the image of the naïve, brash child you see and know that I am not without skill." The words came out more sharply than he had intended, but it was too late to retract them back now.

Della nodded, her own mouth growing tight as she bit off a retort. They rode at a gallop into the hot expanse of desert. Della glanced back at the flock and the male who still floundered in the sand. She wondered how long the mage's power would hold, and looked at Aritian appraisingly as she tempered her surprise. *He is a Ronan after all*, she reminded herself.

Aritian

Chapter Fifty:

The Temple of Darth

They rode through the Ignis Desert with the red eye of Ignathra staring down with unrelenting heat. Sweat drenched their silken robes and their hair hung in gritty, sweaty strands. They both wore their hoods pulled forward, shielding their faces. The gritty, yellow dust that was kicked up by the horses covered them from head to foot. Like a toll claimed for passage, Aritian could feel the desert drawing moisture from him. The Ignis Desert was barren and harsh; the waves of dunes spread ever-outward in a sea predictable and stale in appearance. The silence that pervaded the desert was heavy, and Aritian felt as though they had entered another world; one devoid of life. A hot wind occasionally stirred the dunes, spraying them with biting sand that burned wherever it touched.

Dellacindrael had not spoken a word since they left the nesting grounds. Aritian had been shocked by the elf's admittance of fear, for it wasn't something he had ever expected from such an ancient creature. In all the tales he had ever heard, elves were fearless in the face of terrible evil, bold and brave in a way that defied mortal capacity. They were always wise, unshakable in their good morality. *Perhaps the tales have it all wrong,* he mused, *maybe the elves are not so different than man?*

At one point he even considered himself a fool for being so brazen. *By what right do I know better than she?* He thought, but then he forced himself to view the situation pragmatically. They had survived. Aritian had led them undetected through the flock and had triumphed over the Roc. He had been right holding faith in his power. No, something was there, he knew. Something that had happened to make the elf feel the way she did, and Aritian imagined that if he lived as long as she, he would be faced with experiences that would leave terrible scars that would not soon fade. He did not begrudge her fear, but knew they could not afford to submit to adversity when it did arise. Aritian had been afraid many times in his life, but then mused, *Ignea forces most of its inhabitants to view fear differently; you either overcame it or died young.*

The mare Dellacindrael rode was linked to his mind and Aritian kept the beast close as he led them south. He scanned the horizon for any semblance of shelter. A rocky crag sunken into the sand was the first he spotted in more than five hours. The red rock protruded little more than a dozen feet above the dry sea, and was so weathered that its surface was glossy smooth. Aritian led the horses up the tall dune. It was slow progress and rivers of sand spilled with each step the horses took.

When they reached the apex of the dune, Aritian dismounted from his horse and helped Della do the same. She accepted his hand with a small smile, and Aritian knew then that she had forgiven his harsh words. Aritian let out a shaky sigh of relief as Della walked beneath the scant shadow the rock provided. Aritian removed the horse's packs and hastily set up a crude camp. He watered the horses first, but did not bother securing them; they had been touched by too much of his power to wander off. The beasts were glad of the respite and drank greedily before shuffling against the bluff. After the tent was erected, Aritian and Della entered the shadowed confines.

Aritian wet a cloth with a waterskin and wiped the sweat and sand from his face. He turned to speak to Della, and smiled when he saw that she too was about to speak. Aritian waved her to continue, and her voice grew formal, as she said, "I must apologize for underestimating you. You are a Ronan and from the Oracle's word, a trained assassin of some skill. I treated you as one would a child, and that was wrong of me." She sighed and explained, "Among my own people, I am around those who have endured through many millennia and even among your kin, most have seen several centuries. When I met you, I saw you for your age and little else. I will not do so again." She said, holding his gaze with intense sincerity.

Aritian nodded, accepting her words, before saying, "I am sorry too. I shouldn't have gotten angry." He hesitated, before admitting, "I am still learning to trust myself, so I cannot begrudge your doubt."

A silence fell between them. Aritian pulled bread, cheese, and dried strips of meat from the pack. He passed Della a share of provisions and they ate in silence. Della did not eat the meat and silently passed it back to him without a word. He ate her share without question. When she was finished the elf threw back her hood and began to braid her dark hair.

Aritian stared at the canvas floor for a long moment, gathering his nerve. Without looking at her, he asked, "What happened in your past that makes you fear the Roc so?"

Della's hand dropped from her hair and she stared at him with an unreadable gaze. A long moment of silence, Aritian nearly retracted the question. Before he could speak, Della replied quietly, "Long ago, before the Cataclysm, there was a war. History names it the Blood War, and aptly so, for we fought for the very blood of Adonim." She licked her dry lips, as if gathering her courage, and then said hesitantly, "I am not sure you will understand..."

Aritian met her gaze unblinking and her sapphire gaze fell to the canvas floor. In a quiet murmur, she recounted, "The war lasted a long time, many human lives in length. We of the light battled the vampire, our greatest shame, and the forces of evil that the Dark Lady had gathered. You see, the vampire are not only evil themselves — their very presence brings corruption of the heart like a disease. To be near them is to be tempted to the dark side. The vampire themselves rode Vespires in battle — great, bat-like creatures twisted by dark powers, who scream with the very voice of fear. The corrupted human magi who had fallen to darkness rode the Roc." She shuddered, as the shadow of her fear returned.

In a weak voice she admitted, "When the night sky grew darker than midnight and the whispers of tens of thousands of wings filled the land, we who championed the light learned to fear these creatures above all else. I watched my brother die in the beak of a Roc. He was torn asunder while the human on its back laid waste to our troops with fire and lightning." Della met his eyes then, and said, "I carry the scar of that night forever more." She pulled down the sleeves of her robe, and Aritian saw that the skin on her forearms was twisted and swirled with red.

Aritian nodded stiffly, not meeting her eyes, and carefully said, "I am sorry for your loss. I don't regret our path here, for we had no other choice, but I think you braver than I ever imagined." Della gifted him with a frail smile, and returned to braiding her hair.

Aritian cleared his throat, and asked, "Did the Oracle tell you how Razia and I were to be reunited?" He had thought of little else since he heard the Oracle's promise and itched to sail north with all haste.

Della's deft hands stilled and he could feel her heavy gaze on him. When she spoke her voice was tinged with apprehension. It was as if she was unsure of how he would react and feared his response. "No, she merely showed me a vision of myself telling you the words that I would say when I found you." Aritian nodded stiffly. He hadn't really expected for the elf to know more, but he had to ask. Gently, Della said, "This woman must have been very important to you."

A smile warmed Aritian's face as he thought of Razia. In a whisper he said, "She was everything." He met Della's eyes, and his voice grew faint, as he said, "I doubted her and we had only just reconciled when…" His voice broke, and he looked down at his feet.

After a long pause, Della asked, "How did she die?"

"I killed her." Aritian said without thinking. His eyes clenched, and he took a steading breath, before explaining. "She was a priestess of Ignathra. When Inee fell, the Velon army set the city aflame." The conflagration flashed through his memory, and here in the desert it was almost as he could feel the heat of the flames of that day again. "The fires raged like a hurricane, unnaturally strong, having been augmented by a red powder the gnomes provided. I stopped the flames, froze them, but I couldn't consume such a mammoth force... Razia channeled the flames into herself, but the act killed her." It had been twelve years for him, but still those words came hard. Aritian knew the conflagration wasn't his fault, but he also knew that if he had known then what he did now, Razia wouldn't have needed to sacrifice herself. *She would be alive*, he thought bitterly.

"I am sorry, Aritian." Della said gently into the oppressive silence that had settled in the tent.

Aritian nodded, and stood. "I am too. Get some rest. We have a long night ahead of us, and even a longer day I fear."

Aritian stood beside the shadow of desert rock and looked south across the waves of sand. The ruins were less than thirty miles from their position, if Aritian judged correctly, and they would need to ride hard through the night to reach them by dawn. There was little to be seen in truth, but Aritian knew that the apparent isolation was merely a façade.

There was life here, thriving amongst the harsh conditions, and most of it was quite dangerous. Aritian closed his eyes and spread his arms wide. A soft ruddy mist bloomed from the palms of his hands and spread in a half circle, cupping their encampment against the pocketed shaft of rock. The sand vibrated where his power touched and a line formed, as if drawn by a stick. The fog towered above him and met the rock behind him. Aritian opened his eyes and the red mist dissipated. A shimmer, like refracting light, formed a half dome around the camp, barely visible to the naked eye. The ward would shield them from the eyes of man and beast, preventing either from passing.

Aritian let his senses expand outward, his eyes open and black as night, searching for signs of life. He speedily retraced their steps and found the Warlord's encampment northwest of their location; not far from where they camped now. The Warlord was just a few hours behind them, but Aritian was confident that they would stay ahead of him. Only a fool would travel in the heat of the day. *No*, Aritian thought, *Qurin will travel by torch or moonlight, as will we.*

Aritian turned his mind's eye to the sky, searching for pursuit. The sky was much more difficult to scout as the Roc could fly at great heights, making for an expansive search. Minutes ticked by, but the small flicker of small birds and large bugs was the only sign of life he could find among the clouds. Aritian turned his eye south and allowed his senses to expand to the area where he thought the ruin would lay.

The ruin glared with angry light, alive with activity. A blossom of life stood before him in a landscape where it was found so sparingly. Bile rose in his throat as he sensed the auroras of millions. The auroras were twisted with black and red angry streaks touched by a power that should not be found in the world of man. The life ran deep into the ground before congregating around a single area. Aritian opened his senses further, tasting the air. A musky scent that stank of mold filled his nose and moisture filled his mouth. *Water*, Aritian noted. Aritian expanded his senses deeper, concentrating on the life itself, and the stench of corruption filled his nostrils making his heart pound wildly. This was the feeling he had felt when Devaney had appeared to him. This is what she bade him to seek out.

The ruin was but a gate that led to hundreds of miles of tunnels beneath it. Aritian blinked his eyes, rapidly dropping out of his trance. A drop of sweat crawled along his back and he found himself shaking uncontrollably. He touched his dry lips with a nervous hand and studied the quiet dunes. Barren desert stretched quietly before him, and within its bosom a foul blight hid.

*****

The sky was a murky purple as Aritian and Della crawled on their stomachs through the sand toward the crest of a large dune. The air was cool, as the night's darkness still clung to the sky, but it would be morning soon. They were silent, motioning to one another with hand signals as they waited, looking down upon the ruin of Darth.

The ruin was desolate. The grand temple grounds lay broken and abandoned; the once-green land lay cracked and decrepit. It was hard to imagine that this place had once been bountiful with life. The temple grounds sprawled more than a mile with buildings of a dull-grey, cracked sandstone set in the low dip of land. Sand piled high against the compounds walls, spilling over in several places as the desert fought to reclaim the land.

The forty-foot walls of the compound were not made from sandstone, however, but thousands of bleached bones held together by a grey mortar. The poor fools who had met their end at the Temple of Death remained, guarding until the end of days. Over a dozen small building surrounded the tall pyramid that dominated its center, dome-shaped, and they held staircases at their shadowed doorways that led to underground levels. Sand spilled haphazardly along the deserted roads and courtyards, and only the pyramid's peak stood above the dunes like a solitary sentinel.

The Temple of Darth was a macabre sight. The architecture was old and its five levels were graced with hundreds of archways, each filled with stacks of skulls. The entrance of the pyramid stood before them, facing north. A pair of twenty-foot tall statues guarded either side of the entrance, shaped in the grim visage of a skeleton cloaked in long robes of stone who held great scythes in their bony hands. Aritian eyed steps of the stone pyramid, noting that they were stained brown with dried blood. A shiver ran down his spine, as he thought, *this is a place of darkness.*

There was no movement in the ruin and to all eyes, it seemed as if it had been untouched since it had been abandoned. Time seemed to pass slowly as they waited nervously, but could be marked easily as the night sky slowly brightened and became tinged ruby, citrine, and brilliant pink. A dim rattle filled the air. The noise was loud, but heard from a far distance.

Aritian motioned the elf to look behind them, and they saw a plume of dust rise in the soft light marking the path of the Warlord's approach. The dust curled in the air and as it grew close the rattling noise turned into the distinct sounds that accompanied mounted soldiers: the thud of the horse's hooves, the jangle of armor, men talking in raised shouts. Aritian had carefully disguised their position with magic, warding them from sight, but even still he hunched down lower as the legion rounded the bend of the base of a neighboring dune.

There were more than two-hundred soldiers that rode surefooted, Ignean desert horses. Forty heads of camel ran in the center of the train, grunting and protesting the quick pace that they were forced to endure. All of the camels' backs were heavy with packs, which made their lumbering gait even more awkward.

The soldiers wore the sigil of Utarye stamped in the dark leather over their hearts; a red fist that sat in a circle of yellow fire. White turbans and cowls protected them from the harsh glare of Ignathra's eye. These men were hardened warriors, but Aritian saw that their eyes were narrowed, fearful and fugitive, as they took in the desert land around them.

Qurin rode at the forefront of the horde on a fawn stallion. The Warlord was richly adorned in gaudy layers of gold silk, thick leather armor, and the bejeweled, golden hilt of a massive scimitar flashed at his side. He wore a golden helm that was shaped in the likeness of an eagle and wore a heavy war hammer strapped to his back.

The soldiers rode to the gate of the of temples entrance, kicking up sand and dust as they slowed their mounts. Men dismounted hastily as Qurin yelled a string of commands in a booming voice. The men calmed the camels as soldiers corralled them before the gate. The men seemed uneasy, constantly scanning the dunes around them and the city walls with nervous apprehension.

Several men yelled, pointing to the dune that towered to their right. Aritian and Della whipped their heads to the side looking toward the area that had caught the soldier's attention. Perched on the top of the dune, sitting lazily on its heels, was a large cat. It was no wild feline, but rather looked like an oversized house cat. It had long, black fur and heavy, orange eyes that watched the men below. Della whispered something under her breath and Aritian looked at her sharply. She shrugged. Aritian turned back to the dune and the cat was gone. *A product of pets left behind*, Aritian assumed dismissively.

Many of the men raised their right hand and held four fingers up toward the temple, and then motioned to where the cat had been, warding off evil. This was no place for men and the soldiers below could sense that. Qurin remained mounted, as the majority of his men did. They would not stay long, Aritian could tell. The soldiers worked quickly to unburden the camels, but it took two men to carry every pack they unloaded and each camel held two packs. The ruin remained quiet as a tomb as they worked.

Della turned to him in confusion as they men began to stack the packs at the gates entrance. Her eyes were wide and questioning, and Aritian was filled with the same question. *Why wasn't someone there to meet the Utaryerian's?* He motioned for her to wait with a short hand movement.

Aritian let his eyes fill with black power and looked at the temple anew. So close was the presence of the corruption that he felt overwhelmed. It was as if brimstone and noxious gas filled his mouth, heavy with the scent of death. The creatures hovered, holding their position within the temple unmoving as they waited. *No natural man waits within those walls*, Aritian thought, but he quickly reminded himself, *I don't know that until I see them with my own eyes.*

Aritian let a tendril of power flee his hand. Invisible, his power fled through the arid air and snaked inside the mouth of the temple to touch those within. He tried to reach their minds, but found an alien presence, incompatible to his touch. He didn't want to force entrance, because for all he knew they could be sensitive to such an invasion. Aritian had no intention of revealing himself, and let his power retreat.

The soldiers finished unburdening the camels and speedily dropped the last of the packs with a heavy jangle. The men then turned to the camels and led them toward the entrance of the gate. The soldier's fingers shook as they tied the camel's leads to the gates iron-barred doors and the camels shifted nervously, jostling one another. When the men finished, they dashed away from the gate, and fled to their horses. The men leapt onto the backs of their mounts and began to turn them away from the temple.

Qurin eyed the temple with a red-rimmed glare, as if trying to spy what lay within. He spat to the side and raised a bone horn's golden mouth to his lips. The horn blared, loud and long, reverberating across the sand dunes like a war cry. As the sound of the horn faded, Qurin turned his horse with a yank of his reins and led his men from the Temple of Darth. The horses raced between two sand dunes at a gallop, fleeing the temple with all haste. Aritian and Della turned to watch them go. After exiting the confines of the dunes that surrounded the temple they turned their mounts south, and it was several minutes until they were lost to sight to the dust cloud that followed their path.

Della made to sit up, but Aritian yanked her down by her thin wrist, holding a hand up in warning and mouthing the words: *no, wait.* Della could see the fear in his eyes and nodded her head in understanding. They turned their eyes back toward the temple. The sun had risen while the soldiers delivered the weapons and the shadows that lurked between the compounds buildings slowly receded. Several minutes passed in silence with no movement. Sweat broke out upon Aritian's brow and his long hair clung to either side of his face. Sand slipped into their pale robes, making their skin gritty to the touch, but still they lay unmoving.

When the first beast stepped from the shadows of the temples gate blinking its orange, oversized eyes in the bright light Aritian felt Della recoil at his side. Aritian found himself barely able to draw breath. The beast stood between the two hooded statues that guarded the entrance to the temple, allowing its sensitive eyes to adjust to the light. This gave Aritian and Della an opportunity to take in the measure of its monstrosity. *A Cambion,* Aritian thought with disgust. His heart sunk. He had felt the demonic presence, but had hoped against his better judgment that he was wrong. *Maud must hold a powerful demon for this creature shares little in common with man,* Aritian thought with detached wonder.

The half-demon stood six-feet tall and had an emaciated look. The creature's bones stood out prominently, stretched across hairless skin that was as black as pitch. Its head was crowned with three horns that curved backward over its skull. Resting beneath the horns were small pointed ears, and the place between its high jaws lacked any semblance to a nose. Rows of curved teeth were exposed as a blue, forked tongue flicked the air lazily. The Cambion's chest was more pronounced than a man's and deep slits ran under each of its sixteen ribs that seemed to be where the creature drew breath.

It wore a thick band of rolled silk on its sharp hips, and

fine strands of silk hung loosely to mid-thigh. A long whipcord tail, nor more than three inches in circumference, and more than five-feet in length flicked restlessly side to side as the half-demon stepped from the shadows. The first was soon followed by more than a hundred of its kin. They walked with a weaving gait, swaying slightly on long muscular legs as they walked. Their feet made an odd print in the sand, for while they held five toes like a man, they walked on the balls of their feet and had a heel that was high and flared in a curve.

Aritian found himself unable to look away from their gaunt forms. These were born with the flesh of man and the seed of a far darker world. Aritian was heedful to allow himself to feel the full presence of the creature's demonic taint and took in their detail carefully. The act twisted his stomach with knives of nausea. *I knew Maud was dark, but this goes beyond the realm of Sanguis Nox*, Aritian thought with disgust as he eyed the abomination before him. He could not identify their specific demonic origin, but he knew that there were those among the Ronan who could.

The creatures walked to the camels first, seemingly bewildered and shocked by the sight of them. They blinked owlishly and ran their hands over the breadth of camels, seemingly luxuriating in the softness of the tawny beast's hides. Their blue tongues flicked rapidly and they turned to one another and stared at one another in long pauses, motionless. *They've never seen a camel*, Aritian realized. The camels themselves balked at the creatures' approach, calling out to one another in their long, heavy brays. The Cambion ignored the camels' protest.

The Cambion were easily to distinguishable from one another, if one observed them long enough. Individuals had varying horn length and thickness, some had duller, grey-colored skin, while others had skin closer to a shade of blue-black. They stood at varying heights, depending on age and sex. The females stood nearly a foot shorter than the males and had

519

two sets of small, pert breasts. The males varied in muscular density, although all of the creatures ran gaunt.

The Cambion who had stepped from the temple first ignored the camels and instead walked directly to the bundled packs. The half-demon bent on one knee, his spine clearly outlined as he untied the bindings of a pack. With a casual flick he opened the pack, exposing dozens of swords. The blades glinted brightly in the harsh morning light. He lifted a longsword, one hand cradling the blade reverently while the other gripped the hilt testing its feel. His black lips curled under as he smiled, exposing a purple gum line.

Aritian eye caught movement on the dune across from where they crouched. The black cat stared back at him boldly, its orange eyes unblinking. It held his gaze steadily then turned its eyes down to watch the creatures below. Aritian felt the hairs on the back of his arms stand up, but reluctantly turned his eyes back to the temple below.

The Cambion brandished the sword high and the crowd of his companions turned, blinking their tangerine eyes in wonder, their attention riveted on the blade he held. The male walked toward the crowd, holding the sword parallel to his chest. The creature's whip cord tail stood erect and writhed in an S formation, rippling with excitement. A female stepped forth, her blue-black skin shining dimly in the bright sun. Her lips curled up and down rapidly, and her tail wriggled low. The male cocked his head, eying her challenge. With a quick movement, the sword flashed, cutting her head from her shoulders in a spray of black blood. Della stifled a cry with a hand, as the female slowly sunk to her knees before toppling over.

Aritian touched Della's wrist and she turned her head slowly, meeting his gaze with horrified eyes. The elf had grown as pale as parchment and quivered in terror. Aritian motioned down the dune and Della nodded jerkily. Aritian could tell she was frantic with repulsed shock and Aritian wasn't far behind her. He could witness no longer.

Aritian's heart was torn by furious indecision. He wished for nothing more than to spend his last breath annihilating the corruption below, even if it cost him his life. *These creatures cannot be allowed to survive*, he thought darkly. The other part of him warred against such an act. His heart championing the battle, crying out in despair. *If you do, you shall never see Razia again*, it warned. A cool rationale settled over him as he remembered the Oracle's words. He was not even supposed to speak a word, let alone take to the field of battle. In that moment, he knew that these creatures were beyond him and that the only hope for Ignea lay in raising the Ronan's full strength. To do that, he knew he had to turn aside today and live. It was hard, but he did what he knew he must.

Slowly, and with great care, they moved stealthily down the dune. Aritian felt his blood rushing through his head as his ears strained for any sound that might signify that they had been heard. When they were halfway down and hidden by the mound of sand, they stood, and ran crouched down the dune to the base. Aritian offered the elf his hand and she took it without hesitation. Aritian let the black power ripple like waves across his eyes, and bright cherry light flashed where their hands met. Aritian cursed mentally as boiling welts traced from the Ring of Suppression up his skin to his elbow. The wounds caused by the ring were not quick to fade, nor was the pain.

Aritian gave Della a curt nod, and dropped her hand. They raced through the warren of dunes faster than any man could run, his power fueling their legs, allowing them deep reserves of strength. They weaved silently between dunes for more than three miles and in less than five minutes came upon their horses. The mounts stood unbound, waiting quietly in a low dip between two tall peaks of sand. Aritian and Della both leapt into their saddles and kicked their horses into a quick gallop, both wishing to put as much distance between them and the Temple of Darth as they were able.

*****

Hours later, they rode at a steady pace toward a golden smudged that marked the Roc's nesting ground. Aritian weaved in the saddle, exhausted. He had spent much of his power fueling their race across the desert, and what had taken them a days' ride had passed in three, short hours. Breathlessly, Aritian said, "You must understand, Della, even the Ronan are bound by laws. The Coven has a commandment that forbids certain practices and acts. I can tell you with certainty that Maud has broken one of the greatest of these laws. This corruption, this malignant race she's bred is against all our beliefs. Even among the Order of Onyx, this is sacrilege." Aritian paused, swallowing his fear, as he remembered the taint he had felt in the auroras. "The Cambions must be destroyed." Aritian said this with unbending resolve.

Della nodded, her face was tight with worry. Worriedly, she queried, "You said that Maud has been isolated in Ignea for the last seven hundred years. Do you believe she has been breeding them the entire time?" Aritian grimaced and nodded tightly, his lips pressed together at the thought of such a thing. *She must have, there is no other way their numbers could be so great,* he thought, remembering the millions of creatures he sensed. Incredulous, Della asked, "How has this come to pass? How could no one, not the Ronan, not the elves, not the lesser Seelie Court, no one sense this evil before now?"

Aritian shook his head. He didn't know the answer, but he had his suspicions. He explained them, "I am not sure, but Maud has had almost a millennium to breed and hide this nefarious race. When I was under the compulsion of the Passion Berry I studied her." Aritian didn't admit that while under the influence he been motivated by his admiration of her ruthlessness finesse.

"She was banished from the northern lands in the year

five-thousand nine-hundred and two according to a Remembrance Orb I studied. The magi whose memories imbued the Orb was Cain, her older brother, but he did not say the reason why she was being punished — only that she had been sent to the lands of Amissa. Even after the Sundering she was shunned." Aritian flashed the elf a grim look, and said, "And yet, despite her exile, Maud had enjoyed the backing of every single Archmagus for the last eight hundred years. Her father Cornelius took the throne in the year six-thousand two-hundred and two, after murdering Solomon. Her own son succeeded him, after Ayfe and Mathis murdered Cornelius and Cain in a mage duel." Aritian gave the elf a pointed look. It was obvious to him. The Archmagi had known of Maud's experiments and allowed them to take place. There was no other explanation. No one, not even Maud, could have hidden the corruption this long alone.

Aritian continued, his voice growing with concern, as he said, "Selyni said that the Ronan who sits the Weirwood Throne now is a man named Ultan. I know nothing of him nor his possible allegiance to Maud."

Della asked with surprise, "Selyni was here?" Aritian nodded, yes. Della considered a moment, and then carefully said, "Ultan hails from the Sanguis of Nox, and it was with Maud's blessing that he claimed the title of Archmagus. His ascendancy was greatly contested by a magus known as Felix. Many Ronan whisper that Ultan could not have beaten Felix if it had come to a trial by battle. With Maud's supporting his opposition, Felix repented his claim."

Aritian could only nod. Maud was a master when it came to manipulation and he had little doubt that she had the current Archmagus wrapped around her lovely finger. Suddenly, a thought came to him, and he asked, "The elves are said to have bound the Unseelie court." Aritian closed his eyes, and thought back to a black-bound tome he had once read. He could almost feel the thick vellum pages in his hands. He remembered the silver inlaid title: 'A Telling of the Blood Wars'.

Excitement touched his voice as he recounted, "I read that they are held in some sort of captivity, but before their imprisonment they had bred legions of Cambion. Maybe it is with the remnants of these creatures that she had built this race." Aritian didn't want to consider the alternative.

Della shook her head, and mournfully said, "The Cambions were created and bound before the Great Sundering. They, along with the Unseelie court, remain behind the veil of Cla'ditis on the continent of Carcere. There is but one alternative, Maud has freed a demon upon the world, for only an unbound demon can breed." Della gripped her reins fearfully. Worriedly, she said, "Aritian, such magic is lost to this world." Aritian let a hiss of air escape between his teeth. Silence settled between them as they both grimly considered. Minutes passed by and the yellow smudge of the Golden Plains became distinct. In the silence, Della wondered aloud, "How does she sustain them? The temple lays barren."

Aritian had thought of that, too, and mused aloud, "It would be within Maud's power to divert the underground spring that fed the oasis. I suspect she did so when the demands of her creation grew too great to share the source with the compound above. From what I was able to sense, there is a water source deep beneath the ground." He would not doubt what he had felt, his power could not be deceived.

Della looked at him, and her voice grew suddenly serious, as she asked, "What are you going to do now that you know the truth?"

Aritian gritted his teeth. He was filled with a need to confront Maud, but he knew that such foolishness would only result in death. His voice grew hard as he said, "I intend to trust the Oracle, and heed her words." The memory of her prophecy repeated like a mantra in his head. "I must sail north after my Covenant Trial." Aritian whispered, eyeing the northern horizon. A plan was beginning to form in his mind and he smiled.

Devaney

Chapter Fifty-One:

Prophecy

Devaney knelt motionless, a solitary white-flame alone in the darkness. She was dressed in a stained, flimsy shift. Her arms were bound to the floor by thick curling roots, grey with age. The roots gripped her wrists like a vice, binding her as surely as chains. Blood rolled down her thin hands to softly drip on the dirt floor unnoticed. Though they cut her, she was reassured by the roots. Through them, Devaney felt the minds of many. Her light was unbent against the heavy presence of her adversary. Shadows clung about her, oppressive with heady power, but none could touch her shining figure. A soft luminous cloud hung about her, forestalling Aileen's wicked magic.

Aileen had haunted her relentlessly, but after that first night Devaney found herself in Folsa's dream, she hadn't been able to plague Devaney's mind. That had spared her pain for a time, but soon passed as her captors turned to more mundane forms of torture.

Slowly, but with an ever-increasing tempo, the sound of footfalls filled the tomb. Devaney made no sign indicating she heard and her head remained bent. Wild curls fell over her slim face haphazardly, veiling her expression. Suddenly, ruby light bloomed from one of the shadowed alcoves that stood across from her. Someone approached.

The shadows fled like a cowed dog in the glare of the fiery light and abruptly, the tomb seemed all the brighter. Devaney knew then that the shadowed nightmares had fled. A man appeared. Dressed in black robes, he was neither young nor old, rather he was cast with an ageless visage. He had black hair that was neatly slicked back and fell to the nape of his neck, and a long thin face that held heavy, grey eyes. He was pale, almost sickly so, and his expression stoic. An orb floated, as if by its own accord, over his shoulder casting a long shadow against the tombs dirt walls. The orb of light seemed to be made from liquid fire, and slowly, it swirled; moved by an unseen current.

The man stopped several feet away and gazed down at her silently for a moment. His stormy-grey eyes flicked over her form in cold-assessment, weighing her resolve. Devaney made no movement. The only sign that she still lived was the slow, steady rise and fall of her chest. The man's thin lips curled into a slight frown, as though what he found was to his great displeasure.

His voice came in a whisper, as smooth as silk, as he asked, "Oracle, has your time here given you an opportunity to reconsider or shall more time here be required? I am a patient man, but I assure you that stalling is futile." Devaney ignored him. She hadn't been stalling, she had been learning at the heel of a Fae. Many long weeks had passed within the darkness, but instead of falling further to despair, she had grown braver and more secure. Folsa had opened many doors locked within her mind and with the knowledge had come power. The thought of what Caethe endured for their cause gave her strength to endure the pain that came in this place of darkness.

A moment of silence passed and the man raised a hand casually, threateningly. Still, Devaney remained mute. His fingers flashed with harsh red-light and lightning danced dangerously between his twisting fingers. Still, Devaney's eyes remained downcast in silent defiance. The ruddy lightning crackled from his fingers, leaping across the distance between them to crawl along her form.

With a gasp, Devaney's spine straightened rigidly with a snap and her head turned upward revealing a mask of pain. Her eyes clenched and her lips pressed tightly together as she grunted against the violence that lanced through her. Her entire body trembled and shook as his power coursed across her skin. The man smiled and the lightning flashed brighter. Devaney cried out, and her arms snapped up to her breasts as she struggled against the restraints that held her.

The lightning fled as quickly as it had come and Devaney sagged to the floor with relief. Her breath came in ragged gasps as she tried to swallow the pain that still echoed through her limbs. The man spoke again, his voice remaining coolly detached, as he asked, "I thought we had come to an agreement the last time we spoke? If I ask you a question, you give me the respect and courtesy of answering. I am the Archmagus of the Ronan and your King. You will attend me, Devaney." Ultan's visits were sparing, but always left her shaking with weakness. Far more often he sent one his lackeys, Lilith or Lorchan, to interrogate her. No matter how great the pain, Devaney had made sure that they left disappointed.

Devaney sat tall, gathering what little dignity she was able, as she raised her head to meet the Archmagus's dark eyes with her own white-sightless gaze. When she spoke, her voice was surprisingly deep and filled with rich tones of an almost musical quality. "We both know, Ultan, that you are no Archmagus. The one that was promised has been born into the world. The others may turn a blind-eye or bask in their ignorance of tradition, ancient and hallowed by our Coven, but I know the truth. I cannot pretend otherwise." No longer did she hold her power apart or have to strain to feel its touch; it coiled alive and present within her at all times.

A small, deadly smile crept upon Ultan's face. His voice fell quieter still as he said warningly, "Careful, dear Devaney, lest you commit treason unknowingly. The traditions of old died with the Great Sundering. We Ronan left carry on as we are able. A new age of Ronan has begun." Ultan's grey eyes flicked to the root covered alters, and dryly, he said, "The spirits you commune with are from an age dead and gone. I have been anointed, crowned, and received the oaths. This will be the last time you discuss matters that you cannot possibly comprehend. Do I make myself perfectly clear?"

A broad smile crossed Devaney's face. She had hit a nerve, and uncaring of what wrath she might face, she asked, "Or what, Ultan, you'll murder me like my predecessor?" Ultan raised his eyebrows in mock surprise, and Devaney said, "Oh yes, Ultan, I know about young Hannah. Or will you torture me until my mind is broken, like Aileen?" A wild chuckle ripped from her throat as she threw all caution to the wind, and said, "You're running out of time, Ultan, and you can't afford to wait for another Oracle to rise."

Ultan smiled lazily, and asked lightly, "Am I now? What do you think you know, child?"

Devaney spoke confidently, as she said, "You mock the Fae at your peril, for they have revealed much of our most ancient truths. I know it was Hannah who first gave you prophecy of hope, and Aileen who showed you the black price that had to be paid to achieve it." Ultan's apathetic expression cracked as rage bloomed. Devaney laughed, and asked, "How long do suppose Magrados will continue to bless your reign? You have broken the Accords, Ultan, and it only takes a single magus to claim rights to an inquisition."

Red lightning crackled across the tomb engulfing the Oracle. Devaney fell to the floor, screaming and flailing, as pain raced through her. She lost control of her bladder, staining her sullied gown further. Her sight darkened as she began to fall into oblivion's sweet embrace. The lightning died.

Ultan's voice, while low, had grown deadly as he whispered, "I have done what was demanded of me by the circumstances of my reign. You think you know this power, Magrados, but you are an ignorant fool. I have no fear of Magrados, for the very power guided my hand and safeguards what was taken." Devaney paled visibly, for she had not known this, and Ultan smiled maliciously. Arrogantly, he said, "You are nothing more than a puppet of sleeping shadows, girl. Bide your words carefully, Oracle, for despite my need I will not hesitate to kill you if you ever suggest such fell treason again."

Devaney struggled weakly to sit, and whispered harshly, "We both know you won't. Banish such hollow threats from you slithering tongue, you embarrass yourself." A steely silence settled between them as Devaney stared up at Ultan and he sneered imperiously down at her.

Devaney was the first to drop her eyes. She crossed her legs and smoothed her sodden shift, regaining her calm, and said, "I came to you for sanctuary, Ultan. I was warned of your avarice and callousness, but I was desperate, fleeing the only home I have ever known. You have proven equally as malicious as those I fled."

Ultan's voice changed, softening, as he persuasively said, "This is not what I wished for you, Devaney. You betrayed me. You empowered Caethe, and now you threaten to squander our only hope of freedom." Ultan shook his head sadly, and admonished, "Such brazen disrespect cannot be allowed. If we Ronan are to survive we must be of one mind, one heart, and one soul. We need you Devaney. You are the light that illuminates the future. Bend the knee, swear the oath, and the Coven will embrace you as the respected leader you were born to be."

Devaney remained silent for a time, her head bowed in thought. Ultan smiled, knowing her resistance was failing. She was young and her heart already scorched by deep betrayal. Like a cat with a mouse cornered, Ultan knew he was gaining ground.

Ultan pushed on, saying gently, "You will be treated with care and honors beyond even the dreams of the most powerful royals in the land. You are beyond such mortal dredges, born from the Magrados, magic made flesh. You have but to surrender yourself and everything you came here for, shall be yours. I will embrace you as my own daughter, and no pain of heart or body shall touch you..."

Devaney cut his tirade short abruptly, asking, "What is it that you truly want, Ultan?" Ultan cocked his head in annoyance, surprised, but undeterred by her bluntness. Devaney continued, "We both know you're not here for my oath, so what is that you truly wish to know?"

Ultan grew mild with indignity, as he protested softly, "You are wrong, in part, for I do desire your oath. It is what is natural and expected of a newly born Ronan." He smiled without humor then, and admitted, "But you are right in your assessment, we Ronan have been cursed to exile for far too long and our window of escape draws to a close soon." Ultan turned away, and his black-robes whispered as he walked to stand before an altar.

His voice grew weary and distant as he said, "It is true that Hannah gave me hope and with her vision we were able to put events into action." His voice faded softer still, as though he was lost in thought when he said, "The visions she saw frightened her, and unlike yourself," Ultan looked over his shoulder, his expression not unkindly, before turning back to the altar, "she could not control the visions. For her, it was a never-ending, wave after wave, torrid of sight that drowned her, scattering her sanity to the far reaches of her mind." His voice fell silent.

When he spoke again his voice had turned cold and bitter, "I need the clear vision Hannah denied me and that Aileen is incapable of producing. Now that Caethe has betrayed us, I fear that we shall be lost for all time, exiled here and forgotten. I know you know the answers Devaney. Tell me and I shall grant your freedom from this tomb."

Devaney inhaled sharply, his promise making her forget herself. Devaney's heart pounded. This was the moment she had been waiting weeks on end in the darkness for. She knew what was to come, for she had seen it in her Awakening. In a hesitant whisper, she asked, "If I agree to tell you, will you give me your word?"

Ultan gazed at her with an unreadable glare. It seemed as though his eyes bore into her very soul, searching for any sign or deceit or iota of lingering strength. After a time, he placed his hand over his heart, and a red glow sprung from his palm. "I give you my word Devaney, I shall release you from this tomb should you provide me with a prophecy that will lead our people to freedom."

Devaney breathed shakily, preparing herself. Briefly, she considered letting the moment pass. Her thoughts turned to the future waiting for her should she let fear guide her. Devaney shuddered, shakings her head, refusing to bow to such a fate. Her breath came in harsh gasps as her voice grew fear-laden, as she spoke hollowly, "I know what you seek, Ultan. The answers to the questions that haunt you and those that have yet to shadow your heart." Ultan took a step closer, his eyes growing hungry as their gazes met. "You fear the loss of your power above all else. A dark prophecy is what you now seek, a road so twisted and obscured that the warren of possibilities that follow you cannot possibly fathom, as they number greater than the stars in the night's sky. Following this path with change the course of the future beyond understanding. Do you still wish to know?

Ultan's voice came in a low growl, "Yes."

Devaney nodded, resigned. When she next spoke her voice lost all fear. Fear didn't exist in Magrados. The words passed her lips, falling like drum beats marking the start of a battle, as she said, "The time of Magrados has come. With its child born into the world, magic seeks rebirth. Ware', for that which has slumbered shall stir." Her head rolled on her neck, and her face became obscured by tangled curls. "Two seeds fell from the false king of Magrados."

Devaney's lips grew blue and her breath came with puffs of cold frost, as she said, "One sailed north, resting at the heel of her mother's sarcophagus. Hannah, a visage of purity lay entrapped, frozen in ice by the hand of her lover's embrace. The child's heart damned, clouded by a pall of divine sophism. It is she, blind to her blood, the key to the Ronan's salvation. Beware, should her heart be interred in god's faith, her soul will forever be guarded against Magrados's dynamism. Betrayal is the key to her rebirth."

Silence pervaded the tomb as she let the weight of her words settle between them. Ultan watched her, unblinking, as he drank in all that she said.

Devaney continued, her voice growing deeper and crackling with the hiss of flames, as she followed the prophecy further. "One sailed south, the seed a secret, as mother's fear gave wind to her flight. Brother of the Queen to be, it is he who shall hear her speak the key. Lost at sea, a black storm flung her hope beyond disheartenment. Birthed on sands black as night, a son was born. Forged in the fires of the south, wild as the storm, only he can triumph over the Father's chosen."

A smile crossed Devaney's face, and Ultan frowned, unnerved that she spoke prophesy that made her heart soar so. "Beware, for the princes are heirs to ancient blood untold, and shall shape Adonim with magic beyond reproach. Beware, they shall usurp their father's crown, climbing a twixing, elder branch. Beware, one shall be our salvation, while the other our doom."

Devaney words became feverishly quick, as the effort of speaking so long with Magrados was draining her unto death. "In Magrados's rebirth, blood shall spill as millions meet death's unerring glare. Beware of what you have awoken, for the champion is here. Beware, a millennia of reverie, its power has only grown. What has been sundered can be once again be whole. A spell, grails gathered, a circle drawn, a sacrifice made led by Magrados' soul. Your succor, your claim to power, lays now in the darkest of schemes. To cling to supremacy, listen to whispers promised in her nightly bower, spoken to you in your darkest of dreams. Only then shall you rise as the black-crowned king." Devaney's sightless eyes snapped to Ultan's face, and tears of blood spilled down her cheeks. Her voice came harsh and tortured, as she whispered, "She has laid her hand upon your soul."

Devaney fell silent as she slumped ungracefully to the ground. The prophecy had been torn from her lips from the depths of her soul. Ultan smiled and thought, *Such an unambiguous foretelling comes at a steep price.* The girl had used the last of her strength. She lay there, barely breathing, in the dirt at his feet. Ultan muttered the words, closing his eyes, as he committed the prophecy to memory.

After a moment, Ultan's eyes snapped open, and he straightened. He gazed down at the frail girl with a content smile that rapidly curled into a smirk of malicious intent. With a voice shaking with anticipation, he said, "I gave you my oath Devaney. Look at me and receive your promise."

Devaney lifted her head weakly from her prostrated position, her wild hair shadowing her eyes. Ultan spoke on, "You've been corrupted by the foul usurper's sweet promises and for that betrayal, you deserve my wrath." He paused dramatically, and Devaney's bottom lip trembled, but she dared not speak. Ultan pulled a robin's egg-sized diamond from the depths of one of his deep pockets, and held it delicately before him, as he said brightly, "But an oath, is an oath, my dear." The stone glinted in the red light of his mage fire. He eyed the diamond contemplatively, and remarked casually, "I think your soul will find the diamond's interior quite luxurious compared to this dark tomb."

Devaney voice came devoid of emotion as she whispered, "You swore an oath to free me."

Ultan smile widened, and he said, "I swore to free you from this tomb. I did not swear that I would let you go. A few years within the stone and I will set you free when I have your oath of fealty." The diamond began to glow with an ugly, purple light. Ultan chuckled gleefully, before saying, "Don't fret, dear,

I will find you a much more suitable body then that wraith-like, frail twig you inhabit now."

Violaceous light bloomed brighter than the noonday sun as power thundered through the tomb. Devaney sat up with a jerk. All weakness fled her form, cast away as if it had never been. Iron-will filled her slight face as she raised a thin hand in rebuke. Time slowed.

The changed happened in a fraction of a second, and the only reaction Ultan gave was a dilatation of his pupils. The Archmagus stood before her as still as stone, holding a diamond that shone like a violet star. Its light flooded the tomb, searching for her soul, but the light's bloom had been halted not six-inches from her. The air hummed as the ferocious power keened for release. Slowly, barely perceivable, it moved, inching closer to her.

Devaney rose to her knees, holding her wrists before her. The roots that bound her glowed with blue flames as time raced fearlessly forward. The ancient roots had long lives, touched by magic as they were, but all things met the Shadow; a simple truth that Devaney had clung to while huddled in the darkness. A moment passed and the roots burst into a spray of dust. The lilac light had crawled an inch closer. Devaney stood and gently rubbed her wrists. Where the roots had held her, her skin had aged, darkening and growing wrinkled. Devaney held the mark of ages before her, making sure the sight of them would be imprinted upon Ultan's memory.

Devaney spoke slowly as she took a step backwards, "You are a fool, Ultan. Deceived by your ego and blind to the power that stood before you. I spoke of prophecy, it is true, but only that which I needed you to hear." Devaney smiled as she took another step backward. The corners of Ultan's mouth were turning downward, as anger licked his lips. "I hold no malice for what you have done to me here, within the tomb of Toutha' Da Fae. I have learned much from the slumbering folk and as an Oracle, I understand that what is destined to happen must be allowed to take place."

Devaney smiled grimly, before admitting, "A harsh lesson it is true, but know this: I believe in the solidarity of sacrifices which must be made. You will come to know this lesson well, false king." Her voice dripped with bitter understanding as she promised, "I will do what I must. Trust in that truth, Ultan. The prophecy is alive, and our fates sealed." Devaney took another step back and mockingly bowed with a flair that Lifoy would have been proud of. She turned on her heel and disappeared in a white blur that fled the darkness of the catacombs. Seconds passed and the tomb, and all within, remained still. The only desirable mark of time was the slow creep of the fractured light that bloomed from the diamond Ultan held.

As fast as it had been stilled, time resumed its natural course. Brilliantly bright light flashed across the tomb, encompassing it completely. The diamond's power cut off abruptly, winking out of existence to reveal Ultan. Pale anger flooded his face, and flames of fire bloomed around him as his fury took form. The flames grew until they reached the ceiling, a tempest of red that swirled around him. With an explosion that made the very ground tremble, the flames raced into each shadowed archway that led from the tomb. The flame, like a wild beast, raced through the maze-like catacombs promising death to all it touched.

A moment passed, and flames burst from three points on the island. One raked the edges of the forest with hungry tongues of flame. Another scorched the rocks that led up the cliffside. The last licked the white sands of the beach that lay in the shadow of the mountain, turning it to glass. None of its hungry heat tasted the blood of the Oracle.

Devaney ran on waves of cerulean waters. The waves were frozen as she ran up and down the swells, her feet leaving just the barest of impressions. She leapt over a white crest, and held her breath as she plunged beyond the Curse that held the

Ronan in exile. Its effects fled her in a fraction of a second. Devaney ran so quickly that she appeared as no more than a blur of white, streaking across the surface of the sea.

In the distance she saw a ship. Devaney slowed, her footsteps now deeply marking the water's surface as she eyed the green sails. Upon the sail were three goblin's chained to a black tower; the symbol of Melisoance. Knowingly, Devaney thought, *a Reblyn city that rests on the edge of the Balu Swamp.* She remembered the prophecy she had given Lifoy,

'As Shades Island bathes with the witch king's ire

The blind walk upon cerulean wave

The chameleon uncovers the forsaken liar

Sailing beneath the flag of emerald mire

Due north of the sentinel's cave.'

Devaney raced to the edge of the ship and stood still. Time resumed, and she plunged into the icy-cold waters of the Chalice Sea. Men yelled, hearing the splash, and Devaney floundered in the water waiting for rescue.

Aritian

Chapter Fifty-Two:

Covenant Trials

Sunlight drifted lazily through blue-stained glass doors and spilled across the opulent furnishings of Aritian's apartments. The room was spacious and sprawling. Aritian studied the ribbed ceiling and stone beams that vaulted toward the center, forming a circular design. A curling staircase elegantly crawled upward along the right side of the room, ascending to a private study. The rich trappings of the apartment had become a lonely place, but Aritian had not wanted his companions anywhere near Maud after the Time Vortex.

Aritian sat on the edge of a four-poster bed that lay against the far side of the room. He had not slept and as the moon crept across the sky and the sun broke the morning, he knew that the time he had been waiting for had come. Aritian stood shakily and walked to the birch-wood side table. A stone basin had been filled with cool water and small white linens, embroidered with the image of a golden phoenix, lay neatly folded beside it. Aritian dipped a cloth into the cool water, and washed the morning from his face and the sweat from his body. Afterwards, he opened the doors of a tall wardrobe and dressed with shaking hands. Today was the day he would face the Covent Trials.

Aritian abandoned the casual style of southern dress and instead dressed in traditional magus garb that Maud had provided; long, blue robes that marked him as a Ronan without a claim to any particular Order. The robes were trimmed in gold along the edges of the collar and sleeves, and stitched with a flame-wreathed bird. Rings glinted on four of his fingers: onyx, emerald, and ruby flashed with his quick movements. He wore two necklaces. One held a medallion that was stamped with the image of a phoenix flying in the center of a pentagram of fire. The other held the large chunk of dragonbone that was set in a delicate net of gold. The bone was now inscribed with tiny etched runes. Aritian's bound his long hair in a tight bun at the nape of his neck and secured it with a long-toothed emerald comb.

Aritian closed his eyes briefly, calming the turbulent nerves that rolled like snakes in his stomach, and then walked out of the double doors onto the balcony. He found two guards waiting by the door. They, like all the men here at Maud's compound resembled Hector; with golden skin and crowned with blonde hair.

Aritian gave the guards a nod, and waved to the one on the left, saying, "Lead on, Elijah." The man blinked with surprise, startled that Aritian had known him by name. The soldier recovered quickly, and gave him a polite bow. Aritian was unsurprised by the escort. Maud had made it apparent that he would attend the trials by his own will or without. The Scarlet Witch would not be denied.

The soldiers led him briskly across the courtyard, through an archway, and toward the columned building that acted as Maud's personal residence. The courtyard before it was deserted, no doubt by Maud's command, and they walked up the steps into Maud's reception hall. The hall, much like most of the compound today, was abandoned. The long black veils of silk and the pentagram that had adorned the hall when he entered the Time Vortex were gone, replaced once more by low, velvet couches.

Aritian looked toward the library, but the glowing red power that had marked the silver door was gone. Instead, the door hung open, as normal and unremarkable looking as any door in the compound. Aritian spied the neat bookshelves and low tables, before turning away with a shudder. He had not been able to bring himself to go into that room since emerging from the spell, and the very sight of it now brought frightful memories raging to the surface.

The soldiers walked across the hall to the far right, past a wide archway into what appeared to be a small parlor. Elijah waved the other soldier forward, and commanded, "Open the way, Daichi."

The guard nodded, walked around a low dining table and behind a long bar. He placed his hand on the stone wall, in a space clear of shelves, and began whispering to himself. After a few seconds, Daichi stepped back and the wall faded away to nothing to reveal a wide stairwell. The illusion was powerful, anyone without the proper command could have touched it and felt only stone. Only Maud's descendants, and a scant few among them, could open the way to her hidden sanctum.

Aritian followed the guards past the glamor and felt a thrum of power as the wall hummed back to life behind them. A shiver ran down his spine and he had to grip his hands before him to still their shaking. He had never been to this part of the compound, hadn't even known of its existence. As he considered, he concluded that it suited her to have a lair beneath ground like some desert scorpion hidden from Ignathra's gaze. Orbs of red fire bloomed along the ceiling of the stairwell, paced twenty-feet apart, and illuminated the stairs with the brightness of the sun. Aritian looked down and saw that the stair descended hundreds of feet. He walked down them without pause.

When they reached the landing, Daichi waved to the left, and they walked through a sandstone archway. Unlike the structures above, the walls here were not whitewashed, but left their natural rouge. Aritian followed his escorts down the long hallway. The ceiling arched above, more than forty-feet in height, and the peaks of the ceiling were lost in wash of fierce, bright fire that moved and crackled as if alive. As Aritian walked, he looked to either side and saw that tall archways bloomed with light at odd intervals. Idly he distracted himself with the hall's looking portals that displayed Maud's zoo.

To his left he saw a doorway filled with murky green water. Goblins swam lithely among green algae stalks, flitting before the portal like dark shadows. These were gilled creatures, frilled with long fins, and only slightly smaller than the Gillo variety. In the distance, Aritian could see mounds of floating land that were held up by twisting roots and on them, tall Gaur who stood before huts made of weaved fronds. Schools of silver-finned fish swam here and there among the murk of the tangled roots.

To his right, he saw a desert-scape and what appeared to be a square mile of land. The ground was cracked and white, and the light of the cage blared with potent heat. In the distance, he saw squat creatures leaning on worn staffs of bent wood. They milled among domed hovels made from pale stone and walked ponderously through fields of tall cacti. The creatures wore greenish-brown shells upon their backs, but walked ploddingly on two feet. One turned its long, leathery-grey neck and Aritian saw that it was beaked, much like a turtle. Its beak opened, as if to speak, but Aritian could hear none of the strange creature's words.

They moved on, and Aritian passed dozens more cages. Some were filled with hundreds of creatures, while others seemed abandoned. The geography was controlled by Maud's magic and was as varied as the creatures they held. He passed snow-capped hills, dark forests, and open green valleys. Aritian's paced slowed as he came upon a familiar sight.

Golden grass swayed by an unfelt breeze. Aritian walked to the portal's entrance. The guards made to speak, but Aritian held up a hand, commanding silence and the men swallowed their protests. Aritian placed a hand on the portal and it tingled with vibration, but seemed as smooth as glass to the touch. He called out with his mind, and from across the grass plains a form flitted from the sky on iridescent wings. It was the Insecti queen, and as she settled on the ground before him he met her innumerable red eyes. Her abdomen was flat and as she settled her emerald wings, he saw her young bounding across the grassy plain in a brown tide. Their strange, swaying gait carried them speedily and soon they gathered around her, chirping at her knees in the hundreds. The Queen's antennae twitched excitedly and her thorax's vibrated, but Aritian could not hear the buzzing of her call.

The Queen pressed her head to the portal with a dim thud and snapped her wings shut. Her young fell silent, slowly swaying on their long legs. Aritian could see himself reflected a hundred times in her multifaceted eyes. Aritian touched her mind once more and her thorax thrummed with waves of vibration in response. Aritian nodded to her and her hooked arm slammed against the portal with a boom. Out of the corner of his eye, he saw the two soldiers flinch. Aritian resisted a smile. For a moment they stood like that, his palm to her hooked appendage, separated only by the portal. Aritian dropped his hand and turned away. He gave the soldiers a curt nod, and they led on.

After walking for more than an hour, the guards stopped before a large archway and waved him through. This was Maud's true reception hall, the place she reigned Ignea from with twisted lies and veiled threats. Aritian hesitated, his heart pounding in his chest, and closed his eyes. He did not want to enter. Fear gripped him then and he merely stood there. A whisper floated from the background of his mind, gently reassuring him, egging him forward. Aritian could not deny the voice, so compelled, and stepped within the hall. The soldiers did not follow him.

The hall was massive and soared a full four-stories in height, held erect by twenty-four golden pillars etched with runes of power. Large orbs of red fire floated by their own accord at the ribbed center of the hall just beneath sprawling fiascos that spanned across the ceiling. Mage battles flashing with glaring, cackling powers battled against armies of men and elves and creatures he could not name. The artistry was masterful and vast, and nearly took Aritian's breath away. Every creature was depicted with a sense of realism that belied the human capacity and depicted with starting clarity, from the chainmail spokes of a soldier's armor, to the gleam in the horses' eyes, to the coiling fire, and smallest blade of grass.

The floor, black marble, gleamed with a glossy sheen that reflected the hall above. Ranks of lorith stood shoulder to shoulder, between each pillar, so still they looked like statues etched in scales; only their yellow eyes moved, watching as Aritian walked the expanse of the hall. The lorith were all armed with tall pikes capped with a long serrated blade that flashed in the dancing, red light. The reptiles were outfitted richly, with golden breastplates and leather braces that covered their legs and the base of their tails.

The silence of the hall was akin to a tomb, only interrupted by the clip of his footsteps. At the end of the hall were four slabs of red marble that sat on top of one another, descending in size as they rose. A gold throne sat in the center of the dais, made of clean lines and simple design, with armrests shaped in the form of talons and a high back that stood thirty-feet in height. Flanking the throne to either side was a collection of ancient mirrors framed in silver or gold, varying in shape and size. There were twelve in total, each holding a silver, liquid face that moved languidly, unreflecting. The hall was cavernous, every element carefully crafted to intimidate those who came in supplication.

Maud sat silently, unmoving on the throne. Her dark eyes followed his approach with imperious appraisal. She was outfitted like a queen in a scarlet and black gown with a red corset and a skirt frilled with hundreds of layers of sheer silk. Her hair had been tightly braided, and coiled at the top of her head to sit in the center of the three-pointed crown. In one hand she held her black-diamond wand, and in the other she held a tall, black staff that was capped with a ruby the size of a fist.

Aritian stopped a dozen feet from the throne and looked up at Maud, expressionless and silent. Maud lifted her staff a few inches from the floor and tapped the wooden end against the marble floor, four times. Four plumes of red energy flooded from the staff's head and thudded with a crackle into four of the magic mirrors. The silver faces hissed and twisted in rolling swirls before turning clear. Mirrors on either side of the throne shone with four reflections. They did not reflect the hall, but rather reflected four different rooms in places far from Ignea.

The mirror that sat to the right of Maud's throne was gold and the frame was made in the likeness of twisting fire. The reflection showed a cavernous and dimly-lit reception hall. Twenty-one silver thrones, made in uniform likeness, faced him. The center throne sat nearly five-feet taller than the others, topped with a silver thirteen-pointed star. Four of the thrones were occupied, including the central throne. Maud introduced the magi shown within, and they each nodded when their name was spoken.

Maud waved her hand toward a dark haired man, and said, "Ultan, our king and righteous ruler." The Archmagus sat regally in the central throne wearing long black robes. Ultan looked nearly forty to Aritian's eye, had a nondescript face with plain features and flat grey eyes. There was nothing about his appearance that made him stand out, but even through the mirrors Aritian could feel the heady power that cloaked the man. Ultan gave him a slight nod, his expression unreadable.

Aritian felt a wave of nervousness crash over him as his resolve threatened to break. Once again, that indomitable voice at the back of his mind whispered confidence and provided a wellspring of strength. Aritian buried the feeling of unease in an unreadable mask of composure.

Maud gestured toward a woman, and said, "Aileen, the

Augury of the Onyx." Aileen sat to Ultan's right and wore a simple black gown of lace. She had long, free flowing hair, a thin frame, and sharp features. Her hands, covered with black satin gloves, were clenched before her in excitement. Her slightly-bulging eyes were a pale green and too large for her petite face. Something wild lurked within those eyes, and Aritian could sense that with a little provoking it would burst free to the peril of the one who antagonized her.

"To Ultan's left sits Meinolf," Maud said, waving toward a man who wore simple grey robes, was tall, and crowned with wild, bronze hair. His pale, freckled face held a bored expression and his brown eyes lazily searched for something of interest.

Maud turned from the youth, and waved toward a man with friendly eyes, and said, "Aedus, the Wise." Aedus sat next to his son, and Aritian knew they were related for they shared such similar features as only a father and son do. In Aedus he saw a craggy hardness that belied his soft brown eyes. He looked at Aritian as he stroked his long, red beard thoughtfully.

The mirror to the left of Maud shone with white light and displayed a stark room. Everything in the room was pure white, the walls were whitewashed, and stone marble floors were covered in pale furs. Even the two people displayed wore white, with long sweeping robes, and pale expression. "Ayfe, the eldest of our Coven, and herald of the Order of the Albastella." Ayfe was a thin woman, touched by great age. Her lips were pale and she had a long, pointed nose that gave her a somewhat birdlike appearance. She had blue eyes that sparkled with intelligence, but she wore a frown of deep concern.

Maud waved to the man who sat next to Ayfe on the simple, white bench, and said, "And Mathis, her most trusted advisor, and our Coven's most learned Historian." Mathis had thinning brown hair and an expansive beard that rolled across his wide belly. His brown eyes took in the vision of the hall in a glance before settling fully upon Aritian.

The other two mirrors bloomed with light in rapid succession.

The first mirror illuminated was framed in silver and round in shape. The mirror displayed a dim room that glowed with a pale, emerald light. "Morgana, the witch of the Chalice Sea," Maud said thinly, as if she could not bother to hide her distaste for the woman. Morgana sat on a throne made from a gargantuan seashell that was ribbed with a pale brown. She wore a seafoam green gown that flowed generously from her voluptuous hips and a pearl pendant that rested atop her billowing breasts. She looked no older than Aritian himself, but one look in her knowing blue eyes and Aritian could see the wisdom of ages resting within.

The final mirror was square and large, its golden frame marred by great age. It depicted a massive hall that sat empty but for a simple wooden chair. The hall was open to the grey northern sky and lacked any semblance of a ceiling. Great stone boulders tumbled haphazardly behind the chair; a remnant of the hall's stone roof. Maud waved to the woman with a slight nod of respect, and said, "Gwynevere, granddaughter of Ayfe and protector of the north." Gwynevere sat in full plate-armor that glinted brightly in the steel-grey light that played from the sky above. Her long, blonde hair tumbled loosely in gentle curls to her waist and in her lap lay a great, silver sword. *Gwynevere the gorgeous*, Aritian thought, *with a perfectly sculpted form and a face that would make angels weep*. She had bright green eyes, high cheekbones that were touched by a hint of pink, and a long neck line that held the carriage of a queen.

When introductions were made Maud stood, and walked slowly down the steps to stand before the mirrors. In a clear, bold voice she addressed the Coven, "I, Maud Circe Marie Ronan, welcome you and present Aritian Ronan for his Covenant trials." Maud bowed slightly, before she continued, addressing Ultan directly, "I invite you, Archmagus, to judge this trial, and those who join him to bear witness in accordance of the Covenant so that all might see the truth of Aritian's success or failure." Ultan gave a casual a wave of his hand for the proceedings to commence.

Maud turned from the mirrors and looked at Aritian once more. In a bright voice, she instructed him, "You shall be faced with three tasks. Complete each, and you shall ascend to the rank of Coven member and receive all the rights accorded by our laws. Fail, and you shall be remitted to study and forced to undergo the trial in one year's time. Shall we begin?" Maud asked, her tone remaining neutral. There would be no witty quips today, no biting remarks. The Coven looked on, and a serious air dominated the hall.

Aritian stepped forward, and addressed the Coven in a confident voice, "I willingly submit myself to these trials and hope that I may impress upon you the wealth of knowledge that I have been provided. I thank you for the honor you afford me by bearing witness." He bowed to the mirrors, and then said, "and passing judgment." He bowed lower still before Ultan. "I shall accept any verdict you deem prudent." Aritian said in polite conclusion. The voice reminded him that this was but a formality, whether he passed the trials or not he would sail north. *But we won't fail*, the voice assured him.

Aritian turned back to Maud and she gave him a cold smile. She waved to his hand, and he felt the presence of the Ring of Suppression recede to nearly nothing. "Let it be known that the weight of the Ring of Suppression has been lifted." Maud said in a loud voice that reverberated across the hall.

Maud brandished her staff and red light bloomed from its tip. The hall was thrown dark with ruddy light and began to fill with thick swirling fog. Maud's voice came as if from a great distance, as she said, "Your first task will to be find three golden rings that have been hidden in this hall. Beware, you will face the aversion of magic and the might of the two-hundred and forty lorith who will seek to stall you. You have one hour."

Aritian turned toward her voice, but found that the throne

and mirrors had disappeared beneath a thick cloud of red. Aritian listened closely, cocking his head. Soft scratching sounds began to fill the hall as the lorith began to search for him, their talons clipping across the marble. Aritian closed his eyes and crouched low.

The fog rolled ominously all around him, and he felt despair fill his mind. Aritian breathed deeply, inhaling the fog, and his fear increased. The voice cautioned, *The clouds are poisoned with fear, stay strong in your resolve.* Sweat drenched his skin as if a cold pale of water had been upended over his head and his heart thundered erratically. A chill gripped him. Aritian fought the panic and breathed slowly. When his thoughts no longer screamed for him to flee, he nodded to himself, swallowing the terror.

Aritian found himself before the great door where he kept his power locked away. It stood suspended in darkness, soaring above him. Aritian thoughts raced, but a hand fell upon his shoulder. He did not turn to face the one who stood behind him, but with that touch his mind grew focused, and all his fears and self-doubt burned away.

The figure behind him guided his hand to the door, so that his palm rested against the crystalized surface. Crimson light crackled at the edge of the door, seeking escape like an eager hound. Aritian did not overthink what he was about to do; he simply acted. Lightning raced from his hand, leaping across the surface of the door to fill the runes along its face with bright light. With a single thought, the door imploded and disintegrated to dust.

Burgundy power flooded free. The power wailed like an inferno as it fled its prison, unstoppable and colossal in might. It threatened to drown him and he cried out. Aritian resisted the urge to take shelter or fight it. Instead, the hand on his shoulder pushed him forward, forcing him to embrace it. He cried out again as the torrid power ripped through him like a hurricane. The voice guided him until he gripped the power and bent it to his will. The chaotic power resisted, but his will rippled through the energy and it began to spin above him in a vast whirlwind. As the winds of magic settled, Aritian stepped into the center of the power.

Aritian's eyes snapped open and rolled with power. A shield, burning with blue flames, snapped around him. Lorith charged toward him from all sides, bursting from the writhing fog from every direction. Aritian reach out and touched the fog. The fog ignited as quickly as dry kindling with a tortured scream. Flames shot outward from his shield, rolling across the hall in a great, crackling wave. The lorith howled with fear, fleeing before it. Several fell, writhing in gouts of yellow and orange flames, screaming guttural cries before falling silent. Their blackened bodies spilled black smoke as they stilled. Aritian spared no thought for the dead, the voice that spoke to him and dominated his mind acted beyond pity.

Aritian slipped off the golden ring that was capped with ruby from his left pinky finger and felt its cool surface. He knew he was meant to search the hall by magic, but Aritian would not complete the trial in the way he was expected to, simply on the merit of expectation. Aritian held the golden ring in his palm of his right hand and the ring began to shine as if filled with starlight as likeness called to like. From three different directions silver light flared. Aritian held his left hand up and the silver light flashed toward his palm and with it, three small, golden rings. The metal was hot to the touch, but cooled rapidly in his open palm.

The hall cleared of fog, fire, and smoke as bright light replaced the dim darkness. The throne and mirrors appeared behind him, and Aritian turned to display the rings he held. The first trial had lasted less than two minutes. Aritian stood expressionless, wrapped confidently in the full weight of his power as he eyed the expressions of the watching magi. Meinolf sat forward in his seat, watching intently, his boredom having fled the moment the trial began. The others seemed to hold expressions of mild surprise. Aileen smiled wildly, her eyes gleaming with something that resembled hunger. Only Ultan seemed unimpressed, and he waved a hand imperiously for Maud to continue.

Aritian gave a short bow, placed the small golden rings on a red marble step, and turned toward Maud. Maud raised an elegant eyebrow, but otherwise made no other expression of how she felt. In a flat tone, she commanded, "Your second task is to call forth a Daemon of the Shadow Realm and bind it to your will."

The hall remained unchanged this time. Aritian walked to the center of the hall, past burnt carcasses of the smoking lorith, and turned back to the dais. Aritian raised his right hand, spreading his fingers wide. Silver light bloomed at each fingertip and after a moment, beams of light burst forth to slam into the black marble at his feet with the crack of lightning. A five-pointed star formed around him, cast in silvery-light, followed by a circle that connected each point of the star to one another. Aritian raised his right hand and a line of blood formed down the length of his palm, cut by his will alone. Pain blossomed like fire across his palm, but Aritian held a blank expression as blood dripped into the center of the star at his feet. He would show no weakness before the arrayed Ronan. Aritian curled his left hand in a fist and squeezed. When he opened his hand, the cut had disappeared. Aritian displayed it to the mirrors, before dropping it to his side.

The blood droplets on the floor began to hiss as they crawled across the floor with a life of their own, and two dozen lines of runes were written from the blood in the center of the pentagram by Aritian's wordless command. The runes flashed with light and grey murky smoke began to boil in the primary triangle of the star. Aritian looked to Maud, and a small orb of red light formed in her palm. The orb shot across the hall and disappeared into the grey smoke. *They will witness what transpires in the Realm of Umbrael*, the voice cautioned. The voice guided his mind as Aritian closed his eyes. With a mental twist, his consciousness dived toward the dark fog.

Aritian found himself standing on an abandoned plain. He didn't feel the firmness of the ground, but instead seemed to float just above the surface. The plain stretched as far as his eyes could see. As he looked out, it seemed as though the plain fled into the grey sky, becoming synonymous in the distance. Grey fog rolled along the ground and as Aritian looked down he saw that his body was translucent, painted in grey shades. The only light in the grey expanse of the shadow was the blue-flamed shield that surrounded him. It burned brightly and the very air of the plain seemed to recoil before its touch. Aritian saw the small red orb of Maud's power floating high above. He disregarded it as he concentrated. He had never before astral projected, and only had a theoretical knowledge of what he was now doing.

Aritian raised his hand above his head and a great sapphire-colored orb filled his palm. Aritian let it grow until it was nearly the size of a wagon and, with a grunt, threw it into the sky. The flaming orb shot from his hand as quick as an arrow, fleeing into the grim clouds above. Aritian let the flame explode with a mental touch, and blue bands of light arched across the sky.

Dark grey shadows began to fill the sky. Aritian turned his head upward with a grin, and shouted, "That's right, one of you must face my challenge!" He spoke with the voice that controlled him. A piece of him trembled in the darkest recess of his mind, cowering with fear, but that was no longer who was in control.

A black shadow, nearly the color of pitch fell from the sky in a great rolling cloud. As it landed, the fog wreathing the ground rippled outward in rings. The shadowed form became more distinct, although it remained cloaked in dark, curling smoke. The Daemon stood nearly ten-feet in height, had a muscular build, and was crowned with four horns. Red eyes glared from the shadow, flashing with challenge.

Aritian took a step back, as his mouth went dry. In a whisper, he said, "That's right, come on beast."

Four bat-like wings snapped out, spreading behind the Daemon like a cape of darkness. Gales of wind buffeted his shield, sending tremors through it as the Daemon tested his strength. Aritian smiled, unimpressed by the weak attempt.

Suddenly, black power burst with a hiss from the beast's eyes and slammed into the shield with a metallic whine. Aritian grimaced as he was pushed back a step, and wind gathered about him flowing in strange patterns as it pelted him with fine sand that passed through the shield without pause. The sand burned his skin, and his robes began to disintegrate as the hungry sand sated itself. Silvery cracks crawled along the shield's sparkling surface as it threatened to buckle.

Aritian grimaced and poured more of his magic into the shield. It glowed fiercer, flashing outward with silver beams of light that penetrated the murkiness before him. The Daemon leapt forward, bounding across twenty feet in a flash, and raked its black, dagger-like talons across the shield. Aritian cried out as sparks rained down and fell to a knee.

Aritian gritted his teeth, as he flung his hands outward. Bolts of blue lightning shot from his fingertips to lash the beast like whips of fire. The shadows that clung to the demon's body shuddered and writhed. Aritian could see that it had a lithe body and ran on four legs. The Ring of Suppression burned, and knew he was reaching the limits of power he could safely command. Razia's face floated before his eyes then and he promised himself, *I will not fail.*

He cried out, and lightning screamed through the air. The stench of ozone filled his nose and lances of pain raced along his forearm. The Daemon fell back under his might, roaring. Aritian slapped his hands over his ears as his mind threatened go dark. The Daemon flapped its great wings, sending Aritian's robes dancing as it rose before him.

Aritian raised a hand and a beam of light shot from it, looping around the ankle of the Daemon. The beast screamed again, and its wings flapped furiously as it sought to escape him. Aritian raised his other hand and another beam of light shot forth, catching one of the great wings. Aritian tore downward with a bestial scream, ripping the beast violently from the sky. It slammed against ground, but quickly stood and raced across the plain toward him. Aritian let it come. The beast ran with such weight that it sent tremors through the plane. The shadows that draped it reached out to surround the shield in darkness.

Aritian opened his arms as the beast slammed into the shield, and silver light flashed brighter than a star. The shield expanded with a groaning boom, and the beast was flung to the ground. Aritian's hands worked with dizzying speed, weaving a net of blue fire that trapped the Daemon against the ground at his feet.

The Daemon looked up at him snarling. Aritian could see that it had an elongated snout, one far longer than a wolf's. Its black teeth snapped toward him, not three inches from his foot. Aritian did not move. Its breath was putrid and stank of noxious gas. A voice filled the air like thunder. It did not come from the beast itself, but instead echoed across the plain, as it commanded, "Release me, magus."

Aritian smiled down at the Daemon, and replied calmly, "I command you to tell me your true name." The beast roared, struggling against light that held it with all its might. Aritian did not wait to see if it could muster enough strength to escape. Lighting tore from his hands, racking the Daemons body with hundreds of bolts. It twisted and whined in a high-pitched scream.

It roared, and screamed with the voice of black fire, "I am Yeagrar, the Shadowed Wolf, Tempus of Darkness, Devil of Fang, Banyr of Black Blood."

Aritian let the lightning roll across its body until its grey skin smoked and its mangy fur curled and fled in whips of smoke. Aritian repeated himself, "I command you to tell me your true name."

The Daemon hissed, and Aritian raised his hand threateningly. A low growl rolled across the plain and the beasts red eyes locked with his own. In a whispered of smoke, Aritian heard the words, "Fhygromour'umbra." Aritian felt the word reverberate through his mind, spoken only to him. The Daemon's soul was his now, and he felt a thread connect the two like a chain from his mind to the Daemons. Aritian felt no triumph, merely satisfaction.

Aritian nodded curtly and lifted the dragonbone necklace from his neck. The gold netting that held the raw bone glinted in the harsh glare of his shield. The runes that traced along the dragonbone filled with icy light as Aritian whispered words of binding. The Daemon lost its defined form and turned into a great, swirling cloud of shadow that flooded toward the pendant as if pulled by a strong current, and the dragonbone drank the Daemon's essence with a hiss. Aritian held the pendant in his palm and whispered a command. A flash of blue flame licked his hand, and when it snuffed out, the pendant was gone. Aritian closed his eyes and the corporal projection of his mind fled the Realm of Umbrael.

Aritian opened his eyes and found himself back in the reception hall. Aritian let the power of the pentagram collapse, and the silvery light of its outline faded from the marble floor. Aritian walked back toward the dais and bowed woodenly.

Maud sat upon the throne, her lips pressed tightly together. Aritian knew then that she had not expected him to succeed, had been hoping that he would fail and humiliate himself. Ultan held a slight, but pleased smile.

Ayfe leaned forward, eyes gleaming like two chips of ice as she examined him closely. Her low voice filled the hall, as she asked, "You realize that there is a hierarchy of demon in each realm?" Aritian nodded his head, indicating that he did. "Did you call specifically for a Daemon of the ninth order, or did you simply call allowing any to challenge you?"

Aritian answered without pause, "I called for the ninth order. If you were able to observe the clouds from your vantage point, there was eight Lupibradae that responded to my call. The strongest of those had the right to challenge me... to his folly." Aritian concluded with a small smile. Ayfe nodded in agreement, although her expression remained neutral.

Meinolf spoke, his deep voice rolling from the mirror like thunder, as he asked, "Where did you send the vessel?"

Aritian smirked, but did not answer, and Ultan smile grew wider. Morgana sat forward, her expression incredulous, as she asked, "Before your trials, we were informed that you had been trained for less than three months. Many of us," she looked side to side, catching the eye of Ayfe who nodded slightly, before saying, "thought that holding your trials now would be pointless, as no Ronan has ever passed at such a young age with so little training."

Morgana sat back, and raised an elegant crimson eyebrow, as she said, "Some would consider your prowess the mark of a prodigy and others merely reckless luck. I, for one, believe there is more here than what meets the eye. Maud, would you care to elaborate on his training?" Aritian turned to Maud and adapted a studious expression. He knew that his training had been orchestrated in a way that broke more than one Covenant, and secretly had been hoping that such a question would be posed.

Maud smirked at him, before turning away to face the mirrors. In a measured voice, she replied, "I followed the dictations of the Archmagus. If he would like to extrapolate, then I will of course explain. I find it a trivial matter, of little consequence, and urge the Coven to purge it from their minds. You wanted a weapon forged, and here he stands." She waved toward Aritian. Aritian cocked his head in question, and the voice in his mind asked, *A weapon, huh?*

Gwynevere spoke quietly, but her words dripped with chilling ice, as she said, "Trivial or not, this magus has more training than three months would allow. Either you lied to the Coven about when you found this young man and have in fact raised him from a very young age, or you did something that would expedite his training. In my mind, neither is trivial. In fact, quite the opposite."

Ultan leaned forward, and replied simply, "It was the latter."

Ayfe's voice cracked across the hall, as she asked, "You agreed to this?"

Aritian shifted his feet, nervous under the glare of her attention. In a whisper, he said, "I agreed, although I was ignorant and bore no knowledge as to the true price of such magic." Ayfe nodded, but her frown deepened. Aritian could tell that she was furious, but she did not speak further.

Mathis raised his pudgy hand, and said curiously, "Maud has informed the Coven of your conversion to the southern faith."

Meinolf snorted at this, shaking his head, and asked, "You do know that Ignathra is but one of the great fire elementals? He is not omnipresent, nor could he even touch your soul if he had a mind to do so. The elements are uncaring creatures. Fire only hungers for destruction." Aritian looked at the man baldly, challenging him with his deadpan stare, and Meinolf's lips pressed tightly in disdain as he restrained himself from arguing.

A slight frown touched Ultan's face as he caught sight of Aritian's staunch defiance, before disappearing, fleeing as quickly as it came. "Can you explain your allegiance to the elemental god?" Mathis asked, pressing on, his voice not unkindly.

Aritian was surprised by the question. He had not been prepared to explain his faith, had not thought it would be a point of contention. He shifted his feet nervously as his thoughts whirled. The voice in his head began to whisper to him and Aritian shook his head slightly, unsure. He was aware that the Ronan looked on, but he was at a loss. The mind of the voice surged forward, taking command of his body. The part of him that was meek that sought to appease the powers before him, fell to darkness; his voice falling mute. The ring at his hand burned like a brand, but he hid it in the fist of his left hand, stilling its uncontrollable shaking.

Aritian nodded undeterred, for he held no shame of his faith. It was unsullied by the opinions of others, and proudly, he said, "I serve Ignathra as an acolyte of his will. I have followed his teachings all my life, and I have entrusted by soul to his holy flame. I see no reason why that will ever change." Mathis turned to Ayfe with an unreadable expression and gave her a slight nod.

Aileen stood, her face was pale with anger, and screamed, "Flame bringer, flame kisser, flame father! He who seeks the flame shall be burned by its touch. You may find the flame, but the flame's heart has burned away, away, away. Your tongue will taste only ash. Seek it not, seek it not!" Ultan laid a hand on her arm, calming her. Aritian looked at her amazed, struck by her wild temperament. She sat shakily, whispering to herself with fervent abandon in a tongue he did not recognize. Aritian studied the Augury intently, wondering at her words. *Is this prophetic or merely the ramblings of a mad women?* He asked himself.

Ultan spoke commandingly, "Enough, these inquiries have nothing to do with the present situation. Maud, if you will?" The Ronan grew quiet by his command, and Aritian was grateful that the attention was turned back to the trials.

It was disturbing that his faith was still a question of dispute, for he thought that only Maud held this blatant disregard for the gods. *It seems that all Ronan do*, Aritian mused, uncomfortable by the idea. *They must hold such vehement scorn for the divine*, Aritian thought in realization, *because the gods are beyond even their might and had rebuked them as no other had.* Aritian suppressed a smile, thinking that exile was an appropriate punishment for the greedy creatures who had existed for so long outside the rules of nature and man.

Maud addressed him coldly, saying, "You have one remaining task before you. Are you prepared to face it?" Aritian nodded slowly. A malicious smile spread across her face then, and she said, "Very well. I have placed a sapphire ring at the end of the hall. Retrieve it. You have two minutes."

Aritian turned and his face fell, crestfallen, as he took in the scene before him with a glance. At the far end of the hall, suspended in the air, was Dellacindrael. She wore a white shift and nothing more. He could see the shadow of her form through the thin material. The sapphire ring hung on a silver chain around her pale neck. A pit lay beneath her, sinking into the marble floor twenty-feet. She struggled to speak, her face twisting red with strain, but she could not form words. The bottom of the pit was filled with hundreds of venomous snakes that slithered in a great mass, hissing at one another as they attempted to climb the edges of the pit.

Twenty-seven lorith stood at random intervals between him and the pit, pikes held at the ready. They hissed at him angrily, cursing him in their reptilian tongue. At the pit's edge stood two bearded giants with pale blonde hair that covered their skin in a messy tangle. The giants stood tall, more than three times his height, and broader than four men. They held massive scythes in their meaty grips and were scantily dressed in white loincloths. The giants eyed him darkly beneath heavy brows, and smiled eagerly with deadly intent. Aritian took in the scene in less than two heart beats. The giants roared in challenge, their voices thundering through the hall.

Maud called to him, but her voice was dim beneath the rush of adrenaline that filled his ears, "I know not what you and your fair whore have been up to, but I know it's by no will of mine. You didn't think an immortal could step into my domain and I not know it, did you?" She chuckled throatily, and whispered, "I own you Aritian, and now you shall reap the reward of your defiance."

Aritian's eyes flashed with darkness, just as the power that gripped Della was released. Time slowed as magic thundered through him. Aritian felt his hand burn with lancing pain, but dismissed it. The elven lady fell in slow motion. Aritian began running, pulling the dagger from the scabbard at his side. He sliced his arm with a quick flick of his blade, and where blood touched, emerald fire bloomed. Lighting thundered from his other hand, as his form was lost in a blur. The lightning, directed toward the closest lorith, refracted off an invisible shield and hit the floor, scarring it white. Aritian paused for a fraction of a second and silver fog erupted from his palm with a wailing scream, flooding across the hall. As the fog rolled against the invisible shield it exposed a maze that lay between him and the pit.

Aritian felt his heart beat. He raced into the maze and met the first lorith. The lorith swung its pike toward him in a downward slash. Aritian leapt to the side, kicked off the wall of the shield, jumping over the blurred swing. As he fell, he slammed the blade to the hilt into the lorith's scaled neck and tore its soul free with a flash of yellow light. The lorith was dead before it hit the floor. Aritian's heart beat once more, and he was past the first enemy.

Aritian raced through the maze and avoided the swipe of a blade by slipping underneath the second lorith on his knees. He sliced its left achilles tendon in a jet of blood as he passed. The wound wouldn't normally kill, but he was using no common blade. Aritian threw himself to the side as he stood, avoiding a thrust from the next lorith. Black fire bloomed from his outstretched hand, and filled the maze before him. The lorith's scaly skin cracked and blistered before popping in a burst of ash. Aritian leapt through the flames, trailing smoke as he rolled free and sprang to his feet.

Aritian's heart beat once more. Aritian's eyes snapped toward Della. The elf had fallen more than half the distance, and her mouth hung open in abject fear as her hair trailed wildly behind. Aritian knew then that he would not reach the elf before she met the depths of the pit at this pace. Lightning and fire flooded from his palm, dancing and twisting together in a red and silver stream that crackled and seared the walls of the maze. The shields of power imploded with a terrible force, throwing the remaining lorith to floor like rag dolls. Aritian felt his heart beat.

Aritian raced forward, the maze of shields gone, and his approach straight. Dellacindrael passed beneath the edge of the pit. The giants swung their scythes widely, one swinging high, the other low. Aritian leapt between the blades, twisting his body as he did to avoid the lower blade. The giant's eyes widened slowly in shock as he passed between them. Boiling black fog flooded in a great arc to either side of him, cutting through the abdomen of both giants as easily as butter. They looked down in a delayed response as their spines were severed and blood exploded, spraying from their stomachs and backs. Aritian's heart beat again, and his dive carried him past the edge of the pit.

Aritian watched Dellacindrael descend beneath him as he fell. Her face twisted with anger, and she snarled at him, before her eyes closed. The elf landed heavily in the writhing mass of snakes. Aritian watched as half a dozen sunk their fangs into her pale, perfect flesh. Aritian's heart beat and Della's face began to swell as blood and flesh was torn from her with each bite. Aritian landed in the pit on all fours. Fangs struck him from a dozen different directions, filling his veins with icy-hot venom. Aritian ignored the pain and lifted the slack, mangled body of the elf in his arms. Fire bloomed around him, incinerating the snakes with a hiss. He fell to his knees as poison raced through his blood like insidious coils of fire; intent on reach his heart with malicious speed.

The red flames rolled around him as he held the dying elf in his arms. She tried to speak through bared teeth. Aritian nodded with a smile, revealing the fangs that had extended. The poison of the snakes was absorbed by his power, and he felt his strength grow. Venom dripped down his chin, and he felt his eyes burn. He knew that they were red now, and split like a serpents. He grabbed the necklace that held the sapphire ring and tugged it from the elf's swollen neck. She was alive, but just barely. Her breath came raggedly as she choked on blood, and her frail form seemed to weigh nothing in his arms.

The fire raged in a great pillar above him with such heat the air boiled in glimmering ripples. Aritian leaned down, and whispered in her ear, "Your suffering is but a penance to the betrayals you have paid me." The elf's eyes grew wild with pain and rage. Aritian stood and turned with the elf in his arms. The pit's black, marble wall melted before his eyes. Aritian let the fire burn to either side of him as he walked from the pit, his power melting a ramp into the marble floor, leading him to the dais.

Aritian laid the Della before the first step of the dais and smiled. Della's form shuddered and shook as the poison raged. Her form began to shift and her skin ripple. In seconds, the elfish features were replaced, and Namyr was revealed before Maud's feet.

The boy cried out in pain as he reached out with a trembling hand toward his mistress. His form shuddered again, and the powerful enchantment that hid his true form faded away under the torrent of agony. Black wings sprouted from his thin shoulders, twisting and flailing beneath him, and his young face grew leaner as his features grew sharper. His ears extended and two horns sprouted from the dark curls of his head. The eyes of the Coven stared in horror at Unseelie half-breed before them.

Aritian bowed mockingly to a furious Maud and said triumphantly, "You did not sense my illusion for your own powerful enchantments lay over him. Mine were but a flimsy shell compared to your own, but effective." He smiled, as her face paled. Maud did not speak, and dared not confront him before the Coven.

Aritian threw the necklace to Maud's feet, but she made no move to retrieve the sapphire ring. The astounded eyes of the Coven were locked upon him. Aritian's face was twisted in anger as his split eyes narrowed on Maud's burgundy gaze. A part of his mind, the part that had once been in control, screamed for him to flee, but Aritian ignored it. In a whisper, he said, "I know your secret."

Maud blinked, and four bolts of red lightning seared the air, smashing into the faces of the mirrors at either side. The watching Coven disappeared beneath twisting spirals of silver as the mirrors faces grew still and metallic once more. Namyr choked, and blood spilled from the corners of his black lips. His thin hands were tipped with long, black nails and they dug into the marble, chipping the glossy stone as he struggled for breath. Maud dipped her staff down and touched his chest with its ruby tip. Burgundy light swirled, and Namyr stilled as she fed him power. He would live, Aritian knew. Maud's eyes never left his own. After five seconds passed, she spoke in calm a whisper, "Please Aritian, do tell me, which of my secrets have you discovered?"

Aritian smiled coldly, and said, "The only one that matters."

Maud smiled wide, and it was a wild smile that promised violence. She walked down the steps of the dais and reached up to stroke his cheek gently. In an overly honey-sweet voice, she purred, "I would caution you against any foolish notions, as you're still wearing a Ring of Suppression." She looked down at his hand, where the ring glowed white hot. Ugly blisters popped and wept down the length of his arm as the ring contained the full strength of his magic.

Maud chuckled as she paced away. In a bold voice, she said, "But you have struck against me, nearly costing me my hybrid..." She turned with a sweep of her long train, and pointed her diamond wand at him, as she dared, "So please, speak boldly."

Aritian pulled the dagger from his belt with his left hand, and held his red hand before him. Aritian met Maud's eyes as he slashed down. The blade severed his pinky finger with a searing flash of white light. The ring and his pinky hit the floor, as blood pumped from his hand. Aritian didn't even feel the pain, as he arched his eyebrow, and said, "I am a slave to no one, Maud." His skin itched as the wound knit closed, and with a casual sweep of his hand against his robes, he wiped away the blood.

"Namyr is your son, isn't he?" Aritian asked, eyeing the Unseelie half-breed. Namyr's humanity had been stripped away to reveal the truth. His tanned, green-tinged skin, was greyed, and the veins around his now black eyes stood out prominently. Aritian turned away with disgust. It hadn't taken him long after seeing Maud's Cambions to guess at Namyr's origin. It hadn't been an easy task for the Serpents to subdue Namyr either, but struck mute, wearing the illusion of the elf, Maud had taken Namyr captive when he fled to her manse, wholly unaware of the peril he might face.

Maud followed Aritian's gaze and looked at Namyr warmly. In a whisper, she said, "One of many." She met Aritian's eyes then, and smiled knowingly.

"Tell me, when did you turn your back on the Ronan?" Aritian asked, as he squared his shoulders.

Maud met his gaze with a deadpan stare, and said flatly, "If you have something to accuse me of, don't play coy, accuse me."

Aritian shook his head, and asked, "What do you seek to gain by raising this Cambion army?" There it was said. All was laid bare between them. Aritian expected her to deny it, to attack him, but Maud did neither.

She laughed, long and loud. Aritian's eyes narrowed, as she wiped away her tears of mirth. She straightened, and said breathlessly, "That really was a very stupid thing to say. To allude, sure..." She shook her head, unable to stop the smile that played across her face, before saying, "But to actually say it. To be so bold? I envy the pluck of youth." She climbed the dais once more and sat on the throne.

Maud gazed down at him with a regal pose of a queen ready to pronounce verdict, and said, "I suppose there's little reason not to confess, now that you have so condemned me." Her lips twitched in a smile again, and she said, "When I was a young girl, I lived through the Blood Wars." She flicked her wand up, and said pointedly, "A more appropriate word to describe that time would be *survived*. There was no sibilance of life, and the petty trials you have suffered are but a holiday compared to those dire times." Aritian cocked his head in disbelief, but dared not speak.

Maud's expression grew dark as she stared across the hall and lost herself to memory. She spoke in a whisper, "I apprenticed under my grandfather, Nagfari." She smiled, still not looking at him, and her voice grew humorous as she said, "Now I know, you know that name." Aritian nodded, he did. He felt a cold sweat break upon his brow. "When he made his allegiance to the Dark Lady, I fell under suspicion of course. I was held prisoner, and waited a hundred and thirteen years under lock and key in the lands of Amissa. My trial was held after the Great Sundering under the auspicious eye of Solomon the Great. He proclaimed me guilty for crimes of treason and I was banished."

She twirled her wand casually, and mused, "I suppose I was lucky, for many of the accused did not meet so fine a fate." Again, she smiled, and her voice grew light as she pondered, "But I was young, and the daughter of Solomon's most powerful adversary. He knew to kill me was to risk open war. So I was sent away, exiled from the sight of the Coven. It was then that I began my little experiments."

Maud waved to the Unseelie at her feet, and said proudly, "You see, Namyr was born before my imprisonment, and for him to escape death by Solomon's hand I returned him to his father. He grew in power in the century of his father's tutelage, and much like me, escaped the wrath of his judges. He fled the lands of Carcere just before they fell under the elven spell of binding. Namyr sought me out, and brought me much knowledge, including how to create the half-breeds known as Cambion." Aritian understood then; she would not have otherwise known the dark rites of creation had not her son been a child of the dark ones.

Maud's eyes fogged over with memory, and she said, "I wandered a few centuries. A few failed attempts at true power passed me by and then I found myself here, in Ignea." She smiled with genuine affection, as she spoke on, "I began to build my base of power. I started breeding the Cambion. First with my own body, and then with my female descendants. You see, to control them, they need a fair share of my blood." Aritian shuddered, and he resisted the urge to wail as he was consumed by rage. The small voice at the back of his mind begged insistently for him to flee. Aritian ignored it. "It was when the Curse struck me that I found true power."

Maud's red gaze practically glowed as she said, "I had thought I had it before," she barked a laugh, and said, "but I knew nothing before."

Maud's gaze turned down, and she settled her strange stare on Aritian. Arrogantly, she said, "The others, the Coven, all wonder how I escaped the Curse, but I have never divulged that secret. Do you wish to know?" She asked, with serious intent. Aritian nodded. He was riveted by her words and despite his disgust, couldn't help but listen, entranced.

Maud smiled, nearly with kindness, and said indulgently, "I thought you may. By this time the Faith had learned the Curse well. They did not need to be in close proximity to bind the Magi they sought. They merely needed a true name."

Her voice grew bitter, and her smile died, as she said, "They Cursed me. I was upon a ship, fleeing south when it hit me. Driven mad by the Curse, I was filled with an indomitable need to flee to the exile... to go where they had bound me." Her voice had filled with anguish as she remembered the insanity that had frayed her mind. With certainty, she said, "It would have killed me, for they bound me to a place in the middle of the Virdi Sea." She laughed, but it was ribbed with anger. "Even in my insanity I knew that to relent would spell death."

Maud hit the butt of her staff against the marble floor with a clang, and spoke with fervent quickness as she whispered, "I'm not sure why I did what I did. Maybe it was instinctual, maybe it was an act of last defiance." She shrugged, it mattered not. "I'll never know why. What I do know is that I leapt through a portal, into Umbrael. Not with my mind, but my physical body." Aritian flinched and met her eyes with dismay.

Maud nodded, and said quietly, "Yes, I can see by your expression of horror that you know what happened. After the Sundering, no mage, no matter how powerful, could survive such a feat, and yet here I am." She spread her arms, and looked up to the ceiling. Power rolled around her in a sourceless wind that made her skirts dance and Aritian's hair play across his face, and red fog danced behind the throne, teasing as it crawled down the golden back with crackling sparks of bright energy. Maud reveled in her own might, smiling with such fervent triumph that Aritian felt himself take a step backwards.

Maud stood, and leered down at him, shouting, "I fell through the realms, my physical form unsupported by a lack of magical energy, and found myself before the Abyss. The winds of Chaos raged around me and I was thrown into the very pit." Maud's voice caught in her throat, and her voice fell as she said, "I thought I was ended then. I thought that I would be torn apart, body and soul, to fall into oblivion and sweet nothingness." Maud raised a single finger, and smiled as she said, "But, I have always been a stubborn girl. My survival instincts claimed my mind, and I threw every iota of power I had, and like a lifeline, it clung to the lip of the pit. Chaotic magic ravaged my body and mind, but inch by inch I crawled forth from the Abyss."

Her voice filled with remembered validation, as she crowed, "I lived, reborn, and thus my true name was changed. The Curse's hold fell away with the death of who I once was." Maud nodded to herself, and said, "It was then that I felt the connection to my bloodline. Something happened, something had changed in the madness of Chaos. It was then that I turned my back on Magrados, for I am greater than any mere Ronan."

Maud smiled wickedly at him, so sure and mighty in her confidence. Aritian felt himself recoil beneath her eye. He was drenched in fear-laden sweat, and could only croak the question, "Who knows this?"

Maud answered without hesitation, "You, and no one else. A few have stumbled along the truth, but none of them survived long enough to tell a soul. A shame really, that you must join them now."

She smiled then, and flicked her wand. Aritian reached up and felt his throat. His hand fell away, wet with blood. He choked as his mouth filled with a metallic tang and fell to his knees. His vision careened wildly to the side as his head tumbled from his shoulders and rolled across the floor. He retained consciousness long enough to realized that Maud had cut through his shield, cut through the very core of his power, and decapitated him without him even realizing. His eyes widened as he watched his torso crumple to the floor and then saw only darkness. Maud's head craned back as she laughed.

The color faded from Aritian's face and he grew pale as his body cooled, and still Maud laughed. "Fool!" She screamed across the hall, her shout echoing with jubilation. At her feet Namyr wheezed weakly, enjoying his Mistress' splendor.

A mocking laugh filled the hall, and Maud's cackle died in her throat.

A shadow of a form slipped from Aritian's body and with it, the illusion that had clung. Maud's recoiled on her throne as Aritian's shade rose. Beneath him, Ibriham lay dead. Aritian knew his time was short, and so spoke hurriedly, "I learned much from you, Lady Maud, and for that I am grateful. You have claimed a steep price for such knowledge, but I shall not pay you with my life. Blood, like you said, allows for much," He waved to Ibriham and the deception, and then said, "Before I left for the Temple of Darth, Ibriham was kind enough to share his body with a small portion of my soul and adapt his form in the likeness of my own." The shade of Aritian smiled sadly, and promised, "You secret is safe for now. Goodbye, Maud. We shall meet again in the old lands."

Aritian felt his soul stretch as was pulled toward his body, gone before he could hear the echo of Maud's bloodcurdling scream.

Selyni

Chapter Fifty-Three:

The Spoiled Seed

Selyni stood on the bow of a ship. The green waters of the Virdi Sea rolled beneath her throwing spray and salt into the air. The sun hovered on the horizon, just peaking above the waves in the far distance. The deck behind her was quiet, only a few sailors milled about. A handful absently manned the sails while talking in low whispers, and a bleary-eyed greybeard whistled a quiet tune as he held the stern. Without turning, Selyni said, "I wondered when you would show yourself."

A man stepped to her side. He was a slight youth, dark-haired, with pale grey eyes that shifted nervously. He wore a fine black tunic, a velvet cap topped with a long purpled peacock feather, and grey hose. From his dress, Selyni knew that he was a northerner. *Odd*, she thought, for she had departed from a southern port, and few such men could be found in Ignea.

"There was little reason to draw attention to our connection before now." He whispered softly. His voice was smooth and rich. Selyni shivered; she didn't like the notes that she recognized in his tenor.

"And what connection would that be?" Selyni asked mildly, turning to look at the man more fully.

The man bowed low with an elegant flourish. "I am a corrupted seed sired by your king." He admitted with deference. Selyni nodded tightly. She could see it fully now in his hollow eyes, too-pale skin, and gaunt frame.

"Your name?" Selyni asked, eying him coldly.

Without raising his eyes from the deck, he said, "Pravus

Elijah Shade, my Lady, at your service." Selyni dipped her head, affording the man more respect than he was due. He was a bastard, one of hundreds that called Shades Island home. Most of the bastards born there adopted the last name Shade. Some felt that it paid homage to their more-than-human parentage, but Selyni had always pitied them, for like a shadow, they were lesser creatures.

"I trust you have instruction," Selyni suggested, when the man made no move to speak.

Pravus nodded, and said, "You are to call on the mage known as Lilith. I was given the mirror, your description, and where to find you; nothing more." From a pocket in his tunic he pulled out a small package wrapped with black velvet. He presented it to her with another bow, and Selyni took it with shaking hands.

She looked out over the sea. They were far from the coast. All she could see was the gentle green waves of the Virdi Sea. She knew that soon they would come upon the Balu Swamp, and pass through a string of islands to the Chalice Sea. No more than three days, she guessed. "To be trusted with a Veritas Mirror is a great honor." Selyni said in a low, but not unkind voice.

Pravus nodded, and said humbly, "If you say so, my Lady."

"Where will you go now?" Selyni asked curiously, eying the man out of the corner of her eye.

The man smirked secretively, and said, "Onward, as we all must. Good day, Lady Selyni." He bowed once more and turned away. Selyni frowned, but followed him toward the lower deck where her cabin waited.

Selyni dreaded the tight confines of the four walls and wanted nothing more than to take to the sky and fly, but she wouldn't. She had been forbidden to do so, and so was forced to travel like some commoner. It was infuriating. The ship she was on was named the Greenhawk, and was a stately ship, overly large and made to transport large quantities of goods.

Nothing like a hawk, she thought, irritated. She climbed down the narrow ladder that led below deck, *more like a swine, lumbering and slow.*

When she reached her cabin she closed the door behind her. The room didn't hold much; a narrow bed with a thin, grey blanket, a small trunk that squatted at the foot of the bed, and a rusted mirror that hung on the wall. Selyni sat on the bed, crossed her legs and unfolded the velvet covering that hid the mirror. The mirror was tiny and framed in gold, holding a face that was no larger than the palm of her hand. Selyni laid the mirror on the bed and with the nail of her pointer finger, cut the palm of her left hand. She let the blood collect in her palm and then let the blood drip onto the frosted face of the mirror.

"Lilith." Selyni whispered as the mirrors face began to clear.

Lilith smiled at her lazily, and said, "Selyni." Selyni could not see much of the woman, for her vantage was narrow. All she could see was the woman's beautiful face.

Selyni resisted the urge to sneer at the woman irritatingly high-pitched voice, and nodded her head in deference. "I was told to call on you." She murmured quietly, not wanting to be heard. Doing magic so far into the sea had little risk. They were still far from the lands of Ordu and Afta, where she might be detected, but still she had no desire for the crew to grow suspicious or worse, think her mad.

Lilith flashed her a brilliant smile, and said cheerfully, "Yes, and you are a very good girl to call so promptly. I should have led with that. I know how much you Changelings like praise." She added, chiding herself lightly in a mocking way.

Selyni gritted her teeth, and asked, "What do you want?"

"It's not what I want, it's what Ultan desires," Lilith drawled teasingly.

Selyni rolled her eyes. She hated this woman. Detested her. Though Lilith was her aunt, she had always treated Selyni with disdain. "Very well, what does he want?"

Lilith smiled blandly and said, "The ship you are on is bound for Molveria. Barring any delays, you should reach the capital in less than five weeks. The Archmagus commands you to insert yourself into the royal house..." Lilith paused and bit one of her long nails as she contemplated, before adding, "Nothing presumptuous now, something nondescript. He wants you to move unseen."

Selyni frowned. It would not be easy. Molveria was the kingdom that spearheaded the Ronan exile. Even now, decades later, they would be suspicious of anyone that exhibited any odd behavior. Selyni would have to take great care. "Why have you waited three weeks to tell me this? I could have spent my time preparing, and instead have stared at the wall of my cabin like some mindless idiot." She said, exasperated.

Lilith gave her an innocent look, and gently chided, "Pravus had his orders, and it would be good of you to take note of his obedience. Ultan is very displeased with your performance in Ignea."

Selyni ignored the rebuke. If she was to be punished it would be by Ultan himself, not his lackey. "Once I am in, what then?" Selyni asked, ignoring her aunt's quip.

Lilith chuckled lightly, and it sounded to Selyni like a mouse being tortured. "Goodness me, we are a little slow this morning, aren't we?" Lilith asked, raising an eyebrow.

"Out with it Lilith, I'm in no mood for your games," Selyni warned. She wanted nothing more than to dash the mirror against the cabin wall, but resisted the urge.

Lilith lost all visage of playfulness and grew suddenly serious, as she said, "His daughter will be arriving in the city. You are to attach yourself to her service and guard her person until you have received further instruction. Do not let on that you know her or that you are a Ronan. If you do, you will spoil everything and that would be the death of you."

Selyni nodded, and sighed heavily. She knew that this day might one day come, but she had hoped that she would be lucky enough that someone else would be tasked with the unfortunate orders she was now under. "As the Archmagus commands, so it will be done," she whispered.

Lilith smiled brightly, and said, "Good..." Selyni waved her hand over the mirror, cutting off her aunt's words. She fell back on the bed, and stared at the ceiling. *Why me*, she thought, *why must I be the one to ruin the girl's life?* The wooden planks above did not design to answer.

Aritian

Chapter Fifty-Four:

Departure

Aritian's eyes snapped open. He lay on an old dock in an abandoned part of Creuen. Dark waters lapped near his face. It was night. The trials had last all day. He knew that only a second had passed from the time that he had left Maud's hall and found himself here. His body and mind felt disjointed. Beryl gripped his hand, and Aritian struggled to his feet. "Easy lad," Beryl said softly, with a pleased smile. Aritian gave the short dwarf an appreciative nod, and matched his smile as relief fell over him. He had made it.

Della hurried to his side, and worriedly whispered, "Ibriham?"

Aritian shook his head with a frown, and said, "He would not flee and spoke in challenge against Maud. He forced my hand."

"He sacrificed himself?" Della asked, horrified.

Aritian nodded grimly, but thought, *Brother of mine, I hope you're at peace now. In your last moment you proved your bravery and snubbed one far beyond reproach.*

Beryl, Ori, Azera, Entah, and Rythsar stood around him, their faces glowing with vitality and a joviality that couldn't be dimmed no matter the circumstances. Aritian had fed them power when he returned from the Ignis and they had wakened without mishap. That he had hesitated to use his power to help them recover before seemed ridiculous now and part of him still burned with self-chastisement. Each and every one of them beamed at him with nervous excitement.

Azera stepped forward and grabbed in in a bear hug, and with a voice thick with emotion, choked out, "We were so worried. We thought... we feared..." For a few short seconds Aritian feared she would crush him, but she soon relented, realizing he was struggling for breath.

"It's alright now, I am safe." Aritian assured her, his own voice growing thick. She took a step back and nodded her head, her expression tight as she fought the foreign emotion. Ori touched her arm, and whispered softly to her.

Aritian turned toward the dock's entrance to where the Dranguis guarded. He gave them a deep bow, and said, "I did not express my gratitude for capturing Namyr so stealthily, but I give you my deepest of thanks." They bowed to him in unison, but did not respond as they turned back to face the city. They were extensions of himself; no thanks were necessary, or even appreciated. He looked down and saw his detached pinky. The Ring of Suppression glinted in the moonlight. Aritian kicked both into the murky waters. *I won't let your sacrifice be in vain, Ibriham*, Aritian promised silently.

The spell he and Ibriham had performed had been tied by their blood. Ibriham was able to take his form, even use his magic, for he possessed a piece of Aritian's soul that acted like a doorway to Magrados — but to make the illusion seem real Aritian had been forced to forge a Ring of Suppression for Ibriham. It had not been easy, but without his half-brother they would have never been able to leave the city with Maud unaware. Ibriham had also warned that Maud would have sensed the elf's presence. Dellacindrael herself had come up with the idea on how to use this information to their benefit. Aritian barely believed that it had worked.

A gurgling voice filtered from the water, "If you are ready my Lord, my mistress encourages us to depart with great speed." Aritian squinted toward the water, and saw hundreds of dark heads bobbing just above the surface. The sea creatures were mottled in colors of blue, yellow, green, and white that blended in with the swirling water around them. Some had smooth, scaled skin, while others wore crowns of heavy frills that dripped down their backs to spill down their shoulders. Their eyes were black and large, their mouths cone shaped and lipless, leaving their long, curved teeth exposed. The one that spoke, blinked its double lids as it eyed him. Aritian could see no more of its form.

"What are you?" He whispered in amazement, before he realized that he had spoken aloud.

The voice was light, and gurgled wetly, as it explained, "We are Elmare, Mer Elmare. Come, we must depart. Come, the Sea Witch calls us north." Aritian nodded in agreement and looked around.

Aritian could see no ship, but even as he opened his mouth to question the creature, the dark water began to bubble as something large rose from the depths. A shell appeared, massive in size, to rise thirty-feet above his head. It was spiraled in shape and above him, Aritian could see a dark opening. The seashell was covered in green algae and barnacles, and as it broke the surface the scent of salt and sea wafted across the deck. The bobbing heads of the Elmare disappeared, and Aritian saw the flash of fins as they swam beneath the water. The shell rocked gently as it floated in the water.

Beryl craned his head up and in a dubious voice, asked, "Are we to travel in a conch?"

Aritian grinned, and chuckled. "We are," He said, and he turned back to his waiting companions, "I fear the time has come for me to depart, though I am loathe to leave Ignea in such peril. Rythsar, Aethera." The two lorith looked to him attentively, and Aritian said, "You must remain in Ignea, but not Creuen. You must find the horde, and turn it back to the Pomum. This senseless war with Velon must end. Rong will stay with you."

Rythsar dipped his horned-head, and hissed a whisper, "I despair at the thought of leaving your side."

Aritian continued on as if he hadn't heard the lorith's protests, and said, "Rong will speak with my voice. You and Aethara will serve me better here. Afta is a cold land and your kind will not fair well in such a clime. Rythsar," Aritian paused, and gave the lorith a meaningful stare, before saying grimly, "I am counting on you. Turn the Horde back by whatever means necessary." Rythsar bent his head, overcome with grief, but extended a taloned hand. Aritian clasped it tightly, and for a moment they stood there, two creatures of Ignea brought together by mutual respect. Aritian dropped his hand, and the lorith retreated a step, hissing in his reptilian language to his mate.

Aritian beckoned Rong forward. The long-haired assassin bowed his scaled face, and listened intently as Aritian spoke, "I will be able to speak into your mind and you into mine. Keep me apprised on your progress. Ride to Victes, then to the Kingdom of Spres, and finally Darkryn Hall in that order. The people of Ignea must know the threat of the Scarlet Witch." The assassin nodded once before jogging to Rythsar side. He moved with such grace and speed that belied his near-human appearance.

Aethara bent her pale head in a low bow, but her red eyes flicked nervously to the city. In a nervous trill, she asked, "How shall we escape the city?"

Aritian smiled, and closed his eyes. He sent his mind back along the path his shade had taken. His magic met a familiar mind, and for a moment he saw through her eyes.

A glowing door rested before her, its light reflecting oddly as she held its image refracted a hundred times over. The Loci Queen felt the mind touch her own, and her thorax thrummed with excitement. The Insectis lifted her hooked hand and gazed at the small, emerald stone the mage man had passed through the portal. Without hesitation, she slapped it against the glowing door. With a sizzle, the light faded. Her clutch bounced around her, but she snapped her wings out, quelling their eagerness. Tentatively, the Queen reached through the archway.

Nothing happened.

With a bouncing leap, the Insectis crossed the threshold. Her children raced up the hall, but the Queen turned. Her wings spread open and she flitted in the opposite direction. She landed before the next door and slammed the emerald stone against the light of the portal. A rush of hot air gushed past her, as the shield fell away. She moved on, flying to portal to portal. At each she opened the door.

She flew to the last, a doorway filled with water, she eyed the dark shadows that had gathered at the door. The goblin writhed excitedly in the murky green water. The Queen flew higher, and slammed the stone against the horrid light. A rush of water fled the portal, and the Queen buzzed over the river that now flowed down the hall toward the entrance. Goblins crawled along the walls, screeching in piercing calls of jubilation, and swam swiftly through the dark water that followed after her. Ahead, tall hairy mammoths stomped through the water, led by tall, grizzled giants. In their shadow, maned humanoids with spotted skin raced toward freedom. As she passed above, they roared with feral glee. Thousands of creatures milled in the hall with confusion.

The Queen spun in the air, her emerald wings flinging her toward the entrance. The Loci raced up the steps and found her clutch bouncing eagerly at the door that was a wall. They were not alone, and still more gathered as they sought escape. The Insectis Queen pressed the emerald against the stone illusion. With a flicker, it died, and a stampede of creatures flooded out. In a chirping screech, the queen led them to freedom.

A minute ticked by, and then the dim echoes of screams filled the air. Aritian looked to the south end of the city. Smoke curled in a dark cloud, blotting out the sky. In a hushed whisper, he said, "I gave Insectis Queen the key to Maud's Menagerie, and even now she releases all held within. Use the distraction to make your escape. There will be a man waiting for you in Igri. You will find him in the Blue Viper Inn. He will act as your guide. Go now." Aritian commanded in conclusion. Rythsar held his gaze for a moment more, and then bowed his head. Without a word, the tall lorith slunk down the port toward the city with Aethara and Rong trailing just a few steps behind.

Aritian stared after them until they disappeared down a street and then turned back to the giant seashell. Without another word, he gripped the first rung of the ladder that had been carved into the shell's stony surface and climbed. His companions followed him hurriedly. No one wanted to remain longer than they needed and risk facing Maud's wrath.

Aritian crawled along the lip of the shell's opening. It was dark within, but he didn't hesitate. He slid down the open mouth. As he passed the opening, he felt a tingle of magic. The interior of the shell was as smooth as glass and pure white. He slid down the throat of the shell, following its twists and turns until he came to the bottom. He was deposited into a large open room. It was dark, but he could feel magic pulling him across it. His companions followed, cursing or laughing at the absurdity of it all as they slid into the room close behind.

Aritian felt carefully along the perimeter until his hand felt the back of a throne that was seemingly carved out of the shell itself. He sat in it, and bright green illuminations bloomed awake. Mage lights hung in the air, activated by the presence of his power. The shell hummed with vibration as Aritian looked around.

The ceiling curved above him with a delicate spiral. To either side were benches along the wall; Aritian waved for his companions to sit. He glanced over his shoulder and saw that two more rooms lay deeper in the shell.

Aritian dismissed them for later, however; he had no time to investigate. He looked ahead. Standing on a curved platform was an orb of glimmering pearl that was nearly as large as his head. Aritian reached out and touched it. The vibrations increased, and the shell wall in front of him fell clear. Green light spilled from either side of the transparent portal, and they saw the sea beyond.

The shell began to sink, and quickly fell beneath the green

waves. Ori and Azera gasped in amazement, while Beryl cursed, and Della stood to gain a closer look. The Dranguis remained stoic, unable to care. Entah had begun scribing furiously on a piece of parchment he clutched in one hand while an owl-feather quill bobbed in the other.

Hundreds of Mer Elmare were strung out in a team before the shell. They grasped a length of sea grass that were attached to the front of the ship. Beneath them, Aritian saw a white sand bed that rippled before them like an unending plain and above, saw the curling currents that danced in waves along the surface of the sea.

Aritian felt his breath catch as he took in the majesty of the sea creatures. The Elmare had long slim tails that stretched from their torsos for a dozen feet before ending in wide, pale fins. Beneath the water and bathed in the dappled light of the green mage lights, Aritian discovered that they were far more varied in brilliance then he first suspected. He saw yellows as bright as the petals of a sunflower, blues as cheerful as at the desert sky, and greens as brilliant as emerald gems. They moved through the water with such grace that they seemed to dance through the currents. The gills along their necks pumped furiously as they breathed, and the long frills that crowned their heads and backs writhed in excitement. As the lights disappeared from the rocking surface of the water, the Elmare began to swim forward. Their tails cut through the water with astounding strength, sending swirls of water and jets of bubbles spinning behind them.

The ship began to move, and Aritian laughed, for this was true magic pure, elegant, and beautiful. As they were pulled into deeper waters and away from Creuen, Aritian felt his heart lighten, and he murmured to himself a promise: "I am coming for you, Oracle."

Caethe

Chapter Fifty-Five:

Annihilation

Caethe sat in the center of the cell with his legs folded and his eyes closed. Night had fallen and with the moonless sky, he sat in complete darkness. His two upper arms were braced behind him, supporting his weight, while his lower arms rested lightly in his lap. He breathed long and evenly as he calmed his spirit. His heart slowed until it beat but twice per minute. It was dangerous he knew, to venture so far within himself, but the risk of not was even higher still.

Caethe traveled through the warren of protections that lay around the center of his mind, a maze that kept intruders out and those within, bound. *Tall golden walls rose before him as he stepped from the darkness and found himself at the center of the maze. There, rising before his mind's eye, stood a tower that soared to the highest recesses of his mind. The tower sat in a courtyard above a void of darkness. The darkness was a gate that descended directly into the Abyss. It was mind-numbingly dangerous he knew, creating such a doorway within himself, but those within would not be easily kept. A bridge led from the maze behind him and arched over the darkness, golden and spindly thin. It was wide enough for only one to cross at a time. Caethe walked forward, over the bridge, and the massive double-doors that guarded the tower swung open with his approach. Caethe walked through.*

Caethe found himself in a wide-open, circular room. The room was eighty-feet in circumference and starkly bare. The walls, much like the tower, were made of smooth, glistening gold. The ceiling flooded upward and was lost in the golden glow of the orbs of golden fire that hung suspended in the air fifty feet above. Before him, sitting on a pair of thrones, sat two men.

The throne to his left was black and made from raw onyx cut into a square obelisk. It rose more than thirty feet in height, but the man who sat upon it was eye level with Caethe. The man was old, and desperately so. His face was wrinkled as leather and he had a square jaw that held a long, white beard that pooled in the lap of his black robes. His eyes were jet-black and burned furiously beneath his heavy, bushy brows, and his hands were encased in the stone to either side, as were his thin legs beneath him. The man's lips curled with loathing as he caught sight of Caethe.

The throne to the right was made from a white tree, crowned with star-shaped leaves. Its roots curled around a fair-haired man, binding his arms and crossing his lap. He seemed to be in his early forties, and his face was only lightly lined. His long hair was a mix of silver and gold, and he wore elegant, white robes. The man had a kindly face that was illuminated by brilliant, blue eyes, and his mild expression was serene and calm.

Caethe knew that neither of the magi before him were of lesser danger then the other despite their varying appearance.

Caethe bowed low before them with respect. The old man sneered, barely containing his anger, but the younger mage nodded his head in response. Caethe spoke without preamble, "I have come to tell you that I shall release you from my control shortly and that you shall be free to do as you will. Magrados bound your spirits to my mine so that I might have the power to escape my prison." Caethe paused, and sadness clouded his eyes, before fading away beneath firm resolve. "I have decided that with your power I no longer have need of your knowledge. Neither of you have proved cooperative, and thus you are more of a nuisance than benefit." They both stared at him in silence. Both men were far too ancient to be shocked, but rather their thoughts spun as they sought escape from the damnation his words promised.

The old man's face had gone red with fury, and his deep voice came out in a low hiss as he asked, "So you steal us from our immortal *slumber and now seek to thieve our power?"*

The younger man said reasonably, *"Such perversion is against the Ronan Accords."*

Caethe replied in a calm voice, *"The Accords speak nothing..."*

The old man interrupted him, spittle flying, as he screamed, *"Do not speak to me of the Accords, boy. I wrote the laws of our kin."*

Caethe smiled in the face of the old magi's rage. He paced before them, as he said, *"Be that as it may, I have a prophecy to uphold and I cannot release your power back to you as it is now bound to my core."*

"You could, but it would cost you your life." The younger mage said quietly, his eyes imploring silently with heavy regret.

"Your life is nothing, boy." The older man snarled viciously as he tried to stand, throwing himself wildly against the bindings of stone.

Caethe looked to younger man as anger licked his thoughts, and his voice grew with frustration, *"I seek to correct the mess that you have made. You broke the Bridge of Magrados. Your fate has been sealed, Mangus. You will fade from memory for your crimes against the natural law."* Mangus's pale head dipped, and his shoulders sagged against the accusation.

The old man jerked his head forward, his beard jutting out, as he asked, *"What of me? I am innocent of all wrongdoing."* His black eyes narrowed as he turned to the throne next to him. In a venomous whisper he said, *"My son deserves to have his power stripped from him. He is a murderer, and has broken our most sacred power."* The ancient turned toward Caethe and shrugged his boney shoulders. Adopting a feeble tone, he reasoned, *"I am but an old spirit; free me, and I shall help you bind the bridge."*

Mangus's head snapped up and his blue eyes flashed with lightning, as his voice grew with cold anger, *"Do not color your words with hypocrisy, father."* He then looked to Caethe as he implored, *"Dileethues murdered far more than I, and delved in dark powers that fouled this world. His influence opened the door for such darkness to be born. It was only as Adonim stood on the percipience of destruction that I acted."* Mangus's voice grew hard, and with iron sincerity, he said, *"I had no choice. Adonim would have been consumed."*

Dileethues barked a laugh. His jubilance melted rapidly as his face twisted with vicious fury. The old magus screamed at his son, "I lived before the Dawn of Adonim. You are nothing more than a foolish weasel of a man. I battled gods and feasted upon their flesh as they crawled forth from the Chaos. Do not speak to me of the tides that flood Adonim. If I were free, such torture would I inflict upon..."

"Silence, both of you." Caethe screamed, his voice echoing through the tower with such force that the golden floor cracked. Both magi fell mute. They knew that here, they had no power against Caethe's anger.

Caethe continued, his voice regaining its calm, as he said, "You both committed atrocities and you both were the greatest of our kind in the respective age. You both know that soon the door of healing will close and the Bridge of Magrados will forever be sundered. I must, like you, lead our people." Dileethues snapped his head to the side unwilling to entertain him any longer. Caethe continued, "The Bridge must be healed. Your powers have been forfeited and gifted to me by the blessed Pool of Magrados. Neither shall regain your power. I can offer freedom of spirit, nothing more."

Mangus's façade of humbled contrition was thrown aside then, and when he spoke his voice was strong and confident with spite, "You stand there assured of your actions, but if you succeed the blood of millions will stain your hands. Yet you condemn our souls to be lessened to that of a mere mortal?" He laughed bitterly, his muscular form twisting against the thick roots that bound him as he asked, "You would damn us to the Sea of Aelfmae?"

Dileethues straightened, raising his head, and said proudly, "We are Ronan, and unlike those foolish humans who pray to sticks and fire, there is no hope for sanctuary without our power."

Caethe, ignoring Dileethues, locked eyes unflinchingly with the vast knowledge that was held in the blue seas of Mangus's eyes. Forcefully, Caethe said, "I will gladly pay the price and will trust my soul to Magrados."

Dileethues laughed, his deep voice booming across the hall. With a tongue dripping with condemnation, he explained, "Magrados is not some god who barters with sinners and saints. It is raw energy, boy. If *you aren't an ignorant bastard, then you're an insane fool to look for succor in Magrados's cold embrace."*

Caethe smiled with feral intent, and said, "I never claimed sanity, Archmagus. Prepare yourselves, your time here grows short." Caethe turned on his heel. The doors of the towers boomed open, and Caethe walked through them, smiling.

Dileethues screamed after him, "Betrayer! Bastard! I will end you, boy, this I so swear on...!"

Caethe opened his eyes to find Grigori's leering face not two inches away. Caethe jerked back, which elected a cruel laugh from the priest. It was then that Caethe realized that they were not alone. A group of ten priests stood in the doorway, each grinning eagerly. The expression would more normally be found on a child that was being given a treat. On these elderly men, the gleam in their eyes was disturbing.

Grigori gripped him by the amber collar and yanked him to his feet. "I had thought you had left us once more." Grigori growled in his ear. A knife appeared at Caethe's throat. Caethe stood unmoving in the priest's grip as the blade lightly sliced across his neck with an edge of sharped amber. His blood sizzled and smoked when it met the blade, and the pain he felt was as if someone held a brand his throat. Caethe gritted his jaw tightly, but made no sound other than the quickening of his breath. "I am glad you did not disappoint me," Grigori whispered before throwing him toward the cell door. "Come brethren, the time has come. Take him to the inner sanctum." Grigori commanded in a bark.

Strong arms lifted Caethe from where he had jarred his knees against the stone floor. Caethe's hands were bound behind his back with a coarse rope, and a chain was attached to his collar. Caethe struggled in their grasp viciously, bucking toward Grigori, spittle flying as he screamed, "Why? Does Ordu wish to parade his devil once more? Does he want me to put on another fucking show for the people?" Veins bulged in Caethe's neck, and the men grunted as they tried contain his rage.

Grigori smiled in response to his struggle. It was a secret smile. *He wants this*, Caethe thought in sudden realization, *the sick fuck wants me to struggle. Grigori is enjoying this*. Caethe let his limbs go lax all at once and nearly fell to the ground once more.

A white gag was shoved into Caethe's mouth and tied around his head. Caethe was dragged from the cell into a small guardroom. The room was bare, windowless, and filled with a table set with fine cutlery. The stark, white walls were decorated with weapons crusted in stones of amber. Caethe found the air of the room suffocating. Quickly, he was led down a flight of stairs surrounded by priests of Ordu.

They led him silently down three flights of stairs, but despite the muted air they held the energy around them was charged with excited anticipation. Caethe could see it in their twitching smiles and grasping hands. Caethe's breath came raggedly with fear; he knew what was to come.

Guards were found at each level, but Caethe didn't see past each landing. When they came to the last, two guards wearing silver breastplates stamped with the sigil of Ordu, capes of white, and silvered helms opened a door. A cold wind buffeted the small entryway as the soldiers saluted the priests who passed through the doors.

Caethe was led toward across a stone bridge toward a larger tower that descended toward the dome that sat far below. Snow flurries danced around the stone bridge, and the air was fiercely cold. Caethe shivered in his nudity, but breathed the cold deeply enjoying the biting wind. It made him feel alive, and in that moment he wanted for nothing more. The magi imprisoned within screamed at him then, burning his mind with all the power that they could muster, but Caethe maintained his hold on them. He did not have long, their torture would soon be silenced.

Below, the pyramid of Ordu sprawled to dominate the foothill of the mountain in which it perched on. Far distant, the sleeping city of St. Aleksandru sat illuminated by sparsely-spread light. The city seemed peaceful, nearly too quiet, but here, in Ordu, order reigned supreme. Above him, towers rose like mountainous white pillars that plunged into the night sky with arrogance. The bridge sloped downward, and he was quickly jostled into the adjoining tower.

Bright torches set in heavy iron brackets were spaced along the wall and Caethe was escorted down a long hall filled with ranks of soldiers who stood to either side. They snapped salutes as the priests hustled him by. Their dark eyes glittering beneath their silvered helms as they eyed the creature in the priest grasp: the demon whispered of in Inns and noble halls alike. Caethe saw some tremble in fear, while others gripped the hilts of their swords as though they withheld from striking him down with only the greatest restraint. The priests ignored them, rushing Caethe at nearly a jog, so eager were they in their eagerness.

Off in the distance, deeper in the tower, Caethe could hear the sounds of laughter and merry. At the end of the hall stood another stone staircase that wound about itself as it descended. It sounded as if a feast was taking place close by and as they descended the stairs, Caethe could smell the heady aromas that wafted from the lower levels. His stomach growled hungrily, but Caethe was beyond thought. His mind frozen with panic-borne adrenaline.

At the bottom of the tower, some eight flights down, Caethe was ushered across a stone courtyard toward the domed building. Caethe knew, despite never entering it, that this was the innermost sanctum of Ordu. Around the edge of the dome rested the square bases of the fifteen Towers of Light; places where the Order of Ordu kept their most secret teachings. Caethe could feel his skin tingle and began to burn. This was an unholy place, a place that Magrados could not exist. As they drew close, the inner turmoil fell silent as the magi within weakened.

Priests had filled the courtyard and talked in hushed whispers. Every priest held a white candle, and the flickering light bathed the dark courtyard with a tawny glow. The priests were dressed in sweeping white robes, and one and all held brown, leather tomes tied to their belts. When the priests caught sight of the approaching prisoner, they slapped their fists to their hearts and stepped aside to clear a path. Caethe closed his eyes, his mind numb as he was yanked forward.

The dome loomed before them, standing a hundred feet in height, bare and unadorned. The building was windowless, save for the clear-paned glass that dominated its apex. Their path drew them to a small, dark door that hunched beneath an arch of white marble. Caethe did not resist as the chain that he was led by was handed to Grigori. The priests fell back, remaining outside, and Grigori led him in.

The interior of the sanctum was circled by stepped pews that rose half the height of the dome. The center had been left clear, but for a stone pillar that rose eighty-feet in height. A narrow staircase circled the monolith, reaching the top. Brackets of iron held crackling fire, and filled the pale temple with ruddy, dancing light. The moment Caethe stepped inside, he felt his heart shudder, skipping a beat, as his very life flickered, threatening to sputter and die.

The sanctum was abandoned, save for two men who stood at the top of the pillar and a woman who sat in the upper-most pews on the far side of the room. The woman was young, no more than twenty, and bundled thickly in a heavy, white cloak. Upon her sweat-soaked brow she wore a simple iron crown and beneath, her eyes were swollen and red. The woman's mouth was tightly pressed in a grimace of determination. She was neither fair nor ugly with her blotchy bunched cheeks and golden hair, but held an air of imperious nobility that belied her common features.

The men atop the pillar stood in stark difference. One was dressed in a sweeping, white-mink fur cloak that was clasped closed over his silver and gold armor. He was tall, with a regal bearing, and a soldier's build. His nose was hooked, his skin pale, and his receding hairline blonde. The man standing next to him was old, perhaps the oldest human Caethe had ever seen. Wrinkled and bent, he clung to a white staff for support. The priest's sparse white hair hung about his face in long strands. He smiled, revealing a toothless maw, as he caught sight of Caethe.

Grigori led him to the stone staircase that circled the pillar of marble, and yanked him close by the collar to whispered in his ear, "Climb the stairs. Resist, and I will make you wish you never lived." He cut Caethe's gag free and pulled it from his mouth, before shoving Caethe forward. The chain hanging from Caethe's neck rattled against the steps of the stair as he began his slow ascent.

Caethe did not let himself think. Pure terror rode upon his thoughts, and like a dark wind, obscured all. Outwardly, his expression was calm, nearly serene, as he climbed the winding stair. When he reached the apex, Caethe nearly collapsed in fear. The presence of Ordu was thick upon the air that surrounded the priest and heavy in his eyes. Caethe felt his own power retreat deeper within, fleeing its proximity. Dimly, he heard the spirits within his mind screaming in panic. The priest beckoned him forward with a hooked, age-spotted hand. For a moment Caethe hesitated, unable to force himself to move.

It was momentary. Caethe stepped forward.

"Kneel, spawn of Magrados." The priest said, with a powerful voice that belied the feeble confines of his body. Caethe knelt. The priest stepped forward and Caethe had to resist from jerking back. Sweat slicked his hair and covered his body in a hot sheet so great was his terror. Caethe found his breath ragged and labored. The priest lifted a golden funnel from the pedestal before him, and stepped closer. "Open." The priest commanded. Caethe knew what the priests asked, but could not.

The priest laid his soft hand against Caethe's cheek. Caethe screamed, his back arching as the power of Ordu flooded through him, tearing his very essence asunder. He opened his mouth as tears streamed down his cheeks. The priest removed his hand, and placed the stem of the funnel into Caethe mouth. The stem was long and cold, and Caethe gagged as the priest shoved it down his throat.

The priest raised his staff, and the man next to him threw open his white cloak revealing a small bundle. The priest spoke, his voice taking on a chanting candor, "This night has been blessed by the noble birth of Alexander the 9th. Marking the New Year, he has emerged from the womb at the crux of time. Mighty, he is strong, with a voice that shall one day command armies. The boy is filled with a spirit that sings with Ordu's purity. Long would he reign, and with that strength, lead our people against the hordes of heretical." The priest paused, clearing his throat, and in the silence Caethe could hear the woman's muffled sobs. The priest continued, "But it is not to be. Another will be born in his place, to take up the mantle of the righteous. Filled with Ordu, Alexander will serve another purpose this night. With this holy sacrifice, light will be born into the world of man." The priest concluded, his eyes gleaming with an otherworldly intelligence.

The priest looked to the stoic man. Seconds passed as their gazes locked in a battle of wills. It lasted but a moment. The man stepped forward and pulled a long curved-dagger from the sheath at his belt. He upturned the small bundle he held. Caethe's eyes snapped closed, as the man's blade sliced down viciously. A woman's screams filled the sanctum, and Caethe felt hot liquid pool down his throat. Pain bloomed through his soul as cruel energy raged down to his belly, consuming all in its path. Caethe fell limply to the floor. His eyes stared unseeing before twitching closed.

Devaney

Chapter Fifty-Six:

Sails of Green Mire

Devaney sat cross-legged on a hilly mound. Beneath her, plush green stalks of grass softened the ground, and around her lilies bloomed, filling the air with heady perfume. The Elder Fae lay in the grass before her with an expression of serene peace. A moon dominated half the dark sky above. Here, there were no stars; just the moon and darkness.

Folsa held her wrist gently in her taloned hands. In a whisper, she counseled, "You ride time like a buckling stallion. It is wild as the northern wind, and unpredictable as the sea. Like a rainstorm, the future falls upon you as you seek to steer your steed through a tangled web of possibilities." Folsa stretched casually, arching her back, and sat straight. Her voice grew deeper as she warned, "You cannot dominate time itself. If you try, it will break you. Instead, you must grab small moments, tiny slips of control, that you wrest from the indomitable power before releasing it as quickly as you can."

Folsa leaned forward, playing a talon along Devaney's chin, as she said, "Your body however, is a crux in time. An anomaly, so impossible that it has become possible. Within the confines of your body you are the master of time. This is powerful." Her hands fell to Devaney's lap and gently took her wrists in her hands. She turned them over, eying the leathery scars time had marked her with. Folsa eyes rose from her wrists, and met her gaze steadily, as she commanded, "Turn time backwards and heal your wrists."

Devaney eyed her wrinkled skin. The scars weren't painful, but they were ugly reminders of her imprisonment. Taking care not to address the Fae with a direct question, Devaney said, "I was able to stop time because I used the emotion of fear and anger to fuel my magic as you instructed. I would be grateful to know what emotion keys the reversal of time."

The halo of sapphire light that hovered over Folsa's head, pulsated rapidly. Devaney had come to recognize this was a mark of annoyance. The Fae's voice grew sharp, as she chided, "Emotion is a clumsy tool to wield when no other path lays before you. You have time now. Clear your mind of all thought, all emotions, and you will see the spinning of time marked by the cortex of your power." Devaney settled her breathing, and closed her eyes. In her mind she found the core of her power. It rested at the center of her, swirling above and below with heady potency.

Folsa purred quietly, "The cortex of Magrados that rests within you is different then all others, Ronan and mundane alike. You see it." Devaney nodded that she did, and Folsa continued, "Your power is tied to the source. Like a root, it is connected to the Pool of Magrados, and from its depths you are fed Prophecy. I do not speak in hypothetical, nor of transient connections. This root is physical. It does not come and go. It exists physically within you. Grip it tightly and it slows. Fuel it with energy and it speeds. Drain it of power, and time will turn back upon itself." Devaney nodded. She remembered when she had slowed time, she had gripped her power like a vice. She had done the feat in a gut reaction, using her fear to instinctually act. "Heal your wrists," Folsa commanded again.

Devaney reached out with her mind, and touched the swirling, crystalized purity of her power. She held the image of her wrists in her mind, as she drew power from her Cortex. It was strange. She felt herself draining her own power, but also felt the energy pooling at her wrists. Her skin began to itch and burn. She cracked open her eyes, holding her breath.

White fire raced along her wrists, and the leathery skin began to crack and peel. Fear jumped into her heart, and Devaney looked to Folsa. Devaney nearly dropped the power, fearing she was doing something wrong, but found the Fae smiling. Devaney looked down again, and her breath caught in her throat. The aged skin had fallen from her wrist and new pink skin was being knit. Even as she watched her skin blurred with the swiftness of healing. Devaney let the power go with a sigh, and slumped to the ground. She felt drained, but as she eyed the perfect skin of her wrists she also felt elation.

Folsa nodded her approval, and said, "We will continue this lesson when you next dream of the Moor. Until then, you have fate to meet this night. Wake now, child." Folsa leaned forward, her black fur making her movements difficult to follow, and touched Devaney's brow gently. Blue light flashed before Devaney's eyes.

Devaney woke up, and sat up so quickly that she nearly fell out of the hammock she rested on. The ship rocked beneath her in the gentle embrace of the waves. Surrounding her tiny corner, were shelves of dried produce and barrels of salted fish. Nets wove above her in a tangled knot, hanging from thick hooks that had been driven into the rafters. Quietly, Devaney slipped out of the hammock and walked to the small door of the store room. She had no possessions when she came aboard the ship and none now.

The Melisoance sailors were tradesmen from Reblyn on their way home from the Capital of Molveria with a hull full to the brim with goods. They had taken her aboard with some confusion. Devaney had pretended to be mute as well as blind. After discovering she did not speak they had taken pity on the poor blind girl, provided her with rations of food, and otherwise left her alone. She was glad for their kindness.

Devaney smiled, knowing that soon they would be even more confused by their mysterious guest. She cracked open the wooden door that led to a hall. The door was warped from its many years on the sea, and she had to shoulder it open. The narrow hall beyond was dark. Devaney peered into the gloom. There was no one about, and quietly Devaney crept out of the room. She felt along the worn wall until she felt the rungs of a ladder. Devaney climbed them speedily, with a hand raised above her head, and when she felt the wooden door that led to the deck, she cracked it open.

In the darkness of midnight, she saw little movement on the deck. A few sailors napped in coils of rope, while two others played dice on the floor next to the helm. Devaney pushed the door open further, and craned her head upwards. In the crow's nest, a tanned man watched the sea with narrowed eyes. A shadow passed above him, blotting out the stars, but was gone again before he took notice.

Devaney climbed out of the hull hurriedly, keeping low as she walked toward the starboard side. She gripped the rail and peered over the edge. The ship cut through the blue waters steadily and foam billowed in the crest of the waves. A bird's cry cut the air. Devaney stood straight, gripped the rail, and flung herself off the edge of the ship. She heard a man cry out in fear. The water raced toward her.

Devaney landed on a silvery, feathered head awkwardly and rolled down a crest of feathers until Adwin's thin hands caught her shift. He yanked her toward him, and called over the rush of wind, "Hold on Oracle, I have you!" Lifoy's wings pumped furiously, throwing them into the air. Devaney clung desperately to handfuls of feathers as Lifoy rose above the ship. Devaney found her seat at the base of the Roc's neck with the help of Adwin's steadying hand. Adwin wrapped his arms around her, and she smiled back at him in thanks. "My brother has little sanity, Devaney, but fear not, I shall not let you fall," Adwin promised earnestly. Devaney laughed, elated and surprised by how joyful she felt to share their company again.

She heard Lifoy's voice in her mind, *'As Shades Island bathes with the witch king's ire, the blind walk upon cerulean wave. The chameleon uncovers the forsaken liar, sailing beneath the flag of emerald mire, due north of the sentinel's cave.'* He finished quoting her, and laughed. *You think you could have spoken a bit more plainly? Poor Adwin and I, have been flying up and down the coast for the last week.*

Devaney smiled, and said, "For someone as clever as you, I would have thought my prophecy child's play."

The Roc trilled with amusement, and Lifoy spoke into her mind. *Emerald mire, now that was inspired. I will have to remember that the next time I trade words with a disgruntled Reblynese.* He sighed dramatically into her thoughts, and said, *I do hope it was worth it, pissing off our esteemed Lord as it were. If he catches us, he will do more than bathe us in his ire.*

Devaney smirked remembering, and said, "Oh never fear, I fully duped the poor sap and left him choking on the ashes."

Adwin chimed in, and asked, "Where to, Lady of Time?"

Devaney didn't hesitate in responding, "Fly east, we must make all haste to Endar." She sensed Lifoy's confusion, but didn't explain. She had spent much time in the darkness with her eyes clouded with the weave of prophecy. Devaney knew she had to act meticulously in the coming days.

Lifoy spoke into her mind with a groan, *Dear one, please tell me we are not off to join the disgruntled nobles that I think you are alluding to.*

Devaney smiled secretly, but did not answer. Lifoy flew higher and they broke through the white mists. Dawn was breaking the sky and below them, spread for as far as the eye could see, gilded clouds rolled in a vast array. There was a peaceful isolation here, and Devaney felt a tear trickle down her cheek as she took in the glorious beauty. Silently, she thought, *I will save you, Magrados, I promise.*

Name Glossary

Aegoth A-goth
Aethara A-ther-ra
Aethral Ath-ral
Agsonath Ag-so-nath
Aileen A-lean
Aktymor Shanaid Ak-ty-mor Shan-aid
Amare- A-mair
Amor A-more
Aramubaer Ar-amu-beer
Aritian A-rit-E-an
Arkyn Ar-kan
Aqu Ah-koo
Azera Az-air-ah
Baleyia Bale-ee-ahh
Bellumayr Bell-ooh-may-or
Berko Burk-o
Braugaethrael Brah-gay-thrail
Brath Brath
Britton Brit-en
Bulzaelar Bul-zay-lar
Caethe Aethyon Kay-thay A-thee-on
Calnimor Cal-ni-mor
Ceareena Sar-een-a
Cimexael Ci-mex-ael
Cla'ditis Cla-dee-tis
Cyraque Cy-ra-ka
Daichi Day-chi
Dayvor Day-vore
Dellacindrael Dell-ah-cin-drael
Devaney Dev-uh-knee
Dileethues Deh-lee-thee-us

Dranguis Dran-gu-ees
Ebris E-bris
Ekogina Eek-o-gee-na
Entah in-tah
Eyo- E-yo
Farrin Far-in
Feryium Ferry-um
Folsa Foal-sah
Fronsylia Fron-sil-ee-ah
Golithiel Go-ly-theel
Go'olmarg Go-ol-marge
Grigori Gri-gor-ee
Gwynevere- Gwin-nev-eer
Gythlear Gyth-leer
Gylrna Gleer-na
Ibreal Ib-real
Ignathara Ig-na-thra
Jabari Ja-bar-ee
Jin jen
Jizial Zhi Je-zeal zigh
Jyre- Geer
Kotau Koo-ta
Lifoy La-foy
Lorchan Lor-can
Magatha Mag-ah-thah
Magrodos Mag-rah-dose
Mangus Mang-is
Mial Me-eel
Meave Meev
Mosyna Mo-zee-nah
Nagfari Nag-far-ee
Namyr Na-meer
Naturye Nah-too-rye
Netheria Neth-er-ah
Nyox Ny-ox

Ordu Or-do
Ori Or-ree
Ovstar Ov-star
Qurin Kur-in
Razia Ra-Z-ah
Raelwyn Rail-win
Ronan Row-nan
Rythsar Ryth-sar
Sabizael Sah-bee-zal
Sicaroo Sih-ka-row
Simisola Sem-E-sol-ah
Shethiyae Sheth-eeyah
Shu Zhi shoo Zigh
Sogin So-gin
Solani So-lon-ee
Sythilia Sigh-eel-eeah
Talia Tal-ee-a
Thoriston Thor-is-ton
Trillithi Trill-lith-E
Trescoronam Tres-cor-o-nam
Tooru Tor-u
Ultan Yul-tun
Ugawa ooh-ah-wah
Ugrael U-grail
Wu-rie Du Wer-ree Doe
Xokipilli Oh-ki-pil-ee
Yamiel Yam-i-el
Yeagrar Ya-grah-ar

Glossary of creatures and species.

Banoot (goblin) Ban-newt
Beymalum Bey-mal-um
Daemon (middle realms) Day-mon
Demon (lower realms) Dee-mon
Diamon (higher realms) Dy-A-mon
Divinus Hart Di-ven-us Heart
Elmare El-mare
Feligni Fi-len-gee
Fyrarox Fear-ar-ox
Gaour (goblin) Gay-our
Gillo (goblin) Gil-low
Insecti- In-sec-ti
Lorith (reptilian humanoid) Lore-ith
Mothos Moth-os
Sacti'Avem Sa-ki Ah-vem
Toutha' Da Fae Too-the Da Fey
Yithla (avian humanoid) Yith-la

Glossary of landmarks, continents, and kingdoms

Adonim Ad-o-nim
Aelfmae Sea Aelf-may Sea
Afta Af-tuh
Aftians Aft-E-ins
Allisosian Plain Al-eh-so-si-an
Amissa Ah-Meesa
Aznyr Desert Az-neer Desert
Barathrum Bear-A-thrum
Carcere Car-sir-ee
Castitate Cas-eh-tate
Creuen Crew-in
Dakryn Hall dak-rin Hall
Duladad Do-la-dad
Endar In-dar
Fervite Mountains Fur-vite
Flamae Cideru Flame-A Side-ru
Futu Fu-too
Igidum Sea Ig-gi-dum Sea
Ignea Ig-knee-uh
Igri Ig-ree
Igris Ig-ris
Illustusta Forest Ee-lus-too-stah
Ilvarsomni forest Ill-var-som-ne Forest
Inee in-knee
Krin Kren
Lafrey La-free
Manemia Mane-mia
Melisonce Mel-ee-sonce
Mondeus Mountain Range Mon-di-us Mountain Range
Mortemal Islands Mor-ti-mal Islands
Nimfrael Nem-frail

Novus No-vus
Pateru Pah-ter-roo
Pomum Pom-um
Pontees Pon-tees
Reblyn Reb-lyn
Requiem of Uventae Requiem of Ov-tini
Sandivi Plains San-dee-vi
Sidhe Shay
Somnumexteri Som-noom-ex-terry
Stellum Isles Stel-um
Tenebrosaqa Teen-bros-akah
Tenese Teen-ees
Victes- Vik-tis
Virdi Sea Vir-dee
Vinae Vee-na
Velonians Vee-lon-ee-ins
Umbrael Um-bray-il
Urobor Island Er-o-bor
Utarye U-ta-rye
Yamillia Forest Ya-mil-ee-ah
Zhara Za-har-ra
Zharians Za-har-E-ins

Made in the USA
Middletown, DE
12 June 2019